DEPTH
OF A
SHADOW

TOM DEAN

Published in 2012 by FeedARead.com Publishing – Arts Council
funded

Copyright © 2008 Tom Dean

Second Edition

While some of the events and characters are based on historical
incidents and figures, this novel is entirely a work of fiction.

A CIP catalogue record for this title is available from the British
Library.

For my wife, Beverley and daughter, Stacey, without whose help, patience and encouragement this book would not have made it into print.

ALSO BY TOM DEAN

A Dangerous Windfall

Praise for A Dangerous Windfall

Twists, turns and discoveries are what make a book so good that you can't put it down. And author Tom Dean's A Dangerous Windfall does just that.

The story follows Simon Preston, who is left just over £20million in a will from the late General Crozier.

He is the sole beneficiary, despite never having met the general.

The plot follows Simon's life with the windfall, which soon begins to look like a poisoned chalice after he becomes the target of a psychopathic hit man which leaves him fighting for survival.

He is determined to find out why the money was left to him and who his enemies are.

Fighting back, he continues his quest, opening up a history of death and betrayal stretching back to the First World War.

The book is a pacy historical thriller which keeps you hanging on till the end.

Northumberland Gazette – January 29th, 2009

DEPTH OF A SHADOW

CONTENTS

PROLOGUE	-	Page 1
THE RETURN	-	Page 5
NORTH MOOR	-	Page 105
EXILE	-	Page 365
RETRIBUTION	-	Page 485

DEPTH
OF
A
SHADOW

...................Unable to sleep, he lay staring into the darkness until his thoughts were interrupted by the sound of Mary's drowsy voice. 'Why do pitmen wear such bright clothes on Sundays?'

'I'm not sure,' Henry said thoughtfully. 'I suppose it's because they spend most of their lives working in an underground prison; a twilight world where colour is the depth of a shadow.' He paused, gathering his thoughts before continuing. 'When you spend the best part of your life in the darkness of a mine, you begin to see the world above in a new light. A world where the stars shine brighter, where the grass is greener and where the summer sky becomes an intoxicating blue. I think pitmen express this in their Sunday dress on their one day of freedom from the pit; an attempt to relieve the drabness of their everyday lives.'

Henry stopped, his eloquence making him feel awkward. He sensed Mary moving close to him and felt her lips brush his cheek.

'Those are the most beautiful and touching words I've ever heard you say, Henry Standish, and I love you very much for saying them.' She took his head in her hands and kissed him passionately on the lips with an urgency that surprised him.

PROLOGUE – ENGLAND, 1816

As he regained consciousness, the man chained to the wooden pit props which supported the roof of the mine began to scream. His body wrenched and twisted in a futile frenzy of panic until the iron shackles cut deep into his wrists. Blood ran down his outstretched arms, turning darker as it mingled with the coal dust before congealing in a black, sticky mass into the cuffs of his fine linen shirt.

He felt little pain, spread-eagled across the six-foot wide roadway deep inside the abandoned worked out area of the mine. His mind was numb and his eyes were transfixed in a hypnotic gaze on the flame of the new Davy lamp, recently introduced into the pit, which was placed on the roadway floor a few yards in front of him. Someone had taken off the wire-gauze cover of the safety lamp thus removing any protection from explosion. The yellow flame from the oil wick spouted occasional tinges of blue as it picked up the traces of explosive methane gas, known locally as 'firedamp'.

What he hoped had been a dream was, in reality, his worst nightmare come true. He was trapped and alone with his tormentor, entombed seven hundred feet down in the bowels of the earth, in the mine he hated and feared.

Suddenly, his anger welled up and for a moment overcame his fear. His voice raged and echoed down the deserted galleries of the mine. 'Damn you! Why are you doing this to me?'

There was no reply, only a mocking silence. He began to sob, quietly at first, but gradually growing into an uncontrollable fit of hysteria until it was finally stilled by exhaustion. The only sounds now were the drip of unseen water and the faint hiss of escaping gas from some obscure fissure in the coal seam.

After a while, he could discern the shadowy outline of his tormentor who was squatting on his haunches, pitman fashion, against the wall of the roadway. 'In God's name, what do you want of me?' he again implored.

'Truthful answers to some questions,' the squatting man replied. 'And as you mentioned God, you can regard it as a confessional; a purging of your soul.'

1

'I'm not a catholic and I'll wager you're no priest.'

'No, I'm not a priest.'

'Then why should I confess anything to you?'

'Because you'll die with a sinful conscience if you don't.'

'And you also, damn you!'

'True, but then I'm prepared to die. Unlike you, I'm not afraid.'

'You're mad,' the prisoner screamed. 'Put the cover on the lamp before the pit explodes.'

'Not until you confess your guilt and explain.'

'Explain what? Just what am I guilty of?'

His tormentor rose and moved forward into the light, revealing himself for the first time. He looked accusingly into his victim's eyes. 'Rape, betrayal and murder,' he rasped.

Recognition flickered in the chained man's eyes. 'You!' he whispered. 'I thought you were...' His voice dried up as a spasm of fear convulsed in his throat. Now that he knew the identity of his tormentor, any hope that he might somehow stay alive quickly faded.

The man groaned and slowly sagged on his chains in limp resignation. He listened anxiously to the menacing sound of the oozing gas and his eyes returned, trancelike, to the naked flickering flame of the Davy lamp. He knew his tormentor must have opened up some of the trapdoors and stoppings of the mine, diverting the vital flow of ventilating air and allowing the dangerous methane gas to seep into the disused main roadway. It was now only a matter of time before the gas built up to an explosive level that would be ignited by the unprotected lamp. He could only watch like some helpless rabbit frozen in the stare of a predatory stoat, waiting for death to strike.

The flame of the unguarded lamp was now surrounded by a large blue aureole, indicating the strong presence of gas. From his own pit experience the chained man knew what would follow if the gas ignited. Without warning, the narrow confines of the roadway would be filled with a blinding flash of light, followed by the roar of the explosion as the pit erupted. Then, the searing heat of the fireball would scorch the skin from his body, leaving the exposed flesh charred and blackened. There would be moments of unimaginable agony before death and he froze, terror-stricken, as the realisation took hold.

2

Paralyzed with fear, he lost control and felt the warm, wet patch at his crotch widen and spread slowly down the legs of his trousers. He began to whimper as he waited for the end.

THE RETURN

CHAPTER 1

YORKSHIRE – APRIL 1794

Mary Standish glared at her husband, 'You're a stubborn man, Henry, and pig-headed to the point of being selfish.'

'Selfish! I'm selfish?' Henry was taken aback by his wife's outburst.

'Yes. You show more concern for your responsibilities at the pit than those you owe to me and our son!'

Henry's exasperation rose. 'If trying to protect the lives of the men and boys who work for me is selfish then yes, I suppose I am.'

Mary threw up her hands in angry frustration. 'Damn you and this awful pit village. I'm sick of all the misery and squalor you brought us to. You promised it would be a new start; a giant step towards a better life. But it's just another foul smelling, godforsaken pit village with only rough pitmen and their families for neighbours. What sort of future is this?' she asked bitterly.

'You forget I was once a rough pitman,' Henry countered, stung by his wife's scathing outburst.

'But you're supposed to be a colliery manager now, an under-viewer, second only to Mr Marshall.

'And so I am.'

'Some people wouldn't think so by the way he treats you. You might just as well be the overman, or even the hewer you once were.'

Henry knew his wife was right but the truth still hurt. 'At least I'm better paid and we have a proper house with three rooms. Better than a pitman's one room hovel,' was all he could manage in reply.

'A tenancy tied to the colliery owner and within a stone's throw of his wretched pit village,' Mary hit back.

Henry sighed. 'It's a quarter of a mile away and… oh hell! We're having the same old argument again.'

'Because you never listen to me, or consider my views.'

'I do listen.'

'Yes, but you don't hear what I say. You're too engrossed in your own world of coal pits and pitmen.'

'Because it's what I do – my living.' Henry retorted. 'And it keeps us from starving,' he added coldly.

'Then why can't you just get on with it without constantly quarrelling with your superiors? After all, Mr Marshall is the colliery viewer and he's responsible for the overall management of the pit, not you.'

'Because the bloody man's incompetent.'

'But you're the under-viewer. You can put things right. You said Mr Marshall avoids going underground when he can and you've always corrected his mistakes in the past.'

'Yes, but now he's become dangerously incompetent. He's putting lives at risk.'

'Because there's too much firedamp in the workings?'

'Yes.'

'There's always gas down a pit. It's supposed to be an occupational risk, or so you always tell me.'

'It is, but it can be controlled by good ventilation. Trouble is the owner won't spend the money and Marshall always gives in to him. It's now got to the stage where gas levels are far too high for safe working. Once it mixes with air and coal dust the smallest spark can cause a massive explosion. And remember, every hewer needs a candle to work by.'

Mary tried to understand the dilemma they now faced. It was an impossible situation and she sighed in despair. 'So you're refusing to go down the pit today.'

'Yes.'

'That means you'll be breaking your contract. You could be dismissed and we could be evicted from our home.'

'I don't think it will come to that,' Henry lied. 'I'm not subject to the annual bond like the men,' he added. He was referring to the annual custom known as the binding where a skilled pitman signed, or (more commonly) put his mark, to a legal bond which enslaved him to the owner for the following year. If he broke his bond he could be imprisoned and his family evicted from their tied colliery cottage.

Mary was not convinced by Henry's reasoning and struggled to control her emotions before replying. 'Are the men following your lead? Are they refusing to go down too?'

8

'Some of them.'

'But not all?'

'I think most of them will when it comes to the final decision,' Henry lied again, hating himself for not telling his wife the truth.

'Then you'd better get going. It's nearly four o'clock. They'll all be waiting for you.'

Henry sighed as he pulled on his coat. 'Best you go back to bed, dear. It'll be a while yet before dawn. I'll be back as soon as I can.'

After hearing the front door close, Mary sat staring into the flickering flames of the fire. She felt sick with the fear and uncertainty of what lay ahead. Misery flooded her heart and threatened to engulf her. Struggling to control her emotions she crept quietly up the stairs to her bedroom, trying hard not to disturb her young son Mark in the adjacent room.

The sound of his parents raised voices had penetrated Mark's bedroom driving all sleep from his mind. When he became fully awake he had crept quietly to the top of the staircase to listen, unobserved, to what was being said in the room below. Soon he realised that this quarrel was something different. Previous family arguments had always been brief and quickly and lovingly settled. Now a threatening tone of bitterness had crept into their voices, something he had never noticed before. Unable to understand, he felt frightened and insecure.

Hearing his mother approaching the stairs, Mark quickly tip-toed back into his bedroom. Slipping into bed, he pulled the bedclothes up to his chin. But however hard he tried, sleep would not come. From his mother's room next door he could hear the faint sound of weeping.

As Henry walked down the squalid main street of the village heading towards the pit, he sensed there would be trouble. It was almost four o'clock in the morning and most of the front doors of the hovels that served as cottages for the pitmen stood open. Hewers and their families stood holding candles by the open doors, silent and hostile, their eyes glinting with defiance despite their deep apprehension. Though it was still dark, fires that had been banked up for the night were now stirred back into life, their flickering flames sending dancing shadows across damp, whitewashed walls.

Henry walked on, ignoring the sullen mood of the men and coughing as the acrid smoke which hung low over the village clutched at his lungs. He was inwardly pleased that many of the pitmen, mainly the older more experienced hewers, were making no attempt to follow him towards the pit, where work normally began at four in the morning. At least his warning had been heeded by some of them, though there was no sign of gratitude.

Silently angry at this undeserved rebuff, Henry forced himself to remain calm and hide his resentment. He knew the men blamed him for their dilemma, for he had opened their eyes and minds to the additional dangers forced on them by a greedy, uncaring owner; dangers made worse by the incompetence of an obsequious viewer like Marshall in charge.

The problem was that Marshall was arrogantly proud of his status as viewer and of being a member of the professional class of mining engineers who managed collieries on behalf of the owners. As most of the collieries, called pits by those who worked in them, were owned by the aristocracy or rich landed gentry, Marshall assumed this gave added respect of his profession. It was a misconception which made him unctuous to those he served and contemptuous of those he managed.

It was unfortunate that Marshall's conceit blinded him to his own managerial shortcomings and poor grasp of the essential sciences of mining and engineering. But he had been quick to recognise Henry's exceptional talents and clever enough to realise that these could be exploited to his own advantage. Accepting his viewer's recommendation, the owner had duly appointed Henry to the post of colliery under-viewer and deputy to Marshall.

However, the new arrangement quickly ran into difficulties and tension grew between the two men. Marshall began to resent his under-viewer's superior knowledge and experience and saw him as a threat to his own position. He began to take every opportunity to belittle Henry and undermine his deputy's authority. Matters had now come to a head and in the impending confrontation Henry knew he could not win. But his stubbornness would not let him walk away from the fight. It was not a matter of personal honour but a genuine concern for the lives of the pitmen and the boys he had come to know over the past two years. Their rejection of him had not diminished that.

Henry continued walking and as he approached the pithead, he could see the dark outline of the winding engine and the pithead pulleys silhouetted against the pale, pre-dawn sky. Cast-iron braziers filled with flaring coals were placed around the shaft, casting a lurid glare on the group of men and boys who were waiting to descend. Black smoke from the underground ventilating furnace spewed from the shaft.

The men fell silent as Henry approached and the atmosphere suddenly became tense as Marshall pushed his way to the front. 'Changed your mind, have you?' he said tauntingly.

'No,' Henry replied. 'The pit's too dangerous and you know it.'

'So you refuse to go down, then?'

'Not until we improve the ventilation – make the pit safer.'

'It'll cost too much. You know the owner can't afford it.'

Henry's anger boiled over. 'We're talking about men's lives, for God's sake. What price do you put on them?'

Marshall shrugged. 'Half the men are willing to work.'

'And the other half are not,' Henry countered.

'Only because you've filled their heads with your foolish theories and put the fear of death into them.' Marshall retorted. 'They'll wish they'd changed their minds when we throw them out of their cottages to make way for the new men.'

Henry was appalled. 'That's an abuse of power - virtual blackmail. The men and their families will be homeless.'

'It's legal. The cottages belong to the owner. The men have broken their bond so they've only got themselves to blame.'

'And come the next binding, I'll wager their names will be on every owner's black list.'

'Yes, and yours too my friend, unless you stop this nonsense and tell the men to get back to work.'

'No. I won't have their lives on my conscience.'

A smile of triumph spread slowly over Marshall's face. 'In that case, I have to tell you that your own services are no longer required.

11

The owner wants you off his property within twenty-four hours, otherwise the bailiff moves in.'

It was what Henry had expected, but it still came as a shock. By tomorrow he and his family would be out on the streets with little hope of finding another job.

Marshall turned his back on Henry and shouted to the men. 'Right lads! Let's be having you below.'

Immediately, the first group of men and boys swung themselves onto the chain attached to the end of the winding rope and hung precariously over the smoking abyss of the shaft. At a signal from the banksman in charge of the winding engine the four horses harnessed to the winding drum began their circular trot. The huge wooden drum of the winding engine began to revolve sending the ropes hissing over the pithead pulleys and the cluster of men and boys sank quickly into the shaft.

Exasperated by the final rejection, Henry started to walk away. But after a few steps some instinct made him pause. He turned and looked back at the remaining group of pitmen gathered around the shaft patiently waiting their turn to go underground.

After each descent, the four horses powering the winding drum were turned around in their traces to reverse the engine. Then another cluster of men and boys, hanging like bats from the winding chain, would sink into the acrid darkness of the shaft.

The process was repeated every five minutes without mishap and soon the waiting group had dwindled to a dozen pitmen. Henry began to wonder if he had misjudged the situation. Perhaps he was becoming an alarmist, losing his nerve and exaggerating the danger. But it was too late to change his mind, he thought morosely. Even if he admitted his mistake and made a grovelling apology to the viewer, he knew it would not save his job and home. It was rapidly becoming clear in his mind that Marshall had deliberately manoeuvred him into a public confrontation knowing that a stubborn pride would not allow him to back down.

The final group of men were now ready to begin their descent and Henry caught the look of triumph on Marshall's face as the viewer swung himself onto the winding rope. He made a mocking victory salute in Henry's direction before disappearing into the darkness of the shaft.

Henry felt defeated and stared dejectedly at the turning wheels of the pithead winding engine marking the descent of the final group. He turned and began to walk away heading back to the privacy of his home, a temporary sanctuary to reflect on his misjudgement pending his eviction. He had gambled on his professional assessment and lost. In trying to save lives he had jeopardized the livelihood of those who had heeded his warning and stayed at home. By doing so they had risked all by deliberately breaking their bond. They too now faced dismissal and eviction, perhaps even imprisonment or fines. The tragic irony of the situation was not lost on Henry.

A pale, orange glow began to lighten the eastern horizon as Henry walked back through the village. The men who had heeded his warning and stayed at home were now gathered in small groups and talking in loud, angry tones. The earlier atmosphere of apprehensive defiance was fast changing into one of ill-tempered recrimination as they argued among themselves. Not wishing to provoke a pointless confrontation, he carried on walking trying to maintain a dignified pace.

Henry was relieved to find Mary fast asleep when he arrived home. At least the confrontation he dreaded most could be postponed for a while. He sank wearily into the chair by the fire, gazing dejectedly into the glowing embers as he contemplated his future. His actions had been honourable but he was being blamed and punished for trying to save lives. It seemed so unfair. Yet Mary's words kept coming back to haunt him, '…why can't you just get on with it without constantly quarrelling with your superiors?' A wave of tiredness swept over him. He closed his eyes and drifted slowly into a shallow, disturbed sleep.

The explosion, when it came, was ear-piercing and sudden. The power of the blast sent a strong tremor through the house that rattled the windows and forced open the front door. Henry, his sleep instantly shattered, jumped to his feet, knowing instinctively that the pit must have fired. A wave of anguish and guilt swept through him as images of men and boys who had rejected his advice to stay at home, flashed through his mind. He ran out into the street and on towards the pit. Other people were emerging from their houses in the village swelling the stream of humanity, all running in the same direction with an urgency fuelled by fear.

Henry ran on, his lungs almost bursting from his exertions, and as he drew near to the pithead his worst fears were confirmed – the pit had erupted. A dense column of smoke and ash was belching from the shaft into the early morning sky, and he could see that most of the pithead buildings and machinery had been destroyed. Debris had rained over a wide area around the pithead and scorched and dismembered bodies lay scattered on the ground.

Exhaustion was now slowing him down and as he stumbled slowly towards the shaft something caught his foot and made him look down. There was blood on his boot from the severed head that lay on the ground. Aghast, he stared at sightless eyes sunk in blackened flesh and saw the agony of a terrible death frozen on Marshall's face. He turned away, overwhelmed by nausea as the magnitude of the catastrophe began to sink in.

CHAPTER 2

The stage waggon, drawn by six sweating horses, jolted and swayed over the rutted, pot-holed surface of what, by 1794, the long-suffering English traveller had come to call the Great North Road.

The waggon, its loose canvas cover shaking and flapping to the uneven motion, had descended the road from Chester Common and was now approaching the outskirts of the ancient town of Chester-le-Street in the County of Durham. The June air lay warm and still and the horses, straining at the traces, raised a fine cloud of dust which hung in a low, gentle cloud over the road. Behind the waggon, the twin tracks of the broad-rimmed wheels left an imprint in the loose, dusty surface marking their progress.

It was an uncomfortable ride for Mary and young Mark, but preferable to walking on the poorly surfaced road. Henry had no such inhibitions and was stretching his legs, walking between the waggon and the horse being ridden alongside by Gabriel, the waggon driver, who held a long whip cradled over his arm. Henry had soon discovered that the irascible old waggoner was no angel, but he was a good companion and the two men had quickly formed a bond.

The past two months in Yorkshire had been traumatic for the Standish family following the pit explosion which had killed so many men and young boys. The grief at the loss had torn the village apart and even those who had heeded Henry's warning showed no gratitude.

In the aftermath of the disaster Henry had organised and led the operation to recover the bodies. He subsequently conducted an assessment for restoring the damaged shaft. After completing his report to the owner he was summarily dismissed with one month's salary and notice to quit his colliery house. The final insult came when the owner appointed a new viewer to implement Henry's proposals for re-opening the pit.

Angry at the unfairness of it all Henry had raged at the owner and finally pleaded for an opportunity to prove himself. Being right in his warning of the explosion gave him little comfort, but he had realised that the superstitious owner had come to regard him as a bad omen.

15

Harbingers of death, even those with the best intentions, were never welcome. The implacable owner refused to change his mind.

The family were now on the final stage of their journey from Yorkshire to Newcastle-upon-Tyne, where they were to stay with Mary's older sister Ellen and her husband William. Mary hoped it would only be a short imposition on her sister's goodwill, just long enough for Henry to look for work and allow them to re-build their shattered lives.

The waggon slowly rumbled its way into Chester-le-Street past deserted, shuttered houses that lined the straggling main street leading to the market place. It was here that they first felt the strange atmosphere of melancholy which permeated the town, its invisible presence seeming to extract the very warmth from the sun's rays. It was as if a scent of death, odourless but all-pervading, hung in the still, summer air. Mary shivered and with a protective instinct held her son close.

Their slow progress continued toward the church marking the town square and as they came closer to the church they could discern a large throng of mourners gathered in the churchyard. They were mainly pit folk who had come to pay their last respects to the latest victims of their dangerous trade. Only a week had passed since the explosion at the local colliery at Picktree which had killed thirty men and boys. Two days later, the neighbouring pit at Harraton had exploded claiming another twenty-eight lives. Twenty-seven of the Picktree men were being buried in one mass grave that day, their bodies charred beyond recognition and mercifully hidden by the plain wooden coffins borne by their families and friends.

Gabriel gestured with his whip to the row of coffins lying alongside the large open grave. 'Fiery pits in these parts,' he said. 'Biddick, Lambton, Fatfield, Harraton, there's many a good pitman 'as met his maker in them pits,' he added reprovingly.

Henry nodded in agreement. 'Pits are getting deeper. The deeper you go, the more gas you'll find, so you need better ventilation. Trouble is good ventilation costs money and greedy owners prefer to go on risking other men's lives while they carry on lining their pockets.' His emotional scars from his own recent experience were still raw.

Young Mark, who had been following the conversation, looked quizzically at his father. 'What's a fiery pit?' he asked.

Henry smiled at his son's curiosity. 'A fiery pit is where the coal seams give off a lot of dangerous gas we call firedamp. When it mixes with air and coal dust it becomes explosive. A candle or even one spark can set it off.'

'How do you stop it exploding?'

Henry's smile broadened. 'It may sound daft, but you light a large fire near the bottom of the pit shaft so that the shaft acts as a flue. This sucks out the gas before it can build up in the workings.'

'Doesn't lighting a fire make the pit even more dangerous?' Mark asked.

'Not doing so would make it worse. The gas only becomes explosive when it's allowed to build up in the workings.'

'How do you know when that happens?'

'When the flame of your candle turns blue, but by then it's often too late.'

Mark nodded but did not look too convinced. He was intelligent and quick to grasp a problem having been taught intensively from an early age. Like his father, he had a highly developed curiosity that emanated from a love of books.

Henry looked fondly at his son and his thoughts drifted back to his own childhood. He remembered the unremitting hardship and ceaseless toil that he and thousands of other children were forced to endure in mining communities scattered throughout the Great Northern Coalfield of Northumberland and Durham. With the suffering experienced in his early life and the resentment it caused, came the realisation that learning offered one of the few opportunities to a fairer and better way of life for a poor working man.

He was fortunate when, as a boy, an understanding Methodist preacher who taught Sunday school in his Northumberland pit village recognised a rare intelligence and determination in young Henry Standish. It was a challenge the preacher could not resist and his patience and encouragement, together with Henry's tenacity, finally won through. Against awesome odds Henry learned to read and write, often falling asleep at his slate after a harsh fourteen hour day down the pit. Sunday, Henry had discovered, was a day to be savoured; a whole day to be spent with books without the debilitating effects of working a gruelling shift underground.

The preacher also taught him the rudiments of mathematics and science and when the young Henry had extracted the last grains of knowledge from his tutor, he again had the good fortune to come to the attention of the paternalistic owner of the pit. To the surprise of other less compassionate pit owners in the district he allowed Henry the use of his extensive library and watched with interest as the young man voraciously slaked his appetite for knowledge.

The pit owner was also far-sighted enough to recognise a strong practical streak in Henry and a natural flair for leadership which gained him the respect of his fellow pitmen. Henry was soon made deputy-overman in the pit where he worked, and within a few years, overman at a neighbouring pit. Having risen rapidly through the ranks of lower and middle pit management Henry was eager to develop his ambition to become a viewer and one day manage his own pit as a member of a respected profession. It was to further this ambition that he had left Northumberland, two years earlier, to take up a post of under-viewer at a pit in Yorkshire; an unfortunate decision that was to prove so disastrous to his career.

The stage waggon continued on its journey towards Newcastle and the sombre scene in the churchyard was soon hidden by the neighbouring buildings. The sad sight of so many coffins by the mass grave had rekindled harrowing memories in Henry's mind of the death and destruction he had so recently witnessed in Yorkshire. Twenty men and eighteen boys had needlessly perished on that day, leaving a community traumatised by grief and loss. The carnage had left him with deep psychological wounds and an inexplicable feeling of personal guilt.

The road now began its descent down the slope towards the narrow three-arched stone bridge which crossed the Conebrook. As they approached the bridge the urgent notes of a coach-horn cut through the still air.

Gabriel pulled out his watch. 'Must be the London mail,' he said. 'Leaves the Cock Inn at Newcastle at eleven 'afore noon, so it's late. They'll want the bridge.'

He dismounted from his horse and guided the waggon team into the side of the road just short of the bridge. Mark grew excited and stood on the waggon seat to get a better view. Coming down the turnpike on the north side of the stream he could see the mail coach, resplendent in its livery of red, maroon and black with a perfectly matched team of four horses. He saw the glint of metal as the guard raised his "yard of tin" and blew a call to make sure the bridge was clear. The coachman expertly negotiated the narrow bridge with hardly a pause and the coach thundered past the waggon, stirring up a fine cloud of dust

'Bloody nuisance', Gabriel snorted in disgust. He had seen too many coaches and suffered too much inconvenience to be impressed by these new so called "Kings of the road" who claimed right of way and paid no tolls or taxes.

Henry smiled. 'A nuisance? Not if you're a regular traveller. Newcastle to London in forty-five hours.'

'Aye, if you're rich. Four guineas inside and three pounds ten outside. By stage waggon it's less than a shilling a day.'

'And takes fourteen days,' Henry countered. 'But it's all poor folk like us can afford.'

Gabriel gave a sly grin. 'Worth every penny if you get the likes of me for company.'

'Yes indeed,' Henry said dryly. 'But thank God you don't carry the mail or the Post Office would soon be out of business.'

'Aye, maybe,' the old man reluctantly conceded. Muttering to himself, he led the waggon team across the narrow bridge then, mounting his horse, led the way up the sloping road towards the village of Birtley. When the waggon reached the top of the rise, Henry joined his wife and son on the seat near the front of the waggon. They were now entering the heartland of the Great Northern Coalfield which was concentrated along the banks of the rivers Tyne and Wear and a small area near Blyth in Northumberland.

Gabriel pointed to the east side of the road. 'Picktree' he said, his voice solemn with respect.

Across the fields Henry could see the squalid rows of miners cottages huddled round the pit shaft. The village of Picktree, clustered around the pit, looked empty and forlorn with most of its inhabitants attending the mass funeral in Chester-le-Street. Henry thought of the rows of coffins around the open grave and knew that few of the cottages would be untouched by grief. If tradition was observed the pit owner would allow the widows to continue living in their colliery-owned cottages. The lucky ones would have sons to slave underground and support them when the pit reopened.

During the three-day journey since joining the stage waggon Henry and Gabriel had talked incessantly about the Great Northern Coalfield. The abundant and easily worked coal adjacent to the rivers Tyne and Wear and the ability to ship the coal economically by sea had given the area a monopoly of the lucrative coal trade with London and Europe. Gabriel had delivered goods to pit villages in the area for many years and was a fund of local knowledge.

'The Lambton collieries are going to be short of a few pitmen now,' he said. 'An experienced man like you could do alright,' he added, knowing that Henry would be seeking work.

Henry shook his head. 'I'd rather wait till the binding in October.' He knew a shortage of men would mean increased binding money would be on offer to skilled pitmen willing to sign the bond.

'There's a need for more coal since the war with France.' Henry continued, 'I hear the Tyne owners are looking for more men.'

Gabriel looked at Henry with new respect. 'Aye, now that Wallsend pit's making a fortune for Russell they're all after the high main. Hebburn's just been won,' he added, 'and I hear they're all fight'n for mine leases on both sides of the river below Newcastle.'

'Sounds as though there'll be work for an experienced pitman then,' Henry responded cheerfully. As he spoke he failed to notice the frown that cast a sudden shadow across his wife's face. But the shrewd old waggoner did and, for some unknown reason, this saddened him. He had grown fond of the family.

There was an odd contrast between the rough country speech of Gabriel and the softer, more refined tones of Henry and his family. The occasional use of local expressions and a slight hardening of the vowels gave a hint as to Henry's background, but an overlay of learning and some travel outside the north-east had successfully camouflaged his lowly origins. His wife, Mary, attractive, dark haired and gentle, was the daughter of a yeoman farmer in Teesdale. They had met whilst she was working as a governess in Newcastle and the sparkle and fun of a close companionship quickly turned into a deep and tender love. Their son Mark, with his mother's dark curly hair and searching brown eyes, had brought contentment and a new sense of purpose to their marriage, though this had been severely challenged by their recent misfortunes.

It was, therefore, a poor and socially incongruous family that was returning to the Great Northern Coalfield; one ill-fitted for the rigid socio-economic class order of the day, and the turbulent times that lay ominously ahead.

About a mile past Chester-le-Street the road was crossed by two colliery waggonways that were used to transport coal from the pits to the coal staithes on the banks of the River Wear. Mark stared in amazement at the strange looking waggons which were fitted with flanged iron wheels and ran on parallel wooden rails set about four feet apart. Each waggon was drawn by a single horse. 'Funny looking waggons, father,' he said, his curiosity aroused.

Henry smiled. 'I suppose they are. More like a hopper on wheels. They're called chaldron waggons and can carry nearly three tons of coal to the shipping staithes on the River Wear.'

Mark was impressed. 'It's a huge weight for one horse to pull though.'

'It would be if it was in an ordinary waggon. On a road like this it would take six horses to pull half the weight. But the waggonways are designed to avoid steep inclines and the smooth rails means less friction and no pot holes. Also, because of its shape, a chaldron waggon is easy to unload at the staithes. You just pull a bolt to release the hinged trapdoor at the base and the coal drops through a spout into a keel moored below.' Then, catching Mark's puzzled look, quickly added, 'A keel is a shallow-draughted barge that takes the coal down to the collier brigs waiting in Sunderland harbour.'

Gabriel had listened in to the conversation with growing agitation. 'You'll see plenty of waggonways in these parts,' he cut in dismissively. 'There's scores of 'em along the Tyne and Wear and quite a few in Northumberland.' He turned and spat in the direction of the receding chaldron waggon. 'If they'd spend half as much on the turnpikes as the coal owners spend on their waggonways, I'd only need two horses to pull my waggon instead of six,' he said, cracking his whip at the straining team.

The Great North Road now began its climb over Gateshead Fell, a bleak, depressing place inhabited by tinkers, travelling potters and an assortment of semi-vagrants. The scattered cottages were mostly built of earth and roofed with turf sods.

'A dangerous place for honest travellers,' Gabriel complained. He stretched out his hand and pointed 'that's the spot where Hazlitt was gibbeted in '70 for robbing a coach and a postman. Made an example of 'im, they did and quite right too,' he added.

Mary shuddered and looked away, but Mark was curious to know more.

'How do they gibbet people?' he asked.

Gabriel grinned impishly. 'First they hang 'em,' he said, 'then they cover the body in pitch and cage it in tight metal bars. Then they hang it on a high wooden scaffold like a gallows, built on the spot where the foul deed was committed. Serves as a proper warning to others who might be inclined to rob,' he concluded darkly, evoking a grimace from Mark.

The one compensation for the doom and gloom of Gateshead Fell was the magnificent view it afforded from the summit. Below lay the River Tyne, cutting through its deep, coal rich banks and past the broad reach by the island of King's Meadows until it met the jewel in its crown, the old walled town of Newcastle, which proudly dominated the north bank. A stone bridge linked the town to its smaller neighbour Gateshead on the southern bank.

They continued in silence for a while as the waggon negotiated the long descent towards Gateshead and the bridge which spanned the river. As they approached the junction with the Sunderland turnpike they were held up by a large ragged group of militia coming from Newcastle.

Gabriel shook his head. 'Soldiers! God 'elp us if that lot's all that stands between us and the French.'

When the waggon finally rumbled down Gateshead high street, the grandeur of the north river bank gradually unfolded, until they reached the final descent down to the Tyne Bridge. At this point, a dramatic view of Newcastle suddenly opened up. Henry saw the town rising up the steep north bank of the deep trench cut by the river. It had a picturesque, Elizabethan appearance with rows of brick houses adorned with red tiles and quaint gables. To the east of the bridge lay Sandhill and the seventeenth century Guildhall. On the escarpment above, the Norman Keep of the old castle and the adjacent Half-Moon Battery, monuments to sieges and battles of bygone turbulent times, frowned menacingly across the river. The magnificent lantern tower of the Church of St Nicholas and the towering spire of All Saints formed a backdrop to this breathtaking view.

As Gabriel guided the stage waggon down the steep hill towards the bridge he began to recite:

'Flow on, oh majestic river.
Oft on thy banks I've wandered,
And on thy passing beauties pondered;
Oh, many an hour I've squandered
By bonny coaly Tyne'

Henry smiled at the incongruity of an old man dressed in a waggoner's smock and gaitered breeches quoting poetry.

Gabriel looked across and winked. 'Nice to be home, eh?'

Henry nodded, 'It is indeed.' He suddenly felt a surge of confidence and with it came a new determination. He placed his arm around Mary and drew her close. He was on home ground again and for his family's sake, he would fight his way back to the top.

23

CHAPTER 3

A fine stone bridge, spanning nine arches, linked the small borough of Gateshead to the larger town of Newcastle which stood on the north bank of the Tyne. The bridge was crowded with traffic and the air was filled with the rumble of iron shod wheels and hoof beats, above which rose the curses of the drivers and cries of alarm from those travelling on foot. The unfortunate pedestrians had to weave their way precariously between the horses and a bewildering variety of carts and heavy waggons. There was barely enough room to allow two waggons to pass with any degree of comfort. Those on foot had to constantly shelter in the safety of the angled recesses which were formed at each buttressed pier of the bridge.

Gabriel swore as he manoeuvred the stage waggon across the bridge. 'Should have made it wider,' he complained. 'Only thirteen years since it was built and it can't cope with the traffic.'

Henry nodded, 'They could have added another ten or twelve feet if they'd taken the road out to the edge of the piers.'

'There's been talk of that for years but nothing ever gets done.' It was clearly a subject which irritated the old man.

There were further hair-raising incidents with other road users, often degenerating into a fierce exchange of insults, before the waggon finally negotiated the bridge and turned east into the triangular expanse of Sandhill. This was the commercial heart of the town containing the fine Guildhall with its courts of justice and seat of the town government. The Exchange was also situated here providing a meeting place for merchants, traders and ship owners. Coal fitters, acting as agents for the coal owners, eagerly sought out the collier brig captains who bought their coal for shipment to the major markets in London and in coastal Europe.

Newcastle in 1794 was a bustling, vibrant town, home to a population of twenty-eight thousand with a further eight thousand living on the opposite bank of the river in Gateshead. It was a colourful place built largely of brick and timber with gabled red tiled roofs. The two miles of fortified walls, twelve feet high and eight feet thick, which encircled the town, were still largely intact.

24

Newcastle's prosperity was built on coal. It was the capital of the Great Northern Coalfield which for centuries had exercised a virtual monopoly over the London and east coast markets. Nearly seven thousand pitmen and boys worked down the mines of the Tyne and Wear and many more in ancillary trades. Nearly two thousand keelmen were employed to crew the oval-shaped, flat-bottomed coal barges, known locally as keels, that were used to transport the coal downstream to the collier brigs waiting in the deep water harbour at Shields.

Coal had now replaced charcoal as the fuel for smelting iron, copper and lead as well as for the manufacture of glass, pottery, bricks and in brewing. Newcommen's atmospheric steam engine had revolutionised the mining industry and although inefficient in its use of fuel, this was not a problem in the coal rich areas of Tyne and Wear. Mines could now be drained by steam power and sunk to greater depths allowing new, richer seams to be reached. New pits in the lower Tyne basin were being sunk to previously unimaginable depths of a thousand feet or more. Unfortunately, this had also brought increased danger and death to the thousands of pitmen and boys who worked underground, for the essential technology for ventilating the mines at this depth, had not kept pace with the means of draining them.

The banks of the Tyne were now lined with iron works, lead refineries, soap works, glass factories, rope works, potteries, shipyards and many other manufacturing enterprises. Some collier brigs brought in sand for the glass works and departed laden with coal. In the harbours of North and South Shields, stretching over two miles, a thousand ships could ride safely at anchor.

However, despite this thriving economy, a sullen resentment simmered, directed towards a growing prosperity that only seemed to benefit a select few. The seeds of conflict between capital and labour, fed by a new wave of radicalism, were beginning to grow. Angry public meetings and riotous behaviour added fuel to the fire of dissent. The government of Mr Pitt, ever fearful of a revolution in England, became increasingly alarmed by the rhetoric of leading firebrands like Tom Paine and key members of the well organised and radical London Corresponding Society. They saw radicalism as the enemy within and

Paine as a dangerous rabble-rouser. The Reign of Terror in France and the execution of King Louis XV1 was still fresh in the minds of the people and the shadow of the guillotine had come to haunt the British establishment. The war with France only exacerbated the paranoia and the government's draconian response was the arrest of radical leaders and suspension of Habeas Corpus. The screw was turning ever tighter.

In Newcastle's narrow streets, called chares, which led off from the Quayside and Sandgate, the upper stories of the wretched houses leaned so close that they almost touched. Here, in the gloom that the sun's rays rarely penetrated, lived the poor working class inhabitants of the town. This area, one of the most densely populated in the north was home to more than a thousand tough keelmen and their families, a breed famous for their fighting spirit, ferocious independence and utter contempt for any form of authority other than their own.

In 1794 everyone was expected to know their place in life and the squirarchy, who comprised the appointed magistrates of the ruling establishment, saw it as their duty to maintain the status quo. But, a slow match to the powder keg of radicalism had already been lit and the pent up resentment of years of repression was rising inexorably to the point of explosion.

Two of the busiest of the town's thoroughfares led off from the Sandhill. East lay the Quayside, its cobbled surface stretching some five hundred yards along the riverside, with a forest of masts and rigging ranging skywards from the multitude of sailing craft moored, sometimes four abreast, alongside the quay.

Leading northwards to the upper part of the town, the busy street known as The Side wound its way past the high, overhanging gables of the tall storied buildings which lined most of its length. This was the old heart of Newcastle still throbbing with life and vitality in its crowded shops and markets as it fought a slowly losing battle with the newer and more elegant streets in the upper reaches of the town.

The stage waggon turned into The Side which was crowded with traffic, made worse by the stalls of the shops and market traders which spilled over into the roadway. Seeing a space which would allow him to stop without blocking the road, and so incurring the wrath of other carriers, Gabriel halted the waggon.

'You're heading for Wall Knoll?'

Henry nodded.

'Best cut along the Quayside and up Broad Chare, but watch out for the press gang if you use Broad Chare. The navy's desperate for men now we're at war.'

Henry thanked him and began to unload his belongings from the stage waggon. Allowing Mary and Mark to carry a light parcel each he shook hands with Gabriel and shouldered the heavier bags. An expression of affection passed over the old man's face. He didn't often find a rapport with his passengers but Henry and his family had somehow struck a chord; this is how it might have been, he thought, if his own marriage had not ended so tragically all those years ago.

'Mind how you go,' he said gruffly and turned away.

Henry watched as the stage waggon rumbled slowly up the Side heading towards his final destination, the Bird in Bush yard in Pilgrim Street, where the London waggons quartered. Soon he would be quaffing a glass of old Newcastle ale with his fellow carriers at the Pack Horse or the Nags Head. Old ale was not tapped until it was 12 months old and normally drunk as one part old to three of mild.

I bet he skips the mild, Henry mused, a smile softening his face. The rapport had been mutual.

Henry led the way along the quayside which was seething with activity and crowded with waggons of all sizes. A sedan chair weaved its way incongruously among the bales of merchandise, casks, timber and sacks of corn. Brawny porters, stooping under sacks of grain, walked along the springing planks laid from ships' decks to the quayside. Weather beaten sailors, wherrymen and sweating porters mixed with merchants, brokers and traders to form a heterogeneous throng and the air was filled with a stream of shouted orders, curses and threats.

When the family reached the entry leading into Broad Chare Henry paused, and remembering the old waggoner's warning about the press gang, decided to take the safer route to Wall Knoll.

The headquarters of the Newcastle press gang was at the Plough Inn in Spicer Lane, off Broad Chare, where a room down the yard served as the press room. Danger from the press was always greatest at night when the gang's spies combed the inns and alehouses seeking easy prey, often slipping the King's shilling into the victim's beer tankard when he wasn't looking. Sailors and keelmen were always prime targets, but gangs were not averse to pressing into the navy any healthy young landsman to help fill their quota, especially in time of war.

Wall Knoll was a quiet street near the east wall of the town. The quaint, timbered house of Mary's elder sister stood near the end of the street and looked neat and well cared for. Mary smiled nervously at Henry as she raised the large brass door knocker. At the second knock the door was slowly opened and a small woman of about forty years, with wispy greying hair peeping out from under a lace bonnet, looked warily round the edge of the door. After a few seconds, a smile of recognition spread over her face.

'Why, Mary, my dear!' She clasped her sister and the two women embraced with great affection. 'Nice to see you again, too, Henry.' There was a subtle, almost imperceptible cooling in the welcome as she turned her cheek to allow Henry to kiss her. Finally she addressed Mark. 'Mind how you've grown!'

Mark tried to control his squirming reaction as she kissed him on the head. 'Hello, Aunt Ellen.'

Ellen began to take charge. 'Come in, all of you. You must be tired after your awful journey.'

They entered an oak beamed parlour with panelled walls which led off the small hall.

'Leave your things in the hall,' said Ellen. 'I'll make a nice pot of tea. You can help, Mary, if you feel up to it.'

Mary flashed a mischievous smile at Henry, raising her eyes to the ceiling, as she was led from the room.

Henry looked round the parlour noting its spick and span appearance and the military precision in the way the cushions, ornaments and other decorations were laid out. He winked at Mark. 'I'm almost frightened to sit down. Better be on our best behaviour, eh?'

Mark grinned back. 'I'll try, dad, but I wish we had our own house again.'

Henry put his arm round Mark's shoulder. 'We will, son. Soon, I promise you. We're only staying here a short while, till we find our feet and I can get work. It's kind of your Aunt Ellen to take us in and we mustn't be seen to be ungrateful.'

Mark turned and hugged his father with a fervour that caused a tender, protective wave of emotion to swell up in Henry's throat. He held his son tightly. 'Everything is going to be alright,' he whispered fiercely. 'This is a new beginning for our family and you're going to play a big part in it.'

Little did Henry then realise how prophetic his words would prove to be and the anguish it would cause.

Later that evening, Ellen's husband William returned home from his position as chief clerk in a coal fitter's office near the Exchange. He was a dour looking man of late middle age with the pretentious manner often adopted by those of limited ability who feel they have made their way in life. He wore a threadbare cut-away tailed coat with a white neckcloth soiled by visits to the coal staithes.

After the two families had eaten their simple evening meal in the kitchen and Mark had gone up to bed, William pompously announced, 'Henry and I have important family matters to discuss'. He led Henry into the parlour, and after a nervous pause he continued, 'You must realise, Henry, that your stay here can only be a temporary arrangement. I'm doing this for Ellen's sake and as a duty to my family responsibilities.'

Henry, his pride hurt, struggled to hide his anger and resentment. 'Of course, William,' was all he could bring himself to say.

'However, there is no urgency,' William went on. 'You'll need time to get on your feet again. At least if you find a pit job you'll have a house provided.' William knew the coal trade and this was a clear hint.

'I was planning to wait till the binding in October,' said Henry. 'There'll be a better chance of good binding money then, with all the new pits opening up below the bridge.'

Henry detested the humiliating ritual of the annual binding. The prospect of enslaving himself to an owner for the next twelve months in order to obtain work filled him with shame. "Binding money" was a blatant bribe, when labour was scarce, to encourage pitmen to sell their souls. It also allowed the owners to cleanse the labour market of its undesirable elements each year and now the known malcontents, like radicals and levellers, were becoming prime targets.

Henry was hopeful that the war with France and the extra manpower needs of the armed forces, combined with the increased demand for coal for the production of armaments, would all act in his favour. He was "pit bred" in mining parlance; a trained pitman with management experience, though after working as an overman and an underviewer, he didn't relish the thought of becoming a hewer again. But for the sake of his family and for his own self-esteem he would take any job that was offered.

Of one thing he was certain; he would keep Mark out of the pits whatever that might cost.

William's sanctimonious lecturing broke into Henry's reverie. He realised he was being asked a question.

'Does that mean you'll be staying until October, Henry? Four months?'

'I fully intend to pay you for the rooms. I'm not a pauper.' There was a note of anger in Henry's response.

'I didn't mean to imply that you were,' said William, a conciliatory tone creeping in at the prospect of being paid for the rooms. 'You can stay as long as you wish. We can discuss any financial recompense later.'

'We will discuss it now, if you don't mind.' Henry's anger had not left him and he sensed he could manipulate the situation to his advantage. William's pretentious life style clearly left him short of money.

'I'll pay you one and sixpence a week for the rooms and we'll buy our own food.'

William was obviously pleased with the proposal, but he did not wish to be seen as avaricious where his own family were concerned. Besides, he would have to make his peace with Ellen later and she considered family loyalty to be a Christian virtue, not something to profit by.

'The offer for the rooms is most generous. However, I'm sure we can at least provide the hospitality of our table for a few months without payment, though as you see the fare is plain.'

Henry sensed victory. 'I'm sure our wives can come to some arrangement on that score,' he said.

Later that evening Mary and Henry said good night to their hosts and made their way up the narrow staircase that led to the two rooms they were to occupy on the top floor. The house was on three floors with two rooms on each. The second floor contained Ellen and William's bedroom and a room that William grandiosely described as his study. Above, on the third floor, were two attic rooms with small dormer windows, one which Mark occupied and the other for Mary and Henry.

Mary stopped on the small landing which separated the two rooms and let the light from the candle shine through the partly open door of Mark's room. Satisfied that he was fast asleep she entered the other room, followed by Henry, who closed the door quietly behind him.

The candle cast its flickering light over the low-ceilinged room which contained a chest of drawers, two chairs and a large wooden bed covered by a faded patchwork quilt.

For Mary it was a disappointment that, after so many days of tiring travel, her first opportunity to share her privacy and intimacy with Henry should be in a dreary attic room like this. She turned suddenly and flinging her arms around Henry, nestled her cheek against his shirt which soon became damp with her tears.

'Oh Henry, what's to become of us? I can't stand the thought of you becoming a pitman again. After all you've gone through you deserve better.' Her shoulders shook and she sobbed gently as a wave of despair overtook her.

Henry, frightened and confused by her tears, could only hold her tightly until her weeping subsided. Then, gently lifting her chin, he kissed her on the lips, tenderly at first but with a steadily rising passion as Mary ardently responded.

Slowly, he undressed her and placed her on the bed. Then undressing himself, he lay down beside her and held her close.

Mary felt the slow pulsing of his tumescence against her body and responded by moving closer. She felt a growing excitement as Henry

31

kissed her on the lips then, leaning over her, on her breasts. Her hand gently explored the length and tautness of his full erection before guiding it into the warm, moist home inside her body. Her back arched as he drove deep inside, forcing a delighted gasp of enjoyment. His thrusting became stronger and as the rhythm of his ardour increased, so the old wooden bed creaked and groaned in harmony with their passion.

Afterwards, as they lay contentedly together, Mary's body twitched and she suddenly began to giggle. Henry looked at her in astonishment.

'What on earth....' He felt Mary's hand over his lips silencing him. She was now convulsed with suppressed laughter.

'I just don't know what Ellen and William must think about the noise.' She struggled to control her giggling. 'Their bedroom is right below ours.'

'To hell with what they think,' said Henry. 'Might remind the patronising old bugger what a bed is for.' He leaned over and whispered, 'If it runs in the family, he doesn't know what he's missing. I could go on all night.'

Mary impishly whispered back 'What's stopping you?'

Their second lovemaking was even better than the first. It was erotic with unrestrained, all-consuming passion as Henry thrust faster and deeper with the bed creaking louder and louder in unison. When they finally climaxed they fell back into a spent embrace, their energy sapped but their emotions fully satiated.

Then suddenly, with a resounding crash, the old wooden bed collapsed to the floor in sympathy.

The day after their arrival in Newcastle, Henry and Mary sat down to consider their future and devise a strategic plan of action. Henry did not like leaving things to chance and, now that he had made the decision to return to his roots, he was determined to make the most of any opportunity that came his way. Although he was a Christian in the non-conformist tradition of the mining communities, he had little confidence that Divine Providence would see him and his family through. His past misfortunes had reinforced his belief that Divine help usually went to those who helped themselves. He was determined to make things happen through his own efforts and he knew that this would mean careful planning.

All their furniture and worldly goods, other than those they could carry, had been sold prior to leaving Yorkshire. A quick stock-take revealed that apart from a few changes of clothing and personal belongings, their total resources amounted to thirty-five pounds. At least they could survive without charity for a year, but Henry was ambitious and wanted further schooling for young Mark.

As the weeks went by and June turned to July Henry became increasingly frustrated. He visited pits in nearby Byker, Walker and Heaton as well as those across the river in Gateshead seeking work where his skills and experience could be utilised in a management role. Unfortunately, rejection after rejection left him ever more despondent.

He tried above bridge as far as Scotswood and Blaydon but with equal lack of success. There was no problem in finding work as a hewer, but the suspicions linked to an unemployed under-viewer returning from a failed pit in Yorkshire were proving to be an insurmountable obstacle to Henry's management ambitions. If he had to go back to being a pitman again he would select the best and safest pit and wait until the October bindings.

Mary did her best to console him with love and encouragement, but she knew his pride was hurt, and could only share the pain and resentment that he tried to bottle up inside himself. Yet even the pain she shared had to be concealed and as the weeks went by, living this lie, began to take its toll on their relationship. Even Mark felt an alien pang of insecurity which his young mind could not fully comprehend.

Ellen had also sensed the growing tension between her sister and Henry and after some gentle coaxing, finally persuaded Mary to confide in her. Being fond of her sister and being blessed with a strong practical streak when the occasion demanded, Ellen decided to take some action. Although Mary had begged her not to, she sought William's help in the matter, threatening retribution if he ever let the cat out of the bag.

'We must find Henry some work,' she demanded. 'Surely you must have some influence with the coal fitters, William? You've done their bidding these last twenty-five years.'

William looked unhappy. 'It's not quite as simple as that, my dear. Coal fitting is a rather special trade, and I'm not sure that Henry would be quite suited to it,' he finished weakly, recognising the determined look in Ellen's face.

'Balderdash! There must at least be a clerk's position for a man who reads and writes well and knows the coal trade.'

William saw defeat staring him in the face and decided to give in gracefully. 'I'll see what I can do,' was all he could murmur.

'We must also find a suitable school for young Mark.' Ellen continued, determined to drive her advantage home. 'It will have to be a charity school but All Saints has a solid reputation. Your brother Ambrose has influence with the Trustees. You must talk to him, William.'

The deed was done and three days later, after supper, William led Henry into the parlour for "another little chat".

At first Henry was angry at his brother-in-law's interference but quickly realised that he meant well and it would be selfish, and indeed wrong, to reject his offer of help out of hand. The least he could do would be to discuss it with Mary.

Later that evening, when they undressed for bed in the faded attic bedroom, Henry broke the news to Mary.

'William thinks there may be a clerk's position at his firm of coal fitters.'

Mary's face lit up with surprise and delight. 'You'll take it if it's offered?' There was an anxious note in her voice.

'It might only pay nine shillings a week.' He watched her closely and saw that money didn't matter to her.

'At least it's a job, Henry. And it keeps you out of the pit.'

'There's more,' he said. 'William thinks there may be a place for Mark in All Saints School.'

'Oh that's wonderful.' Her eyes began to moisten with hope and a new-found happiness. 'When would he start?'

'Straight away,' said Henry, then adding after a pause, 'If we send him.'

Mary looked startled. 'But why not? It's a good school surely, even if it is a charity school.'

'It won't stretch him.'

'But we can't afford anything better, can we? At least he can meet other children and learn school discipline.' She was fast becoming exasperated with Henry's obstinate pride.

'I suppose so,' he conceded.

'Henry, you owe him something...' she stopped, biting her tongue, wishing she could retract. She could see the hurt in his eyes. 'I'm sorry...' but it was too late; the damage was done.

'Yes, I should have made a success of things; been a better provider for my family.' His voice was bitter. 'Oh yes, I owe him something. But it's something I haven't been able to deliver.'

'But you've tried, Henry. You've tried so hard and I'm very proud of you.' She looked at him pleadingly. 'I wouldn't change a thing in my life, least of all marrying you.'

She moved across and placed her arms around him. 'Come to bed.'

For a while they lay together in silence each wanting to break the tension but, perversely, hoping the other would make the first move. Henry felt Mary's hand timidly creep across the bed and instinctively turned to embrace her. The tension drained away and he heard her whisper, 'You are a success to me, you grumpy old fool. Don't let anyone take that away from you, least of all yourself.'

He sighed, 'Perhaps you're right, though I can't help thinking that life might have been far less complicated if I'd remained a simple, unlettered pitman.'

Mary snuggled closer. 'Nonsense and you know it! Good night, Henry Standish.'

Her comforting words and warm body pressing closer lifted his depression and he felt lighter inside. He sensed a new and deeper love was creeping back into their marriage, bolstered by a growing optimism for their future together. Tomorrow would be a new beginning.

They made love with a heady mix of passion and tenderness. The sleep that followed was deep, satisfying and untroubled.

CHAPTER 4

The summer of 1794 brought a welcome period of stability into Henry's life. On a cool, blustery Monday morning he arrived with William at the quayside offices of Ivison and Burdon, coal fitters, hopefully to begin his new career. William nervously introduced Henry to Mr Ivison, the head of the firm, and looked put out when the great man asked him to leave.

'Your brother-in-law may be an able and diligent chief clerk, Standish, but I choose my own clerks.' His piercing glance noted Henry's confusion.

'Offered you the job, did he?'

'No, sir,' said Henry quickly recovering his composure. 'He thought there might be a position.'

Mr Ivison smiled. He did not believe Henry but admired his loyalty. 'I understand you have pit experience underground. Unusual for a clerk, eh?' He looked at Henry, eyebrows raised.

Henry briefly recounted his work experience, but his attempts at modesty were defeated by Mr Ivison's persistent and penetrating questioning.

Finally, Mr Ivison motioned to the door indicating that the interview was over. 'Report to my chief clerk. He'll tell you what to do. Nine shillings a week till we see what you're made of.'

After Henry had left the room Mr Ivison sat for a while, deep in thought, as he reflected on the interview.

'He might do,' he murmured to himself. 'He just might do.'

William displayed a mixture of peevishness and curiosity after Henry's lengthy interview with the head of the firm. It was a distinction which he as chief clerk was rarely accorded; most of his dealings were with lesser members of the management. On the way home that evening he bombarded Henry with questions and receiving few satisfactory answers, continued the onslaught over supper.

Henry's response was deliberately vague and evasive and this had the desired effect of increasing William's chagrin. At last he gave up and retired to his study, allowing Henry a smile of amused satisfaction.

Mary flashed him a knowing glance. 'You've got a wicked and mischievous streak in you, Henry Standish. The poor man's at his wits end to know what happened. And so am I.'

During the next two weeks Henry worked assiduously at all the routine tasks of a coal fitter's office. He found the work simple and routine; checking coal shipments and certificates of lading, entering and writing up ledgers. It was less difficult than the work he had done as a colliery viewer dealing with pit accounts and administration, but it was far more tedious.

At the end of the second week Henry was summoned to Mr Ivison's office. The shrewd businessman looked over his gold rimmed spectacles as he entered.

'Sit down, Standish. He looked penetratingly at Henry, 'Coping with the work I see. Not too difficult?'

'It's fairly straightforward, Mr Ivison, but I try not to take things for granted.' Henry didn't wish to sound cocky.

'Easier than the pit accounts, I'll be sure.' Mr Ivison was no fool. His next question took Henry by surprise.

'You'll be back to the pits come the binding in October?'

'I had thought about it, sir, until you offered me my present position.'

'Doesn't pay as well as pit work, though, does it?' Again that shrewd probing look.

'No, sir, but my wife prefers it.'

Mr Ivison nodded in agreement. 'Safer and more respectable,' he said 'but it doesn't pay the bills so easily.'

'No sir.'

An awkward silence ensued, broken at last by Mr Ivison. 'Be a waste if you went back to hewing. You know that, don't you?'

'Yes sir.' Henry was on the defensive, his pride at stake. 'But I have to do what's best for my family.'

Mr Ivison pulled at his watch, flipped open the case and stared absently at the dial.

'I'd like you to join me for supper tonight, Standish. I think it's time you and I had a long and serious talk about your future.

Later that evening William's small house in Wall Knoll was filled with a mixture of excitement, curiosity and envy. Mary shone with elation, and new found hope. Ellen displayed a polite blend of encouragement and curiosity, while William tried, unsuccessfully, to hide his seething envy under a forced expression of casual aloofness.

Henry wore his best coat of dark green cloth and a clean white neckcloth and shirt underneath a yellow waistcoat. With his high crowned hat and polished shoes he looked the part of a gentleman. His tall frame and firm bearing further enhanced the effect. He turned to Mary.

'How do I look?'

'My word, a dandy indeed!' Mary made a mock curtsey. 'You may take my arm, kind sir.'

Henry made an exaggerated bow. 'I wish I could take you with me.'

'Nonsense. It's a business supper to discuss your future, Henry. A wife would only be a distraction.'

Henry left the house and made his way to the quayside where Mr Ivison lived. It was an old house fronting on to the quay, five stories high. The second and third floors had large oriel windows with latticed casements projecting over the street. It was in one of these rooms that Henry sat down to supper, served as the last of the day's sun lit up the corner of the large bay window.

During a pleasant meal, during which Mr Ivison probed deeper into Henry's past, a curious, almost imperceptible mutual understanding began to emerge. Henry's guarded responses became less muted as he warmed to his host. He retained his respect for his employer but gradually lost the feeling of awe.

Later, as the light faded and a chill air crept up from the river, Mr Ivison called for the fire and candles to be lit in the living room. Leaving the dining room they adjourned to the comfortable armchairs placed at each side of the fireplace and, as the fire took hold, the flickering flames cast dancing shadows across the panelled walls. The serious talking now began and the next two hours were to prove a revelation to Henry.

Ivison gave him a long, quizzical look. 'You have an excellent knowledge of the coal trade, Henry, but it's largely confined to producing the coal.'

It was the first time he'd called Henry by his Christian name.

'Most of your experience has been with landsale pits selling to local markets,' Ivison continued. 'The real money in the coal trade is with the seasale pits because only they are able to supply the London and coastal markets including Europe. If you want to put your experience to good use you'll have to learn how this trade is run.

'I'm keen to learn sir.'

'Good, because our world is rapidly changing and we must change with it, something we coal fitters failed to do in the past.'

Henry looked confused. 'I'm not sure I follow you, sir.'

'Then let me explain. Nearly two hundred years ago coal fitters held a monopoly of the Newcastle coal trade. We were called Hostmen in those days, members of a guild which controlled the Corporation of the Town of Newcastle. Whoever controlled the Corporation effectively controlled the coal trade on the Tyne, thanks to a Royal Charter. The Hostmen became a tight-knit cartel and vast fortunes were made.'

'It obviously didn't last,' Henry said.

'It did for a few decades but as the coal trade grew, and with it the profits, the great coal owning families fought back.'

'In what way?'

'They formed their own cartel. The Liddels, Montagues, Claverings, Bowes, Ridleys and other members of the coal owning oligarchy got together and formed a partnership called the Grand Alliance. The "Grand Allies" as they became known soon began to dominate the trade and the Hostmen were relegated to our present status of middle-men, coal fitters acting as agents for the coal owners.'

'You don't seem to be doing too badly, sir, in spite of the changes. With respect, sir,' he added hastily.

Ivison smiled at Henry's frankness. 'I suppose so but I'm a relative pauper compared to the Hostmen of those early days. No large estate and elegant mansion which seemed to be the norm then.'

'You have a very fine house, sir. One that many would aspire to.'

'You flatter me, Henry, but I can find a better use for my money than ostentatious mansions. The coal trade must keep abreast of new developments. The future lies in mining the coal and owning the pits, especially those pits below the bridge where the new rich coal seams lie.

Henry looked astounded. 'You're planning to become a pit owner?'

'In partnership with others, but I'll still carry on as a coal fitter. Don't look so surprised, Henry. I know the cost of sinking a new pit.'

'Yes, sir, but there are other major costs – waggonways to build and maintain, horses to buy and feed, waggoners to pay and staithes to build.'

Ivison smiled. 'In business you must take a broad view and look at the long term benefits. The early pits were near the river and probably paid for the expense of the coal staithes. As the pits moved further away from the river the waggonways were essential to cope economically with the high volume.'

Henry had to agree. A coal waggon operating on poor roads required two horses and two oxen to cope with its seventeen hundredweight load. A chaldron waggon needed only one horse and driver to draw fifty-three hundredweight thanks to the efficiency of flanged wheels running on rails laid on relatively level waggonways. Also, the primitive wain roads were often impassable in the spring when coal prices were at their highest.

Ivison seemed to read Henry's mind. 'Think of it as a simple matter of costs, Henry. If a man and a horse can move fifty-three hundredweight of coal along a waggonway, a keel on the river only needs wind, tide, three keelmen and a boy to move twenty-one tons. That's why the coal staithes are built as far up river as the tide and water levels allow.'

The full economics of coal transport were now beginning to dawn on Henry, and his admiration for Mr Ivison's grasp of the subject grew.

'If we take it a stage further,' Ivison went on, 'A collier brig can transport three hundred tons with a crew of six men and two apprentices. You see, it's all about economies of scale. If the collier brigs could pass under Newcastle Bridge they'd be loading alongside the staithes at Redheugh, Dunston and Derwenthaugh. There'd be no need for keels.'

'I don't think the keelmen would stand for that,' said Henry. He knew the keelmen's fighting reputation.

Ivison agreed. 'No, but the future lies below bridge. The keelmen know it and that's why they keep rioting and damaging the staithes. But you can't stop progress.' I employ sixty keelmen and twenty boys to crew my twenty keels, Henry. Each keelboat costs one hundred and fifty pounds to build tying up three thousand pounds of capital in addition to running costs. Collier brigs cannot pass under the bridge at Newcastle but it's only a matter of time before they are loaded direct from deep water staithes below bridge.'

'You'll still need more capital to sink a new pit below bridge,' Henry insisted. He knew that the further east one travelled, the deeper the main seam ran. 'The pits will have to be sunk to six hundred feet or more and that's going to cost a pretty penny.'

Ivison nodded. 'Yes, below bridge you need steam pumps to keep the pits dry. They're fiery seams too, but the high main has the best coal and fetches the highest prices at the London Gate.'

Henry was not fully convinced. He knew that many of the pits which supplied the staithes above bridge were relatively shallow and had the advantage of free drainage. The rivers Team, Derwent and their feeder streams lay below the level of the coal seams. This allowed sloping tunnels to be dug to drain the pits without the need for expensive pumps.

'It will be hard to compete with pits that have free drainage.'

Ivison was well aware of this advantage. 'It can't last, Henry. Their pursuit of free drainage has taken their pits ten miles away from the river. The advantage of free drainage will soon be lost because of higher haulage costs.'

Henry could visualise the enormous costs involved in the upkeep of almost one hundred miles of sophisticated waggonways located above bridge and the vast army of men and horses that were employed.

'I'm beginning to see the attractions of working below bridge,' he said, 'in spite of the high costs.'

Ivison smiled. 'Russell's reputed to be making a profit of a thousand pounds a week since winning the high main at Wallsend. It's a difficult, fiery pit but he's got two fine viewers in the Buddles. Young Buddle will go far with his father's training behind him, mark my words.'

Henry knew of the Buddles by reputation. Young John Buddle was one of a rising new breed of professional viewers who would have an increasing influence on the future of the coal trade. He felt a pang of envy as he remembered his own ambitions.

Ivison looked at him and seemed to read his thoughts. 'It's high time we put your own talents to better use. I've no intention of sitting back and watching others profit from the exciting opportunities that lie ahead. The old coal owning families have made their fortunes and are now pursuing their political ambitions in London. They buy army commissions and rectories for their younger sons now and trade their heiress daughters to the Whig establishment for political power.'

Henry noted the cutting contempt in Ivison's voice. He clearly had scant respect for the new elite of Tyneside society.

'They'll want to lease their coal deposits in future; find it easier and less risky.' Ivison went on. 'You'll soon see a new breed of pit owner taking over the trade. Men who will recognise the need for capital and see that it is adequately rewarded. They'll see that their investment is properly managed by viewers with practical experience and business sense.'

He paused, looking hard at Henry. 'That's where you come in.'

Henry was taken aback. 'I'm no businessman, Mr Ivison. I think my past record proves that.'

'Rubbish! The failure in Yorkshire was not your fault, Henry. You were far too gullible, but we'll soon change that. I'm going to see that you get some proper business experience and you can start by acting as my runner from tomorrow. I need a strong pair of legs, a young pair of eyes and a quick brain. You can supply those can't you?'

Henry, dumbfounded, could only nod.

'Good, then you can take your lead from me. As my running fitter you'll meet the viewers and other coal fitters. You'll also have to learn to deal with the hard-nosed ship masters who buy the coal. A man with your experience should have ample opportunity to pick up the trade gossip on new pits and pass on the information to me. You understand, Henry?'

'Yes, Mr Ivison.' Henry's voice displayed a mixture of surprise, gratitude and excitement.

'You've got a lot to learn and must absorb things quickly.' Ivison rose and held out his hand. 'We'll start tomorrow with a visit to the coal staithes.'

Henry shook hands and, his mind still in a whirl, made to take his leave. Ivison watched his emotional confusion with quiet amusement.

'You haven't said yes to my offer, Henry.' There was a puckish look in Ivison's eye. 'And you haven't asked what I'm going to pay you.'

Henry paused in embarrassment. 'I'm sure I can trust you to be fair and generous, Mr Ivison.'

'Nonsense. You should have judged my interest and driven a hard bargain. But since you've now accepted my offer, I'll pay you twelve shillings a week, take it or leave it.'

'That's generous of you, sir.' It was more than Henry had expected.

'You'll earn it.'

'I'll do my best, Mr Ivison, rest assured of that.'

'Your best will have to be better than the one you've just shown,' Ivison grinned roguishly. 'I might have paid a pound a week if you'd pressed me. Let that be your first lesson in business.'

Henry felt elated as he stepped out onto the quayside. He heard Mr Ivison's parting instruction as the door closed behind him and smiled.

'Don't tell that brother-in-law of yours about our discussion. Leave that to me.' Henry was only too happy to oblige.

The tide was high and he could smell the sea on the cool night air. The oil lamps on the bridge cast a shimmering yellow light over the dark, swirling waters of the river. Through the masts and cordage of the clustered ships lying at the quay he could see the square, shadowy outline of St Mary's Church tower on the Gateshead bank of the river. Further downstream the ruddy glow of the furnaces at Hawks ironworks lit up the night sky and the sound of the forge presented an audible picture of toiling, sweating men churning out armaments to feed the war with revolutionary France.

Henry drew up his collar against the chill night air. His footsteps echoed down the narrow ghostly chars as he made his way home to Wall Knoll.

Suddenly, the calm and quiet of the night erupted with the bark of shouted commands and the sound of running feet echoing across the pavements.

'This way, men! They're heading for Sandgate by all accounts. Hurry and we'll cut them off.'

A group of shadowy figures came running out of Broad Chare and fanned out along the quayside. Another group appeared from Fenwick's Entry by the low crane, blocking Henry's retreat. He stepped back into the darkness of a warehouse doorway, trying to melt into the background to avoid discovery. His heart began to pound at the thought of being taken by what he presumed to be the press gang.

A cry arose from the group gathered by the low crane. He had been spotted. Three figures detached themselves and made their way cautiously towards him, their leader lifting the shutter of his lantern to light up the doorway. Henry stood rooted in its beam.

'What have we here then?' The leader spoke in a scathing, military tone.

Henry recovered his composure and a feeling of mounting indignation rose inside him. 'Can't an honest citizen walk peaceably to his home without being accosted like a common thief?' His rising anger lent authority to his voice.

The leader, observing Henry's formal mode of dress and dignified bearing, became more cautious. He did not wish to be accused of molesting a gentleman going about his lawful business.

'May I have your name, sir?' The "sir" came almost as an afterthought, a note of respect creeping in.

'Henry Standish. I'm on my way home to Wall Knoll.'

'It's a late hour for a gentleman to be out and about on his own. May I enquire what important business keeps you from your bed?'

'And on whose authority do you ask such questions?' Henry's tone was firm. 'Are you the press?'

'Good lord no, sir.' The man laughed. 'I'm the assistant captain of the watch. These are my men, and a few special constables properly sworn in,' he added.

44

Henry gave a silent sigh of relief. He could now discern the greatcoat, lantern and iron hooked stick which marked the uniform of the town watch.

'You still haven't explained why you're out at such a late hour, sir.' The watch leader's voice was polite but insistent.

'I'm returning from supper and a business discussion with Mr Ivison the coal fitter. His house is on the quayside near the Sandhill. He'll vouch for me, to be sure, if you care to enquire.' Henry decided not to mention that Ivison was his employer.

The leader seemed reassured. 'It's a little late to be disturbing him now, sir. Besides, you don't look like one of those villains we're after.'

Henry was curious. The watch did not often patrol in force and the swearing in of special constables indicated an emergency. 'Has there been some trouble?'

The leader of the watch nodded. 'Those damned keelmen have been at it again, rioting and trying to wreck the coal staithes up river. Now they're trying to get back to Sandgate. Think they'll be safe in that hell-hole of theirs.' He spat contemptuously. 'But we'll get 'em, mark my words.'

He called his men together and they moved off towards the warren of dark, seedy chares that led off Sandgate where the unruly keelmen and their families lived.

It was a relieved Henry who let himself in to the darkened house in Wall Knoll and, creeping quietly upstairs to his bedroom, slid carefully beneath the bedclothes without disturbing Mary.

In the coal fitter's house on the quayside, Ivison sat writing at a small bureau in the upstairs living room. He suddenly felt tired and his writing was becoming laboured. Pausing, he rubbed his eyes trying to ease the headache he felt coming on and irritably pushed the papers to one side.

He sat for a while staring blankly at the wall until his gaze finally focussed on the small drawer at the back of the bureau. He opened it and took out two small gilt-framed portraits. An expression of sadness crossed his face as he stood the portraits on the top of the bureau, propped up against the wall. He looked at them for a long time. One showed the face of a dark haired woman, young and beautiful; the other the freckled countenance of a boy aged about five.

A surge of memories filled his heart with a painful mixture of happiness and sorrow. Almost thirty years had passed since the smallpox had carried off his wife and son, but still the emptiness remained. The boy would have been about Henry's age had he lived, he mused. A gentle sigh escaped his lips as he carefully put the portraits back into the drawer.

CHAPTER 5

Henry arrived at the coal fitter's office on the quayside soon after dawn the next day. He had borrowed William's keys so that he could make an early start and clear his work before making the trip to the staithes with Mr Ivison. He did not wish to provide an opportunity for William, as chief clerk, to accuse him of neglecting his present duties. He was not even sure that he would still have to report to his brother-in-law, but decided not to take any chances. No doubt Mr Ivison would clarify the situation when he talked to William.

The day had dawned wet and sullen, with rain squalls scudding across the river beneath a leaden sky. Henry had almost completed his work when William arrived looking moody and suspicious. He had wanted to talk to Henry over breakfast about his meeting with Mr Ivison and Henry's early departure appeared to be a deliberate attempt to keep him in the dark. His demeanour was one of sullen resentment and jealousy.

Fortunately the early arrival of Mr Ivison pre-empted an unpleasant confrontation. William was summoned to the head fitter's office and remained closeted with Mr Ivison for what, to Henry, seemed an inordinately long time. When William finally emerged he looked angry, his expression a mixture of envy and hate. Ignoring Henry he walked past him and sat down at his own desk making a great pretence of being busy.

Soon after Mr Ivison appeared carrying a high crowned hat and wearing a long travelling cloak. 'Time we were off, Henry. Don't forget your coat.'

The use of Henry's Christian name seemed to infuriate William and he shot a glance of pure venom at the departing pair.

Henry and Mr Ivison made their way to the quayside and boarded a small open boat that was to carry them up river to the coal staithes. The boatman cast off and shooting the inshore arch of the bridge, rowed steadily upstream on the rising tide. Henry and Ivison sat silently in the stern sheets and it was not until they were well clear of the bridge that Ivison spoke.

'That brother-in-law of yours looked a little upset when I told him you were to be my runner; implied that you might not be up to it.'

'I think you may have misjudged him, sir,' Henry said loyally. 'After all, it was he who introduced me to the firm.'

'Because it never occurred to him that you might prove a threat to his own position.'

'But surely I'm not. You'll still need a chief clerk and you have a diligent one in William.'

Ivison looked exasperated. 'You're too trusting, Henry. It's time you learned to recognise people's true feelings. Your brother-in-law is jealous of your new status in the firm and jealous men are not to be trusted. It's just as well you're reporting to me from now on.'

Henry smiled his thanks but decided to ignore Ivison's warning for the present and they continued their journey in silence.

It was several minutes before Henry became aware of Mr Ivison's increasing agitation. His head twisted violently from side to side searching the windswept river. 'Strange,' he kept muttering.

'Is something wrong, sir?' Henry was puzzled.

'The keels, Henry. Where are the keels?'

Henry looked around. 'I can't see any.'

'That's just it. There should be dozens of 'em coming up on the tide to load at the staithes and look!' He waved his arm dramatically. 'Not a keel in sight.'

Henry felt a faint chill of foreboding. He suddenly remembered the watchman's words of the previous evening. Ivison's voice echoed his thoughts.

'The keelmen are striking again; they're withholding their labour and breaking their bond. I hope they don't go further than that.'

'You mean attack the staithes?'

'That's always been their tactics in the past.'

'But why?' Henry couldn't see any purpose in the keelmen destroying the staithes. They'd be destroying their own livelihood.

'It's all to do with the larger staithes below bridge,' Ivison explained. 'That and the use of spouts. Some owners want to load the collier brigs at their deep water staithes using large spouts to feed the coal directly into the ship's hold. 'It's logical' he added, 'saves money by dispensing with keels. But that means no work for keelmen and they won't accept that without a fight. They're a tough breed of men, as you know, and are not to be trifled with.'

Henry sympathised with the keelmen and appreciated their outrage. But in the long term he knew they were fighting a lost cause and the knowledge saddened him. 'They can't stop progress.'

'No,' Ivison agreed, 'but they can and will delay it.'

The river banks above the bridge at Newcastle were crowded with coal staithes. They were huge timber structures built out into the river to allow the keels to moor and load alongside. Coal could also be stored on the upper and lower decks of the staithes. On the south of the river they occupied almost every available site between Redheugh and the point where the river Derwent joined the Tyne.

The boat continued its way past the island of King's Meadows with its lush, flat fields. On the opposite bank the giant staithes at Dunston looked strangely forlorn without the busy cluster of keels alongside.

The river now became wider and more exposed to the gusting wind which sent showers of fine spray over the occupants of the boat. Ahead, they could now see their destination, the great staithes of Derwenthaugh built at the confluence of the rivers Tyne and Derwent and lining the banks of both rivers. The massive wooden structures would normally be crowded with scores of keels, each loading their measure of twenty-one tons before sailing on the ebb tide down to the collier brigs lying at Shields. Today they were deserted, creating an air of abandonment.

The boatman skilfully brought the boat alongside the ladder that led to the deck at the top of the staithe. The river slapped and echoed against the latticework of giant wooden beams that supported the deck structure above.

Henry followed Ivison up the ladder and when he reached the top he could only stand and marvel at the sheer size and sophistication of the complex. There were two adjoining staithes, the larger stretching along the bank of the Tyne for three hundred and ninety yards, the smaller running along the Derwent River for some three hundred and sixty yards. There were berths for twenty-six keels at the Tyne staithes and twenty-four on the Derwent.

The horse drawn chaldron waggons arrived at the staithes from pits up to ten miles distant in the high ground to the south. The waggons were led across the connecting bridges to the staithes and positioned over the square openings that led to the spouts. The bolt was then drawn at the base of the chaldron waggon sending fifty-three hundredweights of coal pouring down the spout into the waiting keel below. In the absence of keels, as on this day, the coal was directed into a large covered storage shed where it could be transhipped by a smaller spout into the keels at a later date.

Ivison led Henry around the staithes introducing him to the staithesman in charge and explaining the various procedures.

'It's important to see that the coal is unloaded as gently as possible. Large coal fetches the best price but every time you load or unload, the pieces get smaller. Coals are like fine wines, Henry. They don't travel well and need careful handling.'

Henry noted the large storage sheds and remarked on them to Mr Ivison. He knew that coal deteriorated rapidly if stored in the open, but these sheds could hold upwards of sixty thousand tons.

'It may seem a lot of storage space and unnecessary handling,' explained Ivison, 'but we're totally dependent on the tides and the weather. A keel can only make one trip on each tide and bad weather often means a shortage of colliers at Shields. We need storage to smooth out the supply without constantly shutting down the pits.'

Henry watched a waggon being unloaded and noted that a series of hinged trap doors built into the spout allowed the staithesman to control the coal's speed of descent to reduce breakage. He could see why Pontop coal brought high prices at the London Gate.

Henry was so engrossed in the workings of the spouts that it was some time before he noted the build-up of men standing idly around the perimeter of the staithes. Some carried heavy looking cudgels. He spoke to the staithesman. 'Are they your men?'

The reply was scathing. 'Not likely. They're a bunch of rascals sworn in as special constables by the owners. Supposed to protect the staithes from the keelmen.'

'Expecting trouble then?'

'Don't know. Never know what to expect from keelmen. I've heard they've been up to Crowley's iron works at Swalwell but Crowley's crew would have no truck with 'em.'

Henry was relieved. "Crowley's crew," as the well organised iron workers were called, ranked close to the keelmen for unruliness and intransigence. He was relieved that they would not be joining the keelmen's fight.

At that moment a small detachment of sweating militiamen arrived in some haste and lined up along the deck of the staithe. The captain in charge spoke animatedly with Mr Ivison. Henry could feel the tension rising as the staithesmen worked on, glancing nervously over their shoulders.

Suddenly a shout went up from the constables on the bank. 'It's the keelmen!'

Henry could see a large body of men wearing blue jackets making their way along the river bank. They moved fast, fanning out to encircle the staithes, halting the chauldron waggons by pulling the bolts and spilling the coal on the rails to block the waggonways. Men with axes began hacking at the wooden bridges linking the staithes to the river bank.

The militia captain spurred his horse forward to face the keelmen, his cheeks flushed with anger. 'I order you to disperse, at once!' There was a quiver of desperation in his voice. The riot act had been read out at Swalwell and soon a decision would have to be made about what action to take.

The keelmen were clearly in no mood to obey and carried on hacking at the bridge supports. A heavy squall of rain drenched the protagonists but did not dampen the keelmen's ardour. Out of the murky waters of the river, unnoticed by those on the staithes, the dark shapes of two keels crowded with keelmen appeared heading swiftly under billowing square sails for the staithes. It was a classic ambush and the keels were alongside disgorging fighting keelmen before those on the deck realised what was happening.

The fighting was vicious and bloody, no quarter being asked or given. The keelmen were well armed with staves, iron bars, axes and a few even carried navy issue cutlasses, souvenirs of past impressments.

The special constables quickly lost their stomach for the fight and the encircled militiamen were being hard pressed. Their officer's horses were of little use on the cramped staithes and the keelmen had long since developed cruel ways to disable them. At the very point of defeat a distant bugle call brought a temporary halt to the fighting. A large detachment of mounted cavalry could be seen bearing down on the staithes at a steady, implacable trot with sabres ominously drawn.

The keelmen quickly realised the hopelessness of their position and began to retreat to the keels still alongside. Three more keels stood off a little way from the staithe as if uncertain whether they should also come alongside.

The sight of the cavalry had given the special constables a new-found courage to rejoin the fight. The keelmen were slowly forced back and their retreat was in danger of becoming a rout when a huge red-bearded keelman hauled himself on to the deck at the far end of the staithe. He was quickly followed by a dozen others, and led a ferocious charge against the constables and militia. His red hair and beard topped an eighteen stone muscular frame and towered above the others involved in the melee. Wielding a heavy stave, he fought his way to a group of keelmen who had been cut off from the main body and skilfully cleared a path for an orderly retreat to the keels below.

The frustrated militia captain led one last charge but it was too late. He could only wave his sabre angrily at the departing keelmen. But at this point a sudden disturbance further down the staithe caught his attention. A wounded keelman had dragged himself to the edge of the deck and was preparing to lower himself into the water below. The captain responded quickly.

'Stop him!'

Only the keelman's hands were visible holding on to the deck. A sergeant moved to stand on one hand; a heavy constable, following suit, placed his weight on the other.

'Hold him!' The captain rushed across and, bracing himself on the edge of the deck, raised his sabre high above his head. The swish of the blade was following by a piercing scream. Blood spurted over the sergeant's boots from the severed hand which now lay limp and bleeding on the deck. The constable stepped back in surprise and the keelman slipped over the side, screaming again as he hit the water below.

Henry and Ivison, who were standing nearby, witnessed the cruel act with horror and disgust. A shocked silence followed before the captain skewered the severed hand on the tip of his sabre and flicked it into the river.

'He won't be sailing keels for a while.' There was a mad gleam in the captain's eyes and a malicious note of satisfaction in his voice.

Ivison, recovering from his shock, berated the captain with rising fury. 'You're a disgrace to your regiment, sir! I'll see that your commanding officer is informed about this barbaric act.'

At that point he was interrupted by a shout from behind. Turning, he saw the giant, red-bearded keelmen leader lifting an empty chauldron waggon clear of the wooden rails. With the fierce MacGregor war cry, "Ard-Choille!" the keelman heaved the waggon across the deck, pushing it in front of him to form a huge battering ram which headed straight towards the captain. The waggon caught the officer square on the chest crushing his ribs and carrying him over the side into the river.

In the confusion Henry saw Ivison, trying to avoid the waggon, lose his footing on the blood spattered deck. Unable to regain his balance, he toppled slowly over the edge of the staithe into the river.

Henry watched in horror then, noting the spot in the water where Ivison had disappeared, jumped in after him.

The water was cold and the shock took his breath away. He could see no sign of Ivison and dived again, swimming through the murky water and groping frantically at every shadow. His hand suddenly touched something solid and he could sense the feel of wool. Tightening his grip he surfaced and saw he was holding the black-cloaked form of Mr Ivison who started gasping and choking for air.

'Are you injured, sir?' Henry was concerned that he might have hit the outward sloping piles of the staithes.

'I don't think so,' came the spluttering reply.

'Let me get this cloak unfastened. It'll drag us down otherwise.'

Henry unfastened the neck clasp and watched the half submerged cloak float away. 'Can you swim, sir?'

'No, dammit! Left it a bit late haven't I.'

Henry could only smile and admire Ivison's courage. 'Turn on your back,' he ordered. Just let your body float. I'm going to try and tow you to the bank.'

The tide was now ebbing fast and the wind and current was taking them into mid-stream. A black squall cloud reduced visibility and rising wavelets constantly hid the shore from view.

Henry kept up a call for help but after five minutes he began to despair. His body felt numb with cold and his swimming became laboured. He received no response to his repeated enquiries to Ivison and tried desperately to keep the older man's face clear of the water.

Suddenly, out of the murk, a large dark mass appeared and quickly bore down on them. Henry felt Ivison's body being torn upwards out of his grip and then strong arms reaching under his own armpits, lifting him clear of the water with effortless ease. He lay gasping on the deck of the keel staring up at a pair of bright blue eyes behind a bushy ginger beard.

The keelmen's leader smiled down at him. 'And how are you, bonny lad. A bad day to be going swimming.' At that point Henry sighed and passed out.

It was some time before he regained full consciousness. When his head finally cleared he saw he was lying in the stern of the keel next to the giant ginger-bearded keelman who was steering the keel sitting on the deck with his feet dangling down the small hatch. Mr Ivison sat on the other side of the deck wearing a borrowed oilskin and appeared to have recovered from his ordeal.

The keelman winked at Ivison, 'Not much stamina in the young 'uns these days. 'Reckon a few weeks as a keel bully in my crew would do 'im the world of good.' Ivison smiled back weakly, but remained silent.

Henry was recovering fast. 'I think we owe our lives to you, Mr...?'

'Rory MacGregor.' The keelman smiled and proffered a hand that dwarfed Henry's in a strong, friendly handshake.

Henry smiled back, 'Henry Standish, and this is my employer Mr Ivison.'

'Ivison and Burdon, the coal fitters?' Rory MacGregor looked surprised, but not displeased. 'Your servant, sir,' he touched his forelock in a gesture that was more teasing than mocking. 'We did your work today, Mr Ivison, if not your bidding. It's a coal fitters' fight as much as a keelman's.'

Ivison responded angrily, 'I don't condone violence, MacGregor.'

'You don't expect us to sit back and watch our livelihood disappear?'

'No, but there are other ways.'

'Not if the coal owners won't listen to our grievances and the courts won't support us. As long as you coal fitters continue to sit on the fence, there is no other way.'

'That's not true. We've tried to argue your case with the coal owners and explain the hardships of unemployment. But taking matters into your own hands like this doesn't help.'

'As long as the fitters own the keels and the keelmen are bonded to the fitters, the coal owners will do as they please. It suits them to have a soft buffer like a coal fitter between them and us,' his voice was full of sarcasm and contempt. 'But it won't work. There'll be other days like today.'

Henry intervened, trying to cool feelings that were clearly irreconcilable.

'At least you didn't allow your grievances to interfere with saving our lives. For that, Mr MacGregor, we are grateful.'

MacGregor grinned, his good humour returning. 'Your employer owes his life to you,' he said dismissively. 'He wouldn't have survived for so long in the water without your help. As for me, I just happened to be passing,' he lied. 'You're also witness to that captain's brutality. There was no need for that.'

'On that point we're agreed,' said Ivison. 'I fully intend to report his appalling behaviour to the authorities.'

'He'll probably receive a commendation.' Posthumously, I hope, Rory added under his breath.

Henry became curious as he remembered the culmination of the fighting on the staithes. 'That war cry; was it Gaelic?'

'Aye, 'twas. Ard-Choille! The war cry of the Clan MacGregor.' There was a fierce pride in Rory Macgregor's voice.

Henry remembered that virtually all keelmen were of Scottish descent. Most were from the Border country but many Highlanders had drifted south to avoid the harsh persecution which followed the forty-five rising. It was easy to see why the authorities looked upon this tough and tightly knit community with a mixture of awe and trepidation.

With a favourable tide beneath them and a brisk wind in their favour, the keel quickly reached the bridge at Newcastle. It passed along the clutter of ships moored at the quayside before nosing quietly on to the soft mud of the Sandgate Shore at a point known as the Swirle, where a small stream flowed into the river.

Henry and Ivison disembarked and led by Rory MacGregor made their way over the soft ground and into the streets of Sandgate, the densely populated stronghold of the keelmen.

'You'll be safe until you reach the quayside. No one in Sandgate will lay a finger on the friends of Rory MacGregor; but I can't say the same for the rest of the town.' A soft chuckle emerged from the red bearded face and he held out his hand.

There was a look of respect in Ivison's eyes as he returned the handshake. 'It's a pity we can't put your talents to better use, Mr MacGregor.'

'But they are, Mr Ivison. Depends which side of the fence you're on.' There was a teasing innuendo in his words which was not lost on Ivison.

Henry felt the firm yet strangely gentle grip of Rory's huge bear like hand. There was an uncanny and mutual flow of empathy between the two men as if an indefinable, yet unbreakable, bond had just been cemented.

'Take care of yourself, bonny lad.'

'And you too, Rory MacGregor.'

CHAPTER 6

The busy months that followed placed heavy demands on Henry's time and energy. His new duties as Ivison's running fitter meant constant travel between the office on the quayside and the staithes to supervise loading and to co-ordinate the keel movements to match the shipping requirements at Shields.

It was long and arduous work but he loved the freedom of movement and the access it gave him to the close-knit group of businessmen who ran the coal trade. His colliery experience was proving useful and his agile, enquiring mind made him a quick learner. He soon developed a competence and even a flair for the wheeling and dealing that formed part of his daily routine and at times his astuteness astounded Ivison. He had good cause to be pleased with the efforts of his protégé which had contributed to the firm's steadily rising profits.

William's reaction remained sullen and resentful and although he tried to hide his pique beneath a veneer of forced politeness, it was all too obvious to Henry. It was even more apparent to Ivison, who determined to keep a careful eye on his chief clerk.

Mark was now attending the charity school at All Saints' Church and proudly wore his free issue blue coat, leather breeches, shirt and bands as well as his cap which perched jauntily on the back of his head. As Henry had suspected, his son was not being stretched. The school was partly run on the monitorial system and the master quickly realised that Mark's talents could be put to good use teaching the other children who were often a good deal older than Mark.

This did not please Henry but he felt there was little he could do at such an early stage. He resolved to keep a close watch on the situation and meanwhile continued to tutor Mark at home in the evenings.

Mark's level of learning was ahead of his age and this created problems for him at school. He became the focus for bullying by the older boys and the butt for taunts from the younger ones. All this he bore with fortitude, remarkable for his age, treating his tormentors with contempt and fighting back aggressively when the occasion demanded. As a result he often took some severe beatings.

His worst persecutors were some of the sons of keelmen's widows who attended the school. Prominent among these was a boy called Colin MacGregor, the nephew of the keelmen's leader. Although only two years Mark's senior he had the physique and strength of a much older boy. Even the thirteen year-olds in their final year at school kept a safe distance from this wild and unpredictable boy who attracted a strong following.

At first, Mark tried to ignore Colin and keep out of his way. This strategy worked during lessons but proved disastrous at playtime and after school. Colin for his part could not understand why Mark did not lie down and succumb like all the others. Whilst he held a grudging admiration for the smaller boy he was determined to exert his dominance. After all, he reasoned, his reputation and tough fighting image would suffer if he allowed Mark to continue to defy him.

As a consequence, Mark took many a beating when a simple submission might have avoided it. And yet, in some strange way, Colin could not bring himself to inflict the maximum pain and damage on Mark, always pulling his punches at the critical moment and allowing his victim to walk away.

This state of affairs might have lasted indefinitely had it not been for an event that would profoundly affect their future relationship.

There were four Church charity schools in Newcastle. They were all run on similar lines to All Saints', each attended by some two score boys with two schools, St Nicholas and All Saints' also admitting girls. There had always been some rivalry between the schools and since young Colin MacGregor had arrived at All Saints' the rivalry between them and their nearest neighbour, St Nicholas School, had developed into something of a feud. This was to have important repercussions for Colin and for Mark.

All Saints' school was situated in the Manors and the girls occupied a house near the entrance to the Surgeons' Hall. Gory tales abounded of bodies of dead felons being delivered to the surgeons for dissection after being publicly hanged on the town moor scaffold. The girls viewed the Surgeon' Hall with a mixture of morbid fascination and abject terror; a place to be avoided.

Colin MacGregor had a pretty younger sister called Ann who also attended All Saints' School. On leaving the classroom one evening to return home she found herself suddenly surrounded by a group of grey-uniformed boys from St Nicholas School. They pushed her, screaming and struggling, inside the entrance to the nearby Surgeons' Hall. She tried desperately to get away but the jeering group of boys kept pushing her back inside, slamming the entrance door in her face. It was somewhat ironic that Mark, who was taking a roundabout route home to avoid another confrontation with her brother, Colin, happened to be in the vicinity and hearing her hysterical cries of distress rushed to her aid.

Mark broke through the crowd of boys blocking the entrance and opening the door, pulled the sobbing girl clear. He was immediately set upon by the frenzied boys from St Nicholas and, though bravely fighting back, was punched and kicked to the ground.

Suddenly, the beating stopped and the boys froze to the sound of a terrifying cry.

'Ard-Choille!'

It was Colin MacGregor, his face contorted with a fury that no boy had ever seen before. Their blood ran cold as they withered beneath his onslaught then, as if their thoughts were synchronised, they all turned tail and fled.

Mark lay half-conscious in a pool of blood with one eye turning purple and the other swelling rapidly. The look on Colin's face had turned to concern as he helped Mark to his feet and began half carrying him down the steep streets towards Sandgate. His sister followed carrying their school satchels.

Mrs MacGregor stood at the door of her house in the narrow char leading off Sandgate, shocked at the sight of the bruised and bloodied boy leaning on the shoulder of her son.

'Go and fetch your Uncle Rory, Colin. Hurry, now!'

She scooped up Mark and, taking him inside the house, laid him gently on a bed in the corner of the living room. His last recollection, before fainting with exhaustion, was of a pair of smiling blue eyes belonging to a giant of a man with a rambling red beard. The wheel of fortune had turned, bridging a generation gap.

*****

59

After the keelmen riots in July, the coal trade had settled down to an uneasy truce which was occasionally broken by sporadic, but minor, outbreaks of violence.

The aftermath of the battle at the staithes resulted in eight keelmen being arrested and committed to Newgate Jail. The authorities, worried about a possible rescue attempt by the unpredictable keelmen, later sent them under mounted guard to Durham Jail.

Rory MacGregor was now a marked man but the close knit society of the keelmen ensured that their leader had a safe haven in Sandgate. The authorities were always wary of entering the warren-like maze of narrow alleyways to fight the keelmen on their own ground. Past experience had shown that the hunters often became the hunted after they had been lured into a well organised ambush in one of these narrow streets. At a pre-arranged signal, men, women and children would jump out of hiding and bring down a barrage of missiles on the unsuspecting constables or press-gang. Anyone caught in these attacks would be severely beaten before being subjected to public ridicule and humiliation. The men would be marched through Sandgate with their jackets turned inside out whilst their officers would be strapped to a long pole to be daubed with dirt and refuse as they were carried through the streets.

Whilst Rory felt safe and confident within his Sandgate citadel, he was careful not to expose himself outside its protective environs. Each sortie into the hostile world outside had to be carefully planned and usually executed at night, often by river. For communications Colin was a trusted go between.

Henry's new-found peace of mind was now about to receive an unexpected jolt which would trigger far-reaching consequences. Returning to the office on the quayside one evening, he found a sturdy young boy waiting for him.

'Mr Henry Standish?'

'Yes'.

The boy looked relieved. 'My name is Colin MacGregor, sir. I have a message from my Uncle Rory.

Henry's surprise turned first to pleasure at the memory of the giant Scot and then to concern.

'He's not been taken, has he?'

'No, sir. He'd like you to come to our house in Sandgate. I'll show you where it is.'

Colin led the way, explaining the reason for the summons as he went and the events leading up to Mark's injuries. Shock and concern knotted Henry's stomach and he quickened his pace so that Colin had to run to keep up.

Arriving at a small house in the narrow, dirty alleyway, Colin knocked on the door.

'Who's there?' The voice inside was filled with caution and suspicion.

'It's Colin, mam. I've brought Mr Standish.'

The door opened and they went inside.

Mark was sitting up on the bed and his bruised and battered face lit up with a smile at the sight of his father. 'Hello dad.'

Henry sat on the bed and put his arm around his son. The instinctive rebuke for his son's foolish bravery died in his throat and he could only hug him with relief. 'Got yourself in a right old mess, eh?' was all he could say.

'You ought to be proud of him.'

Henry turned with a start at the distinctive sound of the booming voice behind him. 'Rory MacGregor! It's good to see you safe and well.' Again he experienced the strange feeling of empathy which he had sensed at their first meeting

He rose and took the big man's hand, as memories of the battle at the staithes came flooding back.

'Thought you'd seen the last of me, eh, bonny lad?'

'Well, I didn't expect to see you parading the streets with the town watch and militia charged to keep a look-out for you.'

'Och, they're easy to dodge. My own spies keep me well posted.'

Henry admired the sheer audacity of the man and warmed to him even more.

'You'd better take this intrepid young warrior of yours home, Henry Standish. He fights like a true MacGregor.' He laughed and his voice took on an outrageously coquettish tone. 'Mind you, when I think of some of the past rogues in the MacGregor clan I wouldn't be surprised to find a drop of MacGregor blood in every English man and woman within a hundred miles of the border.' He winked wickedly at Colin's mother, who blushed with embarrassment.

Colin accompanied Henry and Mark as far as the Milk Market and stood waving as they made their way back inside the town wall through the narrow, congested Sand Gate. From that day on a bond, as strong as kinship, gradually developed between the two families. The feud between the two boys stopped and they became firm friends.

Henry continued to apply himself diligently to learning his new trade, punishing himself mercilessly with hard work and long hours. Some of the leading colliery viewers were now beginning to take notice and in his dealings with ships' masters he was regarded as a tough but scrupulously honest negotiator.

On his visits to the Exchange with Mr Ivison he was treated with respect by the other notables of the trade, a point that did not pass unobserved by his employer. One luminary was overheard to remark that 'Ivison is singularly fortunate in his choice of new running fitter,' which brought a contented smile to Ivison's face as he moved on.

As for Henry, he loved the cut and thrust of the coal trade and seemed unaware of his growing reputation. He appeared equally unconscious of the effect that his new found status was having on his brother-in-law, although this had been noted by Ivison.

The coolness displayed by William towards Henry in the office also now extended to his attitude at home. Henry was always eager to discuss the day's business after supper but William invariably retreated to his study saying he had too much to do.

Mary had noticed the growing estrangement in the men's relationship and it made her feel uneasy. When she raised the matter with Henry, he merely shrugged it off.

'It's just his manner. He means well, but his pride is a little hurt. He'll get over it.' He squeezed her hand comfortingly.

'I'm not so sure, Henry. You're too trusting.'

'But he's been so helpful to us. He gave us a roof over our heads and without his introduction I wouldn't have my present position. He even helped to find a school place for Mark.'

'Only because Ellen forced him. He wouldn't have lifted a finger otherwise.'

'I think you are being a little unfair, Mary.' His voice was gently chiding.

'There you go again!' Her exasperation was clear. 'You think there's good in everyone; that they all share your fine ideals. But you're wrong, Henry, and one day you'll live to regret it.'

The force of her attack stung him and he was taken aback by the fervour she displayed. He stood bewildered, not quite knowing what to say next.

'Aren't you happy here, living with your sister?'

'I don't know. It's not what I want.'

'Don't you get on with Ellen?'

'Of course I do, but it's her house, not mine. She's a good woman and I love her; she understands and tries to help but...,' her voice trailed off to a confused silence.

It was true; Ellen did try to help and understood the anguish going on in her younger sister's mind. She'd even remonstrated with William, telling him not to behave so childishly, but he simply ignored her pleas and carried on as before. Ellen could only respond by involving her sister in the running of the house as an equal, taking her on shopping trips and introducing her to the shops and markets of the town.

Mary had grown to love Newcastle and looked forward to the almost daily excursions through its bustling streets. The town always seemed crammed with a vast horde of citizens and visitors from the large hinterland which it served. In daytime the streets were busy, noisy, thronged and gay with the bright dresses of the ladies contrasting with the sober-suited elegance of their gentlemen escorts.

To Mary, Newcastle was an exciting, cosmopolitan metropolis and she never tired of her shopping expeditions with Ellen. It also meant that for a short time the unhappy atmosphere which unsettled her at the house in Wall Knoll could be forgotten.

She also loved the markets which abounded in the town. Watching the carts of the country folk bringing their produce to market brought back memories of her own childhood. There were markets galore in Newcastle but Mary's favourite was the daily market held in the

Sandhill where vegetables were supplied from the gardens of the neighbouring villages. A regular supply of rabbits came from the warrens on the sea coast as far north as Holy Island. Food was indeed plentiful if you had money to buy it. But that was the rub; in times of dearth, few people had. Prices would rise to levels the masses could not afford, often with calamitous results, as events were soon to prove.

Henry approved of Mary's daily shopping excursions despite the fact there was often little money to justify them. When Mary expressed her own doubts he encouraged her, saying the exercise and fresh air would at least benefit her health. He was aware that the days he found her most depressed when he returned from work were those she had spent cooped up inside the house.

Henry had little time for relaxation and what spare moments he could find were spent coaching Mark. Deep down he knew the situation was unsatisfactory and would not improve. Mary's excursions were palliative and the only cure would be to buy or rent a house of their own. This he would do as soon as he could afford the expense; in the meantime, they would have to make do. After all, he consoled himself, they were better off than most.

Autumn turned into a cold, wet winter. There were freezing mists on the river and the damp, cold air ate into Henry's bones during the interminable boat journeys to the staithes. It seemed a long time before spring came and even then the weather remained wet and stormy.

Ivison could detect the growing strain in Henry's home life and this concerned him. After giving the matter some thought, he decided on a policy of discreet intervention, for he found himself growing increasingly fond of Henry. He was delighted that the talent and ability for the coal trade, which he had sensed were lying dormant in Henry in the early weeks of his employment, were now beginning to flourish.

Having got to know the man, he now had a growing desire to know his family. It was as if a strange, nostalgic yearning for family life had been reawakened inside him, lending a new sense of purpose to his existence. When he took out the gilt-framed portraits of his dead family the pain and emptiness seemed less and in the image of his young son he now saw a likeness to the man in Henry.

After a disappointing spring the weather continued its erratic and unseasonable pattern into the summer. As the days lengthened the farmers' concern for their crops increased and the population at large became more fractious.

At the end of a particularly frustrating day Henry returned to the office on the quayside late one evening to be met by an unusually cheerful Mr Ivison.

'You look out of sorts, Henry. I don't often say this to my employees, but I think you're working too hard.'

'It's just this awful weather, sir. So unseasonable, it makes everyone feel depressed.'

'I have noticed. What with the weather, the war, the price of bread, people have little to smile about. Perhaps it's time I did something about it.' He watched with quiet amusement the puzzled expression spreading over Henry's face.

'I don't quite understand you, Mr Ivison.'

'Of course you don't. I'm planning a surprise.' He was beginning to enjoy himself as he watched Henry's bafflement increase.

'May I ask what kind of surprise?'

'It's my birthday tomorrow; something I don't normally regard as anything special, living alone as I do. I shall be sixty,' he added.

Henry had never discussed personal matters with his employer before and could only offer his congratulations in a sincere but stilted manner.

Sensing Henry's discomfiture and wishing to put him at ease, Ivison quickly went on to explain his surprise.

'I want you and your family to share my birthday with me tomorrow evening. I've booked a box at the Theatre Royal and afterwards we shall have supper together.'

Henry was dumbfounded.

'Oh, and the invitation includes your brother-in-law and his wife,' Ivison added quickly. He was anxious not to widen the rift even if it meant putting up with the company of his pompous social climbing chief clerk.

To everyone's surprise the evening turned out to be an unqualified success, the excitement and glamour of the theatre quickly overcoming any inhibitions or embarrassment.

They entered the theatre by the main door on Mosley Street, a privilege afforded only to those occupying boxes. Access to the pit and gallery was by doors at the side and rear of the building and was altogether less imposing.

The play was popular and the theatre was packed with over thirteen hundred brightly dressed citizen's intent on enjoying themselves. Mary's eyes glistened with happiness and excitement as she sat between Henry and Mr Ivison looking out on the sea of eager faces in the pit below. When the curtain rose and the play began she hung on every word and applauded at the end until the stinging in her palms forced her to stop.

It was an evening to remember and one enjoyed by all. Even William's constant and portentous utterances on the play's message were absorbed with good humour and finally deflated by a slightly exasperated Mr Ivison.

'It was only a farce, William.' Then, to soften the flow he added 'but a damned good one at that.' They all laughed, including William who was suitably mollified by being addressed by his Christian name for the first time.

Afterwards they returned to the house on the quayside where Ivison's housekeeper had prepared a sumptuous supper which was accompanied by fine wines, excellent port and convivial conversation.

The final surprise of the evening was the arrival of sedan chairs, specially ordered by Ivison, to take his birthday guests home. With Mark fast asleep on his mother's lap, the party were transported in style, by the light of flaming torches carried by the escorting bearers, to the house in Wall Knoll.

CHAPTER 7

Mark's new found friendship with Colin MacGregor blossomed and the two boys soon became inseparable companions. As a consequence, the summer months brought a new and exciting dimension into Mark's life as Colin introduced him to the many boyish delights of Newcastle. The friendship also opened up a Pandora's Box of adventure which had been somewhat lacking in his young life. He no longer dashed straight home after school to continue with his studies but sought the joys of normal boyhood pursuits in the company of Colin.

They visited Sandgate Shore and the North Shore where he helped to scrape and clean the bottoms of beached keels and wherries. With Colin's help, he mastered the art of rowing and the intricacies of stern sculling. He learnt to tie reef knots, bowlines and clove hitches with his eyes closed as all good keelmen could.

There were long excursions through Pandon Dene where they followed the burn past the humming water-mills with their dripping wheels turning in the stream. Then on through the steep luxuriant banks and sylvan glades of the valley until they reached the quiet waters of the large millpond above Barrass Bridge. Here, in the rustic shade of the tree-lined pool, they fished and swam, or sailed their home-made boats to re-enact Admiral Howe's famous victory over the French on the "glorious first of June". Colin would be Black Dick Howe, as he was known, and Mark would play the part of Northumberland's emerging new hero, Captain Collingwood. This bewitching paradise lay less than half a mile outside the town walls and there were as many equally enchanting areas within. For Mark, at least, all this led to a growing sense of belonging and a feeling of contentment he had never known before.

There were evenings when the two boys had to forego their play when school tasks or homework had to be done. Mark took to returning home with Colin and they worked together at the parlour table in the small, neatly kept house in Sandgate. On some occasions, Rory MacGregor would leave the haven of his safe house to join them, often regaling the boys with outlandish but exciting accounts of Clan

MacGregor history, or, as Colin's mother sometimes put it, exaggerated folk law.

Rory purported to be related to the clan chiefs and his stories of past clan heroes enthralled Mark. He learned that the clan had been proscribed by King James VI and its members treated as outlaws until 1775. Small wonder, Mark thought, that Rory was in his element leading the tough and equally law scorning keelmen. He sat with rapt attention listening to the tales of the clan's famous freebooter, Rob Roy MacGregor.

'Are you related to Rob Roy?' Mark asked.

Rory shook his head sadly. 'Only in fighting spirit, bonny lad.' He pondered for a moment then went on. 'I'd be inclined to think I've a closer kinship to another clan rascal and rake, Peter Roy MacGregor. It's the way the women are attracted to me, ye ken.' He paused trying to keep a straight face. 'But there's no way an ugly brute like him could sire such a handsome fella like me, now is there?' A spreading grin was soon stifled by a well-aimed dishcloth from Colin's mother which caught him squarely in the face.

Mark's frequent late arrival home was beginning to disturb Henry and Mary. In Henry's case his disquiet was fanned by the nagging feeling that Mark preferred the company of the MacGregors and the excitement of Rory's stories to the dull atmosphere at Wall Knoll. This might change when they lived in their own house, but he wanted to put his mind at rest now. He decided he would visit Sandgate and talk to Rory.

The meeting was friendly but somehow did little to resolve matters. Henry had the distinct feeling that Rory understood the position better than he did himself; as if he were silently trying to tell him something.

Henry didn't wish to offend Rory but he felt he had to make a point. 'I don't mind Mark coming here provided he doesn't impose on you or neglect his studies.'

'Och, he's no trouble and he certainly doesn't neglect his homework. He's a good influence on Colin in that respect.'

'Yes, but I usually set him some extra tasks at home - that is, when he is at home.' Henry wanted to make his point.

'But most nights they're out playing - it's what boys do best in the summer.' There was a gentle, chiding note in Rory's voice.

'Not at the expense of his education.' On this Henry was adamant.

Rory shook his head sadly. 'If ye deny the laddie a proper childhood, he'll no' grow into a proper man. There'll be no laughter in his heart and no contentment in his soul.'

The two men looked at each other and understood. Henry felt no resentment towards Rory, only a feeling of inadequacy in himself. Rory had shrewdly put his finger on the problem and wanted to help. It was an offer Henry was pleased to accept.

It was this unspoken pact that brought the men closer together, and their meetings became more frequent as the summer wore on.

The 8th August 1795 was a date that young Mark would always remember. The town was in a festive mood, for not only was it a Saturday, but there was also to be a public hanging on the Town Moor.

Mark knew that his father did not approve of public hangings and frowned upon those who took a ghoulish delight in watching such spectacles. He decided, therefore, not to seek permission to accompany Colin to see the execution, knowing his father would refuse his request. By not asking he would avoid the dilemma of wilful disobedience that he knew would arise.

Rory on his part had no such qualms for his nephew. Life was cheap as far as the masses of the poor were concerned and with some two hundred capital offences on the statute book this attitude was not surprising. Rory saw no reason, therefore, to protect children from facing up to the sight of death. Whilst he personally deplored public executions, it was because they were degrading to his class and failed in their intended purpose, which was to deter. He also found them boring.

The two boys made their way to the upper part of the town and into the packed mass of people in the Flesh Market where progress was slowed by the carts and market stalls. They carried on into the broad expanse of the Bigg Market, past the fast emptying hostelries which swelled the tide of humanity, all heading for the hanging.

By the time they reached the massive stone edifice of Newgate and the adjoining prison the movement of the crowd had almost stopped as they slowly funnelled through the narrow gate. Once through they spread out climbing the slope of Gallowgate towards the growing mass of people surrounding the gallows. The excitement of the large crowd had been whetted by the fact that there hadn't been an execution since the double hanging at Westgate exactly three years ago.

The boys squeezed their way to the front of the crowd and managed to secure a good vantage point. Soon the increasing roar of the crowd from the direction of the prison indicated that the prisoner was on his way and the boys craned forward to get a better view.

The prisoner, Thomas Nicholson, sat in the prison cart with his hands tied behind his back and accompanied by his guards and town officials. He had been convicted of the murder of Thomas Purvis, who he had beaten to death after an altercation at the Newcastle races. He had compounded his crime by returning afterwards and jumping on the body of his victim. The crowd was not sympathetic.

A large group of pitmen standing at the front of the crowd began to hurl curses and insults.

'Serves 'im right!'

Purvis had been with a party of miners on the day he met his death. There was no compassion in their hearts.

'Make him dance, Hangman. A clean break's too good for him!'

A raucous peel of laughter rang out followed by more insults. Like many of the onlookers, the pitmen had been drinking.

The crowd hushed as the noose was placed round Nicholson's neck. Colin's eyes were wide with excitement but Mark's were now shut tight. A mighty roar from the crowd made him open them and he saw the body convulse before swinging, still and lifeless, the head twisted grotesquely skywards.

After a suitable time had elapsed, Nicholson was pronounced dead and taken down. His body was removed to the Surgeons' Hall for dissection and the crowd began to disperse.

Mark felt sick but Colin was shouting excitedly and tugging at his arm. 'Come on! Rory wants some wood chips for his toothache.'

He dragged his reluctant friend towards the crowd of onlookers who had descended on the gallows wielding knives and other sharp instruments and tearing splinters of wood from the gibbet. Colin rushed to join them. 'Uncle Rory says it cures the toothache.' His knife cut a large splinter.

It was a popular myth that chewing wood chips from a gallows could cure toothache, and tradition lingered strong in Newcastle.

Henry's closer relationships with Ivison and Rory began to crystallize his thinking on social and political matters. Rory was a confirmed radical who believed that wealth and power lay in the hands of a small, corrupt and incompetent oligarchy. He felt there was something evil and intrinsically wrong with a society that tolerated poverty when it had the means to abolish it. Such a society should be changed, and if necessary, by a revolution on the French pattern, but without the bloodshed. The first step would be to ensure that wealth and power were distributed more evenly throughout the whole community.

For his part, Ivison was a philanthropist who believed in reform but who had been frightened off by recent events in France and the current unrest in England. This wish for change was shared by a significant minority of the ruling elite, but self-interest and expediency made them acquiesce to the wishes of the government hardliners, those to whom reform in any guise was anathema.

However, as time passed and reports of the appalling atrocities committed during the Reign of Terror in France filtered back to Britain, many British radicals grew increasingly uneasy. They were men of conscience who found it hard to reconcile such wholesale blood-letting with their belief in liberty, equality and fraternity. A backlash followed against the "English Jacobins", as the supporters of the Revolution were called, who were now seen as enemies of the state and treated accordingly.

However, the demand for reform accelerated with the formation of the London Corresponding Society which was the first artisan-based political movement. It was quickly followed by similar groups in the main provincial cities attracting large working class support.

Agitation and civil unrest reached its peak in the summer and autumn of 1795. The war had halted corn imports from Europe and the poor harvest of 1795 led to shortages and soaring food prices. There was widespread food rioting throughout England where mobs regulated the markets by seizing food and selling it at reduced prices that people could afford. Money from such sales was then handed back to the rightful owner.

These were tactics that appealed to Rory because they gained mass support for the movement and "regulating the markets" had a nice ring of law and order to it. Often the authorities would stand by and not intervene. In April he liaised secretly with the pitmen and keelmen on the River Wear to regulate the market at Chester-le-Street which proved a great success.

The government's response became increasingly repressive. Habeas Corpus had been suspended the year before and secret committees had been set up to investigate radical societies. Government spies and informers were everywhere and loyalist associations to counter the Republicans and Levellers were being set up all over the country.

Rory, like most hard-core radicals, refused to be intimidated and decided to organise an action of protest on his home ground. The opportunity for this came in November when, with the aid of pitmen, lead miners and his own keelmen, the markets in Newcastle were seized and regulated without interference or injury. Butter was sold at eight pence per lb; wheat at twelve shillings per boll and potatoes at five shillings per load, to the great delight of the working populace.

In London the government began to panic. The great demonstrations called by the London Corresponding Society in Copenhagen Fields were drawing ever increasing crowds and the King, going in state to open Parliament, was hissed and hooted and his carriage pelted by an angry mob that thronged the route.

This was the last straw and the government's response was draconian. Two acts were passed by Parliament, one making it a treasonable offence to incite the people against the King, constitution or government; the other banning meetings of more than fifty people unless approved by the Magistracy. Worse was to follow as the government screwed down the lid on dissent.

The result was to create mounting pressure and frustration as the reform movement became locked inside a cauldron of repressive law. The discontent simmered on but finally the radicals were driven underground.

It was at this point that Henry's friendship with Rory began to take on a new perspective. They met once or twice a week and their talk covered a wide range of topics which invariably culminated in a long discussion on radical reform. Henry was introduced to the writings of the leading radicals and read Paine's "Rights of Man" and Godwin's even more revolutionary "Political Justice". He read pamphlets and broadsheets by the score from Cartwright to Thomas Spence, who had once taught at the keelmen's own school at St Anne's Chapel. The shrewd Rory held out an intellectual flame and moth-like, Henry could not resist the challenge.

Henry's sympathetic response to radicalism was not shared by William, whose immediate response was to join one of the Loyalist Associations in support of the government. Henry, remembering Ivison's earlier warnings not to trust William, had wisely decided not to confide in his brother-in-law or mention his growing friendship with Rory. His attitude and refusal to join the association puzzled William.

'You surely don't believe in all this radical and reform nonsense, Henry?'

Henry evaded his question with a shrug. 'I haven't time for politics. Whatever happens the world won't change much for the likes of you and me.'

William exploded with exasperation. 'But these levellers would confiscate all property and share it out with everyone, regardless of any legal rights. That's anarchy - a recipe for chaos if ever there was one.'

'But what if the changes were made lawfully, by a newly elected parliament?' Henry immediately regretted allowing himself to be drawn into the argument. He did not wish to arouse William's suspicions, but his fears proved groundless. William's mind was blinkered and he automatically assumed that anyone with education would support the establishment and the laws of property which to him were sacrosanct.

'Look what's happened in France,' he said. 'No one in their right mind would wish for such things to take place in England.'

Henry nodded in agreement.

'Then it's up to people like us to see that it doesn't happen. And being an active member of a Loyalist Association is the only way.'

There was an arrogant note of finality in his voice. His mind was closed and he could neither understand nor tolerate those who had yet to make up theirs.

Shortly after this futile discussion with William, Henry received another invitation to have dinner with Ivison. These invitations to Henry were becoming more frequent, though occasionally the whole family were invited, including William and Ellen. This was Ivison's subtle way of trying to protect Henry from his brother-in-law's jealousy and envy.

On the non-family occasions Henry and Ivison would spend hours after supper discussing business, politics and the war with France, but more and more the conversation would turn to politics and the worrying unrest being stirred up by the radicals.

Ivison was a fair-minded man but, like William, felt the law of property was inviolable - and being a very rich man, had much more to lose. He was frightened by the extremists in the radical ranks and his initial sympathy for reform began to wane. In addition he now had the opportunity to fulfil a long-held ambition to become an Alderman of the Corporation of Newcastle after his years of service as a member of the Common Council. To the loyal burghers of the town, the slightest whiff of radicalism would quickly put paid to any such ambitions.

On one occasion after an excellent supper, Ivison motioned Henry towards the comfortable chairs by the fire. After a while the conversation turned to the growing state of unrest and the government's increasingly repressive response.

'I see your brother-in-law has joined the Association.' Ivison rarely referred to William by name in his absence.

'Yes, he takes his duties as a loyal citizen very seriously.'

'It seems to amuse you.'

'Only because I can't visualise William with a sword or musket in his hand. I think it's only a token gesture on his part.'

Ivison smiled. 'Yes, I think I see what you mean. I take it you're not a member of the Association?'

'No'.

'Any particular reason, or don't you approve?'

Henry became cautious. 'I don't approve of extremism, whatever guise it takes.'

'Even if it's to protect the King and Constitution?'

'Surely the army and the navy will do that.'

'Didn't do 'em much good in France. The King still lost his head.'
Ivison smiled at Henry's discomfort and the probing ceased.

'You're a strange fellow at times, Henry, but I'll vouch that you're
a loyal and honest man. I think I know which side you'd be on if it
ever came to a fight.'

'I sincerely hope it never does come to that, sir. It will be a sad day
for England.'

Henry was relieved when Ivison turned the conversation back to
business.

CHAPTER 8

During the following year Henry immersed himself in business matters. He worked harder than ever, gaining increasing respect and stature in the coal trade and a growing confidence in himself. But gradually and against his better judgement, he allowed himself to be drawn more and more into the treacherous world of the underground radical movement.

Government spies and informers were everywhere and the meetings of the small core of radical reformers became increasingly dangerous. This did not seem to worry Rory but it caused growing alarm in Henry's mind. On one occasion the group came close to being arrested when the house where the meeting was to be held was raided by the authorities. Only a timely warning had avoided mass arrest and a lingering imprisonment without trial. Henry voiced his fears to Rory.

'Isn't it time for you and your radical friends to lie low for a while?'

'Och no, man. That would be a betrayal of all we stand for.'

'You won't help your cause much by being in prison.'

'Aye, that's true, but you don't give up when the going gets tough. That's when you fight on even harder.' Rory clearly enjoyed the excitement and intrigue of this new type of underground warfare.

Henry was less enthusiastic. 'I don't know that I want to continue to be involved, Rory.' It was a sudden admission, blurted out with embarrassment, which had been building up inside him for some weeks.

Rory, taken unawares looked shaken. 'Don't you believe in what we're doing any more?'

'I'm not a member of your society, Rory.'

'But you support us?'

'Up to a point.' Henry became defensive. 'I support the ideals but I'm beginning to doubt the methods of spreading them. We're breaking the law.'

'An unjust law!' Rory snorted with anger. 'We're forced to break it.'

'No, Rory. You feel compelled to break it and that I understand.' Henry's voice took on a gentler tone. 'But no one is forcing you to do it. There is a subtle difference.'

Rory looked exasperated. 'You're getting soft, Henry. You're losing faith, looking for an easy way out.'

'Then I'm not the only one.' Henry was stung by Rory's attitude. 'There are others who feel as I do, both here and in London. There are other ways of making our voices heard. If we carry on as we're doing we will play right into the hands of the government. There'll be more laws and more repression.'

Rory sensed his own arguments were becoming counterproductive. Henry's sincerity was not in doubt though he was clearly troubled. It was time to soothe rather than argue.

'Och, I know your heart's in the right place, bonny lad. I'm no doubting your intentions and I apologize if it seemed that way. I forget that I'm foot-loose and fancy-free. You've got a wife and family to think of and from what I've heard, good prospects in the coal trade.' He held out his hand. 'But we'll no let it spoil our friendship, eh?'

Rory's good humour was back, his confidence unshaken, and his eyes glinting with steely determination. Henry took his grip and held it, smiling fondly back at the red bearded bear of a man. 'Whatever you do, Rory MacGregor, you'll always be my friend.'

'Then let me ask you one last small favour.'

'By all means. What sort of favour?'

'You're right that we should lie low for a while and let the dust settle.'

'I'm glad you occasionally listen to my advice, Rory. Makes a pleasant change.'

Rory grinned. 'Och, away wi' ye man. I don't ignore good advice, well intended.'

'Then what favour are you asking,' Henry was getting curious.

'I want you to set up a meeting for the group.' He paused, carefully scrutinising Henry's face to assess the reaction to his surprise request. 'It will be the last for some time,' he went on, sensing Henry's reluctance. 'There's lots of loose ends to tie up before we disperse.'

Henry was clearly baffled by the request. 'How on earth can I organise a meeting place? I don't have a home of my own and you surely don't expect me to ask William. He'd have the place surrounded by his loyalist association.'

'No, there's a better venue. One that no one will suspect.' Rory watched the bewilderment in Henry's face.

'Where?'

'Ivison's office on the quayside.' Rory paused to let the shock sink in.

'But it's used every day.'

'Not on Sundays.'

Henry felt he was losing control of the situation. 'It's madness. You'll be seen. '

'There's a quiet entrance at the back. Besides it's the last place the authorities will look. Ivison's the epitome of the law abiding citizen.'

'But you're asking me to compromise him, after all he's done for me.'

'Just this once, Henry, for the cause. Think of it as a gesture to those honest men of principle who now languish in prison because they believe in free speech.'

Henry felt his resolve weakening. 'Just one meeting?'

'Just one, I promise you.' Rory beamed with satisfaction. 'Cheer up, Henry; no one will connect it to you. Have you got a set of keys?'

'Yes.'

'Good, then all you have to do is open the back door on the day and come back later to lock it. I'll give you the time and date when it's all arranged.'

Henry sighed resignedly. 'You make it sound so simple.'

'It will be, I assure you.'

Henry shook his head. A chill feeling of foreboding spread slowly through his stomach. 'I hope you're right,' he said without conviction.

It was to be many months before Rory called in his favour from Henry. The delay was due to Rory's planned visit to London to meet leaders of the London Corresponding Society and other prominent radicals who had managed to avoid arrest and imprisonment. A keel had taken him by night to Shields harbour where a sympathetic collier master gave him free passage to the Thames.

The respite was a great relief to Henry who felt he had been drawn too deeply into the world of radicalism. His sympathies had been mistakenly viewed as active support for the movement and he had become increasingly embroiled, against all his instincts. No matter how hard he tried to distance himself, the danger of his association with Rory fed some deep, indefinable hunger inside him. It was a craving that had to be satisfied and Rory knew the exact dose to administer.

Henry used Rory's absence to deal with other aspects of his life which he had been neglecting of late. He now felt secure enough in his new career to begin looking for a house of his own. The change in Mary when he told her of his decision was startling and he realised he should have made this move much earlier. Mary's expression of sheer happiness at the news was a painful reminder of what she must have been silently suffering during the past few years. He felt angry and ashamed at his failure to understand her distress and the fact that she had borne this without complaint made him feel even guiltier. He determined he would make amends.

'Why don't you look around and see what property is available.'

'What, now?'

'Tomorrow. Make a list and then I'll have a look with you on Sunday. It'll save time.'

Mary threw her arms round him. 'Oh, Henry, I do love you. I just can't wait to have our own home, however small and no matter how humble.'

'You've been so patient you deserve a palace.' He was beginning to realise what a blind, insensitive fool he had been.

Mary looked thoughtful. 'There is a house in the Close but perhaps it's too small. Besides, it belongs to the Mayor.' A cheeky grin spread over her face,

'It may be a year or two before I'm elected,' said Henry joining in the pretence. 'I don't suppose you could wait that long?'

'No.'

'Might save us some money,' he persisted. 'The Mansion House is rent free and there's an allowance too.'

Mary leaned forward and bit his chin then quickly smothered his cry of pain with a kiss. He smiled down at her. 'It's all right, I've got the message.'

The year 1797 started badly for the government. The peace overtures with France had failed and England faced the combined might of France and Spain. Invasion fever was rampant with growing fears about a Jacobin fifth column at home. The country bristled with regular troops, militia, fencibles and various armed defence associations. A shortage of coin caused a run on the banks and a temporary suspension of payments by the Bank of England. The four banks in Newcastle announced they would suspend payment until more coins and notes could be obtained, causing considerable concern and inconvenience to the merchants and traders of the town.

But worse was to come. At the end of February, the French attempted troop landings on the Welsh Coast. In April, mutiny broke out in the British fleet anchored at Spithead which quickly spread the following month to the fleet lying off the Nore, in Kent. Both were put down, the former with leniency, the latter with cruel severity with the ringleaders being hanged.

In July, the last mass meeting of the London Corresponding Society was dispersed by troops and police. Leading radicals were arrested and Rory was lucky to escape. After going into hiding, he returned in secrecy to Newcastle.

Henry was unaware of Rory's return as he made his way to the quayside one September morning, ready for an early start to his work. Dawn was about to break and a chill morning mist hung in the autumn air. As he was approaching the high crane near the bridge, he was startled by a voice calling his name from the grey, shadowy depths of the aptly named Dark Char.

'Who is it?' He stopped and peered cautiously in the direction of the voice.

'I need a word with you, Henry, my bonny lad.' It was the soft but unmistakable voice of Rory MacGregor.

'You must be mad risking your neck like this. The government's crying treason now.' Henry was relieved that his friend had returned safely but concerned at what he might be up to next. 'London too hot for you?'

Henry heard a faint chuckle as he moved into the shadows of the Chare.

'Aye, they started to arrest everyone who might be a threat; radicals, reformers, Jacobins - even the Catholic emancipationists.'

'So you thought it safer to come home, eh?' Henry took the outstretched hand and felt the powerful grip.

'I'm safe enough in Sandgate.'

'Then get yourself back there before it gets light.'

Aye, I will, bonny lad, but first I must ask you to do something for me.'

Henry felt cold inside, though not as a result of the chill morning air. He knew Rory was calling in his favour.

'You want me to set up a meeting in Mr Ivison's office.' His voice was flat with resignation.

'Yes.'

'When?'

'On Sunday evening, nine o clock. It should be dark by then. Just leave the back door open so that everyone can slip in quietly.'

Henry knew it was no good arguing. After all he had promised.

'You swear this will be the last time, Rory?'

'Aye, you have my word on that. I've compromised you enough, Henry. I won't impose on you further.'

'You'll disband and lie low?'

'As a group, yes. But for me, well…' Rory left the answer unspoken, but Henry knew he would fight on with his keelmen.

'Then take good care, my friend.'

'I will that, bonny lad.' Rory squeezed Henry's shoulder. 'We're grateful for all your help and it won't be forgotten.' With that, Rory turned and disappeared into the shadows.

The following week Henry penned a brief note on Rory's behalf to each member of the group summoning them to the meeting at the quayside on Sunday. Some of the notes he delivered himself but most were carried by young Colin. His feeling of unease increased as the

81

week wore on. Following a severe disturbance in the town on Tuesday, there was now a greatly increased military presence on the streets.

The news that Henry and Mary were actively seeking a home of their own pleased William, if not Ellen. Whilst he would miss their financial contribution to the household expenses, the relationship between the two men was now too strained to allow tolerable co-existence. Henry tried his best but William refused to make the slightest effort to meet him half way.

William had also become paranoid with suspicion regarding Henry's relationship with Mr Ivison. He was convinced that they were hatching a plot to dismiss him and now watched every move Henry made.

On the Sunday of the meeting planned for Rory and his radical friends, William detected a growing unease in Henry that became more pronounced as the day wore on. His innate cunning sensed that something was wrong.

After supper Ellen and Mary settled down to some needlework whilst Mark completed some mathematical problems set by his father. Henry took some books into the front parlour in a desultory attempt to kill time, reading words that failed to register in a mind that was elsewhere. William retired to his study on the first floor and leaving the door open, sat listening for sounds from downstairs.

It was getting dusk when William heard the front door close in a quiet, almost furtive, way. He looked out of the window and saw Henry walking quickly along the street and knew, instinctively, that he would be heading towards the quayside. Hastily putting on his coat and hat he quietly let himself out and followed the route taken by Henry. As he reached the end of Wall Knoll he caught sight of Henry who was walking in the direction of the river. He smiled to himself knowing his instinct had been correct. Henry was heading for the quayside and that could only mean one thing. He continued to follow, keeping well back and close to the shadows.

William's suspicions were confirmed when Henry reached the office and let himself in by the rear door. After a while he re-emerged and closed the door, leaving it unlocked, before walking slowly up the narrow back lane in the direction of Butcher Bank. It was not the normal route home.

The mysterious actions of his brother-in-law puzzled William and the enigma fuelled his growing excitement. Whatever the cost, he was determined to find the answers and satisfy his curiosity. Cautiously, he moved out of his hiding place and crossing to the rear door, slipped quietly inside the office and closed the door softly behind him.

It was dark inside as the shutters were tightly closed. As he groped his way into the main office he saw a gleam of light coming through the open door leading into the partners' room. Two oil lamps were lit, one placed on Ivison's desk, the other in the centre of the large polished table. Henry must have lit the lamps in preparation, but for what? Suddenly it became clear to William that there was to be some sort of secret meeting. A wave of excitement coursed through him and he now understood why Henry had been so reluctant to join the loyalist association. He was a bloody Jacobin - a radical!

A faint noise at the rear door startled William and brought him back to the reality of his situation. If this was a venue for a covert radical meeting then he could be in danger. His excitement suddenly evaporated and began to condense into a growing pool of fear as the realisation of his predicament dawned on him. He panicked and looked for somewhere to hide. The partners' room was on the front of the building with a large bay window overlooking the quayside. The heavy velvet curtains in this room were drawn across the shuttered panes to ensure that the light could not be seen from outside. William quickly moved behind the curtains as he heard the sound of footsteps and voices in the adjoining office. He stood, petrified with fear as the voices grew steadily louder with each new arrival. A voice requesting everyone to take their places at the table was followed by the scraping of chairs on the wooden floor.

After a while, William's fears subsided when he realised his presence was undetected. He gently drew the curtains apart until he could see the men seated at the table. He at once recognised Rory and several others who were suspected of radical sympathies. There were three men who he had always regarded as loyal members of the establishment and their presence shocked him.

Rory called the meeting to order and at that point Henry entered the room, having secured the rear door. William's worst fears were now confirmed. His own brother-in-law was a traitor to his country.

After reporting on the break-up of the London Corresponding Society and the problems of similar groups in Sheffield and Birmingham, Rory outlined his plans for keeping in contact while their own group remained underground. An hour later, the meeting ended and William again heard the scraping of chairs on the wooden floor as the delegates prepared to leave. He heard Rory's voice above the soft babble of conversation.

'Those of you who still have Henry's letter and directions had better leave them on the table to be burnt. And anything else that might be incriminating,' he added.

Gradually the sound of conversation dwindled and the voices became more distant as people left through the rear door. After waiting quietly for several minutes, William pulled the curtains a little wider and saw the room was empty. Papers and pamphlets were scattered about the table and he saw some handwritten letters in a small untidy pile at the end of the table nearest to him. He tip-toed across the room, picked up two of the letters and hearing the sound of footsteps, quickly returned to hide behind the curtains again. At this point Henry entered the room from the main office and began collecting all the papers from the table. Then picking up the lamp, he moved across to the fireplace and placed the papers on top of the dead embers still lying in the grate. He held one piece of paper to the top of the lamp and when the flames took hold used it to light the others.

Soon, only a smouldering residue of charred paper remained as evidence of the meeting. After stirring the ashes to ensure they were completely burnt, Henry extinguished the lamps and made his way to the rear exit. William heard the door close and the sound of the key turning in the lock. He was alone at last.

He waited for several minutes before venturing out from behind the curtains, and cursing the darkness, groped his way to the fireplace and ran his hands along the mantelpiece until he felt the tinderbox that was normally kept there. After relighting one of the lamps he took out the two letters he had taken from the table and saw they were written in

84

Henry's distinctive handwriting. He smiled when he saw Henry's signature at the bottom of each letter.

Picking up the lamp he moved out into the main office and went across to Henry's desk. He tried each drawer in turn with a growing confidence that something incriminating would turn up. The bottom drawer was locked but by taking out the drawer above he could gain access to the contents of the locked drawer below. It was Henry's secret store of radical publications, many of which were banned. William took them out and laid them on the desktop, one by one; Paine's Rights of Man and Age of Reason. Godwin's Political Justice, followed by a score of pamphlets by leading radicals and reformers. A smile of triumph spread across his face as he gloated on his discovery. 'Now I've really got you where I want you, dear brother-in-law,' he purred.

Carefully replacing the items in the drawer in the order that he had found them, he returned the lamp to the partners' room, extinguished the flame and then let himself out by the rear door. By the time he reached Wall Knoll everyone had retired to bed and the house was in darkness. This suited him, for he needed time to think; time to plan.

He sat in his study, working by the flickering light of the candle into the early hours of the morning, making notes on the conversation he had overheard and listing those he could identify. Above all he had to decide what to do about Henry. A thin smile of satisfaction crossed his lips. Tomorrow, he would be a man to be reckoned with.

CHAPTER 9

The following morning, before breakfast, William surprised Henry by taking him to one side and asking for an urgent and confidential chat.

'Can't we talk over breakfast?' Henry had a busy day ahead of him and he did not want to waste time on some trivial tête-à-tête with William.

'I think it's imperative that we talk now, privately and before breakfast.' The stern and pompous tone used by William would normally have triggered off only polite amusement in Henry, but on this morning it was a source of irritation.

'It can't be that important, surely.' A note of exasperation began to creep in.

'It can and it is.' William was growing angry. 'I want to talk to you about the events of last night.'

A shock wave surged through Henry but he managed to retain his composure. 'Events of last night?' He feigned surprise and incomprehension. 'What events, may I ask?'

William shook his head and took Henry by the arm. 'Not here. This is something we don't want the ladies to hear.' He led the way into the front parlour and closed the door firmly behind him. 'You can stop playing the innocent. I know all about last night.' He took one of the letters out of his pocket and held it out to Henry. 'You don't deny that that is your handwriting and your signature?'

Henry felt numb as he looked at the letter. 'Where did you get this?'

'It was found at the scene of the crime.'

'By whom?'

'Does it matter?'

'It does to me.' He had to know just how much William knew.

'All right, I'll tell you.' William smirked with satisfaction, pausing to give maximum effect to his coup-de-gras. 'It was me.'

Henry quickly realised he must have been followed to the office by William on the previous night. He suddenly remembered just how suspicious his brother-in-law had been, following him everywhere, rarely letting him out of his sight.

'You followed me to the office?'

'Yes.'

'Alone?' His concern was to protect the others and he needed to know the extent of William's knowledge.

'Now that would be telling.' William smiled at Henry's growing discomfort.

'You have my letters?' Henry was puzzled. He recalled that he'd burnt the letters after the meeting.

'Thought you had burnt 'em all, eh? Well, obviously you didn't'

Henry remembered he was still holding the incriminating letter in his hand. He instinctively thought to destroy it.

'You may as well let me have the letter back,' said William reading his mind. 'Naturally, I have other letters and other evidence.'

There was a long pause as the two men stared at one another each silently trying to assess the strength or weakness of their position. At last Henry decided to call William's bluff and put an end to his taunting innuendoes.

'All right, William. Just how much do you know and what do you intend to do?'

William maintained his look of smug satisfaction. He was thoroughly enjoying his new found role. 'Let me say that I know who attended your clandestine meeting last night. I also know what was discussed and agreed.' To emphasise his control of the situation, he reeled off the names of those attending the meeting which he had written down the night before. 'So you see, my dear, brother-in-law, I have enough evidence to have you all arrested for treason.' He paused to let his threat sink in.

'And is that what you intend to do?'

'It's the duty of every loyal citizen, but....'

'But?' Henry sensed some scheme afoot. Some Machiavellian twist in William's mind.

'I have my wife and her sister to think of,' said William. He pointedly refrained from mentioning any family duty towards Henry. His consuming jealousy had overridden any thoughts of compassion. Henry had become a threat to his own position and now, at last, he had the means to redress the situation and remove that threat. But he must do it with care and circumspection.

'No one has ever questioned your responsibilities as a family man, William,' Henry said cautiously. 'My own family owes much to you and Ellen.'

'And look how you repay me!' William's voice rose. 'By placing my name and reputation in jeopardy and endangering your own family.' His pent up envy and frustration boiled over in a tirade of angry criticism and accusation. 'You're a fool, Henry. A blind, ungrateful fool. Blind because you've allowed yourself to be manipulated by a group of wicked, unscrupulous men. Ungrateful, because you've betrayed the trust that I and - even more importantly - Mr Ivison, placed in you. That a man of your education can behave in such an unprincipled and naive manner is beyond me.' He stopped, too exhausted for words, breathing heavily with anger and emotion.

Henry waited until William became calmer, watching the look of cunning return as his anger subsided. He realised that William had long decided on a course of action. He had just needed prompting.

'So what do you suggest I do, William?'

'You'll have to leave town, of course. It's a bit late in the day but you still have your family to think of.'

'But the authorities need never know.' Henry had no intention of begging but he needed to know how vengeful and implacable William's attitude was.

'Surely, you don't expect me to condone treason!' William became angry again. 'And have you no thought for what this would do to Mr Ivison if it became known that his trusted employee was a member of a proscribed group? His chances of being elected to the aldermanic bench would be slim indeed.'

Henry could now see what William had in mind. 'If I leave town quietly and start a new life as far away as possible, the need to inform the authorities would be removed?

'It might be more discreet and prove less harmful in the long run.'

'But would it placate your loyalist conscience, William?' He couldn't resist one last barb of sarcasm.

'I'm prepared to be magnanimous for the sake of the innocent parties who would otherwise suffer. I can't forgive your crass stupidity and selfishness, Henry, and your cynicism only demeans you further in my eyes.'

You pompous old bastard, Henry thought, but stayed silent.

'Now, to more practical matters,' William went on. 'I'll tell Mr Ivison you're sick and won't be coming in today. That will give you plenty of time to sort out your affairs and pack your things. I want you out of this house first thing tomorrow.'

'And if I don't?'

'I shall inform the authorities about you and your friends and hand over my evidence.'

'And you'd testify against your own brother-in-law?'

'If I have to.

Henry could see this was a well-planned manoeuvre. William knew he would want to save Rory's friends above all and like it or not, he was faced with a fait accompli.

'What do I tell Mary?'

'That's up to you - as little as possible would be my advice.'

'And Ellen? What will you tell her?'

'Nothing. I'm sending her to stay with my brother-in-law in Durham for a few days. When she gets back I'll tell her you just packed up and left.'

Henry looked hard and long at his brother-in-law and seeing the cold, vindictive look of triumph in his face his anger and bitterness boiled over in a furious outpouring at William's infamy.

'You're a pathetic, pompous and malicious man, full of greed and rotting with jealousy. I know it's me you hate so don't cloak your actions in lies and excuses about loyalty and the need to protect others. You'd denounce your own wife if it would further your own ambitions.' As his anger abated he saw William rise and scurry towards the door, fearful he might be attacked. This amused him and restored his composure. He called after him. 'It's all right, William. I wouldn't soil my hands trying to beat the evil out of you.'

William paused at the door trying to rescue his dignity. 'I should start packing if I were you,' was all he could say.

When Henry broke the news to Mary he was met with stunned disbelief which quickly changed to angry recriminations and tears.

'Why, Henry, why?' She kept asking. 'What on earth possessed you to get mixed up with these people?'

He could only shrug his shoulders in mute resignation.

'It was Rory, wasn't it? I knew he'd be a bad influence on you.'

'No,' he re-asserted himself. 'It was my doing. The fault was mine. I won't have you blaming others for my own shortcomings. It was my decision and my judgement however misguided.'

'You place your whole family at risk without telling us. Some judgement.' Her anger was turning into bitterness.

'I'm sorry, Mary, truly sorry.' It was all he could say, yet it sounded so inadequate.

'Being sorry isn't going to help.' She was sobbing in a forlorn, helpless way. He wanted to comfort her and moved to take her in his arms but she pushed him away.

'I can't change things now, though I'd dearly love to,' he said gently.

'You're always being sorry after the event, Henry. It was the same when we had to leave Yorkshire.' It was the first time she'd criticised him for this. It was unfair and he was hurt.

'That was bad luck, Mary. You know it was. You encouraged me to take the job because you wanted me to be a pit viewer one day.'

'And now it's back to being a hewer, I suppose.'

'If needs be. I'll just have to live with the consequences of my foolishness.'

'No, Henry, we will all have to live with them.' She had stopped crying and her voice, drained by anger and frustration, sounded flat and desolate.

'You and Mark can stay on in Newcastle. I'll get work and send you money.' He was desperate to please her.

'No, Henry, we're still a family. If you must leave in the morning then so must we.' Her stoic acceptance of the situation served also as a chilling rejection of his explanations and excuses, a numbing reminder of the consequences of his actions.

Henry felt despair welling up inside him. His mind was filled with an anguish he had never known before as he realised his relationship with Mary would never be the same again. Something had withered and died and he knew it could never be resurrected.

The most frustrating aspect of his betrayal was not being able to tell her about William's despicable part in his downfall. He knew his brother-in-law would keep it from Ellen and he could not bring himself to risk ruining the loving relationship Mary had with her sister. He felt he had destroyed enough already. The irony of the situation stuck in his gullet like a cancerous growth, made worse when Mary berated him on the repercussions of his actions.

'You never gave a thought for the feeling of William and Ellen, did you? Or for Mr Ivison and any embarrassment you might cause him. And after all they've done for us.'

Henry could only remain mute, choking on the injustice of it all. It was at this point that something deep inside him changed irrevocably. His heart hardened as his compassion died and winter entered his soul. From now on he would pursue his own and his family's interests with a relentless single-mindedness, regardless of the effects his actions might have on others. He could now calmly contemplate killing William if it would solve his problems, but too much damage had been done and could not be undone.

However, there were two things he could do to limit the damage. First he wrote a letter to Rory explaining what had happened and telling him to warn other members of the group. He could not trust in William's promise to let the matter rest after he had gone.

The second matter was more difficult. A close bond had grown between himself and Mr Ivison and he had developed a great affection and respect for his employer and mentor. He could not bring himself to leave without some attempt to explain why his departure had been so sudden and unannounced. His first thought had been to go and see Mr Ivison but then rejected this in favour of a long letter. He spent some time marshalling his thoughts before committing his explanations to paper. He wanted his old employer to understand why he had acted in the way he had, and also the hope that his actions would not jeopardise Ivison's prospects at the forthcoming aldermanic elections.

After writing the letters he slipped out of the house and made his way to Sandgate where he left his letter to Rory with Colin's mother. He knew it would be delivered safely, probably by Colin when he returned from school.

On leaving Sandgate he headed for the Post Office in Mosley Street taking the route via Manor Char to avoid the quayside. On arrival he posted his letter to Mr Ivison, addressing it to the office. By the time it would be delivered he would be well clear of Newcastle. He had thought of asking William to deliver the letter but quickly admonished himself for such foolish thoughts. He must not trust anyone, least of all someone like William.

The worst part came that evening when Mark came home from school. The shocking news that he would not be returning and that they were leaving for Northumberland in the morning caused his eyes to mist as he fought back the tears. He looked pleadingly at his father. 'Why can't we stay?'

'Because my work with Mr Ivison is finished and we can't continue to impose on your Aunt Ellen.

'Why couldn't you have told me before?'

'Because I wanted your last days at school to be happy ones.'

'But you must have known ages ago. You could have told me.' The boy's voice was full of accusation.

'I was only trying to make things easier for you. Stop you feeling disappointed and hurt.'

'But I am hurt.' Mark was angry and a little frightened. He could sense a new tension between his parents which had never been there before. In the past they'd always taken him into their confidence and treated him like a grown-up. Suddenly it had all changed and he couldn't understand why. He felt betrayed, and worst of all he did not believe his father's explanation.

'I must say goodbye to Colin,' he blurted out and turned and ran from the room. He continued running past the staring faces of the passers-by and finally into Sandgate with the tears still streaming down his cheeks.

Henry felt wretched. He looked across to Mary for support but she avoided his gaze and walked quickly from the room, closing the door firmly behind her. He listened to her footsteps on the stairs as she made her way to the bedroom and thought he heard the faint sound of sobbing.

CHAPTER 10

It was still dark as Henry helped the carrier's boy to load the family possessions on to the small handcart. A faint paleness in the east indicated the approach of dawn as he closed the door of the house in Wall Knoll for the last time. With a sleepy Mark perched on the handcart they made their way up steep climb to Pilgrim Street which was the starting point of many of the town's long distance carriers. The yard of the Bird-in-the-Bush and all the surrounding streets were crowded with waggons and their long teams of horses. It was a scene of bustle and confusion as goods were sorted and loaded for destinations as far as London in the south and Edinburgh in the north.

After some frantic searching Henry found the Alnwick carrier who was to take them as far as Morpeth. Their few belongings were loaded onto his waggon and soon they were passing through the formidable low arch of Pilgrim Street Gate heading north, rumbling past the shuttered houses and pleasant gardens that lined the handsome and spacious Northumberland Street, now one of the most desirable residential areas outside the town walls. Soon, they were rumbling towards the narrow stone bridge that spanned the sparkling Bailiff Burn which flowed through a deep dene at Barras Bridge on its way to the Tyne.

When the waggon crossed the bridge a pang of nostalgia pierced Mark's young heart as he saw the dawn mist rising from the waters of the mill pond swathing the surrounding tall trees with trailing grey tendrils. He remembered the hot summer days when he and Colin had swum in the cooling waters near the mill, or fought again the great sea battles of the Glorious First of June, or Cape St. Vincent, using makeshift boats with paper sails.

They now joined the Great North Turnpike, the main coach road which ran to the Scottish border and on to Edinburgh. The bustling market town of Morpeth lay fifteen miles to the north where Henry planned to stay whilst seeking work in one of the many local collieries. It was not the ideal geographical centre for his search, but the town had many attractions which would please Mary and Mark.

No one spoke on the journey. Mary sat with her arm around Mark's shoulder staring forlornly into space as Henry walked uncomfortably alongside the waggon. In silence they passed through Gosforth Turnpike Gate and on to Three Mile Bridge which spanned the Ouse Burn, the broad waggon forcing pedestrians to shelter in the recess of the narrow stone bridge to avoid being crushed.

They proceeded in silence as Henry remained deep in his private world of contemplation. Looking east he remembered that the vast expanse of common land stretching from North Gosforth to the coast near Earsdon, known as Killingworth Moor and Shiremoor, had recently been enclosed by two Acts of Parliament. The local small freeholders and yeomen had been elbowed off for only a pittance of its worth. The land, all three thousand and five acres of it, had been awarded to the forty-eight local landlords who were, not surprisingly, also the promoters of the Acts. Their greed had, no doubt, been motivated by the rich coal seams which lay under the common land. Exploratory borings had been carried out and soon shafts would be sunk to extract this wealth of black diamonds. The existing waggonways would be extended and coal would be shipped to the Tyne staithes for sale to the growing London and overseas markets. Coal and gold fever, Henry mused, shared the same common denominator, greed.

The waggon continued its way slowly northwards and as the sun rose higher in the morning sky, so the spirits of the travellers seemed to lighten with its warming rays. Henry's bitterness at his misfortune and the feeling of resentment at the unfairness of it all had begun to ease. In its place was a growing determination to make good the damage done to his life and career prospects. He had stopped feeling sorry for himself and was starting to plan for the challenges that now lay ahead. He was confident he could find work and somehow he would manage to keep Mark in full time education.

Above all he knew he must keep his son out of the pits, a difficult task in the close-knit mining communities where alternative work was a scarce commodity.

Clearing the toll bar, they soon began the long descent into Morpeth. The town was busy and congested with traffic near the narrow, humped-back bridge which spanned two stone arches over the

River Wansbeck. Here, the road turned sharply west into Bridge Street and on to the wide, bustling market place with its elegant town hall, clock tower and market cross.

Morpeth was a popular town with travellers, in particular the carriers and the coaching fraternity. Waggoners appreciated the friendly facilities provided by the fifty or so inns that catered for the travellers' needs. Some of the larger inns had stabling for up to eighty horses and the town was an important posting centre for the stage coaches that plied the great North Road. It was also a major market town with one of the greatest cattle markets in the country, not only for local cattle but also for cattle driven from Scotland.

Henry was surprised at how busy the town was. 'There's almost as many people about as you find on the streets of Newcastle,' he remarked.

'You should see it on a market day,' said the Waggoner. 'Can't move for people and cattle and what with market stalls and farm carts parked all over the place.' His voice dropped off. 'Better off elsewhere on market days,' he warned.

Mary took an instant liking to the town. It had a friendly air and some interesting shops. She felt she could settle here and wished there could be some opportunity to do so. She knew that Morpeth had a grammar school with a good reputation and hoped that a place might be available for Mark to continue his education. She paused in her day-dreaming, angry at herself. If only, if only! Was her life to be dependent on those two words? She forced her mind back into the real world. At best she would have a cottage in some pit village hopefully near enough to Morpeth to allow occasional visits, perhaps on market days. She had experienced the hardships of pit village life before and shuddered, imperceptibly, at past memories which she had tried to shut out of her mind.

Henry found them lodgings in a small house tucked away up a narrow cobbled entrance off Bridge Street. A taciturn landlady led the way up several flights of rickety stairs to two musty smelling attic rooms and departed without saying a word. It was not what Henry or Mary would have wished but they had to conserve their meagre funds until such time as Henry could find employment. Whatever the future held Henry was determined they would face it together. He would make every effort to hold together the fragile family relationship that had been so badly damaged by recent events.

CHAPTER 11

Henry spent the following weeks tramping round the local pits to assess the employment prospects. He rose early each day and walked to the various inns and the ale houses near the pits which served as recruiting offices for the annual binding. His earlier assessment had been correct and there was keen competition, especially from the owners of the new pit at Cowpen, to sign up experienced men.

Henry decided to omit all reference to the time he'd spent in Newcastle with Mr Ivison and referred only to his experience underground at the pits in which he had previously worked. He also carefully avoided giving any impression of being educated. Few pitmen could read or write and those who could were looked upon with deep suspicion by the coal owners and their viewers. An educated pitman was regarded as a potential trouble maker; someone who couldn't accept his God-given station in life.

By the end of September the pits were still short of good men and the score price, the usual method of piece rate payment, had been increased to three shillings. The owners' agents now began to intensify their efforts to persuade the remaining unbound men to sign the bond. As a further inducement the binding money was increased, soon topping three guineas for an experienced hewer. By October, free beer flowed copiously in the ale houses used as recruiting offices by the rival coal owners' agents and the main venues soon became scenes of drunken confusion and debauchery.

Surveying such a scene at a hostelry near Hartley Henry remained aloof from the blandishments and temptations which surrounded him, aware all the time that he was being closely watched by a ferret faced agent standing alone in the corner of the taproom. Henry's quiet but confident demeanour had attracted the experienced eye of the agent. Here was just the sort of pitman a good viewer valued, known in the trade as 'pit-bred'.

After a while the agent ordered two tankards of ale and sidled across to Henry, proffering one of the tankards.

'Drink?' he asked.

'Thank you.' Henry accepted warily.

'You haven't signed the bond yet?'

'No. '

'Any special pit in mind?'

'No, I'm open to offers.'

The agent looked quizzically at Henry. 'You've worked in the pits I take it?'

'Yes.' Henry gave a brief account of his past experience, omitting the time spent with Mr Ivison.

'Just waiting for the best offer, eh?' The ferret face of the agent broke into a smile. 'Come over here and let's talk.' He led the way to a table in a dark corner of the room and sat down, gesturing to the empty chair opposite for Henry to do likewise. 'Are you seeking work in Hartley?'

'Like I said, I'm open to offers,' Henry replied cautiously. 'But the only agents I've talked to so far are binding for Hartley, Cowpen or Plessey.'

The agent took a long, deep draught of ale and then carefully replaced his almost empty tankard on the table. 'How'd you like to work for Mr Forster at North Moor?' He watched Henry closely to study his reaction.

'I don't know the North Moor pit,' Henry said, a note of surprise in his voice. 'There used to be some small landsale pits at the north end of Killingworth Moor years ago but they were all worked out.'

'They've sunk a new shaft to the low main seam at one hundred and twenty fathoms,' the agent said. 'It's a good winning with a seam five feet thick or more. It's a dry pit too,' he added, 'since they put in the new pumping engine.' He deliberately avoided any mention that it was also a fiery pit.

Henry was interested. The pit was only six miles from Newcastle, closer than he would have wished in his present circumstances. However, the area was sparsely populated as a result of the recent enclosure of Killingworth Moor and Shire Moor which lay between the pit and the town.

The agent drew a large, folded document from his pocket and opened it out on the table. Henry recognised it instantly as the standard form of legal bond adopted by the coal owners setting out the terms and conditions that would apply for the next twelve months. It was usually read aloud to the men, often in groups, as so few pitmen could read. Those who wanted to sign would make their mark against their name written at the bottom. Henry noted a few dozen marks at the bottom of the document.

'Want me to read it to you?' The agent automatically assumed Henry couldn't read.

'Can I see it?'

A look of surprise crossed the agent's face. 'The usual terms and conditions,' he said passing the bond across the table.

Henry spread the bond in front of him and using his forefinger as a guide, slowly and clumsily read the lines of legal script wearing an exaggerated frown of concentration. The agent smiled condescendingly, fully taken in by Henry's subterfuge. Here, he thought, was the proud, semi-literate pitman whose pathetic childhood attempts at learning had been destroyed by the call of the pit at the age of six or seven. Only a stubborn pride and the ability to write his name and read a few simple words kept the illusion of literacy alive, though it fooled no one.

Henry's ruse allowed him to read quickly through the document without betraying the fact that he was an educated pitman and so jeopardising his chances of employment. He was also able to calculate his likely earnings by checking the score price against the many harsh penalty clauses in the bond. A score price was the amount paid for twenty corves of coal cut by the hewer. A corfe was a hazel basket that held five hundredweight of coal so a hewer had to produce five tons of coal a day to make a living wage.

But penalty clauses allowed the owners to impose arbitrary fines on the unfortunate hewer who sent under-filled corves to bank or who, inadvertently, allowed a tiny amount of stone to become mixed with the coal. These fines could be levied at the whim of the viewer or his officials whose decision was always final. There was no redress and a pitman could work a full day only to find, on coming to bank to check his tally that the fines imposed had cancelled out most of his earnings.

After examining the bond, Henry calculated that after allowing for some fines plus deductions for the supply of candles, etc. he could probably earn sixteen shillings a week. He would also have a free supply of coal and a pit cottage to live in.

'I take it there's a pit cottage?' He needed to confirm this.

'Are you married?'

'Yes.'

'Any bairns?'

'Just one, a boy.'

'How old?'

'Ten, coming up eleven.'

'Has he worked in a pit?'

'No. '

The agent looked at Henry with a mixture of surprise and disbelief. He'd rarely come across a pitman's son above the age of six without pit experience. 'Is he fit and strong?' he asked. There had to be a good reason for a pitman to refuse the ten pence a day a healthy son could contribute to the family's earnings working as a trapper boy.

'Aye, he's healthy enough,' Henry replied, 'only I don't want him to become a pitman.'

The agent shrugged. 'He's a bit old to start now,' he said, 'but I'll take him on as a trapper if you change your mind.'

Henry shook his head. 'I've got other plans for him.'

'Suit yourself,' said the agent dismissing the matter from his mind. 'I can find you a cottage - a room and loft - but you'll have to sign today.'

'How much binding money?'

'Three guineas,' said the agent.

'Make it four and I'll sign.'

There was a quiet determination in Henry's voice. The two men looked long and hard at each other until, finally, the ferret face of the agent broke into a thin, humourless smile. 'You drive a hard bargain, my friend. I hope you're worth it.'

A quill and ink were produced and four guineas surreptitiously changed hands across the table. Henry then made an exaggerated play of signing his name with slow, ponderous strokes of the quill whilst the smirking agent looked on.

On the long walk home to Morpeth, Henry had ample time to reflect on his actions. He had effectively sold his freedom for the next twelve months since, by signing the bond, he had virtually made himself the legal slave of the coal owner. He would now be dependent on him for his livelihood and the very roof over his head and all would be subject to the arbitrary capriciousness of the owner's agents and officials. Absence from work without permission or a medical certificate was an offence and if he absconded he could be hunted down and sent to prison. Much would depend on the ethics and sense of fair play of the viewer who managed the colliery and if matters went to the courts, the benches were likely to be occupied by the coal owners or their viewers.

Still, he thought, if he worked hard, kept clear of accidents and above all avoided the displeasure of the viewer and his officials, his family would have a roof over their head, coal to keep them warm and sixteen shillings a week. With his experience he could also expect early promotion to deputy overman and he would be back on the ladder of success. He quickened his step, eager to tell Mary and Mark his news.

Darkness was falling when Henry reached the outskirts of Morpeth. As he descended Stobhill from the Shields turnpike he could see the lights of the town below twinkling cosily in the clear autumn air. It was market day and the town was still busy with visiting farmers, drovers and assorted traders who swelled the local population, giving pleasure and profit to the innkeepers. Several farm carts and gigs lined the market square, their empty shafts pointing inwards and resting forlornly on the ground.

Over supper Henry broke the news that he'd signed the bond and that they would soon be moving to a cottage in North Moor. 'We'll be able to buy some decent bedding at least,' he said laying the four guineas binding money on the table and watching for Mary's response.

Her reaction disappointed him. She seemed neither pleased nor displeased. 'I suppose one pit village is much like another.' She said, in a flat, disinterested voice. Henry felt wounded by her detachment but decided not to respond.

Mark reacted with much greater enthusiasm to the news. The novelty of the move to Morpeth was beginning to wane and the earlier excitement had gradually given way to boredom.

'When do we leave, father?' he asked, his eyes sparkling with eager anticipation.

'In a day or so. We'll have to buy some things first, bedding and the like and I'll need some cranky flannel.'

Mark giggled. 'That's the daft name for cloth used for making working clothes to wear down the pit, isn't it?'

'Not so daft. It's hard wearing and it absorbs the sweat when you're working at the coal face, where the real hard work is done.'

'I wouldn't mind working down the pit.' There was a serious, almost wistful note in Mark's voice.

'Nonsense!' Mary cut in sharply. 'A pit's no place for a boy with education. Besides, you haven't finished your schooling yet.'

'I don't want to go to some boring pit village school,' Mark protested. 'Not after All Saints'.' The barb was a reminder of how unjustly he had been treated.

'You wouldn't like working down the pit, believe me,' said Henry trying to defuse the situation. 'There's nothing exciting or glamorous about it; only darkness, dirt, long hours and hard work, to say nothing of the danger.'

'I'd still like to try,' Mark said stubbornly.

'Henry placed his arm lovingly around Mark's shoulder. 'You're still a child,' he said kindly.

'I'm nearly eleven. Some boys go down the pit as young as five or six. You said so yourself.'

'But I also said it was wrong,' Henry answered sternly. 'I don't condone it and never will.'

Mary had heard enough. 'It's time you were in bed,' she said, putting an end to the discussion and over-ruling Mark's protests.

With Mark safely tucked up in bed, Henry sat quietly at the supper table watching the reflection of the candlelight in Mary's eyes as she stared absently at the flickering flame. After a while she sensed his gaze and looked up. A faint, half-hearted smile briefly lit up her face as their eyes met. Henry leaned across and gently took her hand.

'You're not worried about the move to North Moor, are you?'

'No.'

He waited, expecting her to say more but she remained silent.

'I should be able to earn sixteen shillings a week.' He tried to sound enthusiastic. 'At least we won't starve and have to face the workhouse or parish relief.'

'I suppose it's some comfort.'

The toneless brevity of Mary's responses was beginning to unsettle Henry. 'We'll have our own house,' he went on determined to maintain his enthusiasm.

'No, Henry. The house is part of the job. It belongs to the owners, not us.'

But surely it's something to be thankful for at least?' Her attitude was beginning to exasperate him.

'You still don't understand, do you?' said Mary, her voice soft and sad. 'I was an overman's wife when Mark was born and I hoped for something even better for my next child.' She paused as her sadness gave way to bitterness, then went on. 'I didn't expect to be a hewer's wife living in some damp hovel that you call a pit cottage. Do you expect me to be grateful, or even happy at the prospect?'

Henry was stunned by her words. For several seconds his mind remained scrambled and confused as he tried to take in her message. 'Do you mean…are you trying to tell me that we're going to have…" his voice trailed off.

Mary cut him short. 'Yes, Henry, I'm pregnant. We're going to have another child'.

NORTH MOOR

CHAPTER 12

It was on a raw November afternoon two weeks later, that Mary and Mark caught their first sight of North Moor. The hired cart, piled high with their recently purchased belongings, passed through the picturesque North Moor village which straddled the ridge of high ground above the common and for centuries had served the local farming community. Below, about a mile distant lay the pit village. It was known as North Moor Colliery to distinguish it from its more illustrious namesake. The ancient village of North Moor looked down on its pit neighbour in more ways than one.

On the edge of the village they passed the walled grounds of North Moor Hall, the home of Duncan Forster who owned the pit and the North Moor estates. Through the screen of trees they caught a glimpse of the gabled roof and high chimneys of the manor house which sat like a jewel in a landscape of lush parkland and ornamental gardens.

Duncan Forster had been one of the promoters of the Act to enclose the common and his efforts had been suitably rewarded with a grant of ninety-five acres of adjacent common land to add to his large existing estate. What his fellow promoters had not realised at the time was that a rich seam of household coal lay one hundred and twenty fathoms beneath this part of the common, hidden by an old worked out seam above. Coal prospects under this part of the common were regarded as worthless but not to a clever, intuitive coal owner like Duncan Forster. He had drilled secretly below the worked out seam of the old pit and after persevering, to a depth of seven hundred and twenty feet, struck a five foot thick seam of premium grade coal. He then bought another seven hundred acres from the unsuspecting fellow promoters at a vastly discounted price against the read value of the land.

Sinking the new pit had proved difficult and expensive, almost bankrupting Forster in the process. More than half of his estate had been mortgaged to the hilt before the first coal was drawn to bank. After a slow start the pit was ready to make a profit; enough he hoped, to start paying off some of the heavy debts he had incurred. It had been a bold and risky speculation but he felt the gamble had been worth taking. Within six years he hoped to have paid off his bankers and own a debt free pit making a profit of six thousand pounds a year.

All this, of course, had assumed that there would be no geological faults or major catastrophes such as fires, explosions or inundations. But Duncan Forster was a calculating gambler and one of the new breed of professional owners who were steeped in the coal trade. Son of a pit viewer, he had been brought up by his father to follow in his footsteps. But, unlike his father, he was not content to manage other owners' pits and along with some of his more progressive colleagues in the trade, began to take up small shares in the collieries which he managed. He was now a partner in several successful concerns but North Moor was his first venture as a sole owner.

The purchase of North Moor Hall was also the first indication of his social ambitions, although the response from the county's ruling squirarchy had been one of aloof indifference. His pedigree was too short for the small tightly knit ruling oligarchy which had controlled the coal trade for many generations, though they admired his business acumen. As for the landowning aristocracy, Forster was tainted with the twin evils of trade and new money. As such his family was unlikely to be considered seriously for a marriage of convenience which peers, of impeccable lineage and impoverished estates, often sought to restore their family fortunes.

Henry knew little of his new employer as he led the hired cart down the slope towards North Moor Colliery. The pit village consisted of several dreary rows of almost identical cottages standing in parallel lines. The cottages were built of stone from the local quarry and plastered with lime. The roofs were tiled with slate which glistened darkly in the drizzle falling from a gloomy, grey sky.

The village was dominated by the pit, which brooded menacingly over the bleak cluster of cottages like some giant vulture hovering in search for carrion. Black smoke from the underground furnace, which ventilated the pit, belched from the upcast shaft. Whispers of steam could be seen escaping from the tall engine house which contained the pumping engine that drained the pit.

As they entered the village, Henry saw that the first row of cottages were larger and much better constructed than the others. This would be "shiney-row", he thought, the name used sarcastically to describe the best houses in the village which were usually occupied by the overmen, deputies and other pit officials. Henry's own cottage stood in the row nearest to the pit. It was much smaller and had a shabby, run down appearance resulting from years of neglect. A curl of smoke from the chimney suggested his neighbour had kindly lit a welcoming fire for them. It was a good omen, Henry thought, reminding him of the neighbourliness that was endemic to close-knit mining communities. His confidence for his family's future began to grow, lifting the cloud that had shadowed his heart.

Mary stepped down from the cart and stared in dismay at her surroundings. It was worse than anything she had known and the rain served to increase her sense of desolation. The front street was unpaved and surfaced with only a thin layer of cinders on top of the heavy clay soil. Stagnant pools bore witness to the poor drainage which meant the cottages, built without damp courses, would be damper than usual.

The view from the back of the cottage was even more depressing. The rows of cottages were laid out in pairs with their front doors facing each other. The space between the two rows of back doors contained a large ash-heap and dunghill which ran the whole length of the row. There were no privies or drains and the size of the heap indicated infrequent visits by the scavenger cart. The smell of household rubbish and the contents of thousands of chamber pots permeated the air, even on a cold and damp November day. Mary shuddered at the thought of what a hot, fly-infested summer would bring.

She closed the door quickly and turned to survey the single living room which would be her home. It was about fifteen feet square with a steep, unguarded ladder against one wall giving access, through a square aperture in the ceiling, to the loft above. The ground floor was made of clay, sand and lime with a home-made rug placed in front of the large stone fireplace. A huge coal fire blazed brightly, casting a flickering light across the dim room which was reflected from the whitewashed walls that were damp with condensation. At one side of the fire a black, iron kettle was suspended from an iron hook, wisps of steam escaping from the long curved spout.

109

The room was furnished in a typical mining village style with items of furniture purchased by Henry on a previous visit. A pit explosion six weeks earlier had added six more widows to the village population. Three had now left their pit cottages to seek shelter with relatives in other mining communities giving Henry the opportunity to buy a fine four-poster bedstead and a large, brass-handled chest of drawers in matching mahogany. An eight day chiming clock, a table and four chairs completed the furnishing of the main living room. The loft contained a single bed and a smaller chest of drawers. It would be Mark's bedroom.

Henry started to unload the cart, watched by a number of neighbouring women who stood at their doorways displaying mild interest at the arrival of the newcomers. After unloading, Henry paid the cart driver and, smiling at his curious neighbours, entered his new home and closed the door quietly behind him.

'Well, what do you think?' He looked anxiously at Mary who sat slumped in a chair close to the fire.

'I suppose it will have to do,' she replied in a tired, dejected voice. Seeing the hurt expression in Henry's eyes she quickly smiled and added, 'But the furniture is nice. You've gone to a lot of trouble and I'm grateful.'

Henry looked relieved. 'I'm glad you like it. It's a start and by the time I'm finished this place will look like a palace.'

Watching Henry's boyish enthusiasm and his desperate desire to please made Mary wish she had been less reproachful and more supportive. She knew she could have handled things better but Henry's shock revelation of his involvement with the radicals and the urgency of their flight from Newcastle had destroyed her carefully laid plans. She had known she was pregnant some weeks before their departure but wanted to surprise Henry with the news as soon as they had found their own home. Instead, she had been forced to break the news in an attic room of a strange lodging house in Morpeth.

The sight of Mary's desolation tore at Henry's heart. He gently pulled her up from the chair and holding her tight, kissed her with a soft, loving tenderness she had not known before. It was as if a new courtship had begun, eager and uncertain in direction, yet desperately anxious to succeed.

She responded warmly for the first time since leaving Newcastle. Then, pushing Henry into the chair, knelt down beside him with her head pillowed on his lap and felt his warm hands gently stroking her hair. She gazed at the bright dancing flames from the fire, trying to see her future in the flickering ballet that hovered above a stage of glowing red embers. Would her husband's efforts to hew their future from the bowels of the earth be burnt and dissipated, like the coals in their hearth, providing only brief warmth and an ephemeral cheer before turning to grey, lifeless ash?

Her thoughts were interrupted by Mark clambering noisily down the loft ladder after exploring his new bedroom. 'There's a leak in the roof,' he said 'but it's only a small one.'

The announcement returned everyone to the grim realities of pit village life. 'I'll go up and have a look,' said Henry, slowly disengaging his lap from Mary's resting head as he rose from the chair. 'Fetch me that dish, Mark. It'll do to catch the water until I can mend the roof.'

At this point there was a knock on the door and a thin, tired looking woman came into the room and introduced herself as Mrs Dora Hindmarsh, their next door neighbour. She was about thirty years of age, dressed in black and her face drained by the grief of her recent bereavement. In her hands she carried a large pie in a brown, earthenware dish.

'I thought you might be hungry after your journey,' she said shyly, placing the pie on the table.

Mary was pleasantly surprised and stammered her thanks. She had forgotten the kindness of the close knit pit communities and this small, spontaneous gesture warmed her heart.

Mrs Hindmarsh, with painful memories of her husband's recent death, looked poignantly at Henry. 'You'll be starting at the pit tomorrow?'

'Aye, lass, I will.'

'Mind, it's a fiery pit. I bet they didn't tell ye that when ye signed,' she said.

'No, lass, but all pits are dangerous. It's part of a pitman's life.

'My man and five others were killed six weeks ago. Blamed it on a trapper boy leaving his door open, but then they always do, don't they.' She spoke in a sad, matter of fact voice tinged with resignation rather than recrimination.

'The pit's no place for young boys,' said Henry. 'They should be at school learning to better themselves.'

'For what?' There was genuine surprise in her voice. 'There's only pit jobs round here and school doesn't pay a young lad eight pence a day.'

'It's blood money,' was all Henry could reply. He despaired of parents who, because of greed or necessity, allowed their children to be exploited in a way that served only to maintain an underclass in a permanent state of bondage. Only education would change things in the long term, yet learning was the very thing the system contrived to deny them.

'I've seen Mr Wilkins, the viewer, and he's promised to find a job for our Jed,' said Mrs Hindmarsh, ignoring Henry's strictures. 'He's allowed me and the bairns to stay on in the house but taking in washing and things won't feed us. I'll need Jed's money as well to make ends meet.'

'How old is Jed?' asked Henry.

'Nearly seven.'

'And the others?'

'Jim's five and Jane's just turned nine.'

Henry groaned inwardly. At least Mrs Hindmarsh could blame necessity for her actions, although he doubted if things would have changed had her husband lived. The system was insidious and too entrenched to be overcome by the likes of Mrs Hindmarsh. Widows with three or more sons of working age would often receive proposals of marriage within days of their bereavement; such was the earning power of child labour in the pits.

After Mrs Hindmarsh had left they sat in silence eating the pie she had brought and sipping hot, sweet tea. The words 'fiery pit' still reverberated in Mary's brain and the chill sickness she had experienced over the past few days again overcame her. She fought the fainting spell and struggled to hide her discomfort from Henry.

'I think I'll lie down for a while. She gently excused herself from the table and lay quietly on the large four-poster closing her eyes as she fought the nausea. In the back of her mind she could hear the

112

distant voices of Henry and Mark becoming heated, as if in argument, but she felt too tired to intervene.

'I would like to work in the pit with you father.' Mark's plea was firm and sincere. He knew it would be refused.

'You're too young.'

'Jed's not even seven yet and he's going to be a trapper boy.'

'You're too old to be a trapper boy.'

'Then how can I be too young to work in a pit?'

Henry was exasperated by the logic of Mark's argument and tried to explain.

'Trapper boys usually start work when they are six or seven. When they are about eleven or twelve they are promoted to drivers. Then after a few years they become putters and eventually hewers when they are eighteen or older.

'Then why can't I be a driver. I'm nearly eleven.'

'Because you need experience as a trapper boy,' said Henry lamely. He realised his own logic was less convincing.

'Surely I can be a trapper boy even if I'm ten?'

'Yes, but it's not usual. Besides you haven't finished your education yet.' Henry hoped this would clinch the argument.

'There's no school in North Moor; I've asked. The nearest is Benton and that's not very good.

'We'll find something,' Henry said, trying unsuccessfully to sound convincing.

'If I can't go back to All Saints, I'd rather get a job in the pit.' There was a note of quiet determination in Mark's voice. Henry realised his own resolve to keep his son out of the pits was facing a serious challenge. He decided to try a different approach. 'You wouldn't like working down a pit. It's dirty and boring as well as being dangerous. A boy of your education and imagination would never stand the drudgery and the other boys would bully you and make your life a misery. I wouldn't be there all the time to protect you.'

'You can only prove that if you let me try it.' Mark's voice was assured in the knowledge that he had won the debate if not the decision.

Henry realised too late that his tactics had been wrong. His own argument had been defeated by the sheer logic of Mark's case.

113

However, he still felt confident that pit life was not for his son and Mark would soon realise this. The rub was that in order to prove his point he would have to break his long-held vow to keep Mark out of the pits. He looked at his son with a new respect and affection and saw that his determination had not faltered. After a while he sighed and said, 'I'll see Mr Wilkins tomorrow and see what I can do. But within a week I'll wager you'll want to go back to school.'

Mark's look in response made him wish he could retract. Deep down he now knew he would lose and things would never be the same again. He was suddenly filled with foreboding, as if a chill cloud of apprehension had enveloped his heart. Instinctively he reached out and embraced his son, holding him tight. It was a desperate gesture aimed more at comforting himself than reassuring Mark. He heard a disembodied voice, which he realised was his own, speaking in a strange fierce whisper. 'You and your mother are the most precious part of my life and nothing is going to take that away from me.'

Mark gazed up wide eyed and saw an expression in his father's face he had never seen before. It was as though a premonition of doom lurked, deep and menacing, in some dark cavern of private anguish that lay hidden behind his father's eyes.

It was late afternoon before Mary's troubled dozing eased into tranquil slumber as exhaustion gradually gave way to sleep. The lines of tension on her face slowly relaxed and her expression took on a childlike serenity.

Seeing that his wife was sleeping peacefully, Henry decided to take the opportunity to explore the village and examine the pit whilst it was still light. He called softly to Mark. 'Like to take a stroll and see what the place looks like?'

Mark nodded, quietly tip-toeing towards the door so as not to disturb his mother. Once outside he looked up hesitantly at his father. 'Can we go and see the pit?'

Henry paused, as if trying to shake off the inevitable. Then he shrugged and smiled back. 'Why not? It's what I had in mind anyway.'

The village was quite small with four rows of cottages running north to south in parallel lines with the ominous outline of the pit dominating the southern end. The unpaved tracks that served as roads had a thin coating of cinders which did little to absorb the muddy water oozing up from the thick clay below to form cloudy yellow pools. The ash-heaps between each row of cottages emitted a stale odour of urine and excrement which mingled with the acrid, sulphurous smoke belching out from every cottage chimney.

At least pitmen could keep their families warm, thought Henry. They did not have to forage in the countryside for the ever dwindling supply of wood which became scarcer as the war with France dragged on. Free or cheap coal meant every pitman's hearth would be banked up like a furnace. Hot food and warmth, a rare treat for the poor who lived in towns, was the norm for pit families.

As they made their way towards the pit Henry noted the communal brick ovens for baking bread, one for each row of cottages. They were sited at the back near the ash-heaps with a total disregard for hygiene. The well which served the village was also near the ash-heaps. Sickness, fever and diarrhoea would be as familiar to the North Moor as they were to most colliery villages. Some medical men might use strange sounding names like typhus and typhoid to describe such illnesses but for most pit families it was just part of their daily lives. To devout Methodists it was the will of God.

At the end of the row the last two cottages had been converted into an ale house and Tommy Shop. The Tommy Shop sold a varied collection of food and household goods and both establishments were run by the brother of the pit overman. A substantial part of the profits filtered back to Duncan Forster, the pit owner, who supplied the ales and most of the goods through his other trading interests. He also applied the necessary pressure to ensure that his pitmen and their families used the shop and ale house. This was done by using a combination of coercion and easy credit, the latter being deducted from the men's wages. Prices were high and the quality of the goods low. The strong-willed bought sparingly, just enough to avoid being singled out for victimisation. The weak, enticed by easy credit, became hopelessly in debt.

The ale house was unusually quiet. The normal sounds of raucous revelry and drunkenness were strangely absent.

'Must be baff week,' said Henry absently.

'What's baff week, dad?'

Henry smiled at Mark's puzzlement. 'Baff week is the week before pay day. Pitmen are paid once a fortnight and most are spent up by the second week. So it's called "baff week".

Although it was nearly six o'clock the village exuded an uncanny atmosphere of abandonment; almost as though it had been hastily deserted by its inhabitants. There were no sounds of children at play and the streets were empty of human life. It was as if some invisible Pied Piper had seduced the life blood away with a compelling tune played on magic pipes.

The real explanation was more mundane, reflecting the harsh realities of life in a pit village in the closing years of the eighteenth century. Although an experienced hewer could cut and fill his score of corves in seven or eight hours, it took more than twice as long to haul his six tons of coal to the pit shaft and draw it to the surface. The putters, drivers, crane men and onsetters who were responsible for these heavy tasks had to remain below until all the coal was brought out. As trapper boys were usually aged between six and twelve and the drivers and putters between thirteen and eighteen, the youth of the village were compelled to work fourteen hours or more underground. Starting at four o'clock in the morning, young trapper boys and putters were lucky to be home again by six in the evening. The winter months were spent in almost perpetual darkness. The only time they saw the sun was on the aptly named Sunday.

Traversing the short strip of wasteland that separated the pit from the village, Henry and Mark arrived at the cluster of buildings that surrounded the pit shaft. Most were constructed in a ramshackle way using cheap timber. A few were built of stone or brick but even these had an air of utility and impermanence. Pits moved on as new shafts were sunk and building costs were kept to the minimum.

Henry noted that there were two atmospheric steam engines of the Newcomen type. The larger was the new pumping engine with a cylinder diameter of fifty-two inches. The agent had probably spoken the truth when he said North Moor was a dry pit. The huge storage pond of the drainage system confirmed this.

The smaller steam engine powered the winding engine by pumping water from the storage pond into a large cistern which fed a huge double bucket water wheel. This provided the rotary action, using gears and pulleys mounted over the pit shaft which drew the hazel coal baskets from the pit bottom. Each basket, or corfe as they were called in the northern coalfield, held over six hundredweight of coal.

Mark was intrigued by the huge water wheel. He watched with rapt fascination as the water cascaded from the cistern into the large swivelling buckets attached to the perimeter of the wheel. The creaking of the axle and the pulsating roar of tumbling water blended to a strange, hypnotic rhythm.

Whilst Henry's attention was elsewhere, Mark stood transfixed by the water wheel. He was engrossed in watching the ropes, powered by the water wheel, as they slid quickly over the twin pulleys suspended above the pit shaft. The brakesman in charge of the winding engine was raising a corfe from the bottom of the shaft. Henry pulled out his watch and held it in his hand. When the pulleys stopped rotating, Henry closed the lid of his watch. 'Two minutes', he muttered. 'Not bad for seven hundred feet.'

The sound of his father's voice cut short Mark's daydreaming. 'What's not bad?' he queried.

'The time to raise the corfe over seven hundred feet.'

'Is that good?'

'Not good enough with only one pit shaft.'

'Why?'

'Because it'll create a bottleneck in production. They'll be cutting coal faster than they can raise it.'

'Why don't they sink another shaft?'

Henry shrugged. 'I don't know. Probably it's too expensive at this stage.'

Mark was suddenly curious. 'Does that mean the pit will lose money?'

'I doubt it.' To his surprise Henry felt pleased at Mark's probing interest in the pit. 'All the same,' he went on, 'it would have made more sense if they'd installed one of Mr Watts' new rotary steam engines.' Henry's initial assessment told him there was something fundamentally wrong with the pit but he dismissed the matter from his mind for the present. 'Come on, it's getting dark. Time we were going home.'

As they made their way past the pit, a group of boys and youths were being drawn up the shaft. They emerged, clinging in a precarious cluster to the chain attached to the end of the winding rope before jumping clear of the smoking shaft. The older youths greeted their freedom from entombment with shouts of delight and lethargic bouts of horseplay. The younger boys were too tired to join in after fourteen hours underground. Some were almost asleep and had to be carried home on the shoulders of their elder brothers. When they passed the suspended iron grates filled with flaring coals which illuminated the pithead, their eyes shone listlessly from faces grimed with coal dust. Red parted lips disclosed rows of white teeth gleaming in the light of the flaring braziers. The sounds gradually faded into the quickening night as they headed towards the village and home.

Henry and Mark walked on, skirting the raff-yard which housed the stables, fodder store and the pick-shop where the hewers could have their tools repaired and sharpened, but at their own expense. There were also workshops for joiners, masons, smiths, engine-wrights and general labourers; all the trades necessary for the essential maintenance of the colliery. North Moor colliery encompassed the wide range of work skills required for a self-contained community. It also provided employment for nearly one hundred and fifty men and boys.

Crossing the twin tracks of beech rails which formed the waggon way, Henry noted that the pit was still drawing coal and his doubts about the pit's winding capacity increased. The last of the horse drawn chaldron waggons were being led back to the pit having completed the final return journey of the day from the staithes on the Tyne.

As they made their way home, Mark reminded Henry of his promise. 'You will speak to Mr Wilkins in the morning, dad?' His voice conveyed a mixture of determination and apprehension.

Henry sighed resignedly. 'I will, Mark. You know I always try to keep my promises.' He could only cling to a tenuous hope that the viewer might refuse but the words of the ferret-faced agent kept ringing in his ears. 'He's a bit old to start now but I'll take him on as a trapper if you change your mind.'

Mary was still sleeping soundly when they returned to the cottage. The gentle rise and fall of the covers registered her deep rhythmic breathing but her face looked flushed and feverish.

Henry said good night to Mark and watched, fondly, as his son climbed quietly up the ladder to his bedroom in the loft. Then, after checking that the fire was well banked up with small coals, he laid out his crankie-flannel working clothes ready for the morning. He didn't want to be late for his first day back down the pit.

CHAPTER 13

The sound of urgent tapping slowly permeated Henry's deep slumbers and he woke with a start. He stared into the darkness, his body tense with a feeling of vague trepidation. The tapping started again, this time more insistent.

Henry realised it must be half-past three in the morning and he gently slithered out of bed trying not to disturb Mary. The knocker-up, having received Henry's acknowledgement, proceeded on his rounds leaving a trail of dismay as cursing men and boys dragged their tired and aching bodies from the warm comfort of their beds.

Henry groped his way towards the faint red glow of the fire and felt for the poker. Picking it up he plunged it into the coals, stirring until a yellow flicker of flame licked up the back of the hearth. Lighting a candle he began to dress.

Mary stirred and sat up watching as her husband donned the traditional cranky flannel worn by pitmen in the northern coalfield. The breeches were made from coarse, checked flannel cut short at the knees so that they could be drawn easily over the stout, square-toed shoes. The jacket, made from the same material was long with large side pockets and underneath he wore his shirt and a collarless waistcoat of rough felt. At the coal face, he would strip to the waist and wear the waistcoat next to his skin to absorb the sweat.

Mary rose and ignoring Henry's protests, cut bread, cheese and slices of singing hinny, the rich girdle cake made by Mrs Hindmarsh. She made a mental note that she must learn how to make this popular local delicacy. She packed the food into Henry's satchel and filled his canteen with sweet tea. Now, with satchel and canteen slung around his neck and newly sharpened picks balanced over his shoulder, Henry was ready for his first day back down the pit. After such a long absence from hewing, he hoped his strength and stamina would help him survive the hell of his first shift. He knew it would take several weeks before his body became used to the torture of heavy labour in a confined space. He would be relying on the peculiar skills which marked a pit-bred hewer, to see him through the early days of his return to the trade.

At Henry's insistence, Mary returned to her bed. She shivered, though not with cold. Her thoughts were with Mrs Hindmarsh and the other recent widows of the village, a terrifying reminder that North Moor was a fiery pit.

A draught of cold air entered the cottage signalling Henry's departure. He quietly closed the door and stepped into the chill air of an early autumn morning, joining the straggling group of men and boys heading dejectedly towards the pit. Along the darkened rows of cottages doors opened and closed, disgorging families of pit folk to swell the human river that meandered in sluggish melancholy towards the pithead. It was as if the houses were bleeding, with all the life blood of the village flowing in a silent stream to be swallowed by the pit.

Back at the cottage, Mark moved away from the opening in the loft floor where he had been watching and listening. He crawled back, into his bed and drifted slowly back to sleep.

At the pit shaft Henry was greeted with a mixture of curiosity and suspicion by his fellow hewers. He knew they would maintain this reserve until he gained their confidence and respect, and this would take time. Pitmen followed a dangerous trade and their dependence on one another was a major factor in binding pit villages into close-knit communities. Outsiders sometimes mistook this for insularity, often accentuated by the isolated location of most pit villages.

A large, heavily-muscled hewer with long blonde hair detached himself from the group of men waiting to descend the shaft. In the light of the suspended fire baskets Henry could see a long, deep scar running down one side of his face. His blue eyes were intelligent and penetrating as he smiled at Henry and held out his hand.

'I'm Wilf Hindmarsh.' He paused, then seeing Henry's look of puzzlement, added, 'Dora's brother-in-law, she lives next door to you.'

As the connection registered, Henry laughed and took the outstretched hand. 'Of course, Jed's mother. I'm a bit slow on the uptake this time of the morning.'

'Aren't we all,' said Wilf, then putting his hand on Henry's shoulders led him to a group of men by the shaft. 'Come and meet my marras.'

Henry was introduced to Wilf's group of friends and as the names were reeled off he soon lost track....Jack Jennings, Sep Fordyce, Jim Walters, Sam Elliott ... The list went on and on as he felt his hand being shaken and his back slapped. Wilf Hindmarsh was clearly the natural leader of the men of North Moor Colliery.

'He's alright,' said Wilf as if reaching a verdict. 'He's one of us in spite of the way he talks.' This was greeted with grins and laughter.

Henry smiled back. 'Blame it on my spell in Yorkshire; enough to ruin anyone's speech.'

'Mind you, he's got education,' said Wilf winking at the circle of grinning faces. 'He's the only one who could sign his name on the bond so you'd better watch out.'

'He's the one that needs to look out,' warned Sep Fordyce. 'If the viewer or the keeker find out he can write the bugger'l be in trouble. The owners don't take kindly to pitmen with learning.'

There was a chorus of agreement and sympathetic nods in Henry's direction. Wilf's tone became more serious. 'You'll need to watch out, Henry. Sep's right, pitmen with learning are looked on as troublemakers by the owners, especially Forster. His viewer, Mr Wilkins, is not a bad man but he's weak and does what he's told. The one to watch out for is Mulligan, the keeker. He's an evil man if ever there was one and quick to bear a grudge. He'll end up in a ditch with his throat cut one night, mark my words.'

At this point they were interrupted by a shout from the banksman as the winding rope returned to the surface. The crowd of men and boys moved towards the shaft and swung themselves onto the chains attached to the end of the winding rope. Some of the more adventurous boys hung on to the rope above. Henry found himself with his leg through a loop on the chain alongside Wilf who was on the next available perch. Above him, a whole cluster of men and boys dangled precariously over the smoking shaft. There was a shout from the banksman and they began their seven hundred feet descent into the darkness of the pit.

122

It took two minutes to reach the bottom of the shaft and during this time Henry reflected on Wilf's warning about Mulligan, the keeker. In any pit village, the most hated man was the keeker whose job it was to weigh and inspect the coal   produced by the men. He could fine any hewer who sent a corfe of coal to bank that was marginally underweight or contained even the minutest amount of stone. He could also impose penalties if the coal was deemed too small because only large coals could command top prices. The keeker's decision was arbitrary and final; there was no appeal or redress for the men. Also, acting as agent for the owner, he was often paid commission on the number of corves found faulty. He was in an unassailable position of power able to exploit and victimize those who incurred his displeasure.

Nothing had changed, thought Henry; Wilf's warning had been sincere and timely. The keeker was still the most hated man in the village; despised yet feared by the men he abused.

At the bottom of the shaft the men lit their candles and inserted them into a piece of damp clay placed between the first and second finger. Henry followed Wilf along the main roadway that led into the mine.

Like most mines in the northern coalfield, North Moor colliery extracted coal using a system known as bord and pillar. This method was particularly suited to the conditions found in the deep mines of Northumberland and Durham where supporting the roof was of critical importance. Great care and technical skills were called for.

The first task was to drive the main road from the bottom of the shaft into the coal deposits. Then tunnels were cut into the coal at right angles on each side of the roadway and after some twenty yards the tunnels turned left and right to leave large rectangular pillars of solid coal to support the roof.

When the maximum quantity of coal that could be worked away from the shaft in this way had been taken out, the dangerous process of "robbing" the support pillars of coal would commence. The hewers would then work back towards the shaft taking out part of each pillar of coal or alternate pillars and allowing the roof to collapse behind them.

In this way nearly half the coal could be removed in the first working and a further twenty-five per cent by robbing the pillars in the second stage of the extraction process. However, it was a highly dangerous technique, especially in the gaseous or fiery pits such as North Moor. Once the pillars were removed and the roof allowed to fall, pockets of trapped gas could escape into the workings often with disastrous results. The combination of firedamp gas and the naked candles used by pitmen was dangerous and often lethal.

As the group of men and boys progressed along the roadway their numbers began to diminish. Hewers and putters peeled off the main party stooping low to enter the constricted tunnels on either side to take up their allotted work stations at the coal face. Each hewer had his own workspace called a stall, drawn by lot, to ensure that everyone had his fair share of good and bad stalls. The coal seam could vary enormously over short distances and this could have a major effect on a man's earnings.

Near the end of the main roadway a simple wooden crane had been erected to lift the loaded corves of coal from the sledges used by the putters onto a flatbed waggon called a rolley. The roadway had just enough height and width to allow a small horse to pull a loaded rolley containing three corves of coal along to the shaft bottom where onsetters transferred them on to the winding rope to be raised to the surface.

Henry and Wilf were the last hewers in the group to reach their work areas at the end of the roadway. They had been allotted adjacent stalls and stooping low, they crawled along the low passage that led to the coal face.

'The agent at the binding said the seams were five feet thick,' Henry grunted.

Wilf laughed. 'You'll be lucky to see four feet in this part of the pit. You ought to know better than to believe the stories they put around at binding time. They promise you the earth if you sign their bloody bond.'

'At least it's dry,' said Henry. 'He was right on that score.'

'Aye, but make sure you've got a good current of air at the face to clear any gas away. It's a fiery pit, Henry, so keep an eye on your candle.'

'By the time you notice the flame turning blue it's usually too late' said Henry, trying to sound unconcerned.

'True. It's better to rely on a good course of air and the feeling in your gut,' Wilf acknowledged.

During their progress Henry had been carefully noting the pillars of coal left to support the roof. He estimated they were about twenty yards by twelve.

'They haven't left much in the pillars, Wilf. Not for a first working.'

Wilf's crouching figure paused and he looked back over his shoulder at Henry. 'You don't miss much, do you?' There was a growing note of respect in his voice. 'I'll lay you've been more than a hewer in your time.' It was a statement rather than a question.

'Sort of,' said Henry guardedly, 'and I know there's something not quite right with this pit.'

Wilf laughed but there was no humour in the sound. 'Bloody right you are. Forster's trying to do everything on the cheap and it shows.'

Henry nodded. 'He's taking out too much coal for the first working, that's for sure. It doesn't make sense.'

'Why?'

'Because he hasn't put in the winding capacity to cope. The roadways are too small and there aren't enough horses below ground to speed up the haulage.'

'Shrewd bugger, aren't you,' said Wilf approvingly. 'You'll know the answer then?'

'No.' Henry was genuinely puzzled.

Wilf looked quizzically at Henry.

'The story is that Forster's strapped for cash. He's borrowed heavily and the lenders are pressing him.'

Suddenly, everything became clear in Henry's mind. The pit was geared to short term returns but there was not enough investment even to ensure this. In a well-planned and properly financed pit there would have been a better winding engine and a second shaft would have been sunk by now. Wilf's explanation made sense. The pit was being run on a shoestring.

'Now I understand,' said Henry, 'but it doesn't make me feel any better.'

Wilf grinned. 'Nor me, but I've got a score of corves to fill. Can't stand talking to you all day.'

125

Stooped in the cramped confines of the tunnel, Henry muttered back, 'Can't stand being the operative words, I'd say.'

They both laughed and crawled on to their allotted work places at the coal face.

On reaching his work stall, Henry stripped down to his drawers, shoes and socks then replaced the rough felt waistcoat next to his skin to absorb the sweat that would pour from his body during the next eight hours. After carefully checking the air flow, he raised his candle to examine the coal seam. It was important to study the cleat or structure of the coal as carefully as a carpenter would study the grain of his wood. Henry knew that a good hewer, using all his skill, could cut more and better quality coal than one relying only on brute strength.

After a quick scrutiny Henry found he knew instinctively where to cut his first section or jud of coal. He realised, first with surprise and then with pleasure, that his old skills had not deserted him including the knack of working in a confined space. Lying on his side and facing the coal seam he rested his shoulder on his cracket. This was a low, sloping stool on which a hewer placed his thigh when crouching or his shoulder if lying down, to gain extra support. He then made a deep wedge shaped cut along the base of the coal seam using a short headed pick which was pointed at both ends. This was the hardest part of a hewer's job requiring strength and stamina.

After cutting the base of the seam to pre-marked points, Henry changed his position to a crouch and made deep vertical cuts into the seam on either side of the jud or mass of coal he intended to bring down. When this had been done he drove wedges into the top of the jud to dislodge the coal. This was the age-old hewer's art of kirving designed to bring down the coal in large pieces. Small coal was often unsaleable and usually left underground. If it was sent to the surface the hewer risked being fined by the keeker.

Henry had filled his first corfe with coal when the putters arrived. They had the back breaking task of pushing and pulling, or putting as it was known in the northern coalfield, the loaded wicker corves from the coal face along the low, narrow tunnels that led to the main roadway. Each full corfe weighed over six hundredweight and was transported on a crude, wheeled sledge which had to be manhandled through passageways that were often only three or four feet high. When they reached the roadway, the corfe was transferred by crane onto the horse drawn rolleys, flat waggons mounted on crude rails.

Putting was the most physically demanding of any job in the pit and was undertaken by youths and boys. Younger boys of similar age and size would work, or put, in pairs known as half marras. Older, stronger youths would put alone. Where a young boy worked with an older and stronger youth he was known as a foal. He would usually be bullied and beaten by his stronger partner, the headsman, into doing the lion's share of the work. In the underground hierarchy of the pit the hewer was king and thereafter strength prevailed. The strong bully was allowed to prey on the weak and usually did so. Down the pit, oppression fed on more oppression and the most defenceless were the young foals and trapper boys who were exploited unmercifully by the owners and abused by their own kind.

Henry groaned silently when he saw that the putters servicing his stall were headsman and foal. The older of the two was a large sullen youth of about seventeen. The foal was a boy no older than Mark but with a much smaller physique. Henry hated bullying and here was the perfect combination to encourage it. He hoped he wouldn't have to intervene but such sentiments were quickly dashed.

The younger boy working as foal was harnessed to the front of the sledge by two ropes attached round his waist. The older lad acting as headsman took up his position at the rear and cursed at the boy to pull. Henry noted that both putters wore leather aprons to protect the lower spine, but their shoulders were cut and scarred by constant contact with the jagged roofs of the low galleries.

Despite the efforts of the straining putters the sledge remained stationary, its wheels obstructed by the small coals lying on the tunnel floor. With an angry bellow, the older lad edged round the sledge and began to punch and kick the younger boy. Trapped in his harness the young foal could only curl up on the ground and try to avoid the blows.

This proved too much for Henry. 'Stop that!' His voice, icy with menace, transmitted his smouldering anger as he moved to intervene.

The older putter turned defiantly to face Henry but his belligerence quickly crumbled when he saw the steely expression in Henry's eyes.

127

'If I don't bray 'im he won't do his share of the work. Nowt wrong with that, is there?' He said defensively, taken aback by Henry's intervention.

'Would you hit somebody your own size?' Henry asked.

'I wouldn't have to,' the youth said petulantly. 'Somebody my size would do his share of the work, not like this weedy little sod.'

'I'm not a weedy sod.' The young boy had spirit and wasn't going to be cowed. Not in front of his protector at least, though he knew he'd suffer later for his act of bravado.

Henry decided the matter had gone far enough. 'You're costing me money.' He leant his weight to the sledge. 'Come on, let's move it.' His strength added to that of the putters was sufficient to get the sledge moving and he watched as their flickering candle disappeared into the darkness of the tunnel. He knew he should not have interfered, that once out of sight the older boy would vent his spleen on the young, hapless foal.

Henry sighed. It was the way of things and he knew that he alone could not change it for the better. The petty tyranny of the pit was the consequence of the environment and years of neglect. It required a renaissance in attitudes and human understanding to change things. Sadly, this was unlikely to happen unless working conditions were radically improved. He retrieved his pick and carried on working.

After eight hours of remorseless toil every muscle in Henry's body was stretched to breaking point. He was nearing the limits of his endurance and facing an insurmountable pain barrier. He'd worked his body to its limits yet had only sent eighteen corves to bank. It was a depressing start, he thought, though not altogether unexpected. Skill on its own, like brute strength was not enough. Successful hewing demanded a judicious blend of the two.

His private world of agony was suddenly interrupted by a cheerful voice he recognised as Wilf's.

'Still at it, then?' Wilf sat hunched over and smiling, his eyes and teeth shining out from a coal grimed face in the reflected light from his candle.

Henry paused and smiled back. 'It's going to take a bit of getting used to. I'm not as fit as I thought I was.'

Aye, it takes time,' agreed Wilf. He pointed in the direction of his own work stall. I've filled two extra corves. If you put your tally on them it'll make up your score. Then we can get out of this hell-hole and go home.'

Overcome by Wilf's thoughtfulness and generosity Henry could only offer a muted protest which was quickly cut short by Wilf.

'Like I said, it takes time after a lay-off. You can do the same for me one day, if I'm not up to it,' he added in an attempt to defuse any embarrassment.

It would be a rare day, Henry thought, when Wilf was not up to it. The man's kindness and understanding brought a glow to his heart and sent a suffusion of emotion coursing through his veins. Suddenly the pain and misery was all worthwhile. With the friendship and understanding of men like Wilf Hindmarsh there was hope for the future and he felt a new flame of optimism kindling inside himself.

CHAPTER 14

Duncan Forster sat behind a large mahogany writing table in the elegant library of North Moor Hall. The inlaid leather surface of the table was littered with papers and financial accounts relating to his various business enterprises and, to judge from his expression, they made depressing reading. An anaemic shaft of winter sunlight shone through the tall windows but the subdued rays did little to lighten the air of gloom inside the room.

This was reflected in the blackness of Forster's mood as he read the returns charting the dismal progress of his financial investments. His expression darkened further as his anger rose and a strangulated curse escaped his lips. Finally he slammed down the last document and turned to face his son Roland who was standing by the book shelves idly turning the pages of a book.

Roland Forster was a tall youth of nineteen whose slim frame and casual manner conveyed an impression of maturity greater than his age. At first glance he was strikingly handsome, but on closer scrutiny, a number of flaws quickly became apparent. The thick, dark hair was too straight and somewhat dank, the lips were thin and cruel, the eyes languid and arrogant. He was selfish and lazy but women found him strangely attractive.

Duncan Forster looked quizzically at his son. 'Well, what do you think? Will the pit ever make money? I take it you HAVE read the mine reports?' There was a studied emphasis on the word have that bordered on sarcasm.

'Yes, father.'

'Well, then, what do you suggest?'

'I'm not sure, father. Mr Wilkins thinks we're making good progress.'

'Damn it, I'm not interested in what Wilkins thinks. I'll find that out for myself in a moment. I want to know what you think.'

Although Roland was afraid of his father he knew he had some strange hold on his affection. He decided to try and bluff his way out of the situation and risk his father's greater wrath if he failed.

'I think we could cut back on some of the men and reduce our costs.' He carefully avoided his father's eyes.

'And reduce our output and our sales revenue?' Duncan Forster was incredulous. 'Is that the best you can offer?'

Roland knew he had blundered. He wasn't interested in the mine; in fact he hated it. Nor had he bothered to study the accounts. He remained silent waiting for his father to erupt.

Duncan Forster obliged. 'You've had the benefit of a sound and expensive education. You've spent six months apprenticed to my viewer to learn the science of colliery management and you haven't mastered even the most basic elements of how to run a pit. I was only nineteen when my father put me in charge of my first pit and by God I expect you to be able to do the same.'

Roland kept his silence but raised his eyes to meet his father's angry gaze. He saw an expression that frightened him and one he had seen on many occasions. It was a mixture of love and contempt but after a while the look of contempt would usually fade leaving only love tinged with a strange sad longing. He watched anxiously and gave a silent sigh of relief when he saw the softening in his father's eyes.

Duncan Forster had long since recognised Roland's lazy streak. But worse still, he sensed a fundamental flaw in his son's character. It was a weakness that all his son's lying and deceit could not conceal and this worried him. The arrogance and bullying he could condone, but not weakness. After all he was his son and would be master one day and firm action was necessary to keep control over the boy. But despite all his fears and doubts and his contempt for weakness, he loved his son dearly, and it was this that made him persevere against his better judgement. His love for his only son was greater than the contempt he felt. He would continue to forgive Roland's failures whilst striving hard to correct them.

He sighed and turned away. Would it have been different, he wondered, if Martha had given him more sons? He shrugged off his depression and turned again to Roland. 'I want you to put that book away and sit down.' He pointed to a chair in the corner of the library. 'Now if you watch and listen carefully you might learn some basic principles on how to manage a pit. You might also appreciate the

131

financial mess we're in and help me do something about it.' He waited until Roland had sat down then turned towards the library door and bellowed, 'Wilkins!'

The small group of men waiting nervously outside the door jumped at the sound and glanced anxiously at each other. Wilkins, the viewer, rose and made a studied but unconvincing attempt to look unconcerned before opening the door and stepping inside.

Forster carried on sifting and reading documents, totally ignoring his downcast viewer who stood uncomfortably on the other side of the table. It was a deliberate ploy on Forster's part to help him stamp his authority on the interview, especially as it was likely to be confrontational. He sensed the apprehension in his viewer and experienced a sadistic satisfaction as he allowed the tension to mount. At last he looked up, his eyes cold and intimidating and threw the fortnightly pit financial statement across the table. 'Not a pretty picture, is it, Wilkins?'

The viewer nervously moved his weight from foot to foot. 'It's improving, Mr Forster.'

'But not fast enough.'

'We've had problems with gas. Too many blowers.' Wilkins realised he was already on the defensive.

'But I agreed to increase the size of the ventilating furnace to take care of that. There should be a good course of air now.' Forster's tone was scathing.

'The blowers are still causing a build-up of firedamp, the men aren't too happy…'

Forster cut him short. 'The happiness of a pitman is not my concern, Wilkins. They've all signed the bond and that means they'll work when I say so. Is that clear?'

'But it's only a few months since we lost six men, Mr Forster. The men are worried.'

'Nonsense! It's your responsibility to see that the men work when I say so. You're too soft with them, Wilkins, and I won't have you jeopardising my investment.' An icy menace had crept into Forster's voice. He knew Wilkins was a competent viewer but he was too soft on the men and needed propping up in matters of discipline. It never occurred to him that Wilkins was a compassionate man, and if it had, he would have dismissed it as another form of weakness.

Wilkins felt his stomach begin to knot as fear and frustration built up inside him. Most owners left the running of their pits to their viewers but Forster was one of a small but growing number of coal masters who had learnt their trade as viewers. It was this new breed of entrepreneur that was the most difficult to work with, especially the domineering types like Forster who were always impatient to sample the results of their greedy exploitation. He heard Forster's voice cold and probing.

'We only brought up three hundred and forty chaldrons to bank last week.'

'That's not bad for twenty-five hewers, Mr Forster.'

'It's not good enough for me. I need four hundred and fifty chaldrons, Wilkins. Twelve hundred tons of coal each week and every week from now on, understand?'

The viewer gasped. 'But we're drawing coal sixteen hours a day to raise three hundred and forty chaldrons. It'll mean working round the clock to raise four hundred and fifty. '

'So? Is that a problem?' Forster was unmoved.

'The trappers and putters are already working fourteen hours a day underground. You can't expect them to do more.'

'Then what do you suggest?'

Wilkins rubbed his chin thoughtfully. 'We'll have to take on more boys and run two shifts.'

'Rubbish!' We'll take on a few extra but they can all work a sixteen hour shift. Won't do 'em any harm and keep 'em out of mischief.' Forster paused, looking thoughtful. 'We'll need to wind twenty-four hours a day. The onsetters can work two shifts, but only two per shift.'

Wilkins was appalled at the thought of trapper boys and putters working a sixteen hour day. It was too much, especially for their gruelling task. He made one more attempt to water down the proposals. 'We can't cut that amount of coal without more hewers.' He paused, looking anxiously at his employer.

'I've taken care of that,' Forster said dismissively. 'Ask Gibson and Mulligan to come it.'

Gibson, the ferret-faced agent entered first followed by Mulligan, the keeker. They joined Wilkins, forming a nervous semi-circle around the table. Forster deliberately refrained from asking them to sit down and after a pause turned questioningly to his agent. 'Well, how many hewers did you get?'

'Nine put their mark on the bond, Mr Forster.'

'How much did it cost me?'

'Forty pounds binding money, all told,' the agent said edgily.

Forster grimaced and turned to his keeker. 'Hear that, Mulligan?'

The keeker nodded.

'Then see I get it back.'

The keeker looked nonplussed. 'They'll have spent it by now, Mr Forster.'

'I know that, you bloody fool. Do I have to spell it out? Fine 'em. Take it out of their wages and don't take too long about it. I want that money back inside three months. I don't care how you do it.'

Mulligan looked unhappy. He knew he could not take it all back from the new men. He'd have to spread the extra fines among the whole of the existing work force and that could spell trouble.

Gibson, the ferret-faced agent, spoke up. 'We'll need nine cottages for the new hewers, Mr Forster.'

'How many have we got?'

'Only six empty.'

'Then three of the widows will have to go.'

This was too much for Wilkins. 'You promised that the widows and their families could stay on, Mr Forster. It's the done thing when their men folk have been killed in the pit.'

Forster looked irritated. 'A profitable pit is more important. If the pit doesn't make money there won't be a roof over any of their heads, never mind the widows.'

'But we can't go back on the promises we made. It's always been a pit custom.' The viewer's concern bolstered his resolve to argue the case.

Forster's temper was now becoming strained. 'I've kept my promises for six months and given them credit at the shop with little hope of repayment. I've demonstrated my concern but they are not my responsibility. They'll just have to go to their kinfolk.'

'Some of them don't have any kinfolk,' the viewer pleaded. 'Unless, of course, you count their own bairns as kinfolk,' he added sarcastically.

At this point Forster's anger exploded. 'If the profitable running of the pit was as much your concern as mine we might not be in the position we are today. If all I can get from you is obstruction then perhaps it's time I found myself a new viewer.' The threat was delivered with a baleful glare at the hapless Wilkins whose opposition immediately began to crumble.

The keeker had listened with a mixture of relief and enjoyment as the honest viewer was browbeaten into submission. He was a bully like Forster and shared his master's contempt for weakness and equated caring with softness. It was for these qualities that Forster had made him keeker. The viewer's unhappy predicament had brought a faint smile to the keeker's lips, which was spotted by Forster.

'You can take that bloody smirk off your face, Mulligan. I'm none too happy with your work so perhaps a change of keeker at North Moor pit might not be a bad thing either.'

This produced a worried response from the keeker. 'I'm doing my best, sir.' His expression returned to its normal sullen state.

'Oh, we're doing our best, are we,' Forster mimicked. 'Then your best just isn't good enough.' He picked up the pit wages return. 'Not one hewer has earned less than twenty-eight shilling a fortnight. Are you blind, man? Can't you spot small coal and stone?'

'I've fined them whenever I can, sir, but the men have been sending extra corves to bank.' The keeker tried to explain.

'That gives you extra scope to levy higher fines, Mulligan. And try to be more subtle. Some men have hardly been fined whilst others have lost half their wages. Why?'

The keeker was about to answer when Forster cut him short. 'Don't tell me, Mulligan. Let me guess. You fine the ones you don't like; the ones you have it in for? The few you like and the ones you are afraid of you leave alone. Is that it?' Forster knew he was right and so did Mulligan.

'It may seem like that to some,' the keeker said weakly.

'Well, it's going to change from now on.' Forster's voice was curt and authoritative. 'We're paying the hewers far too much. As from now I don't want to see anyone earning more than twenty-four shillings a fortnight. And most a good deal less,' he added.

'If we do that we'll never get them to sign the bond next year,' said the agent intervening. 'Word will get round the other pits too.'

Forster sighed in exasperation. 'I'm well aware of that, Gibson. Three months before the binding date we'll gradually ease the fines until they almost disappear. Pitmen have very short memories and the pill can always be sugared with binding money and a few barrels of ale at the binding.'

Wilkins had listened with growing dismay to a strategy of further oppression and exploitation, a strategy that he would be expected to implement. In doing so he would be seen as a consenting if unwilling party. The situation troubled him even more as he knew he would be unable to face up to the moral dilemma it posed. As in the past he would simply try to shut it from his mind and do his master's bidding. In a strange, irrational way he felt hypnotically attracted to Forster's Machiavellian psyche, and it was this illogical attachment as much as his fear of the man that had turned him into a moral eunuch.

Forster had been watching his viewer's increasing distress with cynical amusement. 'You look unwell, Wilkins. All this too much for that delicate conscience of yours?'

The goading tone sparked an angry response from Wilkins. 'We're playing with the lives of over a hundred men and boys, Mr Forster. The pit's a dangerous enough place as it is; we mustn't make it more so.'

'And just how will making my pit profitable also make it more dangerous?'

'Because if you force boys to work sixteen hours a day accidents will happen. They'll be too tired and become careless. For heaven's sake, Mr Forster, some of them are only children.'

'The hewers can still cut their score in eight hours, can't they?'

'Yes, but the haulage will take longer unless you increase the numbers of putters to match the increase in hewers. It would be better to use more horses underground and fewer boys.'

Forster exploded. 'Rubbish man! A good horse costs fifteen pounds and eats seventy bushels of oats a year plus a ton and a half of hay. It has to be fed whether it works or not and needs a driver when it

136

does. As my viewer you should know this. Have you any idea what it all costs?'

Wilkins was about to reply when Forster cut him short. I'll tell you how much,' he continued scathingly. 'Nearly five shillings a day. The price of fodder has gone through the roof, thanks to this bloody war with France. A boy putter costs me less than two shillings a day and a young foal only half that. And that's only when they're working and before Mulligan here gets his claws into 'em.'

'I still think more horses would improve things,' Wilkins went on doggedly. 'It would speed up the haulage and let us work back to the shaft before other problems start.'

'Other problems?' Forster looked surprised. 'Is there something I should know?'

'We're taking out too much coal in the first working, Mr Forster. I told you it was risky.'

'They're doing the same at Willington.'

'Aye, but we're over a hundred feet deeper. We need to leave bigger pillars.'

'Why?'

'Because the floors in the new workings are getting soft. We'll get creep which can cause fissures if we don't enlarge the pillars in the last section and you know that can lead to dangerous pockets of gas.'

Forster shook his head. 'You're too cautious, Wilkins. We're near the boundary line so we'll be working back robbing the pillars soon. Just leave things as they are. You can take on another half dozen boys but no extra horses.' His tone brooked no further argument.

Roland had followed the discussion with more than his usual degree of interest. He had an idea and the more he thought about it the more convinced he became that it would work. If it did he might redeem himself in his father's eyes and make the others sit up and take him more seriously.

'May I make a suggestion, father?' He tried to sound nonchalant but his voice cracked with excitement.

Forster looked at his son in surprise. 'You, make a suggestion? I don't believe it,' he added incredulously.

A wry smile spread over Wilkins face whilst the agent exchanged a smirking glance with the keeker. They all waited expectantly.

Roland paused, making the most of his moment. 'Why don't we install one of Mr Watt's new rotary engines? It will double the winding capacity and save on the cost of fuel. We could also sink a new shaft.' He waited expectantly hoping for praise. His father's wrath caught him totally unprepared.

'Bloody fool!' Forster foamed. 'Now I know I've sired an idiot.' He glared at his son, trying to control his anger before continuing. 'We can't afford one of Mr Watt's new engines nor the royalties he and Mr Boulton expect for the privilege. As for saving coal? Damn it boy, we've got all the small coal we need free of charge. It's little use for anything else.' He paused, then went on remorselessly, his words beating into his son's wilting brain. 'Get it into your thick skull that it's lack of finance that is the problem, not lack of ideas. Don't you think I would have sunk another shaft by now if I had the money?'

Roland, brow-beaten into submission, remained silent. Forster looked around the room and glowered at each of the men in turn before continuing in the same aggressive tone. 'We'll do things my way from now on. Is that clear?'

There was no further argument and Forster curtly dismissed his employees. Roland was also about to leave the room when his father called him back. 'I want a word with you, Roland. Shut the door.'

Roland returned nervously to the library and waited anxiously for his father to speak.

'I spoke to Mrs Gordon today,' Forster said. 'Would you like to speculate why?'

Roland shook his head, 'No, father.'

'I wanted to know why she'd dismissed Bessie. Any thoughts on the matter?' Forster's voice was mild but tinged with menace.

Roland stayed silent, avoiding his father's eyes.

'Mrs Gordon didn't want to tell me either. Had to drag it out of her. Did you know that Bessie's the third maid to leave our household this year?'

'I thought you said she'd been dismissed?'

Forster's anger rose. 'Don't you try to be clever with me? She became pregnant like the rest of 'em. Coincidence?' His voice rose. 'You've been at it again, haven't you? '

'Why do I always get the blame?' Roland whined.

'Because all your brains are in your cock. You can't control yourself, can you?'

The jibe stung Roland. 'She was a slut, father. She probably opened her legs to half the village,'

'That's all the more reason for you to keep away. I've given you the address of a respectable house in Newcastle which caters discreetly for the randy habits of young bloods like you but you still insist on shitting on your own doorstep. Well it's got to stop, do you hear me?'

'But father....'

'No buts,' Forster cut in. 'If you put the same effort into learning how to run my pit as you put into your fornication I might find it in me to condone, or at least understand, your behaviour. But you don't, do you?'

Roland squirmed. 'No, father.'

'Your conduct is starting to cause resentment. Worse still, you're becoming a laughing stock.' Forster's last words struck home, wounding his son's pride.

'Is that all, father?' Roland's voice was now stiff with anger and resentment.

Forster sighed and gave a weary, dismissive wave in the direction of the door. 'I can see I'm wasting my time.'

'Then if you'll excuse me, father.' Still seething with indignation at his father's treatment and irritated with himself for having been found out, Roland made what he hoped would seem a dignified exit.

On leaving the library he made his way up one of the twin balustrade staircases that swept up from each side of the hall to a long gallery. From each end of the gallery wide passages led to the east and west wings of the house. As he neared the top of the staircase he saw the figure of Mrs Gordon appear at the far end of the gallery. She stopped in confusion and met Rowland's malevolent look which sent a chill of terror down her spine. Struggling to maintain her composure, she hurried down the stairs.

Roland smiled maliciously after her before entering the west wing, heading for his room and a much needed brandy. He was half way down the carpeted passage way when a door opened and an attractive chamber maid in her mid-twenties emerged carrying a coal scuttle. She stood to one side to allow Roland to pass but he stopped and stared rudely at her. He saw she had large breasts and felt a sudden stir of excitement.

'What's your name?'

'Polly James, sir.'

'I haven't seen you around here before.'

'I'm Bessie's replacement, sir.' She could feel his eyes on her breasts and saw the flicker of arousal in them.

'Ah! That explains it. A pretty girl like you wouldn't go unnoticed for long.'

Polly didn't drop her eyes and think of escape. She recognised Roland for what he was and smiled knowingly. His reputation didn't worry her for she'd spent years tendering to the needs of gentry like him. She was interested only in how she could profit from any relationship that might develop.

Roland's arousal increased. 'Why don't you tend to my fire,' he said pointing to his room.

Polly smiled at his double entendre and responded impishly in kind. 'I'm sure I can get a good flame going, Master Roland.' It was the first time she had used his name and she made it sound like the invitation it was.

Roland grinned and opened his bedroom door. This was a clever girl and one after his own heart. 'Allow me,' he said standing aside to let her pass.

Once inside, all Roland's pretence of gallantry disappeared. The coal scuttle crashed to the floor as he made a grab for her.

'Now then, Master Roland, don't be too hasty.' Her feigned attempt at modesty was unconvincing. 'Anticipation is half the fun, I always say.'

He nodded and watched as she stripped, slowly and sensuously. He ogled as the breasts that so fascinated him were exposed, large and purple-nippled. When she had removed the last vestige of clothing, Polly lay down on the bed in a provocative pose that revealed the curve of her hips above long shapely thighs that led invitingly to a large, erotic triangle of pubic hair.

Roland felt a primitive excitement he had rarely known before. A surge of lust pulsated through his loins and he felt his erection bulging out the front of his trousers. Polly's eyes held a harlot's smile of triumph as she watched him tear off his clothes. She uttered a cry of surprise at the sight and size of his manhood. 'My, you are big,' she giggled and let out a gasp as he entered her.

When he had satisfied his craving he lay for a while feeling himself go limp inside her. Finally he rolled over on to his back and stared at the ceiling reflecting on his father's warning. Slowly a smile of defiance lit up his face. 'Bugger you, father. This beats mining any day,' he murmured to himself.

CHAPTER 15

Henry reluctantly kept his promise and asked Mr Wilkins, the viewer, if he would take Mark on. He also put in a word for young Jed at the request of his neighbour, Mrs Hindmarsh.

'I would have asked Wilf, my brother-in-law, to do it,' she had explained, 'but he thinks Jed should have a bit more schooling, such as it is.' the school was an extension of the Sunday school and not held in high regard.

'But Jed's only six,' Henry had protested.

'He'll be seven in a couple of months. Most of the bairns start when they're seven or eight. Besides, we need the money and with Jed working in the pit and young Jim ready to follow, we've a better chance of keeping the cottage.'

Henry began to appreciate her concern. The rumour was spreading that three of the widows were about to be evicted to make way for the new hewers and their families. A widow with two young sons could provide cheap cannon fodder for the pit and therefore would be less likely to be singled out for eviction.

'I'll see what I can do,' he'd finally promised after realising his objections were having no effect.

Henry was fortunate in that his request to Mr Wilkins coincided with the viewer's plans to recruit the six extra boys agreed by Forster to augment the nine new hewers.

'Aye, Standish, I'll take 'em on as trappers. Mind you, your boy's coming on eleven, isn't he?'

Henry nodded knowing what the viewer was about to say.

'He's a bit old for a trapper boy,' Wilkins demurred, 'and he'll need some pit experience before he can go on to putting or driving.

'I've been trying to keep him out of the pit, Mr Wilkins, but he seems determined to give it a try.'

The viewer looked understandingly at Henry. There was something special in this man, he thought, not your ordinary pitman.

'Well, he'll have to start as a trapper but I might be able to move him on to putting when he's had some experience.'

Henry smiled ruefully. 'Thank you, Mr Wilkins.' Inwardly however, he hoped a spell as a trapper boy would prove sufficient to discourage Mark from further pursuit of a pit career.

The hewers were always first out of the pit and Henry and Wilf joined the straggle of tired men, some smoking pungent pipes and others chatting as they made their way to the village. On arrival at their cottages they would strip and bathe in a small tin bath that their wives would make ready for them. It was a daily ritual after each shift and afterwards the cottage doors would open and showers of dirty soap-suds would be ejected into the street outside.

Henry could identify those of his companions who had spent a lifetime down the pit. Their stature was diminutive, their figures disproportionate and misshapen. Their bodies had a strange curvature, with chests protruding like those of a pigeon. Arms long and oddly suspended and the legs bowed. Their faces were equally striking with hollow cheeks and overhanging brows. It was the culmination of years of work in confined spaces compounded by poor nutrition. Henry wondered, sadly, if he would end up looking like this.

That evening, after supper, Henry broke the news to Mark.

'Mr Wilkins has taken you on. You start on Monday as a trapper. He's taken Jed on too.' He watched for Mark's response and any sign of regret but saw none.

'Thank you.' Mark's voice betrayed neither happiness nor disappointment. 'I'll do my best, I promise,' he added with quiet determination.

'I'm sure you will, Mark,' Henry said sadly, 'but it won't be easy for you. The other boys will pick on you.'

'Why.'

'Because you're different. You've got education and you don't talk the way they do. That will make you a natural target for bullying.'

'I haven't had any problems with the lads I've met so far. The boys at All Saints were rough but I managed all right in the end.' Here a note of reproach crept into his voice. He still resented the sudden unexplained flight from Newcastle and the break-up of his friendship with Colin MacGregor that this had brought about.

Henry sighed. 'Well we'll just have to wait and see,' he said resignedly.

143

Mark sensed his father's unhappiness and changed the subject. 'Have you told Jed yet?'

'I'm going to have a word with his mother tonight.'

'Can I come with you?' Mark liked Mrs Hindmarsh and her family and wanted to get to know them better.

'Of course you can. Come on, we'll go next door now.'

The worried face of Mrs Hindmarsh peered from behind the door in answer to their knocking. 'Oh it's you, Henry,' she said, her expression changing into a warm smile of relief. 'I was worried in case it was the agent come to tell me to get out.'

'I don't think it'll come to that now, Dora,' Henry said reassuringly.

'Well come in, both of you.' Dora stepped aside to let them in, smiling at Mark as he passed. 'Jane's doing her letters,' she said pointing to the table where her daughter sat chalking on a slate. 'She's getting quite good at it,' she added proudly.

'You go and sit with Jane,' Henry said to Mark. 'I want to talk to Mrs Hindmarsh.'

Mark needed little prompting. He'd been attracted to the pretty, golden haired girl from the very first day they'd met. Her soft smile and twinkling blue eyes had broken through his initial bashfulness and they had quickly become friends. Jane whispered shyly, 'I'm not half as good as you.'

'I'll help you if you like,' Mark whispered back. He enjoyed spending time in Mrs Hindmarsh house. It was like being with a real family without having to act grown-up all the time. He liked Jed and young Jim; in fact, he thought with sudden surprise, he sometimes felt as if he was an older brother to them.

Henry spoke to Mrs Hindmarsh. 'I've had a word with Mr Wilkins, Dora. He said that Mark and Jed can start as trappers on Monday.'

Dora's eyes lit up. 'Oh, That's grand, Henry. It was nice of you to put in a word for him.'

'It's only eight pence a day, Dora, and a long day at that.'

'It'll be a great help, Henry. I can't make ends meet just taking washing in.' She turned to her son. 'Did you hear that, Jed? A trapper boy at eight pence a day. You'll be the man of the house now.'

Jed smiled sheepishly, 'Yes, Mam,' he said then looked excitedly at Mark. 'Do you think we'll be able to work next to each other?'

Mark shrugged but didn't answer. It was left to Henry to reply.

'I doubt it, Jed. The trap doors you'll be minding might be some distance apart. I'll see what I can do but it will be up to the overman.'

Dora turned to Henry. 'Does Wilf know?' she asked anxiously.

'I don't think so,' he replied. 'I thought it best if you told him.'

'Aye, I suppose so. He won't be too pleased though.' She saw that Henry looked uncomfortable and realised that his sympathies still lay with Wilf even though he'd helped her.

'Don't worry,' she said soothingly. 'I'll soon talk him round.'

Henry changed the subject, trying to ease his embarrassment. 'The boys will need some pit clothes, Dora.' He laid ten shillings on the table. 'That should be enough for the cranky flannel.' She was about to protest and he held up his hand. 'You can sew and make up for both of 'em. Mary's not well and I want her to rest.'

'Are you sure Mary won't mind?' There was doubt in Dora's voice. Pit women were a proud lot.

'No. I'll tell her I asked you.' Henry smiled at her confusion then quickly turned to Mark. 'I think it's time to go home.'

Mark left with the memory of Jane's laughing blue eyes lighting up her parting smile. It was still imprinted firmly on his mind hours later as he curled up in bed and went to sleep.

Mark's first day down the pit was to prove a major turning point in his life. Over the coming years, a chain of events would ultimately transform him as a person and in the process, come perilously close to destroying him. The day signalled a premature end to his childhood and an early introduction to the toil and suffering that was the lot of a pitman. If he avoided death or serious injury he would probably spend the rest of his working life in semi-bondage until his body slowly broke and his spirit withered. But the optimism of youth and the excitement of the challenge meant that such thoughts were far from his mind.

The pre-dawn hours of that fateful Monday morning were clothed in the pitch darkness of early winter. A keen, cutting frost had frozen the stagnant pools between the cottages hardening the path that led to the pit. A bitter easterly wind swept in from the North Sea, whipping across the stone-walled fields of the newly enclosed moor and carrying a smell of salt that was soon lost in the acrid, sulphurous fumes of the pit bank.

Mark and Jed shivered as the biting wind cut through their new pit flannel working clothes. Huddling close together they followed Henry and joined the growing group of men and boys who, with shoulders hunched into their jackets to keep out the cold, made their way towards the pit.

Mark kept close to his father who led the way through the darkness past the pit pond and over the waggonway towards the pit head. The lofty woodwork over the pit shaft looked grim and menacing in the flickering light of the fires from the suspended iron baskets that illuminated the area surrounding the pit mouth. The clanking and sighing of the beam engines, the hiss of escaping steam, the creaking of the overhead pulleys and the sound of the running ropes provided a musical background to the banksman who was calling down the shaft and the faint echoing cries from below.

Jed looked in alarm at the smoke coming out of the shaft. 'Where's that coming from? Is the pit on fire?' There was fear in his voice.

'No, lad,' said Henry reassuringly. The pit's only got one shaft so they've divided it into two with a wooden brattice. The smoke's from the ventilating furnace at the bottom of the shaft. All the smoke and hot air comes up one side, called the upcast shaft and cold air is drawn in down the other side, called the downcast shaft, where it is circulated around the workings to ventilate the pit. Without proper ventilation the pit would soon fill with firedamp gas and explode.'

Jed wasn't convinced. 'How can you be sure it won't explode anyway? It was an explosion that killed my dad.'

'That can't happen again if the pit's run properly,' Henry lied. He wished it were true, but needed to reassure Jed and Mark. He went on to explain their important role.

'It's your job as trappers to see that your trap doors are kept properly closed except when someone's passing through. If you do that, the air will circulate through all the working and prevent any pockets of gas from building up. Most explosions in the past have been caused by trappers falling asleep or wandering off to play, instead of tending to their doors.'

146

There was a shout from the banksman and the crowd of men and boys surged towards the pit shaft. 'Come on,' said Henry placing his arms around the boys' shoulders, 'it's time to go down.'

Mark watched with interest as, every two minutes, a full corfe of coal was drawn up to bank. It was quickly unloaded and the contents emptied over the sloping screens which adjoined the pit shaft. An empty corfe was then hooked onto the chain attached to the end of the winding rope and two or three small boys were placed inside the basket ready for the descent. The men and older boys attached themselves to loops on the chain whilst some of the more adventurous nonchalantly hung onto the rope itself, ignoring the seven hundred feet drop below. A slip invariably proved fatal but this fact did little to deter the more foolhardy.

Soon it was Mark's turn and he and Jed were helped into the basket by Henry and Wilf who rode alongside hooked onto the chain. A cluster of boys clung perilously above. There was another shout from the banksman and a faint answering cry from below. The rope moved over the pulley and they began their descent into the dark, smoking shaft.

Mark gripped the side of the corfe tightly and felt his father's firm grip on his other arm. The acrid fumes from the ventilating furnace made him cough and his eyes began to smart. He watched as the faint light at the top of the shaft receded and quickly disappeared. In the darkness he heard the clanging of the pumping apparatus in the other part of the shaft behind the wooden partition which ran down the centre dividing the shaft in two. There was a rushing sound of falling water as the corfe, now slowing revolving, continued its descent.

After a minute the speed of their descent slowed and Henry felt a sudden tremor pass through Mark's body.

'It's all right,' he said reassuringly. 'We're coming to the passing point.' As he spoke a full corfe of coal scraped past in the darkness on its way to the surface. 'There's not much room in the shaft so the brakesman slows the engine down to avoid damage when the corves pass each other,' Henry explained.

Mark felt the speed of their descent increase and was about to relax when a faint glow appeared in the shaft accompanied by a new roaring sound. He caught a quick glimpse of the glowing brightness of the

147

furnace as the corfe passed the opening of the ventilating drift where it joined the main shaft. After that the smoke cleared and the downward motion slowed and finally stopped. They had reached the bottom of the shaft and in the dim, flickering light of the onsetters candles Mark saw the shadowy entrance to the main roadway leading into the mine.

After lighting their candles, men and boys made their way in by to their allotted work areas. Henry lit a candle and placed it in a sticking of clay between Mark's fingers. 'That's how you carry your candle pitman fashion,' he explained, smiling at his son's bemusement.

Wilf did the same for Jed. 'We'll make good pitmen out of 'em, eh Henry?'

Henry tried to shrug off his feeling of guilt. 'Come on,' he said irritably. 'It's time we took the lads in-by.' He led the way, passing through the cramped passage ways of the pit, explaining the working methods and customs to Mark and Jed as they progressed. Sometimes they were bent double, scraping their backs against the rough stone roof of the mine.

After travelling for a few hundred yards they reached a large wooden trap door nearly six feet square which closed off the whole passage way. A strong cord was attached to the base of the door and ran up through a hook driven into a wooden roof support. The free end of the cord dropped to the floor in front of a shallow recess cut into the side of the passageway. 'This is your door, Mark,' said Henry, 'and that's your trapper's hole,' he added pointed to the recess. 'You can open the door by pulling on the cord from your trapper hole and stay safely out of the way of the traffic. He gave a quick demonstration.

'It's mainly putters that use this roadway,' Wilf said. 'Remember to open the door as soon as you hear them coming or see their light. If you hold them up, they'll bray you. That's a hiding,' he added for Mark's benefit.

'And remember to close the door as soon as they pass through,' Henry said. 'The same goes for you too, Jed. You've got the second door just a little further on down the passage. The idea is not to have both doors open at the same time.'

'Why?' Mark asked.

148

'Because it diverts the air current and could cause a build-up of gas,' Henry explained.

Mark looked concerned. 'How will we know if both doors are open?'

'You won't. You just keep the doors open for as short a time as possible. When you hear the putters coming with a sledge wait till the last moment before opening the door, then close it as soon as they're through. That way you'll be all right.'

The previous occupant of the trapper hole had clearly been smaller than Mark. Henry took his pick and made the recess wider and deeper. He then placed a candle in a nick by the door. 'That should see you more comfortable,' he said. 'Just stay alert and tend to your door and you'll be all right. You'll soon get used to it. 'I'll come and collect you when it's kenner.'

'What's kenner, dad?'

'That's what they shout when it's time to go home.'

Mark settled down in his trapper hole with the draw cord held loosely over his fingers. He watched as his father and Wilf, with young Jed between them, made their way towards the second door which was some fifty yards further on. It was to be Jed's station. Mark continued to stare down the dark passageway until the light from their candles grew faint in the distance. Finally, the light disappeared altogether as the heavy trapdoor slammed shut. He was alone for the first time, seven hundred feet deep in the labyrinth of dark tunnels of North Moor pit.

For a while he could only stare at the black wall of coal in front of him which glistened feebly in the reflected light of his candle. A feeling of loneliness engulfed him as he thought of his mother in the far-off world above.

His thoughts were suddenly interrupted by a faint rumbling noise on the other side of the trapdoor and the sound of distant voices. He gripped his cord tighter as the straining sounds of heavy exertion drew nearer and he heard a hoarse, angry shout from behind the trapdoor. He pulled as hard as he could on the cord and watched the trapdoor rise open to reveal a pair of angry eyes glinting behind a coal blackened face. The eyes belonged to a young putter harnessed to a wheeled sledge which contained a full corfe of coal. He was on all fours straining at the harness ropes whilst an older, stronger boy pushed from the rear of the sledge. As they passed, the older boy cursed and though doubled up with his exertions managed to swing a viscous kick at Mark. 'Get your bloody door open quicker next time,' he shouted.

Mark stifled a cry of pain and felt blood trickling down his grazed shin. He watched with mounting anger as the light from the flickering candle attached to the sledge faded into the distance. Later, he thought he heard muffled shouts and a scream of pain from the direction of Jed's trapdoor. He instinctively rose to intervene then, remembering his father's warning not to leave his post, sank back dejectedly into his trapper hole.

As time dragged on, the sheer monotony and loneliness of his work filled Mark with despair. His despondency increased when one of the passing putters took his candle, leaving him in total darkness. He had to listen carefully to the approaching sounds so that he could open the door in good time and not impede the putter's progress. By keeping well back in his trapper hole he learned to avoid some of the blows and kicks that were frequently aimed in his direction. He consoled himself with the thought that the loss of his candle made him a less visible target.

Mark soon lost count of the number of loaded sledges that passed through his door. He began to dread the return journeys of the putters with their empty corves as they had more time and energy to torment him. One of the older putters, a youth called Herbie Marshall, had taken a particular dislike to Mark and took every opportunity to demonstrate his hostility, both verbally and physically. The sight of Herbie emerging from the darkness on the other side of the trapdoor filled Mark with dismay, though he tried hard not to show it. But Herbie's constant stream of threats created a sinister atmosphere of insecurity which Mark found disconcerting and difficult to banish from his mind.

'Just look at that lah-di-dah little sod,' Herbie said to his marra when passing. 'Useless bugger, isn't he?'

'He is that,' the marra rejoined.

'We'll have to set up a special initiation to sort him out.' Herbie glowered at Mark and lashed out at him with his fist.

Mark deflected the main force of the blow but didn't respond. He remained silent having learned from bitter experience that retaliation only made matters worse. Besides, he was always outnumbered two to one and most of the putters were older and stronger.

'He won't even fight back,' Herbie sneered. 'Frightened little shit.'

Mark continued to ignore the two putters and as a result their sadistic pleasure gained from bullying gradually changed to a mood of frustrated annoyance.

'We'll sort you out at the initiation later,' Herbie repeated menacingly and aimed another blow at Mark's head. They then disappeared through the door on their way back to the coal face.

Sitting alone in the darkness, Mark became aware of sounds that must have been audible before but had gone unnoticed until his candle had been taken away. He heard the gentle oozing of gas escaping from the close-grained coal around him and the steady drip of unseen water. Sometimes the sounds would become feeble, as if their force was spent, but always they returned like an erratic subterranean heartbeat. It was as if the pit lay wounded, gasping for breath and struggling to sustain a life of its own against the rapacious intrusion of man.

Mark had now lost all track of time and the perpetual darkness served to increase his sense of isolation and disorientation. As he stared into the darkness, straining to penetrate its smothering blackness, his eyes were attracted to a faint white object only a few yards away. His heart began to pound as he remembered the scare stories of ghosts of dead pitmen haunting the scenes of their demise. He closed his eyes for a few moments hoping the spectre would go away. When he opened them it was gone and for once he was glad of the enveloping darkness around him. But suddenly it was there again, a faint apparition shining with a feeble luminosity and in exactly the same place.

Mark was now glad of the traffic that passed through his door as each sledge brought a temporary light and a welcome relief which even the bad tempered putters could not fully dispel. But the faint apparition always returned to exactly the place where the light had previously revealed nothing.

Some hours later Mark was startled to see chinks of candle light penetrating through the edges of the trapdoor. He had heard no approaching sounds and quickly pulled on his cord to open the door. He steeled himself for the wrath of the putters which would surely descend if he had held them up. To his surprise and relief he heard the comforting sounds of his father's voice.

'What's happened to your candle?' Henry paused, framed in the doorway, a look of concern crossing his face as he saw Mark cowering in the back of his trapper hole.

'The putters took it.' There was a hint of a sob in Mark's brief explanation.

Henry shook his head in despair. 'I should have warned you. Putting seems to bring out the worst in some lads, but there's no excuse for taking it out on the young ones.'

Henry had been well aware that Mark's candle would not survive long after he had left. He regretted that he had not warned Mark so that he would have been better prepared. 'Was that all that happened?' he enquired, dreading the reply.

'Some of them shouted at me, said they would bray me if I didn't open the door faster.'

'No rough stuff?' Henry asked.

'Not really,' Mark lied.

Henry knew Mark was lying but let it go. 'I told you they would pick on you,' he said gently. 'Besides, trappers don't usually have candles.'

'Why?'

'Because candles cost money and a trapper boy's job can be easily done in the dark.'

'I wouldn't mind the dark if it wasn't for the ghosts,' Mark said.

Henry laughed. 'What ghosts?'

'Over there,' Mark pointed, 'just behind you but it's not there now.'

Henry put down his candle on the other side of the door. 'Close the door,' he said.

Mark released the cord and the door dropped back into place closing off the light.

'Now tell me when you can see your ghost,' Henry said, crouching down beside his son.

After a few moments the pale apparition reappeared and Mark took hold of his father's arm. 'It's over there by the door,' he whispered.

'Right, open the door,' Henry said.

Mark did as he was told and the door swung open. Henry picked up his candle and made a close examination of the spot where the ghost had appeared. 'I thought so,' he murmured and began to smile. 'Come here Mark and meet your ghost. It's only a decaying pit prop, and that's what causes it to shine in the dark.' He placed Mark's hand on the prop. 'Stay there while I close the door and shut off the light.'

Mark stood with his hand on the decaying prop and watched it glow pale and luminous in the darkness.

'So much for your ghost, eh Mark?' Henry laughed but there was kindness and understanding in the sound. 'I'd better go and see if Jed's found any ghosts and set his mind at rest too. I'll be there to meet you at bank when they call kenner.'

'What time is it now?' Mark asked.

'Half-past twelve.'

'What time will they call kenner?'

'Not till well after six, I'm afraid.' Henry could sense Mark's disappointment.

'Are you finished, dad?'

'Yes. The hewers leave when they've cut and filled their score. But the rest stay below until the haulage is done.'

'That doesn't seem fair,' Mark said bitterly.

'I know it doesn't,' Henry said gently. 'There's nothing good or fair about pit work that robs young boys of their proper childhood.' He clasped his arms protectively around Mark's shoulders and held him tight. 'You don't have to do this work, Mark. I've heard there's a good school at Longbenton. You can go there if you like.' He suddenly detected stiffening in his son's body.

'I'm not giving up yet,' Mark said stubbornly. 'If Jed can stick it then so can I.'

Henry sighed. 'We'll just have to wait and see then.' He was disappointed and had hoped that one day down the pit would be enough for a boy of Mark's intelligence and sensitivity. He was also saddened by the thought that he'd failed to appreciate a subtle strength in his son's character. Nor could he understand the perverse motivation which fuelled Mark's determination.

'I'd best be off then,' Henry said quietly. 'I'll meet you when you finish your shift. With that he turned and made to move in the direction of Jed's door. After a few yards he heard Mark calling after him.

'What's an initiation, dad?'

Henry groaned silently. Here was something else he had omitted to warn his son about. 'It's just some daft larking about by the putters,' he lied. 'Don't worry about it.'

Mark watched with a mounting feeling of loneliness as his father's receding light slowly melted into the darkness of the pit. He was alone again and after a seemingly interminable eight hours underground, was little more than half way through his first shift.

He was now feeling very hungry and began groping around in the darkness for his food satchel and water bottle. It took him some time to find them and afterwards he sat in his trapper hole eating ravenously, blissfully ignorant of the coating of coal dust that his fingers imparted to the food. Darkness had some compensation to offer, however small.

When he finished eating Mark felt for a more convenient place to hide his satchel from the marauding putters but one which would not be too difficult for himself to find. He solved the problem by cutting off a piece of the decaying pit prop and using a ball of damp clay, attached it to the wall above the secret cache to mark the spot. This gave him another idea and soon several pieces of pit prop were attached to the roof to form an astronomical display; a milky way in miniature with The Plough as its centrepiece. He could now watch his own star-lit galaxy from his trapper hole and with a little imagination, transport himself seven hundred feet up to the real world above. Suddenly, the dark confines of the pit became less oppressive and a little more bearable.

The day slowly wore on and by six o'clock the traffic using Mark's door began to slacken. By now he was so tired he had to force himself to stay awake, remembering the punishment he would receive if he was caught asleep at his post. Suddenly he heard the sound of voices and pulled on his cord to open the door. The bright light from several candles hurt his eyes and he instinctively half closed them until his pupils became adjusted. When his eyes became fully focussed, he saw the face of Herbie Marshall wreathed in a cruel smile.

'I said we'd sort you out, you little toffee nosed shit.' Herbie's threat was backed by a chorus of shouts from the group of putters who accompanied him. Mark also saw the frightened face of young Jed who was being held by one of the putters.

'It's initiation time,' Herbie said. 'You can't work down the pit until you've signed Old King Cole's bond.' This was greeted by a clamour of raucous laughter which soon changed into a rising chant. The noise rose to a frenzied crescendo which reverberated down the galleries of the mine like the wild baying of a pack of hounds rabid with the scent of blood. Suddenly, Herbie and his marra pounced on Mark and dragged him out of his trapper hole.

Mark fought back furiously but was quickly overpowered by Herbie and his putters. He was frogmarched down the roadway until the group reached a pit refuge. This was a large cove-like structure cut into the side of the roadway and used for the storage of timber and equipment. It was also used by many of the pitmen and boys as a convenient privy to avoid making a journey into a worked out waste area of the mine. The refuge was littered with excrement and stank of urine.

Mark and Jed were pinioned to the floor where their trousers were ceremoniously removed to the howls of amusement from the assembled crowd of putters looking on.

'Who's got King Coal's Beard?' Herbie asked.

'Here it is.' A putter thrust a large sheet of brown paper into Herbiest hand.

'Right then,' said Herbie grinning. 'Now, where's the ink? '

'Here.' Another putter stepped forward holding a shovel which contained a large mound of human excrement mixed with coal dust. With a great pretence of ritual, this was emptied over Mark's genitals to a chorus of obscene remarks on future growth prospects for that part of his anatomy.

Young Jed, who had been crying loudly, seemed to attract more sympathy from the crowd. It was now clear that Mark was their main target and all attention was focused on him. Jed was becoming something of an irrelevance.

155

'Give him a ribbon and get rid of 'im,' Herbie said.

A putter bent down and tied a coloured ribbon around Jed's penis. 'Now bugger off,' he was instructed.

Jed rose, still sobbing and scurried down the roadway in the direction of his trapper door, pulling on his trousers as he ran.

'You keep that ribbon on for a week, mind,' Herbie called after him. 'We'll check it every day.' The crowd of putters laughed then turned their attention to their main source of entertainment.

Herbie took the sheet of brown paper and looked down at the heap of black excrement that covered Mark's genitals. 'Right, you've got plenty of ink on your pen now,' he crowed. 'It's time to sign Old King Cole's bond.' With that he placed the sheet of brown paper over his prisoner's crotch and rubbed the filthy mess into Mark's penis and testicles. A cheer went up from the onlookers. 'You're a proper pit lad now,' Herbie said mockingly, 'but don't get any big ideas.' He gave Mark a vicious look then got up and walked away. The group of putters, subdued now that their fun was over, silently followed after him leaving Mark alone with his humiliation.

After a while, Mark rose and tried to clean off the worst of the mess with his handkerchief before pulling on his trousers. He then returned to his trapper hole and sat down, wishing it would swallow him up and cleanse him of the shame and mortification of the initiation. For the first time he began to cry and as the anguish seeped out from his soul, his body became convulsed with racking sobs of despair.

It was half an hour later when Mark heard the melancholy cry of kenner repeating its way around the pit. He waited until long after the echoing cry had died away in the labyrinth of galleries that surrounded him, for he wanted to be the last to ride to bank.

After a while he observed the approaching flicker of candle-light and saw a frightened young Jed appear at his door.

'Aren't you going home, Mark? They've called kenner.' Mark smiled through eye rims sore with crying. 'In a minute, Jed. I want to wait until the others have gone.'

'I'll wait with you,' Jed said. 'The deputy gave me the end of his candle so at least we'll have a light to see our way out.' He sat down and felt Mark's comforting arm creep round his shoulders.

*****

156

It was dark on the surface and the cold night air carried a hint of rain. Near the pit shaft the figures of Henry and Wilf stood silhouetted against the lurid glare cast by the burning coals in the suspended iron grates. The last of the haulage shift had departed leaving only the onsetters and winding men to bring the last of the day's coal production to bank.

'Where the hell are they?' Wilf muttered impatiently. Henry moved across to the banksman, 'Are all the boys up?' he asked.

'Last two are on their way up now.' As he spoke the rope began to revolve over the pulleys above the shaft and Henry and Wilf stood anxiously waiting. Gradually the short length of chain attached to the end of the winding rope emerged from the shaft and as the winding engine reduced speed, the corfe containing Mark and Jed came slowly into view. Wilf, with traces of anger still showing in his face, moved forward. 'Where the hell have you two been?' he said testily.

Henry took hold of his friend's arm. 'Steady on, Wilf,' he said quietly. 'It's their first day down the pit, remember. I'm sure there's a reason.'

'There'd better be.' Wilf's voice softened as his anxiety gave way to relief. 'What kept you then?'

'We wanted to keep out of the way of the putters after the initiation' Jed explained in a voice that was near to tears.

'So the buggers have started up that nonsense again, have they?' Wilf was becoming angry again. 'What have they been up to this time?'

Henry gently intervened. 'Let it rest, Wilf. The lads are tired and it's time they were home.' He could see by the expression on Mark's face that whatever had happened to him must have been deeply humiliating. He took his son's arm and led him slowly away.

Mark was tired and subdued as they began the short journey home. Henry sensed his son was hurting but refrained from asking questions which he knew would not be satisfactorily answered. When they reached the pit pond Mark paused. 'I won't be a minute,' he said and disappeared into the darkness.

Henry's instinct told him not to follow so he waited by the path. After a short while Mark reappeared, wringing out his handkerchief as he walked. 'Got it messed up a bit,' he explained.

Henry nodded. 'Aye, dirty places, pits.' They walked on in silence.

When they entered the cottage a large fire was blazing in the hearth and Mary was busily pouring hot water into a washtub placed strategically in front of the fire. A relieved smile lit up her face as she caught sight of her son. 'I've got a lovely hot bath ready for you,' she said. 'Then when you've finished there's a nice plate of hot stew waiting.' She moved towards Mark. 'Come on; let me help you take those dirty pit clothes off.'

Henry shot her a warning glance and held up his hand. 'Why don't we pop out for a bit of fresh air while Mark's having his bath,' he said.

Mary was about to protest when the look in Henry's eyes silenced her. 'I'll just get my shawl,' she said quietly. 'There's quite a nip in the air.'

As they stepped out through the door Henry caught an appreciative glance from Mark that carried the unspoken message of a new found camaraderie between them. He suddenly felt immensely proud of his son.

CHAPTER 16

On the day of Henry's departure from the house in Wall Knoll, William experienced a heady mixture of triumph and relief. He was relieved that his brother-in-law's absence would remove what he considered to be a threat to his own position with Mr Ivison's firm. He could now be more sanguine, not only about his continued employment but also for his future prospects, which Henry's departure would considerably enhance. His sense of triumph arose from the knowledge that his ruthless cunning had defeated someone who was his undoubted intellectual superior. As William was a selfish person by nature and totally devoid of moral scruples, his conscience was not unduly disturbed by his despicable act of betrayal.

He watched as the handcart containing his brother-in-law's belongings moved off into the pre-dawn darkness, followed by the dejected and bewildered Standish family. The figures quickly melted into the night and the sound of the handcart's iron shod wheels rumbling over the cobbles gradually faded into silence. He was glad he'd arranged for Ellen to be away otherwise an almighty row would have been inevitable. For a moment he thought of following Henry at a discreet distance to make sure he did leave town, then quickly dismissed the idea. He was losing confidence and knew he must pull himself together. He shivered in the chill morning air and hurriedly moved inside the house closing the door behind him.

It was too early to go to the office so William sat alone in the kitchen and watched the yellow tongues of flame from the re-kindled fire lick their way slowly up the back of the hearth. He felt elated and became increasingly impatient for the day to begin. There was much to do and he needed to move quickly to inform the authorities of the names of Rory's associates. But first there was a pressing need to attend the coal fitter's office on the quayside. Henry's quick capitulation had left him feeling uneasy and he needed to allay his nagging suspicions regarding his brother-in-law's likely reaction to such a major setback.

An hour later, with the first grey streaks of dawn lighting up the sky, William made his way to the quayside to open up the office as he always did. Excited though he was, he was determined to try and act normally and not draw attention to himself. What he was about to do needed a subtle but confident touch if he were to receive credit for his actions without incurring accusations of betrayal and the risk of reprisals. He had a healthy and justified fear of Rory MacGregor.

William greeted the clerks curtly as they arrived and briskly set them to their duties. They sensed his strange and nervous mood and busily kept their heads down at their desks. As time passed they began to cast puzzled glances towards the empty chair at Henry's desk.

Although Mr Ivison's house was only a few doors further along the quayside, he rarely put in an appearance until the morning mail had been delivered and sorted, a task he left to his chief clerk. On this particular morning the mail was later than usual and William's agitation increased visibly by the minute, causing the clerks to exchange sly glances of curiosity and amusement.

When the mail finally arrived William took delivery of it and carried the letters to his desk. He anxiously began sorting through the letters, stopping when he caught sight of the envelope which bore the familiar handwriting he was looking for. His intuition had been right and a smile of triumph briefly lit up his face. He began to open the letter with fingers clumsy with excitement. 'Just as I thought, dear brother-in-law,' he muttered to himself. 'A letter of expurgation, no doubt, hoping for a miracle of forgiveness and absolution.' It was the letter written by Henry to Mr Ivison explaining his sudden departure.

William read the letter then returned it to the envelope. With a smile of smug satisfaction he placed the letter in the private drawer of his desk which he carefully locked before replacing the key in his waistcoat pocket.

Henry's other letter, the one to Rory, was delivered by Colin within the hour. Rory moved quickly, organising a team of runners to warn the group of their probable arrest. Safe houses were prepared and keels made ready to spirit the fugitives aboard friendly collier brigs bound for safe Continental ports.

All went well at first but soon news filtered through that three of Rory's friends had been arrested. The big Scot fumed with anger and swore to seek retribution for William's perfidy. 'He's a dead man when I meet up with him,' he told the assembled keelmen. This was greeted with a chorus of assent and offers of assistance.

William, for his part, was in a quandary. Whilst he could alert the authorities and betray the names of the radicals, he could not explain how he had come by this information without seeming to involve the innocent Mr Ivison.

But unknown to William, the authorities already knew the identities of some of the radicals on his list and had decided to act. A series of arrests were carried out and further incriminating evidence was found in some of the homes of those arrested.

William was relieved by the outcome which conveniently resolved his dilemma without compromising his main objective of getting rid of his brother-in-law. With Henry now removed, his own prospects with Mr Ivison would improve. The thought brought a smug smile of satisfaction to his face.

The suspension of habeas corpus had made arrest and questioning much easier for the authorities who could now hold prisoners for long periods without trial. In these circumstances the welcome revelations which followed the arrests acted as the catalyst which finally decided the loyal burghers of Newcastle that more draconian measures were needed. The canker of radicalism needed to be cut out once and for all. Failure to act now would only serve to weaken the government, now going through a difficult time in its war with revolutionary France. Rory and his keelmen, seen as dupes of the radical intellectuals, were to be the prime target.

The four hundred keels owned by the Tyne coal fitters gave work to some sixteen hundred keelmen who crewed and worked these specialised boats. Like the pitmen, they were bound by an annual bond to their employers. Perhaps because of this they were notorious for their fierce independence of spirit which usually manifested itself in strikes and violent acts of destruction. Sandgate, lying just outside the walls of Newcastle, was home to most of these men and their families who formed a unique and clannish community. They were ignorant, rough, uncouth, often drunken, following a skilled calling that descended from father to son. They married only girls of their own class or girls from the local pit community in Heaton or Byker. They were also fiercely loyal to Rory MacGregor.

Sandgate took its name from the narrow road that led into a gate of that name set in the east wall of the town where it joined the quayside. On each side of this road even narrower streets, called chars, branched off into a maze of dingy, densely populated streets that formed a forbidding warren of seething revolt and a deep hatred for authority. Officers of the law entered it at their peril, and few did. On the south side of Sandgate road, narrow chars ran down to the Sandgate Shore where the banks of the river were lined with a jumble of wharves, warehouses and, incongruously, an occasional house where a keelman could tie up a keel at his door. To the north of the Sandgate road the chars ran up the steep hillside to the new road and open countryside east of the splendid Keelmen's Hospital which stood as a monument to the keelmen's compassion for their own kind and a desire for autonomy in such matters.

It was Sandgate, the keelmen's bastion and inner sanctum that the town authorities decided to attack, and for once they took their task seriously. The magistrates planned the operation with great care and swore in sixty special constables to augment the town watch. In addition a full company of militia was provided as a backup to the civil force with orders to assist in the arrests.

Two hours before dawn on the following morning over three hundred armed men converged silently on Sandgate encircling the area and sealing it off on the landward side. On the river, a dozen boats took up their pre-arranged stations off the Sandgate Shore. At a given signal the constables with their large military escort filed through the arch of the town's Sandgate and moved quickly along the dark Sandgate road. On command, small groups fanned off to the left and right and into the maze of narrow chars where the overhanging roofs almost touched each other. The search and arrest operation had begun.

Although it was a full moon, heavy cloud cover nullified any advantage this might have given to the invaders. In the circumstances, each small group was forced to rely on the feeble light of the single lantern allocated to them in order to find their way through the dark warren of narrow streets.

162

The sounds of loud knocking on closed doors signalled the start of the search operation. Those doors not immediately answered were unceremoniously broken down. But as the separate groups of constables and militia progressed further into the maze of Sandgate, so their puzzlement increased. Each house contained only women and a great many children.

'Must breed like bloody rabbits,' a sweating militia sergeant complained after yet another abortive search of a house teeming with children.

'Immaculate conceptions if you ask me,' a grinning constable replied. 'Can't see any husbands, can you?'

The fears and suspicions of the leaders increased as the constables and their escorts penetrated deeper and deeper into the keelmen's citadel without encountering a single adult male. Only when they were deep inside hostile territory did the reason become plain. Suddenly, guerrilla squads of keelmen appeared unexpectedly around dark corners to attack the invaders. Too late, the authorities realised they had been drawn into a well-laid trap. The hunters had become the hunted. The small groups of constables and militia, who were by now well dispersed and pinpointed by their lanterns, became easy targets for the well prepared keelmen.

Fierce running battles took place as the keelmen, armed with stout staves and eager to fight, tore into the constables and their escorts. The keelmen held the advantage in numbers, knowledge of the territory and the element of surprise. Thanks to Rory and his lieutenants they were well organised and superbly led.

After just twenty minutes of vicious fighting the morale of the constables and the ill-disciplined militia began to break. A slow retreat gradually turned into a rout. The women now joined in the fight, hurling heavy objects and the stinking contents of brimming chamber pots from the upper windows on to the unprotected heads of the retreating invaders. In the panic and confusion some muskets were discharged at unseen targets. Because this presented an equal danger to both sides it was quickly stopped on the orders of the militia officers who were desperately trying to restore discipline and control to their demoralised and retreating forces.

Throughout the skirmishing the keelmen fought in silence on strict orders from Rory. Their faces were also blacked with coal dust with the lower part covered by a neckcloth. This strategy was designed to protect their anonymity and reduce the risk of future reprisals. On the other hand, the women were deliberately vociferous during their part in the fighting in an attempt to add to the confusion.

The authorities were now in full retreat, having lost all stomach for the fight. Wet, cold and stinking of excrement and urine they turned and fled, desperate to be free of their tormentors. At this point the final trap was sprung. Large fishing nets, suspended across the narrow streets from the upper windows of the houses at carefully selected points, were dropped over the retreating constables and militiamen. Instantly the writhing mass of netted men was attacked by women who suddenly poured from the houses wielding staves. Others drenched the trapped men further with a seemingly endless supply of well filled chamber pots.

On the river the occupants of the guard boats gazed nervously shoreward, listening to the noise of the fighting. They were blissfully unaware of the two keels, sailing fast on the strongly ebbing tide and which were now bearing down on them. Suddenly the dark shapes of the keels appeared, towering over the small boats. There were sounds of splintering wood which mingled with the shouts and curses of the startled occupants. The two keels rammed their way through the line of guard boats, leaving a devastating trail of overturned and sinking craft in their wake, before disappearing into the night. Constables and militiamen were left splashing and shouting in the shallow water as they tried to struggle ashore. Half an hour later it was all over. The authorities withdrew their forces, leaving Sandgate in the hands of the victorious and jubilant keelmen.

The following evening, Rory and his fugitive radical friends boarded a keel at the now deserted Sandgate Shore and set sail for Shields. Twenty-five captured muskets were consigned to the bottom of the Tyne River on Rory's strict instructions. His was not an armed struggle but a battle for the minds and conscience of the people. Words and ideas were more potent than guns.

Rory was in a pensive mood on his return to the safe house. Already a marked man his continued freedom would be in even greater jeopardy after tonight's victory, he mused.

At the Mansion House the following morning the Mayor presided over a gloomy post-mortem on the previous night's events. It was a bad tempered meeting, full of angry recriminations.

'MacGregor and his friends must have been warned in advance,' complained the embarrassed colonel of the disgraced militia regiment. 'How else could they have been so well prepared?'

'I think we underestimated their intelligence network,' the Mayor said miserably.

'Perhaps your men made too much noise moving in,' suggested the colonel of dragoons. He was the only regular army officer present and found quiet pleasure in the militia's failings. Militiamen were regarded as bungling amateurs by the regular army.

The militia colonel glowered back at him. 'My men were well briefed and followed their orders to the letter,' he responded. Seeing a look of barely concealed disdain cross the dragoon officer's face he added, 'Your lot wouldn't have done any better, I'll be bound.'

'Gentlemen, please!' the Mayor intervened. 'Exchanging insults and recriminations won't help us to arrest MacGregor and his radical friends. The fact of the matter is that last night's operation was a complete disaster which must not be repeated. We were fortunate that no one was seriously injured.'

The militia colonel's face reddened and he looked as though he was about to choke. 'You can't allow the scum of the town to flout the law,' he spluttered. 'We'll become a laughing stock.'

'I think we already have,' said the dragoon colonel quietly, 'thanks to you.'

The colonel of militia was now almost apoplectic with rage. 'Damn you, sir! It's easy to criticise with hindsight especially when you were sitting in your barracks whilst others were doing the fighting.'

Stung by this censure and feeling his honour impugned, the dragoon officer began to lose his composure. 'Last night's work was not for cavalry,' he said crustily.

165

The Mayor held up his hands wearily. 'Come now, gentlemen, let us stop this bickering. It won't solve the problem.'

'Then I'll solve it for you once and for all,' the militia colonel interrupted, 'but in my own way.'

'And what, pray, might that be?' prompted the dragoon colonel icily. He sensed a chance to display his superior military skills and crush this upstart militiaman.

'We'll do the job properly by going in at full strength in daylight. 'I'll use the whole regiment this time with orders to shoot if there's any resistance.'

'Good God, man, you can't be serious.' The dragoon colonel was amazed at the militia commander's stupidity. 'This is England; you'll have a full scale riot on your hands that will end in a bloodbath.'

'I need to recover the muskets we lost last night,' the militia colonel said stubbornly, 'unless you know a better way 'he added sarcastically.

The Mayor again intervened. 'We received a message to say the muskets were dumped in the river. I've got boats out there now dragging the spot. The message came from MacGregor, by the way,' he went on quietly. 'Not quite the action of a military rebel, wouldn't you say?'

This final piece of information finally silenced the warring colonels.

'I think' concluded the Mayor, 'we'll have to consider some new tactics if we are to catch MacGregor and his friends. In the meantime I would prefer it if the troops were to maintain a low profile and keep to their barracks for a while.'

The meeting broke up and the two colonels, feeling somewhat disgruntled, were the first to leave. Standing on the Mansion House steps, the militia colonel watched enviously as the immaculately uniformed dragoon officer mounted his magnificent horse. Catching his gaze the dragoon colonel turned and smiled. 'Better keep the windows open when you confine your men to barracks. They say the place smells like the town midden.' With that he saluted and trotted off, passing through the wrought iron gates of the Mansion House and into The Close. Speechless with anger, the militia colonel could only gape after him unable to reply.

*****

166

In the week that followed his brother-in-law's sudden departure from Newcastle, William was subjected to a daily inquisition by Mr Ivison. The old man seemed devastated by Henry's strange behaviour and unable to comprehend the reason for it. Their relationship had become close and his disappointment was all the more bitter because Henry had not confided in him. He felt bewildered and betrayed.

William did his best to appear equally surprised at the turn of events but somehow he could not quite satisfy Ivison's constant stream of questions. Each morning the interrogation would continue.

'He must have said something to you,' Ivison probed.

'No sir, only that he was feeling unwell and unable to go to work. When I returned home the whole family had gone without leaving a message.'

'Wasn't your wife at home?'

'No, sir, she was spending a few days at her sister's house in Durham.'

'Strange', Ivison pondered. 'Did they take anything with them?'

'All their belongings were missing', William said, 'I assumed they'd taken them with them.'

'And you are sure there was no message?'

'No, sir. I looked everywhere.'

Ivison shook his head in disbelief. 'And no word since?'

'None, sir.'

Ivison looked crestfallen and stared morosely out of the window. William waited nervously and at last Ivison spoke. 'I think you had better take over Henry's duties for the time being. You'll have to delegate some of your own work to your clerks but I'll leave you to sort that out.' He raised his hand signalling an end to the conversation and William quietly withdrew, experiencing a mixture of relief and satisfaction at the outcome.

Ivison continued to gaze out of the window but what he saw did not register in his mind. His thoughts were elsewhere filled with memories of Henry and his family and a deep sense of loss, like the ache he had felt at the loss of his own wife and son so long ago. He suddenly looked tired and defeated, as if all purpose had gone from his life.

*****

167

William returned home that evening in a jovial mood, his spirits lifted by his morning interview with Mr Ivison. He'd been given his opportunity for advancement and was determined to make the most of it. His betrayal of Henry had been worth it and even his fear of Rory's revenge was beginning to ease. Perhaps he had been imagining things after all, and he was not being watched and followed. He decided he must get a grip on himself and regain his confidence. After all, his star was surely in the ascendant and he was now a man to be reckoned with.

He walked up Wall Knoll with a jaunty step to match his mood. Whistling softly he approached the house, his hand deep in his pocket searching for the door key. Suddenly he froze and a stab of fear left his skin dry and tingling. The large brass door knocker was draped with black crepe and hanging from it was a crude wooden plaque shaped like the headstone of a grave. He moved closer to read the carved inscription in the fading evening light. 'In memory of a Judas whose death will serve as warning to all traitors.'

William stood transfixed, his new found confidence rapidly draining away to be replaced by a gnawing terror.

As the days passed, William's fears increased. He saw danger lurking in every dark doorway and took to walking in the centre of the street, preferring to risk the perils from the traffic rather than face the threat of unknown shadows. He was convinced he was being watched.

On his way to work one morning William passed a boy he thought looked familiar. He paused, looking back at the retreating figure, trying to link the memories that had been triggered by the sight of the boy. Suddenly he remembered. It was Colin MacGregor, Mark's school friend. He also recalled that the boy was the nephew of Rory MacGregor and ran errands for his infamous uncle. Slowly an idea took shape in his mind and he smiled at its cunning and simplicity.

The more William thought about the idea, the more he liked it. Finally, he decided to act. He sent a carefully worded message to the Mayor, who he knew was also the chief magistrate, saying he had information that might lead to the whereabouts of Rory MacGregor and requesting an interview.

In normal circumstances, such an exalted personage as the Mayor would not take a message of this nature seriously. The matter would have been delegated to a clerk and an interview would have been out of the question. However, past events had left the authorities grasping at straws and the Mayor needed all the help he could get. He granted William's request and an interview was arranged.

It was a confident William who entered the Mayor's office and even the disdainful glances of some of the grandly uniformed aides did not dampen his spirits. The Mayor coolly surveyed William but did not invite him to sit down. After a short silence he spoke. 'So you think you know the whereabouts of MacGregor?'

William began to feel uncomfortable. He had expected a warmer welcome. He began nervously, 'No your worship, I don't know where he is at this moment.'

The Mayor frowned. 'But your letter said you had such information.'

'No, I didn't mean that sir, but I think I have the means of finding out where he is.'

The Mayor's frown turned to a look of puzzled irritation. 'I think you had better explain yourself,' he said impatiently.

William began to outline his scheme anxiously watching the Mayor's expression as he spoke, trying to judge the reaction to his words. The Mayor listened silently, his face betraying no emotion. When William had finished the Mayor remained silent as if deep in thought, gently tapping his fingers on the table. At last he spoke.

'So you think that by carefully watching the boy he will eventually lead us to his uncle?'

'Sooner or later, yes,' said William.

'And just how do you think we can watch and follow the boy without being noticed?' The Mayor's voice was tinged with scepticism. 'We've tried putting spies into Sandgate before but it's always proved to be a waste of time.'

Realising the Mayor was not convinced, William's confidence began to wane. He desperately played his last card. 'There's a woman who lives near MacGregor's sister-in-law, the boy's mother,' he explained. 'Her husband was a keelman until he was taken by the

169

press about a year ago. She's heard nothing more of him since he was put on board a King's ship at the Nore. I think she might help.'

The mayor looked incredulous. 'Don't be ridiculous, man. The keel folk are all inter-married and stick together like glue. They'll never betray one of their own kind, least of all MacGregor. The man's a saint in their eyes.'

'She's not one of them, sir,' said William. 'She's Irish and since her husband was taken she's been shunned by the other keelmen's wives. Some say she tipped off the press to take her own husband after a family row so that she could claim the bounty.'

'And did she?' The Mayor was intrigued.

'No one knows for sure but the keel folk are convinced. Personally, I feel she's innocent.'

'Can you trust her?'

'I think so, sir. She feels no love or loyalty towards the keel folk now and the hundred pounds reward on MacGregor's head would be a fortune to her. She could return to Ireland and live in some style.'

The Mayor sat back and studied William. He decided that he didn't like the man and deplored his shiftiness and lack of moral scruples. But he had to admit there was a Machiavellian cunning in the plan. 'Tell me,' he enquired, 'how did you learn that the boy carries messages for his uncle?'

'He's a close friend of my nephew,' William replied.

'Your brother-in-law also works for Mr Ivison, I believe?'

'He used to,' said William cautiously.

'Used to?' The Mayor's interest was aroused.

'Yes, sir, but he left town with his family just over a week ago.'

'Did he give a reason?'

'No sir.' William began to feel uneasy.

'Doesn't that seem strange to you?' the Mayor probed.

'It came as a complete surprise, sir.' William was beginning to worry at the line of questioning.

'Where did he go?'

'I don't know, sir. He didn't leave any message.'

'I see.' The Mayor sat deep in thought for a while. Finally he looked up and stared hard at William. 'Was he involved with the radicals?'

'No sir,' William lied. 'At least not to my knowledge,' he added. He felt compelled to defend Henry so that his own reputation would not be tarnished by association.

'He lived with you, I believe?' The Mayor continued.

'Yes, sir.'

'And did your brother-in-law regularly meet with MacGregor?'

'Not that I'm aware of,' William replied trying not to sound evasive. 'If he had any contact it would only be because of the boy's friendship with MacGregor's nephew.'

'Indeed.' The Mayor was still not fully convinced.

William made one last effort. 'My brother-in-law is a loyal and law abiding citizen, your worship. He has no interest in politics and I am certain he does not espouse the radical cause.'

The Mayor remained unconvinced but decided, for the sake of expediency, to give William the benefit of the doubt. He now disliked the man more than ever but his instinct and experience told him that William could be useful. His scheme might just work where all else had failed. He decided to give it a try but first needed to clarify a few nagging doubts in his mind.

'This Irish woman you mentioned. How did you come to know of her?'

Not wishing to raise further doubts, William thought carefully before replying. 'It was through my brother-in-law,' he said cautiously.

'Was he accustomed to visiting Sandgate?'

'No, sir, but his son was. Colin MacGregor was his best friend. '

'So where does the woman fit in?' the Mayor persisted.

'I think my brother-in-law felt sorry for her and wanted to help.' The MacGregors were sympathetic too but couldn't do much to change the Sandgate women's attitude. They don't like the Irish, you know.'

The Mayor nodded. 'Yes, I had heard.'

'My brother-in-law found some work for her. She did some cleaning and washing at Mr Ivison's house and the office. '

'The Mayor's manner suddenly changed. 'So her journeying between Sandgate and the Quayside would be seen as normal.'

'Yes sir. That's why I suggested using her. She'll be able to pass on information without raising any suspicion.'

'Yes, indeed,' the Mayor agreed. His mind was now made up. 'We must move quickly. It will be your responsibility,' he said pointing a finger at William, 'to put the plan into action. But I don't want her to think the authorities are involved, it might put her off. You must convince her you have other motives. Use the hundred pounds to gain her confidence rather than as Judas money.'

The word Judas caused William to quail as he remembered the warning message tied to his door. 'That won't be difficult,' he said eagerly. 'I have every reason to see MacGregor locked up behind bars and the sooner the better.'

It took a week for the plan to work and eight men to subdue the big, bearded Scot when he was arrested. Newgate prison in Newcastle was notoriously insecure, especially for such an important prisoner as Rory MacGregor. To safeguard against any attempt at rescue by the keelmen Rory was moved, under heavy escort, to Durham gaol.

A few days later, after a short bout of high living, the body of the Irish woman was found floating in the Tyne. Her throat had been cut from ear to ear.

After many months of fruitless interrogation by the authorities, Rory was arraigned before the summer assizes and sentenced to four years imprisonment with hard labour.

CHAPTER 17

A light powdering of snow had softened the bleakness of North Moor colliery, covering the muddy cinder roads with a pure white blanket that glowed faintly luminous in the pale moonlight. Even the pit looked less threatening, as if it too welcomed the approach of Christmas.

It had stopped snowing and on the high ground to the north, the lights of North Moor village shone brightly in the crisp night air. The grounds of North Moor Hall were lit with coloured glass lanterns which were hung from the trees. The village green adjoining the church was illuminated in a similar fashion. The sound of organ music drifted from the church as the organist practised for the midnight service that was the traditional start to Christmas Day.

North Moor Hall was ablaze with light from the candlelit crystal chandeliers that hung from the ornate ceilings of the principal reception rooms. The smell of melted candle wax mingled with the aroma of cooking that rose from the kitchen below.

As squire and magistrate, Duncan Forster was patron of the village church and provided a stipend of one hundred pounds a year to support the vicar. After the service he would follow the custom of hosting the annual Christma   §99s supper, an event which would be attended by the lesser dignitaries of the manor together with his agents, managers and some of the local yeoman farmers. The estate workers would attend a less sumptuous gathering below stairs.

Duncan Forster hated these social obligations that were incumbent on his position as squire and lord of the manor. At heart he was a coal master and businessman and hated the triviality of these occasions which distracted him from his real work. Besides, all the people who would be present were his social inferiors and could be of little use to him in furthering his ambitions. He had bought North Moor Hall mainly for the estate's mining potential and access to further land following the enclosure of the moor. He also hoped it would enhance his social status with his peers, but was realistic enough to know that, as a newcomer who had bought his way into the squirearchy, it would take generations before his family would be accepted by the county establishment.

To save wasting an entire evening, Forster instructed his business aides to attend a meeting at North Moor Hall before the service. Roland grimaced when he heard the news.   'But it's Christmas Eve, father, 'he protested.

'They're coming to the supper after the service, aren't they?'

'Yes, but...'

'Then they can bloody well sing for it,' Forster interrupted impatiently and seeing a smirk appear on Roland's face added, 'and that applies to you too.'

Roland's confidence sagged. 'But surely, father, there aren't any pressing matters that can't wait until after Christmas?'

Forster looked at his son, his expression registering a mixture of disappointment and exasperation. 'The trouble with you, Roland,' he said icily, 'is that you're so damned lazy that you wouldn't recognise a problem if you saw one. You should be well on the way to becoming a fully-fledged viewer by now, but just look at you. Wilkins can run rings round you, Gibson and Mulligan have no respect for you and as for the men ....,' he stopped almost choking with frustration, '...the men think you are a laughing stock.' His voice rose. 'You can be a joke by all means, Roland, but not at my expense. I won't warn you again.'

Roland was stunned by his father's outburst and for a while was unable to speak. When he recovered he excused himself and went up to his room fuming with anger and exasperation at what he considered to be his father's unreasonable attitude.

Polly James watched behind a half closed door at the end of the west wing passage as Roland, flushed and angry, entered his room and slammed the door behind him. She waited for a few minutes then walked quietly to the door and knocked.

'Who is it?'

'It's me, sir, Polly James.'

After a few moments the door swung open and Roland's face, still flushed and angry, stared down at her.

'I was going to tend the fire, sir,' she lied, 'but I can come back later.'

Roland's anger evaporated and he stood back leering at her. 'It's all right, Polly. Come in.'

She moved across to the fireplace, her hips swaying provocatively. She bent down to bank up the fire, using tongs to transfer the lumps of coal from the brass coal scuttle. She smiled as she felt Roland's hand move up inside her skirt and fondle her thighs. 'That's naughty, Master Roland,' she said but made no move to stop him.

He pulled her roughly towards the bed and she could see by the swelling at his crotch that his needs were urgent. She wished he had more finesse in his sexual demands and came to the conclusion that he needed taking in hand. She'd given way to his coarse urgings many times in recent months, but now she decided it was time to educate him in the true art of lovemaking.

Roland was by now fully aroused and impatient for Polly to remove her clothes. He made urgent attempts to undress her tearing clumsily at her dress and undergarments. She pushed him firmly but gently down on the bed and began to undress him, her fingers sensuously exploring his body as she did so. He lay squirming with excitement, until he was completely naked, his manhood standing proudly erect.

Polly slowly undressed herself, flaunting her large breasts as she leaned over him. He watched in fascination as her head came down to his swollen member and felt her soft, brown hair tumble over his stomach. He lay moaning quietly as her head moved gently up and down. When he was near bursting point she paused. 'Don't stop,' he pleaded.

'The best is yet to come,' she said, smiling triumphantly at her conquest. She quickly straddled his hips and gently guided him into the moist paradise that lay between her thighs. Slowly and expertly she rose and fell watching his eyes glaze over with ecstasy. She felt his hands cup and fondle her breasts squeezing them erotically to the rhythm of her own movements. He groaned as his passion finally exploded and she felt the warm flow of his seed inside her as she convulsed to her own climax.

She remained poised over him for several minutes while he recovered. Finally, she twisted off and lay down beside him. 'Now wasn't that nice?' she said, flashing him a wicked smile.

'Bloody marvellous,' he replied in a drained but satisfied voice. He looked at her quizzically. 'Tell me, Polly,' he said nervously, 'we've been doing this for months now and yet you're showing no signs of...er..' he paused in his embarrassment.

'Becoming pregnant,' she finished for him.

'Well, all the others did,' he said sheepishly. He was proud of his virility and worried that his procreative powers might be on the wane.

'I'm not like all the others,' she responded darkly. 'I've learned a thing or two, I have.' She could see Roland was curious but wasn't going to tell him she couldn't have children even if she wanted to. That would destroy the illusion. In some perverse way she hoped he might fall in love with her, although her common sense told her otherwise. She knew there was no possibility of marriage even if he did fall in love with her. But she had a faint hope that as he grew older, he might wish to formalise the arrangement and set her up as a proper mistress. There would be money in that.

At this point her ambitious musings were brought sharply down to earth. Roland slapped her hard on the backside and said, 'Come on, missy, it's time to go. Father's called this bloody meeting before the midnight mass. It's going to be a long night.'

Suddenly her fragile dream had been callously shattered leaving her feeling angry and bitter.

The group of men in the library stood nervously awaiting the arrival of Duncan Forster. They were dressed formally for the forthcoming midnight service and their high, stiff collars were wet with sweat, adding to their discomfort and feelings of apprehension. The tension rose when Forster entered the room. He walked over to the writing table ignoring his edgy lieutenants.

For a while he did not say anything and no one else dared break the silence. At last he spoke. 'Good evening, gentlemen.' It was a growl rather than a greeting.

'Good evening, sir.' The response was subdued and unenthusiastic.

'Evening, father.' The lone voice was Roland's trying to make the point that he was not one of his father's lackeys. He was quickly put in his place.

'I'm surprised to find you here on time, Roland. In fact I'm surprised to find you here at all,' his father added caustically. The others exchanged quiet glances of relief and satisfaction that some of their master's wrath was being directed at his son. But their relief proved short-lived.

'To business, gentlemen,' and he turned to his viewer. 'We're not raising enough coal, Wilkins, and what we are bringing up to bank is costing too much.'

Wilkins shuffled uneasily. 'It's the weather, Mr Forster. The collier brigs cannot sail when it's like this. There's nearly a thousand of 'em loaded and cooped up in the Tyne at Shields.'

'We can store coal at the staithes, can't we?'

'Yes, sir, but all the covered area is full. The coal soon deteriorates if we store it in the open.'

Forster glared at him. 'I'm well aware of that, man. I was running pits before you could walk.' He turned to his agent, Gibson. 'How many more brigs can we expect next week?'

'None, if this weather keeps up, sir. We'll have to lay men off soon, like most of the other pits.'

Forster snorted with frustration. 'It's the same every damned winter,' he raged. 'A few weeks of bad weather and the whole bloody Northern Coalfield has to close down. It's high time the corporation did something about the river entrance otherwise we'll lose the London markets.'

'The other owners are facing the same difficulties,' Gibson said soothingly.

'But they don't have my problems,' Forster pointed out irritably. 'I need to keep the cash flowing to secure my investment.' He felt like telling them just how precarious his financial position was, but refrained. He didn't want word to get round that if his mining gamble didn't succeed, he'd be facing bankruptcy. All his other assets had been mortgaged to finance his North Moor venture. He turned to Wilkins. 'How long can we go on drawing coal before all the covered storage is used up?'

'A week, I'd say, perhaps eight days if we're lucky,' Wilkins replied cautiously.

Forster thought for a moment. 'I suppose we'll have to pay the men if we lay them off?'

'Yes, unless we can find them other work,' Wilkins said. 'It's in the bond.'

'We don't have to pay them unless they're laid off for more than three days, Mr Forster.' It was Mulligan, the keeker, speaking for the first time.

Forster looked as his keeker with new respect. 'Indeed we don't, Mulligan. Thank you for reminding me.' Then turning to his viewer he said, 'There's your answer, Wilkins. We can work them for two days and lay 'em off for three. That way we can keep the pit going for three weeks without increasing our costs. By then the weather may have improved.'

'But that's immoral, sir.' Wilkins was appalled. 'The bond shouldn't be used in that way. They're forced to go down the pit when there is work so it's only right that they're paid when there's none.'

'You're too squeamish, Wilkins. We won't be the first to interpret the bond to our advantage. It's not illegal is it?'

'No, but that doesn't make it right,' said Wilkins stubbornly.

Forster began to lose his temper. 'Don't you dare lecture me on how I chose to run my business. You're far too soft, Wilkins. Perhaps it really is time I found myself another viewer.'

Wilkins' resistance collapsed. 'It still seems a bit unfair, sir. The men won't like it,' he added lamely.

'Of course they won't,' Forster snapped. 'But I don't run my pits to pander to the likes and dislikes of the men. We'll lay them off three days at a time without pay until we can resume normal production. Is that clear?' He looked in turn at everyone in the room to ensure that they all understood.

Wilkins plucked up courage to make one final protest.

'I think that will be the last straw for the men, sir.' He said in a voice that was tense with unhappiness. 'For months now Mulligan has been fining very heavily and without justification. Even the best hewers can barely make fourteen shillings a week and they have to watch while their bairns work a seventeen-hour day to draw the extra coal we've been cutting. If we add to their misery by laying them off without pay, they'll break their bond and refuse to work at all.' He paused, waiting for Forster's anger to erupt.

'That's exactly what I want,' Forster said quietly.

Wilkins looked at him in astonishment. 'Why?'

'Because if they break their bond they don't get paid. Don't you see man; I might have to lay them off for more than three days eventually and I'd be forced to pay them for the privilege under the terms of the bond. This way I can force their hand if it suits me.'

'If we force them to withdraw their labour we'll have a hard time getting them back to work,' Wilkins continued doggedly.

'Then I'll just have to fine them for breaking their bond and go on fining them until they come to their senses. I'll put the ringleaders in prison if I have to. Believe you me, I'll soon have 'em back at work when it suits my purpose, but not before.'

There was a long silence and Forster could see that his lieutenants were shocked at his tough stance. Even the hardened keeker was somewhat taken aback. Sensing their misgivings he decided it might be worth sugaring the pill a little by hinting at some of his ambitious plans for North Moor colliery.

'Gentlemen,' he said smiling at them for the first time, 'I understand your concerns but believe me, this is not the time to go soft on the men. We all know that a second shaft must be sunk and I would like to install one of Watt's new winding engines. But all this costs money, so the pit must pay its way by whatever means are necessary. Your futures are linked to mine and if you follow my instructions you'll all be well rewarded for your efforts.' Here his voice hardened. 'But understand this; I'll brook no disloyalty from anyone. I expect your full support.' He waited to let his words sink in. 'Well now, gentlemen,' he went on, adopting a more jovial tone, 'I think it's time we made our way to the church.'

The men, looking dazed but relieved, filed slowly from the room. Roland was the last to leave and his father called him back as he reached the door. 'A brief word with you, Roland,' he commanded.

Roland felt his mouth go dry at the sound of his father's voice. He knew by the tone that he was in serious trouble and prepared himself for the worst. 'Yes, father,' he answered resignedly.

'You haven't kept me informed as to what progress you're making in your negotiations for the new landsale contracts.'

'There's not much to report yet, father,' Roland said guardedly.

'Exactly what do you mean by not much?' Forster persisted.

'I haven't seen all the people you asked me to contact.'

'Have you seen any of them?'

'No, father, but I'm planning to.'

'You've made some appointments then?'

'Well, er...no, actually,' Roland trailed off weakly. He waited apprehensively for the storm to break.

'I see, but you're planning to.' The voice was icy with sarcasm.

'Immediately after Christmas, father. I promise.'

'But I instructed you on this matter nearly two weeks ago. Don't you realise just how important it is? If we can't ship our coal by sea we need to look for new landsale markets – local markets like salt making, brewing, glass making, iron, soda. They all need coal, damn it! And I'm prepared to cut my prices to the bone to supply it. I gave you a list of people to see didn't I? What could be easier for you?' He stopped, overcome by his anger and frustration.

'Well I have been busy at the pit lately,' Roland said lamely.

'Nonsense, boy, you're hardly ever there; even Wilkins has been complaining.'

'That's not true.'

Ignoring his protests, Forster railed at his son. 'You've been drinking and whoring again haven't you. Skulking off to Newcastle to spend your time in those dens of iniquity run by those disgraceful madams.'

'But you encouraged me, father,' Roland complained, aggrieved at his father's inconsistency.

'Only to stop you fornicating with the servants in my own home; not for you to go bedding brothel tarts four or five times a week.'

'You've been having me watched, haven't you?'

'Yes, but only to confirm what I already suspected. Now that I know for certain, it's got to stop, understand?'

'And if I don't?' Roland ventured cautiously.

'Then I'll stop your allowance and confine you to the house and the pit until you come to your senses.'

Roland knew he was beaten and looked at his father with a mixture of defiance and contempt tinged with fear.

But because of Duncan Forster's loving blind spot for his son he mistook the look as one of parental respect from a high spirited young man. He knew he would be proud of Roland one day. All it needed was a firm but loving hand. He began to soften. 'I don't want to be hard on you, Roland, but you must realise it's for your own good.'

'Yes, father.' Hope rose in Roland as he rediscovered his father's weak spot.

'You must try and understand my problems too. I've got great plans for North Moor,' he went on. 'There are thousands of acres and tons of quality coal out there but sinking a new pit and putting in one of Watt's winding engines will be very expensive. To pay for it I've mortgaged the last of the estate and this means everything depends on the pit being a success. If it is, you'll have an inheritance to be proud of.'

'And if it isn't?' Roland gasped.

Forster shrugged. 'I never contemplate failure,' he said dismissively.

Roland stood aghast as he contemplated the folly of his father's reckless gamble, but Forster again misinterpreted his son's expression as one of admiration for his boldness.

'You mustn't breathe a word to anyone that the rest of the estate is mortgaged,' he said.

'I won't father,' Roland acknowledged wearily, 'but is it worth the risk?'

'Of course it is. Let me tell you why. Back in seventy-eight, a Newcastle family of Quakers named Chapman began sinking a shaft on land leased at Wallsend. They encountered innumerable difficulties like water and quicksand and began to borrow money to carry on. The firm that loaned them the money was that of Messrs Russell, Allen and Wade of Sunderland. But before the coal seam was reached the Chapman's ran out of cash and the mortgage was foreclosed. Allen withdrew directly after the foreclosure leaving the pit to William Russell and his brother-in-law Thomas Wade.

The rest is history. Coal was reached almost immediately by the new partners at a depth of six hundred and sixty feet. The seam proved six and a half feet thick and house coal of the highest quality. As you know, Roland, Wallsend coal fetches the highest prices at the London Gate. Since then William Russell, as the senior partner, has made a fortune and last year bought Brancepeth Castle from Sir Henry Vane Tempest for a reputed £75,000. A remarkable achievement in just ten years.'

Forster paused, envious but at the same time, inspired by his own prospects. 'North Moor could be another Wallsend, Roland, and the fortunes of the Forsters' will soon match the Russell's.'

Roland turned away bewildered and dismayed at his father's foolishness. 'They might also match the Chapman's,' he muttered unhappily to himself.

CHAPTER 18

In North Moor colliery the preparations for Christmas were more muted and on a scale less grand than in its namesake village on the hill. The only exception was the ale house where loud singing, intermingled with bursts of raucous laughter, spilled out into the cold winter night.

At the other end of the village, Henry, Wilf and a small group of men were putting the finishing touches to the new Methodist chapel. The building had been converted from two adjoining pit cottages provided by Forster on condition that the cost of conversion would be borne by the men. A fund had been raised to buy the materials and the men had undertaken to do the work themselves.

Forster had been reluctant to help at first but pressure from the vicar, who had recently taken over the village church, finally persuaded him to go along with the idea. The vicar was a willing member of a ruling establishment that chose to distance itself from the mining villages. Like many priests he felt distaste for pits compounded by a complete ignorance about their workings and the lives of the men who were employed in them. It had once been suggested to the government's Home Department that pits would make suitable places for punishment where convicts, removed from view, would reflect on their misdeeds in perpetual darkness whilst the hard labour punished their bodies. In the Northern Coalfield, which contained one of the richest dioceses in Britain, the established church seemed happy to abandon the pitmen to the welcome arms of the Methodists.

Inside the chapel Henry and Wilf had finished whitewashing the walls and stood back to admire their handiwork. The gleaming white surface reflected the candlelight cast by the smoking tallow candles, creating a cosy atmosphere that had seemed absent before. Coal fires burned in the twin hearths that had once warmed two cottages. Fixed high on the wall at one end of the room was a large wooden cross that had been intricately carved by Sam Elliott.

'Not a bad job, eh Henry?'

'Certainly brightens the place up a bit,' Henry agreed.

They sat down on one of the simple wooden benches that had been dragged into the centre of the room to avoid being splashed by the painters' efforts. The benches had been painstakingly fashioned out of scraps of old timber taken from the carpenters shop at the pit together with wood from broken chaldron waggons and various pieces of timber collected at staithes and shipyards on the Tyne.

'Well, it's nearly ready for Sep to conduct his first meeting on Christmas Day, like we promised,' Wilf said, a note of deep satisfaction creeping into his voice. 'It's maybe not as good as the fine church in the village, yonder, but it's ours.'

Henry nodded. 'And we won't have to put up with the villagers looking down their noses at us on Sundays. So much for love thy neighbour?'

Wilf laughed. 'And the vicar wonders why so few pit folk attend his services!'

Their short rest was suddenly interrupted by the voice of Sep Fordyce calling from the other end of the chapel. 'Stop carping you two, and come and give me a hand.' He was carefully removing a protective blanket from a large, beautifully made pulpit which was clearly his pride and joy. 'We can move it into position now, ready for tomorrow's meeting.'

When this had been done to his satisfaction, he slowly mounted the two steps and stood leaning contentedly over the broad wooden rail gazing proudly round his new spiritual home. 'This Christmas will be the happiest in my whole life,' he said, beaming down at the assembled group of helpers. 'Our own chapel at last!'

Dora Hindmarsh and her daughter, Jane, were putting the finishing touches to the fine tapestry fringe that was to decorate the specially made lectern. On it would be placed the large Bible, a gift from the Methodist circuit that North Moor Chapel would now become part of.

Finally, the preparations were complete and the chapel was laid out to Sep's satisfaction ready for the inaugural Christmas meeting which he would conduct proudly. The tired but satisfied helpers slowly began to drift away to their cottages and the rare treat of a night's rest that would not be interrupted by the three o'clock call to the pit.

Outside in the crisp night air the bells of the distant village church could be heard as they rang in the dawn of Christmas Day. Wilf stopped to light his pipe, using a burning splinter taken from the dying embers of the chapel fire. When it was drawing to his satisfaction he turned to Henry. 'Old Sep's like a bairn with a new toy,' he said through teeth clenched firmly over his pipe stem.

'It's probably the best Christmas present he's ever had,' Henry responded, 'and well deserved too.'

'Aye,' Wilf agreed. 'He's been preaching too long without a proper home. Let's hope he can save a few more souls now that it can be done in comfort, so to speak.'

'He'll have strong competition from the ale house,' Henry reminded him.

Wilf grinned. 'I doubt if that will worry old Sep. He was the hardest drinking, most foul mouthed sinner in the northern coalfield until he saw the light. To him the ale house is a challenge and no match for the Lord's wine.'

'Yes, I think you're right,' said Henry said smiling back at Wilf. His new friend constantly surprised him with his intelligence, compassion and good humour. 'I think you and Sep have a lot in common except that you still enjoy a glass of ale and as for seeing the light...?' He broke off with a teasing smile.

Wilf chuckled. 'You might be right about the ale but I truly have seen the light.' He suddenly became serious. 'The trouble is, the light that I've seen is at the end of a very long tunnel. It's more a torch for freedom, justice and decency that I see. It shines bright at the end of September when the old bond expires and burns dim in October when the new bond is signed. There has to be a better way of doing things, Henry, but I'm not sure what it is.' He broke off, embarrassed by his soul searching and outpouring.

Henry was taken aback by the eloquence of Wilf's words and the change in his demeanour. Suddenly a vision of Rory MacGregor, large and smiling behind his bushy red beard, floated before his eyes and with it a strange feeling of déjà vu. As it disappeared he saw the same earnest idealism in Wilf's expression, only it lacked Rory's confidence. Wilf was a leader in embryo, fervent but uncertain as he grappled with his metamorphosis. Rory came from a long line of rebellious chiefs where leadership came naturally and effortlessly, but Wilf's confidence would surely grow.

185

'Sep would explain everything by saying that God moves in mysterious ways,' Henry said brightly, trying to stir Wilf out of his gloomy mood.

'But why make people suffer, especially poor working folk?' Wilf persisted.

'I suppose it's God's form of punishment,' Henry said soothingly.

'But the owners never seem to suffer. Are we the only sinners?'

'No, of course not.'

'Then there has to be a better way. Just relying on God won't solve our problems, not in this world it won't. Our bairns have to work seventeen hours a day in conditions not fit for animals. The ventilation is bad for such a fiery pit and there's no sign of a second shaft being sunk. We'll have another explosion soon, only this time we'll be lucky if we end up burying just six men.' He paused, feeling the scar on his cheek, a permanent memento to his bravery when leading the rescue operation after the last pit explosion. It always throbbed when he became angry.

'Have you spoken to the viewer about the men's grievances?' Henry asked.

'Yes, but he only does what Forster tells him. The trouble is that we are weak and disorganised and Forster knows this. If we could only stick together and form a united front we might get somewhere.'

Henry shook his head. 'That's the rub, Wilf. The men are just simple, unlettered folk, afraid of being fined or imprisoned. As long as their families don't starve most of the men will put up with anything and seek solace in the ale house. Come the next binding, the owners only have to dangle a coin or two and pour some ale and most of them are hooked for another year.'

'Then we must try and change things. We just can't go on like this.' There was a growing determination in Wilf's voice.

Henry could understand Wilf's frustration but he also knew that there were no short term solutions to the age-old problem of exploitation. As long as there were pits needing men and pitmen willing to enslave themselves, nothing much would change. The most pernicious injustice was the annual bond and this the owners were determined to keep. He turned to Wilf and gently tried to explain but

186

stopped when he saw the steely look of determination that reminded him again of Rory MacGregor.

'We must start now, Henry. Organise the men.'

'But it will take years to educate simple pitmen to stand up and fight for their rights.'

'If education's the answer then the sooner we start the better,' Wilf persisted.

'I think it requires more than that,' Henry countered. 'It needs a reformation in human attitudes and understanding and a new breed of pitmen to lead it. Social revolutions take time. Look how long the radicals have been at it and for what?'

'Then let's make sure our children have the education to take advantage of the opportunity when the time comes.'

'How? Their parents send them down the pit when they're six or seven. By the time they're ten they'll have forgotten all they've learned. Besides, we haven't got a school. '

'We've got the Chapel.'

'You'll also need books, paper, slates and chalk. Most of all you'll need a teacher.'

'You're an educated man, Henry. More so than you've made out. Young Mark's quite a scholar too, I believe, so Dora tells me. I expect that's largely due to you.'

'I'm not a teacher, Wilf, and even if I were we haven't the money to support a school.'

'But it can be done, don't you see?' Wilf's excitement rose and the plan that had been incubating in his mind for many months began to pour from his lips. 'I've been doing a lot of thinking,' he went on fervidly, 'that as individuals we're pretty powerless. But if we act together then we'll be a force to be reckoned with.'

'The owners will see that as a combination, a conspiracy to subvert their rights as masters,' Henry cautioned. 'You might all end up in gaol.'

'Not if we form a Friendly Society to look after the welfare of the men and their families. If we can collect two pence a week from each working man it will provide an income of over one hundred pounds a year for the society. That's more than enough to provide a school and other benefits.'

187

'If they all pay up.' Henry tried to curb Wilf's enthusiasm but without success.

'They'll pay up,' Wilf went on, brushing Henry's doubts to one side. 'The chapel can be a schoolroom and meeting place as well as a house of worship. We'll form a committee to run the Friendly Society and act as an unofficial leadership body for the men. That way we can start planning for the future.'

'Does Sep know what you have in mind?'

'No, but it's legal, isn't it?'

'I think so.'

'Then Sep won't object. He wants a Sunday School anyway so a proper daily school will seem like a blessing from the Lord.'

Henry smiled at Wilf's bubbling enthusiasm. 'It will have to be more than just a Bible class, you know. You'll need someone who can teach reading, writing and hopefully, some arithmetic.'

'But surely you'll be our teacher, Henry? We can run the classes in the afternoon after work. Ted Mason, the pit clerk can read and write. He's a staunch Methodist, I'm sure he'll help if you show him how to go about it.'

Henry demurred. 'I'm sorry, Wilf, I can't do it. If Forster finds out that I've got some education I'll be singled out and watched. Come the next binding I won't be taken on and likely as not I'll be blacklisted at the other pits.'

Wilf was taken by surprise at Henry's genuine reluctance to help. Their engrossing midnight discourse had taken them through the village and out by the pit where the iron fire grates sent shimmers of light across the snow covered ground. Wilf turned and studied his friend's face. 'I never thought you were the sort of man to be frightened off by the likes of Forster.' There was a mixture of sadness and disillusionment, verging on contempt, in his voice. 'A good pitman can always find work, Henry. I was blacklisted from two pits before I came here but I don't regret it.'

'It's not that I don't want to help,' Henry said desperately, 'I just can't take any more risks.'

Wilf sensed there might be other reasons for Henry's refusal. He wondered if he had misjudged him? Henry had been something of a dark horse since his arrival at North Moor and he was clearly a cut well above the normal pitman. 'Been in some sort of trouble, have you?' The question was put gently with an implied offer of help. 'Sort of,' Henry said evasively.

'I thought so.' Wilf sighed resignedly. 'And here's me thinking what a fine leader you'd make. The ideal chairman for our Friendly Society.'

Henry felt the anguish of his position as never before. He was torn between his desire to help Wilf and his promise to Mary and himself never to get involved in this kind of situation again. He stood, silent and downcast.

Wilf sensed the torment that was racking through the mind of his friend. 'Like to tell me about it?' he said softly.

Henry suddenly felt an irresistible urge to unburden himself and gradually, as his private dam of bitterness was breached, the story of his involvement with Rory and the radicals came pouring out. When he'd finished he felt a surge of relief and a strange reawakening of something deep inside him.

Wilf listened in silence until Henry finished talking then his face broke into a crooked smile. 'You've certainly led a busy life,' he said, a note of respect and admiration returning to his voice. 'And to think I nearly misjudged a man who'd won the confidence of Rory MacGregor.'

'You know him?' Henry was surprised.

'No, alas, only of him. Some say he's something of a freebooter, but I think not.'

'He's an honourable and generous man, I can assure you.'

'I know. And the men at Walker pit think so too. But then they would, wouldn't they, seeing as half of them are related to keelmen.'

'How do you know that,' Henry asked in surprise.

Wilf laughed. 'Walker was my last pit.'

They walked on past the pit shaft which was still drawing the last of the coal from the day's shift which had ended hours ago.

'Forster's determined to get the last ounce out before Christmas,' Henry remarked.

'Greedy bastard!' Wilf spat in the snow to emphasise his contempt.

Henry decided to change the subject. 'You believe in sharing, don't you Wilf? Helping those in need?'

189

'Course I do,' Wilf responded, surprised at the question.

'Good, then you can help me carry some water home from the pumping cistern.'

'You're not still doing that, are you?' There was mocking disbelief in Wilf's voice. 'What's wrong with the water from the village well?'

'This water is pumped up from a freshwater feeder six hundred feet down. It's sweet and pure.'

'There's nowt wrong with the well water,' Wilf countered. 'It's never done me any harm.'

'That's because you've got a cast iron stomach. I think the village well is foul and the cause of most of the fevers, especially in summer.'

Wilf laughed. 'You get used to it in time. Everyone thinks you're daft carrying water all the way home from the pit when there's a well at the end of your street.'

'We'll see,' was all Henry would say.

The two men borrowed pails from the engine house after Henry promised the engineman that he would return them before the shift ended. After rinsing and filling the pails, the two men staggered off towards the village.

'Do you use this water for everything?' Wilf asked.

'Only for drinking and cooking. We don't mind the well water for washing.'

'You're mad,' Wilf grunted.

When they reached Henry's cottage the pails were placed carefully on the ground. Henry thanked his friend and after an awkward pause, went on. 'I think you're right about trying to change things, Wilf. It's time we stood up for our rights.'

Wilf was taken aback at Henry's sudden change of attitude. When he recovered, he grinned and clasped Henry's shoulder. 'Then you will help?'

'I'll do my best but in my own way.'

'What does that mean?'

'I won't be chairman of your Friendly Society or your leader.'

'Why not?' Wilf's bafflement was turning to dismay.

'Because that's your job, Wilf. You're the natural leader of this pit. I've seen it. I've watched the men. They listen to you and because they respect you, they'll follow you.'

Wilf, red with embarrassment, tried to argue but Henry cut him short. 'Education in itself doesn't make a leader. It helps sometimes but it's not essential. I'll provide you and the others with whatever help you need. I'll write letters for you setting out our grievances, provide a draft for a new bond, if need be, but it will be in the name of a committee representing the men. That way it will be more difficult for Forster to single out anyone for victimization.'

Wilf looked at his friend with eyes dancing with excitement. 'By God you're right, Henry. We've got something to build on at last.'

'It won't happen overnight. Remember that when things get rough.'

'I know, Henry, but we need to make an early start. Word is that the collier brigs are not sailing so we'll have the usual winter lay off soon.'

'But that's when the bond is in our favour, surely? The owners must pay us two and sixpence a day if we cannot work. That's more than we've been getting these past few months with all the tricks the keeker's been up to. Mulligan will end up with a knife between his shoulders if he goes on like this much longer.'

Wilf remained sceptical. 'I somehow can't see Forster paying us fifteen shillings a week for not working. Especially if he's strapped for cash like they say he is.'

'He's got no option, Wilf. It's in the bond.'

'It hasn't stopped some owners in the past. They only have to pay if we're laid off for more than three days. Mark my words, Forster will try to stretch it out.'

'He can't. All the collier brigs are loaded for sea and he's running out of covered storage.'

Wilf shook his head, still unconvinced. 'I think we may have to stand up and fight a lot earlier than you think, my friend.'

Henry could see there was no point in continuing the argument. 'We'll just have to wait and see,' he concluded. He turned to open the cottage door. 'Good night, Wilf, or rather good morning.'

Wilf laughed. 'Why not Merry Christmas?'

'Good Lord, I almost forgot with all your sanctimonious lecturing.' Henry turned and smiled fondly at his friend. 'Why not indeed?

Merry Christmas, Wilf.' The two men shook hands and the special bond between them was even stronger.

Wilf set off for home but after a few yards he turned and retraced his steps to Henry's door which now stood closed. He tapped quietly but urgently and it was quickly reopened.

'What now?' Henry said with feigned irritation.

'Just a small favour to ask.'

'Then ask it and let me get to my bed.'

Wilf stood looking awkward and embarrassed as he groped for the right words before finally blurting out, 'Will you teach me to read and write? Private like, without the others knowing.'

Henry saw that Wilf was serious and quickly smothered a smile. 'Of course I will. You'll be my star pupil, Wilf. That I promise you.'

CHAPTER 19

Wilf's mistrust of Forster's motives proved well founded. As the church bells tolled in the first day of 1798, the pit was laid off for three days without pay. This was followed by two days of paid employment and then a further three day lay-off. Forster intended to continue this pattern for the next few weeks until all the available covered storage was exhausted. His financial future was at stake.

The fledgling committee of the Friendly Society met in secret at the new chapel. The discussions were acrimonious with the men loudly demanding a complete withdrawal of labour. Henry argued strongly against this course of action on the grounds that this would play directly into the hands of Forster. He was supported by Wilf and Sep.

'We must stay within the law,' Wilf insisted.

'But Forster's breaking his part of the bond, isn't he,' some of the committee men complained.

'No,' Henry intervened. 'He's abusing it but he's not legally breaking it.'

The grumbling continued. 'Abusing it or breaking it, that sounds the same to me,' Jim Walters said. 'I say we stop at home until he sticks to his side of the bond.' There was a mutual chorus of agreement from most of the men present.

'No,' Henry persisted. 'That's exactly what Forster wants. If we withdraw our labour we'll be breaking the law. We won't get paid and he can take us to court and have us fined.' He paused looking at each in turn before adding, 'And some of us may not get our jobs back.'

'Henry's right,' Wilf cut in. 'If we stop work now we'll only be doing Forster's dirty work for him.'

'But we can't live on six shillings a week,' Sam Elliott complained.

'It's better than nowt,' Wilf retorted.

'Now, lads,' Sep intervened, 'let's not fight among ourselves.'

'It's only a matter of time before Forster has to lay us off,' Henry said. 'Then he's got to pay us two and sixpence a day as laid down in the bond.' He placed a copy of the bond on the table to emphasise his point before going on, 'The time to withdraw our labour and act together is when the new binding comes up in October. We can ask for the three day layoff clause to be taken out of the new bond.'

There was a chorus of approval at this suggestion and Henry and Wilf exchanged a fleeting smile knowing they had won the day.

'That's it then,' Wilf interceded quickly. 'We do as Henry suggests and sit tight. All agreed?' A quick show of hands signalled unanimity and following some good natured banter the meeting broke up.

After the meeting Henry and Wilf walked home in silence, their shoulders hunched up inside the upturned collars of their jackets to give some small protection from the icy wind. Wilf appeared deep in thought.

'Penny for them, Wilf?' Henry asked softly.

Wilf grinned self-consciously. 'I was just thinking how right you were.'

'In what way?'

'That it would take time to educate the men. And I don't mean the reading and writing stuff,' he added awkwardly.

'I know what you mean, Wilf,' Henry said gently. 'The men need educating in leadership so that they can act sensibly as well as responsibly. But we've made a good start.'

'We nearly lost it tonight, though.'

'Nearly, but not quite. You did a good job in there, Wilf. You retrieved the situation.'

'It was your suggestion, Henry.'

'But your leadership, Wilf, and that's what counts at the end of the day.'

Wilf smiled. 'I'm not much of a drinking man but this calls for a celebration. Fancy a glass of ale?'

'Why not? It's New Year so I can't think of a better time. Lead on, my friend.'

The ale house was not as crowded as usual because of the short time working at the pit. The landlord's scowl gave way to a look for surprise when he saw Henry and Wilf. They were not regulars and he wondered if he might glean some useful information to pass on to his brother who was overman at the pit. Any scraps of intelligence deemed to be worthwhile would be passed on to Forster.

'Evening gents. What can I get you?' He leaned over the counter exhaling a stream of foul smelling breath through broken, yellowing teeth.

'Two glasses of your watered down ale,' Wilf said, grinning provocatively.

'I don't water my ale,' the landlord growled, glaring back at Wilf.

It was a lie but Wilf let it pass. 'Then two glasses of your unwatered ale,' he retorted, in tones of feigned amazement.

The landlord was about to retaliate when Henry intervened. 'Take no notice of him. He's been listening to one of Sep's sermons and he's feeling a bit holier than thou at the moment. Needs a few beers to get it out of his system.'

'He won't get 'em in here if he keeps insulting my ale,' the landlord said, still bristling.

Henry quickly changed the subject to divert attention away from Wilf. 'It's a bit quiet in here tonight. Not much money about just now I expect.'

'Aye, but things will change next week when the contract workers arrive,' the landlord said knowingly.

'Contract workers?' Henry and Wilf spoke the question in unison.

'You haven't heard then?' The landlord's voice took on a superior note.

'No, you tell us.'

'I don't know if I should.' The landlord was enjoying his new found advantage.

'I expect a man in your position gets to know most things that happen around here,' Henry said, adopting a fawning tone. 'Come on, you can trust us,' he cajoled.

'Well...,' the landlord hesitated, 'I suppose it will all be out soon. 'I've heard that Mr Forster is going to build twenty new cottages for the sinkers.'

'For the sinkers!' Wilf exclaimed. 'Then he must be going to sink the new shaft at last.'

'About time too,' Henry muttered.

'This place will be bursting with drinkers next week,' the landlord went on cockily, 'just you wait and see. And when the builders are finished the sinkers will move in. You know how much they can drink,' he said rubbing his hands. 'Thirsty work is sinking. All that digging and hauling inside a shaft.'

Sinkers were a tough itinerant breed with an awesome reputation for drinking and a capacity to match.

Wilf and Henry took their ale to a table in the corner out of earshot of the counter. The landlord watched with annoyance as he realised he had parted with useful information and had received nothing in return. 'What have you lot been doing up at the chapel, then?' he shouted after them.

'Nowt much,' Wilf answered. 'Just listening to one of Sep's sermons on the joys of temperance and the evils of drink.' He quaffed his ale and winked slyly at Henry. The landlord shot him a malevolent look before retreating to his storeroom at the back.

'So Forster's finally got round to sinking a new shaft,' Henry said thoughtfully. 'That means when the sinkers move out there'll be more hewers moving in.'

'Sounds like shit or bust to me,' Wilf said coarsely.

Henry smiled. 'You're probably right but I wouldn't put it in such crude terms. Forster must be confident he can sell the extra coal in spite of the vend.'

'How do you mean?'

'The owners operate as a cartel to control prices by limiting the sale of coal from the seasale pits. It's called the limitation of the vend. Each owner is allocated a production quota and if he exceeds it he pays a fine to the cartel. '

Wilf was surprised and fascinated by Henry's knowledge of the coal trade. 'So you think Forster has a good quota?'

'Either that or he plans to go it alone and ignore the other owners.'

'Can he do that?'

'It's been done before. Owners are a rapacious breed, Wilf, and money is a prime motivator.'

Wilf gave Henry a puzzled look. 'What does rapacious mean?'

'Greedy and grasping.'

Wilf nodded approvingly. 'That's a coal owner alright'.

'One thing is certain,' Henry said. 'Forster will want to squeeze every penny of profit from the pit to pay for the new shaft. He'll probably have to put in a new winding engine to get the extra coal out and that will cost him some.'

'That means he'll try to screw every penny he can out of our wages to pay for it all,' Wilf growled. 'The fines will get worse and we'll be lucky to earn two shillings a day. The men won't stand for it much longer.'

Henry looked thoughtful. 'We need to change the conditions in the bond, Wilf. It shouldn't be the keeker's decision alone to fine a man for cutting a few pieces of stone or sending up an underweight corve. We should have our own man there when the coals are laid out to act as a check on Mulligan.'

'Fat chance of that ever happening,' Wilf snorted. 'It would put the keekers out of business and the owners out of pocket. They know that every hewer puts an extra half hundredweight or more in each corve to try and avoid a fine. But the keekers still fine 'em for being short and the owners get the extra coal for nowt.'

'We can but try, Wilf, and the time to do it is when the binding comes up in October. We can refuse to be bound unless the bond is changed. Forster won't want to see his pit laid idle, will he?'

'Not when it's done legal like, he won't,' Wilf grinned. 'You're a genius, Henry.'

'Don't get carried away,' Henry cautioned. 'It won't be easy keeping the men together and Forster will use every dirty trick in the book to try and break us.'

'Then we'll have to use the committee to educate the men to our way of thinking, like you said. We have to make sure that every man joins the Friendly Society and that way we can keep 'em together.'

Henry lifted up his glass. 'To the Friendly Society.'

'Long may it prosper,' Wilf responded, downing his ale in one large gulp.

There was a mixed response at North Moor pit to the short time working imposed by Forster. It was bitterly resented by most families who were suffering real hardship as a result of the reduction in wages. But to those few families that had some savings the break in their harsh routine came as something of a welcome relief. For the children,

197

the release from being woken at three o'clock in the morning for the start of a fourteen or seventeen hour day was like the paradise promised by the preachers without the disadvantage of having to die first.

Henry's family was one of the lucky ones who had some money put away and were able to enjoy the enforced rest. Although Henry's body had become hardened to the gruelling pit work and his muscles could now stand the torture each shift imposed, he still found it difficult to adapt to the sheer monotony of it all. His educated mind cried out for something more stimulating. Therefore, he welcomed the opportunity that gave him the time to pour his energies into helping Wilf and Sep set up the school and organise the Friendly Society.

Wilf was despondent at first. 'The men haven't any money to pay into a Friendly Society,' he complained. 'We're wasting our time.'

'No,' Henry admonished. 'Now's the time to sell the idea and prepare the men for the next lay-off. Just think, Wilf, if we had funds now we could help those who need it. The men won't save if we leave it to them. We have to give them leadership and organisation. That way we can provide sickness benefits to those who get injured and can't work and give everyone some help when the pit's laid off.'

'Henry's right,' Sep said. 'He always told us it wouldn't be easy.'

'Aye, he did indeed,' Wilf agreed.

'Time and patience change the mulberry leaf to satin,' Sep intoned. 'That's what the old proverb says. Sound advice that is.'

'The important thing is to keep up the morale and motivation of the committee members,' Henry reminded them. 'Without their enthusiastic support we'll never be able to sell the idea to the rest of the men. We must take heart and keep up the pressure.'

It was one of the many exhortations that he would be called upon to give over the coming months.

CHAPTER 20

Mark welcomed the pit layoffs more than anyone. It provided a lifeline that kept his spirit afloat when it was perilously close to being drowned. When the pit was closed it reduced the opportunities for the constant bullying to which he was subjected when he was underground. The pit was a trap from which there was no escape; a trap where he was forced to endure the merciless persecution inflicted on him by the putters led by the chief tormentor, Herbie Marshall.

On the day of the first lay off, Mark had woken at four in the morning in a cold sweat thinking he was late. Groping round for his pit clothes he hurriedly dressed and crept to the trapdoor opening where the loft ladder led down to the room below. On looking down he saw, in the faint glow from the banked up fire, the sleeping forms of his mother and father. A feeling of intense joy and relief suddenly began to surge through his body as he realised the pit was not working that day, nor for the following two days. He quickly undressed, returned to his still warm bed and drifted off into a deep and tranquil sleep. It was one of the happiest moments in his young life.

In the weeks that followed the children of North Moor pit revelled in their new found freedom. Makeshift toboggans appeared on the slopes and fierce snowball fights took place between the pit children and the offspring of their haughty neighbours from North Moor village. Mark reluctantly excluded himself from these activities as his appearance invariably sparked off a hostile response from any putters who were present. Instead he spent most of his time with Jane Hindmarsh, helping her with reading and writing exercises in preparation for her joining the new chapel school.

Most of the pupils who had enrolled so far were under the age of seven. Above that age there were few boys as most parents hoped to obtain pit jobs for their elder sons, especially as word got round that the pit would be expanding. Henry had devised a syllabus based on a simple study of the three r's and a small number of books had been obtained to form the nucleus of the school library. Large roof slates, smoothed and polished by the men and framed in the pit carpenters shop were to be used for writing.

At the end of January, coal storage was exhausted and the pit ceased production. Apart from the essential maintenance staff and the furnace men needed to keep the pit ventilated, all the men were laid off. Much to his chagrin, Forster was forced to pay the men two and sixpence a day and could only fume and fret as the pit lay idle waiting for the weather to improve. For many of the younger pitmen the novelty of their enforced idleness soon began to wane. Freed from the rigid discipline of a strenuous work routine, boredom quickly set in. The rougher element could now afford to visit the ale house and fights between them and the workmen building the new cottages began to break out. These became more frequent and vicious when the tough sinkers joined in. Getting fighting drunk after a hard and dangerous day in the new shaft was preferable to sitting in their cold, temporary shacks.

Mark enjoyed being with Jane. He found her increasingly attractive and enjoyed her impish sense of humour that could gently tease without offending. She was also extremely intelligent. He discovered a new happiness in being with her that eased the pain of the putters' cruel persecution. His patient tutoring drew grateful smiles from her sparkling blue eyes that melted his young heart. He wished fervently that the pit would remain closed forever.

Some week's later Henry took Mark to the pit to show him the improvements that Forster had put in hand.

'They're making good progress on the new winding engine' he remarked.

'What was wrong with the old water wheel engine?' Mark asked.

'Not powerful enough and a bit cumbersome,' Henry explained. 'The new engine is based on Mr Watt's design although I doubt if Forster will be paying any royalties.'

'Why not?' Mark knew about patents and royalties and wondered how Forster could avoid paying.

'Because Boulton and Watt's patent expires soon. He probably sees little risk in going ahead with his own pirated design.'

'Will it really be worth all the money and the risk?'

'I think so,' Henry said, looking closely at the partly completed engine. 'You see,' he went on, 'the new engine works entirely on steam pressure and not just on atmospheric pressure like the old

Newcomen engines. It's double-acting; that means the piston both pushes and pulls, so it's far more efficient. A crank converts the lateral action into rotary motion and so you have your perfect winding engine. It'll raise three corves of coal in the same time that the old water driven engine took to raise one.'

'Will Mr Watt's engines replace all the old Newcomen types?' Mark queried.

'I doubt it. Not for pumping anyway.'

'Why not?'

'Because the old engines are simple and reliable. They use a lot more coal than the Watt engines; important if you're running a mill or a tin mine and don't have cheap coal on hand. But here in the Northern Coalfield small coal comes free.'

Mark could now see the economics behind it all. 'If the pit can raise three times the amount of coal it now produces Mr Forster will have to bind more hewers to cut out the extra coal.'

'You've got the right idea, Mark. It looks as though North Moor pit is going to grow. Hewers and their families will move into sinkers row when the sinkers leave. Come on, let's go and see how they're getting on.'

They walked the half mile to where the new shaft was being sunk and saw the new cast iron tubbing being fastened in place at the top of the shaft. 'What's that for?' Mark asked.

'To make the shaft water tight,' Henry explained. 'They line the shaft with tubbing so it looks like the inside of a barrel or tub. They used to use oak, that's why it's called tubbing. Now they've started to use cast iron segments bolted together. The shaft's lined like that until it reaches the impervious strata, usually about two or three hundred feet down. That way the shaft can be kept dry although the water from the feeders still finds its way to the bottom of the shaft and has to be pumped out.'

They watched the sinkers with their strange tarpaulin hats which hung down their backs to fend off the water and sludge which constantly fell into the shaft during the sinking operation.

'If you think being a pitman is a hard life you should be glad you're not a sinker,' Henry said. 'It's hard, dangerous work and you spend your life drifting from pit to pit like a nomad. It's as bad as being a navvy working on the canals.'

The sight of the wet, mud stained sinkers made Mark shiver and he suddenly felt hungry. 'Can we go home now?' he asked.

'Of course.' Henry put his arm around Mark's shoulders and together they walked back to the village.

When they opened the door of the cottage they were met with the warm, appetising aroma from the girdle cakes browning by the fire. Mary smiled at them. 'I thought I'd give you a treat now that we're getting the two and six a day.'

'Smells delicious,' Henry said, kissing her gently. 'But you shouldn't be doing too much in your condition.'

'Nonsense, I've got nearly six months to go yet. Besides, I'm feeling a lot better.'

'No more sweating and sickness?' Henry enquired anxiously.

'No. My insides seem to have settled down and the headaches have stopped.' She gazed fondly at her husband before adding, 'Stop worrying, Henry, I'm all right.'

'Good.' There was a mixture of relief and joy in his voice. 'It really is a treat to see you looking your old self again after the fever. I was worried, I can tell you.'

'I wasn't the only one, Henry. Half the women and children in the village seem to be down with the fever. They say Mrs Cooper and her little girl are at death's door.'

Henry shook his head. 'It's the well water that's causing it. It's foul, I'm sure.'

'Don't be silly, dear.' Mary said smiling patiently. 'Everybody drinks it but they don't all become ill, do they? It certainly doesn't seem to affect the men.'

'That's because most of them drink the pit water at work and nowt else but ale when they aren't. Wilf thinks you can get used to anything in time.'

'Is the pit water all that special, Henry?'

'It tastes a lot sweeter than the well water. That's why I carry it home for you to drink.' He stopped and a worried look crossed his face. 'You are drinking it, aren't you?'

202

'Of course I am. So are you and Mark.' She flashed a soothing smile. 'It's nice of you to carry it home but I don't think it's really necessary.'

'Your fever's gone hasn't it? You said you feel better. It's only happened since you stopped drinking the well water.'

'Others have got better without changing to pit water.'

'Not as quickly as you have,' he persisted.

'That's because they haven't had such kind and loving husbands to look after them,' Mary said brushing a kiss lightly across his cheek. 'Anyway, supper's ready so let's hear no more about it.'

'Just so long as you promise me not to drink the well water,' Henry said stubbornly.

Mary sighed philosophically. 'I promise.'

After tea, Henry set off for the chapel to attend the first committee meeting of the newly formed Friendly Society. Mark slipped next door to fulfil an eager promise, made earlier in the day, to help Jane with her composition.

After clearing away the table, Mary sat down in the chair by the hearth and stared wistfully into the glowing embers of the fire. Occasionally her expression deepened and her sadness changed to rancour as she reflected on the unfairness of past events and what life might have been had they stayed in Newcastle.

She could have reconciled herself to a life trapped in a pit village if she thought Mark and Henry could be happy. But she knew that the injustice of it all would eventually corrode their intelligent sensitive minds and ultimately destroy them. In the process, she would be destroyed too. Mark's suffering was already almost more than she could bear and made worse by his refusal to discuss the problem or seek help.

Mary sighed and felt the stirring of the child inside her. Suddenly her eyes moistened and warm tears rolled slowly down her cheeks as she wept for the future.

CHAPTER 21

By the end of February the weather had improved enough to allow the collier brigs to clear the dangerous entrance to the River Tyne, and North Moor pit was back in full production.

Still smarting from his defeat in having to honour the bond and the subsequent financial cost of being forced to pay his men while they were idle Forster was determined to recoup his losses without delay. He berated his keeker and instructed him to enforce a rigid regime of heavy fines on the hewers. 'No one must earn more than two shillings a day until I get my money back for paying the lazy bastards during the lay off,' he stormed. 'That way, I'll have my money back inside three months.'

The keeker was aghast. 'The men won't stand for it,' Mr Forster.

'Ah yes they will if we handle it right.'

'You'll push 'em too far,' the unhappy keeker cautioned.

'No, Mulligan. Just far enough for what I want.' Forster smiled enigmatically as he saw the keeker's puzzlement. 'We'll keep the pressure on until August and after that they can earn the full three shillings a score. By then I'll have my money back and more.'

'You'll have trouble binding them in October, Mr Forster.'

Forster laughed. 'They've got short memories, Mulligan. By October they'll be used to earning three shillings a day and won't want to give it up. Besides, I'll be able to offer a bit of binding money if needs be, seeing as they'll have paid for it by then.'

'I hope you're right, sir,' the keeker said dubiously.

'I usually am, Mulligan. Just do as you're told.'

When the unhappy keeker had left, Forster turned to Roland who had remained silent during the discussion. 'You can make yourself useful for once.' His voice carried a weary sarcasm that was becoming habitual when he addressed his son on business matters. It irritated Roland.

'In what way?' Roland's voice was sullen with resentment.

'By keeping a close eye on Wilkins. The men are bound to complain to the viewer and I don't want Wilkins going soft and overriding the keeker's decisions. If we let that happen he'll undermine Mulligan's authority.'

'Why don't you just tell Wilkins what you want, like you told Mulligan?'

'Because he'll turn if I push him too far. He's a good viewer and I don't want to lose him. Not yet, anyway. Not until I've got somebody ready to replace him.' Forster looked pointedly at his son.

Duncan Forster fretted over his losses and sought his revenge through the financial rape of his workforce. At the same time, Henry, Wilf and the other leaders of the Friendly Society were making steady progress in their attempts to bring education and social awareness to the inhabitants of North Moor colliery. The day school at the chapel was now well attended and the Sunday school classes were growing at a slow but promising rate.

But the government of Mr Pitt had now imposed a heavy stamp duty on newspapers, making them a luxury beyond the reach of the poor. Throughout the country, dog-eared, disintegrating copies, often months old, were eagerly passed from hand to hand among the few working people who could read. Like most progressive thinkers, Henry knew that the dissemination of news and information was essential to the promotion of political and social awareness, especially among the poor. The new newspaper tax made them prohibitively expensive.

In North Moor Colliery, newspapers and broadsides were purchased by the Friendly Society and read aloud to excited audiences in the Chapel by the small band of volunteers who were able to read. However, Henry took care to purchase only those papers and tracts that were not too extreme in their political views to avoid incurring the attention of government agents. In the event this proved to be a minimal constraint as most newspapers were proud of their independence and exercised a healthy criticism on matters of State and the conduct of the war.

As the year wore on and the threat of invasion increased war fever began to grip the nation. General Bonaparte had been summoned to Paris to take command of the army charged with the task of invading and conquering England. The wildly cheering Paris mob was convinced that Napoleon, the Victor of Italy, had only to set foot in England for that country to fall.

In February, Bonaparte made an inspection visit to the channel ports where his invasion fleet was being prepared. Fortune smiled on England when a secret agent, employed by Lord Castlereagh, had the good luck to meet the General on the road to Dunkirk. As a result he was able to send back interesting details on the number of flat-bottomed boats ordered at Ostend, and about those already on the stocks at Rouen, Le Havre and Calais. Every useful tree on the roadside near Lille had been felled. He also sent details of an army of fifty-five thousand men within twenty-four hours forced march of the coast. This, he estimated, would be only a quarter of the available force likely to be deployed.

At first, the news was received in England with a mixture of apprehension and defiance, but this was soon converted, with some adroit help from the government, into a wave of mass patriotism. This became manifest in the scramble to form volunteer corps and armed associations for the defence of the realm. The press played its part by publishing lurid accounts of enormous invasion rafts being built that were like floating fortresses. But those members of the public with a nervous disposition were perhaps comforted by news of the new semaphore system which could signal an early warning of an approaching invasion fleet. Transmissions from Yarmouth to the Nore and from Portsmouth to the Admiralty took little more than five or six minutes; assuming, of course, that Bonaparte would have the decency to invade in clear weather and during the hours of daylight.

As spring gave way to summer drills and parades were the order of the day. New volunteer corps, many picturesquely named and attired, sprang up throughout the land. Military tailors did a roaring business.

In Newcastle the inhabitants formed an armed association for the defence of their town. In July eight companies, wearing their blue jackets and white trousers, paraded on the Town Moor. Military encampments sprouted up along the coasts of Durham and Northumberland, and during the summer the area bristled with armed troops of every description.

As squire and magistrate, Duncan Forster played his part by forming the North Moor Volunteer Company, but his motives were more practical than patriotic. He hoped his actions would cause the ruling establishment in general and it's aristocratic elements in particular to regard him favourably. He also thought it might protect his workforce from the twin threats of militia levies and the brutal activities of the press gang. Few pitmen could afford the going rate of twenty to thirty pounds to pay for a substitute.

In May news of the uprising in Ireland gave a further fillip to the volunteer corps recruitment. Apprehension turned to relief as word of the Irish rebels' defeat at Vinegar Hill began to filter through to England. But relief turned again to anxiety when news of French troop landings in Ireland was confirmed. Tension remained high and rumours abounded until the news of General Humbert's surrender to the British Commander, Lord Cornwallis, became known. The capture of the hot spirited Irish revolutionary, Wolfe Tone, was received with quiet satisfaction. There was little sadness outside Ireland when he died in a Dublin prison in November after cutting his own throat.

But General Bonaparte had long since decided that the invasion of England would be too big a risk to his reputation. He turned his attention to Egypt and the Levant.

With the approach of summer Henry grew to dread the eight hours he had to spend down the pit each day. It was not the physical aspects that bothered him; by now he was used to the hard work. But he found it almost impossible to cope with the mental torment created by the boring, repetitive nature of the work. His mind cried out for creative stimulation to ease the monotony of it all.

For relief, he threw himself into the new challenges offered by the Friendly Society and the Chapel school, and as his interest grew so did his determination. He no longer worried about being singled out as an agitator, although he still kept a low profile and refused to become a committee member.

On Saturdays he would journey into North Shields to purchase books, newspapers and any interesting broadsheets. He had kept well clear of Newcastle since his enforced departure and knew nothing of the events that had followed his brother-in-law's betrayal. But as the months passed and his confidence grew he yearned to visit the town again and re-establish contact with Rory. He was envious about what changes time may have brought about. Finally the urge became irresistible and on a Saturday afternoon early in May he set off at a brisk pace, in a south-easterly direction, to walk the seven miles to Newcastle.

The sun shone out of a cloudless sky and the absence of a breeze made the day seem warm for late spring. Henry soon reached the outskirts of Killingworth village and, maintaining his brisk pace, headed south past Longbenton. The landscape was picturesque and not yet significantly spoiled by mining activity. The road was lined with tree-dotted hedgerows beyond which cattle grazed in lush green pastures. Early crops were sprouting in the fields and he returned occasional greetings from perspiring farm workers.

The road now joined the Newcastle to North Shields turnpike and Henry turned right and headed towards Newcastle. The traffic was now much heavier and he had constantly to step aside to avoid the numerous gigs and carts that travelled the busy road. Passing the lodge gates that led to Heaton Hall he began the long descent from Byker Hill and the final mile of his journey.

Below lay the panoramic vista of Newcastle and its environs. Steeples, towers and the red tiled gabled roofs of the houses shimmered in the heat haze that lay over the town. In the distance the afternoon sun hung over the Ravensworth hills beyond the Team valley casting a dazzling reflection on the waters of the River Tyne as it curled its way past the town. On the Gateshead side of the river the sails of the windmills which dotted the ridge of hills behind the town stood motionless in the still air as if frozen on an artist's canvas.

Henry paused to take in the beauty of the view. He suddenly realised how much he had grown to love the old town and how much he had missed its infectious vitality and the cut and thrust of its fast growing coal trade.

Though still medieval in appearance the town was now spreading outside its strong defensive walls. New streets were already beginning to creep outside the walls to the north and west and two of the town's seven gates had been dismantled to ease the flow of traffic. Ancient walls and gates were now obsolete and a brake to further progress.

Shrugging off his pensive mood, Henry crossed over the bridge which spanned the Ouse Burn and, after passing St Ann's Chapel, he entered the teaming streets of Sandgate.

It was Colin's mother, Fiona, Rory's sister-in-law, who opened the door in response to his urgent knocking. A look of suspicion gradually changed to a surprised smile of welcome as she recognised Henry. 'They didn't find you, then?' Her voice was tinged with relief and pleasure.

'I don't suppose they knew where to look,' he said, smiling at her.

She opened the door wide and beckoned him inside. 'You never know who's watching these days,' she said, quickly closing the door and sliding home the bolt.

As they sat down Henry saw the lines of stress on her face and her eyes betrayed the tell-tale signs of sleepless nights and much weeping. 'Where's Colin?' he asked.

'He's working on the keels now, with Rory's cousin.'

'And Rory?'

Her eyes clouded over and a look of pain spread over her face. 'You haven't heard, then?' Her voice quivered as the harrowing memories flooded back.

Henry felt a chill of apprehension. 'Has he been caught?' His voice was thick with emotion, his mind dulled with foreboding.

'Rory was arrested six months ago.' Fiona paused, struggling to control her emotion. 'He was sentenced to four years in prison and now they've taken him to London so that the government people can question him.' Tears began to form as she added, 'I think they were worried in case the keelmen marched on the prison to try and release him.'

Henry sat in shocked silence as the appalling news sank in. When he spoke there was anguish in his voice. 'But didn't Rory get my letter?'

'Yes, but it was too late to save some of the group.'

'So William betrayed us after all,' he said bitterly. 'Did he inform the authorities?'

'Yes, but he wasn't content to leave it at that. He had to take matters further.'

'In what way?'

'He wanted to destroy Rory and take the credit for himself, but without any risk. The man's an evil, cowardly monster.' She went on to explain the course of events that had taken place since Henry's urgent departure from Newcastle seven months ago. The night attack on Sandgate and the defeat of the authorities, followed by the final betrayal of Rory which had led to his capture and imprisonment.

As Henry listened, a cold fury built up inside him as he began to comprehend the full extent of William's infamy. When he finally spoke his voice was brittle with anger. 'The man deserves to die for what he's done.'

Fiona smiled wistfully. 'But that won't help Rory, will it?'

'No, but it might satisfy those who have suffered because of his betrayal. Rory won't shed any tears.'

She shook her head. 'It won't solve anything and I think you know that. Besides, Rory wouldn't want you involved. He thinks very highly of you, Henry, and feels guilty enough as it is for all the trouble he's caused you.'

'It was my decision to get involved,' he said gently.

She gave him a perceptive smile. 'Rory could be very persuasive, couldn't he?'

He nodded sadly and suddenly the realisation came that she knew Rory better than anyone. She understood him as only someone in love could understand, and he began to comprehend the depth of her suffering and despair.

'You must miss him a great deal.' He was trying to be comforting and sympathetic but somehow the words sounded clumsy and sterile.

'We were very close,' she said quietly, and then looking proudly at him added, 'We were more than just relatives in law, you know.'

Her words still came as a surprise though he tried not to show it. 'I can see that now,' he responded warmly.

Seeing that he understood, she went on 'When my husband died, Colin was just a baby. I suppose Rory felt some responsibility for his brother's family; you know how protective keelmen can be towards their own.'

210

Henry nodded, encouraging her to continue.

'Rory became a father to Colin, and as you know there's a strong bond between them. Rory loves Colin as much as if he were his own son. Things just grew from that and over the years we became closer and closer until...' She paused in embarrassment before going on. 'We were planning to get married until this...' She broke off, unable to continue as her eyes filled with tears.

Henry gently took her hand. 'He'll survive, I promise you. He's strong and above all he has the inner courage and conviction to see him through all this. You and Colin will give him the added will to survive if he needs it.'

She smiled back through her tears. 'I know, Henry. I know he'll survive, but I don't know if I can.'

'You will, Fiona. You're strong too. Stronger than you think and you'll have Colin to help you.'

She knew he was right, and somehow his words comforted her. 'Perhaps I will, but it's going to be such a long wait.'

Suddenly, her expression changed and she jumped up. 'I'm not being a very good hostess sitting here moping about my problems. I bet you haven't eaten? Rory would be furious with me.'

Henry smiled. 'I had something before I left North Moor.'

'North Moor? Is that where you live?'

'Yes.' He was about to explain when she stopped him.

'In a moment.' She held a finger over her lips. 'You can tell me when you've got something to eat in front of you.'

She disappeared into the small kitchen at the back of the house and after a few minutes, returned with a plate of bread and cheese and a mug of strong ale.

'Get this down you,' she ordered 'and you can tell me all that's happened to you and Mary. Colin will want to know how Mark is. He never stops talking about him.'

Henry did as he was told and between mouthfuls of food he described their journey north to Morpeth and how they had finally settled down at North Moor Colliery. Her face lit up with pleasure when he told her that Mary was expecting her baby soon.

'That's the most wonderful news I've heard for a long time,' she said, but the pleasure in her voice was tinged with a note of longing.

211

She wanted a child by Rory but wondered if she would be too old by the time he was released.

Henry sensed her anguish. 'How's Colin?' he asked, trying to divert her thoughts.

'He's fine,' she replied brightening up a little. 'He's quite grown up now and takes his new role as man of the house very seriously. I'm very proud of him and don't know what I would have done without him.'

'Will I have a chance to see him?'

'He won't be back till the evening tide. About ten o'clock he said.'

Henry was disappointed. 'Then it will have to be another day. I've got a seven-mile walk home when I'm finished here.'

'You're not going into Newcastle?' There was concern in her voice.

'I am, but I'll be careful. I think the authorities will have forgotten me by now.' It was ironic that neither of them was aware that William, for his own perverse and selfish reasons, had kept his word and not betrayed his brother-in-law.

As Henry prepared to leave he noticed a new resolve and confidence in Fiona. Perhaps his visit had had something to do with it, he hoped. As she drew the bolt she turned and smiled. 'I'm glad you came, Henry.'

'So am I. I would have come sooner if I'd known what had happened.'

'Yes, I know you would. Give my love to Mary and Mark.'

'I'll do better than that; I'll bring Mark with me on my next visit. We'll make it a Sunday so we'll have more time.'

'Good. Colin will be at home then.'

Henry hesitated wondering if he should raise the question uppermost in his mind. Finally he decided he must. 'Will the authorities allow you to visit Rory?'

'I hope so. The keelmen have raised some money for a lawyer in case it will do any good. One of the collier brig captains has promised me a free passage to London and back.'

'Good. It's important that Rory knows his friends haven't forgotten him.'

'Four years is a long time to remember.'

'The keelmen aren't fickle, Fiona. You of all people should know that. They have long memories and strong loyalties. Rory's become a legend in his own lifetime. They won't forget, believe me.'

Fiona smiled at this mild rebuke. 'I'm sorry. You're right, of course. I must stop feeling sorry for myself.'

After leaving Sandgate Henry made his way into Newcastle using the less conspicuous Low Way which ran alongside the river. As he passed the Sandgate midden he was assailed by the overpowering stench which hung in the warm, still air. He wondered why he'd recoiled from the smells of North Moor Colliery yet, until now he'd been oblivious to the even more obnoxious odours of Newcastle middens. Here, human excrement was mixed with horse and cattle droppings which were further enriched by the blood and offal from the many slaughterhouses in the neighbourhood. It was sold as a potent fertilizer.

Avoiding the main streets where possible, Henry continued his furtive progress into the town keeping to the shadows of the overhanging buildings and being constantly jostled by the large crowds attending the many markets. He felt exhilarated by the bustle that always seemed present, especially on market days, and which gave Newcastle its unique character. In the bookshop he browsed happily among the shelves before purchasing the books and tracts he was seeking. Then, as the clock of St Nicholas' Church chimed six, he set off for the long walk home to North Moor.

It was almost dark before the light, cast by the pit head braziers, came into view. The night air had grown chill and as Henry opened the cottage door a waft of welcoming warm air fanned his face. He saw the large fire burning in the hearth, sending long fingers of yellow flame flickering up the chimney. A blackened kettle was suspended at the side of the fire and a thin wisp of steam escaped from its spout.

Mary was resting on the bed and her face lit up when she saw Henry. 'You're late. I was beginning to get worried.'

Henry placed the newspapers and tracts on the table. 'I'm sorry, dear. I was browsing through the bookshop and I lost track of time. You know what I'm like with books.' He crossed over to the bed and kissed her. 'Where's Mark?'

Mary smiled. 'Where do you think?'

213

He grinned back at her. 'Next door with Jane. I needn't have asked.'

'They're becoming inseparable. He spends more time next door with Jane and her family than he does with me.' There was a faint hint of jealousy in her tone.

'They're becoming like brother and sister, aren't they?' Henry said approvingly.

'Mark's growing up a lot faster than you think,' Mary responded. She could see that he had no idea of his son's true feelings for Jane. She doubted whether Mark would fully understand them yet, though the passing of a few years would change all that. Her instincts as a woman and a mother left no room for doubt in her own mind. Mark would marry Jane one day and, much as she liked the girl, the thought of it made her strangely unhappy. The premonition of being trapped permanently in a world of coal pits lurked deep inside her mind.

Henry watched with concern as her face clouded over. 'He might have a sister of his own to fuss over soon,' he said cheerfully.

'No, it will be another boy,' she spoke with a conviction that brooked no further argument. Seeing his unease, she forced a smile and quickly changed the subject. 'Did you enjoy your trip to Shields?'

'Yes.'

'Still no problems?' She was concerned for his safety when he left the village.

'None. I think past events have been forgotten,' he lied. He decided not to mention that he had visited Newcastle instead of North Shields. Nor would he tell her of Rory's arrest and imprisonment. He knew she would only be more distressed and this would destroy the fragile harmony that he had carefully built up over the past few months. He would tell Mark in due course, but swear him to secrecy for his mother's sake. The boy would understand and the prospect of the renewal of his friendship with Colin might compensate for his unhappiness at the pit.

He sat up late into the night while Mark slept soundly in the loft above and Mary stirred fitfully on the bed. The fire, kept low in the summer and banked up for the night, gave no illumination to augment the poor light from the cheap tallow candle. His eyes began to feel the strain and he put the newspaper to one side. Leaning back in the chair, he contemplated on the day's events. He felt a restless discontent gnawing inside himself, for his visit to Newcastle had reawakened memories of happier days working for Mr Ivison. He could feel his earlier aspirations being rekindled, but also the wretched frustration of knowing they could never be fulfilled.

He thought of Rory languishing in some dark gaol, far from his family and friends. He wondered if his proud, exuberant spirit would succumb to the privations of four years' incarceration, or whether it would be crushed by the harsh punishments inflicted by a regime of hard labour, which would be directed with cruel indifference by the prison authorities. Henry suddenly realised that, paradoxically, he too was serving a prison sentence but his own gaol lay seven hundred feet below the earth's surface. He also concluded, sadly, that his was a life sentence.

Dejected by his thoughts, Henry snuffed out the candle and trying hard not to disturb Mary, slid gently into the bed beside her.

CHAPTER 22

It was still dark the next morning when Henry opened the door of his cottage and stepped out into the cinder covered street. Accompanied by Mark, he joined the straggling groups of men and boys making their way towards the pit. The early morning air was warm and muggy foretelling the approach of another hot and humid day. As they approached the pithead they joined Wilf and Sep who stood beneath the flaring braziers waiting their turn to go down the shaft. There was an atmosphere of discontent and murmurings of anger from the hewers, especially the older, more experienced men.

'Everyone seems to have got out of the wrong side of the bed this morning,' Henry observed.

Wilf nodded. 'And small wonder. They're opening up the new workings and the lads driving the main roadways say the place is full of gas blowers.'

'There's nowt new in that,' Sep said dismissively. 'This pit's always been full of firedamp and it should have had a second shaft right from the beginning. It's a wonder we're all still alive.'

'But these are more than just ordinary blowers,' Wilf said. 'The seams are full of trapped gas and the lads think that the pit will fire soon, now that we've started working 'em.' There was deep concern in his voice.

'They won't finish sinking the new shaft until next year.' Henry reminded them.

'By then it might be too late,' Sep muttered darkly.

'Might explain why there's a few hewers missing this morning.' Wilf said. 'Some of the old timers are staying at home, saying they're sick.'

'Forster will still fine 'em, sick or not,' Sep retorted.

'Maybe so, but the old hands recognise the danger. They'd rather be fined than dead.'

Henry agreed. 'They know Forster's been taking out too much coal for a first working. He's not leaving enough in the pillars, and the seams are softer in the new workings.'

216

'That means we'll have creep and more gas,' Wilf said. 'No wonder the viewer looks so worried.'

'Aye, he's not a happy man,' Sep acknowledged, 'but he dances to Forster's tune just the same.'

'They all do,' Wilf said spitting to emphasise his contempt.

At this point their turn came to descend the shaft and seeing their hesitation Henry held Mark back. 'Well, are we going down or not?' he asked.

Wilf looked troubled and placed his arm around young Jed. 'I don't know. I suppose we could always come out again if things aren't so good underground.'

They stood undecided until the press of men and boys forced them towards the pit shaft, as if making up their minds for them. Soon the loops on the chain and the rope above were crowded with clinging men and boys and with a shout from the banksman they began their descent into the smoking shaft.

On reaching the bottom they made their way cautiously to their work stations, testing the airflow as they went. It was weak and intermittent and left them worried and uncertain. Wilf paused then, as if making up his mind, shrugged and said, 'We'll give it a try but keep your wits about you.'

The pit soon became a hive of activity as production commenced and the flow of coal from the honeycomb of hewers stalls quickly built up. Candles bobbed and flickered like fireflies along low narrow tunnels as straining putters moved the corves of coal from the stalls to the main roadways. Here, where space was less confined, horses drew the loaded rolleys along the crude plate rails to the shaft bottom.

Deep inside this subterranean maze of tunnels Mark and Jed and the other trapper boys raised and lowered their trapdoors, allowing traffic through, but maintaining the vital flow of air that would ventilate the pit and keep it free from firedamp. In the vaulted brick-lined chamber of the ventilating furnace a worried fireman watched the flames grow and then subside as pockets of gas, which had been swept out from the workings, became mixed with the return air.

At one point of the new workings, where the weak air current had left it undisturbed, the dangerous gas had been steadily accumulating, silent and invisible. Gradually increasing, the gas slowly and

217

imperceptibly crept along the narrow passage to where a hewer sweated and toiled in the light of a naked candle. From time to time the flickering flame became tinged with blue, indicating the presence of gas. But the hewer, engrossed in his labours, failed to notice the danger and carried on kirving the coal seam.

At precisely eleven o'clock, the pit exploded in a fireball of destruction.

The hewer who had toiled on, oblivious to the danger, took the full force of the blast and was instantly scorched into a blackened corpse. The fireball raced on through the narrow tunnels of the pit, increasing in fury as the coal dust sucked up by the blast also ignited. Sweeping on through the mine, the raging inferno wrought death and destruction. The sudden change from the dim glow of candles to the blinding light of the explosion was the only warning, but by then it was too late for those in its destructive path.

In less than two minutes the holocaust was over, leaving the wreckage of broken sledges, timber, dead horses and mangled remains of men and boys. Some were burnt beyond recognition; others, with singed hair and torn flesh, died with the imprint of their final agony frozen on their face.

It was the hewer's practice to draw lots for their place of work so that everyone got a fair chance to work some of the better stalls. The system had proved providential for Henry and Wilf and they were both working in a safer part of the pit some distance from the site of the explosion. They heard the sound of the blast and felt the rush of hot air which extinguished most of the candles. It was the brief and dreadful warning that every pitman feared. Immediately they all dived into whatever cover they could find to protect themselves from the fireball that would accompany any further explosion. After a few minutes, Henry picked himself up and groped his way through the darkness to the adjoining stall. He called out anxiously, 'You all right, Wilf?'

'Aye, I think so,' came Wilf's relieved response.

Henry felt heartened, then spoke urgently. 'We'd better find the boys and get out quick. Let's hope we can make it to the shaft before the after-damp does.'

They both recognised the even greater danger now faced by those who had survived the explosion; the insidious spread of the dreaded after-damp. The combustion of the explosion created a deadly by-product, a gas known as after-damp or, more appropriately, choke-damp. It was lethal and as it spread through the pit it would kill all in its path, silently and without warning.

Both Henry and Wilf knew that a speedy escape from the mine was their only hope. They had to reach the shaft before the invisible slayer overtook them. But first they had to find Mark and Jed and any others still alive. Fortunately, the boys were working nearby in the same section of the pit.

'Come on,' Henry said grimly, 'let's find 'em. We haven't much time.'

Henry led the way, groping frantically through the darkness. His mounting fear for his son gave added strength to his efforts as he crawled faster through the low, narrow tunnels in the direction of Mark's trapdoor.

They reached the new rolley-way where Mark and Jed had been working and Henry cursed. The rolley-way was in darkness and seemed deserted. But since it was a horse road, they could at last stand up and stretch their aching backs which were now raw and bleeding from contact with the jagged roofs of the low passageways. However, without a tinderbox to light a candle they could not see the extent of the damage, and worse still, they were unable to see any colleague who might be trapped and in need of help. They would have to rely on their senses of smell, touch and hearing, to guide them to safety.

With growing concern, Henry and Wilf systematically searched the low tunnels that led off from the rolley-way, shouting out the boys' names. Henry's anxiety mounted as he found increasing evidence of a stronger blast in this section of the pit. Suddenly he stopped and rubbed his eyes. He thought he'd seen a faint light ahead. He looked again and the feeble, distant glow was still there. Bent double to avoid the rough surface of the low roof, he hurried forward and reached the damaged trapdoor. A candle still burned in a sheltering niche cut into the wall near the door frame. It was Mark's door but the trapper-hole was empty and the passageway deserted. An empty food satchel, which Henry recognised as Mark's, lay crumpled on the ground. He called out, shouting Mark's name into the darkness of the tunnel but the only response was a faint, mocking echo.

Weariness, fuelled by anxiety and frustration, washed over him. He picked up the candle and Mark's satchel and made his way despondently back to the roadway. Presently, Wilf joined him. 'Any luck?' He asked.

Henry shook his head. 'No sign of 'em, but at least we've got a light.'

Wilf lit another candle from the flame, looking hesitantly at Henry. 'The firedamp's already exploded so another candle won't make any difference. It's the choke-damp we've got to worry about now.'

Henry didn't seem to hear him and spoke his thoughts aloud in a laboured monotone, as if seeking reassurance. 'They must be still alive. They're probably trying to find their way to the shaft.' A dead body would have extinguished all hope and so far he had been spared that. His confidence began to rise a little. He felt a touch on his shoulder and heard Wilf's urgent tones. 'Come on, Henry. We haven't got much time.'

The force of the explosion had diminished by the time the blast reached the area where Mark and Jed were working, but it was still strong enough to cause considerable damage. It was fortunate that Mark was sitting deep inside his trapper hole to avoid the kicks of passing putters when the blast stove in the door. He curled up in terror at the back of his trapper-hole and covered his face as the whirlwind of hot, acrid air swept around him. Suddenly all was calm again and his candle, placed out of reach of the putters, spluttered and fought for life before settling down to a steady flame.

Mark had never experienced an underground explosion before, though he'd listened to many graphic descriptions of such events. He knew this was a major blast and not just the firing of a small blower. He also realised that, having survived the blast, he was now facing serious danger from the after-damp. He recalled listening to the lurid tales of old pitmen telling of the relentless spread of suffocating gas after an explosion, remorselessly and silently killing all in its path.

Recovering his wits, Mark grabbed his candle and made his way to Jed's trapdoor, his stomach knotting at the thought of what he might find. As he approached the door he saw the yellow candle-light coming through the broken woodwork and heard the sound of crying. He was relieved that Jed was still alive, but fearful of what injuries he might find. As he crawled through the door he saw Jed lying curled up in his trapper hole, his body racked by hysterical sobs of fear and desolation.

Mark moved closer and called out, 'Jed, it's me.'

The sobbing stopped and Jed looked up. Then, as recognition dawned, he crawled out of his hole and put his arms around Mark and hugged him fiercely. Presently the sobbing started again but it was gentler and became more subdued as Mark held him tight. 'We'll be all right, I promise you,' he said quietly, 'but we must be quick and get to the shaft. Bring your candle,' he instructed.

Jed followed him to the rolley-way where Mark told him to remain while he returned to his own trap-door to replace his own candle in the niche.

'Where's your candle?' Jed asked when he returned.

'I left it by my door as a message for my dad,' Mark explained. He'll come looking for us with Wilf.'

'Then shouldn't we wait for them?'

'No.'

Mark could not face the fact that his father and Wilf might be dead and did not want to convey his fears to Jed. He knew that if his father had survived the explosion he would come to find him. But he also knew that time was running out and replacing the candle and leaving his satchel was the only message he could think of. 'Come on,' he said. 'It's time we made a move. Follow me and stay close.'

Holding the candle, Mark cautiously led Jed along the rolley-way knowing this joined the main roadway of the pit which in turn led to the shaft. They tried to run but broken timber and roof falls impeded their progress and slowed them to a walk.

Mark continued to lead, shielding the candle with his cupped hand and praying that it would stay alight. Suddenly, he heard a strange sound ahead and saw a shadowy outline of a large object. Part of the shadow seemed to be moving. Easing slowly forward he saw it was a

221

pit pony, its tail switching nervously, standing harnessed to a rolley containing three corves of coal. The pony snorted again and gave Mark a welcoming nuzzle. 'Easy, boy.' Mark said, patting the pony's neck.

'Where's the driver?' Jed asked.

'Probably ran out after the explosion,' Mark replied.

'And left his pony?'

'Not much else he could do. You can't drive a horse up the shaft.' Mark was bemused by Jed's concern for the pony when their own situation was so dire. 'Come on, we haven't any time to lose.'

He was about to lead on when he heard another sound coming from inside one of the low tunnels which led off the rolley-way at the place where the horse had stopped. It was a tormented sound; a cry of pain mixed with terror and despair. It was also a human sound, which probably explained why the horse had not bolted.

Mark's instinct for the survival of both himself and Jed told him to ignore the sound. They were fast running out of time if they were to escape the killer after-damp now permeating the workings of the mine. Their only hope was to reach the shaft quickly where, if it had not been destroyed by the blast, they could be drawn to safety. But his heart and his conscience held him back. He agonised over his decision and it was his compassion and humanitarian feelings that finally won the day. 'Make your way to the shaft,' he instructed Jed.

'What are you going to do?' Jed asked anxiously.

Mark pointed to the tunnel. 'Someone in there needs help.'

'I'll go with you.'

'No. There isn't enough time.'

'I'm not going to the shaft without you,' Jed said stubbornly.

'Then stay with the pony and hold on to the bridle. A horse can always find its way out.'

Taking the candle, Mark bent down and crawled into the tunnel heading in the direction from which the sound had come. Progress was slow for the roof was little more than three feet high and the tunnel was partially blocked in places. After a few more yards, he came across signs of greater destruction. Some timber supports had been blown away causing a major roof collapse. He stopped at the edge of the fall and raising the candle, saw that further progress was impossible. A pile of stone and coal completely blocked the tunnel.

Mark was about to turn and head back to the rolley-way when he heard a spine chilling groan that seemed to come from inside the cave-in. Moving closer, he could see what looked like a wheel and part of the wooden frame of a putter's sledge protruding from the fall. He shouted and heard a choked response and by what appeared to be a small movement among the rubble of stone and coal. He saw a blackened hand with nails that were strangely luminous. A further slight movement dislodged some more coal revealing two bright, terror stricken eyes shining out from a black coal grimed face. Mark held the candle closer and recognised the unmistakable features of his arch tormentor, Herbie Marshall. The black grimed lips opened revealing rows of shiny teeth that seemed to sneer back at Mark. The look of terror slowly changed to one of cocky contempt. 'Well if it isn't the toffee-nosed shit. Can't expect any help from you, can I?' Despite his fear, Herbie remained unrepentant.

'No, but you're going to get it.' Mark replied ignoring Herbie's insults. He quickly set to work clearing the fall where Herbie lay trapped. After a while he felt a tug on his sleeve and turned to see Jed squatting behind him. 'I told you to stay with the horse,' he said impatiently.

'I was scared so I tied it to a pit prop and followed you.'

Mark groaned in exasperation. 'Well make yourself useful and help me clear the fall.'

As Jed moved closer he recognised Herbie's face. 'We're not helping him,' he shouted.

'We are,' Mark said firmly.

'Leave him,' Jed screamed. 'We haven't time.'

Mark became angry. 'Either help me or get out,' he shouted.

Jed calmed down and together they dug furiously at the rubble of the fall. Soon, only Herbie's legs remained trapped and they started to pull him out. Herbie screamed with pain as they dragged him clear of the fall and Mark saw that both legs were broken. Jed also realised that something was amiss. 'We won't be able to carry him out, will we? We've wasted all this time and risked our lives for nothing.'

'Shut up,' Mark ordered. 'Get hold of this and when I tell you, pull as hard as you can.' He handed Jed one of the harness ropes from the half buried sledge and took the other one himself.

'Now pull.'

Slowly, the four-wheeled wooden sledge began to move until it was clear of the fall. Mark examined it and found it undamaged. 'Now help me lift Herbie on to the sledge.'

Herbie screamed again as they half dragged and lifted him onto the sledge. Then, with Jed harnessed at the front and Mark pushing at the rear, they manoeuvred the sledge out of the tunnel and into the wider, loftier rolley-way.

Mark heaved a sigh of relief when he saw the horse was still tethered to the pit prop. 'Here, hold the candle,' he instructed Jed and, one by one, he toppled the three loaded corves of coal from the flat base of the rolley waggon.

'What are you doing that for?' Jed asked in surprise.

'We're not going to push him all the way to the shaft on a sledge when we've got a rolley waggon and a horse to do the hard work,' Mark replied.

It was a difficult task transferring Herbie from the sledge to the slightly higher rolley waggon. Herbie shouted and screamed for them to stop but they ignored his protests. Soon he was overwhelmed by the pain and passed out. At last, nearly exhausted by their efforts, they succeeded in lifting the limp, unconscious form onto the rolley and were ready for the final journey to the shaft. 'Gee up!' Mark commanded and taking the bridle led the horse in the direction of the shaft with Jed riding on the rolley beside the still unconscious figure of Herbie. Mark's remaining hope was that they would reach the bottom of the shaft before the deadly choke-damp gas caught up with them.

Now that they had a candle to help them see their way and enough room for them to stand upright, Henry and Wilf made good progress along the rolley-way.

'Let's hope the shaft isn't damaged,' Wilf muttered.

'We're not there yet,' Henry responded. He was desperately anxious to find Mark and could only pray that he'd managed to find his way out.

'The bairns are probably ahead of us,' Wilf said, as if reading Henry's mind.

'Aye, you might be right.'

They proceeded in silence, both fervently hoping that they had read the signs correctly and that the boys were safe. They had almost reached the junction where the rolley-way joined the main roadway of the pit when Henry stopped. 'There's something ahead of us. I can see a light.'

Quickly moving on they could soon discern a horse and saw it was harnessed to a rolley. Two small figures stood motionless a few yards in front of the horse. As they drew nearer Henry felt a surge of relief pass over him as he recognized Mark and Jed. 'Mark,' he shouted and started to run.

Mark turned and a smile of recognition lit up his face. He felt his father's strong arms around him in a tight, loving embrace. The pent up dam of emotional anxiety burst as stifled fear gave way to relief and joy. The same scene was repeated between Wilf and Jed.

When the euphoria abated, cruel reality set in. The rolley-way was partially blocked by a roof fall. It was this obstacle that had held up the boys' progress. Henry and Wilf examined the debris blocking their way. 'We can get through on this side,' Wilf announced, a note of relief creeping into his voice. 'But we'll have to dig first.'

They all set to work furiously tearing at the rubble with their bare hands. Finally, they managed to clear a gap just wide enough for them to squeeze through, but not the horse.

'What are we going to do?' Jed wailed. 'We can't leave the horse.'

'We haven't any option,' Henry said gently. 'We couldn't get it up the shaft even if we got it that far.'

'What about Herbie?'

'Leave him to me,' Wilf said, gently lifting the injured putter from the rolley. Herbie let out an agonised scream before passing out again.

'Come on,' Henry ordered. 'We're running out of time.'

One by one, they squeezed their way past the fall watched by the sad, brown eyes of the horse. As they cleared the fall, Jed began to sob uncontrollably.

They saw more signs of major destruction as they reached the main road leading to the shaft. Debris and overturned rolley-waggons littered the way but the roof was still intact. As they neared the shaft, they could see lights ahead and a group of men and boys, crouching apprehensively by the entrance, waiting their turn to be wound up to the surface.

They reached the scene in time to see the winding rope descend to the shaft bottom. It was instantly covered with survivors who clung to the chain loops and any other part that they could get hold of.

'That's enough, now,' the overman shouted. 'You'll overload the winding engine if any more of you try to get on.' He signalled the brakesman to start winding and the cluster of men and boys disappeared up the shaft, leaving the last handful of survivors behind.

'Trust us to be last,' Wilf growled.

'We'll make it on the next haul,' Henry said, trying to sound confident.

The five minutes that passed before the winding chain reappeared at the bottom of the shaft, were the longest in Henry's life. No one had to be reminded of the urgency of their situation and within seconds the remaining group found a place on the chain. Wilf, with Herbie over his shoulder, was given the safest perch and the ascent to safety began.

CHAPTER 23

The first indication to those on the surface that the pit had fired was a large increase in the volume of black smoke pouring out of the upcast section of the shaft. This was instantly followed by the low rumble of the explosion, which sent a strong tremor through the surrounding earth that could be felt for more than a mile.

In the village, women drawing water from the well and those baking at the communal ovens looked at each other in alarm. They recognised the chilling omens of impending disaster which so often in the past had proved to be a harbinger of death. Cottage doors were flung open and women and children ran out into the streets. All eyes turned towards the tall framework surrounding the pit shaft and saw with dismay the column of black smoke rising ominously in the still, summer air.

At once, as if their actions were triggered by the same sense of foreboding, people began to make their way to the pit-head and soon almost the whole population of the village who were not underground, stood in silent vigil around the shaft. The women waited, tight-lipped with the strain of holding back their emotions, their thoughts with their loved ones, husbands, sons and brothers who might be trapped and dying seven hundred feet below.

Wilkins, the viewer, was on his way to North Moor Hall to see Forster when he heard the muffled sound of the explosion. He turned his horse and spurred him into a gallop back towards the pit. As he edged his way through the crowd he saw Roland sidling towards the pit office and trying hard not to draw attention to himself. After glancing furtively around, he entered the office and closed the door quietly behind him. An expression of fury spread over the viewer's face. Dismounting, he quickly made his way to the office and angrily kicked open the door. 'Master Roland!'

There was no answer, but he heard a faint scuffling sound from behind the desk. Moving across the room, he saw the quivering figure of the assistant viewer hiding behind the desk. 'Get up, Master Roland. We've got work to do.' His voice was icy with anger and contempt.

'I'm not going below.'

'Yes, you are. There are men down there who need help and it's our job to see that they get it. Now for God's sake, get up and act like a man.'

Roland shook his head. 'It's madness to go down before the after-damp has had time to clear.'

'Damn it man, it will be criminal if we don't. We have a responsibility to the men. The whole village is out there and they expect us to show some leadership.'

'I'm not going.'

Wilkins' anger exploded. He realised he was holding his riding whip in his hand and raised it to strike Roland. As he was about to bring it down he felt a firm grip on his raised arm and looking round, saw the grim face of Duncan Forster.

'I won't have you chastise my son like this,' Forster took the whip from Wilkins' hand.

Roland looked up and smiled ingratiatingly at his father. The smile quickly turned to terror as the descending whip cut a deep welt across his cheek.

'I won't have a son of mine behaving like a coward, either,' Forster snarled. The whip rose again and again, the swishing and cracking being punctuated by loud screams of pain from the unfortunate Roland.

'Now get up or I'll thrash you to within an inch of your life,' Forster barked.

Roland slowly rose, holding his hands to his face, trying to stem the flow of blood which ran through his fingers. The two Forsters looked at each other; the son with an expression of fear and hate, the father with a strange mixture of love that had become malignant with contempt and despair. Then, as if dismissing the unpleasant scene from his mind, Duncan Forster turned and left the room, calling for Wilkins and Roland to follow him. His tone brooked no argument.

From then on, Forster took control of the situation. With skill and firmness, he set about organising the rescue operations, selecting the team that he would lead in the recovery attempt and sending men scurrying for special equipment. All the men who had escaped the blast volunteered to accompany him down into the pit and he selected

228

a small team that included Henry and Wilf. A quick check revealed that seven men and six boys were unaccounted for.

After checking the winding gear which showed surprisingly little sign of damage, Forster and Wilkins led the first rescue party and descended the shaft to examine the condition of the mine. Soon the all clear signal was given that the pit bottom was free of choke damp and the rest of the rescue party was lowered down the shaft.

Moving cautiously forward, they methodically began to search the roadways and workings of the pit. As they approached the scene of the explosion, they saw increasing signs of destruction with timber, sledges and debris wedged together by the force of the blast. They passed the wreck of a broken rolley-waggon and saw the body of the horse bulging in the harness. Nearby lay the singed, headless body of the driver, ominous portents of the carnage yet to be revealed.

It was in one of the narrow galleries that they came across the most moving and tragic sight of all. The burnt body of Joe Winship, the deputy overman, lay face down on the ground. Ahead the huddled forms of four boys who had miraculously escaped the blast, lay placid in death with not a single facial muscle distorted, as though in a deep and peaceful sleep. It was clear that the deputy, though badly burnt himself, had been trying to shepherd the boys to safety until they were all overcome by the lethal after-damp. A choking sob came from one of the hewers in the rescue party and bending down, the grieving pitman gently picked up the body of his son. Holding him close and sobbing quietly, he turned and carried the limp figure away in the direction of the shaft.

Pressing on, the rescue party finally reached the site of the explosion where they found the remaining bodies, scorched and blackened by the fierce blast. Their faces bore the expression of men who had passed away in agony.

Only the mournful task of bringing the bodies to the surface now remained. This was largely carried out in silence as the trauma of their gruesome discoveries took hold. When the rescue party eventually reached the surface they were greeted by a large and silent crowd. It had been a vigil of despair, with only the faintest hope that anyone would be found alive. At the sight of the blackened corpses, even this tenuous hope died. The sounds of weeping steadily began to grow as

229

mothers and wives, fearing the worst, gave vent to their pent up emotions.

As the sombre group of rescuers emerged, the crowd swept forward and surrounded the pit shaft. Harrowing scenes took place as bereft relatives searched for their loved ones and took charge of the bodies. Hysteria set in as attempts were made to identify the corpses that were severely scorched and almost beyond recognition. A sobbing mother found her eight year old son and took his cold, lifeless body in her arms. Hugging the pale, limp frame she sank to the ground and began to rock back and forth as if desperately trying to will her son back to life. At length she was led gently away by her grieving husband who, because he had survived the blast, felt consumed with guilt.

Mary and Dora had also waited anxiously in the crowd, their eyes fixed on the shaft and the winding rope. Their apprehension had increased as more and more men and boys were hauled to the surface with still no sign of their own loved ones. Even the warm sun could not dispel the chilling numbness they felt as they silently waited and watched. When Henry and Wilf had finally appeared, accompanied by Mark and Jed, anxiety turned to joy and tears of relief.

Now they waited once again for Henry and Wilf to emerge from the pit they had come to fear and hate. There had been no remonstrations when, after the ecstatic and tearful reunion, both men had announced their intention to go back down the pit with the rescue party. It was expected of them as part of the pitmen's tradition of loyalty and support for each other, especially in times of danger and distress.

It was a responsibility accepted without fuss and in a quiet spirit of solidarity. Mary and Dora were still waiting two hours later when Henry and Wilf appeared with the last of the rescue party. They watched as the grisly remains of the last victims were handed over to their families, provoking further scenes of heart rending grief.

The crowd started to disperse as people made their way home. The lucky ones, chastened by the experience, were grateful for their deliverance and walked with a quiet, sombre dignity. The others, racked with grief and in a state of shock, were gently led away and comforted by their relatives and friends.

*****

It was the custom of pit village life that, in order to come to terms with the tragedy, proper recognition of the corpse was required when possible. This meant that recovery of the bodies was essential and now that this had been done the village could at last begin to mourn. The funeral would mark the end of the disaster and then the long and painful healing process could begin.

The pit, looking grim and forbidding, was now largely deserted. Its brooding presence looked down on the last of the departing crowd, baleful and unrepentant. It was as if some graven image, having received its blood sacrifice, still craved for more.

The village now lay quiet under the late afternoon sun with doors closed and curtains drawn. The sad ritual of preparing the dead for burial had begun. An air of melancholy pervaded every street as a small group of women, hardened and experienced in the grim task of laying out bodies, made their mournful rounds. In one cottage they found a grieving widow desperately trying to wash the scorched body of her dead husband and going slowly mad as she watched the blackened skin peel away from his flesh. Sobbing hysterically, she was led gently away.

Two days later the bodies of seven men and six boys, the youngest aged seven, were borne to the church in North Moor Village for burial. The vicar eulogised the dead and admonished the living and the victims were laid to rest in a far corner of the churchyard reserved for the pit-folk of North Moor Colliery. Three days later the pit reopened and life for most returned to normal.

The disaster itself went largely unreported. The cosy cabal between the coal owning establishment and the newspaper proprietors prevailed and only a brief announcement appeared in the local press. There was no mention of the number of deaths and the accident was referred to as an Act of God.

CHAPTER 24

The weather continued hot and sultry for the rest of May and this lasted into June. Life in North Moor Colliery became even more unpleasant as the unrelenting stench from the ash heaps and middens grew stronger in the heat and the swarms of flies and insects multiplied. Rodents became a familiar sight and rats took on an unfamiliar insolence, holding their ground until the last moment when any human approached, before reluctantly retreating to a safe distance.

Disease struck down the young and the infirm. Soon almost a quarter of the population was infected with a severe enteric fever which swept through the village. The fever surprised no one and only the severity of it gave rise to comment. In later years, doctors would diagnose such an outbreak as a typhoid epidemic, but to the inhabitants of North Moor it was just a normal hazard of daily life.

Henry blamed the well water for most of the afflictions, though he could not explain why. Wilf and Sep disagreed, pointing out that they and their families drank the well water and were not affected. Henry had to admit that the fever struck indiscriminately and there seemed little pattern in the spread of the illness. But he still insisted that the well was to blame and continued to carry water home from the pit, much to the amusement of his friends and neighbours.

Conditions at the pit became harsher and the hours of work longer as Duncan Forster tried to squeeze every pound of profit from his colliery in a desperate effort to keep his enterprise solvent. Exploitation of the men increased and the keeker, Mulligan, continued to impose unjust and heavy fines on the hewers. He ignored the threats of reprisal, for his fear of Forster was greater than the fear of retribution from those he oppressed.

The mood of discontent festered on and the pitmen's smouldering anger frequently burst into flame, with protests to the viewer and a refusal to work the longer shifts. Wilkins was sympathetic, but was overruled by Forster who insisted that the bond be honoured and threatened to imprison those who broke it. Fights between pitmen and the itinerant sinkers working on the new shaft erupted in the alehouse, and some wives and children suffered arbitrary beatings as some tormented hewers vented their frustrations on their families. But the fines and inequities continued and the resentment smouldered on.

Some of the more militant pitmen were for wrecking the shaft in retaliation for the unfair fines imposed on them. Henry knew this would serve no useful purpose and would only make matters worse by destroying what livelihood remained to them. It would also bring down the wrath of the law through the iron hand of Duncan Forster, who was the magistrate for the district.

Henry also realised that the men now needed strong leadership if the growing number of hotheads were to be contained. He counselled moderation, self-discipline and the need to comply with the law. He channelled his ar   guments through Wilf, whose support was critical in controlling the men's anger. Wilf was a popular leader, well respected by the men. His heroic efforts in the aftermath of the explosion, which had killed his brother and five other men and left Dora a widow, were not forgotten and he was held in high esteem by all. The death toll would have been much worse but for Wilf's courage and leadership in the rescue operations. He had almost forfeited his own life to save one man and this would long be remembered in North Moor.

Preaching restraint was neither easy nor popular. Henry persuaded the more intelligent men to restrain their anger by expounding his vision of the future. This he outlined at meetings of the Friendly Society held in the chapel. 'We need to keep close contact with other pits in the Northern Coalfield,' he explained. 'We need unity, for our strength lies in numbers. But we must use this unity for a common purpose. We must act as a brotherhood to improve the lot of all pitmen.'

There was general agreement to this, but also many doubts and fears as to how it could be achieved. 'Trouble is,' said Wilf, 'we never know what the other pits are up to.'

Sep nodded in affirmation. 'And when we do find out it's usually too late to do anything worthwhile.' There was a chorus of support from the men.

'But that's the whole purpose of having a brotherhood,' Henry declared, 'so that we can understand each other's problems and speak with one voice.'

233

'And how do we do that?' Sam Elliott asked.

'By meeting regularly with men from the other pits to exchange ideas and co-ordinate our activities.'

'It's over thirty miles to some of the other pits,' Jim Walters said dubiously. 'Some of the men won't walk three miles let alone thirty.'

Henry smiled. 'I'm not suggesting all the men meet; only one appointed delegate from each pit. And the meetings should be held at a central point like Newcastle,' he added.

'Makes sense to me,' Wilf said.

'Me too,' Sep added and there was a murmur of agreement around the room.

'I'm glad,' Henry said smiling at Wilf, 'because I propose that you be elected as the official delegate for North Moor.'

Henry's nomination was greeted with murmurs of approbation and Wilf's face flushed red with embarrassment. He held up his hands in protest. 'No. A job like this calls for a man with education. Someone like Henry, here.'

'You can read and write can't you?' Henry responded brightly, recalling the long hours spent fulfilling his promise to make Wilf his star pupil.

Wilf's face reddened deeper. 'A bit,' he acknowledged sheepishly, hoping Henry would not betray their secret.

'You're a bit of a dark horse,' Sep said looking at Wilf in astonishment.

'I think he's been listening in to Mark coaching Jane,' Henry cut in, skilfully deflecting any further questions and grinning back at Wilf as he saw the look of relief on his friend's face.

'I still think Henry's our man,' Wilf resisted stubbornly. 'It's his idea and he's the one with the real education.'

Henry saw the others begin to waver, and it was now his turn to look to Wilf for support, 'I can't do it for reasons that I...' he paused awkwardly, 'that I can't explain.' He looked pleadingly at Wilf; the only man present who knew about has past.

'I'll do it,' Wilf said quickly, 'but only if Henry will help me draw up a proper case.'

'You have my word on that, my friend,' Henry said with relief, shaking Wilf by the hand. There was a roar of agreement and the matter was settled.

'We'll need a set of rules and a manifesto,' Henry said.

'What's a manifesto?' Wilf asked.

'It's a statement setting out our aims - a list of grievances, if you like, to put to the owners.'

'That'll take some writing up,' Sep scoffed. 'You'll end up with a book bigger than the Bible.'

'Not if we concentrate on the key issues,' Henry explained, 'and seek general agreement on those. We can then go to the owners as a united front to negotiate better terms and have them written into the bond.'

'And what if the owners don't agree?' Wilf asked.

'Then we don't sign the bond,' Henry replied, smiling at the dubious faces around him. 'If we present our demands just before the binding in October, We'll take the owners by surprise. The magistrates can't gaol us for breaking a bond if we haven't signed one. So we can withdraw our labour legally and the pits will have to close.'

'But we won't have any wages,' Wilf countered.

'Nor any binding money,' Sep added.

Henry smiled in acknowledgement. 'I agree. Times will be hard but there is a way round the problem. First we must organise a benefit fund to support those in most need. Then, if we can all stick together, some of the pit owners might break ranks and agree to our terms. Forster isn't the only owner strapped for cash, and news of a stoppage will cause coal prices in London to rocket. That will tempt the greedy ones and those facing bankruptcy.'

'But what about the others?' Wilf asked. 'I can't see the Grand Allies backing down nor the rich owners of large collieries like the Brandlings, Bell, Russell, Ridley and the Delavals.'

'And don't forget Vane-Tempest, Lambton and Lord Scarborough on the Wear,' Sep reminded.

'I never said it would be easy,' Henry said defensively, 'but if enough owners break ranks and agree to our terms, we can levy a charge on the wages of the men they employ to be paid in to the benefit fund. That way the rest of the men can last out longer without their families starving. Remember, the owners, particularly the owners of large collieries are rich because they are greedy and they won't stand by and see the smaller pits making a killing at their expense. The main point is not to be too greedy ourselves otherwise we will frighten off the smaller owners and stiffen the resolve of the larger ones.'

For a while no one spoke as they all digested Henry's plan of action. At last Wilf broke the silence. 'I think it will work,' he said thoughtfully. 'In fact I'm bloody sure it'll work,' he went on enthusiastically grinning broadly at the others. Gradually, the expressions on the faces of the doubters changed from brooding scepticism to smiling confidence as the logic of Henry's clever strategy began to sink in.

'It's damn well brilliant,' Sam Elliott said admiringly and shook Henry's hand. Wilf looked around the room and seeing there was unanimous support, felt his own determination strengthen in a surge of new found confidence.

Henry looked into the smiling faces of the men as, one by one, they came up to shake his hand. And as they did so he could discern a look of pride in their eyes, as if a new spark of hope had been kindled in their hearts. In a strange way he felt his own spirit lighten, as though a flickering flame of ambition had entered his own heart too.

That evening as he walked home from the chapel with Wilf, Henry realised that he had been running away from the unpalatable aspects of his life. He had allowed the setback of his brother-in-law's betrayal to crush his spirit and used the need to protect his family as an excuse for not fighting back. It had taken the hardship of others whose misfortunes were worse than his own to rekindle the vital spark that had lain dormant inside him. He realised this was the only road back to regaining his self-respect. Suddenly, he understood why he now relished the challenge of the coming struggle and welcomed the dangers that would accompany it. He turned and spoke to his friend. 'You'll be our official delegate, Wilf, and by God I'll attend all the meetings with you to give my full support.'

'Are you sure that's wise?'

'Probably not.'

'The owners will mark you down as a troublemaker and blacklist you.'

Henry laughed. 'What the hell, trouble seems to find me anyway. We'll write this manifesto together, Wilf. We'll add your experience to my vision and we'll put both our names to it. The teacher and his star pupil! Let it be our epitaph when we depart this unjust world.'

The two friends walked on in silence for a while before Wilf spoke. 'Talking about trouble, how about a pint of ale with the sinkers?' There was a hint of mischief in his voice.

Henry smiled. 'Why not? We need to learn how to live dangerously.'

As they approached the alehouse it suddenly erupted into a brawl of volcanic proportions, spewing fighting pitmen and sinkers into the street.

'I think we'll give it a miss,' Henry said.

'Some other time,' Wilf agreed.

They threaded their way carefully through the melee of drunken, fist swinging brawlers and continued their journey home.

Fired with enthusiasm in the weeks that followed, Henry and Wilf set to work on drawing up the manifesto, using most of the time remaining to them after a gruelling shift down the pit. A small consultative committee was formed and everyone agreed to keep their deliberations secret.

Wilf was all for talking to the other pits immediately. 'We need to spread the gospel straight away. We can visit the local pits in the evenings and the others at weekends.'

'No,' Henry cautioned. 'There's no point in visiting the other pits until we've drawn up a list of our grievances and some solutions for putting them right. That way we'll have something to sell.'

Wilf demurred at first. 'We've only got three months before the binding in October. We need to move fast.'

'It may take longer than that,' Henry cautioned.

'Why?'

'Because it's not just a case of agreeing and setting out our demands to the owners,' Henry explained. 'We also need to ensure that every pit has a proper Friendly Society and those that haven't must be shown how to set one up and run it accordingly to the law.'

Gradually, Wilf began to see the reasoning and wisdom of Henry's arguments and they concentrated their efforts on completing the manifesto. This proved more difficult than Wilf had imagined and he realised how far-sighted Henry was in his thinking. His admiration for his friend grew, and with it the knowledge that Henry, rather than himself would ultimately prove to be the real leader.

Mary noticed the change in Henry and watched with pleasure as he regained his zest for life. The changes were subtle at first; his smile reached his eyes, his mood became lighter and there was a new spring of confidence in his step. She also noticed the increasing respect in which he was held by his fellow pitmen and for some reason, for she both hated and resented all the aspects of his pit life, this acknowledgement of her husband gave her considerable satisfaction.

She thought of Mark, too, and how the past few weeks had changed him. She had been afraid that the pit explosion would have unnerved him but, since then, he'd become more relaxed and cheerful. Perhaps he had become accustomed to the dangers and long hours. Perhaps everyone did in time, she thought, if they had nothing else to look forward to.

All this helped to take her mind off her pregnancy which was proving very difficult. She frequently felt ill and was confined to bed more than she would have wished. The baby was now overdue and still the contractions would not come. She hated having to lie in bed; it made her feel lazy and useless.

Mary watched with growing irritation as Dora's sister, Alice, began preparing a meal in readiness for Henry and Mark's return from the pit. Alice was helping out that day but, unlike Dora, she was slovenly and did not keep herself, her children, or her house clean. Mary tried hard to tolerate Alice on the few occasions she stood in for her sister, for she had grown fond of Dora and didn't wish to upset her. But on this particular day her patience was being sorely stretched. To make matters worse Alice had brought her two youngest children along, boys aged two and five, and the heat was making them fractious and noisy.

The large girdle cake that Alice had made was now cooling on the table and the children were tearing pieces off with their dirty hands and stuffing the food in their mouths. A package of sugar had been opened by tearing out a piece of the paper at the corner. From time to time the children stuck their dirty, sticky fingers inside the packet and withdrew them coated with sugar which they then sucked noisily. Mary closed her eyes to hide her annoyance and disgust, choking back the angry words that rose to her lips.

Mistakenly reading Mary's expression of distaste as a sign of distress Alice crossed to the bed, a look of concern creeping over her face. 'You all right, pet?'

Mary opened her eyes and seeing Alice's anxious gaze, her anger softened. 'I'm just tired, Alice. And lying here like this makes me feel so useless.'

'Because you're not well, that's why. Stands to reason you're tired. Can I get you something?'

'Just a drink of water, please.'

Alice retreated to the small lean-to which Henry had built onto the rear of the house for additional storage. She remembered Dora's instructions that all drinking water should come from the wooden pail with the lid. A lot of nonsense, she thought as she dipped the cup into the water. There's nowt wrong with well water, she told herself as the carried the cup back to the bedside.

Mary sipped gently on the water made tepid by the summer heat. There seemed little comfort left in her unhappy world, she reflected. She could only see squalor and unending wretchedness stretching away into the future. She buried her face into the pillow and silently began to weep.

The banksman cupped his hands around his mouth and leaned over the pit shaft. 'Kenner! Kenner! He bellowed down into the smoking darkness. His cry was taken up by the onsetters at the shaft bottom and passed on echoing through the myriad of working tunnels throughout the mine. What to a stranger might have sounded like a dirge was to the men and boys in the pit the music of paradise, for it signalled the end of the day's work.

When the faint cry filtered through to Mark he heaved a sigh of relief. He rose and groped his way to the section where Jed was working and found him crouched in his trapper hole in darkness. Candles were expensive and now that they were both used to the pit, a candle would be a rare luxury. 'Time to go,' Mark said. 'Follow me and stay close.'

They had almost reached the main roadway which led to the shaft bottom when Mark spoke again. His voice was quiet and serious. 'No problems today, Jed?'

'No.'

'Putters leaving you alone?'

'Yes. Why do you ask?'

'Just wondered.'

Jed grinned. 'They're becoming quite friendly, these days. I think it's because we helped get Herbie Marshall out of the pit after the explosion,' he added thoughtfully.

'I suppose that might have something to do with it,' Mark said. 'They're not picking on me any more either. In fact one or two have become quite pally.'

'But not Herbie? Jed's voice carried a mixture of bafflement and pique.

'No, not Herbie, 'Mark acknowledged. 'He just ignores me now.'

'And me,' Jed said. 'Still, it's better than being kicked every time he passes the trap door.'

'Aye, it has to be an improvement,' Mark agreed. He had pondered a great deal about Herbie's strange behaviour since the accident; more especially since his former tormentor returned to work after his injuries had healed. Herbie's attitude had been one of surly acceptance, as though he resented being under any obligation to Mark and Jed for saving his life. Perhaps he felt it diminished his authority over the other putters, Mark thought. But it didn't make sense. He shrugged and tried to dismiss the matter from his mind.

They had now reached the main roadway, dimly lit by the occasional candle. As they neared the shaft bottom they saw a large group of putters and trappers waiting to be wound to the surface. Most sat resting on their haunches, with knees to their chins and their backs leaning against the wall, the common repose of a resting pitman. A

240

few of the boys, despite a fourteen hour shift, still had enough energy for boisterous horseplay. As Mark and Jed approached, they were welcomed by friendly shouts and greetings from most of the group. Herbie remained stubbornly silent and ignored them.

'What's your fettle, Mark?' one of the squatting putters said, his eyes smiling up at Mark through a coal blackened face.

'I've felt better,' Mark replied. 'And you?'

'Knackered.'

'Me too.'

'Sit down here, man.' The putter waved to a space at his side.

Mark squatted down alongside his new found companion just as the chain attached to the winding rope reached the shaft bottom. He made no move to rise for he could see that there were too many people waiting for the available space that the capacity of the winding engine allowed. He would wait for the next lift.

The crowd of men and boys scrambled forward to seek a place on the winding rope. Some attached themselves to the loops on the chain, others just grabbed hold of the chain itself. There was a signal up to the surface and the cluster of swaying bodies disappeared slowly up the shaft on the seven hundred feet journey to the world above.

Some minutes later, the winding rope returned to the bottom and it was the turn of the final group to begin their ascent. Mark and Jed each found a loop on the chain near the bottom and the last two places were taken by a young putter and his six year old brother who had just started as a trapper boy. There was a shout to the man at the top of the shaft, followed by an answering call from the surface, and the last of the shift began their ascent.

The group was halfway up the shaft, coughing in the darkness with smoke stinging their eyes, when Mark realised that the young putter and his brother riding below him were in trouble. He heard the trapper boy shout to his brother, 'I'm slipping.'

'Hang on to me,' his brother ordered. 'Put your arms around my neck and wrap your legs around my waist.'

The young trapper tried to follow the instructions but only managed to wrap his arms around his brother's waist, leaving his legs dangling unsupported. After a while the extra weight began to tell, forcing the putter to lose his grip on the chain.

'I can't hold on!' he screamed.

'I'm still slipping,' his brother wailed back despairingly.

Mark acted quickly. He uncoiled his feet from the chain and swung himself upside down forcing his feet through the leather loop he had been holding on to with his hands. He called out to Jed, 'Keep your feet round the chain and put both your hands around the loop. Careful, now,' he warned. 'Keep the loop tight so my feet won't slip through.'

Jed did as he was told and gripped the loop tightly. Mark took a deep breath and let go of the chain and hung upside down, suspended from the loop by his feet. He extended his arms, searching for a handhold on the putter who was still hanging on to the chain below him. After a few seconds, he managed to grasp the putter's jacket and straining hard, took up some of the weight.

The young trapper, holding grimly on to his brother, screamed again, 'I'm slipping!'

'Hold on!' his brother screamed back.

There was a short silence which was broken by an agonised cry from Jed, 'I can't keep the loop closed.' Mark felt his feet slip a little. 'You've got to, Jed.' He called back, 'just a little longer, we're almost at the top.'

Suddenly, Mark felt strong hands gripping the loop, closing it tight around his ankles. He heard a voice above, 'Leave go, I've got him.' It was the voice of Herbie Marshall.

Mark's relief was short-lived. There was an intolerable strain on his arms as he desperately fought to hold the combined weight of the putter and his young brother hanging beneath. Suddenly the strain eased and the shaft was rent by a terrified scream. The young trapper had finally lost his grip and fell almost seven hundred feet to the bottom of the shaft. The scream echoed up the shaft for several seconds until it was suddenly silenced. There followed a faint splashing sound as the body of the boy hit the water in the sump at the base of the shaft.

Mark felt the cool air brush over his face as the winding rope reached the surface. A wave of relief passed through him as strong welcoming hands lifted him to the safety of the pit bank. He lay gasping, waiting for his pounding heart to ease. But elation at his own escape was muted by the sadness and horror of the fate of the young trapper, whose brother sobbed uncontrollably nearby.

A rescue party was immediately sent down the pit. They returned with the mangled body of the boy whose skull had been crushed during the fall mercifully sparing him the agony of a slow drowning in the cold, dark water of the shaft sump. An oppressive sadness fell on the crowd of onlookers who had gathered at the pit head.

Mark stood up and watched as the rescue party dispersed and the boy's family tearfully carried his body home. Suddenly, he realised that Herbie Marshall was standing next to him. Mark turned and held out his hand. 'Thanks, Herbie. You saved my life.'

Herbie cocked his head and grinned back. 'That makes us quits then.' With that he placed his arm around Mark's shoulders and together they made their way back to the village.

The accident caused little stir or comment outside North Moor colliery. Such accidents were seen as just another hazard of a pitman's trade.

CHAPTER 25

Early in the afternoon on the 1st August 1798, off the coast of Egypt, the seventy-four gun ship of the line *Zealous*, the most easterly of Admiral Nelson's squadron, signalled the sighting of the French battle fleet anchored in Aboukir Bay.

Nelson ordered his squadron of fifteen ships to set course for the bay to seek action with Admiral Brueys' squadron. Soon the two fleets were heavily engaged in a battle that would last until the early hours of the following morning.

Just after ten o'clock that evening, the French flagship, the mighty three-decker *L'Orient* mounting one hundred and twenty guns, exploded in a huge conflagration as fire reached her magazine. Just prior to the explosion the brave Admiral Brueys, having lost both his legs, had been seated in an armchair on deck with tourniquets on his stumps, directing the action when a cannon-ball from *HMS Swiftsure* almost cut him in half.

The spectacular loss of *L'Orient* marked the turning point of the action which was to lead to a British victory by dawn. But it would be two months before the news reached England.

At about the same time on that same August day, but over three thousand miles away in North Moor Colliery, Mary reached a turning point in her own long drawn-out battle. After forty-two weeks of a most difficult pregnancy, she finally gave birth to a healthy son to the satisfaction of the village midwife and the relief of Dora who had been assisting her. The news was conveyed to Henry and Mark waiting anxiously next door. 'You can go in now,' Dora said smiling. 'It's a boy and they're both all right.'

Henry and Mark hugged each other and then they both hugged Dora. 'That's the best news I've had for a long time,' Henry said. 'And my thanks for all you've done for us. '

'Haddaway with you, man. There's nowt special in helping a bairn into this world. It's the mother that does all the work and takes all the pain.' Dora felt herself colouring with embarrassment. 'You'd better get yourselves next door and cheer her up. And mind you don't tax her too much,' she called after them as they hurried out through the door. She shook her head and flopped down wearily in her chair.

Mary held her baby proudly in her arms, her eyes glistening with motherly love. She looked up and smiled when she saw Henry and Mark enter the room. 'I think we'll call him Ralph,' she announced.

'Yes, I like that,' Henry said, crossing over to the bed. He stood there smiling fondly down at mother and baby whilst Mark sat gingerly on the other side of the bed. He saw the look of exhaustion on Mary's face and realised just how difficult and painful the birth must have been. He asked, 'Can I get you something?'

'Some water if it's cool.'

'I'll get it,' Mark said sliding off the bed and disappearing into the lean-to.

'May I hold him? Henry said awkwardly.

'Of course.'

He gently took the baby in his arms and gazed proudly into the tiny, wrinkled face. 'You're a beauty, just like your mam.'

Mary watched in amusement, forgetting her pain and discomfort for a moment. 'I would rather he grew up handsome like his father.'

Henry laughed. 'A bit of both and the world's his oyster.'

'More likely an underground dungeon,' she retorted her face clouding over. 'Black diamonds instead of pearls.' She saw the hurt in Henry's eyes and immediately regretted her words. 'I'm sorry, I shouldn't have said that.'

Henry shook his head. 'No, you're right to say what you feel.' He was about to add a vow that his second son would not have to work down a pit when he remembered that he'd made the same promise for Mark, only to see it broken.

He met Mary's eyes and saw her compassion; saw that she understood the hopelessness of his position and suffered the same feelings of frustration and despair as he did. But Mary also saw the true reality of their situation and, being a pragmatist, was prepared to face life as it was even though it was not as she would have liked it to be. Her eyes pleaded with him to do the same but somehow, deep inside himself, he knew he could not come to terms with a world that held no hope. He knew his only salvation was to believe that things could be changed and to fight on to see that such change came about.

And now he had an even more powerful reason to try and improve his world; to keep his second son out of the pits.

Mark returned with the water and they watched as Mary drank. 'It's not very cold,' she said, not meaning it to sound like a complaint.

'Water doesn't keep cool for long in this weather,' Henry chided gently. 'I'll get you some fresh from the pit if you like.'

'No, I'm all right.' She smiled her thanks at him. 'I think my son and I will have a little rest, now.' She held out her arms and Henry realised he was still holding the sleeping baby. Gently he placed the soft, warm bundle that meant so much to him into Mary's tender arms. 'I'll get some fresh water anyway. The bucket's nearly empty.'

'Don't be silly,' Mary remonstrated. 'It's nearly eleven o'clock. I don't like you wandering round the pithead in the dark.'

'There'll be plenty of light from the braziers. Besides, the walk and fresh air will do me good after all the excitement.'

'Can I come?' Mark asked.

'No,' Mary cut in firmly. 'You have to be up at three in the morning and you need your sleep even if your father doesn't.' Henry ignored this parting shot and slipped out of the house, leaving a disconsolate Mark to climb wearily up to his bed in the loft.

As Henry headed towards the pit a familiar looking figure loomed out of the darkness. 'Watcha!' It was the unmistakable voice of Wilf.

'Hello, Wilf. You're out late.'

'Same can be said for you.'

'I've had a long and anxious wait and need some air.'

'Aye, so I gather,' Wilf said grinning. 'Congratulations. A boy isn't it?'

'Yes.' Henry grinned back, grasping Wilf's outstretched hand. 'How did you know?'

'Dora sent a message up to the chapel.'

'Chapel? I didn't know there was anything on tonight.' Henry sounded surprised.

'We didn't want to bother you,' Wilf said awkwardly. 'We thought you had enough on your plate, what with the baby coming and all.'

'What was the meeting all about,' Henry quizzed. 'You don't sound too happy.'

'I'm not. Word is that Forster is going to evict all the widows to make way for the new hewers and their families.

Henry was stunned. 'But it's always been the tradition that the widows of men killed in the pits keep their pit cottage rent free. Some owners give free coal too.'

'But it's not the law,' Henry. 'They don't have to follow the custom if they don't want to.'

'No, but very few break it.'

'Well, Forster is going to by all accounts. Not right away mind you,' Wilf said sarcastically. 'Forster's a generous man. But they'll all have to be out before the binding in October, so I've heard.'

'That means Dora too...' Henry paused as the shock of the news began to sink in. 'It's not right,' he went on angrily. She has three young children and Jed's already working down the pit.'

'There are other widows with better claims than Dora,' Wilf said gloomily 'but if I know Forster, he won't let sentiment stand in the way of profit.'

'But the new shaft won't be ready by October,' Henry countered.

'It won't be far short, according to the sinkers,' Wilf said. 'Forster will use the extra hewers to drive the new roads while this shaft is being finished off. It'll be cheaper than using contractors.'

'We've got to find a way to stop this,' Henry fumed. 'This is the sort of thing we need to write into our manifesto.'

'Aye, but it will be too late to keep a roof over Dora's head and the bairns.' Wilf said gloomily. 'They'll be out on the streets by then.'

Henry made a quick calculation. 'There must be up to a dozen families involved. Where will they all go?'

Wilf shook his head. 'God knows. The lucky ones will be taken in by relatives; the rest will probably end up in the workhouse.'

'We can't let that happen to Dora,' Henry said despairingly.

'I don't intend to.'

Henry looked at Wilf in surprise. 'Are you going to take Dora and her family in?'

'No. We haven't room, what with the old folk and my two younger brothers.'

'Well, what then?' Henry was puzzled.

'I'm going to live with Dora.'

Henry was dumbfounded at Wilf's naivety. 'But living in sin will only make matters worse in Forster's eyes, he being the pillar of the church and all. It won't stop her being evicted,' he added seriously.

'It will if I marry her,' Wilf said quietly.

There was silence for a while as the two friends looked at each other then a broad grin spread over Henry's face. 'You sly old devil. I never thought you had it in you.'

Wilf grinned back. 'I've always had a soft spot for Dora even before she married my brother, and more so since he was killed. The kids sort of take me for their father now,' he added proudly.

'Have you proposed to her?'

'No, not yet.' Wilf's face clouded.

'Then don't you think it's time you did?'

'I suppose so, but I'm worried. She might think I'm asking her out of pity.'

Henry shook his head. 'If you think that, my friend, then you don't understand Dora. She's very fond of you; don't underestimate her.'

'I suppose you're right,' Wilf muttered, then suddenly looked anxious. 'I take it a man can marry his sister-in-law?'

'Yes, providing she's legally free to do so. And also assuming she's been asked,' Henry added provocatively.

'What if she turns me down?' Wilf panicked.

'Then she'll demonstrate she has good taste.' Henry's expression was deadpan.

'You're needling me, aren't you?'

'Yes, and I'll go on needling you until you propose to the poor woman.'

'I'll ask her now,' Wilf said, as a new-found confidence flooded through him.

'Don't be so bloody stupid, man. She's tired and probably asleep by now. You can do your asking tomorrow after work. I'll find an excuse to take the bairns out of the way so you'll have the house to yourself.'

'I don't know how to thank you, Henry.'

'You can make a start by helping me carry some water from the pit,' Henry said handing him a bucket.

For once Wilf didn't scoff at his friend for his crazy ideas on drinking water.

Four weeks later on a fine Saturday afternoon, Wilf married Dora in the old, grey stone church at North Moor village. It was a colourful occasion and the wedding was attended by over fifty guests dressed in their Sunday finery. Most of the men were resplendent in the unique Sunday garb worn by the pitmen of the Great Northern Coalfield: shining blue velvet breeches over a white linen shirt with long stockings drawn up to the knee and bright buckled shoes. Coats were also shiny blue, with even brighter linings. And their hats had bands of yellow ribbon stuck with flowers. But their greatest glory was the beautiful brocade waistcoat, a posy jacket, cut short to show an inch or two of shirt above the waistband.

Set against all this peacock flamboyance, Henry's dark cutaway coat looked positively drab, Mary thought.

The wedding party lasted well into the night as, mercifully, the pit did not seek its pound of flesh on the Sabbath. Henry, as best man, was obliged to stay the course but at last he, and an even more exhausted Mary, took their leave of the merry bridal pair and made their way home. They found Mark dozing on the bed and the baby sound asleep in his crib. Henry gently roused Mark. 'Off to bed with you,' he said softly.

'Was it a good party? Mark asked drowsily.

'Aye, it was that,' Henry said, 'and I expect there'll be a few sore heads in the morning to prove it.'

As Mark disappeared into the loft, Henry slowly undressed, looking as he did so at his own sober dress. Mary, watching from the bed, seemed to read his mind. 'Not as bright as some of the others,' she whispered, her eyes sparkling.

'No,' Henry mused, 'but at least I can wear this for funerals as well.'

Mary laughed. 'Come to bed,' she instructed, holding the covers back. Henry smiled and quickly slipped into the warm space beside her, feeling the sensual smoothness of her naked skin as he leaned across to nip out the candle. He knew it was too soon after the birth to

249

make love, but they held each other close with a special tenderness. Unable to sleep, he lay staring into the darkness until his thoughts were interrupted by the sound of Mary's sleepy voice. 'Why do pitmen wear such bright clothes on Sundays?'

'I'm not sure,' Henry said thoughtfully. 'I suppose it's because they spend most of their lives working in an underground prison; a twilight world where colour is the depth of a shadow.' He paused, gathering his thoughts before continuing. 'When you spend the best part of your life in the darkness of a mine, you begin to see the world above in a new light. A world where the stars shine brighter, where the grass is greener and where the summer sky becomes an intoxicating blue. I think pitmen express this in their Sunday dress on their one day of freedom from the pit; an attempt to relieve the drabness of their everyday lives.'

Henry stopped, his eloquence making him feel awkward. He sensed Mary moving close to him and felt her lips brush his cheek.

'Those are the most beautiful and touching words I've ever heard you say, Henry Standish, and I love you very much for saying them.' She took his head in her hands and kissed him passionately on the lips with an urgency that surprised him.

CHAPTER 26

Duncan Forster was in a foul mood and the sound of his temper tantrums echoed through the elegant rooms of North Moor Hall. An atmosphere of acrimonious tension permeated through the house and was reflected below stairs in the prickly exchanges between the servants. Harker, the butler, having just suffered a tirade of abuse from Forster for responding too slowly to his ring was, in turn, venting his spleen on the unfortunate footmen and maids who happened to be in the servants' hall. Mrs Binns, the cook, was having none of this and, after a testy exchange of views, beat a hasty retreat to the housekeeper's room to solicit Mrs Gordon's support.

Harker's satisfaction at his small victory was interrupted by the ringing of the front door bell. Cursing, he made a less than dignified exit from the servants' hall and raced up the stairs that led to the main hall before slowing to the steady walk that befitted his station. He opened the door to admit Mr Wilkins, the viewer and Mulligan, the keeker. 'Mr Forster is expecting you, sir,' he said to Wilkins, taking his hat and coat. He studiously ignored Mulligan who, he felt, had no right to use the front door and led the way into the library.

Duncan Forster was seated behind the large mahogany writing table and he glared balefully at the two newcomers as they entered the room. Wilkins noted that the ferret-faced agent, Gibson, was standing nervously by the window and Roland Forster, seated at the side of the table, was affecting an exaggerated but unconvincing display of boredom to hide his anxiety. There was no invitation to be seated, a standard ploy when Forster was in a bullying mood. With a sinking spirit, the viewer realised that the meeting was destined to be extremely unpleasant. After a long silence, Duncan Forster spoke. 'You've probably gathered by now that I'm not satisfied with the progress we're making sinking the new shaft.' He paused, letting his words sink in.

'We're ahead of schedule, Mr Forster,' Wilkins responded, trying to sound confident.

'Of course we are,' Forster said irritably. 'The contractors always overestimate when they bid to sink a shaft. Allows them a bit of leeway, but it doesn't fool me.'

'They're doing a fair job in my view,' Wilkins said doggedly.

'But not in mine,' Forster cut in. 'I reckon they're running two weeks late. That means we won't be ready to draw coal before the end of November at the earliest.'

'Does that matter?' Wilkins sounded surprised.

'It does when I'm planning to take on an extra twenty hewers at the October binding.' Forster paused to let his shock announcement sink in.

'But we won't have work for another twenty hewers in October,' Wilkins gasped.

'We will if they drive the new roadways.'

'But that's normally done by the contractor.'

'There's nothing signed yet,' Forster persisted. 'While the sinkers are lining the shaft and excavating the sump we can use the extra hewers and putters to drive the new roadway. That way we'll be ready to draw coal by the beginning of November in time to catch the high prices before winter.'

'But we haven't got contracts for the extra coal,' Wilkins argued.

'My fitter assures me he can place an extra three hundred chaldrons a week on the London market.'

'If the vend will allow it. The other owners might not agree,' Wilkins pointed out. The vend was the maximum amount of coal each colliery owner was allowed to sell.

'I won't ask 'em. By the time they find out, the coal will be shipped and the collier brigs will be laid up for winter. 'Time to argue afterwards when money problems might not be so pressing.' Forster smiled at his own deviousness.

'The committee will fine you,' Wilkins warned. The cartel of owners which limited the sale, or vend, of coal from seasale pits took a dim view of owners who deliberately exceeded their allocated production.

'Then let them fine me,' Forster said dismissively. 'I won't be the only owner to exceed his vend, I'll be bound.'

Wilkins knew this to be true and remained silent. Owners often broke their agreements to keep to their allocated vends as and when it suited them. Their short-term greed frequently sabotaged the long-term strategy of the Limitation of the Vend, as the cartel was known. The cartel's aim was to maximise the price of coal by limiting the supply to the demand, but this often proved an uphill struggle.

'What you must understand, Wilkins,' Forster continued, 'is that North Moor coal sells for only three shillings a chaldron less than Russell's Wallsend. With a premium like that and collier masters willing to buy, I'm not going to lose any sleep over the vend.'

Wilkins had to admit that North Moor coal was as good as anything that Wallsend colliery produced. Yet Wallsend was synonymous with best quality household coal on the London market and always fetched the best prices. Coal from other pits often had to be discounted by up to forty percent to find a buyer. Everyone knew that Russell was making a fortune out of Wallsend and some owners, Forster in particular, were deeply envious. Given the time and money to invest, Forster felt sure he could turn North Moor into another Wallsend. But he knew he was in danger of running out of both time and money.

Gibson had been listening to the exchange between Forster and his viewer with growing unease until, at last, he felt forced to intervene. 'You might have a problem binding enough hewers,' he said nervously.

Forster gave Gibson a withering look. 'If you can't find an extra twenty hewers then I'll find another agent who can.'

Gibson stood his ground. 'There won't be many hewers going spare come the binding in October, he said quietly. 'The war with France has seen to that. The press have taken over two thousand men from Shields and Newcastle for the Navy since '93, so I've heard. And there's the militia levies.'

'The Navy is only interested in seamen and keelmen,' Forster growled. 'They haven't much time for pitmen.

'They get taken just the same when they're caught drinking with the sailors or the keelmen.'

Forster snorted impatiently. 'Are you telling me, Gibson, that you can't find me twenty extra hewers?'

'No,' the agent answered looking uncomfortable, 'but it's likely to cost you a fair amount of binding money.'

'How much?'

'Three or four guineas a man, maybe more.'

'More?' Forster gasped in disbelief.

'You're not the only owner looking to bind more hewers, prices being what they are.'

'I'm not paying that sort of money. It's blackmail.'

'You'll have competition from the new pits,' Gibson warned. 'Mr Barnes needs more men for the new King pit at Walker and I've heard that Mr Buddle has reached the High Main seam at Percy Main Colliery. There's also Hebburn B pit across the water. They're into the High Main now. I reckon they'll all be seeking extra hewers.'

Forster raised his hands. 'All right, Gibson. I take your point. But can you guarantee me twenty extra men if the binding money's right?'

Gibson hesitated. 'I think so, but...' he tailed off awkwardly.

'But what, man?' Forster's ire was rising.

'Well, sir, the word's getting round that North Moor is not a happy pit. Too many fines to make a decent living,' he added looking accusingly at Mulligan.

'I'm only doing my job,' the keeker responded bristling.

'Aye, but true bred pitmen are a close lot and these things get talked about,' Gibson countered. Then turning to Forster he added, 'I think we might have problems getting some of the existing men to renew the bond in October.'

This last comment visibly shook Forster. He rounded on Mulligan 'I told you to ease up on the fines before the binding.'

'I was about to, sir,' Mulligan said falteringly.

'About to!' Forster's voice began to rise. 'Good God, man, it's only four weeks to binding. Do you expect them to sign a new bond if they feel hard done by?'

'You said pitmen have short memories,' Mulligan said lamely.

'Not that short, you idiot,' Forster snarled.

'I'm sorry, Mr Forster, I just didn't think.'

Forster exploded. 'I don't pay you to think, Mulligan. Just to follow my simple instructions. I don't know why I bother keeping you on.' He glowered at the unfortunate keeker before calming down.

'Now listen carefully,' he went on. 'I want all the fines you've got marked up now cancelled, do you understand?'

Mulligan nodded.

'Yes, Mr Forster.'

'And no more fines whatever for anyone between now and the binding, do you hear me?'

The keeker shook his head vigorously. 'Yes, Mr Forster.'

'And see that the prices in the Tommy shop are brought down until everybody has signed the bond. I'll make up the difference until they can be put back up again. And see that everyone has as much credit as they want, even the bad payers. They'll need a job to pay off their debts and we can get it all back later.'

Wilkins saw that Forster was worried. Carefully measuring his employer's mood he decided to raise an issue he would otherwise have let lie. 'If we don't evict the widows it will do as much as anything to improve the men's mood,' he said quietly.

'I'll have to build more houses for the new men if I let them stay.'

'We'll need extra cottages anyway if the pit keeps on growing,' Wilkins persisted.

'But not just yet,' Forster demurred. 'I'll need every penny to pay for a new winding engine. The one we've got won't cope with the increased production when the new shaft opens.'

'I think Mr Wilkins is right, sir,' Gibson interceded. 'There's been a lot of bad feeling expressed at other pits about the evictions. Hasn't done North Moor's reputation any good.'

Forster looked surprised. 'I'm amazed that other pits have got to know about it so quickly.'

'Word gets round fast, Mr Forster,' Gibson said. 'There's a lot of kinfolk in other pit villages. If you let the widows stay it will make my job a lot easier. That and good binding money,' he added.

Forster was not happy but he saw the logic of the argument. 'All right,' he agreed reluctantly. 'They can stay on.'

Wilkins smiled. 'A wise decision, if I may say so, Mr Forster.'

'An expensive one,' Forster grumbled. 'Nevertheless, I'm still puzzled how word of the evictions got round the other pits so quickly.'

255

'The men are getting more organised,' Gibson said. 'They're trying to set up Friendly Societies at every pit in the coalfield and some of our own people have been pretty active.'

I've heard tell there's some sort of secret brotherhood being formed,' Mulligan broke in.

Forster suddenly became interested. 'For what purpose?' he asked.

'To draw up a list of grievances to present to the owners, I think,' Mulligan said scratching his head. 'Sort of united front, like,' he added.

'Sounds more like a conspiracy to me,' Forster said thoughtfully, his magistrate's mind coming into play. 'And an illegal one at that. Do you know who's behind it at North Moor?'

'Wilf Hindmarsh and Sep Fordyce are leading lights on the Friendly Society committee,' Mulligan said. 'They meet up at the chapel.'

'Isn't Fordyce the lay preacher?' Forster asked.

'Yes, and he organises the schooling.'

'Schooling?' Forster laughed. 'Can he read and write?'

'A bit, but he gets others to help him, so I understand.'

'Ah!' Forster became more interested. 'Who?'

'Henry Standish for one.'

Suddenly Gibson's head lifted as a memory triggered his mind. 'Standish? That name rings a bell.' He nodded and went on. 'Aye, I remember now; signed him up last October. Different, he was, a cut above the rest. No mark, signed his own name. Even read the bond, though I thought he was pretending at the time.'

Forster's fingers began to drum on the table. 'We'd better keep close eye on those three,' he murmured. 'And that will be your job,' he added looking pointedly at Mulligan. 'Find out all you can.'

The keeker smiled ingratiatingly. 'Leave everything to me, Mr Forster. I'll find out what's going on.'

'If I left everything to you I'd be a ruined man,' Forster said coldly, wiping the smile of Mulligan's face. 'Just watch and listen. Don't frighten them off with a lot of questions.' He turned to his agent. 'Can we close the chapel?'

'It will be difficult,' Gibson said warily, 'since the building was gifted to the village. They have every right to use it as a chapel and a school.'

'But not as a meeting place for radicals to conspire.'

'We'd have to prove that,' Wilkins intervened, 'I'm sure there's more good than harm coming out of that chapel. Besides, it's easier to deal with intelligent leaders who can control their men than hotheads who can't.'

Forster gave him a withering look. 'God preserve me from educated pitmen and soft viewers,' he said scathingly. With that he dismissed Gibson and Mulligan but signalled for his viewer to stay. 'You wanted to talk to me about the new winding engine, Wilkins. I hope we're not behind schedule?'

'No sir.'

'Then what's the problem?'

'I think we're infringing Boulton and Watt's patent with the new steam engine.'

'More than likely,' Forster said unperturbed. 'And probably Pickard's as well if we go for a crank arrangement. '

'Then you already know?'

'Of course I know, Wilkins. What do you take me for?'

'Then you'll be paying the royalties?'

'Damned if I will. Our design is sufficiently different; or so I will maintain.'

'But isn't that dishonest?' The viewer was appalled.

'It's good business, Wilkins, and that's all I'm interested in. Watt's patent expires in a year or two so why bother. I'm not the only one to stretch a point and there's no reason why Boulton and Watt should find out, is there?' He glanced pointedly at Wilkins.

The viewer shrugged unhappily. 'Be it on your own head, Mr Forster.' With that he turned and left the room.

When the door had closed Forster rounded on his son who had remained seated and silent during the meeting. 'Thank you for your profound contribution to the discussion, Roland,' he said sarcastically. 'Your grasp of detail never fails to astound me.'

Roland shuffled uncomfortably. 'I thought you were very much in control of the situation, father,' he said ingratiatingly, trying to dampen any further criticism.

'I usually am, and I don't need you to tell me that,' his father replied, refusing to be flattered. 'But what really annoys me,' he went on, 'is that you have no inkling of what's going on at the pit. Why do I have to learn it first from Wilkins or Mulligan?'

'I thought Wilkins would keep you informed about the fines.'

'He's too soft and doesn't stand up to Mulligan.'

'Because the keeker's your man, father. Anyway you always seem to know what's going on,' he finished lamely.

'I do when I'm here. But these past few weeks I've been away attending to urgent business to secure the expansion of North Moor pit and with it our family fortune. You're supposed to be my eyes and ears when I'm not here.'

'I do try, father.'

'Do you, indeed.' Forster sat back and looked at his son. Again he felt the familiar and frustrating emotions of fondness and disappointment suffuse slowly through his body. He sighed. 'If you could only apply yourself to business with the same determination as you try to impress the ladies, and I use that word advisedly,' he added, 'I'd be a proud and contented man.'

Roland said nothing. He sensed the worst was past and that it might be a good time to take his leave. He rose and crossed to the door where he paused with a puzzled expression on his face. He turned and looked at his father. 'Are you really going to let the widows stay on?'

Forster looked up wearily. 'Of course not. Just until everybody signs the bloody bond.'

Roland grinned. 'For a moment I thought you'd gone soft like old Wilkins,' he said before closing the door.'

'Imbecile,' Forster muttered.

CHAPTER 27

Towards the end of September, Henry's new found confidence was being put to the test. His optimism took a battering as disputes began to emerge over the draft manifesto. Other pits in the area showed less enthusiasm for a confrontation and differences began to surface as the binding time approached. The men smelled good binding money and as usual their greed overrode their common sense and unity.

A poorly attended meeting of the Friendly Society, held in the chapel, listened glumly to the committee's report.

'The feeling is that most owners will be offering at least four guineas binding money,' Wilf said.

'I've heard that the Wearside pits are offering five,' Sep added.

'Forster's hinting at five guineas,' Wilf continued, 'and isn't it strange that nobody's been fined for nearly a month now?' he added. 'Some men are earning over twenty shillings a week and most are taking home eighteen. '

'And the widows have been allowed to stay on,' Sep reminded them. 'Strange that one, since he hasn't brought the builders in yet.'

'Nor will he,' Sam Elliott growled.

'But why can't the men see all this,' Henry said despairingly. 'Don't they realise that once they've signed the bond we've lost all our bargaining power?'

'They don't want to see,' Wilf said. 'They're blinded by the binding money and they tell themselves that Forster will keep his word.'

'But everyone knows he won't'

'Yes, but they just keep on hoping. Five guineas buys a lot of hope around here, Henry.'

'And a lot of misery when the hope runs out,' Henry countered.

'Aye, but most of 'em are just plain pitmen with no learning and a lot of mouths to feed,' Wilf said, trying to console Henry. 'You have to remember that.'

'Yes, I know. But sometimes their gullibility is beyond my understanding.'

'You said yourself it would take a long time.'

'Yes. I think I'm just beginning to appreciate how long. The hard bit is coming to terms with it.'

'It's the reality of pit life, Henry. Things are as they are and not as you'd like 'em to be.'

Henry looked at Wilf and smiled ruefully. He suddenly realised that Wilf was more in tune with the men than he could ever be. His own intellectualism had created a subtle void between his own thinking and that of the men he wanted to help. He now knew that he could only bridge that gap with Wilf's help and looking at his friend he saw that Wilf also understood. He smiled at Wilf. 'This will require a lot more time and patience than I'd bargained for.'

Wilf smiled back. 'Time and patience change the mulberry leaf to satin.' He repeated, remembering their recent long discussion on philosophy and proverbs.

The meeting broke up in a mood of despondency and a quiet group of delegates made their way homewards, peeling off as each one reached his home street. It was left to Wilf to keep everyone's spirits up and this he did with a blend of determination and satirical humour. 'Cheer up lads. It's not the end of the world just yet. That takes place on Sunday after Sep's fire and brimstone Chapel sermon.'

Mary was asleep when Henry arrived home. Her face was flushed and her breathing quick and shallow. He felt her forehead which was hot and covered in perspiration. 'You all right?' he whispered. There was no answer.

He undressed quietly and slid gently into bed beside her. A strange feeling of foreboding stirred inside him and remained until he sank into a troubled sleep.

Mary was still asleep when Alice arrived at the cottage the next morning and her smile quickly changed to a frown as she moved towards the bed.

'You all right?'

Mary opened her eyes at the sound of Alice's voice. 'Oh, yes...' she faltered, realising she must have gone back to sleep after feeding her baby.

'And how's my little nipper today, then,' Alice crooned, bending over the wooden cradle that had been lovingly carved by Henry.

'Asleep, I hope,' Mary answered quickly, hoping that Alice had not woken her son. She had had a difficult night.

'Dora asked me to pop in and see if you're all right. She's been worried about you.'

'I'm just a little tired, that's all. Nothing to worry anyone. Had a bad night with young Ralph, here,' she added, wishing she could be left alone.

'Aye, bairns can give you a hard time but they're worth it,' Alice said, clucking like a broody hen over the cradle.

Mary closed her eyes to hide her feelings. She found the close neighbourliness of pit communities too cloying, although she appreciated the good intentions behind it. Somehow, she felt she would never come to terms with being a pitman's wife, try as she may.

'Dora says you're to stay in bed today. I'll get the meal ready for your man.'

Mary groaned but she knew it was no good arguing. She decided to make the best of it and pretended to fall asleep. The ploy worked and Alice's chatter ceased and she moved more quietly around the room. Soon Mary didn't have to go on pretending and dozed off into a shallow sleep.

Not wishing to disturb Mary's rest, Alice decided to prepare the meal in the small lean-to at the back of the cottage. It was a bit cramped but any noise would be less likely to wake Mary and the baby. She reached down to the wooden water pail with the lid used by Henry to store the water he carried home from the pit. Alice had been given firm instructions by both Henry and Dora that only this water was to be used for cooking and drinking. The pail was placed in an awkward position behind the two carrying buckets and Alice tried to slide it out to gain easier access. As she tugged on the handle the pail suddenly toppled over, spilling the contents. Alice watched in dismay as the water quickly soaked away into the earthen floor of the lean-to. 'Shite,' she muttered to herself.

Alice lifted the pail and saw all the water had disappeared. She shrugged and picked up one of the buckets and then, after checking to see that Mary was still asleep, made her exit by the back door and headed towards the village well. She walked along the path between the ash heaps and the cottages, oblivious to the swarms of flies and the appalling stench made even worse by the long hot summer. A life spent in pit villages like North Moor had left her immune to discomforts like these. At the well she joined the small group of women waiting to draw water.

'Bloody well's running dry with this weather,' one of the women grumbled as she hauled up the bucket. Soon it was Alice's turn and as she emptied the well bucket into her own she saw that the water had a dark, brackish look. She hoped Henry and Mary wouldn't notice, then shrugged off her concern. A lot of nonsense anyway, she thought, carrying water all the way home from the pit. There was nowt wrong with well water. Everybody else drank it and it didn't do them any harm.

She arrived back at the cottage and poured the water from her bucket into the wooden drinking pail. She noticed that with the lid prised half open, it was difficult to see the colour of the water. She decided she would not tell anyone about the accident. 'What the eye can't see, the heart don't grieve over.' She muttered to herself and carried on preparing the meal.

It was two hours later when Mary woke and she lay for a while feeling hot and drowsy.

'Can I get you something, pet?'

Mary opened her eyes and saw the plump, kindly face of Alice smiling down at her. 'Can I have some water please? I'm so thirsty.'

'You do look a bit flushed, pet.'

'It's this awful heat.'

'And the bairn. You've had a bad time of it what with being so late and all. I'll just get your water.'

Mary sat up and sipped the water, which was warm and tasted awful. But she had a raging thirst and, after closing her eyes, drained the cup as quickly as she could, trying hard not to taste the water. She shuddered and sank back onto the pillows.

'The bairn will want his feed directly,' Alice said.

'I'll wait until he wakes up,' Mary's voice sounded drained and her eyes were listless.

Alice returned to her cooking, using half the remaining water to fill the kettle and to top up the stew she was preparing. They'll never know the difference, she reflected. Then, as if on an afterthought, she opened the back door and emptied out the remaining water in the pail. She knew Henry would bring home a fresh supply when he returned from the pit.

Two days later on his return from the pit, Henry was met at the door by a worried Dora. 'I'm glad you're home, Henry. Mary's ill. I think she's got the fever.'

Henry hurried inside and saw that Mary lay in a troubled sleep, tossing and turning in the incongruous setting of the four poster bed. Her breathing was rapid and her face flushed. Suddenly he saw the empty cradle and froze. 'Where's Ralph?'

Dora took his arm. 'It's all right, Henry, Mrs McBride's taken him. Mary couldn't feed the poor bairn so we had to find a wet nurse.'

'Is he all right?'

'He hasn't got the fever, if that's what you're thinking. He'll be fine with Mrs McBride for now.'

Henry looked down at his wife, his heart chilled by an anxiety he had never previously experienced which was made worse by his feeling of utter helplessness. He felt a gentle tug on his arm.

'It's best to let her sleep,' Dora said softly. 'I'll sit with her while you get yourself cleaned up.'

'I suppose you're right. Thank you, Dora. You're a good woman and I won't forget it.' He went into the lean-to, stripped and washed himself before putting on a fresh shirt and trousers. Returning to the room he was struck by the maddening normality of it all; the stew pan simmering quietly over the low fire with wisps of steam sliding from under the lid, the rhythmic tick of the eight-day chiming clock and the steady swing of the heavy pendulum, the glint of polished, brass against dark mahogany. The very domesticity of it all seemed to mock him. He sat down gently on the bed, silently smiling his thanks to Dora as she slipped quietly out of the house. The movement disturbed Mary and she opened her eyes and stared dully at her husband.

'Are you all right?' Henry asked, trying hard to hide his anxiety.

'I've got an awful headache. It's driving me mad.'

'Can I get you something for it?'

'Just some water, please.'

Henry filled a cup from the container in the lean-to and returned to the bedside. 'I brought some fresh water home with me. It's still nice and cool.'

Mary sipped the water slowly then sank back on the pillows. A frown of pain crossed her face and beads of perspiration began to form on her forehead. Suddenly she sat up. 'Where's my baby?' The anguish in her voice shocked Henry.

'Ralph's all right,' he said soothingly and held her close. 'Mrs McBride's looking after him until you're well again.'

'Is he ill?' She began to panic.

'No. He's safe and well, I promise you. You'll have him back again as soon as you're better.'

Mary was not fully convinced but felt too tired to argue. She lay back and closed her eyes.

Henry watched her for a while then rose and went into the lean-to. He found a square of clean, soft flannel and a large basin which he filled with cold water. Returning to the bed he began to bathe Mary's face, constantly dipping the cloth to keep it cool before replacing it across her brow and temples. 'Is that better?'

'Yes.' Mary managed a wan smile at her husband before closing her eyes to hide the pain.

Henry had noticed that Mary's tongue was furred and her mouth looked dry. 'Would you like another drink?' he asked anxiously.

'Yes, please.' She drank deeply this time.

Henry continued to nurse her until she finally drifted into a shallow, restless sleep. He gently rose from the bed and taking a plate from the table spooned some stew from the pan which was still simmering on the hearth. When it cooled, he ate slowly with little appetite. Mark could finish it off when he got home from the pit, he thought and pushed the plate away.

Over the following week Henry and Dora watched with growing concern as Mary's condition continued to deteriorate. Her abdomen was distended and there were violent discharges of foul diarrhoea tinted with blood. They remained by her bedside constantly and Henry began to realise just how much he was indebted to Dora for her unfailing support.

He was also worried about Mark's reaction to his mother's illness. His son was clearly concerned, but managed to maintain a remarkable control over his feelings that seemed unnatural for a boy of his age. Perhaps his son was growing up faster than he'd realised, Henry thought. Mark had now taken to eating next door with Dora and her family and was developing an even closer relationship with Jane. In the circumstances it was a situation which did not displease Henry. Jane was mature beyond her years and could help Mark through a difficult period.

At the beginning of October, news of Nelson's great victory over the French at the battle of the Nile reached England. It was received with relief and gratitude by King George and all his subjects and celebrations took place throughout the kingdom.

On the 5th October, an illumination took place in Newcastle in honour of the victory. Many depictions were displayed throughout the town lit by candles and lamps.

But as the festive lights burned bright in Newcastle, darkness descended over a small cottage in North Moor colliery, where a single candle flickered and dimmed as the life ebbed from Mary. By a cruel coincidence, her life, the life that had given birth to a son on that first day in August, the very day of Nelson's great victory, ended on the day that the news of that triumph was being celebrated in Newcastle.

Something died in Henry that night. Grief stricken, he held the lifeless body of his wife and wept. Dora, blinded by her own tears, left him to grieve alone and slipped quietly next door to break the news.

Mary was buried in a quiet, sunny corner of the village churchyard away from the area normally reserved for pit families. A gold coin from Henry's hard earned savings found its way into the sexton's greedy hands in order to secure this privilege, but Henry was determined to fulfil what he felt would have been Mary's last wish. He knew that she had hated pit life and longed to be away from it all. He had failed her in life but, in death at least, she could lie at rest among the families of yeoman farmers and the like. He commissioned a beautiful marble headstone and paid for this with his five guineas binding money.

CHAPTER 28

May 4th, 1802, was the day appointed by the magistrates of Newcastle for the formal proclamation to the local populace of the peace between Great Britain and France. Duncan Forster was participating in the ceremony with a detachment of North Moor volunteers and to everyone's surprise, declared the day a holiday. To the even greater surprise of the pitmen he employed, they were to receive two shillings and sixpence to compensate for their lost pay.

'He'll take it back in fines,' Wilf growled suspiciously. 'You see if he doesn't.'

'Don't look a gift horse in the mouth,' Sep said soothingly. 'The good Lord may have persuaded Forster to change his ways.'

'And pigs can fly,' Wilf retorted.

'We'll just have to wait and see,' Henry broke in, trying to calm things down. 'Anyway, it's a paid holiday and I'm going to make the most of it.'

'Me too,' Wilf said. 'I expect there'll be some right shenanigans going on in Newcastle after they've read the proclamation. You ought to come along as well, Sep.'

'I've got better things to do here,' Sep answered reprovingly. 'There'll be far too much drinking and fornication when all the parades and speeches are finished.'

'Sounds as good a reason as any to go,' Wilf said, winking at Henry.

'You're a married man,' Sep said scoldingly. Then, seeing his rebuke ignored, he stormed off in disgust.

'See what you've done?' Henry sighed. 'You shouldn't bait him like that. It's the wrong subject to tease him about.'

'I know, but he takes life far too seriously. I'll apologise when I see him again.'

The holiday dawned fine and clear with the promise of warm sunshine to come. Henry and Mark, along with most of the inhabitants of North Moor, were heading for Newcastle. Their intention was to visit Fiona and Colin to seek news of Rory, whose release from prison was now imminent. Their restrained manner was in sharp contrast to

266

the boisterous, festive mood of the other travellers on the road that morning who waved and shouted ribald greetings to one another.

As they approached Newcastle, they could hear the church bells ringing to mark the occasion and the crowds grew thicker as they passed through the outskirts of the town. Once inside the walls, they found the streets thronged with people, also in a gay, festive mood. The volunteers and militia headed for their muster points, their uniforms and accoutrements sparkling from their parade ground preparation. The main event was to begin at noon at Sandhill and this left Henry and Mark plenty of time to visit Fiona and Colin in Sandgate.

Colin answered the door and gave them a warm, welcoming smile. He looked resplendent in his best keelman's shore attire, the short blue jacket and belled trousers emphasising his tall, strong frame. But seeing the sober dress of the visitors he suddenly felt overdressed and coloured in embarrassment.

'Looks like you'll be making the most of the celebrations, eh?' Mark said grinning.

'Aye. There won't be many keels sailing the river today,' Colin replied, self- consciously.

'Mind if I come along?' Mark sensed he would have more fun in Colin's company than with his father. Almost seventeen, he wanted to sample a man's world, a world beyond the confines of a pit village.

'Sure, if it's all right with your dad?' Colin looked at Henry.

'Of course,' Henry said, 'but watch what you're doing.'

'You'll have something to eat, first,' Fiona cut in. 'It'll be a long day so you'd best start with a full stomach.'

Half an hour later after a simple but satisfying meal of cold meat, cheese and coarse bread, the two young men set off in high spirits for the Sandhill, where the start of the day's celebrations would take place.

Fiona handed Henry a glass of ale. 'Drink that while I clear these things away.'

Henry watched as she busied herself around the house in a burst of nervous energy, as if trying to hide her unhappiness and frustration. 'No news of Rory?' he ventured at last. 'It must be nearly time for his release.'

Fiona paused for a moment. 'He should be released any day now but the authorities are being evasive.'

'Why?'

'I don't know, but they won't give a firm date.'

'But he's served his sentence. They can't keep him locked up without good reason.'

'Do they need one?'

'Of course. We're a civilised country and believe in the rule of law. Now that we're at peace with France the government can't use public safety as an excuse to lock up their opponents.'

Fiona looked at him despairingly, 'Then why won't they release him?' Her eyes began to fill with tears.

Henry held her gently. 'I don't know, but I'll go to London to find out.'

She shook her head. 'His friend, Jamie Drummond, sailed two weeks ago for the Pool. You may remember him; he's the master of a collier brig, the *Lady Morag*.'

Henry nodded. 'Yes, I remember meeting him a long time ago. Wasn't he a member of the radical group in Newcastle?'

'Not really, but he sympathised with Rory's radical beliefs. I've written to Rory to tell him Jamie's brig will be lying in the Thames, somewhere between Woolwich and the Pool, for two weeks during the time he should be released. If he doesn't turn up, Jamie will instruct a London lawyer to seek Rory's release through the courts.'

'Then we must hope that Jamie's mission will be successful.' Henry could see that Fiona was close to breaking point. He gently took her hand. 'He'll be back aboard the *Lady Morag*, you'll see.'

She smiled at him, bravely fighting back her tears. 'I hope you're right, Henry. I do so hope you're right.' Then, brightening a little she asked, 'How are you coping at North Moor?'

'Not too badly, thanks mainly to Dora.'

'And how's young Ralph?'

'Growing up fast. He'll be four in August and looks more like his mother every day.' She could see the hurt in his eyes at the recollection of Mary and felt guilty for burdening him with her own problems.

'You've suffered more grief than I these past four years, and borne it much more bravely. Yet still you call on me and listen to my woes without complaint.' She smiled and squeezed his hand as her heart went out to him. 'You're a true friend, Henry, and I can see why Rory thinks so highly of you. '

He smiled back at her. 'Now you're making me feel embarrassed.'

'Then we'll talk about something else. Tell me how Mark's getting on.'

'He's fine. He's a fully-fledged putter now and ready to move on to hewing. Young Jed's working with him as his foal.'

'That's good progress at sixteen, isn't it?'

'Aye, but with his education he shouldn't be working down a pit.'

'Neither should you.'

'Perhaps not, but I had little option.' He paused in confusion hoping she would not think he was blaming Rory.

'We're all victims of circumstance.' She flashed him an understanding smile.

'I suppose so, though hostage might be more apt'

'Are you and Mark getting on all right?'

'Yes. Why do you ask?'

'You don't seem to be as close as you were.' She was about to add 'since Mary died,' but stopped herself. 'You haven't had a quarrel?' She went on awkwardly.

Henry looked surprised. 'No, we get on fine. He's growing up, that's all. I suppose things change a little when that happens.'

Fiona tactfully changed the subject. 'I'm pleased he gets on so well with Colin.'

'Aye, There's quite a bond between those two, isn't there?' Henry beamed. 'Colin's turned out to be a real credit to you.'

'And Rory. He's been a father to the boy.'

'He has indeed. He's made him into a proud MacGregor like himself. It's a good thing to keep your family heritage alive and pass it on to the next generation.' His voice took on a wistful tone.

Fiona laughed. 'Rory doesn't just keep it alive, he exaggerates it. I sometimes think the clan history is just a game to him, even though he is the son of a clan chieftain.'

269

'There's no harm in that,' Henry said. 'Better to be born a penniless gentleman than working pitman.'

She detected a yearning for some fulfilment in his life that had been unfairly denied to him. She wondered if this was the cause of the slow but progressive change in Henry that she had observed since Mary's death. She had discerned a strange, almost imperceptible distancing in Henry's relationship with Mark and her intuition and mother's instinct told her it was not just a question of a son growing up. It was more serious than that and it made her sad and uneasy.

'You're looking very serious.' Henry's voice cut across her thoughts.

She smiled at him. 'I was just thinking that if we don't leave soon we'll miss the proclamation ceremony,' she lied.

Henry stood and held out his arm. 'Then allow me to escort you, ma'am,' he said with all the gravity he could muster.

Fiona giggled. 'By your leave, kind sir.'

The ceremony proclaiming the peace began at the Sandhill at noon with the assembly of the corporation in all their regalia, attended by officers of the police. The Newcastle Volunteers, the Armed Association and the Gateshead Volunteers paraded with their bands and the sounds of military marches filled the air. Then, after a fanfare of trumpets, the Royal proclamation was read out to the crowd by the Town Marshall. After that, the celebrations began and throughout the day the merry-making gathered pace.

At three o'clock Henry and Fiona returned to Sandgate feeling tired and subdued. They had had enough of the celebrations and the gaiety and laughter of the crowds reminded them of their own loneliness, emphasising the void caused by the absence of their loved ones. Fiona saw that Henry had remained outside the open door. 'Aren't you coming in?'

'No. I think I'll make my way back to North Moor, if you don't mind.'

'But aren't you going to wait for Mark and Colin?'

'I reckon it'll be dark before those two get back,' Henry said smiling. 'They'll be looking to sample some of the delights of the grown-ups, I'll be bound.'

She responded with a wan smile. 'I suppose you're right. They aren't boys any more, are they?'

'Life moves on, Fiona, and so must I. Mark can make his own way home. Tell him not to be too late.'

She watched as he walked away, heading for Byker and the North Shields turnpike. She noticed for the first time that his shoulders seemed to droop a little.

Dora Hindmarsh was busily preparing supper when she heard the door open. Glancing up, she saw a tired looking Henry enter the room to be greeted by an excited young Ralph. 'Have you brought me something, dad?'

Henry smiled fondly at his son as he fished in his pocket for the present. 'There,' he said, handing Ralph a small notebook and pencil. 'And there's one for Jane and Jimmy, too.' Jane smiled and thanked him.

'Jane's notebook is bigger than mine,' Ralph complained.

'That's because she writes more than you do. Anyway, you're still using a slate. When you can write as well as Jane you can have a larger notebook.'

Henry looked at the books scattered around the table with a feeling of nostalgia as he recalled the days when Mark used to tutor Jane and Jed. Now it was Jane's turn to stand in as tutor to Ralph, and her young brother Jimmy, when he, or Mark, could not find the time. He suddenly realised that the girl was almost a woman, and one of great beauty, he thought. Her long hair hung down in golden profusion to her shoulders, providing a perfect frame for her fine boned cheeks and sparkling blue eyes.

'Jane's been offered a place at Highfield Hall,' Dora announced proudly. 'Mrs Gordon, the housekeeper at North Moor, put in a good word for her.'

'That was very kind of her,' Henry said. 'I hope Jane's pleased.'

'Aye, I think she is, but she's got this thing about not wanting to leave me here to manage on my own.'

'You can't look after three working men and two boys all by yourself, mam,' Jane cut in. 'It's too much for you.'

'I can manage; others have to,' Dora responded tartly, 'though I'll grant I'll miss you. Anyway, young Jimmy's been promised a job at the pit by Mr Wilkins, so that'll leave only young Ralph to look after during the day.'

Henry groaned inwardly. More pit fodder, he thought angrily, but managed to hold his tongue. He didn't want to upset Dora, for she had been a godsend to him and his family since Mary's death, acting as a surrogate mother to Mark and Ralph. Living next door to each other also had mutual and practical advantages. Jed and young Jimmy now slept with Mark in Henry's house which allowed Jane to have the other loft room to herself; Dora and Wilf shared the matrimonial bed in the living room.

Jane looked pleadingly at her mother. 'Are you sure you want me to go?'

'Of course I do, pet, if it's what you want. It's a chance for you to get into service, perhaps become a lady's maid one day.'

'I'll be starting in the kitchen, mam. It's a big jump from a skivvy to a lady's maid.'

'But you've got some education now, thanks to Mark.'

'Sometimes that can be more of a hindrance than a help. Best to keep quiet about it.'

Dora began to bristle. 'Education is something you should be proud of. There's no need to go hiding it.'

'Some gentry prefer servants without education,' Henry cut in gently, trying to calm the situation. 'I think Jane shows a lot of common sense to understand that.'

'Why? Surely servants who can read and write are more useful than those who can't.'

'A lot of gentry still think that education for working folk like us only breeds troublemakers.'

'Well, education or not, Jane's going into service. It's a better future than she'll find here.' There was a note of finality in Dora's voice that brooked no further argument.

'I'm sure she'll be happy,' Henry said, 'and if she isn't she knows she's got a loving family to come home to.'

Dora turned to her daughter, her eyes moist. 'Aye, remember that pet. If things don't work out, you come straight home.'

'I don't know what Mark will think of it all,' Henry said pensively.

'He doesn't know yet,' Jane said.

'Then he's in for a surprise. He's going to miss you.'

Her eyes clouded over. 'I'll miss him too.' Then, brightening up, she added, 'but I'll be able to visit home once a month on my day off.'

'That should ease any pain.' Henry said dryly. 'When do you leave?'

'Next week.'

'You'd better tell him as soon as possible then. Give him time to get used to the idea. '

'I'll tell him tomorrow,' Jane promised.

Henry's response was interrupted by the sound of angry voices in the street outside. The door flew open and Wilf entered, looking flustered and annoyed. When he saw Henry he smiled and tried to compose himself. 'Did you enjoy the fun and games in Newcastle then?' There was a touch of chagrin in his voice.

'Not much. I really went to see Fiona to find out if there was any news of Rory's release.'

'Has he been set free then? Wilf's tone was more conciliatory.

'Not yet, as far as we know. The authorities seem reluctant to give any information.'

'Sounds like they're looking for an excuse to keep him locked up.'

'That wouldn't surprise me,' Henry said bitterly. 'But they haven't got any legal grounds for doing so.'

'Since when did they need 'em? The usual excuse is a threat to public safety.'

'But not now the war's ended.'

Wilf scratched his head in puzzlement. 'Aye, you'd think they'd live and let live. Wipe the slate clean, like.'

'Well, we'll know in a few weeks.' Henry explained that Jamie Drummond's collier brig had sailed for London and hoped to rendezvous with Rory on the Thames.

'I hope he has better luck than I've had today,' Wilf said wearily. 'The trip was a bloody waste of time.'

'Trip?' Henry sounded surprised. 'What trip?'

'To Willington and Wallsend pits to talk to some of the men. Sep and a few of the committee went along as well.'

'I didn't know you'd planned a recruiting drive.'

'Because you don't attend many committee meetings these days.' He spoke with a gentle note of recrimination. 'We've seen more of young Mark this past year. Getting quite keen, he is.'

Henry looked a little put out. 'I would have gone with you if I'd known,' he said peevishly. We need all the recruits we can get.'

'We weren't recruiting,' Wilf answered crustily. 'The Combination Laws put a stop to the idea of a coalfield brotherhood and our pitmen's manifesto. You should know that.'

'Yes, but not Friendly Societies,' Henry countered.

'Aye, but we needed your help today. Once the Wallsend men started to ask questions that we couldn't answer properly they soon lost interest.'

'Is that what you were all arguing about out there?'

'More or less. We usually end up arguing when you're not there, which is pretty often these days.'

It was a rebuke that Henry knew he fully deserved and it made him feel guilty. He had let the men down and worse still, he felt he'd undermined Wilf's authority and leadership. He looked at Wilf and saw, in his friend's eyes, not anger but sadness tinged with just a little impatience. There was sympathy for his loss, but four years had passed since Mary's death and to Wilf, this seemed an unnaturally long time to grieve. Henry was about to speak when Dora intervened.

'Come and sit down you two. Supper's ready and the children are hungry even if you aren't.' She continued in a worried whisper, 'There's been no falling out between you, has there?'

Henry smiled. 'No, of course not. In fact I think your husband has just done me a great service by telling me a few home truths.'

Dora looked at Wilf who was now grinning happily. 'Well that's a comfort to be sure. But you could have fooled me the way the pair of you have been going on lately.' The relief in her voice took the sting from the intended chastisement.

They sat and ate for a while without talking. But it was a silence of contentment, as if some hidden obstacle to their friendship had now been removed. Henry began to reflect on the four years that had passed since Mary's death and his descent into a world of despair he had never known before. In the months following his bereavement, his grief had been almost too painful to bear and only his love for Mark and Ralph helped him to carry on. The desire to make up for a mother's love that had been taken away from his children became all consuming. Over the years his interest in the men's cause had slowly begun to wane, despite Wilf's strenuous efforts to keep it alive. The task of drawing up the manifesto which he had once found so exciting suddenly became a chore which no longer enthused him. The passing of the Combination Act by Pitt's government back in '79, which prohibited combinations of workmen for the purpose of obtaining better conditions, had dealt a hammer blow to his cherished plan to form a brotherhood of pitmen. But with Mary's death, the bright fervent flame of his idealism had been snuffed out, so it did not seem to matter anymore.

'Are you still with us?' The sound of Wilf's voice interrupted his reverie.

Henry smiled sheepishly. 'I was just daydreaming.'

'That's a relief,' Wilf said. I thought I'd upset you. '

'No. What you said needed saying. I've been wallowing in self-pity for too long.'

'You're letting your food go cold,' Dora interrupted. 'Aren't you hungry?'

'Yes, of course I am.'

'Then eat it up. You've been neglecting yourself again.' There was kindness and concern in her voice.

'I've been neglecting a lot of things lately, Dora, but from now on things are going to change.' He looked at Wilf and saw in his friend's answering smile that he understood, what he had meant.

It was nearly dark when Mark arrived back at North Moor. He had walked for more than two hours but his body did not feel tired. His mind, still fired by the revelry and excitement of the day, was intoxicated by elation rather than alcohol. He had taken some ale but decided he did not really like the taste and watched with growing amusement, as Colin and his keel bullies sank pint after pint. The word bully had always puzzled Mark until he learnt that it was a keelman's term of endearment akin to brother. So he felt proud to be one of Colin's bullies.

Colin had been somewhat the worse for wear when Mark finally got him home. After supper, presided over by a slightly amused but disapproving Fiona, Mark took his leave and set off for home, taking the same route his father had taken several hours earlier.

It was the sight of the pithead, grim and forbidding against the darkening sky, that finally brought him back to earth, and his feeling of euphoria quickly began to evaporate. His attitude to pit life had recently taken on a confused love-hate relationship, but it was an ambivalence he had not yet come to terms with. He was proud that his courage and determination had won him the respect of his fellow pitmen and he appreciated the special camaraderie to be found among the pit folk. But deep inside, he knew he was wasting his talents, and the thought of spending the rest of his life as a pitman was something he just couldn't contemplate. Yet he could see no alternative in the immediate future.

He had known, without fully understanding it at the time, that his mother had been unable to adjust to pit life. She had tried hard to live with the situation, but it was like a malignant cancer eating away inside and slowly killing her. Part of his own childhood had also been killed by the soul-destroying nature of pit life, and with the death of his mother the rest had died too. At first, he blamed the baby for her death and refused to take any interest in his young brother. But gradually the helpless innocence of the child won him over and the baby became a sort of memorial to his mother's memory.

As Mark's love of his baby brother grew, his relationship with his father gradually became more distant. He now found Henry's obsessive attention cloying and slightly embarrassing. He took to spending more time next door with Jane and her family and almost became one of them. He also realised that the men's cause was in trouble and the Friendly Society, on which many hopes were pinned, was struggling to survive. Wilf, Sep and the rest of the committee, who needed Henry's help so much, could no longer rely on it. Whilst this caused Mark some dismay at first, he soon began to take a personal interest in the affairs of the society, extracting as much information from Wilf as possible after each committee meeting. He helped Wilf to complete the draft of the manifesto and surprised his adopted uncle with his knowledge and intuitive grasp of the problems. He also took over Wilf's tutoring which Henry had begun to neglect. They became an unusual yet oddly compatible pair.

Henry was reading when Mark came home. He looked up when he heard the door open. 'You're late.' It was a greeting rather than a censure.

'Yes, I stayed on with Colin and his friends for a while.'

'Drinking?'

'Not much. I don't really like the stuff.'

'Have you eaten?'

'Yes. I had supper at Colin's house before I left.' He moved towards the loft ladder to join Jimmy and Ralph who were sleeping in the loft above but Henry indicated that he wanted to talk. Mark sat down opposite his father at the table. There was an awkward silence before Henry spoke. 'Things haven't been much fun for you these past few years, have they?'

'Nor for you, dad.'

'No, but I could have helped you more than I did after your mother died.'

'But you did help, only…' He was about to add that nothing could have eased the pain at the time, but stopped short.

Henry sighed. 'I know, mothers are special. I felt the same when my mother died. But I shouldn't have been so selfish, bottling things up and thinking I was the only one really hurting.'

'It hurt me too, dad, but I've learned to live with it now. '

'And I haven't.' It was an admission rather than a question.

'I suppose you have in your own way.' There was an implied criticism in Mark's reply, though he hadn't intended it to sound that way.

'Could have done better if I'd tried a little harder, eh?' There was wry humour in Henry's response.

'That's not for me to say, dad.'

'But you're right, son. I should have tried harder instead of wallowing in self-pity. I not only let you down I also failed Wilf and Sep, to say nothing of the others.'

Mark smiled. 'Hallelujah! I'll tell Sep you've seen the light at last.'

Henry laughed. 'As bad as that. Well better late than never, but things are going to be different from now on.'

'I'm pleased to hear it, dad,' Mark said happily, 'really pleased.'

Henry stood up. 'You know, Mark, I think I shall go to bed feeling at peace for the first time in years.'

Mark rose slowly. 'I think I will too, dad.'

Then, as if possessed by a mutual and irresistible compulsion, they clasped each other in a long-continued embrace. 'We should have done this four years ago when your mother died,' Henry said, burying his face in Mark's hair to hide his tears.

CHAPTER 29

The morning of the 4th May, 1802 also dawned bright and sunny over the City of London, with a cool refreshing breeze blowing upriver from the Thames estuary. A few fleecy white clouds caused an occasional shadow to be cast as they slipped between the sun but as the day wore on the sky became a vast expanse of blue.

A lone figure stood by the steps of the stone-walled jetty used by the watermen who acted as pilots to the incoming shipping. He was a big man with intense blue eyes that stared out with a steely gaze from a red bearded face. His complexion had an unhealthy pallor resulting from four years of incarceration in dark, evil smelling gaols on an inadequate diet. But his stance was firm and upright and his eyes still carried the glint of an unbroken spirit.

Rory MacGregor turned as he heard the waterman's approaching footsteps and held out his hand. 'Good day to ye.'

'You my passenger, then?' The waterman winced under the strong grip.

'Aye, I am that.'

'That's her out yonder.' He pointed to a smart collier brig of some 200 tons anchored inshore of the main stream. '*Lady Morag*, she's called. D'ye know her?'

'No, but I know Jamie Drummond, her master.'

'He expecting you?'

'I'm no' in the habit of boarding strange vessels without being invited,' Rory said smiling.

'Sorry. It's just that most of the colliers unload up at the pool first before they take on passengers. Unloading's a dirty business and usually takes a week or more,' the waterman added as if trying to explain his inquisitiveness.

'The ship's master and I are old friends and we haven't seen each other for a long time. And if we stand here chattering much longer we'll miss the tide.' Rory smiled again but the humour had faded from his eyes.

Sensing his curiosity had gone too far, the waterman hurried down the steps and untied the painter of a small skiff that was moored there.

Holding the boat steady, he motioned for Rory to board. Rory did so with the practised ease of a skilled seaman, displaying a surprising lightness and dexterity for such a big man after four years of harsh imprisonment. He sat down in the stern sheets, observing that the waterman had been suitably impressed.

They rowed out to the *Lady Morag* in silence. As they drew near, Rory noted with approval the brig's clean lines and ship-shape condition that would have done credit even to a King's ship. Indeed Jamie Drummond, the ship's master, might well have ended up serving in His Majesty's Navy but for their chance meeting nine years ago. He remembered that it was his fierce intervention with the press gang back in '93 that had saved Jamie from being taken. The recollection of the senseless bodies of the impress men lying sprawled out among the wreckage of the taproom brought a smile to his face, especially the memory of old Josh, the landlord, bewailing the damage to his establishment. Old Josh had been a long standing pimp of the impress service so he deserved no sympathy. It was this event that had forged the start of a friendship between Rory and Jamie that had grown ever stronger over the intervening years.

The boat came alongside the *Lady Morag* and Rory clambered up onto the deck. He was met by the tall, skeletal figure of the master. 'Avast there you heathen Highlander.' James Drummond smiled and held out his hand.

'Why, you lowland apology for a Scotsman. Remember you're speaking to a MacGregor. 'Ye ken, a Drummond is only one step up from an Argyle,' Rory grinned back.

Friendly insults exchanged, they embraced like long lost brothers. Jamie was shaken by his friend's appearance. 'Man you're no' looking so well. You need feeding up.'

'Aye, the cooking hasn't been too grand these past few years.'

'We'll soon put that right when we reach the Pool.' Jamie promised.

Rory watched with growing interest as the crew bustled around the deck and the topmen went aloft to unfurl the sails. The waterman's skiff was made fast astern and the *Lady Morag* weighed anchor and came into the wind. The ripple of water along the hull and the creak of timbers and spars was music to Rory's ears after four long years in prison. Keelmen were superb seamen, which was why they frequently attracted the attention of the press gangs. Soon, Rory could remain idle no longer and joined in helping the crew as the *Lady Morag* completed the last leg of the voyage. A few hours later, the large wooden-stocked anchor splashed into the foul mud off the Pool of London and the brig waited her turn to unload.

Rory remained on deck, taking in the sight of Europe's most exciting port. The wharves stretched away in panoramic confusion on both banks below the Tower at London Bridge and as far as Hermitage stairs. They were a mixture of medieval timbering and gimcrack seventeenth century weather-board interspersed with the occasional more substantial Georgian brick and stone. There were hundreds of craft lying in this crowded stretch of the river, each vessel to its own anchor.

'Why are there so many ships in this short reach of water?' Rory asked.

'Because you can only land dutiable cargoes at Legal Quays or Sufferance Wharves, and most of 'em are here in the Pool.'

'Then why don't they put proper moorings down?'

'God only knows. We've been asking for 'em long enough.'

After supervising the stowage of the sails and checking the general appearance of his ship, Jamie went below to change into his best shore-going clothes. He wanted to impress the factors at the Coal Exchange who held a monopoly on the London market. A collier master was more than just a ship's captain. He was also the owner, or part owner, of his ship, responsible for buying and selling his cargo and needed to look the part. So, suitably attired, Jamie reappeared on deck with a leather satchel containing the various ships papers and custom's documents ready to be rowed ashore in the waterman's skiff. He paused by the rail to speak to Rory. 'Ye'll join me for dinner when I get back.' It was more a friendly order than a request. 'I've arranged something special for ye.' With that he disappeared over the side.

Later that evening in the stern cabin of the *Lady Morag*, Jamie kept his promise. The soft light of the oil lamps cast a warm glow over the dark mahogany of the cabin table and their reflections glinted off the fine glassware that had been brought out for the special occasion. Looking out through the stern windows, Rory could see the riding lights of anchored ships dancing like a swarm of fireflies on the dark water. He sighed contentedly and pushed away his plate. 'It's been a long time since I tasted beef like that, Jamie, to say nothing of fresh vegetables and bread hot from the galley oven.'

Jamie smiled. 'We're not finished yet.' He reached behind him and placed a bottle on the table. 'Ye'll tek a we dram,' he said pouring a large measure. Then raising his glass he looked fondly at his friend. 'To freedom and your future happiness.'

'I'll drink to that,' Rory responded 'and to my friends who made it possible and worth waiting for.'

'Do ye want to talk about it?' Jamie asked gently. 'It might help.'

'Aye, it might indeed. Exorcise the soul, as the preacher would have us believe.'

'No. Just talk to a friend. I promised Fiona and Colin I'd bring ye back a new man, as good and sound as the day ye were taken.'

'It's easier said than done if you're a vengeful man like me. Perhaps it'll be easier when I've settled some scores.'

Jamie saw the steel in Rory's eyes and knew it would be useless trying to dissuade him from whatever course of action he had in mind. 'Just remember that Fiona and Colin are waiting for ye, as are hundreds of your friends.'

Rory smiled. 'Don't worry, I'll try not to jeopardise my new found freedom. Believe me; I value it too much to start taking risks. But I'll no kowtow to anyone and those who've crossed me had better watch out. In prison you learn how to wait.'

Jamie laughed. 'Well ye can start now because it will take us a week to unload. Then, wind and tide willing we'll hope for a speedy voyage home.'

Rory settled back in his chair. 'Then I can count my blessings. I was expecting a much longer voyage as a guest of his Majesty's Navy.' Seeing the look of surprise on Jamie's face he went on to explain. 'When I finished my sentence the prison authorities handed me over to the press.'

Jamie was outraged. 'But that's illegal. They had no right to do that.'

'They said I'd volunteered. I suppose it suited their purpose to keep me out of the way for a few more years.'

'Didn't you protest?'

'Och, man, of course I did. But it takes more than that for the navy to let a keelman go.'

'Then how did you escape?'

'I didn't.'

Jamie threw up his hands in exasperation. 'Then explain yourself, man.'

'They transferred me to a navy hulk moored in the Medway, guarded by marines. They kept shipping pressed men in but nobody was transferred out to navy ships. After a few weeks the hulk was crammed full of pressed men and dregs from the gaols who'd taken the King's shilling. Then one day we were all released and put ashore. I made my way to Woolwich as planned and thank God you were late in arriving.'

'We were held up by the weather for nearly three weeks. Couldn't clear the Tyne. I wouldn't have raged on at the crew if I'd known what happened to you.'

'Well perhaps the good Lord has decided to look after me from now on,' Rory chuckled.

'Why did the navy let you go?' Jamie enquired.

'They didn't say at the time. But I've since heard that with the peace treaty signed, the government's decided to reduce the size of the navy. There's a lot of ships being taken out of commission, so they don't need as many men.'

It was indeed true. Since Addington had become Prime Minister following Pitt's resignation the previous year, he had wasted no time in ruthlessly cutting military expenditure.

Jamie shook his head. 'I don't think the peace will last. Bonaparte won't be satisfied with being First Consul. He'll want to become Emperor just like the Romans.'

'Bonaparte might well become a dictator but he's no Augustus,' Rory said dismissively.

'Don't ye underrate him,' Jamie warned.

'We'll see. Anyway, enough of politics. Tell me what roguery you've been up to that makes ye master of a fine brig like the *Lady Morag*?'

'Honest endeavour, my friend,' Jamie said smiling. 'But she's a fine ship, is she not?' he added proudly.

'She's no' a ship if she's only got two masts,' Rory said mischievously. 'What's happened to all the barques in the collier fleet? They were proper ships with three masts.'

'Aye, they were that, but they needed a crew of ten men and a couple of apprentices. Ye can sail a collier brig with only six hands, although I prefer seven. With fewer men to pay and feed there's more profit. Most of the colliers are brigs nowadays.'

'Times are changing, and fast' Rory sighed.

'But for the better as far as colliers are concerned,' Jamie said. 'A two hundred ton brig draws well under sixteen feet which means she can clear the bar at either Shields or Sunderland and sail up the Thames as far as the Pool.'

Rory was impressed. 'You're a clever laddie in spite of being born a Drummond.'

'Aye, clever enough to be sole owner of a four year old brig,' Jamie responded. 'Bought out the last of my partners this year,' he added proudly.

'Man, ye must be worth a fortune.' Rory really was impressed now.

'It's not been easy.'

'Aye, the coal trade is a one-way business. Not many return cargoes to the Tyne, eh?'

'Only ballast, and I have to pay Trinity House one shilling per ton for it plus sixpence a ton for putting it aboard. Then when I get to the Tyne, it costs me another ten pence a ton to dump it at the ballast quay.'

'Ye poor, wee man,' Rory said in mock sympathy. 'So ye have to take paying passengers on board as well just to make a living; the ones who won't spend five pounds on a three day coach journey.' He shook his head. 'And all the commissions and commercial transactions you're paid to carry out while your ship's unloading?'

Jamie laughed. 'If anyone knows the tricks of a collier master it's a keelman. I can see I'm wasting my time trying to impress ye.'

'But ye do impress me,' Rory said seriously. 'As a friend and a generous one at that. I'm grateful to ye for bringing Fiona to London and seeing her safely home when they wouldn't let her visit me in prison. And I'm grateful to ye for this voyage.'

'Away with ye, man. Ye haven't had ma bill yet,' Jamie said to hide his embarrassment. 'Ye'll be singing a different tune then.'

'Since when did a MacGregor ever pay a bill,' Rory retorted entering into the mood with a display of shocked disbelief. 'Still, I might make an exception for ye, seeing as the Clan Drummond did fight for Bruce at Bannockburn and for Prince Charlie at Culloden.'

Jamie laughed. 'You're still an unrepentant Jacobite, I see.'

'Some things never change, my friend. But it's getting late and I'm sore tired.' With that he rose. 'I'll bid ye good night, Jamie.'

'Sleep well, Rory.'

In the week it took for the *Lady Morag* to unload its cargo, Rory made several trips ashore to buy newspapers, books and various other publications in order to catch up with the events of the past four years. He used some of the money sent by the keelmen and entrusted to Jamie for safekeeping.

Reading voraciously to make up for his four lost years, Rory soon realised that Jamie might have been right about Bonaparte after all. The man was clearly a military genius with political cunning to match, he thought. The more he read the more convinced he became that there were turbulent years ahead for England.

Once the actual unloading of the *Lady Morag* had begun, after several days of waiting, Rory found the noise and dust too disturbing for him to be able to concentrate on his reading. The team of coal-whippers, working in the hold and on the deck unloading coal into the lighters moored alongside, were matched by similar teams on the other colliers moored in the Pool. Coal dust filled the air, blackening masts and yards and creating a haze which often hid the dome and cross of St Pauls from view. The river also stank from the untreated sewage of London's huge population which had now grown to almost nine hundred thousand, the largest for any city in Europe. To escape, Rory took to spending more time ashore exploring various parts of London. He visited the more reputable taverns and coaching inns where the cosmopolitan clientele provided an informed commentary on the political and social events of the day.

Rory learned that the Treaty which had blossomed into the Peace of Amiens on March 27th was proving to be a source of irritation or even downright anger. Most of the people he talked to thought that England had made too many concessions to France and her allies. It was an unsatisfactory compromise and few thought the peace would last.

Two days later, the *Lady Morag* took on ballast and sailed on the ebb tide for the Thames estuary and the voyage north up the east coast of England. The weather proved fine and settled and with a steady, reaching breeze from the west, the brig made a fast and safe passage to the Tyne. After waiting for a few hours for the tide, the brig entered the river on the flood and dropped anchor off the town of North Shields.

Rory had sent word ahead by another Tyne-bound collier which had left London a week before the *Lady Morag*. Within minutes of their arrival, the brig was surrounded by keels and the wildly excited keelmen gave a tumultuous welcome to their returning leader.

Half an hour later, a small flotilla of keels, with flags and bunting flying from their masts, rounded Whitehill Point and headed towards the *Lady Morag*. As they drew nearer, Rory noted that the keels had been scrubbed clean and the decks holystoned to a state that would have done credit to a man-of-war. The crews were colourfully dressed in the keelman's best shore attire of short blue jackets, slate-coloured trousers, yellow waistcoats and silk hats with flat brims.

As the fleet drew alongside the brig, Rory's heart suddenly leapt. Standing on the foredeck of the leading keel was a familiar figure, the memory of which even four years of absence could not dim. It was his nephew, Colin, now eighteen years old and almost a man. He stood tall and proud, his strong, sinewy frame bearing witness to the five years he'd spent as a keelman on the river.

Overcome by the welcome, Rory turned to Jamie, he eyes misting over. 'I thought they'd have forgotten me after four years.'

'Not after all the fighting you've done for them. Have ye no faith in yersel, man?' Jamie chided warmly.

'Aye, but...' Rory shook his head.

286

'Och, away with ye. Your gear's been taken aboard the keel, yonder.' Jamie pointed to one of several keels that now lay alongside. 'I ken there's somebody a wee bit anxious to meet ye.'

Rory turned to see Colin vaulting over the ship's rail and the two men clasped each other in a warm embrace.

'Good to see you, Colin.'

'And you too, uncle. It's been a long time.'

'Aye, it has indeed. You were a boy when I left and now you're a man. And a fine one at that.'

Colin blushed. 'Well, you haven't changed much.'

'Och, no. The rest's done me good,' Rory lied, and changed the subject. 'How's your mother?'

'She's fine. Can't wait to see you when we get back to Sandgate.'

'Then what the hell are we standing here for!' With a wide grin he leapt down onto the deck of the keel and the war cry of the Clan MacGregor echoed across the water. 'Ard-Choille!'

As if anticipating events, the wind had backed steadily into the south east, providing the keelmen with a "sailors wind" for the return voyage up river to Newcastle. The fleet proceeded in triumphal procession upstream on the flood, reaching the Sandgate shore as the sun was setting in a golden glow above the hills of Dunston.

As the keels stood in towards the Swirl, a large crowd of keel men and their families surged down to the foreshore to welcome Rory. He was carried triumphantly ashore to the tune of The Keel Row, played by an impromptu band of fiddlers, fifers and drummers. Rory scanned the crowds lining the shore, looking for the one face whose image had kept him sane over the past four years. He felt a tug on his sleeve and saw Colin smiling and pointing into the crowd. Then he saw her, the shining chestnut coloured hair billowing over the fine cheekbones, as she waved to attract his attention. 'Fiona!' he shouted, and struggled through the back-slapping throng towards her as she, in turn, made her way eagerly towards him. She was as he remembered her, tall and slim with a beauty and composure that had always created a special attraction. When they came together, there was the briefest pause before they were in each other's arms and their lips met in a kiss that embodied four years of pent up love, longing and frustration.

Somewhere in the distance the strains of The Keel Row could be heard and the crowd took up the refrain.

'As I came through Sandgate
I heard a lassie sing:
'0'weel may the keel row,
The keel row, the keel row,
0'weel may the keel row,
That ma laddie's in.'

But Fiona and Rory were oblivious to it all.

CHAPTER 30

Rory MacGregor's jubilant homecoming inspired a new confidence into the hearts of the Tyne keelmen, who had sorely missed their leader. More and more spouts were being constructed at deep water staithes on the Tyne to enable the collier brigs to load the coal directly into the hold without the need for keels. This was putting the livelihood of the keelmen at risk as more and more collieries to the east of Newcastle began to build waggonways to the lower Tyne. Rory knew that unless a stand was made, keels would eventually be confined to working the staithes above Newcastle, where the low bridge over the river prevented the collier brigs from sailing further upstream.

The authorities viewed Rory's return with some misgiving and mindful of the past, an atmosphere of watchful unease began to develop. But in the small house in Wall Knoll, the atmosphere was one of sheer terror as William tried desperately to come to terms with his own fragile future. The man he had betrayed four years ago was now free and he knew that Rory MacGregor would not rest until he had extracted retribution. He remembered the crude wooden plaque, shaped like the headstone of a grave, that he'd found hanging from his door knocker. The words that were chiselled in the wood were now carved permanently in his mind, *In memory of a Judas whose death will serve as a warning to all traitors*. Suddenly, he realised why no-one had tried to harm him these past four years. Rory MacGregor's revenge would be a personal matter between the two of them; all the precautions he had taken whilst Rory was in prison had been a waste of time. He began to tremble and felt his blood run cold.

Ellen looked up from her embroidery as William's involuntary movement caught her eye.

'Feeling cold, dear?'

He looked at her, uncomprehendingly. 'Cold?'

'You're shivering.'

'Am I?' He paused trying to gather his wits and control his trembling. 'It is a bit chilly,' he said absently. 'I think I'll go upstairs to my study. It'll be a bit warmer up there.' He sensed, though he did not look at her, his wife's puzzled expression as he left the room.

Once safely in his study he sat down to think. He needed to be calm and rational to plan his future course of action, but his overriding fear made this difficult. His instincts urged him to cut and run, but his common sense told him that it was impractical and would solve nothing; sooner or later, Rory would find him. He thought of seeking out Rory and confronting him, but quickly dismissed the idea. In the end, as his fear subsided a little, he decided to carry on as before, keeping a sharp lookout for the unusual and staying alert at all times.

In the coal fitter's office Mr Ivison began to notice William's strange and nervous behaviour. He had grown to rely on his chief clerk since Henry's abrupt departure, but somehow he could not bring himself to like the man. There was none of the rapport which had drawn him to Henry and his family and for some unknown reason, he could never quite bring himself to trust William. Now, his clerk's edgy manner was beginning to irritate him. 'What's the matter with you, man? Seen a ghost or something?'

The question startled William. 'No, sir. I haven't been sleeping too well lately and it's making me feel a little tense.'

'A large glass of port before you go to bed is what you need. Never fails to do the trick for me.'

'I don't like port.'

'Then try a glass of brandy.'

'I don't drink alcohol of any sort, Mr Ivison.'

The coal fitter looked long and hard at his chief clerk. 'Then perhaps it's time you did.' William didn't respond and Ivison turned towards his office, muttering softly to himself, 'pompous bloody fool.' As he was about to close the door he called to William. 'You'd better get yourself up to Dunston. We're loading ten keels today.'

'Yes, Mr Ivison.' William answered in a miserable voice. He detested the river and everything connected with it. In particular, he hated visiting the coal staithes.

Rory flung the newspaper violently down on the table. 'We'll get no support from this rag, that's for sure.' The rag in question was the Tyne Mercury, Newcastle's latest newspaper, which had started publication in June.

Henry smiled at his irascible friend. 'What do you expect? They'll offend most of their readers if they side with the keelmen.'

'But they can surely tell truth from fiction,' Rory said scathingly. 'We're not wreckers by choice.'

'Damaging the spouts is breaking the law. No newspaper can be seen to be siding with lawbreakers.' Henry pointed out gently.

'Are ye tellin' me that it's all right to break a man's life by taking away his livelihood? Are people less important than the law?'

'No, of course not. But I sometimes wonder if you're protesting in the right way.'

'Och man, we've tried talking, but nobody will listen. And when you're livelihood's threatened, you've got to stand up and fight.'

The friendly, but sometimes heated argument had been going on all morning. Rory, refreshed and more determined than ever since his release from prison, argued with the burning conviction that had never deserted him, not even in the darkest moments of his incarceration. On the other hand, Henry, his faith in the pitmen's cause now restored, argued with the more muted zeal of a born-again reformer anxious to maintain his resolve and not fail again.

The debate was brought to a premature and conclusive close by Fiona, who'd had enough of their arguing for one day. After a month of being properly married to Rory she still could not get used to the endless debates and arguments that always seemed to surround her new husband. She placed some bread and cold ham on the table and ordered them to eat. 'No more talk of politics and confrontation, please. You can have a glass of ale if you promise.'

'Now that's an offer a man can't refuse,' Rory said, grinning.

'Agreed,' Henry said, pleased at the prospect of some respite.

They ate in silence for a while until Rory spoke, raising a subject which Henry would have preferred to forget. 'Have you seen anything of that brother-in-law of yours?'

'No.' Henry answered cautiously.

'Doesn't he concern you any more?'

'No. It's all in the past now.'

'He concerns me.'

'Let it rest, Rory.'

'Like hell I will.' There was a steely malice in Rory's voice which perturbed Henry. 'There'll be an old clan saying,' he went on, 'an unsettled score's like a festering sore.'

'It will serve no useful purpose.'

'What won't?'

'What I think you have in mind.'

'But I need to heel ma sores, bonny lad. I canna heal with him carrying on with his life out there and his wickedness unpunished. Don't you see, Henry. I'm no' a forgiving man like ye. There's too much poison inside me.'

'It's past, Rory. Can't you forget?'

'Not when you've spent four years festering inside a prison. It was the thought of revenge that gave me the strength to see it through.'

'Not Fiona and Colin?' The words were out before Henry could stop them.

Rory looked sadly at his friend. 'That was below the belt, Henry.'

'I'm sorry. I should have known better.'

'Fiona and Colin kept me alive through my memory of their love. But it was hate for that man which stopped them breaking me.'

Henry tried once more. 'Please, Rory. It'll do you no good. It won't change anything.'

Rory sighed. 'That's a matter of opinion, but we'll say no more on the subject, eh?'

'If you wish.'

'And we're still friends?'

'Of course.'

They looked at each other and smiled. But Henry knew that Rory's mind was made up and nothing he could do or say would change that. Rory MacGregor had a score to settle.

CHAPTER 31

All through the long winter months, William waited and fretted for the reprisal that never came. There were times when he wished Rory would make his move and end the suspense which left him in a constant state of fear. But when spring came and there was still no reprisal, his hopes began to rise and his confidence picked up. He knew Rory would never forgive him for what he'd done. Perhaps, on reflection, he'd decided that trying to kill him was simply not worth the risk. He began to smile again and to the surprise of the office clerks, was occasionally heard to hum softly while he worked.

But William's euphoria was not to last. As the spring days began to lengthen his suspicions were once more aroused and his doubts and fears returned. He knew he was being followed again, but no matter how hard he tried, he could not spot the person who seemed to dog his every footstep and yet managed to remain unseen. But he knew that he was being watched. He also knew that the person watching him could only be Rory MacGregor. The day of reckoning was drawing close.

When he returned home that evening he was almost out of his mind with fear. At supper, his hand shook and he spilled his food as he tried to eat. Ellen was visibly shocked at his appearance. 'What on earth is wrong with you, William? You look ill.'

'It's nothing, just a chill,' he mumbled unconvincingly.

'You ought to see a doctor or the apothecary.'

'I'll be all right. It's just those damned journeys to the staithes. You know how I hate them.' Her questions were beginning to irritate him.

'You've been like this for months now and it's getting worse.' Ellen spoke with genuine concern.

William's patience snapped. 'Can't you stop your carping, woman? Why do you keep going on about it again and again?' With that he stormed out and, stumping upstairs, locked himself in his study. Shocked by this unusual temper tantrum, Ellen burst into tears.

William stayed in his study all evening staring listlessly at the wall and ignoring Ellen's knocking and entreaties to come out and talk. Eventually she went to bed alone and cried herself to sleep. At midnight she awoke, her pillow wet, and found she was still alone. She rose and crossed the landing and knocked on the study door.

'William, my love, come to bed. It's past midnight.' There was no answer. She knocked again. 'Please, William.'

There was a muffled, tortured sound from inside the room followed by a shouted, 'Go away, damn you. Leave me alone.'

Ellen, hurt and bewildered, stumbled back to the bedroom, sobbing as though her heart was breaking.

The following morning, William left early for the office on the quayside to avoid another confrontation with his wife. He walked quickly down Broad Chare, glancing anxiously behind him as he went. When he turned into the quayside he kept well clear of the narrow entries to the warren of chares that led off it until he reached the office near Sandhill. After quickly closing the door behind him he sat down at his desk feeling his heart pounding wildly against his ribs. When the clerks arrived they noticed his agitated state and began to whisper to each other, sniggering, as they sat at their high stools. William shot them a withering glance. 'Stop that silly whispering and get on with your work,' he barked. The clerks immediately bent over their ledgers and the office was suddenly transformed into a hive of activity.

Later, when Mr Ivison arrived, William received his instructions for his visit to the staithes and left the office in a foul mood. It was a task he detested, for he hated the boat journeys, particularly those to the up-river staithes above bridge where the broad, windswept reaches of the water often made him seasick. He also found the constant climbing up and down ladders difficult, for he had no head for heights.

William set off to visit the large staithes on the south side of the river first, calling at Dunston and then the large complex at Derwenthaugh. On the return journey he called at Benwell and Elswick. The boatman that day was a swarthy, taciturn fellow he had never seen before and, apart from giving directions, William avoided any further conversation during the journey.

The river bustled with activity, even though the upper reaches were restricted to craft which could negotiate the low arches of the Tyne Bridge at Newcastle. In addition to the numerous fleets of keels, there were also a variety of wherries, lighters and barges and a profusion of small rowing boats including the ubiquitous "comfortables", as these small covered passenger boats were known.

It was late afternoon before William completed his business at Benwell. The boat took the North Channel past King's Meadow Island, where cattle grazed on the lush grassland, then headed for the shore. At the spouts serving Elswick colliery only one keel was moored at the staithes and there appeared to be no sign of activity. When William climbed up onto the deck of the staithes he found it deserted. A line of chaldron waggons loaded with coal stood parked on the rails that let across the deck, the first of them positioned near the large aperture of the spout.

William's puzzlement now turned to irritation and he called out, 'Hello!' There was no answer from the staithesman's hut where he assumed everyone had gone. 'Hello there!' he called again, and moved towards the hut. The buggers are resting in there, he thought, instead of working. He opened the door of the hut and stepped inside, but the hut appeared to be empty. A feeling of foreboding crept over him; something was wrong and he decided to get away as quickly as possible. As he turned to leave the hut, he sensed a movement behind the door. Before he could cry, out a sack was pulled over his head and his world was blacked out. He felt strong arms encircling his waist, pinioning him like some errant child, before he was lifted and carried outside the hut. All he heard was the sound of his captor's footsteps as he was carried across the deck of the staithe. He experienced the awful sensation of being upended and feeling his shoulders being pushed through some opening on the deck. Then, with a scream that was muffled by the sack over his head, William tumbled down the spout and landed with a sickening thud in the hold of the keel that was still moored alongside the staithe. As he lay unconscious the sack was quickly removed from his head.

On the staithe's deck shadowy figures emerged to join Rory, who stood in triumph over the spout entry. For a moment his resolve weakened, but as memories of his own long incarceration returned, his desire for revenge gained strength. He turned and, pushing the first chaldron waggon over the spout opening, pulled the bolt which released fifty-five hundredweight of coal to cascade down the chute into the hold of the keel, burying the now semi-conscious William in its painful, suffocating embrace. The men on deck then pushed the remaining chaldron waggons, aligning them one by one over the spout, before pulling the bolt. Ton by ton, the coal thundered down the chute and over the inert body of William until the keel had received its full load of twenty-one tons. It then cast off and drifted into the river to join the fleet of keels awaiting the ebb tide that would carry them downstream to the waiting colliers anchored at Shields.

Night had fallen over Shields harbour as the fleet of keels converged on the waiting collier brigs. Rory's keel made fast alongside a brig and the arduous task of casting, shovelling the coal from the keel into the hold of the brig, began. The shovellers sweated in the flaring light of the coal braziers that were hung from the brig's rigging to provide illumination. A cool, soothing breeze came in from the sea caressing the aching muscles of the keelmen as they toiled in steady rhythm. When the last coal had been shovelled through the gate in the collier's bulwarks, Rory gave the order to cast off. The keel began to drift into the darkness of the river and when it was well clear of the colliers, Rory lifted the crushed and blackened body of William on to the deck of the keel. After staring at the lifeless form for a moment he pushed it over the side into the river, where it floated away on the last of the ebb tide.

Two days later William's body was washed up on a beach further down the coast. His skin, scoured pale by the sea, was covered in black ringed abrasions which were a source of puzzlement to the authorities.

Mr Ivison was both concerned and puzzled by the sudden disappearance of his chief clerk. It was so out of character, he thought, for a man of William's precise habits and boring attention to detail, to vanish without a word of explanation. It was only when the body was found that he suspected something more sinister was afoot, though he refrained from saying so when he broke the news to a shocked and tearful Ellen.

Later that day, after dismissing the clerks early, he paused by William's desk on his way out. On a sudden impulse, he sat down and tried to open the top drawer of the desk, but it was locked. Typical of

296

William's thoroughness, he thought. His curiosity now increased and he returned to his own desk for William's office keys, which had been found on the body and returned to him by the authorities.

Making his way back to William's desk, he sat down and opened each drawer in turn, carefully searching through the contents of each. He found nothing unusual until he opened the last drawer and stared in astonishment at what lay there. The drawer was full of radical tracts and literature including Payne's "Rights of Man" and lying on top was a letter addressed to himself. The handwriting looked vaguely familiar.

Ivison took out the letter and opened it. He saw it was dated September 1797 and written by Henry. A lump came into his throat as he started to read it. It was a letter of apology, giving a full explanation of Henry's actions and his subsequent sudden departure from Newcastle five years ago. As he read, he began to appreciate that Henry's decision to leave had been an act of unselfish generosity, intended to avoid him any embarrassment during the aldermanic elections of that year. The letter was made all the more poignant by William's appalling betrayal. He put the letter down and thought of all the years during which he had been denied the talents and the company of a man he'd grown to love like his own lost son.

For a long time Ivison sat quietly contemplating events. Then finally he rose and placed the letter carefully in his pocket. He now knew what he had to do. He must find Henry and try to make amends for the injustice of the past five years. His instincts told him that Rory MacGregor would know where to look.

The uneasy peace with France that had lasted for just over a year was now showing signs of strain. War clouds were gathering and much resentment was directed at the French for not honouring the terms of the peace treaty signed at Amiens. The British Government who were beginning to regret their hasty run down of the army and navy, decided to take action.

In the second week of May, Lieutenant Frazere, a naval officer of the Impress Service living in Newcastle, opened his mail and began to read. *'In Pursuance of his Majesty's Order in Council, dated the twentieth Day of April, 1803, We do hereby impower and direct you to impress so many Seamen, Seafaring Men, and Persons whose occupations and Callings are to work in Vessels and Boats upon Rivers, as you shall be able, in order to serve on Board his Majesty's Ships, giving unto each Man so Impressed One Shilling for Press-Money. And, in the Execution hereof, you are to...*

It was an impressment warrant ordering a hot press to be carried out on the Tyne and Wear. A week later, Aldington's government rediscovered their resolution and declared a resumption of war with France.

The press gangs wasted no time swooping on Shields harbour, where scores of keelmen and other sailors were taken. In spite of all the protests and the herculean efforts of Rory, fifty-three keelmen were held for the Navy and sent to the receiving ship.

The coal owners and fitters were incensed by the Navy's cavalier attitude and took a hard line. A shortage of keelmen could cause havoc in the coal trade, and there had always been an unwritten understanding that keelmen would not be hounded by the press gangs.

A meeting was called to consider what action the coal owners and their fitters could take and Ivison made an unorthodox but ingenious suggestion which was immediately accepted. The following day, his message was delivered to Rory MacGregor, and within the hour the two men stood face to face,

'It's been a long time, Mr Ivison,' Rory said warily. 'I hope you've got something worthwhile to tell me.'

'I think I have, but first let me say that I had nothing to do with your arrest all those years ago.'

'No, but one of your employees did.'

'Yes, I realise that now but...' he paused and took out Henry's letter and passed it to Rory. 'I found this two weeks ago, locked in the drawer of my chief clerk's desk. It must have lain there since William intercepted it five years ago. I think you should read it.'

Rory took the letter and began to read. Gradually, his face darkened as the extent of William's double betrayal was revealed to him. 'He even betrayed his own brother-in-law. Why?'

'Jealousy, insecurity, who knows?'

'But his own kin! What sort of man does that?'

298

'I think he resented Henry being much cleverer than he was. He probably felt he was being pushed aside which, I suppose, in a way he was.'

Rory frowned. 'And here was I thinking Henry ran away to save his own skin, even though it was my fault for leading him on. Yet all the time he wasn't thinking of himself. He was trying to save your reputation.'

'Yes, I can see that now.'

'So what are you going to do about it?'

'Find him, with your help.'

'And then?'

'Bring him back to Newcastle.'

'To do some more clerking for you?' There was a faint note of scorn in Rory's voice.

'No. I owe him something better than that.'

'He'll no' take your charity, man.'

'I won't be offering him charity. It's a partnership I'm proposing and I'm offering it because he'll be an asset to the firm.'

Rory thought for a moment. 'Aye, he will that and he's earned it too.'

'Then you'll help me find him?'

Rory laughed. 'I'll do better than that. I'll introduce you when he comes to see me on Sunday.'

The surprise of Rory's statement left Ivison completely nonplussed. 'Then you've kept in touch with him all these years?'

'Aye. Henry's the sort of man you can rely on.' Seeing the hurt in Ivison's eyes he added gently, 'He had your best interests at heart, misguided though he was. You must remember that.'

Ivison nodded. 'Indeed, I will.'

Rory smiled. 'I'll see that you do,' but there was no threat in his voice.

'There is one other thing I'd like to discuss,' Ivison said, adopting a more serious tone.

'What would that be?' Rory's caution returned.

'It's to do with the keelmen.'

'You're no' asking me to mend my ways are you?'

It was Ivison's turn to smile. 'Now that would be something. No, I've got a proposition to put to you on behalf of the coal owners and fitters.'

This time it was Rory who was nonplussed. 'A proposition for me?'

'For you to put to the keelmen. I think you'll find it generous and to the keelmen's advantage.'

Rory was intrigued. 'Go on.'

'I understand that fifty-three keelmen were taken by the press this week.'

'Yes.'

'And the navy won't release them?'

'No. We asked them nicely and they refused. So our next request won't be so polite,' Rory said pointedly.

'I wouldn't advise you to take the law into your own hands, not with the navy.'

'Then what would you advise?'

'Offer to find substitutes if the keelmen are released.'

Rory laughed. 'And where would we find the money to pay for substitutes? It'll cost at least fifty pounds a man. '

'The coal owners and fitters will pay.'

Rory was astounded. 'On what conditions? That we behave ourselves and stop attacking the deep water spouts?'

'There are no conditions.'

Rory was surprised and bewildered. 'You're right, Mr Ivison. It is a generous offer.'

'Then you'll accept?'

'I'll put it to the men. I'm sure they'll agree, if there's no catch in it.'

'You have my word on that.'

'Yours is the only word I'd trust from an owner. You at least are a man of honour. I'm afraid I can't say the same for the others.'

The two men shook hands, knowing there was respect and trust between them. What Rory did not know was that Ivison was putting up most of the money himself.

CHAPTER 32

April, 1810

The war with France had now dragged on for seventeen years and the people of the Great Northern Coalfield were as disillusioned and war-weary as the rest of the population. But for the inhabitants of South Shields there was the prospect of some spectacular light relief to come when coal owner Simon Temple announced that the grand opening of his new colliery in the town would take place towards the end of April. Like the opening of his other major colliery at Jarrow, seven years previously, it would be an impressive affair, and invitations were sent to all the leading families in Northumberland and Durham.

The day itself dawned fine and the event was greeted with gun salutes and the ringing of bells. There was the customary festive procession of waggons to the coal staithes, accompanied by the band of the East York militia and watched by an excited crowd of onlookers. Then, at one o'clock, some one hundred and fifty gentlemen adjourned to nearby Hylton Castle and sat down to an excellent dinner. At eight o'clock, a grand ball commenced, attended by four hundred guests who included the social cream of the two counties. After a late supper, the dancing continued until nearly six in the morning. Clearly, the gentry were bearing up better under the strains of war than their less fortunate employees, whose energies had been sapped by the arduous conditions of the past year.

Henry and Mr Ivison joined the guests for dinner, but politely declined the invitation to the grand ball. They left Hylton Castle and returned to the river to catch a river boat that would take them back to Newcastle on the evening tide. They discovered they were the boat's only passengers for the journey.

'I'm getting too old for dancing,' Ivison said, sitting down and stretching his legs. 'But you should have gone, Henry. You might have met an attractive young lady,' he added mischievously.

'If you're too old for dancing then I'm past the age for attractive young ladies,' Henry parried. 'Besides, I don't dance and I've no social graces.'

'Is that a rebuke?' Ivison asked peevishly.

Henry smiled. 'No, of course not. But you're always hinting that I should make more effort to meet the fairer sex.'

'Well, Mary's been dead these past twelve years and you're still a comparatively young man.'

'I'm forty six,' Henry said patiently, 'and I'm beginning to feel it.' They had had this sort of discussion before.

'Young Ralph needs a mother's influence at this time in his life,' Ivison persisted.

'His Aunt Ellen has been a mother to him for seven years now. She dotes on him as if he was her own and he loves her too. He'd resent a stepmother.'

Ivison accepted defeat. 'I suppose you're right. Ellen's a wonderful woman and she's been a godsend since she came to live with us. Never could understand what she saw in William, though.'

'I think she loved him in her own way,' Henry said. 'It might have been different if they'd had children.'

'She got over his death quickly enough, just the same,' Ivison countered.

'Now you're being unkind to her. One minute you're full of praise, the next you disparage her. You're getting crotchety in your old age,' Henry reprimanded gently.

Ivison chuckled. 'You're right. I'm sorry.'

It was quite dark now and they sat in silence for a while, trying to pick out the shore lights as they continued their journey up river. Henry began to reflect on the events of the past seven years with a mixture of pleasure and sadness as he pondered on the cruel ironies of fate. The partnership with Ivison had rescued him from the misery and frustration of a pitman's life, but it had not brought him true happiness. His own salvation should also have been Mark's, and he recalled again the trauma of that fateful day when Mark had told him he was not leaving North Moor.

They had argued for hours but, to Henry's bewilderment, Mark had stood firm. He had pressed his son, asking for a reason but Mark, at first, had refused to give him one. Henry persisted. 'Why?' he had kept on asking. 'Just tell me why?' It was then that his bewilderment had turned to pain.

'Because there's a cause to be fought here that's worth more than the comforts of a safe calling in Newcastle.' The sword had struck deep and now the blade was turned. 'Without your help the men's spirit and resistance will crumble. All that's been built up will wither and die.' He had accused his father of surrendering his principles and running away.

'Is that a good reason for you to stay?' Henry had asked. 'You're only seventeen for goodness sake.'

'Age hasn't anything to do with it. Wilf and the men need help. If you won't stay then I must. I'll be starting as a hewer next month.'

Henry recalled again that final ultimatum as though it were yesterday, for the pain still lingered as a constant reminder. Deep down, he knew that he'd failed Wilf, Sep and the others, the very men who had never let him down even in his darkest hour of need. He recalled Wilf's inspiration and help on his first day down the North Moor pit and the support and companionship that he and the others had offered, unstinting and unasked. Yet in their own hour of need he'd been found wanting and had allowed a substitute to take his place. It didn't even cost him the proverbial thirty pieces of silver, but it had almost cost him a son. He stared morosely into the dark waters of the river, feeling the millstone of his guilt hanging even more heavily around his neck.

'I won't offer you a penny for them. By the look on your face they're not worth it.' Ivison's voice cut through his reverie.

I'm sorry,' Henry said sheepishly, 'I was thinking.'

'I can see that. Thinking of what?'

'Of Mark.'

Ivison sighed. 'That explains it.'

'Explains what?'

'That strange, haunted look on your face. I've seen it before and it worries me. It's as if you're still longing for something that, deep down, you know you've lost forever.'

Henry smiled. 'You're not so far from the truth.'

'I know, I've been there myself and I know the heartache. But let it go, Henry. It's the only way.'

'I can't, though God knows I've tried.'

'Mark still loves you. Can't you leave it at that?'

'No. I need his respect too. Without that our relationship is too fragile.'

Ivison frowned. 'Then I don't think I can help you.'

'You said you'd been there yourself?'

'Yes, but that was a long time ago.'

'Tell me,' Henry pleaded. 'It might help.'

Ivison looked at him for a while as if undecided, then shrugged. 'As I said, it was a long time ago. I'd been married, happily I thought, for eight years when my wife left me, taking our only son with her. I was too wrapped up in my business and she could no longer bear my neglect for my own family, however unintentional. When I found out it was too late to make amends. They were both dead, carried off by the smallpox, and I've been saying sorry in my heart ever since. Don't let that happen to you, Henry. You at least can still say sorry in person.'

Henry looked at his friend and mentor with a new, protective tenderness. He watched as a tear rolled slowly down the old man's cheek and felt his own eyes moisten in sympathy. 'The portrait...' he prompted, hesitantly. 'Is that why you keep it locked away most of the time? To stop you remembering?'

'I suppose so.' He sniffed, trying to hide his embarrassment.

'Then can I offer you some advice?'

'I can see you're going to anyway,' replied Ivison.

'Take the portrait out and put it in a place of honour where everyone can see it. Then perhaps we can both come to terms with our past and lay a few ghosts in our memories.'

Ivison smiled. 'Perhaps it's worth a try. It might not hurt so much now.'

It was nearly ten o'clock when the boat landed them at the steps leading up to the quayside at Newcastle. It began to rain as they came ashore. The few street lamps cast a feeble glow on the wet cobblestones as they hurried past the dark shapes of ships moored, sometimes three abreast, alongside the quay. The shadowy outlines of masts and rigging reached upwards before disappearing into the darkness of the night sky.

Once inside the house, they were greeted by Ellen and an excited Ralph who was impatient for an account of the day's events. Ellen

304

shushed the boy's questions. 'Let Mr Ivison and your father get out of their wet clothes first,' she chided gently. 'Then you can talk by the fire while I prepare some supper.'

They sat in the comfortable armchairs by the inglenook fireplace, watching the glowing coals as Henry recounted the day's events to his son. Ralph was approaching his twelfth birthday but he possessed a maturity beyond his years. He was tall for his age, with a slim figure that belied his growing strength. His hair was fine and dark but less curled than his father's had been at his age. The high cheek bones and clean-cut features were like those of a young patrician, but the humorous sparkle in the dark brown eyes showed no trace of arrogance. In a few years he would be categorised as a handsome, eligible and intelligent young man; the type much sort after by the more discerning mothers with daughters of marrying age.

From time to time, Ralph interrupted his father's account of the day's events to ask some deep and searching question. To Henry's surprise, most of these were directed at the technical and commercial aspects of Mr Temple's colliery venture, rather than the pomp and ceremony of the occasion. He began to realise that this was a reflection of the emphasis he had placed on some aspects of his son's education and of his careful selection of schools and tutors.

In the normal course of events Henry, like most successful merchants, would have opted to send his son to the Grammar School. However, these schools by law could only offer a classical education and this he did not want for his son. So Henry turned to the private academies that had sprung up to plug the gap in the market by offering a more rounded curriculum, designed to meet the needs of business and commerce. After careful thought, he chose Bruce's Academy in Percy Street, a school with a growing reputation run by a progressive visionary called John Bruce.

Although Ralph had received some grounding in Latin and was making good progress in the French language, he was now discovering a strong aptitude for mathematics and science where his insatiable curiosity made learning easy for him. However, his real talents lay in the application of maths and logic to business and economic matters, helped by a natural ability to argue his case. Even at this early age a latent entrepreneurial flair, that hungered to be given free rein, was apparent. It was an aspect of his son's character that Henry was beginning to appreciate, and he smiled with pleasure at the future possibilities.

After supper Ellen and Ralph retired to bed, leaving the two men to enjoy a glass of port. As they contemplated the dying embers of the fire, there was a long, contented silence before Ivison spoke. 'That boy's a credit to you. He's growing into a fine young man and I think he'll go far.' There was a note of quiet pride in his voice.

'I hope so,' Henry responded, pleased with the old man's compliment. 'I've tried to give him the best possible start in life by ensuring that he has a modern education that will be of some practical use.'

'Plus love, understanding and stability,' Ivison added pointedly .

Henry nodded, acknowledging Ivison's finely honed barb and the subtlety and accuracy of its delivery. He looked quizzically at the old man. 'Is that where I went wrong with Mark?'

'No. I think you gave him all those things, but...' He stopped, undecided.

'But what?' Henry prompted.

'Perhaps you weren't consistent enough with your feelings, or in the way that you expressed them. Perhaps you understand Ralph in a way that you never really understood Mark. Fathers rarely have exactly the same feelings and affinity for all their sons. There'd be fewer black sheep if that were so.'

'You're not suggesting that Mark's the black sheep of my family are you?'

'No, but there's a clash of minds between you that seems to create a barrier. There's something about Mark that puzzles and intrigues me and I'd love to know the answer. But one thing I do know is that he loves you in his own strange way, probably every bit as much as Ralph does.'

'He certainly has a peculiar way of showing it,' Henry said wryly. 'There are times when I almost despair of him.'

'Because you're on different sides of the fence now,' Ivison gently reminded him. 'We're also partners in two colliery ventures, so Mark sees you as an owner as well as a coal fitter. Remember we employ both miners and keelmen now, all subject to the annual bond.'

'Enlightened owners, I hope,' Henry rejoined. 'We don't abuse the men or tolerate excessive behaviour by the keekers in our pits. Not in the way the likes of Forster do.'

'No. But I doubt if you'll convince Mark that we're not out to exploit them. We're still part of a system that's led to the growing confrontation these past few years, and Mark has so far shown little sign that he's willing to compromise.'

'He has to carry all the men with him now, not just those of North Moor,' Henry said, trying to defend his son's actions. 'He's seen as the leader of all the pitmen on both the Tyne and Wear.'

'But he's antagonised the coal owners, especially the hardliners like Forster. They are insisting on January being kept as the new binding month and won't go back to October.'

Henry sighed. 'Then the men will withdraw their labour and we'll have a full-scale strike on our hands.'

Ivison shook his head. 'The owners will see it differently. In their eyes the men will be breaking the bond, as well as the Combination laws, if they act together. Mark my words, they'll prosecute and seek to imprison the men. '

'What! All of them?' Henry voiced his disbelief.

'No. They'll pick out the ringleaders first and that will certainly include Mark.'

'It's strange,' Henry said bitterly, 'that we as coal owners can invoke the Combination Act to stamp out any threat by a concerted action of the men. Yet we ourselves, as coal owners, can combine with impunity.'

'In what way, Henry.'

'We have our own Combination. We've had it these last five years since the Joint Durham and Northumberland Coal Owners Association was formed. We combine to control prices. We combine to control production by limiting the vend, even fining those owners who exceed their allocation. Worst of all, we combine to impose an annual bond on the men with ever harsher conditions. Do all these things not constitute a combination? If so, why are we not prosecuted?'

Ivison was taken aback by Henry's vehemence. 'I think you're placing a very literal interpretation on things, Henry. The Coal

307

Owners Association is purely a trade organisation, no different from a Guild.'

'It's a cartel,' Henry said flatly.

'I can see you won't be convinced,' Ivison said touchily. 'It's as well that I attend the Association meetings and not you.'

Henry realised he'd upset the old man by the fervour of his support for the pitmen rather than the owners. Yet, he himself was now an owner and he had happily accepted the advantages gained through being a member of the Coal Owners Association. He suddenly felt a fraud. 'I'm sorry,' he said, looking at Ivison. 'I suppose you think I'm a hypocrite, criticising the Association on the one hand whilst accepting the benefits with the other.'

Ivison smiled with relief. 'Put it down to being an enlightened owner. It's a hard cross to bear, but I'm glad we haven't fallen out over it.'

CHAPTER 33

Jane Hindmarsh was rapidly coming to the conclusion that her return to North Moor had not turned out to be the success she'd hoped for. She felt the frustration of her situation gnawing away inside her, strangling her customary light-hearted nature and making her feel depressed. Three months after starting work at North Moor Hall, she still felt a stranger and sensed a growing antagonism towards her from her colleagues below stairs.

It was all a far cry from the many happy years she had spent at Highfield Hall, she thought, and was now beginning to regret her decision to leave. Her only consolation was that she was nearer to Mark and her family. She was an attractive woman now, but Mark seemed so wrapped up in his work for the Brotherhood that she sometimes felt neglected. Yet he remained in her thoughts every day.

Mr Harker, the butler, and Mrs Binns, the cook, clearly resented her appointment as personal maid to Mrs Forster, particularly as they felt they had not been properly consulted as they would have been in a proper gentleman's household. They were also jealous of her friendship with Mrs Gordon, the housekeeper, who had been largely instrumental in obtaining the position for Jane.

'There'll be trouble with that one, mark my words,' the butler had announced darkly.

Cook sniffed in sympathy. 'Stuck up young madam she is. Thinks she's almost a lady herself 'cause she's got a bit of learning. Not one of us, that's for sure.'

Harker nodded sadly. 'I don't know what the mistress was thinking of, taking her on in the first place. She never asked for my opinion.'

'That randy Mister Roland's been eyeing her up, though,' Cook said mischievously. 'Fair drooling over her, he was.' Turning to Polly James she added, 'You'd better watch out for her, pretty Polly. Knock you off your perch she will.' She let out a shrill cackle of laughter as she saw the pun strike home.

'Stupid fat hag!' Polly shouted, and stormed out of the kitchen.

'You shouldn't have said that,' Harker admonished. 'Polly's got her talons into the girl already. The blood'll start flowing soon.'

'Mister Roland will have his last fling with both of 'em before he gets married next month, you'll see.' Her face broke into a bawdy grin at the thought.

'Mister Roland will have to learn to control his urges,' Harker said pompously.

'He'll have to stop messing on his own doorstep, that's for sure,' Cook responded crudely. 'He'll have to visit the Madam in Newcastle, like all the other young rakes do when they feel the urge coming on.'

Harker winced at Mrs Binns' coarseness and was about to reprimand her when Jane entered the kitchen. She was greeted with a frosty silence as she walked to the sink and put down the tray she was carrying. 'Mrs Forster's getting all worked up about the wedding arrangements,' she said brightly, trying to break the ice. There was no response. She tried again. 'I suppose it's only natural in the circumstances.' Then she stopped, acknowledging defeat.

Mrs Binns walked across to the cupboard at the other side of the sink and started to take out some baking dishes. She deliberately ignored Jane while she did this and then returned to the kitchen table, making an exaggerated show of being busy. At that point the bell rang and, looking up at the display panel above the kitchen door, Jane saw with relief that it was Mrs Forster who had rung. She ran quickly to the door and hurried upstairs.

As she entered the Hall, she saw Roland standing on the long gallery that joined the two staircases which swept down from the first floor. She slowed down, watching from the corner of her eye to see which staircase Roland was making for, then headed for the other. Roland spotted her move and dashed across to the other side, a look of triumph spreading over his face. This changed to a lecherous leer as he moved down the staircase towards her. He stopped, blocking her way. 'The charming and delectable Jane,' he said mockingly. 'You've been avoiding me, my dear, and that won't do.'

'I've been very busy, sir,' Jane said, trying to slide past him.

'Too busy to spare a moment for me?' He moved closer and she felt his hand on her thigh. 'My mother must be a martinet to keep you so heavily occupied. You need some relaxation.'

A mixture of fear and revulsion transfixed her for a moment. 'Please, sir, I must go,' she blurted, as she desperately tried to squeeze past him.

He saw the look of loathing in her eyes and knew she would never willingly be his. She wasn't like Polly or the others, but her rejection of him made him all the more determined to have her. By God she's beautiful, he thought. If she wouldn't come to him willingly, he'd have to go to her. He smiled at the prospect and stood to one side to let her pass. He watched her disappear in the direction of his mother's room and decided he'd have to act quickly, before his wedding became too much of an obstacle. Humming to himself, he ran down the staircase two steps at a time.

Unobserved at the other end of the gallery, Polly James watched the encounter on the stairs with mounting fury. She had long since accepted the inevitability of Roland's forthcoming marriage. There was little she could do about that. After all, his fiancé was a baronet's daughter and heiress to an estate that would add five thousand acres and three collieries to the Forster empire, so she'd been told. But she was plain and dull so Polly knew Roland would continue to need relief from what promised to be an extremely boring marriage. The question was, she asked herself, would he seek it from her or this new upstart? She would have been more confident if the new girl wasn't so damned beautiful.

She decided she couldn't just let the matter rest in the hope that things might end in her favour. She would have to act and do something to resolve her problem once and for all.

Over the next few days, Polly James redoubled her efforts to make life difficult for Jane. It was now open warfare and the servant's hall was full of intrigue as Polly enlisted the willing help of most of the other servants. Jane suddenly found that things she needed for Mrs Forster would mysteriously disappear without explanation. Trays of food, which she had painstakingly prepared for her mistress, inexplicably became contaminated, usually with dead flies or insects which, in other circumstances, might be seen as unfortunate accidents. But she knew they weren't. She could tell by the cruel shrieks of laughter that

311

followed her when, driven to despair, she ran sobbing from the kitchen to escape her tormentors.

Fortunately, Mrs Forster had taken a strong liking to her new maid and this, together with the support and protection of Mrs Gordon, the housekeeper, made Jane's position almost unassailable. Polly slowly began to recognise this and decided that more drastic measures were called for. In time, her innate cunning and devious opportunism would find a way, and she had long since learned the art of waiting for the right moment.

That moment eventually came on the day a grand dinner party was held at North Moor Hall. It was a day that would trigger momentous events and cast long, tragic shadows into the future.

Jane was on her way to the seamstress's room to collect Mrs Forster's dress, which was having a small alteration made in readiness for the evening's festivities. As she entered the corridor which led to the bedrooms in the west wing of the house, she saw Polly staggering under a pile of bedding and linen sheets which swayed violently from side to side. At that moment, Polly seemed to trip and the pile of bedding tumbled to the floor in an untidy heap. Jane moved forward to help, warily at first, expecting a refusal. To her surprise, Polly smiled up at her from where she knelt. 'Can you help me pick this lot up?'

'Of course.' Jane knelt down beside her.

'I'm a right butterfingers,' Polly said.

'Me too,' Jane responded, pleased that Polly hadn't rejected her. 'Where're you taking this lot?'

'In here.' Polly opened the door that led into a large bedroom and Jane followed her inside.

'Is this for one of the guests? Jane asked.

'Sort of,' Polly replied, evasively. There was a thin smile of triumph on her face. 'Put the bedding down there,' she said, indicating where she'd placed her own pile of sheets and blankets.

Jane did so. 'Do you want any help to change the bed?' She was now eager to consolidate this new and unexpected friendship.

'In a moment. I just need to collect a few more things first. Shan't be long.' With that, Polly left the room, closing the door quickly behind her. She paused, looking up and down the corridor before taking a key from her pocket. Then she turned and gently and quietly locked the door leaving the key in the lock. She walked back to the gallery at the head of the twin staircase and saw Roland watching from the hall. He flashed her a villainous smile as he acknowledged her signal and, as Polly descended one staircase, he bounded quickly up the other.

Jane examined the bedroom with interest. It was clearly a man's bedroom, judging by the number of masculine objects scattered around and the faint aroma of brandy and tobacco. She was more familiar with the other wing of the house where Mr and Mrs Forster had their rooms, and she'd avoided the west wing because of ...a stab of fear ran through her ...because of Roland! As her thoughts began to crystallise, she knew this must be his room. She began to panic and ran to the door, but found it locked. She twisted and pulled frantically at the handle with growing alarm. Where was Polly? Why had she locked her in? Suddenly, she heard footsteps coming along the corridor. The sounds stopped outside the door and she backed away, trembling with apprehension. She froze as she heard the key twisting in the lock and saw the handle slowly begin to turn. The door opened and Roland stood there, framed and smiling, the excitement of his lecherous intent gleaming in his eyes. 'Well, Well!' he leered. 'What a pleasant surprise.' He moved inside the door, closing it firmly behind him.

'I'm just waiting for Polly, sir,' Jane blurted out nervously, as she backed further away.

Roland followed her. 'My word, what a succulent young morsel you are, my dear. Are you my special hors d'oeuvre for this evening?'

'No, Sir. I was just...' She broke off as he lunged at her, and turned to run. Roland laughed as he caught her by the shoulder and spun her round.

'Please, sir!' Jane gasped, struggling to fight him off. But he ignored her pleas and pushed her towards the bed, tearing at her dress as he did so.

'I like a woman with a bit of spirit,' he said. 'Makes for good sport, but don't overplay your hand.' He bent down and tried to kiss her, but she turned away and twisted out of his grasp. Feeling herself free, she ran to the door, opened it and almost collided with Polly, who had been listening outside. Jane ignored her and fled downstairs to the kitchen, rearranging her dress as she ran.

When Roland recovered he cursed and followed her through the doorway, only to find Polly barring his way. She smiled seductively. 'Let's go back inside,' she cooed. 'I have a special tasty treat that will please you.'

Roland ignored her invitation. 'Out of my way, you stupid wench,' he roared and flung her violently against the wall. 'You're not on the menu today,' he added viciously before following after Jane.

Polly leaned weakly against the wall, dazed and perplexed at the turn of events. It wasn't meant to be like this, she thought. She had expected that Roland would have his way with Jane, as he had done with all the others. She had also assumed that, in due course, Jane would become pregnant, just as all the others had, and be forced to leave. Then, Roland would have been hers again. It had all seemed so simple at the time. But she had misjudged Jane she realised. She wasn't like the others.

When Jane reached the kitchen, she was relieved to see that cook and two of the kitchen-maids were busily preparing the food for the special dinner that evening. The aroma from the pans simmering on the kitchen range and the presence of other people reassured her and calmed her fears. She felt a wave of tiredness pour over her and sank down on a chair, thankful to have escaped Roland for the present but worried for the future. Mrs Binns shot her a quizzical glance before carrying on with her work.

Suddenly, the kitchen door burst open and Roland came staggering in and moved across to block Jane's line of escape. He screamed over his shoulder at Cook and her startled maids, 'Get out, all of you!' Cook and the maids scurried off quickly. Roland was noted for his tantrums, especially when he'd been drinking, but they'd never seen him like this before. He was like a man possessed and Cook decided that something terrible was about to take place. She quickly ushered the two frightened maids out of the kitchen and ran to tell Mrs Gordon what was happening.

Roland advanced menacingly towards Jane, his eyes wild with lust, his breathing rasping with pent-up excitement. Jane quickly backed away until she had the large kitchen table between them. Slowly, they circled the table, eyeing each other with fierce intensity; the hunter stalking his prey, moving in remorselessly for the kill.

Suddenly, Roland dived across the table with a speed that took Jane by surprise. She tried to run but he caught her in a vicious grip and pulled her towards him. 'Got you, my little beauty. Quite the vixen, aren't you, he growled, his hands again tearing at her dress. Jane saw the cruel intent in his eyes and knew she had to escape or risk being violently raped. She made one more frantic effort and broke away, running between the table and the kitchen range towards the door. Roland followed, pausing only long enough to snatch a pan of simmering stock from the range, before continuing the chase.

With mounting hysteria Jane fumbled at the door handle. Glancing over her shoulder she saw Roland poised, with the pan in his outstretched hand, ready to throw the boiling contents at her head. 'You won't be so pretty when I've finished with you,' she heard him scream. He moved a step closer and she could only stand, paralysed with fear, as she watched the pan begin its arc of deadly destruction.

Without warning, the kitchen door burst open knocking Jane to one side. Polly walked into the kitchen and, too late, tried to turn away. She let out an agonised scream as the side of her face took the full, scalding contents of the pan.

CHAPTER 34

Mark returned home after a long day visiting pits in the lower Tyne basin. He was tired but elated, as he sank contentedly onto his bed and lay with hands clasped behind his head. His euphoria stemmed from his successful negotiations with the leaders of the pits he had visited that day, and similar discussions with other pits which he had visited in the preceding weeks. He now had thirty-one pits firmly committed to the Brotherhood and all determined to act in concert to refuse a January binding. If the owners would not agree to revert to the traditional binding month of October, then every pit would stop work. There were also other demands that would be put to the owners at the same time.

It had taken seven years of hard work, persuasion and often disappointment, to get this far. He now felt vindicated and extremely proud of the Brotherhood that had been created largely through his own untiring efforts, with the loyal support of Wilf and Sep. At last, he had an organisation he could lead through the elected delegates from each of the thirty-one pits who were members of the Brotherhood. Decisions could now be made quickly at meetings of the delegates, knowing that word would be passed back to each pit. For the first time they could act together swiftly and strike hard in unison if it came to a fight. And in his heart he knew that, sooner or later, it would come to that and the battle would be hard and bitter.

Already Mark was paying the price for his vision of the future. He was now a marked man, blacklisted by the owners. This had become clear at the last binding, when pit after pit refused to have his name on the bond. He'd been forced to take up his father's offer of financial support, so that his dream of a united brotherhood of pitmen could be realised. But, he accepted only what he would have earned as a hewer and felt no qualms in taking from one owner, albeit his father, what the other owners had unjustly denied him. He'd moved out of the Hindmarsh's pit cottage at North Moor, to avoid endangering Wilf and his family and now rented a small, run down farm cottage nearby.

His new home consisted of a single, large living room with a lean-to scullery attached to the rear. A ladder led to a dusty, cobwebbed loft. The living room contained only a table, two chairs, a single bed and a chest of drawers which served to emphasise the sparsity. The lack of comfort was compensated by an excellent fireplace complete with range with ample fuel supplies provided by his friends at North Moor colliery.

As Mark contemplated the struggles of the past few years and the way in which the small successes had always seemed to be followed by disappointments, he was thankful for one piece of good fortune. Jane's decision, three months previously to return to North Moor meant that he now saw her at least once a week, instead of the fleeting, monthly visits he had had to accept during the years she had worked in Highfield Hall. He had always been especially fond of Jane but, over the years, his passionate quest to unite the pitmen had absorbed all his time and energies. By the time he realised he was in love with her, he felt it was too late to burden her with a proposal of marriage. He could not ask her to share his precarious existence, which was becoming more tenuous with each month that passed.

His response was to bottle up his desires and feign a close brotherly type of love in an attempt to hide his true feelings. Perhaps one day, he thought, he would tell her the truth; tell her how much he had always loved her, but not yet. Perhaps by then she would be married to someone else. After all, she was twenty-two now and very beautiful. His stomach turned cold at the thought and he desperately tried to dismiss the prospect from his mind.

The knowledge that he would be seeing her again on the next day revived his flagging mood. As his depression began to ease and as a little of Cupid's optimism crept in and he vowed he would try to see more of Jane from now on. Who knows, he thought, what the future might bring.

Jane knew she could never return to North Moor Hall. There was an evil in Roland that terrified her and the thought of meeting him ever again filled her with dread.

'You haven't eaten much,' Dora chided as she saw Jane's food remained almost untouched.

'I'm not hungry, mam. I keep thinking of poor Polly.'

317

'It wasn't your fault the girl got scalded. The gentry at the hall think they can do as they wish with the likes of us.'

I'm not going back, mam.'

'You're still upset, pet. You'll feel different in the morning.'

'No I won't.' Jane was adamant. Dora looked at her in surprise. 'You're serious then?'

'Yes.'

Dora sensed her daughter's unease. 'There's something else, isn't there? Something's troubling you?'

'Yes.' Jane stared at her food feeling the embarrassment welling up inside her.

'That Mr Roland?' Dora persisted. 'Has he been bothering you?'

'He won't leave me alone, Ma. The tears began to form and she wiped them away angrily with the back of her hand.

'Aye, I can see why. You're a beautiful bairn, but you're not like the others. He should have seen that.'

'He thinks we're all the same,' she answered bitterly. 'Thinks he just has to click his fingers for any servant girl to come running. And when we don't...' she broke off, trying to eradicate the trauma that was still fresh in her mind .

Dora remained silent for a while as she grappled unhappily with a problem that was beyond her. Then she sighed, her mind made up. 'Aye, pet. I think you're right. There is no going back.'

'Can I stay here for a bit, then?'

'Of course you can, pet. You can stay as long as you want, till you sort yourself out, like.'

Jane got up and hugged her. 'Thanks, mam. I'll do the washing and help you keep house.'

Dora smiled. 'Oh aye, you will that, lass. Three men in the house take a bit of looking after, believe you me. But Wilf will be pleased to see you back home. Got a soft spot for you he has, so mind you don't go telling him too much about...' she paused in embarrassment, 'about Mr Roland's goings on. You know how worked up he gets about these sort of things, and he's got no time for the Forsters.'

'I won't, mam, I promise.'

'Does Mark know you're not going back?'

'No. I wasn't sure myself until now.'

'You'd better tell him, then.'

'I will, tonight. I'm meeting him at the cottage.'

'See that you do, pet. He's got an even bigger soft spot for you than Wilf.' Dora had always hoped that Jane and Mark would marry one day. For the life of her, she could not understand why it had not happened already, but she lived in hope.

Mark listened with growing indignation and horror as Jane recounted the events that had taken place at North Moor Hall. His indignation gave way to outright anger when she told him of Polly's scalding. 'Bloody coal owners!' he fumed. 'Think they can treat everybody like cattle. And the Forsters, don't even have the excuse that they're gentry, though by God they do their best to ape them. At least gentry know no better, though it doesn't excuse them either. But the Forsters were once pit folk like us.'

'Not anymore,' Jane said. 'Roland's set to marry a baronet's daughter.'

'Aye, for her money and family connections,' Mark countered scathingly. 'But the true gentry will still laugh at them behind their backs. If Russell can't get accepted after all the money he's made out of Wallsend colliery, then what hope have they?'

'They say the Russell's live in great style since they bought Brancepeth Castle and the estates from Sir Henry Vane Tempest,' Jane said, proud of the gossip she'd picked up during her years in service.

'True, but Russell's son was rejected by the Durham voters when he stood for parliament ten years ago. The old landed classes saw to that. Even old man Russell's fortune couldn't buy his son that seat. Had had to buy another pocket borough in the end.'

'Why do the old gentry hate the likes of Forster?' Jane asked. It was something she had always thought of as odd.

'They don't hate them; they merely despise them which in a way, I suppose, is worse. But the impoverished old families are content enough to marry new money if there's no alternative.' Mark had watched with contempt as the increasingly wealthy coal owners sought to make their wealth respectable by buying country estates and marrying up the social scale.

319

'Then I suppose Mr Roland's made a good match,' Jane said thoughtfully. 'He's marrying into money as well as a good family.'

'It would seem so,' Mark replied, slightly perplexed. 'But the chances are that by the time his wife inherits, the Forster estates will still be mortgaged to the hilt.'

Jane sighed. 'It must be nice to have a future to look forward to, just the same.'

Mark looked at her and felt a tender and familiar yearning stirring inside him. He suddenly realised how beautiful she was and how much he loved her. But then again, he experienced that perverse reticence which always seemed to intervene when he felt like this, a strange inner battle which, in the end, always stopped him from telling her his true feelings. Was he afraid of rejection? Had they become too much like brother and sister? His thoughts made him feel depressed and apprehensive. One day he would lose her.

Jane's voice penetrated his melancholy. 'Why so sad? You look as though you're carrying all the cares of the world on your shoulders.'

Mark smiled. 'I sometimes feel as if I am.'

'Well, looking miserable doesn't help. I found that out a long time ago.'

He looked at her with new respect and understanding. He realised how lonely and miserable her life must have been over the past few years, yet her cheerful optimism and bubbly spirit had always shone through. It made him feel guilty and ashamed. 'What are you going to do with your life, Jane?' He asked. 'You won't go back to North Moor Hall, will you?'

'No, I shan't do that. But there doesn't seem to be any alternative. I can't stay with my mam forever.'

'You could get married.'

'Yes, if somebody would ask me.

'You could marry me.' It slipped out before Mark realised he had said it.

An emotional shockwave struck Jane as the implication of Mark's unexpected words registered in her mind. She looked at him in surprise. 'Is that a proposal?'

'I suppose it is,' Mark said after a bewildered pause.

An impish urge suddenly took hold of her. 'Sounds more like an afterthought to me.'

'No it isn't,' he answered quickly, a slight sense of guilt creeping over him. 'I think, deep down, I've always wanted to marry you.'

'You have a funny way of showing it, Mark. I don't even know if you love me,' she added coyly.

Mark panicked. 'But I do. You....you must know that,' he stammered.

'You've never told me so before.'

'I'm telling you now.'

Jane tried hard to look serious and suppress the happiness that welled up inside her. 'This is not how I imagined a proposal of marriage would be.'

'How did you imagine it?' Mark asked anxiously.

A mischievous smile crept over Jane's face. 'Oh, I thought the man would first of all go on his knees…'

Mark was instantly on his knees in front of her. 'And then?'

'He would ask me properly, with sincerity and looking into my eyes as he said it.'

He looked up nervously. 'Jane, will you marry me?'

'Oh Mark! You make it sound so casual, like asking me the time of day. Have you no romance in your soul?' She was struggling hard now to keep her face straight.

'Please Jane, will you marry me?' he implored.

The mischief gave way to laughter. 'Of course I will, you silly fool.' Then, looking rapturously into his eyes she said, 'What took you so long, Mark?'

'I don't know,' he replied, a look of happy bemusement lighting up his face. 'I suppose I was afraid you'd say no.'

Jane's eyes sparkled. 'Idiot! As if I would.'

A pensive look returned to Mark's face. 'You do realise that I can't offer you much of a future now that I've been blacklisted by the owners and their viewers?'

'Oh yes, you can,' she retorted. 'I think you're very special and so must the owners if they've made you a marked man. That's a good enough future for me.'

'I suppose we could seek a new life elsewhere,' Mark said. 'America, perhaps,' he added hesitantly.

Jane looked aghast. 'And abandon the Brotherhood? After all you've achieved?'

'Wilf and Sep could carry on.'

'Not without you, Mark. It's your vision and leadership that holds the Brotherhood together. Without you it will slowly wither and die. In your heart you must surely know that?'

Mark looked uncomfortable. 'Yes, but...'

'But what? That being married to me will hinder you? Is that what you're saying?'

'No.

'Then why the doubt? Don't you believe in what you're doing any more?'

'Of course I do.'

'Then you must carry on, Mark. For your own peace of mind and for the sake of all those men who believe in you, who look to you for a better future. If you give up now it will only lie on your conscience. It will be like a cloud constantly hanging over us. I don't want that, Mark.'

'Neither do I.'

'Then there must be no more talk of giving up the Brotherhood.'

'If that's what you really want.'

'It is, Mark,' she answered fervently. 'You can achieve great things if you want to. I just know you can.'

'No, Jane,' he corrected, gently taking her into his arms and burying his face into her soft, golden hair. 'I can't do great things any more, not on my own. But with you I can, if you really believe in me.'

She looked up at him, her eyes shining. 'Of course I do, Mark, and I always will. I wouldn't marry you if I thought any other way.

Mark held her tightly as an unexpected feeling of guilt threatened to overwhelm him. He suddenly realised that he had been ready to walk away from the Brotherhood for the sake of Jane and their future happiness together. Ready to betray the men for greater security for himself and a more comfortable lifestyle. That was the very same betrayal he had so bitterly accused his father of all those years ago. He felt a complete fraud.

Jane noticed the change in Mark and saw the distant look of anguish in his eyes, like a sudden shadow on a summer day. 'A penny for your thoughts?' she said softly.

The request startled him out of his reverie. 'Oh, it's nothing, really,' he said vaguely.

Jane quickly sensed the evasion and looked up into his eyes. 'Please, Mark, no lies. No secrets between us. Not now, not ever,' she added pleadingly.

He sighted resignedly. 'I feel so guilty, that's all.'

'Why?'

'I suppose I've just realised what a complete charlatan I am.'

Jane smiled in disbelief. 'In what way may I ask?'

'Because I've been living a lie, telling myself that the Brotherhood was the only purpose in life that really mattered to me, its success my only worthwhile ambition. And now I'm suddenly confronted with the truth. I was prepared to walk away and leave the men to fend for themselves. My only thought was to protect our own future.'

'Isn't that a natural reaction for a man suddenly faced with the responsibilities of marriage?'

'No. I was being selfish, putting our own future happiness before the interests of the men.'

'But we will be happy, Mark, and you will still lead the Brotherhood. That's what I want; what we both want, surely?'

Mark smiled ruefully. 'Yes, I know that now. But seven years ago I accused someone of betraying a sacred trust and now, after all these years, I suddenly find myself prepared to do exactly the same.'

'Was that someone your father?'

Mark hung his head. 'Yes,' he muttered.

'I thought so,' Jane said, pulling him close to offer comfort. 'I'm glad you finally told me.'

Mark looked surprised. 'You knew already.'

'No, I only guessed. Is that why you see so little of him?'

'Yes.'

'He must feel very hurt. You were so very close, once.'

'I suppose we were.'

'Tell me what happened, Mark. All of it. I'd really like to know.'

323

He smiled down fondly at her eager, upturned face. 'It's a long and complicated story, Jane. I promise I'll tell you all about it, but not now. There's a meeting of the Brotherhood at the Chapel tonight. I promised Wilf and Sep I'd be there, and there's something else I must do.'

Jane spoke firmly. 'I really do want to know, Mark. It's important to me. Important to us.'

'Yes, I know.'

'Then I won't let you forget. Remember, no secrets.'

'No secrets,' he agreed, taking her in his arms.

They kissed, tenderly at first as if in disbelief at their sudden good fortune; then with a fierce passion as their smouldering love finally burst into flame, quickly overcoming any remaining doubts or inhibitions.

The setting sun was low in the sky when Mark left the cottage and headed for North Moor village. It was warm for late Spring and the faint scent of newly scythed grass hung in the still, evening air. As he approached the village he could see the colourful mass of blossom on the fruit trees that rose behind the high stone walls surrounding the vicarage and the adjoining orchard.

Passing through the lychgate, he entered the churchyard and skirted round the ivy-clad, stone church until he reached the main burial ground at the back. Here, a path lined with green elms and purple hued copper beeches, wound its way past the grassy mounds of graves and moss-hung tombstones.

When he reached his mother's grave, he smiled as he caught sight of the bunch of fresh wild flowers placed at the foot of the marble headstone. Dora was still making her regular visits, he thought, then his smile faded as twinges of shame seeped into his conscience. His own visits, he realised, had gradually become less frequent as his work with the Brotherhood made ever increasing demands on his time.

He squatted on his haunches gazing at the headstone in deep contemplation. He hoped his mother would approve of his plans to marry Jane. At least she would be happy that he was at last out of the pit, the pit she had always hated. It was ironic, he mused, that it was his black-listing by the owners that had finally allowed his father to redeem his broken promise.

The rays from the dying sun were casting long shadows across the churchyard and in the distance, the soft trilling of a turtle dove could be heard. But Mark was oblivious to the sound and remained motionless by the grave, his mind travelling back in time, harvesting memories from the past.

Things had never been quite the same after they had left Newcastle, he recalled. The quarrels had started then. Real quarrels; not the commonplace and quickly forgotten disagreements that had been there before. Even later when they had settled down in North Moor Colliery, the ostensibly happy family atmosphere often seemed threatened by some hidden tension lurking in the background. He wondered if the seeds of his estrangement from his father had been sown then.

The sun had now sunk beneath the horizon and a cool breeze brushed gently over the churchyard grass like a fond caress. Mark shivered and stood up to stretch his aching limbs. It was almost dark but the white marble headstone still glistened in the dewy dusk. On impulse, he stooped down and lightly kissed the stone.

'I still miss you, mother,' he whispered. 'Rest in peace.'

As he rose, he reflected on his father's last tender gesture; the beautiful headstone and the bribe to the sexton in order to secure her a special plot in the churchyard. At least her final resting place was among the families of yeomen farmers and the like, well away from reminders of the pit life she had always hated. That would have pleased her, he thought, and he felt himself warming towards his father. Perhaps now was the time to start healing old wounds.

It was quite dark when he left the churchyard and made his way towards North Moor Colliery for his meeting with Wilf and Sep. As he passed the wrought iron gates guarding the entrance to North Moor Hall, he noticed that coloured lanterns had been hung in the trees lining the long drive leading up to the house. Preparations for Roland's wedding were clearly well advanced.

Jane had told him that over three hundred guests had been invited and there would be music and dancing after the sumptuous wedding feast. He had a vision of smart carriages sweeping up the drive to the portico of the house where they would be met by liveried footmen in powdered wigs. He imagined the old hall, brilliantly illuminated for the occasion, pulsating to music and dancing until the early hours of the morning.

He smiled and moved on. His own wedding would be a much more modest affair, he mused; positively spartan compared to Roland's. But at least his would be a marriage of true love and not a marriage of convenience to secure more money and power. And Jane was beautiful, too.

He felt more at home when he reached North Moor Colliery, despite all the drabness and poverty which now surrounded him. He made his way to the new shaft and stood in the shadows, just out of range of the blazing braziers illuminating the pithead. For Wilf and Sep's sake, he did not want any news of his visit to the Colliery to reach the ears of Forster.

He watched as the new steam winding engine drew three fully laden corves to bank and realised just how large the pit had grown since he had first gone underground. The old water driven engine could only draw one loaded corfe at a time, he recollected.

Forster must have made a fortune, he thought, but none of this wealth had been shared with the pitmen, who helped produce it. It was the same sorry tale throughout the Great Northern Coalfield of Northumberland and Durham, but the Brotherhood would one day change all that, he determined.

Suddenly, he heard the familiar cry of kenner echoing down the shaft. He could almost sense the relief of those still toiling below as the call would be taken up and passed on through the workings. Most of those still underground would be trapper boys, some as young as six, and putters barely into their teens. The hewers, mainly older men, would have finished their shift hours ago.

Soon the first group of men and boys were being drawn up clinging to the chains attached to the end of the winding rope in a precarious black cluster as they emerged from the shaft. He saw tired, red rimmed eyes and white teeth glistening from blackened faces, accentuated by the dancing light from the braziers. Some of the younger boys stumbled with exhaustion, almost asleep on their feet after their sixteen hour shift below.

Mark knew that most of them would be carrying injuries, many with their bodies lacerated from the jagged roofs and walls of tunnels cut too narrow and too low in order to save money. Accidents were a daily occurrence and accepted with a stoicism that had always amazed him.

His anger rose as he contemplated their future. Within twenty years, these boys would be pigeon-chested and bow-legged like their fathers, their growth stunted by long hours working in impossibly cramped conditions in the glimmer of a single candle. Many would inevitably suffer from the eye and lung diseases that were endemic to coalmining communities like North Moor.

It was a grim prospect, he thought; a life of squalor, injury, disease and an early death. A life of bondage, tied to a coal owner and slave to the whims of a ruthless viewer and his keeker. A life of constant danger, made worse by the greed and callousness of owners like Forster.

'No!' he suddenly cried out as his anger flared again. 'There has to be a better way.' He stood, clenching his fists in sheer frustration.

His involuntary outburst left him feeling slightly ridiculous and exposed. He turned and began to walk back to the village, cautiously keeping to the shadows. He knew the answer was now in his own hands and in the hands of men like Wilf and Sep. The future lay with the Brotherhood. It would require patience, strict discipline and involve many sacrifices. But, in time, it would bring about the desired changes and create a new and better world for the men.

Suddenly his heart felt lighter. He had a cause worth fighting for and hope for the future. Soon, he would be married to the woman he loved and who loved him. She was someone who would always be there when he needed her and who would bring happiness and stability to his life.

He would also make his peace with his father, something he now found himself looking forward to. A roguish smile crossed his face. Perhaps one day he would make Henry a proud grandfather.

As he headed towards the chapel for his meeting, he thought of his friends. Of Wilf and Sep whose loyalty and support had been a tower of strength since his blacklisting. Of Rory and Colin who had championed his cause and had always provided a safe haven in

Sandgate when he visited the pits on the Tyne. Of young Jed who was like a brother to him, more so than Ralph, his own kin. And there was Dora who had unstintingly filled the enormous emotional gap left after his mother died. With friends like these the future could only be a bright one.

He squared his shoulders and struck out towards the chapel, his step firm and his determination renewed.

CHAPTER 35

The summer months brought a new dimension to Mark's life. He experienced happiness and contentment beyond anything he'd ever felt before. As his love for Jane grew he cursed himself for the wasted years of self-doubt and his past failures to face up to his true feelings for her. But all this was behind him now. He was a man reborn through love and he worked with a new found zest which surprised everyone.

Jane brought a woman's delicate touch to the cottage, adding a bright new homeliness to the previously drab interior. Curtains appeared at the windows, flowers decorated the once spartan living room and a cheerful patchwork quilt soon added warmth and colour to the matrimonial four-poster. The impressive bed and a fine mahogany dresser, wedding presents from Henry and Mr Ivison, gave a touch of elegance to the otherwise humble cottage.

But this brief, idyllic period in their lives was soon to be threatened by the gathering conflict around them. The dark clouds of strife began to mass ominously when the coal owners decided to change the annual binding date to January. This was the quietest time of the year for the coal trade because bad weather seriously interrupted coal shipments by sea to the prime London and continental markets. This created severe problems for the owners in maintaining steady coal production in their pits.

The pitmen, led by Mark and the Brotherhood, were equally adamant that the traditional binding of October, the busiest time of the year, should be retained. As October approached, with still no sign of a breakthrough, so the tension remorselessly increased.

The first real test of Mark's leadership came when he called a meeting of delegates from all the thirty-one pits supporting the Brotherhood. As he set off to walk the seven miles to Newcastle, accompanied by Wilf and Sep, the first seeds of doubt began to grow in his mind. Could he really lead the men to victory, he wondered, if it came to a fight? He knew there was a deep anger that had spread to every pit in the northern coalfield, but was he the man to harness it to their cause? Could he take the aspirations of a largely uneducated, inarticulate group of men and focus them into a united struggle against the owners? Could he give them their self-respect and a ray of hope for the future? Could he convince the other leaders from the Durham pits? Or was his new found happiness with Jane making him go soft through fear of the risks involved? All these questions and self-doubts he pondered as he walked his own personal road to Damascus.

'Feeling all right, Mark? Wilf asked anxiously. 'You're looking very glum.'

Mark gave a startled smile. 'Yes. I was just thinking over what I should say to the men.'

'Well put a better face on it,' Wilf advised. 'They'll need all the confidence they can get if it comes to a fight.'

'But am I the one to give it to them, Wilf?'

His companions stopped in surprise. 'You've given the men organisation and leadership,' Sep said earnestly. 'You can't stop now, Mark. The men need you, they believe in you. You've given them faith and they'll follow you to the ends of the earth.'

'Or to an even greater hell than the one they know now,' Mark countered. 'It won't be pleasant if it comes to a fight, we all know that.'

'There's nothing lost if we fail,' Wilf argued. 'Didn't some philosopher say that it was better to try and fail than not to try at all?'

'Philosophers are very rarely called upon to demonstrate their theories. If they were they would probably be a lot less to quote from,' Mark answered sardonically.

'You've demonstrated your own theories,' Wilf persisted. 'You've given the men a cause and a leader they can respect. Above all, you've given them hope. Don't desert them now, Mark.'

Mark looked at his two friends and knew they were right. There was no turning back, no running away as his father had done. He forced a smile. 'I suppose you're right. If they'll follow my ideals to the ends of the earth, then I'd better bloody well lead them there myself!'

Wilf slapped him on the back. 'They will, bonny lad, they will. You can take my word on it.'

The meeting that took place that afternoon was a triumph for Mark, though not without some initial hiccups from a few wavering delegates. 'Why can't we stay with the January binding?' asked a querulous delegate from one of the Lambton pits.

'Because it suits the owners,' Mark replied. 'In January most of the collier brigs can't sail because of the weather. So what happens?' He paused to let his next words sink in. 'The pits are laid up aren't they? And when the pits are laid up there's no rush to bind any men. That way the owners don't have to pay for idle time when we're laid off and there'll be precious little binding money on offer.

'The owners say they'll keep their word and bind any man who wants to work,' the Lambton man insisted.

A groan of derision greeted this and there was a growing feeling that the Lambton man had been planted by the owners. 'Since when did the owners ever keep their word?' Wilf shouted.

'Only when it suits them,' Sep yelled, joining in the cat calls.

'That's true,' Mark said raising his arms for quiet. 'In October the London market needs all the coal it can get and the prices are usually high. We all know that high prices means greedy owners, so we have a stronger case if the binding is held in October, like it always was. It'll mean better binding money, too.'

There was a roar of approval and Mark knew he'd carried the day. 'All those in favour of an October binding,' he shouted. A sea of hands was raised. 'Then I say the motion is carried,' he declared to the wildly cheering men.

After the meeting had been formally closed, Mark joined Wilf and Sep for a glass of ale and a pie whilst he chatted to some of the delegates.

Later, the three friends set off for North Moor, Wilf and Mark slightly the worse for wear, having eaten and drank too much. Sep admonished them on the evils of over indulgence keeping up a running commentary of chastisement as they made their way home through Newcastle.

They were passing the Cattle Market when Wilf spotted the public necessary. 'I need to go,' he said abruptly.

The others also felt the need. 'Must have been the pies,' Sep muttered as he followed Wilf and Mark inside. As they squatted down on the five hole bench of the privy, an old woman trader came in and said, 'My apologies gentlemen, but I've been caught out. And them as is needful cannot be mindful.' With that she hitched up her skirt and sat down beside an embarrassed Sep, who looked away in confusion as she dropped. He continued to stare away with diplomatic aplomb until he felt a tugging at his shirt. He turned and saw the old woman holding his shirt tail in her hand. Before he could utter a word, she wiped. Then rising, she pulled down her skirt and turned to Sep. 'I reckon your folks will be washin' before mine.' With that she bid them goodnight and left, leaving the three friends totally nonplussed. Sep's howl of indignation was suddenly drowned by an explosion of hysterical laughter from Mark and Wilf.

'It's not a laughing matter,' Sept wailed trying to control his sense of outrage.

Wilf turned to Mark. 'It's a bloody miracle,' he said between paroxysms of laughter. 'The sun really does shine out of Sep' arse. You can tell by the sunburn on his shirt tail!' He doubled up in a fit of uncontrollable laughter.

Duncan Forster glared malevolently at his fellow-owners. 'We can't negotiate with this rabble.' He spat out the words with venomous distaste.

'They're not a rabble,' Mr Forster, the secretary responded wearily. 'They are surprisingly well organised and are in a very determined mood.'

'Nonsense,' Forster snapped. 'If we negotiate it will lead to anarchy.' There was a half-hearted murmur of assent around the room.

'Then just what do you suggest we do?' the secretary asked, a note of irritation creeping into his voice. John Buddle had been secretary to the Joint Northumberland and Durham Coal Owners Association since its formation in 1805. For this he received a salary of one hundred pounds a year, but he was much more than just a paid official. He was now one of the most eminent and respected head viewers in the coal trade and a part owner in several pits. His work, as a consultant viewer to many of the leading colliery owners, was reputed to earn him over one thousand five hundred pounds a year and he was fast becoming the acknowledged expert in his field. He also kept his ear to the ground and because he understood how true pitmen felt he also gained their respect. He had an aversion to the crude, avaricious owners like Forster, who put short term profits before the long term interest of the coal trade, and this was beginning to show.

'It's time we took a hard line,' Forster insisted. 'The men are acting as a combination to improve their wages and conditions. This is unacceptable and it's illegal. I say we invoke the full force of the law before things get out of hand.' There was a murmur of approval from some of the owners, but others were not so sure.

'Are we not acting as a combination ourselves?' Buddle asked pointedly. 'I fancy the men might have a better legal case against us than we against them.'

'Nonsense, we're a legitimate trade association,' Forster spluttered. 'You have to be united and firm when you're facing mob rule.'

'I think that's putting it a bit strong,' Buddle responded. 'All the men are asking for is a return to the traditional binding month of October.'

'Because it places them in a stronger position to make further demands on us. They'll be telling us how to run our pits next, if we accede to this.'

'You make it sound as if there's some great conspiracy being hatched against us by the men.' Buddle said, a note of disdain now colouring his scepticism.

'That's exactly what is happening,' Forster said. 'I know and so does Lambton,' he added dramatically.

'How?' The others were suddenly more interested.

'We have informers in the enemy camp. Pitmen who want to protect their livelihood by safeguarding our property.'

'You're not suggesting that the men will try to wreck the pits if we don't agree to their demands? Buddle's tone was almost scathing.

'They've done it in the past,' Forster reminded them.

'But only in localised disputes,' Buddle countered irritably. 'Isolated incidents perpetrated by a few hotheads.'

'This is more serious,' Forster persisted as his anger rose. 'There's an organisation, known as the Brotherhood, which is creeping into every pit in the coalfield. This hasn't happened before. It's like a secret society and there's something sinister about it. We need to act quickly to stamp it out before it's too late.'

'But how do we do that?' A worried owner asked.

'By arresting the ringleaders. If you cut off the head the body will die.'

'And who are the ringleaders?' Buddle enquired.

'They're all listed here.' Forster threw a sheaf of papers on the table with a theatrical flourish. 'I've made copies for each of you.'

The owners studied the list of names in silence until, eventually, it was broken by Buddle. 'Most of the names that I recognise are staunch Methodists,' he said thoughtfully. 'Many of the others are involved with the Friendly Societies.'

'Exactly!' Forster exclaimed in triumph. 'The perfect cover for an illegal organisation, wouldn't you say? I told you there was something sinister behind it all.' He looked challengingly around the table eyeing each owner in turn. 'Now, gentlemen, are we going to do something about it, or do we just abdicate our responsibilities and wait for something to happen?'

There was a flurry of conversation, mostly in support of Forster. Buddle could see that things were not going his way and any appeal for caution would not be heeded. He tried once more to prevent things getting out of hand. 'We can't go out and arrest all these so called ringleaders,' he said. 'We've no proof that the men are planning any action against us, whether it is unlawful or otherwise.'

'I tell you they'll withdraw their labour and shut our pits if we don't agree to an October binding,' Forster shouted, determined to press home his argument. 'I say we should act now before it's too late.'

'In what way?' Buddle asked tersely. 'You'll have to be more explicit if it's a resolution you're proposing.'

'By arresting all the ringleaders on that list, 'Forster said firmly. 'Most of us sat around this table are magistrates, are we not? Surely the most sensible way to preserve the peace is to issue warrants for the arrest of those troublemakers who set to break it. Then they'll have to stand trial and prove their innocence.'

'Surely the onus will be on us to prove their guilt,' Buddle said sharply. 'And for that we'll need proof.'

'I'll find you all the proof we need if you'll all back me up,' Forster promised confidently.

'And how shall I minute the proposal?' Buddle asked forcing the issue.

'I think it should remain an unofficial matter for the time being, until I provide you with the proof you need. In the meantime, I suggest we honour our duty as magistrates. You all have a copy of my list.'

'Then are you suggesting it's not an Association matter?' Buddle queried, worried by Forster's deviousness.

'Let's just say we have a gentleman agreement for the moment. As you implied yourself, Buddle, we mustn't be seen to be acting as an owners' combination must we?' Forster's smile of smug satisfaction was a further irritation to Buddle, but he let it pass and said nothing.

Jane watched with growing anxiety as Mark became more and more embroiled in the impasse over the binding. In October, the tension rose as the owners refused to listen to the men's request for an October binding. Matters finally reached a head by the middle of the month and Mark decided to call a meeting of the Brotherhood. On the 16th October delegates from nearly every pit in the coalfield converged on Longbenton in a grim but determined mood. After a lively discussion, it was resolved that the men in every pit would withdraw their labour unless the owners agreed to revert to the traditional binding on the 18th October. This the owners flatly rejected, triggering off a long and bitter strike.

Duncan Forster and many of the hard line owners, wasted no time in issuing arrest warrants and hunting down the known leaders of the pitmen. Special constables were sworn in to assist the militia, and soon the gaols began to fill as the strike leaders were rounded up and committed to prison. Those that remained free kept on the move to avoid arrest, sleeping at friendly houses to elude the militia and the growing numbers of informers and special constables.

Mark knew he was now a prime target of the owners, along with Wilf and several others. He and Wilf became fugitives, forced to travel in secret, seeking out the ever dwindling number of safe houses where they could rest and eat. Although Sep was also a marked man, he refused to leave his beloved chapel and to everyone's surprise, he was not arrested. Duncan Forster had a special reason for this. He knew that any attempted contact with the men of North Moor colliery would be made through Sep, and arranged for a close watch to be kept on the chapel as well as the homes of the men. He also ensured that Mark's cottage was kept under regular surveillance.

As the weeks went by, more and more delegates were arrested and life became increasingly difficult for Mark. He was now confined to furtive meetings, at secret rendezvous, with the remnants of the delegates from the original thirty-one pits who still supported the Brotherhood. The few leaders, who remained free, reported that the men were still loyal to the cause and determined not to give in to the intimidation of the owners. Mark learnt that so many pitmen had been arrested that the gaols were overflowing, and some prisoners were now being transferred to the Bishop of Durham's stables.

'What else would you expect from the Church,' Wilf said disdainfully. 'Half the magistrates seem to be clergymen, the other half coal owners.'

Mark nodded in agreement. 'That's because the government recognises the power of the pulpit as a propaganda weapon. The lower orders can't read, but they can listen. So the Church Acts for the establishment and preaches its message of law and order, regardless of right and wrong. Why else do the clergy teach fear of God before love of God?'

'They'll have you for blasphemy if you're not careful,' Wilf said, grinning.

'Well at least they don't burn you at the stake anymore,' Mark responded with a tired smile.

'They would if Forster and his likes had their way.'

'I suppose trying to starve us into submission is almost as bad,' Mark said.

'Wilf nodded. 'But the greedier owners are beginning to get worried. Coal prices are starting to rise because of the shortage and they don't like losing their juicy profits.' There was a murmur of assent around the room.

'We must remain united,' Mark said firmly, 'and keep good order. We need public support,' he reminded them, 'so no law breaking, no matter how much we are provoked.'

It was dark when the meeting closed and Mark and Wilf walked together, keeping well into the shadows, until they reached the point where their ways parted. Mark turned to his friend. 'Take care of yourself, Wilf. They've taken another ten of us this past week. I fear there's still a Judas in our midst.'

'You're the one with a price on your head. Wilf spoke with concern. 'Without you, we'd be lost and the owners know that.'

Mark shook his head. 'No one is indispensable, not even me. You, Sep and young Jed are doing an equally fine job. '

'It was your idea to recruit the putters as runners and use the chapels as clearing houses for our messages.'

'But you and Jed are making it work.'

Wilf snorted. 'Our brawn would be no good without your brain. It's because of you that we've remained firm for so long.'

'Well, tell Jed and Sep to keep a sharp lookout for informers. And no messages in writing,' he warned. 'There must be no evidence that could be used to show we're acting as a combination.'

'Don't worry, everybody's been fully briefed. Verbal messages only. There's not many of us can read anyway,' he added.

Mark smiled and held out his hand. It seems a long time ago since you were my father's star pupil, Wilf.' He felt the fervour and strength of Wilf's grip.

'Take care of yourself, my friend,' Wilf said warmly. 'Remember, we need you.'

'Don't worry, I'm heading for Sandgate. I'll be safe enough there with Rory MacGregor and his keelmen.'

'Aye, you will that,' Wilf agreed.

The two men turned and walked away, melting into the shadows of the night.

Duncan Forster was in another of his foul moods as he paced up and down the room waiting for his son to appear. Outside the room, the servants hurried to find Roland. Inside the room the ferret faced agent waited, with the controlled calm of twenty years' experience, for his employer's next outburst. It came when Roland finally entered the room. 'Where the hell have you been?' Forster demanded. 'I sent for you ten minutes ago.'

'I was busy, father,' Roland equivocated. 'I didn't realise the matter was urgent. '

'There's only one urge that ever makes you move fast enough,' Forster said with heavy sarcasm.

Roland ignored the innuendo and sat down. He'd long since given up arguing with his father when he was in this mood. 'Well I'm here now,' he said genially.

Forster scowled at his son before he continued. 'As you know, I attended a meeting of the Coal Owners Association yesterday.' He paused to emphasise what was to follow. 'I regret to say I detected signs of weakening on the part of some of the owners. They are worried over the loss of trade and are contemplating talks with the men, or their so called leaders. I counselled against this course of action but I fear my advice will be ignored.'

There was a short silence before the agent spoke up. 'Then, with luck we might see an end to this sorry dispute. Negotiation is the only way it can be resolved.'

'Is it?' Forster cut in. 'As I see it, if we negotiate with the men it's tantamount to abdicating our rights to manage our own pits. That I won't allow.'

'Then what do you propose to do, father?' Roland asked. 'I don't see that there's any alternative.'

'Oh yes there is,' Forster growled.

'What?'

'Destroy this damned conspiracy once and for all. Eradicate this secret brotherhood that's poisoning the men against us.'

And how do we do that? Most of their leaders are locked up already but they still refuse to work.'

'We haven't arrested the real leaders yet. Not the one who really matters.'

'And who would that be?'

'Standish!' Forster spat out the name. 'The troublemaker who used to work at North Moor before I refused to bind him and had him blacklisted.'

'Standish,' Roland repeated, rubbing his nose thoughtfully. 'Strange fellow, that one. His father's a partner with Ivison, isn't he? Must have fallen out with his son, though'

'They're both troublemakers,' Forster said. 'Ivison's one of those whose gone soft. Probably been brainwashed by his partner's radical views.'

A look of remembrance flitted over Roland's face. 'Wasn't young Standish the fellow that married mother's maid? Pretty young thing she was, too, if I recall.'

'You should remember,' Forster said irritably. 'You tried hard enough to bed her and caused mayhem in the servant's hall to boot.'

Roland remained silent, allowing a picture of the beautiful maid to re-focus in his mind. His groin began to ache again at the thought of the pleasure he'd missed. She was one of the few that had escaped his advances and the memory of it still rankled. 'So you think this fellow Standish is the key to the problem?'

'Yes. If we can get rid of him the whole conspiracy will collapse. The problem is how?'

'He must be a cunning fox to stay free this long.' Roland mused.

'Because the hounds haven't caught scent of him yet,' Forster said, irked by his failure. 'I deliberately let that Fordyce fellow remain free because I knew that chapel of theirs was being used to pass messages. I've had it watched, as well as the cottage where Standish lives, but so far we've drawn a blank.'

Roland remained deep in thought as an idea took shape in his mind. After a while he spoke. 'I think I might be able to snare this troublesome fox of ours, father.'

Forster looked dubiously at his son. 'And what makes you think you can succeed when everyone else has failed?'

'Because I think I know the man's weakness; his Achilles' heel.' As Roland spoke he knew his father was still unconvinced and smiled. 'Put it down to my unrivalled knowledge of the fairer sex, father. It's a talent I knew would come in useful one day.'

'I think you'd better explain yourself before I lose my patience.' Forster said irritably.

'It's very simple, 'Roland replied calmly. 'If you want to lure your fox into the chicken coop, you need some enticing bait. Standish rents a farm cottage which we can use as the coop, and that beautiful young wife of his certainly makes juicy bait. All we need to do is to trigger his protective instincts, and you can safely leave that to me'

'You're not to harm that girl,' Forster warned. 'If you physically molest her in any way, you'll answer to me for it.'

Roland smiled coolly at his father. 'You're forgetting that I'm a happily married man now, father.'

'Leopards don't change their spots either,' Forster retorted. 'Remember, you've been warned.'

Roland ignored his father's threat and started to outline his plan. 'You still have a man watching the cottage, I believe?'

'Yes. '

'Then call him off. He's too obvious. Everyone knows he's there so they'll know when he's called off.'

'The whole idea was to keep Standish on the run,' Forster spluttered.

'I don't want him on the run, father. I want him back here where we can catch him. I'll give him a reason to come back, but don't ask me what,' he added enigmatically.

'But if we don't watch the cottage we won't know if he does come back.' Forster was rapidly losing confidence in Roland's plan.

'We will watch it, father, but not so obviously. We'll put our best gamekeepers from the estate on the job to watch all the approaches. They're woodsmen who know how to keep cover and stalk their quarry. Not some bumbling special constable who's probably half asleep or drunk most of the time.'

Forster suddenly began to see the devious ingenuity of the plan and liked it. He looked at his son with a new respect. 'It's worth a try, I suppose. But no harm must come to the girl. It's her husband we're after, so just you remember that.' He had hoped that marriage would help settle his son down but, deep inside his mind, there lurked a nagging doubt that Roland would never change his ways.

The plan was put into action immediately and the special constables were withdrawn. Word soon got round that the pressure was off and the news eventually filtered through to Wilf and Mark. No one saw the four gamekeepers who took over the surveillance. Armed, and working in pairs, they built clever, strategically placed hides. Then, totally unobserved, they began their twenty-four hour watch on all the approaches to Mark's cottage.

CHAPTER 36

The repercussions of the dispute struck hard at Jane. She missed Mark terribly and the loneliness was almost unbearable. But the hardest thing to come to terms with was not knowing if Mark was safe and well.

Her brothers brought her messages from time to time, but the news was always several days late by the time she received it. Jed was now a hewer, a grown man and courting strong. Young Jim was a putter but hoped to be bound as a hewer when the strike was over. There was a close family bond, and the two brothers looked after their sister with a fierce protectiveness that she found both flattering and endearing.

Jane visited North Moor colliery several times a week, partly to ease the pain of her own loneliness by talking to her mother, and partly to comfort her. She knew Dora was also suffering by being parted from Wilf. But she always returned to the cottage in the evening, for she knew that if Mark came home, it would be at night. She stayed up as late as she could manage and always left a candle burning when she went to bed. Often, she would cry herself to sleep and the pillow would still be damp in the morning. She was blissfully unaware that the cottage was still being watched.

One evening, as Jane was about to lock the door for the night she heard the sounds of a horse coming up the narrow lane that ran past the cottage. She left the bolts undone and ran to the window, hoping it might be Mark. Pulling back the curtains, she saw the outline of the rider and, even in the dusk light, she knew it wasn't Mark. As the horseman drew up outside, she felt a stab of fear as she suddenly recognised the man in the saddle. She rushed back to the door but, before she could push home the bolts, it was flung open. She backed away in horror as Roland entered the room. His smile could not hide the menace in his demeanour and his eyes had the wild look that she remembered was always present when he'd been drinking. 'Please excuse the intrusion, my dear,' he said. 'I was anxious to see that no harm had come to you.'

'Thank you, sir, but I'm quite well.' She tried to sound calm and added, 'Who would harm the likes of me anyway?'

'A beautiful girl like you might attract the attention of undesirables,' Roland said, the smile still oiling his face. 'Especially since your husband's no longer here to protect you,' he added pointedly.

'My brothers are quite capable of looking after my safety. They visit me every day,' she lied.

'I'm sure they do but it must still be lonely for you without your husband.'

'I can thank your father for that,' she replied spiritedly.

'He's only doing his duty as a magistrate,' Roland said, moving closer. 'After all, your husband's been going around inciting the men to break the law and neglecting his pretty wife in the process. Both serious crimes in my book.'

'He's seeking justice for the men. I don't see that as a crime, no do I feel neglected,' she said trying to keep away from him.

'You're putting on a brave face, my dear, but you must be feeling lonely.' He suddenly stepped close to her and she felt his hand on her arm pulling her towards him. His breath reeked of spirits and his skin was moist with sweat.

'Please leave me alone,' she begged.

Roland saw the revulsion in her face and anger flared in his eyes. 'Still the uppity little tart, I see. Prefer a criminal to a gentleman, eh? Perhaps we can change that.'

Jane struggled to get away from him, anger and loathing mounting inside her. After toying with her for a while, Roland laughed and pushed her away. 'Not tonight, I think. I must get back for my guests. His voice took on a silky venom. 'But I'll come again soon. Just to see that you're properly taken care of.'

Mark read Jim's letter with mounting anger and frustration. But his anger was suffused with apprehension and a feeling of impotence that he could not properly protect his wife from the evil attentions of Roland Forster. He turned to Jed who'd delivered the letter. 'Is the cottage still being watched?'

'I don't think so,' Jed replied. 'There used to be a special constable or two watching the place but we've seen no sign of 'em these past few days.'

Rory MacGregor read Mark's mind. 'Don't go, laddie,' he warned. 'Take it from an old hand like me, it's a trap to entice you back.'

'I can't just leave her there on her own with a monster like that preying on her. What sort of man do you think I am?'

'A sensible one, I hope,' Rory answered calmly. 'Don't let feelings of love and gallantry blind your common sense.'

'But the bastard's been to see her twice,' Mark said, his anguish plain to see.

'And twice he's left her alone,' Rory countered. 'They're trying to smoke you out and using the oldest trick in the world to do it.'

'I can't just wait and do nothing,' Mark said doggedly.

'You can and you will,' Rory answered with equal determination. 'I'll send Colin and some of his keel bullies up to keep an eye on things for a few days.'

'I'll help too,' Jed said. 'I'll ask some of the other men as well,' he added. 'Between us all, we can keep a regular watch on the place.'

'Jane's my responsibility,' Mark said, still irritated by his own inadequacy.

'You've also got a responsibility for the men and their cause. Without your leadership it will fail.' Rory spoke with conviction.

Mark began to see the logic of the argument. 'I suppose you're right,' he conceded reluctantly. 'I'll keep away for a few days.'

'You'll stay away until this whole thing's been settled,' Rory ordered.

Mark smiled. 'If you insist my friend,' he said without conviction. But he knew he wouldn't be able to stay away from Jane for very long. Rory also knew this and he recognised it as a fatal chink in Mark's armour.

Jane locked the door of the cottage and pushed the bolts firmly home. After drawing the curtains, she lit a candle and stirred the dying embers of the fire until a small flame burst through the cinders and licked slowly up the back of the hearth. Later, she added more coal before retiring to bed.

She lay for a while, willing herself to relax, but sleep wouldn't come. She watched the dancing shadows cast by the flickering candle and thought of Mark. Was he safe, and when would she see him again? She felt the tears begin and sat up to blow her nose and wipe her eyes. Crying herself to sleep was not the answer, and she must learn to control her emotions, she told herself firmly.

She was about to lie down again when she heard a sound outside the door. She froze, thinking it must be another of Roland's dreaded visits. Please God no, she prayed. Though he hardly touched her, the menace of his presence unnerved her and left her a trembling wreck. She heard the noise again. It sounded like a loud whisper, as if someone was calling her name. Gathering all her courage, she got up and went over to the door. 'Who's there?' she asked, her voice hoarse with fear.

'It's me, Mark,' came the whispered reply. 'Put the candle out and open the door.'

Joy and relief overwhelmed her. She snuffed out the candle and hurried to unbolt the door. Within seconds Mark was inside, closing the door quietly behind him and gently easing home the bolts. Then she was in his arms, responding passionately to his kisses as he held her tight. She began to weep but this time it was tears of joy that ran down her cheeks. 'Oh, I've missed you so much, Mark,' she sobbed clinging to him fiercely, as though she were afraid it might only be a dream.

'I've missed you too,' he answered, before silencing her with another long, sensual kiss.

She felt his arousal and responded with urgent anticipation. 'Come to bed,' she pleaded.

'That's the best offer I've had in weeks,' he said grinning.

She undressed him urgently and shamelessly, pushing him down on the bed before loosening her night dress and letting it fall to the floor. Mark gazed at her lovingly, then gently drew her down beside him on the bed, pulling up the blanket to cover their nakedness. Soon, their bodies were entwined and in the faint light of the dying fire, the shape beneath the covers rose and fell with quickening intensity as they nourished the hunger of their love.

It was late and most of North Moor Hall was in darkness. But the lights were still burning in the dining room where Roland had remained, drinking heavily, after a silly but vicious disagreement with his wife. There was a quiet knock on the door and Harker, the butler, entered the room. 'What the hell do you want?' Roland snapped. 'I didn't ring.'

'My apologies for disturbing you, sir,' Harker said nervously, 'but the gamekeeper, Reid, is waiting outside. Says he has a message for you and it's rather urgent.'

'Rather urgent, eh?' Roland mimicked. 'It bloody well better be at this time of night.'

'Said it was confidential too,' Harker added hesitantly.

Roland sighed. 'All right, Harker, you'd better show him in here.'

A few moments later, there was a further knock on the door and Reid stepped anxiously into the room, as though he was walking on eggs, and stood nervously twisting his hat.'

'Come in, man!' Roland barked, 'and shut the bloody door. Don't want that confounded butler listening in.' Harker beat a hasty retreat with all the dignity he could muster.

Roland adopted his father's tactics and left the unfortunate Reid to stand and wait for a while before he spoke. 'Well?' he suddenly barked. 'What's this urgent news that won't wait for a more civilised hour?'

'I've just come from the cottage, sir.' Reid paused for effect. 'He's back.'

'Is he, by Jove!' Roland was suddenly consumed with excitement. 'Did he see you?'

'No, sir. He just went inside.'

'Do you think he knows the place is being watched?'

'I'm not sure, sir. He approached very cautious like.'

'And you're absolutely sure he didn't spot you?'

'No, sir.' There was a firm pride in Reid's reply.

Roland gave a crooked smile. 'Can't keep away from the nest, eh! That's the trouble with the lower orders, they can't control their urges.'

'Can't say as I blame 'im, sir. She's a fine looking woman.'

'H'mm,' Roland intoned irritably, remembering his own rejections.

'Do you want us to arrest him, sir?'

'Has my father sworn you in as constables? All of you? '

'Yes sir. Just give the word and we'll take 'im.'

'No. I want to be there myself. I take it Crombie's still watching the cottage.'

'Yes, sir, like you ordered. A constant twenty-four hour watch.'

A cruel gleam flickered in Roland's eyes as a plan began to take shape in his mind. He realised he now had the opportunity to extract a double revenge and the thought made him glow with anticipation. He knew what he must do. 'I want you to go to the stables, Reid,' he ordered, 'and tell the groom to saddle my horse. Then you go straight back to Crombie at the hide. I'll join you there later.'

After riding as close as he dared to the cottage, Roland dismounted and after tying his horse to a tree, set off to walk the last three hundred yards to where the hide was situated. It was so well camouflaged that it was difficult to locate in daylight, and impossible to find in the dark. Roland had followed the directions, but it was only a whispered challenge from the two gamekeepers that confirmed he was there. 'Is he still inside?' he asked, peering anxiously into the darkness in the direction of the cottage.

'Aye, sir,' Crombie confirmed. The gamekeeper had spent twenty years searching woodlands at night for poachers. His instincts and eyesight were those of a forest animal. 'Do you want us to go in and take him, sir?'

Roland thought of his plan. 'No. You can take him when he leaves the cottage but wait until he's well clear.'

'It's a bit risky, sir,' Reid cautioned. 'He might give us the slip. Best if we take him inside. '

'No. Do as I say. You're armed aren't you?'

'Yes, sir, but...'

'Shoot him if you have to, but I would rather he was taken alive and unharmed.'

'We'll do our best, sir.' The two gamekeepers were baffled and unhappy with Roland's strategy, but said no more.

They waited two hours before Crombie's urgent whisper jerked Roland out of his dose. 'There's a light in the cottage, sir.'

Roland strained his eyes but could see nothing. 'I can't see a bloody thing,' he muttered irritably.

'It's a shaded candle and the curtains are drawn,' Crombie said. 'Two things can happen now, he went on. 'If he's cocky, he'll leave the light on when he opens the door and you'll see the chink of light. If he's not, the light will go out when he's ready to slip out. Either way, that's when we move in.'

Roland waited, staring into the darkness. Suddenly he saw a brief glimmer of light as the cottage door opened.

Mark woke with a start, fearing he had overslept. He felt Jane's warm, soft body snuggling up close to him and he listened contentedly to her slow, rhythmic breathing. The blissful night of love had relaxed him but, as he contemplated the coming dawn, he began to tense a little as his caution returned.

His eyes had now become accustomed to the darkness and he detected a faint glimmer from the remains of the fire. Easing himself slowly from the bed, he crossed to the hearth and knelt to gently stir the embers, blowing on the hot cinders as he did so. Gradually, the dull red glow brightened until he was able to light the candle. Shading the light, he dressed quietly, trying not to disturb Jane, but the absence of his warm, comforting body intruded on her subconscious mind, and soon she was awake too. She sat up, thinking something was wrong. 'Is there someone coming?' she whispered anxiously.

Mark moved back to the bed and smiled fondly down at her before kissing her gently on the lips. 'Nothing to worry about,' he said as he rose. 'It's almost dawn and time for me to go.'

'Will you be safe?' she asked.

'It'll be an hour before it gets light. I'll be halfway back to Sandgate by then.'

'There may be someone still watching the cottage.' Her voice quivered with apprehension for his safety, and misery at the thought of his leaving.

'I think they've given up on that,' he said confidently, 'but I'll keep a sharp look-out.'

She followed him to the door and they clung together for a while in a lingering, passionate farewell kiss. 'Take care,' she whispered. The door opened and he was gone.

It was still dark outside, but a hint of the coming dawn began to soften the blackness of the night. He moved quietly down the lane, keeping close to the deeper shadow of the overhanging trees, listening for sounds and watching for any sign of movement. He'd gone almost a hundred yards and was starting to relax when the challenge came. A dark shape loomed out of the night and he felt strong hands grasping at his shoulders. Then the shouted command. 'Stop! You're under arrest!'

Mark's first reaction was one of panic as he felt the grip tighten. Then he began to relax, as if he'd given up, and felt the grip relax also. Suddenly, he twisted free and started to run down the lane. He heard a gunshot behind him and the sound of the ball passing in the darkness, but he kept on running. Then, from out of nowhere, another shape rose and he felt a tremendous impact that knocked all the breath from his body. As he fell to the ground, the triumphant voice of Crombie filtered through his dazed brain. 'Gocha, my lad!'

Still winded and confused by the blow, Mark heard the sounds of running footsteps followed by voices, one of which he recognised as the clipped, mocking tones of Roland Forster. 'So this is the fellow who's been causing us all the trouble.' Roland turned to the gamekeepers. 'Have you got the irons?'

'Yes, sir,' Crombie said, pleased he'd been proved right.

'Then see he's properly manacled. We don't want him running off again do we?'

When the shackles had been made fast to Mark's wrists and ankles, Roland ordered one of the gamekeepers to go and fetch his horse. To the other he said, 'keep him here while I go and visit that charming young lady who has a penchant for entertaining felons.' With that he walked back in the direction of the cottage.

*****

As Mark slipped quietly out of the cottage, Jane quickly slid home the bolts and stood for a while, leaning against the door as she savoured the lingering imprint of his tender farewell kiss. Then she crossed the room and climbed back into bed, looking forlornly at the rumpled pillow where Mark's head had lain such a short time ago. Once more she felt a wave of loneliness creeping over her as her depression returned and her spirits sank. Angrily, she forced back the tears and chided herself for her weakness. She needed to be strong for Mark's sake and vowed that, from now on, she would stop feeling sorry for herself.

Her thoughts were interrupted by the sound of voices from outside. She strained her ears and heard what she thought were angry shouts. Suddenly she stiffened as the explosive crack of a gun being fired reverberated through the still night air. She jumped out of the bed and ran anxiously to the door, instinctively calling out Mark's name as she drew the bolts. Opening the door, she froze in terror as she gazed into the cold, cruel eyes of Roland Forster. He smiled sardonically and pushed the door wide open with his foot. 'My apologies for disturbing you at such an early hour, but your nocturnal habits intrigue me somewhat.' He pushed his way inside, kicking the door shut behind him.

Jane backed away and sat down gingerly on the edge of the bed. 'What do you want?' Her voice was a mixture of fear and defiance.

'What do I want?' he repeated, taunting her. 'Now let me see. I already have half of what I want but I'm not sure if it's the right half.'

Jane looked puzzled. 'I don't know what you mean.'

'Then let me explain,' he went on in the same mocking tone. 'The half I already have is your husband. He's under arrest and being held prisoner outside. But I might be persuaded to exchange that half for the other half which I don't possess.'

She suddenly understood his meaning. 'The other half?' she repeated. 'You mean me?'

He laughed. 'How astute. You learn quickly, my dear.'

'And the exchange. What do you have in mind?'

350

'Your husband's freedom, or rather his escape. You'll appreciate that I can't withdraw the arrest warrant, but I'll try to persuade my father.'

'What if he refuses?'

'Your husband can at least escape back to Sandgate. He'll be relatively safe there. Better than five years in the house of correction.'

'And what do you want of me in return?'

'Ah, my dear. Now I think you're being a little naive.' He shook his head tauntingly. 'It's very becoming but a little disingenuous of you, don't you think?' His eyes suddenly became excited as he added, 'You know exactly what I want.'

She did and the thought numbed her. But she knew from past experience that Roland was not to be trusted. On the other hand, if Mark had already been arrested, then a long prison sentence seemed inevitable. If he could be set free, there would at least be a chance that she could join him later and perhaps they could start a new life together elsewhere. But first, she had to be sure that Mark had been captured and was not dead, or wounded. She remembered the gunshot. 'How do I know my husband's still alive?' she asked. 'And if he is, how can I trust you to set him free?'

Roland was compelled to admire her thoroughness. 'You can see him and also witness his escape. You have my word on that. Now, madam, do I have yours?'

She couldn't look at him and had to force out the word. 'Yes,' she answered.

Roland allowed a thin smile of triumph. 'Good. You can watch through the window, but you must stay inside and keep quiet. I don't want him to see or hear you before he escapes. He might change his mind.' He walked to the door, then turned. 'Stay on the bed until I return. When I come back you can watch, and you'll see that I'm a man of my word.' With that he went out and closed the door behind him.

It was still dark outside. Roland paused to allow his eyes to adjust, before walking away from the cottage. He kept to the centre of the narrow lane that cut between the woods on either side. He'd gone less than a hundred yards when lie heard Crombie's voice. 'Over here, Mr Roland.' God, the man really could see in the dark, he thought. As he came closer, he saw the shadowy outlines of the two gamekeepers and his horse. 'Where's the prisoner?' he snapped anxiously.

'Behind us, sir,' Reid said. 'We've tied him to a tree.'

'Good,' Roland sounded relieved. 'Now come over here,' he ordered, leading the two gamekeepers out of earshot of Mark. 'Now listen carefully, both of you.' He slowly and meticulously explained his plan to the two bemused men whose bewilderment gradually changed to consternation.

A few minutes later, Roland mounted his horse and rode the short distance back to the cottage. He was followed by Reid, the gamekeeper, closely guarding his prisoner. The leg irons had been removed but Mark's wrists were still manacled and a leather gag was tied tightly between his teeth. The other gamekeeper, Crombie, had slipped off quietly into the night heading in the opposite direction down the lane.

When Roland reached the cottage, he dismounted and went inside, leaving the horse untethered. Once inside, he lit a small oil lamp, using the candle that was still burning. He turned to Jane who was sitting nervously on the edge of the bed. 'You can watch from the window now. But remember, no noise.' With that he picked up the oil lamp and went outside. He walked up to Mark and held the lamp up to illuminate his face and turning, saw a faint movement of the curtains at the cottage window. Then, on a signal from Roland, Reid leaned forward and whispered into Mark's ear. 'Now's your chance, lad. When I let go, make a dash for the horse.'

Mark quickly tried to assess the situation. Why allow him to escape, he wondered. Was it a trap? His hands were manacled in front of him which improved his chances slightly, but he was not much of a horseman. But then there was only one horse. If he could manage to mount safely, there would be little chance of pursuit. His mind was made up. As soon as Reid released his grip, he made a dash for the horse and managed to get his foot inside the stirrup at the first attempt. Swinging up into the saddle, he pressed his heels into the horse's flanks and spurred it into a gallop.

Roland smiled and stood listening to the hoof beats fade into the night, as horse and rider sped down the narrow lane. Then he turned and went back inside the cottage, closing the door firmly behind him.

Mark felt the cool night air brushing his face as he clung desperately to the galloping horse. He was a poor horseman and wisely decided that the best course was to let the excited animal have its head. Two hundred yards on, he hit the twin ropes strung across the road by Crombie and was catapulted from the saddle. Winded and dazed, he tried to rise but was immediately felled by a blow from Crombie. When he regained consciousness he found himself gagged and lying across the jolting horse, his hands now manacled behind his back and his legs tightly bound together.

The gamekeeper led the horse back up to the lane in the direction of the cottage, stopping well short of the building where they were joined by Reid. After tethering the horse, they carried Mark between them the rest of the way to the cottage. Then, as instructed by Roland, they held their prisoner up at the lighted window. The curtains had now been drawn back, allowing him to see inside the room.

Inside, Roland had lit two more candles which he'd placed strategically around the room, greatly improving the level of illumination. He turned to Jane, who was still sitting on the edge of the bed looking resigned and apprehensive. 'Now, my dear, it's time for you to keep your side of the bargain.'

Jane looked up at him with one last despairing plea. 'Please...'

He stopped her with an angry gesture. 'No! We have an agreement.' He began to undress excitedly and soon stood naked, his huge erection protruding, rampantly. When he saw that she'd made no attempt to remove her nightdress he became angry. He'd waited a long time for this and wasn't going to be thwarted now. 'Get it off, damn you,' he snarled.

Slowly and reluctantly, Jane removed her nightdress and lay back naked on the bed.

'And smile, damn you, smile,' he shouted savagely. 'You may as well enjoy it.'

She forced an agonised smile that was more of a grimace, before closing her eyes. She lay, tense and afraid, waiting for the final humiliation.

At first, the shame and disgust of her violation numbed her. The sheer odium of the act fell like an anaesthetic curtain over her mind, blotting out even the pain of Roland's urgent penetration. Waves of wretchedness consumed her as Roland's lustful thrusting continued until his seed finally surged inside her.

All this Mark watched with anguished disbelief until finally, a sound of animal despair rose in his throat and forced its way passed the gag tied tight between his teeth. Then, a dark tide of desolation swamped his soul and he struggled violently to free himself from his tormentors.

Crombie's initial feeling of erotic titillation at what he'd seen had quickly given way to revulsion. He saw the pain in Mark's frenzied struggles and a feeling of pity overwhelmed him. The blow he struck was one of compassion, the act of a gamekeeper putting a suffering animal out of its misery. Mark sank into the soothing oblivion of unconsciousness.

CHAPTER 37

The first grey streaks of dawn were lighting up the sky when Roland finally emerged from the cottage. He looked flushed and pleased with himself as he swaggered over to the two gamekeepers. When he saw the unconscious form of Mark lying on the ground, his look of smug satisfaction changed to annoyance. 'I told you to make him watch,' he said angrily.

'We did, sir,' Crombie answered, 'but he went berserk and I had to clobber 'im.'

Roland's look of anger gave way to a wicked grin. 'The excitement proved a bit too much for him, eh?'

'Something like that,' Crombie lied.

'What are we to do with 'im now, sir,' Reid asked, pointing to the limp figure lying on the ground.

'Put him on my horse and take him up to the hall.' Roland said. 'You can lock him in the tack room until I get there. When you've done that, you can bring my horse back.' As he turned to go back inside the cottage he grinned and added, 'I'll enjoy my dessert while I'm waiting.'

As the two gamekeepers made their way back to North Moor Hall, the enormity of what they had been party to began to sink in. Both men felt a growing shame at their own collusion in Roland's appalling act, and a gnawing fear as to the consequences of their involvement, left them feeling uncomfortable and afraid.

When they arrived at the hall, they placed the still unconscious Mark in the tack room, locking the heavy door behind them as they left. They were watched by Gibson, the agent, whose ferret face twitched with curiosity. He moved across the stable yard to intercept them. 'What's been going on?' he demanded.

The two gamekeepers, anxious to relieve their guilt, began to unburden themselves, blurting out the story of the night's events. When they'd finished the agent remained silent for a while, deep in thought. When he spoke, there was concern in his voice. 'Are you sure it was rape?' he asked.

355

'Well she didn't put up much of a struggle,' Crombie said hesitantly, 'but then she wouldn't, would she, if she expected her husband to go free.'

'So you think Mr Roland tricked her?'

'It looks that way to me. You know what he's like, sir.'

The agent pondered on this for a while. 'You'd better come with me,' he said and led the way across the stable yard towards the hall.

After listening to the agent's account Duncan Forster called in the two gamekeepers and subjected them to a rigorous cross examination before dismissing them. 'Stay in the stables and see that no one goes near the tack room,' he ordered. 'I may want to see you both later. '

After the two gamekeepers had left the room, Forster turned to his agent and exploded. 'The bloody young fool! What the hell does he think he's doing?'

'Seems as though he lost control of himself,' Gibson responded. 'I think he may have gone too far this time.'

'Tell him I want to see him as soon as he comes home.' Forster's voice contained an icy venom that Gibson had never heard before.

The confrontation that followed was short and very heated. It ended in the total annihilation of Roland's defence until he was reduced to an abject, humiliating silence. 'You brains are still in your cock,' Forster stormed at his son trying to elicit a response. 'You never learn do you?'

The silence seemed to goad him further. 'This time you've left two witnesses who can confirm rape if she complains. Her father-in-law's not without influence, you know. He can afford the best lawyer if it comes to a trial. Think what that means. Even if you win, which is doubtful, there'll be the stigma of the publicity that will remain with you for the rest of your life.' He sat down, finally exhausted and at his wits end.

'Perhaps I should go abroad for a while,' Roland said dejectedly. 'Lose myself in the colonies.'

His son's cringing response was about to invoke another tirade when Forster paused. Suddenly, an idea took shape in his mind and he knew what he must do. 'I want this Standish fellow taken down to the Tyne,' he said.

Roland looked blankly at his father. 'The Tyne?'

356

'Yes, the Tyne,' Forster said irritably. 'Put him in a chaldron waggon and take him down the waggonway to the staithes.' He sat down at his desk and began to write furiously. When he'd finished, he put the letter in an envelope and addressed it to the Regulating Officer of the Tyne and Wear Impress Service. He gave the letter to his agent. 'Get one of the grooms to ride into Newcastle on a fast horse and deliver this.' Turning to Roland he said, 'Wait at the staithes until the navy's boat arrives then hand young Standish over to the press. That should keep him out of circulation for a few years and, with luck, he might never return.'

A look of understanding and admiration crept into Roland's face. 'A capital idea, father,' he acknowledged, smiling for the first time.

'You'd better take this,' Forster said handing Roland a small leather pouch filled with coins. 'There's a hundred guineas in there. Give it to the officer in charge.'

Less than four hours later, Roland and the two gamekeepers stood on the deserted staithes with their still unconscious prisoner, awaiting the press gang. Soon a naval cutter appeared out of the early morning mist and tied up alongside the staithe. A middle-aged lieutenant with a slight limp clambered up the ladder to the deck of the staithe, followed by a tough looking bunch of sailors. He doffed his hat to Roland. 'Lieutenant Morgan at your service, sir. I believe you have a volunteer for me?'

Roland took the lieutenant by the arm and led him to the other side of the staithe out of earshot. 'I have fifty guineas in this purse,' he said offering the leather pouch to the lieutenant. 'The two men guarding the volunteer also have a yen to join His Majesty's navy. I'd be much obliged to you if you could help them achieve their ambition.'

The lieutenant grinned knowingly. 'It's as good as done, sir.' He called over the petty officer in charge and whispered a few words in his ear. The petty officer saluted and went back to the press gang and whispered hurried instructions. 'Right, men,' he ordered, 'take 'em on board.'

Crombie was the first to realise that something was amiss, but it was too late. Despite the gamekeepers' struggles and protestations, they were beaten and manhandled aboard the cutter along with Mark.

357

Roland watched with a glow of satisfaction as the cutter headed downstream for Shields and the receiving tender. His fingers played with the fifty golden guineas in his pocket that he had surreptitiously removed from the pouch. After all fifty guineas was half a year's pay for a lieutenant and he had three volunteers instead of one. Besides, he felt sure he could find a better use for the other fifty guineas than a middle-aged lieutenant with a limp. His father need never know.

When Duncan Forster learned that Roland had betrayed the two gamekeepers, his immediate reaction was one of outraged anger. But, on reflection, he realised that for once his son had responded sensibly to what had been a delicate situation. It had been a despicable act but, in the circumstances, a rather astute one from the Forster family point of view. It had removed two key witnesses from the scene and should the young girl now cry rape, there would be no one to support her accusations. Few people would give credence to the word of a servant girl against that of a gentleman, especially a servant who was married to a known troublemaker. Perhaps he'd misjudged Roland, he thought. Maybe the boy had grown up at last.

The main cause of Duncan Forster's initial anger over his son's actions had been the fear that Roland's criminal infidelity would jeopardise his marriage settlement. The legal matters of the various property transfers had not yet been finalised and he wanted no last minute hitches if news of his son's appalling behaviour became known to the world. In the longer term, Roland could well endanger his inheritance prospects if he continued with his wayward and indiscrete lifestyle. He decided it was now time to put a stop to it, once and for all, something he should have done years ago. After all, he thought, the boy's wife was the only child of a wealthy baronet and there could be further rich pickings in the future.

After careful consideration, he decided that the only course of action open to him was to protect his son against any charges that might be levelled, even if it meant the betrayal of his magisterial oath. With the key witnesses now out of the way, only three other people, apart from the girl herself, had knowledge of the rape. He'd pondered for a while on Gibson's reliability but finally decided that he could count on his agent's loyalty out of self-interest. Clearly, Gibson had nothing to gain and everything to lose by speaking up.

But from now on he would watch Roland like a hawk. He was becoming sick and tired of his son's inherent character deficiencies; a weakness he now knew could never be eradicated. But, by God, he would neuter the boy if he had to.

Gibson had been agent to Duncan Forster for over twenty years and had watched his employer's rising fortunes with a mixture of awe and envy. In the early years, he had admired Forster's energy and single mindedness in pursuing his ambitions, but as his success had grown, so his master's greed had multiplied in direct proportion. Gibson's admiration began to wane as Forster became obsessed with wealth, power and status and in the process his business dealings became more ruthless and unprincipled.

For several years now, Gibson had felt a growing dissatisfaction with his employer's methods and had become more and more reluctant to accept his instructions. He was honest enough to admit that he'd allowed his own moral standards to be corrupted and must, therefore, share some of the blame for the excesses committed by Forster over the years. But Roland's appalling act of rape and betrayal had been too much for him to stomach.

As he reflected on his predicament, he realised that there was very little he could do to right the terrible wrong that had been done. If he spoke out he could prove nothing and would only incur the wrath and enmity of both Duncan and Roland Forster. At first, he decided it would be better to let matters rest for a while and try to forget about the incident. But after five weeks of agonising, his conscience still troubled him and he resolved to try and do something to redress the situation.

The following day, he spent most of the morning dealing with problems of running the estate and trying to fill the gap caused by the absence of his two best gamekeepers. He had already assured the men's families that they could remain in their cottages and lied to them that efforts were being made to find the missing men. As agent, he was determined to see that no more innocent people should suffer for the Forsters' crimes. Then, after calling for his horse to be saddled, he rode out of the stable yard and headed for Newcastle. He had decided what he must now do.

That evening, Gibson knocked on the door of Ivison's house on the quayside and asked to see Henry Standish.

'Who should I say is calling?' Ellen asked.

'John Gibson,' he replied and seeing her blank look added, 'Tell him that I have important news that will be to his advantage.'

A still mystified Ellen showed him in and went to seek Henry.

When the two men met, there was a glimmer of mutual recognition as their minds went back to the meeting in the ale house thirteen years ago. I was right, Gibson thought, there was something different about this man.

'I believe you have some news for me,' Henry said, smiling politely.

'Yes, I have some information about your son.' Gibson saw the shock register on Henry's face.

'Do you know where he is?' Henry spoke with a mixture of caution and surprise. Wilf and the colliery delegates, who were still free, assisted by Rory and his keelmen, had scoured the coalfield looking for signs of Mark, but without success. He'd hired lawyers to check the court files for any record of his son's arrest but again to no avail. And now, here was a man associated with Forster who said he had information about his son. 'Do you know where he is,' he repeated guardedly.

'No, but I know what happened to your son.' Gibson replied.

'And you want some payment first before you tell me,' Henry said scornfully.

'No.' Gibson looked quite shocked.

'Then what?' Henry persisted, still suspicious of Gibson's connections with Forster.

'I simply thought you'd like to know.'

Suddenly, Henry realised the man was genuine and began to feel a little ashamed. 'I'm sorry,' he said awkwardly. 'I just assumed you were a messenger with some nefarious proposal from your employer.'

'He doesn't know I'm here,' Gibson replied.

Henry began to feel uneasy and braced himself for bad news. 'I think you'd better tell me what you know,' he said.

360

As Gibson recounted the events of Mark's arrest and Jane's rape ordeal, Henry struggled to contain his anger. When he heard the details of the betrayal to the press gang, he finally lost control. 'A monstrous and odious act of treachery,' he shouted. 'I'll never forgive Forster for this. He must be brought to book.'

Gibson gave a rueful smile. 'How are you going to do that, Mr Standish?'

'You must speak to my lawyer. You must testify in court.'

'But I wasn't a witness.'

'You can't let Forster get away with this shameful evil.'

'My evidence is only hearsay. The courts won't accept it.'

'Then you'll do nothing? Henry looked at Gibson in exasperation.

'No. I'm afraid I can't help you in that way.'

Henry became angry. 'Have you no sense of honour, man?'

'It was a sense of honour that brought me here tonight, sir, belated though it may have been. But I won't jeopardise my position for no purpose.'

Henry realised that Gibson was talking sense and began to calm down. 'I'm sorry. You're right, of course.'

Gibson looked at Henry with sympathy and understanding. 'There's only one person who can take any action and to succeed, she'll need witnesses.'

'You mean my daughter-in-law.'

'Has she told you what really happened?' Gibson saw the hurt in Henry's eyes.

'No.'

'She may wish to keep it a secret. Without the support of her husband and the gamekeepers, she would be wise to do so.'

Henry now realised all too clearly why Jane had not told anyone about her terrifying ordeal. The shame of the rape and her outrage at the trickery which followed must have hurt her deeply. Yet, in spite of this, her only concern had been for Mark. Suddenly, a new and terrible knowledge struck him. The poor girl couldn't have known that Mark had been forced to witness her rape. What would she do if she found out? And how would Mark react to it all. As the agonising questions bombarded his mind, he covered his face with his hands. 'Why, in God's name, did you have to tell me all this,' he groaned.

'Would you rather I hadn't?' Gibson asked.

Henry slowly shook his head. 'No. It's right that I should know.'

'What will you do now?'

'Contact the Admiralty and try to find my son. Then I'll move heaven and earth to secure his release.'

'I wish you well, Mr Standish, but I understand that false names were given to the press gang. It may complicate matters.' Gibson rose and held out his hand. 'I'm sorry I had to bring you such bad tidings.'

When the agent left, a wave of despair overcame Henry and he sat for a long time with his head cradled in his hands.

The following day Rory MacGregor confirmed Henry's worst fears. The navy tender with the pressed men had left Shields harbour almost five weeks ago. 'He'll be on a receiving ship at the Nore by now. He may even have been transferred to a man-of-war,' Rory concluded despondently. 'I think you will have to face up to the fact that you might not see your son for a very long time.'

As the weeks went by without any news of her husband, Jane's fear for his safety began to grow. Her initial joy when Henry told her that Mark was alive had been quickly dampened by the knowledge of his impressment into the navy. It was a fate feared by most ordinary men, particularly in time of war, for the navy was not a popular service.

Each time he called at the cottage, Henry begged her to come and stay with him in Newcastle until Mark's return. He was now in the invidious position of having knowledge that he couldn't share with Jane and he also feared for her safety. Living in his house in Newcastle, she would at least be beyond Roland Forster's reach. The man was so morally corrupt and unprincipled that he clearly felt himself to be above the law. As long as his father continued to turn a blind magisterial eye to his son's behaviour, Roland would present a continuing threat to Jane and Mark. But, try as he may, Henry could not persuade Jane to leave the cottage she had shared with Mark since their marriage. It contained the memories of her fleeting happiness with the man she loved and her mind had stubbornly blotted out the trauma of her rape. It was the calm acceptance of her violation that worried Henry as much as the on-going threat posed by Roland. Her composure seemed unnatural to him and he again pleaded with her. 'Come and stay with me in Newcastle. You'll be well looked after and I'm sure it's what Mark would wish.'

She smiled and shook her head. 'I appreciate your concern but I want to stay here. I think Mark would understand,' she gently contradicted him.

Henry saw that her mind was made up. 'As you wish, my dear, but I'll see that someone keeps an eye on this place.'

'I'll be quite safe,' she assured him, touched by his concern.

'Let me know if you need anything.'

'Only news of Mark,' she said.

'I'll let you know the minute I hear from the admiralty,' he promised.

She waved to Henry as he rode off down the lane, his expression sad and apprehensive. As he rounded the bend in the lane, the trees hid him from sight and she went inside, closing the cottage door behind her. She stirred the fire into a cheery blaze and sat down by the hearth staring into the dancing flames. Her hand crept over her stomach in a soft, caressing movement. She now knew she was pregnant. But by whom, she anxiously wondered.

EXILE

CHAPTER 38

The movement of the cutter coming alongside the Impress Service tender at Shields, stirred Mark back to consciousness. He slowly opened his eyes and discovered he was lying in the stern sheets alongside the prone figures of Reid and Crombie. Their hands and feet were bound and a mean looking petty officer was watching them closely.

A rope with a bowline tied at the end was thrown down into the cutter from the deck of the tender. This was placed under the arms of the prisoners who were then hauled up on deck. The navy took no chances with pressed men and the lieutenant in charge had a special reason for seeing this trio securely on board the tender. His hand kept returning to his pocket to caress the fifty golden guineas given him by Roland and he smiled with satisfaction.

Once they had been landed on the deck of the impress tender, they were quickly bundled below into the hold. The hatch cover was then closed and locked firmly behind them. The tender's hold was in fact a prison, and through the grating Mark could see an armed sentry standing guard on deck. There were already a dozen men imprisoned in the hold and they were instructed to untie the newcomers.

Mark rubbed his wrists and ankles to help restore the circulation. His head ached and his fingers gingerly searched his scalp and felt the dry, matted blood from a deep cut above his forehead. The only light was from the wooden grating above and the cramped space and the foul smell of bilge water made him feel sick.

On deck, the order 'make sail' was given and the tender proceeded to sea. After clearing the bar, she turned south and headed for the Nore. Two days later, after a fast but uncomfortable passage, the tender entered the Thames estuary and sailing up river, moored alongside the receiving ship. The pressed men were then brought up on deck, in small groups under heavy guard, and transferred to the old floating hulk which served as the receiving ship.

Conditions on board the receiving ship were appalling. It was overcrowded, damp and filthy. The stench rising from the hulk's bilges mixed with the odours of hundreds of unwashed bodies, creating a humid, fetid atmosphere between decks that was a perfect breeding ground for disease. Less than half the pressed men were seafarers or watermen. The rest were landsmen sprinkled with the sweepings of the local gaols known as quota men who had volunteered rather than serve a prison sentence.

The gun ports of the hulk were closed and secured. The only light was that which filtered down through the gratings in the deck. The pressed men were allowed out in small, heavily guarded groups in order to visit the heads in the bow of the ship. This puzzled Mark and he remarked on this to his neighbour, a seasoned sailor with past service in the navy. 'How can the navy possibly operate if pressed men have to be guarded all the time to stop them running?'

'Ah, that's just while we're on board the receiving ship,' came the reply. 'Once we're transferred to a man-of-war, those with seagoing experience will be rated able or ordinary seamen, the rest as landsmen. Then our names will be entered into the ship's muster book and from then on, we're subject to the Articles of War.'

'So we're not in the navy proper, yet?'

'No. The civil law still applies, but you'll have the devil's own job to make use of it.'

'I suppose once we're at sea we can't jump ship,' Mark said.

'Not unless you're a bloody good swimmer. They'll pick you up from the water if they can, and if you're still alive, they'll flog the hide off your back for jumping.'

'What about when the ship's in port?'

'You'll be confined to ship and sentries will be posted in case you try to swim ashore.'

Mark looked incredulous. 'Are we not allowed shore leave?' he asked.

The old sailor laughed. 'I can see you're a landsman. Shore leave is as rare as fresh bread and water in His Majesty's navy. And if your ship's taken out of commission, you'll be transferred straight into another, like as not. Take it from me, matey, you'll be stuck in the navy until the war's over unless, of course, you get yourself killed first. Best make the most of it, I say.'

But making the most of it came hard to Mark in his present bitter state. The events of the morning of his capture had left him deeply traumatised. The two day voyage to the Nore on board the tender had given him time to brood on his misfortune. The initial anger and desire for revenge had gradually given way to a deep, numbing despair. He found he could no longer contemplate his future and his thoughts and functions became purely mechanical. He tried not to sleep, for when he did, the nightmare returned. He saw the rampant loins and the evil, gloating face of Roland in his dream. But it was the expression on Jane's face as she lay naked on the bed ready to receive Roland that really haunted him. Her strange smile, the absence of any resistance and her apparent acquiescence of the act, returned again and again to torment him. He still loved Jane, of that he was certain, but something precious in their relationship had now been destroyed forever. He felt a burning hatred for Roland that he'd never felt for anyone before.

Mark's feelings towards Crombie and Reid were a mixture of contempt and pure malice. He was determined to see them punished for their part in his misfortune despite the fact that they'd also been duped by Roland. But his rancour was partly assuaged when both gamekeepers approached him and apologised for their actions. Then, prompted by anger at their own betrayal, they explained the subtle cruelty that lay behind Roland's Machiavellian scheme.

The revelation only added further anguish to Mark's tortured mind, making him feel guilty for ever having questioned Jane's fidelity. He now knew that she'd sacrificed her honour to save the man she loved, and the knowledge that he'd doubted her consumed him with guilt. All this did little to ease his deep feeling of desolation. It did, however, rekindle his desire for revenge and with it a determination to see Roland punished for the evil he had done.

The two gamekeepers looked questioningly at Mark. 'If there's anything we can do to try and put matters right? Crombie ventured awkwardly.

Mark forced a wry smile. 'It's a bit too late for that. The damage is beyond repair and all the tears in the world won't wash away the evil that's been done. There's only retribution left now, and there you can help me.'

'Just tell us how,' they both answered eagerly.

'Swear out an affidavit to what you witnessed. It might help put Forster in gaol, though he deserves to be hung.'

'How do we go about that?' Crombie asked.

'I'm not sure. We probably need a lawyer or someone with legal authority like the captain.'

'Fat chance of that while we're cooped up here,' Reid said.

'I'll make a start by drafting out something you can both attest to as soon as I can lay my hands on pen and paper. We can see about the legalities later when we're transferred to a ship.' Mark didn't feel too confident but at least it was a beginning. 'The real answer,' he continued, 'is to bring Forster to court and for both of you to give evidence as witnesses.'

'It may be a long time before we're quit of the navy, but you have my word on that,' Crombie said.

'And mine,' Reid added.

Crombie held out his hand. 'No hard feelings, eh?'

Mark forced another smile and took the proffered hand. 'I'll try, but it won't be easy.'

Later that day, another large contingent of pressed men was taken on board the receiving ship and conditions became unbearably overcrowded. Amongst the newcomers were more quota men, the dregs from the local prison where gaol fever had been rife. Many of these men were heavily infested with lice and in the congested conditions of the hulk the other men were quickly contaminated.

Typhus was generally known as camp, ship or gaol fever, depending on where it broke out. It was a disease associated with filth, overcrowding and lice. After feeding on the blood of the infected quota men from the gaol, the lice drew the typhus micro-organisms into their stomachs, where they began to multiply. This would kill the lice within twelve days but not before they had transferred themselves to non-infected men, defecating live organisms on the skin of their hosts as they fed.

That evening, as Reid scratched irritably at his itching body, he rubbed the deadly typhus organism into his ruptured skin and the incubation process began.

*****

After spending four days on the hulk, Mark and the two gamekeepers, together with another dozen men were transferred to the 32-gun frigate *Phoebe* anchored at the Nore. On arrival, they were mustered on deck whilst the barber was sent for. Their heads were shaved and after being stripped naked, they were escorted to the bow of the ship where they were sluiced down with sea water and scrubbed clean. Their clothes were destroyed and they were issued with standard seamen's attire from the purser's slops, the cost of which would be deducted from their future pay.

Next, they were rated and entered into the ship's muster book. Mark and the two gamekeepers were rated as landsmen. Against each name in the muster book were details of the man's appearance; his measurements, colour of eyes and hair and any identifying marks or tattoos. The details would be circulated if a man jumped ship, for the naval authorities were ruthless in hunting down deserters.

As a pressed man, Mark was invited to volunteer his services and so have the letter "V" rather than "P" for pressed man against his name. He refused and persuaded Crombie and Reid to do likewise, even though it meant forfeiting any bounty money. He'd reasoned that being a volunteer, even a coerced one, would weaken his case in any future legal action against Roland. It would also ruin any hope of early release, tenuous though this may be. In theory, the navy could only legally press experienced seamen but, in practice, they turned a blind eye and took any able bodied man they could lay hands on. Mark's refusal brought frowns from the captain and angry scowls from the first lieutenant.

The seasoned sailor who had befriended Mark on board the receiving ship was rated as a volunteer and able seaman. He and Mark were assigned to the larboard watch and allocated the same mess number. He grinned at Mark and held out his hand. 'Jack Suggett's the name, from Whitby. I reckon you're from the Tyne by the sound of it.'

Mark took the proffered hand. 'Mark Standish and you're right about the Tyne.'

'And a man of some learning, too, I suspect.'

Mark looked guardedly at his new shipmate. 'What makes you say that?'

'Heard you talking to those other two,' he said, pointing to Crombie and Reid. Something about an affidavit. I know you're not a lawyer 'cause you wouldn't be here if you were.'

'No, I'm not a lawyer,' Mark conceded.

'Lawyer's clerk then?'

'No.'

'You've got learning, though. You can read and write, can't you?'

'Yes.'

'Then what do you do?'

'I was a pitman.'

The look of disbelief on Jack's face made Mark smile.

'Some pitmen can read and write just as some seamen can,' he chided.

'Aint many of 'em in my experience,' Jack replied. 'And them as can should best keep quiet about it.'

'Why?'

'Cause learning on the lower deck breeds troublemakers, according to some officers. Take my advice and keep quiet about it or you'll only draw attention to yourself. And that, my friend, usually means the lash.'

Mark was dismayed. 'But I must write to my wife and my father to let them know where I am.'

'Then do it privately and try not to be seen.'

'Some chance in a crowded ship like this.'

Jack sighed. 'I can see you're going to need some looking after,' he muttered to himself as they were led below. He made a sudden decision that, for better or for worse, he would take Mark under his wing. Somehow the idea appealed to him.

On deck the first lieutenant spoke to the master-at-arms. 'I think you'd better keep an eye on that fellow,' he said pointing to Mark's retreating figure. 'Something about him that bothers me.'

When they reached the deck below, Mark was astounded to see that there were scores of women on board. It was a bawdy scene bordering on debauchery, with obscene shouts and raucous laughter ringing through the confined space of the lower deck. Jack saw Mark's consternation. 'Ships wives,' he said grinning. 'They daren't give the men leave 'cos most of 'em will run. So they let the "wives" come aboard for a few days and if they behave themselves, the captain turns a blind eye.'

'Are they really married?' Mark asked.

Jack smiled at Mark's naivety. 'A sailor has a wife in every port, didn't you know?'

Mark suddenly realised the obvious. The women were prostitutes, though he later discovered that there was a small sprinkling of genuine wives among them. 'Some of them are very pretty he whispered.

'That's because the bumboat men only bring out the youngest and best looking women. That way, they're sure of getting paid.'

Mark learned that when a ship arrived in port, after a long commission, the crew were often owed several years back pay. The men would collect this in their hats with the amount chalked on the rim. To a sailor, it was a fortune even though the navy always withheld six months' pay. As few men were ever allowed leave, the navy deemed it prudent to allow wives on board. These were brought out to the ship by the bumboat men who only received their three shillings fare if the ladies they carried succeeded in attracting a sailor. Great care was taken, therefore, in selecting only the prettiest and best turned out prostitutes. Those that were rejected were returned to shore, usually amid scenes of mutual recrimination that often ended in foul-mouthed slanging matches. A dirty old crone who slipped through the net, would usually be rejected by the lieutenant or master-at-arms, who had the ship's reputation to think of.

The day's work was over and the crew had been piped to supper. The women and their "fancy men" could now make merry until the call to quarters for the evening muster. Mark and Jack found their allotted mess and joined the other six members who were seated on forms and sea chests around the mess table, which was hung by ropes from the deck beams. Three of their messmates also had wives and their coarse chatter and bawdy behaviour was echoed by the scores of other women scattered around the mess deck.

The food was revolting but the meal was enlivened by the evening issue of grog. Each man received a gill of pure rum mixed with three gills of water twice a day, one tot at noon and the other between four and five in the afternoon. However, the spirit ration had been swelled by the large quantities of rum that the women had managed to smuggle on board despite the watchful eyes of the master-at-arms and the ship's corporals. To most sailors, the attraction of a wife was the bladder of rum she brought on board, as much as for her sexual favours. After supper pandemonium broke out on the mess deck as drunken wives and their fancy men began to quarrel. Others, in their drunken stupor, made clumsy attempts to fornicate, oblivious to anyone watching.

Mark turned to Jack in disbelief. 'I thought the navy prided itself on its discipline?'

Jack grinned at his friend over his mug of grog. 'Oh it does, matey. Just wait till we put to sea. You'll see a difference then.' He laughed and took another unsteady swig from his mug that had been replenished with most of Mark's tot. He was pleased that he'd guessed right when he decided to take Mark under his wing. It was good to have a friend who didn't drink much, especially aboard a man-of-war where grog was the unofficial currency of the lower deck.

The knowledge that he was now trapped in the navy filled Mark with despair. His urgent need was to write to Jane and his father to reassure them and let them know where he'd been taken. He had to do this before the ship sailed, but first he needed paper, quill and ink. He turned to Jack. 'Where can I find writing materials?'

'You'd best try one of the ship's clerks or the purser's steward.'

'Where can I find them?'

Jack shrugged and waved his arm. 'Among that lot, somewhere,' he said indicating the length of the crowded mess deck.

The lower deck was about one hundred and thirty feet long with a maximum beam of thirty-five feet. The whole width of the after end was taken up by a large cabin, called the gunroom, where the ship's officers lived. It had a large table down the centre and tiny cabins down each side where the commissioned officers slept. Forward of the gunroom there were more small cabins against the ship's side which provided accommodation for the warrant officers, the bosun, gunner and carpenter. A further large cabin formed the midshipmen's berth. Immediately forward of the officers and warrant officers accommodation, the marines slung their hammocks. They formed a barrier between the officers aft and the seamen and petty officers, who slung their hammocks further forward. There was no natural light on the lower deck save for that which managed to filter down the hatches and companionways. In the evening it was lit by lanterns and candles, known as "pusser's glims".

It was whilst searching for writing materials among the drunken sailors and their raucous women that Mark discovered the true value of drink as a ship's currency. Paper, quill and ink could be provided in exchange for four tots of grog, though it was a bargain that would not please his friend Jack Suggett.

Mark also sought out the two gamekeepers to tell them he would mention their own circumstances in his letter so that their families could also be informed. Crombie, who had now accepted his fate with a dull resignation, nodded his thanks. Reid said nothing and didn't seem to hear what Mark was saying. He lay propped up against the ship's side with his eyes closed, sweating profusely and breathing heavily.

Mark became concerned. 'How long has he been like this?'

Crombie shrugged. 'Soon after we came on board the frigate.'

'Didn't the surgeon notice anything?'

'Obviously not, but he wasn't so bad then. The scrubbing seems to have made him worse.'

Mark took a closer look at the sick man and pulled back his shirt. 'He's got some sort of fever. He's coming out in a rash.' There were large purple and brown skin eruptions on Reid's shoulders spreading down to his body. 'I think we should get him to the sick bay and ask the surgeon to look at him.'

When the ship's surgeon was called, he removed Reid's shirt and after a quick examination, pronounced ship fever. He ordered Reid to be put ashore immediately and taken to hospital, then went aft to consult with the captain.

After the evening muster hammocks were piped down and Jack showed Mark how to sling his from the wooden cleats nailed to the beams above the deck. Each man was allotted the regulation space of fourteen inches between hammocks.

'A man can't sleep in that narrow space,' Mark protested.

'You'd better get used to it,' Jack said. 'It's all you'll get.' Seeing Mark's look of shocked disbelief he added, 'It's not so bad when

375

we're at sea. There's always one watch on duty so you'll have double the space. You'd better get in quick before the others,' he advised.

Following Jack's instructions, Mark climbed into his hammock and was soon wedged in so tight by his neighbours that he couldn't move. The men on each side of him had wives which added to the pressure as well as his embarrassment. The frigate was well manned by wartime standards with only a dozen men short of her complement of two hundred and twenty. Soon, the lower deck was festooned with hammocks slung from the beams above, like a large colony of bats hanging from the roof of a cave.

Mark soon realised that a man-of-war in port was no place for the squeamish. As he lay in his hammock, wedged firmly between his neighbours, he could hear the sounds of lovemaking all around him. Some of it sounded violent with excitement but most of it was subdued, even to the point of being laboured, as the effects of the alcohol took hold.

The seaman on Mark's left was too drunk to make love, as was his woman. The man on his right, lying with his wife on top, made a valiant effort to co-operate before falling asleep. Fascinated, Mark raised his head and saw the woman's naked buttocks rising and falling in a steady rhythm. Suddenly, she stopped and cursing loudly, tried to wake her man, but without success. Then, sensing she was being watched, she peered out over the edge of the hammock and her drink-fuzzed eyes met Mark's. 'You all alone, luvvy?' she said, grinning wickedly.

Mark smiled back weakly, careful not to offend but equally anxious not to encourage. 'She's gone to the heads,' he lied.

The woman gave him a strange look and sank back on top of her man. At that point the call came for lights out and Mark settled back in his hammock and tried to go to sleep. But misery and despair overwhelmed him and sleep wouldn't come. He lay staring into the darkness until he sensed a sudden movement from the next hammock. He felt a hand beneath his blanket gently exploring his body until it found his crotch. It was an expert hand and it began to manipulate gently, slowly coaxing an erection. Mark groaned and closed his eyes. He hoped the hand belonged to the woman, but he was too tired and miserable to care.

At four o'clock in the morning the prolonged shrill of the bosun's call echoed down the main and fore hatches to the lower deck. This was followed by the shouts of the bosun's mates as, with lantern in one hand and a rope colt in the other, they made their way through the rows of close packed hammocks on the mess deck. 'Rouse out there, you sleepers! Show a leg! Out or down!'

A leg that was shown over the edge of the hammock that looked smooth and feminine allowed the occupant to remain undisturbed. Otherwise, it was everybody out. Any laggard had his hammock unceremoniously cut down with the sleeper still in it.

Mark sighed and hauled himself out and on to the deck. He heard the order 'lash and carry' and struggled to unsling his hammock, at the same time watching to see what the others were doing.

'Not like that.' Jack's voice brought relief and reassurance. 'This way, now watch carefully.' He showed Mark how to correctly lash his hammock with seven turns of a cord called a hammock lasher. This transformed the hammock into a tight roll, like a long sausage. It was then unhooked and slung over the shoulder to be taken up on deck and stowed in its numbered place in the hammock nettings. These ran round the upper part of the ship making a protective bulwark for the marines and small arms parties.

The ship's routine now followed its normal daily pattern with the scrubbing and cleaning of the main deck.

Hand pumps were rigged over the side sending streams of water over the deck, whilst lines of men with brushes scrubbed the surface clean. The deck was then sanded and holystoned until it reached the pristine condition that would satisfy the standards set by most captains. It was hard work. The holystones were large pieces of Portland stone which had to be dragged back and forth across the deck by ropes. In the areas which were too narrow for the holystones, smaller hand stones, called bibles, were used.

At daybreak, drums beat out from every ship anchored at the Nore, the sound echoing across the water until a man "could see a grey goose a mile". Each ship then hoisted her colours.

After breakfast, which was burgoo, a kind of porridge which tasted foul, the task of taking on board the final shipment of stores began.

All day long the provisions arrived and had to be hoisted from the supply boats moored alongside and stowed in the frigate's hold. Most of it was in casks, salted beef, pork and casks of water, beer and rum. Bread, or ship's biscuit, was supplied in two hundred and twenty-four pound puncheons and one hundred and twelve pound bags and stored in the bread-room, a large apartment lined with tin, and artificially dried by hanging stoves. The biscuits were baked at the royal bakeries attached to the dockyards and were mostly made from wheat and pea-flour. As each man received one pound of biscuit a day, an incredible amount was needed to provision a ship at the start of a commission. The *Phoebe* carried over twelve tons.

'Looks as though we're in for a long cruise,' Jack mused as he contemplated the bulging hold. 'I reckon we're for the Channel or the West Indies.'

'What makes you say that?' Mark asked.

'The rum.'

'The rum?

'Because if we were headed for the Mediterranean we'd be taking on more black strap. That's wine,' he added, seeing Mark's puzzled look. 'A seaman's allowed a pint of grog a day or a gallon of beer. But in some places, like the Mediterranean, they give us a pint of wine, usually red. We calls it black strap,' he said contemptuously.

Mark suddenly realised that if the ship was bound for the West Indies, he'd better get a letter off as soon as possible. But who could he trust to post it, he wondered. It was a casual observation from Jack which helped to concentrate his mind.

'You'd best keep your head down,' he advised.

'Why?'

'I think you're being watched. The master-at-arms, or one of his ship's corporals, has been keeping an eye on you all day. Haven't you noticed?'

'No. Why should they be interested in me?'

'Depends on what you were up to before you were pressed.'

'Just a small dispute with the pit owners.'

'And somebody wanted you out of the way?'

'Yes.'

'That somebody's had your card marked, shipmate. And like I said, officers don't trust a man with learning on the lower deck. They'll have you marked down as a troublemaker, so keep your head down,' he repeated.

Mark decided that if he was being watched, he'd better follow Jack's advice. It was also possible that his letters would be intercepted, assuming he was allowed to write home. He fingered the four shillings in his pocket, the money held been carrying on the day he was pressed. He would ask one of the women to post his letter when they were sent ashore. Four shillings would be more than enough, especially as the postage charge was paid by the recipient. He knew his father would be more than happy to pay and also arrange delivery of the letter to Jane which he would enclose.

After supper that evening, Mark obtained his writing materials and wrote a long and detailed letter to his father. He then set about the difficult and sensitive task of composing his thoughts into a letter to Jane. His words were consoling and tender with love, for he knew what she must be suffering. He tried to impart a confidence he didn't feel, for he knew he had to give Jane faith and with it, hope for the future. After sealing the letters, he placed them safely inside his shirt next to his body.

The following day, all wives were ordered ashore along with the pedlars who had been allowed on board to sell their trashy wares to the sailors at exorbitant prices. There were some surprisingly tender scenes between some of the men and their temporary wives when the time came to bid farewell. But the departure of the pedlars caused considerable acrimony, as many men refused to pay for their rings, watch chains, shoe buckles, waistcoats and the vast range of rubbish that was usually sold at five times more than the goods were worth.

Mark looked at the departing women and tried to seek out one he thought looked reliable enough to entrust with his letter. His eyes finally lit on the woman who had shared the hammock next to his own. After three days of debauchery on board, she looked surprisingly pretty.

The woman caught Mark's gaze and smiled back. 'You've left it a bit late, luvvy. I can't do much for you now.' Her hand lightly grazed his crotch as she fluttered her eyelashes. 'Pity really, 'cos I really fancied you.'

'You can do one thing for me,' Mark pleaded, trying to maintain his composure.

'What's that?'

'Post this letter for me when you get ashore. It's very important to me. I'll give you four shillings.'

Her eyes widened. 'It must be important to be worth four shillings. You married?'

'Yes.'

'I thought so.'

'You'll do it then?'

'Of course I will, luvvy.' She guessed he'd not long been married, which explained his reticence. He's not queer after all, she thought, and this pleased her.

Mark handed over the letter and the four shillings. He guessed that the woman was illiterate, so he carefully-explained what she had to do when she got to the post office in Sheerness. He watched to see that the woman was safely over the side and into the waiting wherry. He continued to watch until the boat was a dark speck near the shoreline.

By late afternoon, the last of the bumboats had cleared the ship and the crew were put to cleaning up the mess on the lower deck. Mark could now detect a sharp change in the ship's routine as the rigid discipline of a man-of-war was re-imposed on the men.

That evening, the ship's surgeon returned to the *Phoebe* after visiting the hospital and the crew learned that Reid had died from the fever. The news caused little comment, for few had known the man. Reid's death brought neither sorrow nor satisfaction to Mark; only an angry frustration that a key witness to Roland's crime was now lost to him.

The following morning, the ship was fumigated by pouring sulphuric acid and the powder of nitre on heated sand. After subjecting the crew to a thorough medical examination, the surgeon reported to the captain that he was satisfied there were no further cases of fever. With relief, the captain ordered "make sail" and the *Phoebe* proceeded to sea.

Jack was soon proved right; the frigate was to escort a convoy of merchantmen to the West Indies. 'You can say goodbye to England for at least six months,' he announced to his disconsolate friend.

Mark could only nod bleakly as he gazed astern at the receding shoreline.

When the bumboat landed the wives at Sheerness, word quickly spread that a large number of solders, drinking in the nearby hostelries, were seeking female company. The women immediately began to range in on their new targets.

The one entrusted with Mark's letter dithered at first, but decided she could always call in at the post office later. But the corporal who took her fancy proved a demanding customer with a better head for drink. Six hours later, as she lay in a drunken stupor, he took her money and left. When she awoke, all she had left was Mark's letter. Screaming and cursing, she tore up the letter and threw the pieces on the filth strewn floor. Then lurching through the door, she staggered off in pursuit of the corporal.

CHAPTER 39

Convoy duty was hated by the navy and Captain Ash, of the *Phoebe*, showed his resentment by imposing a strict ship's routine backed up by harsh discipline. Mark soon realised that the daily pattern of a ship in port bore no resemblance to that of a man-of-war at sea. At any one time, half the crew were involved in sailing and working the ship. The watch system meant four hours' work and four hours rest, but in bad weather the call "all hands" brought everyone up on deck.

Each morning, just before dawn, the ship beat to quarters to the sound of the marine drummer tapping out the tune Hearts of Oak. Each crew member had his allotted task and station which was detailed in the ship's "quarters, watch and station bill". This listed every task to be carried out in a ship under way, in battle or in an emergency. As the men hurried to their posts, two lookouts were sent aloft and the decks were sprinkled with wet sand. The thin bulkheads which formed the officers' cabins were dismantled and taken into the hold, along with any furniture, to give a clean sweep of the deck fore and aft. The topmen securely stopped the top-sail sheets, rope preventer lifts and slung the lower yards with chain. Gun crews cast their guns loose from their lashings, struck the ports open and ran out the guns. All this activity was carried out silently and in a matter of a few minutes. This was the navy at its disciplined best, running like a well-oiled machine. Mark could not help but be impressed.

As soon as it became light enough to report horizon clear, the ship reverted to the normal day's business. Scrubbing the upper deck removed the sand which had been sprinkled earlier, sails were adjusted and halyards slackened, or taken up a few inches, to ease wear and tear by minimising chafing on the sheaves of the blocks. The galley fire was lit and the cook started to prepare breakfast, whilst the crew carried on with the multitude of tasks aimed at keeping the ship clean and tidy. At half-past six, the off duty watch was called and the ritual of lashing and stowing hammocks took place. Then, at eight o'clock the hands were piped to breakfast, sitting on forms either side of the mess table which was slung from the deck beams above. Breakfast was the usual burgoo, made from a portion of each man's weekly ration of three pints of oatmeal boiled into gruel. This would sometimes be supplemented by ship's biscuit and a meagre ration of butter and cheese.

Half an hour was allowed for breakfast, and then it was back to the routine of ship cleaning and maintenance. At nine thirty, the men paraded for divisions under their respective lieutenants. Then, at eleven o'clock, the boatswain's mates piped "all hands to witness punishment" and the men trooped aft where the marines were drawn up with their muskets and the officers were present wearing formal dress. The master-at-arms, the ship's policeman, then brought the accused men before the captain and stated their crimes or misconduct. Mark had long since discovered that the captain of a man-of-war was "God" on board his own ship. His word was law and in matters of discipline and punishment, he was both judge and jury. On his whim, a man might be reprimanded or given six dozen lashes of the dreaded cat-of-nine-tails.

At half past eleven came the most pleasant order of the day, "clear decks and up spirits". Each mess member took it in turns to act as mess cook for a week. On hearing "up spirits", the cook dashed to the rum butt carrying the mess blackjack, a small tub which held the mess grog ration. After receiving the grog from the master's mate he returned to the mess table to the accompaniment of banging plates and cheers from his messmates. The ritual of sharing out the grog then took place and debts were settled and new favours agreed.

The afternoon was taken up with exercises for the watch not on duty and at four o'clock hands were piped to supper where the second issue of grog took place. After supper the drum beat to quarters and all hands hurried to their action-stations. The guns were cast loose and the lieutenants and midshipmen made a careful inspection of the men and gear under their charge.

'Stand straight,' Jack whispered to Mark, 'and don't look the officers in the eye,' he added.

'Why?'

'You'll draw their attention. Remember you're a marked man and they're watching for signs of being drunk. It's a flogging offence and the master-at-arms is always on the look-out to arrest the man who's unsteady on his feet.'

It was an anxious wait for Mark as his heart-beat quickened.

The first lieutenant saluted Captain Ash. 'All present and sober, sir, if you please.'

Mark struggled to stop himself sagging with relief.

After the evening muster, the drum beat the retreat, hammocks were piped down and at eight o'clock lights were extinguished on the lower deck and the first watch went on duty. Weather permitting, the ship settled down for the night, the quiet only being broken by the creaking of timbers and tiller ropes, the sounds of straining canvas and the occasional cry of "All's well" from the sentries.

At first, Mark found it difficult to cope with the monotony of the daily routine. The tedium of each day was only matched by the repetitiveness of the food, a large amount of which he found inedible. Each man received a weekly ration of seven pounds of bread in the form of ship's biscuit. He also received four pounds of salted beef, two pounds of salted pork, two pints of peas, one-and-a-half pints of oatmeal and a few ounces of sugar, butter and cheese. The meat was mostly made up of bone, fat and gristle supplied by corrupt contractors and was often found to be rotten when the casks were opened. The butter soon became rancid and the cheese turned so foul that few could eat it.

Water in the casks became stagnant after a few weeks and Mark learned to mix vinegar with it to make it palatable. He traded some of his grog for vinegar to supplement his weekly ration which was only half a pint. Occasionally, he obtained some tea or cocoa which helped to disguise the foul taste of the water.

After only a week, the beer had run out and rum became the regular daily issue. Mark found the grog to be a much more valuable currency in which to trade. He now began to understand why men sold their souls for grog and hoarded their daily ration so that they could get drunk once in a while. To some, it was the only escape from the hardship and misery of a sailor's life and well worth the risk of a flogging if discovered drunk.

Captain Ash had the advantage of being the son of a wealthy landowner and Member of Parliament. He was a perfectionist with an obsession for smart sail drill and good gunnery. His promotion from master and commander to post captain, and command of a fifth rate, fuelled his ambition. He was now determined to make his name as a fighting frigate commander in the style of his hero, the brilliant Lord Cochrane. Ash was only twenty-six and, as promotion from post rank was purely by seniority, he could confidently expect to reach flag rank in the fullness of time.

In contrast, Mr Urquhart, the first lieutenant, came from a poor Scottish family with no political or social influence. This explained why, at the age of thirty-eight, he was still a lieutenant, and why he now held a grudge against the service in which he had served since he was a twelve year old midshipman. His bitterness had made him bad tempered and allowed a cruel streak to surface. He was disliked by his fellow officers and greatly feared by the crew. It was fortunate that the Admiralty only allowed a ship's captain to order punishment and Captain Ash, being a fair and humane man, was able to curb the worst excesses of his second-in-command.

Both captain and first lieutenant were superb seamen and it was this mutual respect that helped them maintain a reasonable working relationship. But Captain Ash disliked flogging as a punishment and used it sparingly. This annoyed the first lieutenant who saw it as a sign of weakness. Under Captain Ash, flogging was reserved for serious crimes, such as mutiny, desertion, striking an officer, wilful disobedience and theft. However, he made an exception to this rule if a man was regularly found to be drunk. Drunkenness was always a problem in a man-of-war and, if left unchecked, could hazard the safety of the ship.

The animosity between the two men came to a head six weeks into the voyage when Captain Ash forbade the further use of starting the crew. "Starting" was a brutal form of coercion that had long been practiced by the navy as a means of expediting an order. On the order, "start that man", a bosun's mate, wielding a "colt" made from a length of rope with the end strands unlaid to form three knotted tails, would lash the unfortunate offender until ordered to stop.

It's indiscriminate and cruel use did little to improve efficiency and only bred resentment among the crew. It had recently been proscribed by the Admiralty but some captains still turned a blind eye once at sea. Captain Ash had allowed it for a specific purpose which he now felt had been achieved. Not so his first lieutenant.

'I must protest, sir!' Urquhart exploded as they reached the limited privacy of the great stern cabin.

'Protest, Mr Urquhart?' Captain Ash raised his eyebrows. Are you questioning my orders?'

'With respect, sir, I think we're being too soft of the men.'

'You mean I'm being too soft.'

Urquhart remained silent and Ash took this to mean yes. He felt his anger rising but kept it under control. 'So you think we should continue with starting the men?'

'Yes, sir.'

'Even though the Admiralty forbids it?'

'The Admiralty forbade any captain to award more than twelve lashes until 1806, but few captains took any heed of their lordships. And flogging must be entered into the log,' he added, to reinforce his point.

Captain Ash sighed. 'I don't have to explain my actions to you, Mr Urquhart, but I will make an exception just this once. I don't agree with starting and never have. But because more than half the crew are landsmen, and with precious few able seamen among the rest, the safe handling of the ship might have been in jeopardy. I therefore agreed to allow starting to continue in the hope that it might speed up the training process.'

'It has, sir. It's the only way and all the more reason to continue, unless.....' Urquhart broke off, uncertain how to phrase his next point.

'Unless I order more floggings?' Ash had read Urquhart's mind.

'It's the only way to enforce discipline,' Urquhart said doggedly.

'I disagree,' Ash answered firmly.

'Some men only respond to starting or the lash,' Urquhart persisted.

'Regrettably that's true but that only applies to a small hard core of men. Most of the crew will respond to fair treatment and good leadership.'

With respect, sir, some will see it as a sign of weakness.' Urquhart was still unconvinced. Officers could order a man to be started but only the captain could order a flogging. He resented any restriction on his own power to bully the crew.

Captain Ash was fast losing patience with his first lieutenant. 'Let me make myself clear, lieutenant. Starting the men will cease forthwith. If I see a petty officer carrying a colt, let alone using one, he'll be instantly de-rated. Do I make myself clear?'

'Yes, sir.'

'And let me make myself equally clear on another matter. The sight of a thirteen year old midshipman beating a sailor old enough to be his father disgusts me. He knows that because he is a junior officer, the sailor can't retaliate and that is abuse of his position. I won't have it, Mr Urquhart, and I expect you, as first lieutenant of this ship to see that it doesn't happen again.'

Urquhart was almost speechless with frustration. Then, seeing the captain's steely look as he awaited an answer, muttered a reluctant 'Aye, aye, sir.'

'And finally,' the captain went on, 'I'll only order a flogging if it's absolutely necessary. In my book the lash is a cruel and ineffectual form of punishment. It makes a bad man worse and breaks the spirit of a good man. I hope I made myself clear.'

'Yes, sir.' Urquhart now knew that further argument would be futile and counterproductive. His dislike of Mark and his determination to have him flogged now seemed doomed to permanent failure.

Captain Ash appeared to read his first lieutenant's mind. 'You seem to have a down on this landsman fellow, Standish. Is he a malcontent?'

'I think so, sir. He refused to volunteer.'

'That's no crime, surely?'

'No, sir, but he's got some education and I don't trust a man with learning on the lower deck.'

'What did he do before he was pressed?'

'He was a pitman, I believe.'

'Was he, by God!' Captain Ash was astounded. 'Unusual that, an educated pitman. How did he come to be pressed? We're only supposed to take seamen and the like.'

'Seems he was the leader of a pitmen's strike. I expect the owners wanted him out of the way.'

'Well they certainly got their wish. Must have been quite a thorn in their side for them to go that far.'

'More than likely, sir, from what I've heard.'

387

Captain Ash was even more curious. He didn't normally take a personal interest in a member of his crew as insignificant as a newly pressed landsman. But his curiosity was aroused and he determined to keep an eye on Mark. Then, sensing that his first lieutenant was still unhappy, he changed tack. 'Now that our business is over, Mr Urquhart, perhaps you'll join me for dinner. I have an excellent Madeira I think you might enjoy.'

The prohibition of starting, which under Lieutenant Urquhart had got out of hand, was welcomed by the crew. It came as a special relief to Mark who had been subjected to a campaign of persecution by the first lieutenant since the *Phoebe* had left the Nore. Urquhart wanted to see Mark flogged and had him carefully watched for any sign of drunkenness. But success was denied to him by Mark's fortunate decision to trade his grog rather than drink it. In this Mark was helped by the veteran master-at-arms who, though a strict disciplinarian, was unusually fair and honest. If a man was not drunk, he refused to place him on report and no amount of pressure by the first lieutenant could persuade him otherwise. Besides, he knew that Captain Ash was watching the situation and he had no desire to incur his displeasure. He knew the captain could disrate him; a godly power denied to the first lieutenant.

Unfortunately for Mark, the younger midshipmen were not so scrupulous, and their fear of the first lieutenant was such that they were happy to co-operate in making his life a misery. But he always remembered Jack's advice. 'No matter how much they provoke you, don't strike back. The young bastards are officers, so if you do it's a flogging for sure.' Mark took the youngsters blows without defending himself and somehow managed to control his temper. But this did not save him from being started at every opportunity and his arms and shoulders were heavily bruised by the colts wielded by the bosun's mates. The dreaded order "start that man" was immediately followed by a welter of blows from a burly bosun's mate and there was no redress. The banning of this cruel custom came as a timely relief to him, for the degradation was such that, sooner or later, he knew he would lose control and retaliate.

Gradually, the trauma of his impressment began to ease as Mark slowly adjusted to shipboard life. But his hatred of Roland became obsessive as the injustice of his position continued to fester in his mind. He also missed Jane and his longing for her grew with every day that passed. And yet, though his heart ached with love for her, a corner of his mind was still tortured by doubts that, try as he may, he could not entirely dispel. It was as if a precious link in the golden chain of their love had been fractured, leaving the strength of the chain uncertain.

To alleviate his mental turmoil he concentrated his efforts on becoming a good sailor. In the process, he developed a keen interest in the ship's guns and discovered an aptitude for gunnery. This was quickly spotted by the gunner, an amiable and respected warrant officer from Kent called Brewis.

Captain Ash regarded gunnery as a science and deplored the Royal Navy's preference for short guns. Long guns, as favoured by the American Navy, were far more accurate at a distance and when laid point blank, or horizontal, could be fired with great precision at targets up to three hundred yards. For this distance, the short gun had to be elevated and this greatly reduced its accuracy. But the Admiralty preferred commanders to engage at close quarters where the short gun usually proved more destructive.

The Royal Navy was also frugal in the issue of powder and shot, which inhibited the opportunities for gunnery practice. However, keen and wealthy captains, like Ash, could overcome this problem by personally paying for extra supplies. Because of this the *Phoebe* could enjoy the luxury of daily gunnery practice, with the guns being fired live at targets, usually a beef-cask with four feet square of canvas attached. Each gun was expected to load, run out and fire to within five yards of the target, every minute, to meet the required standard. Only at close quarters would speed of fire become paramount.

After two months of convoy escort, Captain Ash now felt he could relax a little. His strategy of allowing starting for the first six weeks of the voyage, together with a regime of strict but fair punishment, was beginning to bear fruit. The ship was now being handled with smartness and efficiency. Even the gunnery was improving, though not as much as he would have wished. He was pleased to see that many of the landsmen were becoming proficient and some were developing into good seamen. A few even indicated a potential for promotion and Standish, he noted, was the most prominent of these, though he doubted if the first lieutenant would agree. A large part of the overall improvement was due to Ash's insistence that the landsmen's duties should not be confined to the dull and menial tasks that were usually given to them on board a man-of-war. By a judicious rotation of duties, the more intelligent received training in all aspects of seamanship.

As the convoy approached Barbados, Mark was promoted to ordinary seaman and his monthly pay was increased from the landsman's twenty-two shillings and sixpence to twenty-five shillings the rate for an ordinary seaman. His aptitude for gunnery had also been noted by Captain Ash and he was made captain of his gun crew. He was also transferred from the waist of the ship to the afterguard which further enhanced his status among the crew.

When Mark had joined the *Phoebe* he was quickly made aware of the social hierarchy that existed on the lower deck of a man-of-war. The crew were divided into five groups, each with its clearly defined place on the social pecking order. First, there were the sheet anchor or forecastle men, selected from the older and more highly skilled able seamen. Their duties involved working the anchor when weighing and anchoring and tending to the foresail and jibs. Next came the topmen, young and agile able seamen, whose duties were carried out above the lower yards. These two groups formed the elite of the lower deck and slung their hammocks at the forward end of the mess deck.

The third group were known as the afterguard, comprising mostly of ordinary seamen and landsmen, who worked the after braces, main, mizzen and lower stay-sails. Then came the largest group, called waisters, who worked in the waist of the ship handling the fore and main sheets. They were also the scavengers, swabbers, pumpers and doers of the ship's dirty work. Waisters were made up from landsmen who were unfit and untrained for other duties and became the butt of the other groups.

Lastly, came the idlers whose name, like the waisters, bore little relationship to their tasks. They were made up from the carpenter, gunner, sail maker and their mates as well as the ships servants, clerks and cooks. Unlike the other four groups, they did not have to stand watches and were on duty from dawn until eight in the evening. Even the waisters could join the rest of the crew in looking down on the idlers.

Mark celebrated his promotion by taking a small tot of grog at supper, much to the chagrin of Jack who was hoping for his usual extra free ration. The meal was spartan and unappetising, it being what sailors called a "banyan" day, one of the three days in the week when meat was not issued. Instead, each man received a few ounces of sugar, butter and cheese to add to their peas, oatmeal and the inevitable ship's biscuit. The heat had turned the butter liquid and the cheese was rotten.

Deciding that the cheese was inedible, Mark took a bite out of his ship's biscuit and started to chew. After a few moments, an expression of extreme distaste contorted his face. Quickly cleaning his mouth, he threw the rest of the biscuit on the mess table.

Jack looked up in surprise. 'What's up?'

'What the hell are those?' Mark spluttered, pointing to the biscuit.

'Bargemen.'

'They look like maggots to me.'

'They are, but we calls 'em bargemen.' Jack said, grinning at Mark's discomfort.

The maggots were large and white with black heads. They were fat and cold to the taste but not bitter. Mark shivered at the thought. 'How can we be expected to eat biscuits that are full of maggots?'

'Best eat 'em in your hammock after lights out. You can't see 'em in the dark' Jack added, winking at the other members of the mess.

'You're not serious, are you?' Mark said in surprise.

'There's nowt wrong with bargemen,' Jack retorted. 'Full of goodness they are. Just wait a few more weeks till the bloody weevils get in. Now those little bastards really do taste rotten.'

Mark groaned as the misery and helplessness of his life on the lower deck returned. He knew he would never be able to come to terms with serving in His Britannic Majesty's Navy, yet to abandon hope was to surrender to a downward spiral of despair. It was only his love for Jane and he deep hatred of Roland that gave him the will to go on.

CHAPTER 40

The stalemate of the binding strike continued for the rest of the year with little sign that either side would give way. Hundreds of pitmen had now been imprisoned including most of their leaders and, to the exasperation of the owners, they resolutely continued to refuse the new bond. The men who were still free also refused to negotiate whilst their colleagues remained incarcerated. To break the impasse, the Reverend William Nesfield intervened and by January, 1811, a compromise was reached. Four of the pitmen's leaders, replying on behalf of the thirty-one collieries involved in the dispute, agreed to a compromise and acceded to an April binding bringing the first major co-ordinated strike in the great northern coalfield to an end.

But as the hard frosts of winter eased into the showery breezes of spring, Jane's thoughts were no longer with the pitmen's brotherhood, which she now saw as the prime cause of her misery. As the months passed, with still no news of Mark, her fears grew and her despondency deepened. At first, she had visited Dora several times each week and even spent a whole week in Newcastle, staying at Henry's house. But as the summer approached, she began to go out less and spent almost all of her time cooped up in the cottage, to the great concern of Dora and Henry. Outwardly, Jane appeared self-possessed, almost to the point of being cheerful, but there was always a strange look of melancholy in her eyes which disturbed those close to her. They watched in helpless dismay as she increasingly withdrew into her own strange world of detachment.

Henry pursued his efforts to seek news of Mark and harried the Admiralty incessantly, fuming at their evasive tactics and procrastination. By June, more than six months after Mark's impressment, he was still without firm information. But he now felt more certain than ever that his son was still alive. Unfortunately, without clear confirmation of this fact, he was unable to convince Jane.

'Why hasn't he written to me?' she asked.

'If he's at sea aboard a man-of-war, it will be difficult to send a letter,' Henry explained. He refrained from adding that a King's ship could be abroad on active service for several years.

Jane looked at him, her eyes filled with despair. 'I might never see him again. I don't think I could live with that.'

The tone of her voice and the anguish in her expression shocked Henry. 'You mustn't abandon hope,' he said, trying to encourage her. 'Mark's a survivor. I just know he'll be all right.' But he saw from the look on her face that she didn't believe him.

Despite Jane's protestations Dora and her sister, Alice, took it in turns to stay with her during the final stages of her pregnancy. At the end of August, as the summer days began to shorten, Jane gave birth to a son and named him Michael.

It had been a difficult birth, as if Jane was reluctant to co-operate. But finally a tired but exultant Dora, smiling happily down at her daughter, gently placed the baby in Jane's arms. 'He's a real bonny bairn, just like his dad,' she said.

Jane made no reply and lay holding her baby as if she were ashamed of her new found motherhood. Dora's smile slowly faded as she saw the look of indifference in her daughter's eyes. 'Are you all right, pet?' she asked anxiously.

'Yes, Mam. Just a bit tired and sore,' Jane answered. But she knew it was more than that. There was no heady feeling of joy at giving birth, only a strange emptiness that left her feeling wretched and lonely. She forced herself to look at her baby, trying to seek out the signs she desperately wished to see. But what she saw only intensified her doubts, for she discerned only the features of Roland in the sleeping child's face. She watched as the baby stirred, momentarily opening his eyes, and her doubts increased. She wanted to love her baby, convince herself it was Mark's child, but somehow the emotion wouldn't come. The odious picture of Roland still lurked in her mind and with it a loathing at her own complicity. The guilt of her rape on that fateful night still lingered, corroding her confidence. Was it really her fault, she wondered? Tears welled in her eyes and a cold desolation swept over her.

Dora stayed for the rest of the day, fussing about the cottage and finding things to do until it was time to leave. She'd watched with growing unease as Jane's strange, subdued mood showed no signs of changing. She couldn't quite put her finger on it, but the relationship between Jane and her baby wasn't as it should be. She paused at the door before leaving. 'You sure you'll be all right now?'

Jane smiled for the first time since the birth. 'Of course I will, mam. You get yourself home and feed those hungry menfolk of yours.'

The smile reassured Dora a little. 'I'll send them up later to see the new addition to the family,' she said proudly. But as she walked home, her doubts returned. There's something wrong, I'm sure, she thought.

As the weeks went by, Jane gradually recovered her physical strength but her mental turmoil would not go away. She fed and looked after her baby, but her actions were perfunctory rather than truly maternal. She tried hard to love the child, welcoming its trusting dependence on her and, at times, almost convincing herself that she was a loving mother. But her heart told her otherwise and she wept tears of shame and frustration at her failure.

The days began to get colder and soon the early autumn leaves began to fall, covering the ground in a russet coloured carpet that would soon dampen into leaf mould. With still no news of Mark, Jane finally lost all hope and retreated further into her protective cocoon of delusive indifference. It was a defensive measure, a self-induced detachment that helped her to remain aloof from a world that only brought her pain and unhappiness. She now took to walking aimlessly in the woods surrounding the cottage, carrying her baby cradled in her arms. It was preferable to being cooped up in the cottage with all its painful memories. Having abandoned all hope of ever being reunited with Mark, the cottage was fast becoming a prison. It was on one of these walks that she again met Roland.

It was a chance meeting, for Roland had no wish to flaunt his father's final ultimatum to stay away from Jane. Their paths crossed in a clearing in the woods when Roland, mounted on a fine hunter, suddenly rode out of the trees. They watched each other in stunned silence for a while before a twisted smile crept over Roland's face. He doffed his hat in an exaggerated gesture. 'Good morning, my dear. What a pleasant surprise.'

Jane's shock turned to a mixture of fear and anger. 'Stay away from me,' she shouted, backing away from him.

'His smile vanished. 'Indeed I shall,' he snapped back at her. Then noting the bundle she carried was a baby, he added 'Is that yours?'

'Yes.' There was more defiance than pride in her answer.

He leered at her. 'Is it mine too?'

'If he grows up to be a cheat, a coward and a man without honour, then the answer is yes.

Roland's sardonic humour turned to anger. 'More likely he'll turn out to be a troublemaker like your husband,' he snarled.

'Then my husband will have cause to be proud of him when he returns.'

'If he returns,' Roland corrected.

'And why shouldn't he?' Jane demanded, but without conviction.

'You really do want him back don't you?' he said, tauntingly.

'That was a stupid question, even from you,' she flared.

Her insolence made him angry and knowing he couldn't have her again, he wanted to retaliate in a way she would never forget. So, determined to hurt her, he rashly told her the truth of how he'd lied to her on the night Mark was taken. How he'd tricked her into being raped and made her husband watch. 'Judging by your performance, my dear, I doubt if he thought you were an unwilling partner.' He laughed at her distress before delivering a vicious coupe de grace. 'You must be mad to think he'd want to come home to a slut like you.' With that he spurred his horse and galloped off, leaving her numbed with shock. She leaned weakly against a tree for support, feeling a rising nausea inside her. When it finally subsided, it left her feeling dirty and cheapened.

The following day, Jane wrote two letters. One was addressed to Henry and the other to Duncan Forster. She made sure that each letter was correctly addressed, before carefully sealing them. She then went to considerable trouble and expense to ensure that the letters would be properly delivered.

When she returned to the cottage, she sat down and wrote a long letter to her mother. When she finished it, she carefully read it through, folded it and put it down on the table. Then, after feeding baby Michael, she wrapped him up well and set off for North Moor to see Dora.

'My, this is a nice surprise,' Dora said as she opened the door. 'Come in, pet, and I'll make us a nice cup of tea. '

'It's all right, mam,' Jane said. 'I won't be staying long.'

'Long enough to have a cup of tea before you walk home.' Dora spoke in a voice that brooked no opposition. 'Sit yourself down, pet.'

Jane sat down, holding the sleeping baby on her lap, and took the proffered cup from Dora. 'Ta, mam, but you shouldn't have bothered.'

Dora looked quizzically at her daughter. 'Are you all right, pet? She asked. 'Nothing bothering you?'

Jane smiled back. 'Stop worrying, mam. I'm a little tired, that's all, but I'm managing fine.'

The smile partly reassured Dora. Perhaps Jane was coming to terms with her misfortune at last. But there was still a lingering unease at the back of her mind. There was something different about her daughter, she thought. She couldn't quite put her finger on it, but Jane seemed strangely distant, almost as if she were in some kind of trance. 'Drink up then and have something to eat,' she said, pointing to the girdle cake on the table.

Jane shook her head. 'Thanks, Mam, but I'm not hungry.'

'You need to feed yourself properly for the bairn's sake,' Dora admonished.

'But I do,' Jane protested. 'I cook when I have time.'

'When you have time!' Dora snorted. 'Why don't you let me help?'

'You can, mam. You can come and help me whitewash the cottage tomorrow.'

'It's the wrong time for spring cleaning,' Dora said, surprised and mystified by Jane's request.

'I want it nice and clean for young Michael, here,' Jane explained, glancing down at the baby. 'Can you come first thing tomorrow morning?'

'Impatient to start, aren't you?' Dora said, unable to hide her curiosity.

'You said you wanted to help,' Jane countered.

'I'll have to get the menfolk off to work first.'

'But you'll come?' There was a note of pleading in Jane's voice.

'Of course I will, pet. But it'll be seven o'clock before I get there.'

'That's all right, mam.' Jane sounded relieved. 'I'll have everything ready.'

After her daughter had left, Dora sat for a while feeling puzzled and uneasy. Finally, she gave up trying to unravel her thoughts and turned her attention to the many chores still to be done. But the disquiet in her mind lingered on.

Jane returned to her cottage and after feeding Michael, spent the rest of the day in a frenzy of house cleaning. In the evening, she ate a plain supper of ham and fresh bread that Dora had given her. She then banked up the fire for the night, for the late autumn evenings were now turning cold, and lit a fresh candle. Crossing the room to the tall chest of drawers, she pulled the bottom drawer open and took out two white dresses, placing them on the table. The smaller garment was the baby's christening dress; the other was her own wedding gown, worn on that special happy day that now seemed so long ago.

Baby Michael woke and began to cry for attention. She picked him up and gave him his evening feed then wrapped him in his christening dress. He soon fell asleep and she returned him gently to his crib. Then, taking the letter which she had written to Dora that morning, which was still lying on the table, she placed it in a prominent position inside the baby's crib.

Returning to the table, Jane picked up her wedding gown, letting it unfold as she did so. Stripping off her working clothes, she changed into her wedding gown and stood in front of the small mirror to adjust the bridal veil. Then she slipped quickly out of the cottage, closing the door quietly behind her.

A gusting wind sweeping in from the North Sea chilled the night air. It caught her dress, swirling it around her as she walked giving her the appearance of some phantom figure from the past. The moon was almost full, lighting up the lane that led from the cottage like a thin ribbon of silver.

She walked towards North Moor colliery but turned off to the west as she neared the village, and headed towards the original North Moor pit that had been abandoned nearly twenty years ago. A sudden fierce rain squall drenched her, causing her dress to cling to her body, but she felt no cold or discomfort. The fixation in her mind blanked out all other feelings.

She could now pick out the dark shapes of the ruined building around the disused mine shaft, silhouetted in the moon's pale light. The pit shaft had been boarded in but the timbers were now shrunken and rotten. She pulled at the boards until she had made a gap big enough to squeeze through. Slowly, she felt her way to the edge of the shaft. For a while she stood staring into the blackness beneath her feet then, after taking a deep breath, she jumped.

She made no sound as she fell seven hundred feet to the bottom of the shaft, not even when she struck the shaft lining at the start of her fall. She was still conscious when her body hit the deep water that had flooded the shaft bottom. She felt its cold embrace, soothing and purifying, filtering the turmoil from her mind. Her final thoughts were of Mark and the sudden realisation that, at last, she felt clean again.

Wilf read Jane's letter to a tearful Dora. His voice choked over the last few lines as his emotions overwhelmed him ... *'My baby is an innocent party, yet I feel no mother's love and this makes me even more ashamed. I seek no forgiveness, for what I am about to do is beyond that. I know it will be hard for you to understand and if you cannot, so be it. But please, keep me in your thoughts and pray for me. Your loving daughter, Jane.'*

It was two days before they found Jane's body. A sudden intuitive memory stirring in Jed's mind finally led the searchers to the old mine shaft, a secret and daring scene of their early childhood. Her body was laid to rest in the tranquil corner of North Moor churchyard alongside the grave of Mary. Henry felt sure that Mark would want his wife to be buried near her family and he knew that Mary would have approved. But it took a very large sum of money to convince the vicar and his sexton that the manner of Jane's death would not defile the sanctity of the church ground.

*****

Duncan Forster read Jane's letter with a mixture of anger and alarm before throwing it down on the desk. The contents left him feeling distinctly uncomfortable and exposed. After pacing up and down the room, deep in thought, he picked up the letter and again began to read.

"........*Roland is most certainly the father of my child. I cannot prove this but all my maternal instinct convinces me that he is. No doubt your suspicions will conclude that I am seeking money from you, but this is not so. By the time you read this, I shall have ceased to be of any consequence to you or this cruel world. But I do wish for you to understand, if you don't already know, that in Roland you have sired a despicable and cowardly pervert for a son. He is clearly beyond redemption and you will have to live with his failures for the rest of your life. In this, your own suffering will ultimately prove much greater than mine.'*

Though the letter failed to achieve Jane's primary purpose, for he already knew about the rape, it nevertheless disturbed him more than he cared to admit. His feeling of discomfort grew as he began to comprehend the truth of Jane's prophesy. 'Damn the boy,' he muttered angrily to himself.

Jane's letter also disturbed him in other ways. He was puzzled by some of the oblique references to her future. Was it a suicide note, he wondered. It certainly had that strange lucidity often associated with a deranged mind. He took the letter and, placing it on the fire, watched it burn and curl into a blackened ash.

For the next two days Duncan Forster experienced a growing desire to see and talk to Jane. He wanted to question her on a number of things and, above all, he felt a compelling urge to see the child. When he received the shock news that her body had been recovered from the disused mineshaft, the urge to see the child became overwhelming.

He ordered his horse to be saddled and, accompanied by a mounted groom, set off for North Moor colliery.

As they rode through the squalid pit village they saw that the cottage occupied by Wilf and Dora was marked by a small group of mourners who stood quietly around the door. When they saw Forster approaching, they respectfully drew back and watched silently as the

399

two riders dismounted. Forster handed the reins of his horse to the groom and, after a peremptory knock on the door, entered the cottage.

The small group surrounding the coffin turned at his entry, their surprise changing to hostility as they recognised Forster. Henry was the first to recover. 'You're intruding on our privacy,' he said angrily. 'You, of all people, have no right to be here.'

Forster forced himself to control his temper. 'I've no wish to intrude on your grief,' he replied, attempting a conciliatory note. 'I would like to offer my sincere condolences.'

'And you think that will assuage your conscience?' Henry taunted, his voice filled with contempt at Forster's affrontery.

'No. My conscience is clear, and if it weren't it's no concern of yours.' Forster's natural hauteur was returning.

At this point Wilf intervened. 'I'd like you to leave, sir. This is a private family mourning.' He spoke respectfully but firmly.

'I'm sorry if my presence offends you,' Forster said, realising he'd overstepped the bounds of good behaviour. 'I will leave, as you wish, but first I would like a private word with Standish here, if I may.'

There was a short awkward silence as Wilf looked first at Dora and then at Henry. It was Dora who broke the impasse. Taking Wilf by the arm, she led him out through the back door. 'Just a few minutes, mind,' she called back over her shoulder.

When they were alone Henry looked at Forster. 'Well?'

'May I see the child?'

The request took Henry by surprise. Then he saw the agitation in Forster's eyes and knew the reason. 'You think it might be Roland's? And you said your conscience was clear.'

'It is, but my curiosity is not. I need to know. I must see the child.'

The two men walked over to the crib and looked down at the sleeping child. After a while, Forster moved away.

'You're not sure are you?' Henry said.

Forster shook his head then looked at Henry. 'I don't think you are either.'

'We'll never know.' Henry replied. 'But the child will be raised as a Standish, and when Mark returns, your son will have to answer for his crimes.'

'We shall see,' Forster retorted, unmoved by the threat.

The two men glared at each other with unconcealed hatred.

CHAPTER 41

The passage to the West Indies was an unusually slow one due to the light winds which at times almost becalmed the fleet. Normally the voyage would have taken no more than nine or ten weeks, but it was well into the thirteenth before the convoy reached Barbados. Here, the convoy split up, the Leeward Islands ships heading north whilst the Jamaica ones sailed on across the Caribbean. The *Phoebe* escorted the Jamaica bound ships on the final thousand miles of the voyage.

Following his promotion to gun captain, Mark took an even greater interest in the ship's great guns and developed a close rapport with the gunner and gunner's mate. The frigate, like all men-of-war, was designed primarily as a sailing gun platform and all other design considerations, such as crew comforts, were of secondary importance.

The *Phoebe*'s main deck was dedicated to her great guns. She was armed with twenty-six 12 pounders, mounting thirteen along each side of the deck. She also carried four 6 pounders on the quarter deck and two on the forecastle. In addition, there were two 24 pounder carronades, known as smashers, for use at close quarters. The captain was the only man to live on the main deck, occupying the great stern cabin which ran the full width of the ship. But even this spacious and elegant cabin was home to two of the guns and would be quickly stripped bare when the ship went into action.

In the daily gun practice, which continued over the last leg of the voyage to Jamaica, Mark's gun crew consistently scored better than any of the others. But in spite of this, he was not satisfied, nor was Captain Ash. Even Mark's gun could only average a sixty per cent success rate at the point blank range of three hundred yards. Beyond this range, when the gun had to be elevated, the accuracy fell away alarmingly. Mark was sure he knew the reason for this and set about finding an answer to the problem. The following day he sought out the gunner, Mr Brewis, to outline his ideas.

Brewis was an experienced gunner of the old school. He knew everything there was to know about guns, but little about the science involved in firing them accurately at long range. He'd been schooled in the Nelson theory of close engagement which favoured placing the

402

ship alongside the enemy at the first opportunity. In this position, speed of fire was more important than accuracy.

The rapport between Mark and Brewis was mutual, and the old gunner was flattered to have such a willing and intelligent pupil as Mark, eager to pick his brains. However, being steeped in his ways, he was less than enthusiastic as he listened to Mark explaining his theories about long range gunnery. They were talking by the gun beneath the quarterdeck rail, unaware that Captain Ash was standing within earshot on the deck above.

'A good gun captain doesn't need sights,' Brewis argued. 'At close quarters you only have to look along the barrel and point the gun at the target. '

'Only if you can see through all the smoke,' Mark countered. 'And what if you're not at close quarters?'

'Then you don't waste powder and shot.'

'But you can cripple your enemy at long range if your gunnery's good enough,' Mark insisted. 'Then you go in for the kill. It minimises damage to the ship and that means less casualties.'

'It won't work. You don't open fire until you're within three hundred yards,' the gunner repeated irritably. 'Like I said, lad, it's a waste of shot.'

'Not if we fit gun sights and practice how to use them,' Mark said stubbornly.

'We haven't got any sights. I don't know of any ship that has.'

'We can make our own. I've worked out how to do it.' Mark produced some sheets of paper with rough sketches and measurements. The sides of the paper were covered with calculations. 'Here, let me explain,' he said, he voice eager with enthusiasm.

The old gunner sighed with exasperation. 'I'm too busy now, lad. We'll talk about it later.

The matter may well have ended there but for Captain Ash. He'd listened to the conversation with growing interest and needed to satisfy his curiosity. He leaned forward over the quarterdeck rail. 'Mr Brewis!'

'Sir!' The gunner straightened up and saluted.

'I couldn't help but overhear your conversation. Seems to me there might be something in this fellow's idea. Standish isn't it?' He added, looking at Mark.

'Yes, sir,' Mark acknowledged, standing stiffly to attention.

'I'd like to hear more and have a look at those,' Ash said, pointing to the papers in Mark's hand. 'It'll be more comfortable if we discuss it in my cabin.' With that he descended the ladder that led down from the quarterdeck and, indicating for the gunner and Mark to follow, led the way aft to the great stern cabin. The marine sentry on guard outside stamped to attention as the three men entered, relaxing as he heard the door close firmly behind them.

Ash walked across to the large mahogany table placed near the stern windows of the cabin. 'Now then,' he said, motioning for the gunner and Mark to join him, 'Explain this intriguing idea of yours.' He smiled encouragingly at Mark to try and put him at ease.

'Well, sir, it's just an idea at this stage, but I'm sure it will work.' Mark spoke cautiously, not knowing what support he might get from Brewis. He didn't want to antagonise the old gunner, whose help he would need if his ideas were to be implemented.

Ash sensed Mark's difficulty. 'Good ideas are usually motivated by the desire to improve something; and our gunnery does need improving. I know Mr Brewis agrees with my sentiments entirely and will support any new proposals that might lead to better standards. He knows a good pupil when he sees one.'

The backhanded compliment pleased the old gunner who smiled happily in appreciation. 'At the rate he's learning, there'll soon be little left to teach 'im, sir,' Brewis said, pleased to support his captain.

'And all credit to you, Mr Brewis.' Ash turned to Mark. 'Well then, let's hear about your idea.'

Mark spread his papers on the cabin table. 'I've made some sketches and worked out some calculations, sir. Without sights, the gun captain just aims along the top of the barrel in the general direction of the target. But the guns are short and have a considerable taper towards the muzzle. This means that the line of aim is always at a different angle to the true line of fire. That's why I think our gunnery gets progressively more inaccurate at distances over one hundred yards or so.'

404

Captain Ash nodded in agreement. 'I can see the problem, Standish, but what do you propose for the answer?'

'Fit dispart sights to the guns, sir.'

A bemused smile crossed Captain Ash's face. 'I think you'd better explain further.'

Mark pointed to his sketches. 'The dispart is the difference between the semi-diameter of the gun at the base ring and the muzzle. The dispart sight corrects for this inaccuracy so that the gun aimer's sight is always in line with the direction of the bore of the barrel. That way the guns can be fired more accurately, especially at a distance.'

Ash listened with growing interest as he began to appreciate the significance of Mark's idea. He looked at the sketches and checked the calculations. 'It's an excellent concept, Standish. We must see if it works in practice. Can we make some sights?'

'I think so, sir. The gunner's mate used to be a blacksmith. If I can borrow some instruments, I think I can draw my sketch to scale.'

'I'll see to that,' Ash promised. 'You can also use my clerk's desk and let me know if there's anything else you need.'

'There is something else, sir.'

'Yes?'

'A quadrant and plumb-bob.'

Ash looked puzzled. 'Why?'

'It's not good having an accurate sight on the gun without an exact way of elevating them. Above three hundred yards, the guns have to be elevated for the shot to carry to the target. You need a quadrant for that and a plumb-bob to make sure the deck is level when you take a reading.'

'I see,' Ash said thoughtfully. He looked at Mark with new respect. 'You really have put some imagination and effort into this. Well done, Standish.' Then, turning to the gunner, he added. 'You certainly know how to pick a fine pupil, Mr Brewis.'

The gunner, who was feeling a little put out by all this, suddenly felt reassured. He smiled back at his captain. 'Thank you, sir.' Then, catching Mark's eye, he gave a sly wink. Ash noticed this and, with difficulty, stopped himself from smiling.

'One more thing, if you please sir,' Mark said.

'Yes.' Captain Ash was all ears.

405

'If we cut some compass lines into the deck by each gun, they can be swivelled more accurately to take account of the ship's bearing. With the smoke on the gun deck, it's sometimes difficult to see a target, but the officer sailing the ship can call out the enemy's bearing.'

Ash was really impressed now. 'By gad, that really is something,' he said excitedly. 'The sooner we start on this the better.' Then, turning to the gunner he said. 'I'll leave this in your good hands, Mr Brewis. See that Standish has all the help he needs. You have my full support.'

Mark followed the gunner to the cabin door, but before they could exit Captain Ash called after them.

'By the way, Mr Brewis.'

'Sir?'

'You're still short of a quarter gunner, I believe?'

'Yes, sir.'

'Then you'd better take Standish here. I'll enter him into the muster book as from today. He can also come off watch and join the idlers.'

'Thank you, sir,' Mark stammered.

Ash smiled. 'You've earned it, or you will if your ideas work.'

'They will, sir. I promise.'

As Mark followed the gunner on to the main deck he suddenly realised he was now a junior petty officer in charge of four guns. His pay would go up to nearly two pounds a month and coming off watch would mean eight hours sleep most nights. He smiled at the thought.

'You can wipe that smile off your face lad,' the gunner cut in. 'We've got work to do.' Then he held out his hand and grinned. 'Well done, Mark. You made quite an impression in there.'

Mark's new found status as a petty officer entitled him to an outside berth on the mess deck, with more space to sling his hammock. As an idler on day duty, he now had more time to develop his ideas on gunnery and prove his theories to Captain Ash. With the assistance of the gunner's mate, who proved to be a very skilful blacksmith, Mark made dispart sights for the four guns under his control. It was now time to put his theories into practice.

406

The first gunnery exercise using the new sights sent a wave of excitement through the ship. The target was dropped overboard and Captain Ash wore the ship round so that the target came up on the starboard beam at a distance of some three hundred yards. The new dispart sights had been fitted to two guns on the larboard side and two on the starboard so that each watch could learn how to use them. Mark sighted and fired the first two guns and scored a direct hit with each shot. The *Phoebe* then wore round to allow the larboard guns to fire and again Mark scored two direct hits.

The men began to cheer, as if they had captured an enemy ship that would make them rich in prize money. Captain Ash, directing the fire from the quarterdeck, beamed at the gun crews. 'Well done. Now we'll increase the range. Reload and run out!'

Long distance gunnery required the guns to be elevated so that the shot would carry to the target. This was where the use of quadrant and plumb-bob became extremely important. But even at distances that previously would have been considered a waste of shot, the new sights proved remarkably accurate.

Captain Ash turned to his first lieutenant. 'I think Standish has proved his point, Mr Urquhart. From now on, I want every gun captain to be trained in how to use the new sights. They can practice in turn with Standish. When we reach Jamaica, we must find materials to fit sights to all the guns.'

Urquhart's response was a sullen, 'Aye, Aye, sir.' His dislike of Mark had not abated and the success of the new sights only served to increase his irritation. The fellow was making an impression on the captain, he thought, and it's time he was cut down to size. He was now determined to find a way of doing this.

Two days before the *Phoebe* reached Jamaica, the happy atmosphere on board was marred by the boatswain's mates piping, 'All hands aft to witness punishment.' The officers were on deck in formal dress, wearing their swords, and the marines were drawn up aft with their muskets. The ship's company fell in as best they could immediately forward of the main mast.

Mark stood beside Jack, feeling sick inside as he watched the wooden hatch gratings being dragged aft in preparation for the flogging. One grating was placed flat upon the deck with the other upright on top of it and secured to the ship's rail. The two prisoners were then brought on deck under guard and led aft. After a few moments, Captain Ash appeared holding the slim volume of the Articles of War. He and the crew then removed their hats as the Article appropriate to the offence was read out. The first man was to receive a dozen lashes for persistent drunkenness, the second two dozen lashes for thieving. This was a heavy punishment by Ash's standards, though light to the point of weakness in Urquhart's eyes. Thieving was considered a serious crime aboard a man-of-war and Urquhart had served with some captains who would have awarded six dozen lashes. But when he'd protested that he couldn't be expected to maintain discipline without the threat of a flogging, Ash had merely smiled and said, 'Nelson and Collingwood did; and their crews would follow them to hell and back.'

The first man to be punished was the drunkard, a tough sailor who regarded a dozen lashes as a worthwhile price to pay for the pleasure of getting blind drunk. On the order 'seize him up', his shirt was stripped off and a leather apron was tied around his waist to protect his lower back. Mark noticed that the man's back was badly scarred from many previous floggings, though this was his first aboard the *Phoebe*. Next he was spread-eagled against the upright grating and secured to it by his wrists and ankles. The boatswain's mate then took the cat of nine tails from the red baize bag and ran the tails through his fingers. The cat was made up of nine tails, each two feet long, and tucked into a rope handle.

On the order 'Do your duty', the boatswain's mate stepped up to the grating and commenced to flog using the full sweep of his arm with all his strength behind it. He knew anything less could result in a disrating. The force of the blow knocked the wind from the man's lungs and he let out an involuntary gasp. The blow also left a deep welt across his back and a small trickle of blood appeared where the skin had been broken. After each stroke, the boatswain's mate ran the tails of the cat through his fingers to clear them of the flesh and blood which would otherwise have deadened the next blow. When the dozen lashes had been delivered, the sailor's back was a grisly red slough.

After the first sailor was released from the grating, the man found guilty of thieving stepped forward to be seized up in his place. In accordance with custom a new cat was brought out, for the same cat was never used twice. In this case, it was a thief's cat, with the tails knotted at three-inch intervals. Thieving was the only offence for which the dreaded knotted cat was used.

A fresh boatswain's mate stepped up to administer the second flogging. After the first dozen lashes, the man was screaming in agony and at the end of the second dozen he was almost unconscious. His lacerated back resembled a piece of scorched meat with the ivory glint of bone showing through in places. The crew watched in sullen silence as the thief was taken below to have his wounds attended to. As he dismissed the crew Captain Ash noted the subtle change in the men's attitude and silently cursed the navy's brutal acceptance of flogging. He was now more than ever convinced that, as a punishment, it was counterproductive and felt trapped in a tradition he no longer believed in.

The floggings had deeply affected Mark and as his feeling of disgust subsided, it was replaced by one of anger. At dinner, he turned to Jack to express his frustration.

'How can a country which professes to be civilised allow such barbarity to be inflicted on its own people?'

Jack shrugged. 'There's always been one law for officers and gentlemen and another for the likes of us. It's always been like that and always will be,' he added philosophically.

'But it doesn't have to remain that way,' Mark retorted, irritated by Jack's acceptance of his lot. 'Things can be changed for the better. The Americans and the French have proved that.'

'Aye, but only through bloody revolution,' Jack lowered his voice. 'You'd best hold your tongue, matey. If Urquhart or his spies hear you talking like that he'll have you hung for treason.'

'But how can you, of all people, go along with such a cruel and unjust system,' Mark persisted. 'I've seen your back. Those are flogging scars aren't they?'

'Aye, I took four dozen once, but never again.'

'So you think fear and brutality make for good discipline? '

'I dunno', Mark. A flogging puts the fear of God into me. I think it would destroy a thinker like you.'

Mark reflected on Jack's words and decided he was probably right.

When they docked at Jamaica, the gunner's mate was sent ashore to supervise the making of extra gun sights at the naval dockyard in Port Royal. A substantial payment to the yard officials by Captain Ash, from his own pocket, ensured the yard's co-operation.

The *Phoebe* was due to join the North American squadron after replenishing her stores. As time was short, the gunner's mate was instructed to remain ashore until the gun sights were ready. This proved to be an unfortunate decision, for he contracted yellow fever and was laid low in hospital when the ship sailed for America. The misfortune of the gunner's mate turned out to be good luck for Mark, for he was promoted in his place.

Immediately after their arrival in Jamaica, Mark had written letters to Jane and Henry. He knew that the Post Office packet service provided a fast, regular service between Falmouth and the West Indies and Captain Ash had arranged for mail to be sent on board the next packet which was due to sail two days prior to the frigate's departure for America. He'd been bitterly disappointed to find that there were no letters waiting for him in answer to those he'd sent to Jane and Henry before the *Phoebe* sailed from England. But, on reflection, he realised there would not have been enough time to reply.

After only a week in Jamaica, the *Phoebe* weighed anchor and proceeded to sea. Captain Ash was instructed to keep a close look out for French privateers who were wreaking havoc on unescorted merchant shipping. Two homeward bound packets had been taken over the past two months and this was causing concern at the Admiralty who used the Post Office packet service for their dispatches. Recent intelligence indicated that a much larger, well-armed privateer was now operating in the Caribbean with orders to attack the mail packets and so create havoc in the navy's main line of communication.

As soon as the coast of Jamaica dipped beneath the horizon, Ash ordered extra lookouts to be posted. 'We may soon have the chance to practise some gunnery on that French privateer if we keep a sharp watch, what say you Mr Urquhart?'

'Likely as not the Frenchie will be too fast for us, sir,' Urquhart responded moodily. He was still sulking over Ash's decision to ban starting.

'Nonsense, man,' Ash answered sharply. 'It's ten guineas to the first man who sights her. Pass the word round.'

'Aye, aye, sir.' Urquhart saluted and watched as Ash went below to his cabin on the main gun deck. His eyes were sullen with resentment.

The quartermaster at the wheel grinned behind Urquhart's back and whispered to the master's mate standing beside him. 'There'll be an almighty bust up between those two one of these days, just you mark my words.'

'My money's on the Captain,' came the whispered reply.

Thirty-six hours after leaving Jamaica the *Phoebe* sailed through the Windward Passage, which ran between the islands of Cuba and Hispaniola, and headed north to rendezvous with the North American squadron. Soon, the long chain of the Bahama Islands were left to the south as the frigate continued north with the coast of America hidden more than two hundred miles over the horizon to larboard. But, apart from fishing boats and local craft the only ships that were sighted proved to be British or American merchantmen. A frustrated captain and a disappointed crew had to make do with gunnery practise using canvas targets rather than the elusive French privateer. Ash's only consolation was that all his guns were now fitted with dispart sights and he was determined that every gun captain should learn how to use them.

After ten days at sea, the *Phoebe* sighted the North American squadron cruising off the coast of Virginia. After acknowledging the Admiral's signal, Ash went aboard the flagship, a 74-gun ship of the line, to deliver his dispatches. Later, over dinner with the Admiral and the squadron captains, he learned that relationships between England and America were becoming more tense and acrimonious. The arbitrary methods adopted by the British navy in enforcing the trade blockade of France were deeply resented by neutral countries. There was now a rising storm of protest from America whose merchant fleet had suffered severely at the hands of His Britannic Majesty's navy.

'It'll end up with war between us if this goes on, the Admiral prophesied darkly. 'Yet if we stop searching American merchantmen how will we know if they're trading with Boney?'

'But do we really have to press American seamen when we search them, sir?' Ash enquired.

'We don't impress Americans,' the Admiral corrected testily. 'We only take back British seamen and most of them are deserters. It's an easier life on board an American ship with better pay and that's what attracts the British seaman.'

'But most of them have protection as American citizens, sir,' another frigate captain interposed. 'Yet we ignore them.'

'And rightly so,' the Admiral snorted. 'The protections are false. Some of the seamen are no more American than you or I. The American authorities just turn a blind eye when they issue them.'

'They're not worth the paper they're written on,' another captain haughtily agreed.

'It's absolutely essential that we maintain our blockade of France and her allies,' the Admiral went on, 'and to do that successfully we must insist on the right to board any neutral ship that may be trading with Boney.' His tone brooked no further argument and the subject was diplomatically dropped.

The following day, the *Phoebe* took on board dispatches for Jamaica and headed south for the Caribbean. Captain Ash plotted a course that would allow him the maximum opportunity to intercept any French privateer that might be preying on unescorted merchantmen or mail packets. But fortune failed to smile on him and, after an uneventful passage lasting two weeks, the frigate dropped anchor again at Port Royal.

On going ashore Ash learned that the gunner's mate, who had contracted yellow fever, had died. When he returned on board the *Phoebe*, he confirmed Mark's promotion to gunner's mate from an acting to a permanent basis, which increased his pay to two pounds two shillings and sixpence per month. More important, it reinforced Mark's status as a senior petty officer in the eyes of the crew.

The following day the *Phoebe* weighed anchor and proceeded to sea. Ash's orders were to call in at the Leeward Island to deliver dispatches to the British base on Antigua, and then sail back across the Atlantic to Lisbon. Ash knew this would be their last chance to come up with a French privateer and again posted extra look-outs. He also doubled the prize for the first sighting of an enemy ship to twenty guineas so that many duty lookouts were reluctant to hand over to a fresh pair of eyes and had to be ordered down on deck.

Excitement rose to fever pitch as the *Phoebe* approached the Leeward Islands and with it the crew's expectations. But when the frigate left Antigua astern, with still no sign of the elusive French privateer, the euphoria subsided into despondency as the prospect of prize money began to fade. It was when disappointment was at its lowest ebb that the cry came from the masthead lookout. 'Deck there, sail ho!'

The ship was immediately galvanised into a ferment of excited speculation as the off duty watch joined their mates on deck. All eyes searched the horizon for a glimpse of white sail.

Captain Ash hurried on deck. 'Mast head there!'

'Sir?'

'Where away the sail.'

'Off the starboard bow, sir.'

'What does she look like?'

After a long pause the lookout answered. 'A large square rigged ship, sir, standing towards us.'

Ash turned to the first lieutenant. 'All hands to quarters, Mr Urquhart. Clear the ship for action.'

'Aye, aye, sir.'

The marine drummer beat out the tune Hearts of Oak as the crew quietly made the ship ready for action. Bulkheads were quickly dismantled and struck below, the guns were run out and the decks damped down and sprinkled with sand.

'Deck there!' All eyes focussed on the masthead lookout. 'She's seen us and she's turning away.'

Ash felt his scalp tingle under his cocked hat. 'Make all sail, Mr Urquhart. That's the Frenchie we've been seeking or I'll be damned. Thank God we've just got the windward gauge.'

Crowding on all sail, the *Phoebe* slowly began to close the gap on the unidentified ship. Ash noticed that their quarry was desperately trying to claw her way to windward which allowed the *Phoebe* to draw even closer. Soon he could make out the outline of the other ship's hull.

'She's a Frenchie, all right, sir,' the first lieutenant said. 'A big 'un too, by the look of her.'

The French privateer, seeing the British frigate inexorably closing the gap between them, suddenly altered course.

'She's bearing away, Mr Urquhart,' Ash murmured. 'Thinks she can outrun us.' He picked up his glass and brought the French ship into focus, studying her carefully. 'Gad, you're right, Mr Urquhart. She is big.' He began to count. 'Pierced for 22-guns on her main deck. Same as a sixth rate frigate.'

'Should give us a good fight, sir,' Urquhart replied, smiling at the prospect.

'She will indeed. Likely as not she's armed with nine or twelve pounders. Gives us an excellent opportunity to test our new gun sights in battle conditions.' Ash lowered his glass. 'Ask Mr Brewis and Standish to lay aft, if you please. '

When Mark and the gunner reported to the quarterdeck, Ash gave them strict instructions. 'I want you both to supervise the loading of each gun on the main deck. You take control of the larboard guns, Mr Brewis and Standish can look after the starboard. I want every gun to be single shotted with the proper cartridges that we've been using in target practice.' Turning to Mark he added, 'The starboard guns will fire first. I want you to personally aim and fire a gun in turn at 600 yards range. Mr Urquhart will give the signal on my command. We may get lucky and slow the Frenchie down. In any event, the shots should be close enough to make him nervous and shake his confidence.'

Urquhart was about to protest when Ash cut him short. 'At four hundred yards we'll open fire with broadsides, each gun captain to aim and fire independently. Then we'll close to three hundred yards. I'll call out the distance and direction.'

The first lieutenant, who'd listened to Captain Ash's instructions with growing unease, finally lost patience. 'Aren't you being too

414

cautious, sir? Surely we must engage the enemy at close quarters. If we lay ourselves alongside the Frenchie, she'll soon strike.' Urquhart's tone was almost scathing.

'We'll fight yard arm to yard arm when we have to, Mr Urquhart,' Ash replied icily. 'My purpose is to defeat the enemy with minimum casualties to ourselves. Remember, we're up against a privateer and she'll be carrying extra crew to man prizes. We'll be outnumbered when we board her.'

Urquhart opened his mouth to protest further, then changed his mind. If the French privateer managed to escape, the Admiralty might interpret Ash's actions as being too cautious and lacking in resolution. It could well be seen in some quarters as bordering on cowardice. He smiled at the thought as he followed the gunner and Mark down on to the main gun deck.

However, Ash had no intention of letting the Frenchman escape. He would lay his ship alongside at the first opportunity, but first he wanted to test the *Phoebe*'s gunnery at long range to prove the accuracy of the new gun sights in combat conditions.

The French privateer gradually wore away, testing the *Phoebe* on each point of sailing in her attempts to escape the British frigate, until finally, both ships were running before the wind. This was what Ash wanted and as the two ships closed to within six hundred yards he headed the *Phoebe* into the wind to allow the starboard guns to train on the Frenchman's stern. Then, after carefully checking the distance, he passed the word to open fire.

On the gun deck, Mark squinted through the dispart sight then signalled the gun captain to pull the lanyard that would trigger the flintlock and ignite the powder cartridge inside the breech. He leapt to one side as the gun roared, belching dense, acrid smoke from the muzzle before violently recoiling inboard until brought up by the breaching. The shot fell ten yards short of the Frenchman's stern sending up a plume of water to mark the spot.

Moving quickly to the next gun, Mark called on the gun crew to increase the elevation. Hand spikes were inserted under the breech to adjust the angle. When he was satisfied, he forced home the quoin to maintain the correct position of the gun. Then, taking careful aim, he signalled for the gun to be fired. There was another deafening explosion followed by more pungent smoke, some of which drifted back inboard through the open gun port causing Mark's eyes to water. A cheer went up from the watching ship's crew as the second ball smashed through the stern window of the privateer. The celebrations were promptly cut short by a bellow from Urquhart ordering silence.

The French captain now realised that he could not out sail the *Phoebe* and brought his ship into a parallel course with the frigate ready to do battle. At five hundred yards the *Phoebe* fired a full broadside and several shots found their target. The Frenchman replied but all the shots fell short. As the range shortened to four hundred yards, the accuracy of the *Phoebe*'s fire began to tell and shot after shot tore through the privateer's hull.

At three hundred yards, the Frenchman's fore and main topmasts fell as the pounding from the *Phoebe* continued. At this point, Ash wore the *Phoebe* round and brought the frigate across the privateer's stern so that the larboard guns could rake her as she made her pass.

Being raked from astern was the most dangerous position in which a ship's captain could find himself. Enemy shot coming through the vulnerable stern could sweep the length of the decks and create carnage. The French commander realised this, but first he wanted to destroy the evidence of his privateering activities in which three Post Office Mail packets had been taken. He was stuffing the captured mail and admiralty dispatches into a weighted bag, to be thrown overboard, when shot after shot crashed through the unprotected stern. A huge wooden splinter pierced his neck, almost severing his head. The blood gushing from the wound soaked the bag as the dying captain fell slowly to the deck.

Ash had expected the privateer to strike, but the French continued to fight on bravely. He turned to the master. 'We'll board her, Mr Straughan. Prepare to lay us alongside, if you please. I'll give you the word.'

'Aye, aye, sir.' The master saluted and grinned.

Ash then called over the junior midshipman. 'My compliments to Mr Urquhart. We'll close and board the Frenchman. I want all starboard guns loaded with canister but he's to hold his fire until we're within fifty yards.' Ash knew that at this range the canisters, filled with lead shot, were lethal and would clear the enemy's deck.

The young midshipman hurried off to seek out the first lieutenant, but before he could reach the gun deck a shout range out. 'She's on fire, sir!' Ash looked at the crippled privateer and saw the glow of fire lightening up the thick smoke that bellowed from the Frenchman's deck below her mainmast. He turned to the master. 'Belay there, Mr Straughan. I want a safe distance if her magazine blows.'

The *Phoebe* luffed up into the wind and the gap between the two ships steadily widened. There was intense activity on the privateer's deck as the crew fought desperately to prevent the blaze from spreading. But the fire had taken a firm hold and soon tongues of flame could be seen licking up the sails and rigging.

In the wrecked stern cabin, flames had begun to lap the body of the French captain, which still lay on the deck clutching the weighted bag containing the captured documents. The bag began to smoulder then burst into flames as the contents ignited. Among the many burning letters inside, was the one written by Mark to Jane and posted in Jamaica nearly two months earlier.

A few minutes later, the fire reached the privateer's magazine and the ship exploded in a volcanic fireball. Burning debris showered the *Phoebe*'s deck and the crew had to work frantically to extinguish the many small fires that were started.

The frigate hove to whilst her boats searched among a sea strewn with wreckage and bodies. Only seven French survivors were picked up. The *Phoebe* had received little damage and casualties were light, with only two members of the crew suffering minor splinter wounds.

A contented Ash ordered 'Up spirits' to the cheers of his crew. Then, turning to the master, he ordered, 'Lay her on course for Lisbon, if you please, Mr Straughan.'

CHAPTER 42

It was August before the *Phoebe* made a landfall off the coast of Portugal and edged her way slowly into the magnificent natural harbour formed by the Tajo estuary at Lisbon. The anchorage, four miles wide in places, was crowded with craft of every description, ranging from massive ships of the line to small coastal vessels. Most of the ships were merchantmen and navy transports, part of the large fleet needed to supply and reinforce the Peninsular army commanded by Lord Wellington.

Mark was disappointed when he heard that there was no mail awaiting the *Phoebe* though, like most sailors, he was now inured to the absence of news from home. Immediately after the frigate anchored, a cutter came alongside to collect the *Phoebe*'s dispatches and deliver new orders to Captain Ash. As soon as they had taken on water and provisions, they were to sail and join a squadron of the channel fleet blockading the French port of Brest.

The news did not please the crew and Jack expressed his disgust in forthright terms to the rest of the mess at dinner. 'Bloody channel gropers', he stormed. 'Worst bloody job in the navy.'

"Channel gropers" was the disparaging term given to the Channel Fleet, in particular the squadron engaged in blockading the French port of Brest. When the wind blew in a direction which allowed the French fleet to leave harbour His Britannic Majesty's navy had to remain on station in order to engage the enemy if they should put to sea. When the winds were unfavourable, or too strong, the blockading squadron could sometimes withdraw to Plymouth Sound or Torbay, leaving only a screen of frigates to keep an eye on the French fleet.

Frigates were the glamour ships of the navy, the eyes and ears of the fleet. They were too light to form line of battle, yet were fast cruisers able to inflict heavy damage on enemy ships of similar size and on merchant shipping. This allowed greater opportunity for prize money, always an attraction to the English sailor. But the glamour of a frigate was often more apparent than real and when orders called for convoy duty, or channel groping, this was driven home with a vengeance.

Mark could see that Jack was still angry. 'It can't be that bad, surely,' he said, trying to calm his friend down.

'Oh can't it,' Jack roared. 'You've never spent a winter thrashing up and down the Brittany coast in freezing rain when it's blowing a gale. Week after week of wet clothes, wet hammocks and wet nursing the Admiral, watching his signals and running his errands.'

Mark knew better than to argue with Jack in this mood. 'We'll survive, my friend,' he said, smiling consolingly as he passed his grog across the mess table.

Jack grinned back as he sheepishly accepted the proffered mug. 'Aye, I'll drink to that.' He took a long quaff before adding 'And damn the bastard's eyes who thinks we're channel gropers.'

After three months of blockade duty and with the onset of winter, Mark began to realise why Jack had been so vehement in expressing his distaste for the miseries of channel groping. Early December had brought with it a succession of strong north easterly gales, forcing the blockading squadron to seek shelter off the English coast, leaving a small screen of frigates to keep watch on Brest.

As the squadron rode at anchor, Mark gazed miserably at the English coastline, his spirits sinking lower as he contemplated what might be happening at North Moor. There was still no word from Jane or Henry and the sight of England, so near and yet so impossibly far, caused his despondency to deepen into utter despair. Had the fleet been anchored in the Thames estuary, he would have attempted to jump ship to seek out a friendly collier captain returning north to the Tyne. He felt a gentle hand on his shoulder and turned to see Jack, whose wry smile was warm with sympathy.

'Don't even think of it, my friend. This is not the time nor the place, as you'll see.'

Mark forced a smile. 'So you can read my mind, eh?'

'Aye, and the rest of the crew as well. All thinking how easy it must be to swim ashore past the guard boats, and then freedom.'

'Yet so few do?'

'Thinking about it is easier than doing it. You'll see why tomorrow.'

Jack's cryptic remark was explained the following morning when news quickly spread that there was to be a flogging through the fleet. Two seamen had tried to desert by swimming ashore. One had drowned in the attempt whilst the other had been captured soon after landing. He'd been sentenced to receive three hundred lashes through the fleet. As was the custom, the number of lashes was divided by the number of ships in the fleet, which were fifteen. This meant that twenty lashes would be laid on alongside each ship in turn, with the whole ship's crew turned out to witness the punishment, a calculated ritual which aimed to deter.

Mark was appalled and turned to Jack. 'Will he survive it?'

'Best if he doesn't. If he does, he'll be a broken man, that's for sure.'

That night the deserter died. In accordance with custom, his body was rowed ashore the following morning and buried in the mud below the tidemark, without religious rights.

The winter months passed slowly and uncomfortably under leaden skies in cold, windswept seas, off the French port of Brest. Mark celebrated the first anniversary of his impressment into the navy, frozen by a fierce westerly gale as the *Phoebe* desperately clawed her way off the island of Ushant. There was still no news from home.

In the early summer of 1812, the *Phoebe* was ordered south to join the squadron patrolling off Rochefort, between the Ile de Re and the Gironde estuary. Captain Ash posted extra lookouts and sailed close to the Brittany coast as he headed south. By standing close inshore he hoped to tempt out any French frigate that might be anchored in one of the many harbours that abounded on this stretch of the French coastline. Off Lorient, with a good wind from the north, north east, there was a shout from the masthead lookout. 'Deck there! Sail off the larboard bow.'

Ash was quickly on deck. 'Masthead!'

'Sir?'

'What does she look like?'

'She's square rigged, sir. Big with three masts, I think. '

Ash tensed with expectation. Three masts meant a ship, and a large ship could well be a frigate. He ordered a young midshipman aloft with a glass, and within minutes the call came down.

'Deck there. She's a large frigate by the look of her. I think she's flying the tricolour.'

A tremor of excitement ran through the decks as the ship beat to quarters and cleared for action. Gun crews raced to their allotted stations and cast loose their guns. Bulkheads, furniture and all lumber disappeared into the hold to give a clear sweep of the ship fore and aft. Decks were wetted and sanded and damp cloth screens were rigged around the hatches. Mark made his way to the magazine to help supervise the issuing of powder and cartridges to the powder monkeys who served the guns.

Ash noticed that the enemy ship was making no effort to avoid coming into action. He rightly surmised that the French frigate could out sail him, yet her captain refrained from making more sail. As the two ships drew closer, Ash realised why. The French frigate was considerably larger and heavier than the *Phoebe*. He slowly lowered the telescope before passing it to the first lieutenant. 'I think we've got a real fight on our hands this time, Mr Urquhart.'

The lieutenant focussed the glass on the Frenchman. 'We have indeed, sir. Carrying 44-guns, I'd say, and a lot of troops, too,' he added.

'I'll wager she's armed with eighteen pounders,' Ash said thoughtfully. He now recognised what he was up against and realised that the odds were very much in favour of the Frenchman.

'They obviously want to engage, sir.' Urquhart spoke calmly.

'Then we mustn't deny them,' Ash murmured, refocusing his glass. 'We'll keep it at long range if we can. If it comes to boarding, we'll be vastly outnumbered with all those troops she's carrying. Must be a hundred of 'em.'

At eight hundred yards, and a little astern of the Frenchman, Ash eased the *Phoebe* into the wind and opened fire. The months of specialist gun training now paid off and several shots found their mark, with no reply from the enemy. The range steadily narrowed to five hundred yards when suddenly, the French frigate shortened sail and luffed up, turning to rake the *Phoebe*. Ash barked orders to the helmsman and the *Phoebe* swerved violently to larboard and then, the moment the French broadside was fired, back to starboard. But the long eighteen pounders of the Frenchman proved accurate and lethal, upending one of the *Phoebe*'s guns and killing two members of the gun crew. Three other men received splinter wounds and a falling spar narrowly missed Ash.

'Firing at the rigging as usual,' Urquhart growled as he looked up at the torn and peppered sails. 'Typical Frenchie tactics.'

'He certainly knows how to fight and handle his ship,' Ash said, a note of respect creeping in.

The two ships, now three hundred yards apart, ran before the wind keeping up a furious cannonade. Though the *Phoebe*'s rate and accuracy of fire was better than their opponents, the sheer weight of metal from the French frigate's heavier and more numerous guns began to take its toll. There was carnage on the *Phoebe*'s gun deck and, as the destruction continued, the casualties rose. But still the two ships fought on. After half an hour, the *Phoebe*'s main topmast was brought down and the Frenchman forged ahead. Ash kept his head in the confusion that followed and quickly wore his ship round to rake the French ship's stern with devastating effect.

Then disaster struck the *Phoebe* when her mizenmast came down, smashing the wheel as it crashed across the quarterdeck. The frigate lay helpless for a while as the crew worked desperately to bring the ship under control. Seeing his chance, the Frenchman moved in for the kill.

As the two ships closed, Ash could pick out the massed uniforms of the soldiers lining the decks and tops of the French frigate. They would fire a final volley from their muskets before joining the boarding party that would sweep across the *Phoebe*'s deck, like a human tidal wave. He shouted orders down to the first lieutenant on the gun deck. 'Grape shot and canister, if you please, Mr Urquhart. Fire when I give the order.' Ash knew that, outnumbered as they were, their best chance was to fire a devastating broadside of lethal grape and canister whilst the enemy boarders were massed on their own deck. Timing would be vital.

Watching closely, Ash realised that the two ships would collide at an angle, bow to bow, and that the rebound would bring their quarters together. 'Hold your fire, Mr Urquhart,' he instructed. 'Wait for my order.'

The bows crashed together with a juddering impact, followed by the tortured sound of grinding timbers. As Ash had surmised, a small gap opened up between the two ships as their bows parted and their quarters came round. 'Fire!' he ordered.

The *Phoebe*'s broadside tore into the French frigate, carving a bloody swath through the massed ranks of the boarding party lining her deck. 'Same again, Mr Urquhart,' Ash ordered.

The second broadside virtually cleared the Frenchman's deck and brought down her mizenmast. The two ships, still firing furiously at each other, slowly drifted apart as the crews struggled to bring them under control. Ash watched as the *Phoebe*'s mizenmast was cut away and cleared over the side. He turned as Mr Straughan, the master, came to report. 'Tiller ropes repaired and manned, sir. We can steer her again.'

Ash's relief was quickly tempered by the fact that the French frigate had also regained control and her long eighteen pounders were again battering the *Phoebe*. Suddenly, a cry went up from the deck. 'She's turning away!' Ash stared in amazement as the Frenchman began to wear round and head back towards the Brittany coast. 'Pon my soul, he's had enough,' he murmured in surprise. But a call from the masthead soon provided an explanation. 'Deck there! Two sails to starboard.'

Ash ordered a midshipman aloft with a glass and after an agonising wait, his call floated down. 'Deck there! A two decker and a frigate.' Then after a further anxious pause, 'They're British, sir!'

A surge of relief ran through the ship and everyone began to relax as the approaching ships drew nearer. Ash sent the first lieutenant and the master to assess the damage and report on casualties. Slowly, the ship's routine returned to normal as the excitement of the battle began to subside.

The *Phoebe* had suffered considerable damage to her hull and rigging as well as losing her main topmast and mizenmast. The wheel had been smashed beyond repair. Worse, she'd suffered severe casualties with seven men killed and twenty-one wounded. Among the dead were the *Phoebe*'s gunner, Mr Brewis, and Crombie, Mark's only remaining witness to the rape of his wife.

*****

423

For several days after the engagement with the French frigate, the atmosphere on board the *Phoebe* was a mixture of elation and sadness, tinged with a vague feeling of frustration. Some of the crew had wept openly as their dead comrades were committed to the deep in a moving ceremony conducted by Captain Ash. But as their grief started to ease, and their elation at being alive subsided, a vague feeling of frustration began to pervade the lower deck. The action had proved indecisive and its premature ending left a nagging discontent in the minds of the crew. Pride and confidence, nurtured by nearly two decades of victory at sea, had been undermined by a feeling that the *Phoebe* may have come off worse in the engagement.

Mark was slowly coming to terms with the loss of Mr Brewis, the gunner, who had become his friend and mentor; also, the shock of being promoted to acting gunner in his place. He now occupied the gunner's small cabin forward of the gunroom, and whilst he appreciated the seclusion it afforded, a rare privilege in the navy, he couldn't quite dispel the feeling that he was somehow trespassing on a dead man's privacy. This sense of intrusion was reinforced by the fact that the ship's boy, who now acted as his servant, had also served Mr Brewis. The gunners' white-lined blue coat, with its blue lapels and cuffs and gold anchor buttons, hung on its peg as if daring him to try it on for size.

Mark recalled Ash's warning. 'I can only promote you on an acting basis, Mr Standish.' He'd noticed the Captain's use of "Mr" for the first time. 'The appointment can only be confirmed by the Navy Board', Ash added, then seeing Mark's look of puzzlement, went on, 'the Admiralty appoint commissioned officers for the duration of a ship's commission. The Navy Board appoints the standing, or warrant officers, who stay permanently with the ship, unless promoted. You'll have to pass a "viva voce" examination before a mathematical master and three able gunners,' Ash explained. 'You must also have at least a year's experience as a petty officer, which you now have. I don't think you'll have any problems with the maths,' he added, smiling.

As a warrant officer, albeit acting, Mark found himself on a par with the boatswain and carpenter. Though not of wardroom rank, or gunroom in the case of a frigate, he was nevertheless an officer with major responsibilities, holding an important place in the hierarchy of the ship. As a result, his relationship with other members of the crew began to change. It was as if an invisible barrier had been raised, and with it came an awkwardness in the crew's attitude towards him which had never been there before. Only Jack remained unchanged and summed up the situation in his usual blunt style.

'You're an officer now, my friend. One of them.' He laid emphasis on the word "them".

Mark didn't ask him to explain.

After two weeks patrolling with the squadron off Rochefort, it became clear that the *Phoebe* had suffered substantially more damage than had first been thought. She was taking in a good deal of water well below her waterline and no matter how hard the carpenter worked, the problem became progressively worse. Soon, the pumps were almost permanently manned and it was clear that the frigate needed to be taken into dry dock for repairs.

The rear admiral commanding the squadron reluctantly ordered Ash home, and after taking on board mail and dispatches, the *Phoebe* took leave of the squadron and set a north westerly course for Ushant. After rounding the island, and with a spanking south westerly behind her, she ran up the English Channel heading for Plymouth.

News that the *Phoebe* would be going into dry dock sent a buzz of speculation through the ship. Mark wondered if the crew would be given leave and voiced his thoughts to Jack. 'Think we'll be allowed ashore when we reach Plymouth?'

Jack shot a bemused look at his friend. 'Not a chance,' he said dismissively. 'We'll be put aboard an accommodation hulk till the ship's ready to sail again, likely as not. Or we might be transferred to another ship,' he added.

'Does the navy ever allow leave?'

'Some captains do, but most don't. Especially in England.'

'Because they think we'll desert?'

'Wouldn't you, given the chance?'

Mark thought about it for a while. 'I suppose I would,' he said guardedly. In fact he knew damn well he would, given half a chance of seeing Jane.

'As Acting Gunner you might be allowed ashore until they appoint a permanent one. There's a lot to be done. '

425

'Ash wants me to take the "viva voce" examination,' Mark said.

'Aye, but there'll be dozens of other qualified gunners, who've served on sixth rates and unrated sloops, all looking for promotion. If you get your warrant it's likely you'll be given another ship.'

'No chance of getting this one?'

Jack smiled. 'Don't bank on it, my friend,' he said kindly. 'The navy can knock you back just as quickly as it can promote you.'

Jack's prophetic warning proved to be well justified. The day after the *Phoebe* dropped anchor in Plymouth sound, a dozen members of her crew, including Mark and Jack, were transferred to the 38-gun frigate *Macedonian*. Their new ship was under orders to reinforce the West Indian station and ready to put to sea. Soon after being taken on board, they found themselves heading back down the English Channel and out into the broad waters of the Atlantic.

CHAPTER 43

The *Macedonian* was a fairly new frigate, much larger and more heavily armed than the *Phoebe*. But she was not such a happy ship and had changed captains several times in recent years. One previous captain, whilst commanding the *Macedonian* had figured in a notorious court martial and had been dismissed from his ship. His successor, Captain Waldegrave, was equally notorious, but as a flogging captain.

It was in this strained atmosphere among a new and wary crew of two hundred and fifty-four men now commanded by Captain Carden, that Mark and Jack suddenly found themselves. As an experienced able seaman, Jack was immediately assigned to the forecastle elite. Mark's assimilation into the crew proved more difficult as the *Macedonian* already had a gunner and gunner's mate. Eventually, impressed by Ash's letter of recommendation, Captain Cardin rated Mark as a quarter gunner.

Mark had shot Jack a wry smile as they made their way down to the lower deck to stow their gear. 'What did you say about the navy knocking you back?'

Jack grinned. 'Could have been worse. You're still a petty officer - just!'

When Mark examined the 18-pounders, he saw that there were no dispart sights fitted. As the ship headed south into the Atlantic, gun drills were infrequent and by the *Phoebe*'s standards, Mark considered the *Macedonian* to be a fairly slack ship. There was certainly none of Captain Ash's strict, professional approach and constant quest for fighting efficiency. Rather complacency, bordering almost on arrogance, as if any frigate of His Britannic Majesty's Navy would automatically prove more than a match for any enemy ship of comparable size.

By the summer of 1812 other momentous events began to unfold around the northern hemisphere. The roads across Germany and Poland thronged with horses, guns and waggons as the Emperor's *Grande Armee* of more than half a million men, mustered for the invasion of Russia. On June 24th, Napoleon crossed the Niemen on his fateful road to Moscow. As he contemptuously turned his back on the Europe he had conquered, the Peninsular army of Wellington captured the fortress of Badajoz, kicking open the final gate from Portugal into Spain. After defeating the French at Salamanca, Wellington entered Madrid to the pealing of bells and the ecstatic welcome of the populace. But an event that would have a significant impact on Mark's future also occurred in June, when the Congress of the United States of America finally lost patience and declared war on Great Britain.

The crew of the *Macedonian* knew nothing of these events, and the news that Britain was now at war with America was deliberately withheld from them for some time. When it was finally announced, it was greeted with mixed feelings by most of the men and outright dismay by the Americans on board who had been pressed into service despite their claims to American citizenship.

Mark sympathised with the American seamen on board. 'Surely they can't be expected to fight their own countrymen?'

'You'd best keep your opinions to yourself,' Jack warned. 'If any of the officers hear you you'll be on the grating with your shirt off feeling the cat peel the skin off your back.'

'It's still not right,' Mark persisted.

'Stow it!' Jack snapped. 'The captain's told the Americans he'll shoot any of 'em that won't fight. So don't go making trouble for yourself.'

Though they were poles apart in intellectual outlook, Jack valued his friendship with Mark and kept a protective eye on him. But there were times when he despaired of his friend's humanitarian and liberal views and his frequent lack of discretion in making them known. Jack was a product of his age, accepting cruelty, hardship and injustice as part of his everyday lot. He simply couldn't comprehend why Mark could not do the same, and this lack of understanding sometimes irritated him. Perhaps it was because, reluctantly and subconsciously, he recognised the logic of Mark's arguments, but his conditioned mind could not rationalise a suitable response. Such thoughts made him feel uncomfortable and he reacted, as he always did, by concentrating his mind on how to survive another day.

*****

428

Sunday, October 25th, 1812, found the *Macedonian* sailing west and midway between the Canary Islands and the Arzores. After calling in at Madeira to take on board a supply of wine, the crew had scarcely finished breakfast when the masthead lookout shouted 'Sail ho!'

Breakfast was quickly forgotten as many of the crew ran up on deck. Captain Carden had also heard the shout and appeared on the quarterdeck, squinting aloft at the lookout. 'Masthead there?'

'Sir.'

'Where away's the sail?'

'On the leeward beam, sir.'

'What does she look like?'

'A square-rigged vessel, sir.'

Most of the crew were now on deck and a buzz of excited chatter rose from the rails as they speculated on the identity of the strange ship. This was soon cut short by an angry order from the quarterdeck. 'Keep silence, fore and aft.'

After a few minutes the captain again hailed the lookout. 'Masthead there!'

'Sir!'

'Can you make her out yet?'

'Looks like a large ship standing towards us, sir.'

A midshipman was quickly dispatched aloft. After a tense wait of several minutes, his call came floating down. 'Deck there! A large frigate bearing down on us, sir!'

A whisper of excitement again broke out among the crew as word spread that the sighting was not a Frenchman but an American man-of-war. The *Macedonian* hoisted her private recognition signal and, receiving no reply, the order was given 'All hands clear the ship for action!' The rhythmic tap of the drum beat to quarters as bulkheads were taken down, decks dampened and sanded and wet frieze screens fitted round the magazine hatches to prevent any sparks penetrating.

Mark and his gun captains went to the gunner's store room to collect the cartouche boxes containing the powder tubes for insertion into the touch-holes of the guns. Whilst they were doing this, the gun crews were casting the guns loose from their lashings and clearing away the side-tackles, preventer tackles and breechings. The tampions were removed from the gun muzzles and crows, handspikes and sponges laid out ready for use. The cheeses of wads were made ready and rope rings containing the round shot were placed between the guns.

Mark returned to his crew and hung the powder horn, full of priming powder, above the gun. He then stuck his priming iron inside his belt ready for use. Powder boys hurried up handing out cartridges from their salt-boxes ready for the first broadside. From the quarterdeck above, the clump of heavy boots could be heard as the marines, with muskets and side arms, lined the rails ready to pick off the topmen and sail trimmers on the opposing ship.

Soon, the colours of the approaching ship could be seen, confirming that she was an American frigate. This was received with mixed feelings by the *Macedonian*'s crew for they had assumed that any enemy would be French. American frigates were generally bigger, more heavily armed and carried larger crews than their British counterparts. Mark also had an uneasy feeling that American standards of seamanship and gunnery might prove superior to their own. British overconfidence and a neglect of gunnery had compromised their fighting capability. This was typified by the sloppy complacency that he'd witnessed since joining the *Macedonian*, a far cry from the high levels of professional efficiency demanded by Captain Ash aboard the *Phoebe*.

As the two ships converged, it became clear to all on board the *Macedonian* that they faced a formidable opponent. The American ship was one of a class of heavy frigates built to the concept of Joshua Humphreys, a man recognised as the ablest shipbuilder in the New World. She was the 44-gun *United States*, one of the first of this new and powerful breed of super-frigates, destined to write a new chapter in the history of naval warfare. Based on the long, slim Baltimore clippers, she could out sail almost anything afloat. With an overall length of two hundred and four feet, a beam of over forty-three feet and a displacement of two thousand two hundred tons, she was considerably larger than the *Macedonian*.

Although rated a 44-gun ship, the United States in fact carried fifty-six. Her armament consisted of thirty long 24-pounders on the main gun deck and twenty four 42-pounder carronades on the quarterdeck and forecastle, plus two long 24-pounder bow chasers. To withstand the extra strains of such heavy armament, she was stoutly built with twenty inch side planking, at least five inches thicker than in contemporary frigates. For the past four years the *United States* had been commanded by Stephen Decatur, an able and experienced officer who had made a name for himself through distinguished service in the Mediterranean.

On board the *Macedonian*, Captain Carden realised that his only hope was to engage the enemy at close quarters as quickly as possible. With only 18-pounders against the American's long 24-pounders, and a crew of two hundred and fifty-four against a likely four hundred and sixty on board the *United States*, he knew he would be considerably outgunned and outmanned.

The two frigates passed on opposite courses at long range. The *United States* fired two broadsides from her long 24-pounders; the first fell short but the second found its mark and did some damage. The *Macedonian*, out of range, remained silent. Captain Carden tried desperately to close the range but Decatur, determined to retain his advantage, skilfully manoeuvred his ship and continued to pound the *Macedonian* at long range, inflicting considerably damage.

Crouched over his gun on the main deck, Mark waited for the order to fire. He could hear the sound of rushing wind above, like a sail being torn apart, as the enemy shot passed overhead. The crash of the shots which found their mark made the ship tremble.

Some of the *Macedonian*'s larboard guns had begun to open up when the curt order came, 'Cease fire! You're wasting shot.' Then the order was given, 'Wear ship,' which brought the starboard guns to bear. Mark sighted along the gun barrel and pulled the lanyard, jumping clear as the gun recoiled violently inboard after firing. Even with two degrees elevation, he saw that the shot fell a little short. The results of the other gun captains were even worse, most of the shot falling well short of the target. What little gun training they'd received had been restricted to firing at point blank range, where speed of fire was considered more important than accuracy.

Mark now appreciated how right Captain Ash had been to make good gunnery his top priority on board the *Phoebe*. With the same high level of training and the proper use of dispart sights, the

Macedonian would have been in a much better position to fight the well-handled American super-frigate.

But it was too late for that now. All they could do was to fight like lions against a superior foe, which they manfully did. Soon, gun smoke and the acrid smell of gunpowder filled the cramped space of the gun deck as broadside after broadside was discharged at the enemy. The amount of physical effort required to run in the guns, swab and load, then run out again, was immense. Knowing this, the gun crews had discarded their jackets and shirts and fought stripped to the waist, with a handkerchief bound round their heads and over their ears to avoid being deafened by the roar of the guns.

After nearly an hour of action, the smoke filled gun deck had become an infernal scene of slaughter. The flash of guns lit up this shadowy hell, like lightning accompanying a thunderstorm. The ear-splitting crash of heavy shot striking home was followed by screams as scattered splinters of wood scythed through the deck, killing and maiming in the confined space. The river of blood which had stained the deck red had now congealed into a greasy, odorous mess which made the surface slippery to walk on.

Many of the guns in the waist of the ship were now damaged and some overturned. This part of the ship, known as the slaughterhouse, always took the brunt of the enemy fire and suffered the most casualties. One man had his hand cut off by a shot; another had lost his leg. A third lay writhing on the deck, clutching his bowels which had been torn open. A powder boy, running to serve his gun, suddenly screamed as his powder caught fire, burning the skin of his face. The dead were immediately thrown overboard and the wounded carried below to the cockpit to receive the attentions of the ship's surgeon.

The sound of spars falling on deck and the sluggish motion of the ship indicated to Mark that the *Macedonian* was now badly damaged. Suddenly, the hail of enemy fire stopped and this was immediately followed by an order from the lieutenant to cease firing. An eerie silence descended on the *Macedonian*'s gun deck as the gun smoke slowly began to clear.

The British frigate was now a wreck and lay disabled, wallowing in the Atlantic swell. Her topmasts and main yard had been shot away and her mizzenmast hung over the stern. Over a third of her crew had been killed or wounded. The unthinkable had finally happened. His Britannic Majesty's frigate *Macedonian* had struck her colours and was now a prize of the American frigate, *United States*. The battle had lasted only an hour and the *Macedonian* had been crippled at fairly long range, beaten by a larger foe employing superior gunnery and better fighting tactics.

The *United States* sent over a boarding party to take control of their prize. Though badly damaged, the *Macedonian* was in no danger of sinking and the task of repairing her, so that she could be sailed back to America, was begun immediately. Mark was assigned to a working party charged with cleaning up the foul mess that marked the aftermath of the bloody engagement. The greasy, red carpet of congealed blood had to be scrubbed and swabbed from the decks before the ship could be cleansed and disinfected with vinegar and brimstone to remove the smell of death. Torn off limbs were thrown overboard and human fingers prized out of the ship's side as the working party proceeded with their grisly task.

When the running repairs had been completed, most of the *Macedonian*'s officers and men were transferred to the *United States*. A small number remained on board to help work the ship and look after the wounded. Mark was delighted to find Jack alive and well and they exchanged stories as they waited to be taken on board the American frigate. But it was a sombre gathering of chastened men who learned that thirty-six of their shipmates had been killed in the battle and sixty-eight lay wounded below. In stark contrast, the American frigate looked very little damaged and her casualties were only five killed and seven wounded.

Captain Carden was relieved to discover that he was not the first British man-of-war to strike after a single ship to ship engagement. That honour had gone to another British frigate, the 38-gun *Guerriere*, which had been beaten into submission two months earlier by the American frigate *Constitution*, a sister ship of the *United States*. Worse was to follow before the British navy learned its lesson and accorded the small, but efficient, American navy the respect it deserved.

A few weeks later, the *Macedonian* entered Rhode Island Sound and sailed into Newport with the Stars and Stripes flying proudly over the British ensign. The victorious Decatur reached New London with the *United States* on the same day. The crew of the *Macedonian* now faced an uncertain future as prisoners of war.

CHAPTER 44

The *Macedonian* was brought down Long Island Sound for a refit at New York. A captain and crew were appointed to her, but when she and the *United States* were ready to put to sea they found the exits blocked by British ships. Though several attempts were made to break out, all proved unsuccessful. The *United States* was destined never to get to sea again during the war and the *Macedonian* never to be used against the British.

To his surprise, Mark found life as a prisoner of war remarkably pleasant. Conditions were lax and he felt that their captors were not quite sure what to do with them. Soon, he began to enjoy the anomaly of freedom as a prisoner of war; or so it seemed after two years of oppressive discipline in the British navy. He also came to like the Americans and their proud, independent ways. The differences between the labouring and ruling classes appeared far less marked than in England. Even in their mode of dress, the merchants and gentlemen did not try to adopt a superior style that would mark them out, unlike their counterparts in England. Relations between rich and poor seemed altogether more relaxed and egalitarian, and there were surprisingly few beggars in the streets.

Jack was also enjoying his new lifestyle in America and had made several rather dubious contacts with the local population. 'Beats the navy any day,' he confided after completing another shady deal, the details of which Mark didn't want to know.

'It's not quite what I expected prison life to be,' Mark confessed. 'It's almost as if they're embarrassed and don't know what to do with us.'

'You're right. Two more lads escaped this week and they've made precious little effort to recapture them.'

'Perhaps it's because they didn't want the war in the first place.'

'Why do you say that?'

'Because most of the merchants and traders are in New England and support the federalists. The war's hitting their pockets.'

Jack looked puzzled. 'Then why did they declare war on us?'

'Because President Madison and the Jeffersonian Democrats are in power and they are anti-British.'

Jack looked thoughtful. 'And the New English states are pro-British?'

'More or less.'

'That explains it then.'

'Explains what?'

'The rumours that the Connecticut men on their side of the Thames River send secret signals to the British ships every time the American frigates try to leave.'

Mark smiled. 'I doubt if even the most ardent federalist would go that far to betray his country.'

'Well whatever happens, I'm not going back to England when the war's over,' Jack said firmly. 'This is the country of the future and I want to be part of it.'

'You like the Americans, then?'

'Don't you?'

'Yes, I do but...' Mark was not sure how to go on.

'You don't sound too convincing, my friend.'

I do like them but, for a nation that prides itself on freedom and independence, they seem to have an awful lot of black slaves and treat them very badly.'

'There's no law against that. And anyway, the British navy presses men into slavery. White men at that.' Jack added to reinforce his argument.

'Slavery is a moral argument, Jack, not just a legal one,' Mark said patiently. 'I don't condone what the British do and I know we still allow slaves in our colonies. But the American Declaration of Independence states, and I quote: *That all men are born equal, that they are endowed with unalienable rights, that among these are Life, Liberty and the pursuit of Happiness....*' He paused, and then added, 'If you're white, that is.'

Jack sighed and looked fondly at his friend. 'You take life far too seriously. You're a dreamer, Mark, and it will take more than dreams to change this rotten world. Anyway, if you create a heaven on earth you'll ruin the church. They won't have anything left to peddle to the likes of us.'

Mark laughed at the absurd logic of Jack's argument. 'You may have a point there, my friend, but I doubt if we'll ever have the opportunity to prove it.'

'Maybe so, but I reckon there's a better chance of a good life here in America than back home in England.'

'I think you're right. The problem is will the Americans let you stay?'

'Why shouldn't they?'

'Because we're British. We're enemy prisoners of war, remember?'

Jack looked crestfallen. 'I never thought of it in that way, they being so easy on us like.'

'You'll improve your chances if you volunteer for their navy,' Mark said, encouragingly.

'Not bloody likely! If the British navy ever catch up with you, they'll string you up from the nearest yardarm for treason.'

'You'd be in good company. They say that half the American navy is crewed by British deserters.'

'More fool them, I say.'

'It would take a ship of the line to beat one of their heavy frigates.'

'I'm still not risking it. The Royal Navy's bound to learn from their mistakes sooner or later. I don't want to be aboard an American ship when that happens.'

'Then volunteer for the American army. There's fighting in Upper and Lower Canada.'

An expression of exasperation crossed Jack's face. 'Why volunteer at all? I'm quite happy here in New England.'

'Because I've heard that all volunteers will be given three months' pay and a quarter of land when they're honourably discharged after the war.'

'A quarter of an acre isn't much,' Jack sniffed contemptuously. 'Hardly worth risking your life for.'

'It's quarter section – that's a quarter of a square mile - one hundred and sixty acres, Mark corrected, smiling at his friend's astonishment. 'Americans think big, and what's more,' he added, 'you don't have to give one tenth of your crop to the parson.'

'What! No church tithes?'

'No. '

Jack looked thoughtful. 'Now that puts a different slant on things. It's worth thinking about.'

'It certainly is,' Mark agreed.

'Then why don't we both volunteer for the army?'

'Unlike you, my friend, I don't want to stay in America.'

'Why not?'

'Because I have a wife at home and some unsettled business to attend to. I need to stay alive.'

'Then you won't volunteer?'

'No. But don't let me stop you.'

'I'll think about it,' Jack said non-committedly.

Two months later Mark received a letter from England, the first since his impressment. It was from his father and, clumsy with excitement, he fumbled it open and started to read. Then, as Henry's words registered in his brain, his whole world began to fall apart.

Mark awoke from his recurring nightmare, bathed in perspiration. He lay, with his eyes tightly shut, trying desperately to erase the images which stubbornly lingered in his mind to torment him. The look on Jane's face as she lay naked across the bed. The leering face of Roland, obscene with lust and evil, as he prepared to mount her. Opening his eyes, he tried to control the cold spasms of shivering which the nightmares always brought on.

It had been like this since the day he'd read the letter. His father's words, so painfully put to paper, were meant to comfort. But, numbed by the shock of Jane's death and the manner of it, Mark's anguish was inconsolable. The pain had cut deep into his heart leaving a void of desolation in place of the tenuous strands of hope that he'd nurtured since his impressment. Hurt, he'd withdrawn into a reclusive mental world where he could brood and plot revenge. In the ensuing months, his desire for retribution had steadily grown until it became an obsession.

To the casual observer, Mark was a man who stoically bore his grief, compensating for his misfortune by pursuing a ferociously active lifestyle to keep his mind occupied. But Jack knew his friend was

438

hurting, and his inability to help had left him feeling frustrated and useless. All he could do was to stay close to Mark and try to protect him from the consequences of his often brave, but usually reckless actions. It was almost as if Mark had entertained some death wish and since their enlistment in the American Army, Jack's loyalty and watchfulness had, on more than one occasion, saved his friend's life. In the process, their friendship strengthened and it was this special bond that enabled Mark to survive the darkest months of his anguish. It also helped him to control the pent up anger that constantly simmered inside him.

Mark's decision to enlist in the American army had taken Jack by surprise. In their many conversations on the subject, Mark had always dismissed the idea and his sudden change of heart caught Jack off balance. Knowing his friend's state of mind, he'd gently quizzed him. 'You sure this is what you want to do?'

'Yes.' Mark had smiled, but there'd been no humour in his eyes. 'I can't stand the monotony of being a prisoner any more. I need something to do.'

'You said you didn't want to stay in America.'

'I'm not sure that I do.'

Jack, looking confused, had asked, 'So you'll go back to England when all this is over?'

'Yes, but not to stay.' Mark's voice had sounded cold and detached.

'Just attend to the unfinished business, eh?' Jack had prompted, anxiously.

'Yes, but that can wait.'

'You might get yourself killed.'

Mark had shrugged. 'Then my problems will die with me. '

Jack had remained silent for a while, and then asked 'Do they still give you one hundred and sixty acres on discharge?'

'No.'

'I knew there'd be a catch in it somewhere.'

'They've upped it to three hundred and twenty acres if you enlist for eighteen months,' Mark had gently corrected, his voice carrying a trace of mischief which was not lost on his friend.

Jack had grinned back. 'Sounds all right to me.'

'There's also an enlistment bounty of one hundred and twenty-four dollars and the pay's ten dollars a month.'

Jack's grin had widened. 'It gets better all the time.'

'The problem is,' Mark had cautioned, 'you have to earn an honourable discharge.' For the first time in many weeks, his expression had shown a teasing flash of humour.

'Then I'll just have to enlist with you to make sure that you behave yourself,' Jack had countered, beaming back at his friend. 'Besides, you always did need looking after.'

And so it was that, in the early summer of 1813, they had both enlisted in the United States Army and to their surprise, they were not sent to the Canadian front but in the opposite direction to join the forces of General Andrew Jackson in the south.

CHAPTER 45

The war of 1812 proved to be a strange conflict, one that most Americans and most Britons did not seem to want. In the end, neither side could claim to have won but the southern "War Hawks", led by Henry Clay of Kentucky and John C. Calhoun of South Carolina, saw war with England as an opportunity to seize more land by invading Canada in the North and the Spanish held Floridas to the south. It was also an opportunity to deal, once and for all, with the Indian problem.

The Indians had always been an obstacle to westward expansion. Their refusal to assimilate into the American way of life infuriated Indian haters like General Jackson, who viewed such behaviour as irresponsible. The Indians were happy to co-exist and co-operate with the American government, but only as tribal nations within the United States. They wanted to preserve their customs and culture and this required vast areas of land in relation to the size of the Indian population. The restless, land hungry white settlers saw this as extravagant and wasteful. Under white ownership the land could be productive and highly profitable.

The Louisiana Purchase of 1803, whereby Napoleon had made over eight hundred and twenty-eight thousand square miles of French claimed territory to the United States, had more than doubled the size of the country. And all for the ridiculously low price of fifteen million dollars, less than four cents an acre! A vast, relatively unpopulated land now lay west of the Mississippi, ripe for settlement. It would ultimately make possible the creation of thirteen new states and lay the foundations for a century of rapid economic development. However, there were more attractive opportunities for the white settler nearer home. In the South, vast tracts of rich tribal lands were still owned by the most advanced group of Indians; the Creeks, Cherokees, Choctaws, Chickasaws and Seminoles, long regarded as the Five Civilised Tribes. Such lands were ideal for growing the new wonder crop, King Cotton.

Eli Whitney's simple, but efficient, cotton gin had transformed the plantation economy of the south and the expanding cotton mills of industrial England wanted all the cotton America could supply. The era of cotton mania had begun and fortunes were there for the making.

But, Virginia, the Carolinas and Georgia were largely tobacco growing states and less suited to cotton. However, a new Deep South beckoned in the lower Mississippi Valley, if only the Indians could be persuaded to move.

It was the war of 1812 which provided America with a convenient excuse to apply such persuasion. The vast area of the new Mississippi Territory lay between Georgia and the Mississippi River, with Tennessee to the North and Spanish held East and West Florida to the south. It contained large areas of Indian tribal lands and some of the best belonged to the Creek Indians. Following Chief Tecumseh's attempts to form a confederation of Indian tribes to drive the whites from their lands, most Indians were now regarded as hostile and none more so than the militant Creek Indians. To make matters worse, the British had armed and trained four thousand Creeks and Seminoles who were now equipped with muskets, carbines, rifles and pistols together with a large supply of powder and shot.

Taking their cue from Tecumseh, the Creeks launched an attack on the American settlers who retreated into the grandly named Fort Mimms, which was just an acre of ground surrounded by a log fence with slits for muskets and two gates. Despite advance warning of an impending assault, the gates were left open when the Creeks attacked. The result was a massacre and five hundred and fifty-three men, women and children were brutally slaughtered. Only fifteen whites survived to tell of the carnage; of men and women scalped and children seized by the legs and killed by battering their heads against the stockades. Of how pregnant women were opened up, whilst still alive, to see their embryo infants let out of the womb.

The massacre had taken place on 30th August, 1813 and when the news filtered through, Andrew Jackson, a major general of militia in Tennessee, was ordered to take his men south to avenge the disaster. It was at this point that Mark, Jack and their small detachment of regulars had joined up with the motley army of militiamen and local volunteers which was being hurried south by the impatient General.

Although the American regular army had been considerably expanded during the war, it was still a relatively small force thinly spread over several fronts. Mark discovered that most of General Jackson's army was made up of a rag tag of state militia and local

442

volunteer units, with only a small core of regulars. The tiny contingent of British volunteers, many of whom were deserters, were treated with some suspicion at first.

But, it sometimes happens that a death wish seems to bring its own immunity, and so it was with Mark. His many acts of bravery, often imprudent and headstrong, began to affect the mood of his American comrades. An attitude of mild distrust for the British volunteers gradually began to change to one of grudging acceptance. And as Mark's standing and popularity grew, so the reluctant acceptance of the British contingent changed to one of open respect. Mark and his fellow Britishers eventually became accepted as true American compatriots, save for a few diehards who maintained a lingering mistrust of all things British.

Having been used to the rigid, brutal discipline imposed in the Royal Navy, Mark and Jack found life in the American Army something of a revelation. The egalitarian nature of this young nation was manifested in the army's approach to discipline, which was less harsh and more humanitarian than that practised in the British Army. In 1812, congress had outlawed flogging in the American Army but the British soldier could still receive up to three hundred lashes for misbehaviour. Most southern Americans regarded the whip as punishment suitable only for black slaves.

Though Mark had always abhorred flogging as an ineffective and dehumanising practice, he had to admit that the American militia and local volunteer units appeared sloppy and ill-disciplined. And the motley bunch of fringe-shirted, fur-hatted frontiersmen, who formed part of Jackson's army, seemed to be a law unto themselves. He wondered what would happen if they ever came face to face with Wellington's peninsular veterans, now rumoured to have pushed the tough French army of Marshal Soult out of Spain and poised to invade France.

Yet it was with these freewheeling frontiersmen that Mark learned the basics of woodcraft and Indian fighting skills that were so essential deep inside the hostile territory of the Creek nation. He soon learned that this was no conventional war. There were no formal rules of engagement in this vast inimical land where no country's writ stood firm. The fact that Mark was a remarkably quick learner, seemingly without fear and blessed with a rare military flair soon caught the attention of a noted sharpshooter, Davy Crocket, and the two men quickly became friends. But Mark found it difficult to come to terms with the way the frontiersmen treated the Indians. Having fought them, on and off, for most of their lives, they regarded the Indians as savages and showed them no more humanity than that which they extended to the animals they hunted and trapped for furs.

Two months after the massacre at Fort Mimms, General Jackson's army had moved deep into Creek territory in a multi-pronged campaign, building roads and forts as they went. Early in November, they surrounded the hostile village of Tallushatchee and Jackson ordered his friend and partner in land speculation, General John Coffee, to move in with one thousand men and destroy it. Up until then, Mark's war exploits had been confined to scouting and foraging, where he'd only been involved in minor skirmishes with small Creek war parties. Tallushatchee was his first major engagement and it totally sickened him. It was revenge for Fort Mimms, and bloody it was. Coffee's men killed every male Indian in the village, one hundred and eighty-seven in all. Only eighty-four women and children were spared and taken prisoner. As Mark fought his way through the village, his stomach revolted at the sight of charred bodies and the smell of burning flesh. He counted eight half consumed bodies in one cabin alone. Later, when he heard his friend Davy Crocket boasting about shooting the Indians like dogs, he could hardly restrain himself from swinging a punch at the Tennessee sharpshooter.

'You all right, son?' Davy had asked, puzzled by Mark's distress.

Mark spat out an oath and walked away.

'You did well in there,' Davy shouted after him. 'Take any scalps?'

Mark kept his silence and carried on walking. He heard a burst of ribald laughter from the bunch of frontiersmen surrounding Davy and realised that the war was just a game to them; an excuse to shoot Indians and an opportunity for booty. So Mark directed his anger at General Jackson for allowing his men to behave in such a barbaric way. But even this became muted when he learned that the General had adopted a ten month old Indian child who'd been found clutched in his dead mother's arms. He'd sent the boy back to the Hermitage, his fine estate near Nashville, to be taken care of.

The General's strange mixture of tenderness and savagery both puzzled and fascinated Mark. He suddenly wished he could have the opportunity to get to know this tall, thin, angry looking man with the blazing blue eyes and iron will. A man with a ruthless streak, said to be loyal and generous to his friends, remorseless to his enemies. Little did Mark realise that fate would soon allow his wish to be granted.

Within a week of the slaughter at Tallushatchee, General Jackson won what was virtually a pitched battle against a force of one thousand Creek warriors near the village of Talladega, killing two hundred and ninety Indians for the loss of seventeen of his own men and a further eighty-seven wounded. To Jackson's annoyance, seven hundred Creeks broke through his encircling troops and made good their escape.

But after the battle, the picture began to change and soon the General was facing problems of a different kind. The threat of famine had always worried him more than fighting the Creeks. Feeding an army numbering nearly two thousand men in difficult and hostile Indian Territory was never going to be easy, and hungry men would have little stomach for fighting. Now, with no rations left to feed his men, Jackson's army threatened to disintegrate.

To make matters worse, the militia were only obliged to provide ninety days service and this was about to expire along with the one year enlistments of some of the volunteers. Added to this, an expedition by the Alabama Volunteers under General Claiborne had ended in disarray and General Floyd's Georgia Militia had lost two hundred men following an attack on their badly posted camp, forcing him to pull his troops out of the war. Now, the men had had enough and wanted to go home. The General was given an ultimatum. The army would either march home under Jackson, or mutiny and march home without him.

Under any other commander, the whole campaign might well have petered out. But an angry Jackson was having none of this and refused to give in to what was now becoming a military rabble. He skilfully played off the volunteers against the militiamen and used his few regulars to intimidate both. However, this was not enough and only his indomitable will could save the day. He posted General Coffee and a few loyal troops along the road with orders to shoot any mutinous soldier who tried to march home. Then, back in camp, he faced an entire brigade, his right hand clutching a musket which rested on his horse's neck, his left arm still in a sling as a result of his duel with Benton three months earlier. He stood alongside his horse holding the mob in his fierce glare, as if daring them to disobey.

Mark, recently promoted to Sergeant, seeing the General's danger, ordered his squad of regulars to form up behind Jackson, their muskets loaded and at the ready. The combination of the General's iron will and the small but determined bunch of regulars lined up behind him, was enough to defuse the crisis. The militia, still in a surly mood, slowly broke up leaving an atmosphere of unease hanging over the camp.

As the General turned his horse his eyes rested on Mark and a thin smile broke through his pain-lined face. 'Well done, Sergeant.'

Surprised, Mark could only mutter an embarrassed, 'Thank you, sir.'

The General handed his horse and musket to an aid and walked up to Mark. 'What's your name, Sergeant?'

'Standish, sir.'

'You sound a bit British.'

'I am, sir.'

'A deserter?' The General's voice sounded a little less friendly.

Mark stiffened. 'No, sir. I was a naval prisoner of war for nine months until I volunteered.'

The General could see that Mark had been stung by his unfair insinuation. His smile returned. 'Stand easy, Sergeant. My apologies if I've upset you. I'm proud to meet a genuine volunteer and I won't forget what you've done today.' With that, he turned and walked back to his horse and after painfully mounting, rode off without a backward glance.

Mark's bemused thoughts were interrupted by the sound of Jack's voice. 'Not often a Sergeant gets an apology from his commanding General. Especially that one.'

Mark smiled. 'You think it's my lucky day?'

'At least you're in his good books. He's not a man I'd want to pick a fight with.'

'Why?'

'They say he's killed a few men in his time. Fought his first duel when he was twenty-one, they reckon. The last one was less than three months ago. That's why his arm is still in a sling.'

Mark shrugged. 'He'll have forgotten me by the time he reaches his quarters.' He tried to dismiss the General from his thoughts, yet somehow the strange charisma of the man lingered in his mind and refused to go away.

But General Jackson had not forgotten Mark. Something about this Britisher, who'd exchanged a safe and easy life as a prisoner of war to join the American Army, intrigued him. He felt impelled to find out more about the man.

Three weeks later, the spectre of another mutiny began to raise its head. This time it was a group of volunteers who were discontented. Their enlistment time had also expired and they wanted to go home. It was another tense impasse as an angry Jackson again faced up to the mutineers after rejecting their demands. Realising that the General was outnumbered and outgunned, Mark called to Jack and a group of militiamen and together, they dragged two small pieces of field artillery into position.

'Grape shot,' Mark ordered in a deliberately loud voice. He took charge of one cannon and ordered Jack to oversee the other. After loading, he ordered both guns to be trained on the mutinous volunteers. 'Cannon ready, sir,' he called to the General.

Jackson gave a brief acknowledgement but kept his fierce gaze on the mutineers. When they did not respond to his repeated orders, he called out to Mark, 'Fire at my command.'

The seconds of tension which followed seemed like hours, as if time had stood still. Finally the men yielded to the General's iron will and, muttering among themselves, they slowly dispersed. After watching for a few minutes, the General spurred his horse and rode off without a word.

Half an hour later, Mark was ordered to report to the General's quarters. On arrival at the command tent, he stood to one side as a

447

number of staff officers began to leave. Then, the General's personal aid beckoned him to enter before he also made his exit.

The General was seated on a camp chair having his wound cleaned and dressed. Mark was staggered at the damage to the General's body. There were scars on his chest, a legacy to an earlier duel and his shoulder was a mess where the ball from his last duel had entered before lodging in the bone. That this man had been such a dynamic and tireless leader during three months of hard campaigning, despite his wounds, was testimony to his immense will power and his ability to live with constant pain. If ever there was a born leader of men, Mark thought, Jackson must surely be that man.

The General gestured with his good arm. 'Sit down on the bed there, sergeant, and watch this butcher ply his trade.

The surgeon ignored the insult and began to probe the wound, causing the General to grimace with pain. 'Keep still, General, or you'll make matters worse.'

'And I suppose you can make them better?' the General responded through gritted teeth.

'Yes, if I could only prise out the ball.'

'Then do it, for God's sake.'

'I can't. It's embedded in the bone.'

The General sighed. 'Then let it stay. It'll be company for the other one.' He was referring to the bullet that was still lodged in his chest as a result of a duel with Charles Dickinson in 1806. He'd killed his opponent, but Dickinson's bullet had broken two of his ribs before burying itself deep inside his chest. That Jackson had lived was attributed to his wearing a heavy, loose fitting coat which impeded the bullet. Unfortunately for the General, the bullet had also carried pieces of cloth into the chest cavity causing a lung abscess which would cause him decades of pain.

But General Jackson had learned to live with pain and discomfort and as soon as the surgeon was finished, he was summarily dismissed. The General turned to Mark. 'That was a smart move with the cannon, Sergeant.'

'Seemed the only thing to do at the time, sir,' Mark answered, awkwardly.

448

'Yes. Grape shot would have made a mess of those insubordinate bastards at that range.'

'I'm glad it didn't come to that, sir.'

'It would have served them right if it had. This army still has an important task to finish and I won't allow a few misguided mutineers to stand in my way.' There was an awesome vehemence in the General's voice which startled Mark.

'Then you would have given the order to open fire? Watched your own men die in cold blood?' Mark's voice was strained with shocked disbelief.

'Yes.' The blazing blue eyes were now fixed on Mark. 'The question is, Sergeant, would you have obeyed my order?'

The question took Mark by surprise. He'd never seriously believed it would be necessary to fire the cannon.

But what if it had been? He knew the General would have stood firm. But what of himself? He shook his head. 'I honestly don't know, sir.'

A faint smile crept over the General's face. 'Then perhaps it's just as well we weren't put to the test, eh Sergeant?'

Mark remained silent but, somehow, he felt the General already knew the answer to his question.

'I expect you were wondering why I sent for you,' Jackson said, suddenly changing tack.

'I was a little surprised, sir.'

'But not curious?'

'Both, sir. More curious than surprised, in fact.'

'Then let me put your mind at rest. I've been making some enquiries about you, Sergeant. I see you served aboard the frigate *Macedonian* until you were taken prisoner. You also served as a gunner on another frigate, the *Phoebe*.'

'Actually, I was only acting gunner, sir,' Mark corrected.

'Nevertheless,' the General snapped, 'That was rapid promotion by British Navy standards, wasn't it?'

'I was just lucky, I suppose.' Mark suddenly felt embarrassed.

'I think not,' the General went on. 'My information tells me that you're extremely knowledgeable about guns. Pity the *Macedonian* didn't make better use of you, though I doubt if Stephen Decatur would agree with me.'

Mark's embarrassment suddenly changed to anger. 'A lot of brave men died on board the *Macedonian*. The outcome might have been different if Captain Ash had been in command.'

The General smiled, acknowledging Mark's spirited defence. 'Tell me why.'

Mark explained how the superb standards of professionalism had been achieved on board the *Phoebe* under Captain Ash's leadership. 'It was the reverse on board the *Macedonian*,' he added.

You have a great deal of faith in your Captain Ash,' Jackson said, warming to Mark's loyalty. 'But I doubt if any British ship, other than a ship of the line, could take on an American frigate in a one-to-one engagement and win.'

'Captain Broke of the *Shannon* did,' Mark quickly countered. 'And with a smaller ship and fewer crew,' he added, ramming his point home. 'He did it by making sure his gun crews were properly trained and professionally led. He and Captain Ash were pioneering a new approach to naval gunnery. To them, gunnery was a science and they treated it as such.'

The General was impressed. 'You seem to be remarkably well informed, Sergeant.'

'I read a lot of newspapers when I was a prisoner of war. Mainly American ones but sometimes old copies of the London Times brought in by merchant captains.'

'So you have some education, eh? Unusual for a British sailor.'

'I was taken by the press, or rather,' Mark paused, uncertain whether to continue. 'Go on,' the General prompted.

'I was foolish enough to trust someone who I knew to be untrustworthy,' Mark said, deciding his personal affairs were no concern of the General.

'And you were betrayed?'

'Yes.'

Mark's pained response warned Jackson that he'd touched on a highly emotive private issue. Though curious, he thought it wise not to pursue the matter. Another time, perhaps, but not now. He quickly changed the subject. 'So you claim to have been well trained in the science of gunnery? '

'I believe so, sir.'

'Then I think it's time we made proper use of your talents, Sergeant.'

Mark looked surprised. 'In what way, sir?' You don't really need artillery to fight this kind of Indian war.'

'No, but we'll need cannon to arm the forts that we'll have to build, if we're to hold on to the territory when the settlers move in. That will require men to be trained in their use. '

'And that will be my responsibility?' Mark asked.

'One of your responsibilities,' the General corrected. 'There are others of greater importance. Come over here and I'll explain.' He led the way to a table on which lay several rolled up maps. Taking one, he unrolled it and placed heavy objects on the edges to stop it coiling up again. The General's finger traced a line across the map, stopping at a spot some one hundred miles south of the Tennessee border. 'This is our present position on the Coosa River,' he said. His finger travelled a further seventy miles southwards on the map before pausing and stabbing at the spot. 'This is the Creek's main fortress at Horseshoe Bend on the Tallapoosa River. My scouts reckon there's a thousand or more of Red Eagle's best warriors camped there inside a hundred acre peninsular formed by the river. It's surrounded by water on three sides with a fortified stockade built across the narrow neck of land which is the only way in. They say the position is almost impregnable.'

'And you think artillery will prove it's not?' Mark said. 'I doubt if our six-pounders will be heavy enough to breech a well-built stockade.'

'They will if they're properly sighted and the fire is accurately concentrated on one part of the stockade. They tell me you're good at that.'

'I'll need the services of a blacksmith to make some sights. Also, a good supply of powder and shot. It takes a lot of practice to knock a gun crew into shape.'

451

'That will be entirely up to you since I'm now putting you in charge of my entire ordnance,' the General paused, smiling at Mark's confusion, before adding, Lieutenant Standish.'

'Lieutenant?' Mark stammered in surprise.

'That's what I said, the General's tone brooked no further argument. 'You'll be joining my staff so you'd better see if the commissary can fit you up with a more presentable uniform.'

'Thank you, sir,' Mark gasped, still overcome.

'You can also pick your own men, regulars or militia. But they'll have to stay on until this war's finished. No more talk of going home.' The last words were spoken with a vehemence that was unnerving.

'I'll do my best, sir,' Mark said, standing to attention in anticipation of being dismissed.

But the General ignored the hint and again turned to the map. 'Easy, Lieutenant. I haven't told you about the rest of my plans.' His finger stabbed at the bottom of the map. 'See the Floridas?' he said, motioning Mark closer. 'East and West Florida; like a pistol pointing at the heart of America. Whoever controls the Floridas can threaten the whole lower Mississippi valley. If the British take them they'll turn them into an American Gibraltar.'

Mark was impressed with the logic of the General's strategic thinking. 'Then it's a good thing the Floridas belong to Spain, sir.'

'Yes, but Spain is an ally of Britain now. She can't be trusted. We need to push a road through from Georgia to Mobile so that we can fortify the town and the seaward approaches to keep the British out.' His finger stabbed the map again. 'For the same reason, we must also occupy Pensacola.'

'But that means fighting the Spanish!' Mark said, aghast at the political implications. 'They have a garrison at Pensacola.'

The General shrugged. 'That's my problem, Lieutenant. Yours is to procure enough heavy guns to fortify Mobile and anywhere else I decide. It will be your task to get the guns there, site them and train the men how to use them. It's the only way to protect New Orleans, our jewel in the Mississippi crown. That's where the British will head for, sooner or later, take it from me. And the way the war's going in Europe it's likely to be sooner than we think.'

Mark was impressed with the General's foresight and the sheer audacity of his plans. 'I think you could well be right, sir.' His voice carried respect for the wily Jackson.

'Damn it. I know I'm right!' the General said testily. 'But most of our army is bogged down on the Canadian fronts. Washington stupidly thought Canada would be a soft target. They forgot that French Canadians are ultra-conservative Roman Catholics who support the Bourbon Restoration and regard Bonaparte as a usurper, same as the British. The British also give them special political and cultural privileges that they know would not be tolerated if they became part of the United States. So if the British come south we'll have to fend for ourselves.'

'No more regulars?'

'I won't be banking on it.' Reading Mark's expression, he added, 'Yes, Lieutenant, I've got a lot of work to do to train and discipline this rabble to stand up to Wellington's veterans. And believe you me, those redcoats will come pouring across the Atlantic as soon as Napoleon falls. But first we have to beat the Creek Indians and most of my blasted army still wants to go home.'

The nadir of General Jackson's desperate struggle to keep his army in the field was reached at the end of December, 1813. He received a letter from Governor Blount of Tennessee advising him to evacuate his fortified camp on the Coosa River and retreat back to Tennessee. This, the General angrily refused to do and he sent a blistering reply to Blount which shamed the Governor into sending Jackson another eight hundred raw militiamen.

With characteristic single-mindedness, Jackson now set about rebuilding his army. He put a stop to whisky coming into the camp and intensified the training and, in order to frustrate the Indian dawn raids, the men were made to get up at 3.30 a.m. His own staff were to rise half an hour earlier. Inefficient officers and those who protested against the new regime were sent home under arrest.

Jackson's harsh discipline reached its peak when an eighteen year old militiaman refused an officer's order and grabbed a gun to resist arrest. The General had no hesitation in court-marshalling him for mutiny and had him shot by firing squad in front of the entire army. This effectively put to rest the myth that, whatever the offence, a militiaman could not suffer the death penalty. It also reinforced army discipline for, although many men now hated Jackson, they feared him even more.

Under the General's iron rule the army, paradoxically, began to attract more volunteers. It was also reinforced by regulars of the 39th Infantry and soon the force was five thousand strong. Earlier, with his smaller army, Jackson had moved in on the Creek stronghold at Horseshoe Bend only to be repulsed three miles short after two fierce engagements that almost ended in disaster. Now, with men to spare, he felt confident to try once more.

In March 1814, the General again marched his men south to the Tallapoosa River and confronted one thousand Creeks defending their natural fortress at Horseshoe Bend. As Mark manoeuvred his cannon into position, he began to realise just how strong the Creek position was. It was a hundred acre peninsular broken by gullies and almost covered by thick brush. It was surrounded by water, save for a three hundred and fifty yard breastwork across its neck. The breastwork was between five and eight feet high with double rows of firing holes. It would be difficult and costly to take by direct assault, he thought, but there seemed to be no other option. He now knew why the General had placed so much emphasis on cannon.

At ten-thirty in the morning, Mark's six-pounders opened fire, concentrating on one section of the breastwork to try and make a breech. But Jackson was becoming impatient. He wanted a decisive victory to bring this stubborn Creek war to an end. At twelve-thirty, he ordered one thousand infantrymen, spearheaded by the 39th, to storm the breastwork. As they charged the smoke-shrouded barrier, Major Montgomery of the Regulars fell back dead, but Ensign Sam Houston, sword in hand, leaped up after him and led the first wave of troops into a murderous melee on the other side. The Creeks refused to surrender and broke up into small bands to stand again and again among the broken terrain. Trapped by the river, they fought on until they were virtually wiped out.

When Mark followed the victorious infantry into the fortress, he was appalled at the carnage. This quickly turned to disgust when he saw soldiers cutting off the noses of dead braves to keep a body count. Others were cutting strips of skin from the bodies to make harness for their horses. It had been a bloody encounter which had lasted until dusk. Jackson had lost forty-nine men and a further one hundred and fifty-seven were wounded. The barbarous body count showed that five hundred and fifty-seven Creek warriors had died, and it was estimated that many more were drowned in the river.

The Creek resistance had now been broken and many chiefs of the hostile Red Stick faction of the tribe had fled to neighbouring Spanish territory. But Jackson was in no mood to relent. He began a ruthless campaign of terror, burning Indian villages, confiscating food supplies and destroying crops. Relentlessly, he pushed through the Creek heartland building roads and forts as he went.

On 18 April, 1814, Red Eagle surrendered to Jackson. He arrived unarmed and was taken to the General.

'General Jackson?'

'Yes.'

'I am Bill Weatherford, Chief Red Eagle. I have come to surrender. Do with me as you please, for I am in your power.'

'You are not in my power,' the General said, surprising those listening. 'I wanted you brought here in chains but you have come of your own accord. You see my camp, my army and you know my object. If you think you can prevail, return and lead your warriors against me.'

Red Eagle sighed. 'I have done you and the white people all the harm I could. If I had an army I would contend bravely to the last. But, I have none and I cannot animate the dead. My people are gone and I can only weep over the misfortune of my nation.'

To the astonishment of his staff, Jackson shook hands with Red Eagle and, after pouring him a cup of brandy, allowed him to go free. The astute General wasn't just being magnanimous in victory. The wily lawyer in him also knew the influence that Red Eagle could exercise in persuading other recalcitrant chiefs to surrender. A drawn out guerrilla war was something he wished to avoid.

By the beginning of August, at a fort named after him, General Jackson faced thirty-five frightened chiefs and imposed a Carthaginian peace on the Creek nation. Showing no mercy, his treaty forced the

Creeks to surrender half their lands, twenty-three million acres in all. Lands that would ultimately form three fifths of the new state of Alabama and add another fifth to the state of Georgia. The fierce and unrelenting General left the chiefs in no doubt as to what would happen if they failed to sign.

The treaty broke the Creeks as an independent nation. It was now only a matter of time before they, and the other civilised tribes, would be forced to give up the rest of their lands and move west of the Mississippi.

Some of Jackson's men, blooded in this Creek war, would go on to greater things and help expand the United States. But to Mark, it was a wanton, brutal waste of human life.

CHAPTER 46

Back in Nashville, Jackson found himself something of a celebrity. He received a hero's welcome, followed by a state banquet and the presentation of a ceremonial sword. A mistrustful administration in Washington reluctantly promoted him to the rank of Major General in the Regular Army and gave him command of the 7th Military District, which covered Tennessee, Louisiana and Mississippi Territory. However, the War Department cautioned him against any new incursions in the South and reinforced this by ordering him to demobilise all but one thousand men.

An angry Jackson, impatient with Washington for dragging its feet, demanded urgent action to secure the new frontier with fortified farms. He wanted the vast new lands, taken from the Creeks, to be offered to able-bodied settlers at two dollars an acre, payable over two years with interest. In this way, the spoils of victory from the Creek war could be fully exploited.

'It's good cotton land,' he'd enthused to Mark one day.

Mark had merely shrugged. 'I'm not a farmer, sir. I wouldn't know where to start.'

The reply seemed to irritate Jackson. 'You buy yourself a section at the Government price of two dollars an acre. Then you clear the land and plant it. If you don't want to farm it, just clear it and sell it on to the plantation owners at a profit. It's as simple as that.'

Mark just smiled, 'I can't see myself as a land speculator, sir.'

'Why not, Lieutenant? Half the officers on my staff are. Why me and John Coffee have been knocking up land deals together for longer than I care to remember.'

Mark had heard many stories of Jackson's wheeler-dealer exploits in land speculation which had earned him enough money to further his legal and political career and help found the new state of Tennessee. 'I don't think I have a head for that sort of business, sir,' he said. Besides, I don't have any capital.'

The General's mild irritation now turned to benign amusement. 'Lack of money never stopped me, nor John Coffee, as I recall. In any case, you can't go wrong buying up the land we've taken from the

457

Creeks. Like I said, it's good cotton land. It'll give you two hundred growing days free from frost and twenty-three inches of rain a year. That's what you need for cotton. If you buy land that gives you access to a good river, and there are plenty of those in the territory, then you can't go wrong. This land will yield one and a half bales of cotton an acre. That's four hundred and eighty thousand pounds of the stuff from a section of six hundred and forty acres. At ten cents a pound, you'll make forty-eight thousand dollars a year from a good cash crop.' He paused, smiling at Mark's astonishment before continuing. 'Take it from me, Lieutenant, you can't go wrong buying land in this part of the territory. Inside ten years, it will become the state of Alabama. Just you wait and see.'

Mark smiled at the General. It was the first time he'd found him in such a benevolent mood. 'I might take you advice, sir. But first, I must return to England as soon as the war is over.'

'Why? You're a traitor to the British. They'll hang you if they catch you.'

'I doubt if the British have access to American Army muster rolls. Anyway, it's a risk I'll have to take.'

'Sounds like mighty important business you have back home to warrant the risk, Lieutenant.' Jackson's earlier curiosity about the events which had led to Mark's impressment had now returned. He sensed that this might be the time to pursue the matter. 'Would it have anything to do with the man who betrayed you?' he probed gently.

'Yes, sir. It has everything to do with that man.' There was bitterness and venom in Mark's voice.

'Like to talk about it?' The General said quietly.

Mark remained silent.

'It sometimes helps just to talk to someone about it,' the General went on, coaxingly. He looked at Mark and smiled before adding, 'Or you can forget I'm a General and tell me to mind my own business and go to hell.'

The kind twinkle in the General's eyes suddenly broke down Mark's barriers. He warmed to the man and felt a compelling need to unburden himself and talk about his problems. As the story poured forth, some of his bottled up anguish was released, but the hatred for Roland remained deep inside his heart.

458

The General listened, prompting occasionally, but saying little that might stop the flow. He could see that Mark had suffered his torment for too long and needed to lighten the burden.

When Mark finally stopped talking, he was suddenly overcome with embarrassment. He began to apologise, but the General cut him short. 'No need for that, Mr Standish. You've been badly used.' He shook his head in angry disbelief before going on. 'I can't think of a more dastardly betrayal. Only a so called British gentleman could humiliate a man in that way.' There was an icy hatred in the General's voice.

'You obviously don't like the British, sir,' Mark said. It was more a question than a statement.

'Indeed I don't. In fact I detest the British ruling class, as I'm sure you do. We both have good reason.'

'Surely being at war with a nation's rulers doesn't necessarily require you to hate its people?' Mark reasoned.

'No, but my father was Irish.'

Seeing the look of sympathy and understanding on Mark's face, Jackson smiled. 'Not Catholic Irish,' he corrected. 'Ulster Scots. A lot of Ulster Presbyterians came to America before the Revolution. The Cumberland Valley was full of them. Some, including my father, settled in the Waxhaws in South Carolina. After years of exploitation by absentee landlords they came to America to seek a new and better life. So you see, Lieutenant, the Ulster Scots have as much reason to hate the British as the Irish Catholics.'

'Yes, but I think it's wrong for one generation to hand down their prejudices and hatreds to the next. A civilised society must look to the future, not the past.' There were times, Mark thought, when the violent hatreds of this bellicose General bordered on madness.

For a moment, Jackson looked angrily at Mark, as if about to reprimand him. Then his mood changed. 'My hatred of the British wasn't just handed down, Lieutenant,' he said quietly. 'My father died just before I was born, so I never knew him. My mother raised me and she hated the Anglican bigots who persecuted her church. She taught me to stand up for myself and fight like a man. When I was twelve, I enlisted in the militia and fought the British in the Revolutionary War. One of my brothers was killed in that war and I was captured by

British Dragoons and taken to a British jail at Camden, South Carolina.'

The General paused for a moment and his face began to cloud over with sadness. It was as if painful memories of the past, that couldn't be laid to rest, were reluctantly being recalled to mind. Mark remained silent, fearing that anything he said might destroy the magic of the moment. For he suddenly realised that this enigmatic, volatile yet lovable man was close to baring his soul.

When the General spoke again, his voice was filled with sadness. 'My mother also died in that war. She was struck down with jail fever while nursing American soldiers who were imprisoned on a British hulk in Charleston harbour.' His voice suddenly rose. 'Do you see these,' he said angrily, pointing to the scars on his head and on his fingers. 'They were caused by a sabre blow from a British officer while I was a prisoner of war. And do you know why he struck me, Lieutenant? Because I refused to clean his boots.' He glowered at Mark until his anger subsided. 'So you see,' he went on, 'my hatred of the British is not just inherited. I've suffered from their arrogance and savagery, just as you have.'

There was a long silence as the General regained his composure. Finally, a thin smile crossed his face and his eyes fixed on Mark. 'I take it you'll call this Forster fellow out when you return to England?'

'What! Challenge him to a duel,' Mark's voice and expression registered complete astonishment.

'Of course. It's a matter of honour, surely.'

'Roland Forster knows me only as a common pitman, not a gentleman. He won't accept a challenge from the likes of me. '

'Then you must either force him to fight you or kill him,' the General said, a note of exasperation creeping in.

'I intend to, but it won't be easy.'

'Why?'

'Because he's a coward and his father is a magistrate.'

'What difference does that make?' The General's exasperation was turning to annoyance.

'He'll hide behind his father's authority,' Mark said scathingly. 'If he feels threatened, he'll find a way of laying charges and have me imprisoned.' He tried to explain the methods by which the English

460

authorities maintained their control over the labouring classes, but soon gave up. He realised that it all sounded nonsense to an autocrat like Jackson, brought up in the ways of the frontier and who, despite his authoritarian ways in military matters, still believed in the rights and freedom of the ordinary American citizen.

The bemused General sighed. 'But you will confront him?'

'Yes, but in my own way.' Mark said firmly. There were some things he couldn't confide in the General. He knew that he had to question Rowland before he could contemplate killing him. There were memories which still haunted him and only Roland could provide the answers which might help him lay the ghosts that still tormented him.

The General's voice cut through Mark's thoughts. 'You'll come back to America, I trust? After you've settled your business? There can't be much future in England for someone like you.'

Mark smiled. 'Yes, sir. I'll be back.'

In the months that followed the Battle of Horseshoe Bend, Mark had been heavily engaged in a procurement programme to obtain guns, powder and ammunition for General Jackson's army. In the course of this assignment, he'd travelled thousands of miles through Mississippi Territory and the new state of Louisiana. His procurement search unearthed an astonishing range of old guns, some of which were still serviceable and others which could be made so. On Jackson's instructions, he'd also surveyed a number of old forts that were situated in strategic positions and which might be reopened and garrisoned.

Mark completed his report at the beginning of August and within hours of submitting it, was summoned to General Jackson's quarters. He found the General in a pensive mood, seated behind a large map strewn table. He gestured impatiently to a vacant chair and Mark placed his worn leather shako on the table alongside the General's huge bicorne with its solid gold eagle set in the cockade. As he sat down, Mark noticed that the General was wearing a new tailored uniform with gold buttons and intricate herringbone embroidery on the coat. The gold epaulettes displayed the insignia of a Major General, the highest rank in the American army. Mark felt distinctly shabby in his plain blue coat, with only a silver epaulette worn on the left shoulder to indicate his rank of Lieutenant.

The General motioned to Mark's report lying on the table in front of him. 'Excellent assessment of the situation, Lieutenant, but gloomy reading. We're still short of guns, especially heavy cannon.'

'I agree, sir. We'll just have to make sure we're better gunners.'

A bleak smile flickered in the General's eyes. 'And how do you propose we achieve that?'

'By being more professional. Better training and daily gun exercises,' Mark answered confidently.

'I admire your optimism, Lieutenant, but I'm not sure we'll have the time. Now that Napoleon has abdicated, Wellington's disciplined veterans will be pouring across the Atlantic. They've been hardened and corrupted by twenty years of fighting the French. Most of my army is made up of raw militiamen.'

'They proved themselves against the Creeks, sir,' Mark countered.

'Fighting Indians is one thing,' the General snapped. 'Doing battle with the British redcoats is another. You of all people should know that.'

Mark realised that glib assurances were wasted on the General and accepted the implied reprimand in silence. He could see that Jackson was frustrated and this was fuelling his ill-temper. He waited until the General had calmed down before offering another suggestion. 'Laffite seems willing to help. He's got ships and guns at Barataria Bay and his men know how to handle cannon.'

'He's a pirate, according to Governor Claiborne. I won't associate with bandits.'

'The Creoles like him,' Mark said, adding, 'he only attacks Spanish ships.'

'That doesn't legitimise his actions,' Jackson snorted. 'He's still a pirate.'

'He's refused to help the British,' Mark persisted.

'Because he's afraid the Royal Navy might hang him. Let it rest, Lieutenant, the answer's no.'

'Then we'll just have to make the best use of what we've got, sir,' Mark said, accepting defeat.

'Exactly so. And this is how we'll do it.' The General spread out a large map across the table and pointed to the Gulf of Mexico. 'We must occupy Mobile and strengthen its defences. Your report mentions an abandoned fort that might be garrisoned?'

'Yes, sir, Fort Bower. It's on a long east-west spit of land south of the town.' Mark indicated the spot on the map. 'As you can see, sir, the spit almost closes the mouth of Mobile Bay.'

Jackson studied the map closely. 'So it does, Lieutenant. If we armed the fort with cannon, it would make the bay almost impregnable.' He gave a broad smile. 'Make life difficult for the Royal Navy, eh?'

'It would indeed, sir.'

'How many guns would it take?'

'At least twenty, probably more.'

'Twenty is all we can spare. I'll appoint Major Lawrence to command the garrison. We can rely on him to get things done.'

'Do you really think the British will attack Mobile, sir?' Mark asked, his voice sounding strangely hesitant. He was finding it increasingly difficult to talk about his countrymen in this detached way.

'Yes, I do, Lieutenant? It would certainly appeal to someone like Rear Admiral Cockburn. He's been raiding at will up and down the Chesapeake, commandeering provisions and cattle to feed his men.' The General had an excellent intelligence network which kept him well informed of events far removed from his own sphere of operation in the South.

'He's plundered so much tobacco,' Jackson continued, 'that he had to keep it in a special store at his base on Tangier Island. He even uses captured American schooners to ship it off to Halifax.'

Mark thought he detected a reluctant note of admiration in the General's voice. 'The Royal Navy always has an eye for prize money,' he said.

'Exactly,' Jackson said. 'And if a man like Admiral Cockburn can accomplish what he has with only five hundred marines, imagine what he might do with five thousand veteran troops. There's richer pickings further south.'

'You mean New Orleans?' Mark's voice echoed his surprise.

'Why not, Lieutenant. There's a fortune in cotton, tobacco and sugar lying there. Enough prize money to attract even the most cautious Commander-in-Chief. And New Orleans could be the strategic Achilles heel of this whole damned war.'

'Surely the British need to reinforce Canada first. They haven't got five thousand troops to spare for an attack further south.'

'Not yet, but it's only a matter of time before they do. My information is that Admiral Cochrane now has a large fleet of warships and troop transports at Bermuda. That means, with Napoleon safe on Elba, the British are already redeploying their troops from Europe to America. They won't all be bound for Canada.'

Mark could now appreciate the logic that lay behind the General's thinking. 'So that's why you want to fortify Mobile?'

'Yes, Lieutenant. If we allow the British to take it, they could strike inland to the Mississippi here at Walnut Hills.' Jackson's finger stabbed at a point on the map two hundred miles upstream from New Orleans. 'A small army could forage and live off the land, cutting off our own supply lines. They would attract dissident Indians and it would only be a matter of time before they linked up with the Spanish Floridas in the south and took New Orleans. If that happened, it would drastically weaken our bargaining position at the peace talks in Ghent.'

Mark looked at the map. 'If New Orleans is the objective, what's to stop the British from sailing straight up the Mississippi to attack the town?'

'Because New Orleans lies over one hundred miles upstream from the delta. Our batteries at English Turn are strong enough to make even the Royal Navy think twice about that option. Our only weak spot,' he went on, pointing to the map, is Pensacola, right next door to Mobile.'

'But that belongs to Spain, sir. They're not at war with America.'

'No, but they're allies of Britain. I'll take Pensacola rather than let the British use it as a base.'

'Isn't that risky, sir? Diplomatically, I mean. They also have a garrison there,' Mark wondered if the General had thought out the political implications of such a move.

Jackson smiled, as if reading Mark's mind. 'The Spanish will huff and puff with indignation, Lieutenant, but the truth of the matter is that

Spain is too weak to hold on to Florida and too proud to admit it. There'll have to be a reckoning one day.' The General folded up the map and sat back in his chair. 'In the meantime, we march south. There's much to be done.'

In the months that followed, Jackson seldom rested, driving himself and his staff with a ruthless determination. Few dared to object or complain, for the General's iron will and obsessive refusal to be denied was fast becoming legendary. He was now known to his men as "Old Hickory" and the Indians called him "Sharp Knife" and "Painted Arrow." Before the end of August he had occupied Mobile and garrisoned Fort Bower. His intuition proved right and when the British sent in four men-of-war to try and take the town, they were repulsed with the loss of one of their ships.

When the shock news came that a small British force had occupied Washington, burning the Capital and other Government buildings as well as the President's House, Jackson was incensed. His rage increased as further stories of American incompetence and cowardice began to filter south. 'Winder had six thousand men at Bladensburg, yet he allowed himself to be routed by a single brigade of Ross's redcoats,' he stormed at his staff officers, most of whom were still stunned by the news.

'The British had four thousand seasoned troops, sir,' one staff officer timidly interceded.

'But less than two thousand were actually used,' the General roared. 'When our men saw them advancing, they simply turned and ran. There was no battle,' he spat the words contemptuously. 'The wits are already calling it the Bladensburg Races. Only Commodore Barney's flotilla men stood and fought.'

'It seems they're blaming General Armstrong for the defeat,' a senior staff officer ventured. 'There's rumours that he's about to resign. '

'And so he should,' Jackson snapped. 'As Secretary of War he must accept some responsibility for the debacle.' He gave vent to a long, angry sigh. 'I just cannot understand why nearly one and a half million white Americans, who live within fighting distance of

Washington, could allow four thousand British troops to spend so long in their midst without any serious hindrance.'

'Our men were mostly raw militia, sir,' an aide reminded.

'Nonsense!' the General flared. 'That's defeatist talk. We'll be facing British regulars soon in the South and most of my army is made up of volunteers and militiamen.' He paused, glaring at this staff. 'Well, gentlemen, I'm going to prove that an American soldier is as good a fighting man as any in the world.'

When confirmation came a few days later, that General Armstrong had resigned and President Madison had appointed James Monroe as acting Secretary for War, in addition to his role as Secretary of State, Jackson's mind was made up. He'd also received disturbing intelligence that a small British force had landed at the main Spanish base at Pensacola and Admiral Cochrane was gathering his invasion fleet for a new assault in the South. It was time to act.

Taking advantage of the government's confusion following the fall of Washington, Jackson marched into West Florida with a force of almost four thousand men. At sunrise on November 7 his army stormed Pensacola and by the afternoon the town and the forts of St Rose and St Michael had capitulated. The small British garrison withdrew to ships anchored off shore after blowing up Fort Barrancas, the town's last remaining bastion. The fact that Spain and America were not at war did not inhibit a man like Jackson. He was determined to deny the British any base from which an attack on New Orleans might be launched.

By December, Jackson was in New Orleans working with furious determination, despite recurring bouts of fever and dysentery, to organise the city's defences. The major problem was the bewildering maze of approaches to the city other than the direct ascent of the Mississippi, which he'd already discounted. West of the river the Bayou Larfourche snaked inland from the coast, as did many of the waterways extending north from Barataria Bay. To the east, the River Aux Chenes penetrated deeply from the Gulf. Further east lay Lake Borgne, linking the Gulf with Lake Pontchartrain, with many meandering creeks that approached almost to the outskirts of the city.

To try and solve these problems Jackson sent out teams of axe men with orders to block the watercourses with fallen trees. Deciding that Lake Borgne was too shallow for the British fleet and would involve them in a row of over sixty miles to land an army near New Orleans, he left the lake guarded by only five small gunboats. It was a decision he would later come to regret.

Whilst strengthening the city's defences the General also worked feverishly to expand his army. He sent for Coffee to join him from Baton Rouge with his eight hundred sharpshooters. A few hours after Coffee's arrival a flotilla of riverboats, with three thousand Tennessee militiamen on board, made a welcome appearance. They had put their time to good use on the long river journey from Nashville by casting fifty thousand lead cartridges. Jackson now had something in excess of five thousand men to defend New Orleans, with a further two thousand Kentucky volunteers still to arrive. Yet his restless energy would not allow him just to sit back and wait. He knew that a large British invasion fleet was now lying at Jamaica and all the intelligence reports pointed to an imminent attack on New Orleans. But exactly from where, and when?

Mark could not but admire the General's intractable spirit and his dogged refusal to let any obstacle deter him from his ultimate objective. But the strange bond between them, forged on a mutual and enigmatic curiosity about each other, continued. Yet, on the surface, the two men seemed to have little in common. Although Mark was only a junior staff officer, the General sometimes discussed his innermost thoughts with him, often to the annoyance of his more senior aides. Mark wondered if it was because he was British, a race the General purported to hate and with good reason. He also wondered why Jackson took such an unusual interest in his plans to confront Roland when he returned to England. It was almost as if he envied Mark his right to seek retribution for his appalling suffering at the hands of the Forsters.

As the days wore on the frustrations of waiting began to surface. Whispers that some of the leading Creole families were sceptical of Jackson's chances of success and preferred a secret deal with the British, soured relations between the General and the city he was determined to defend. This, together with his illness and the constant

467

pain from his wounds, made the General even more tetchy than usual. It was something of a relief, therefore, when Mark received orders to travel to Barataria Bay to meet with the Laffite brothers and ascertain the strength of their pirate force.

'We need more guns and men that can use them,' the General growled. 'If I have to ally myself with banditti,' he went on acidly, 'I want to be sure that it will be worthwhile. I need to know how disciplined they are. Above all, I need to know how reliable they are.'

It seemed clear to Mark, as he rode south, that accepting help from a group of pirates was repugnant to the General. However, Jackson's determination to deny the British the rich prize of New Orleans was so strong that he was prepared to swallow his distaste if it would help him save the city. As he rode on in silence, Mark's fingers idly touched the silver epaulette which he was now wearing on his right shoulder to indicate his new rank of Captain. His surprise promotion, he reflected, was probably Jackson's idea, with the aim of giving him added status and authority for his dealings with Jean Laffite, the leader of the Barataria pirates.

A sudden chuckle from Jack, riding alongside, interrupted Mark's thoughts. 'You've been awfully quiet since your promotion, sir. It must be a heavy responsibility being a Captain.' Jack spoke the words "Sir" and "Captain" with theatrical emphasis.

Mark turned and smiled at his friend. 'You're not doing so bad yourself, Sergeant, thanks to me,' he responded, emphasising the word Sergeant. 'You're dressed up like one of those fancy Creole Volunteers,' he added, pointing to Jack's spanking new uniform.

'Jealous are you, sir?' Jack said with studied disrespect.

'Laffite will think you're in command,' Mark said, grinning. 'Hope you can handle it.'

Jack stared critically at Mark's uniform which, though still smart, had clearly seen better days. His own was that of an artillery Sergeant, with gleaming brass buttons and twin fringed, yellow-worsted, epaulettes on his tight fitting blue jacket. His shako was plumed and tasselled and he wore a Sergeant's scarlet worsted sash around his waist. He carried a new brass hilted sword. Mark, in contrast, looked distinctly dowdy. He wasn't even wearing the crimson silk sash of an officer. Jack decided he'd better tone down his appearance before they

468

reached Barataria Bay. After all, he didn't want to embarrass his commanding officer who'd need all the help he could get. 'You may not look quite like an officer, but at least you act and talk like one,' he concluded gracefully.

They rode is silence for a while before Jack spoke again. 'What I can't understand is why the British haven't asked Laffite to join them.'

'They have,' Mark answered.

'Then why doesn't he?'

'Because he doesn't trust them.'

'Why not?'

'Because if the British gain control of Louisiana, he knows that the Royal Navy will put a stop to his piracy and smuggling. '

A sly grin spread across Jack's face. 'And the Americans will turn a blind eye, eh?'

'They have up to now,' Mark said. 'I think Laffite feels more comfortable with the Americans than the British, and the Creoles like him.'

'Should make your job easier then.' There was a note of relief in Jack's voice.

Mark smiled. 'We shall see, my friend. We shall see.'

CHAPTER 47

When Mark returned to New Orleans he found the city in a ferment of activity. The shock news that the British had landed and against all the odds were now within eight miles of the city had galvanised the General into action.

The British had attacked through Lake Borgne, quickly capturing the five gunboats that Jackson had left to guard it. This not only deprived the General of his "eyes", but also gave Admiral Cochrane five desperately needed shallow-draught vessels to add to his meagre collection of flatboats. The British were able to ferry their troops through the shallow waters of the lake and set up an advance base on Pea Island. When a Spanish fisherman showed them the Bayou Vienvenu, the only waterway leading to New Orleans that hadn't been blocked by Jackson's axe men, Admiral Cochrane knew his luck was in. By ten-thirty on the morning of December 23rd, a force of one thousand six hundred men under Mayor General Keane were in a field of cane stubble by the road leading to New Orleans, having captured the American pickets guarding the bayou and seized the Villere plantation.

Jackson was furious when he received the news. 'Why wasn't the Bayou blocked like I ordered?' he seethed as the alarm was sounded. 'By the eternal, they won't sleep on our soil,' he vowed to a hastily called staff meeting as he outlined his plans. 'Gentlemen the enemy are below and within eight miles of the city. We must attack them tonight.'

Mark was sent to oversee the arming and preparation of two large schooners, the *Caroline* and the *Louisiana*, which were to be used against the British. He picked the best of Laffite's artillerymen to man the cannons and reported back to Jackson as soon as the *Caroline* was ready.

The battle plan was simple. 'I want the *Caroline* to slip downstream as soon as it's dark,' the General ordered. 'When she's in position she'll rake the British left flank. As soon as she opens fire our troops will attack their right flank.'

By five o'clock that evening all Jackson's available troops were on the march. It was a heterogeneous army of two thousand one hundred men made up of Colonel Hinds' Mississippi dragoons plus regulars of the 7th Infantry in their tight blue jackets and Brigadier-General Coffee's tough Tennessee volunteers. It also included a battalion of New Orleans militiamen in their peacock finery; a company of freed black slaves; and a handful of painted Choctaw Indians.

'May I join the *Caroline*, sir?' Mark requested.

The General shook his head. 'No, Captain Standish, I wish you to remain here with me.'

'But, sir!' Mark protested. 'The *Caroline* needs a naval gunner, and that's my speciality.'

The General was unmoved. 'You said yourself that Laffite's men were good cannoneers. Well, now they've got a chance to prove it.'

'They will, sir, but they'll be even more effective if I stay in command,' Mark persisted.

'The answer's still no, Captain.'

'But why?' Mark's tone echoed his frustration and disappointment.

Jackson sighed. 'Do you recall the events that took place a year ago, when the troops threatened to mutiny, and you came to my aid?'

Mark nodded. 'You mean the incident with the cannon?'

Jackson looked at Mark and his expression softened. 'Yes. You stood there, manning a loaded cannon pointed at my men, waiting for my order to fire.' He paused, watching Mark. 'I would have given that order. You know that now, don't you?'

'Yes. I think you would.'

'And you, my friend, would have hesitated; waited until we'd lost that vital moment. Then it would have been too late.' A smile, kind and understanding, hovered briefly in the General's eyes. 'I don't want to put you in that position again; for your sake, for my sake and for the sake of America.'

Mark was aghast. 'You think I'm a coward?' he flared.

The General placed his hand gently on Mark's shoulder. 'No, you're not a coward. We both know that. But you'd be giving the orders to fire on your own countrymen.'

471

'And you think I couldn't?' Mark was crestfallen, for he knew the General was probably right. He'd never stopped to think the matter through.

'If you did,' Jackson said gently, 'you'd be riven with guilt for the rest of your days. You're a man of honour; an idealist with a strong humanitarian streak. Those are qualities that don't sit well with being a soldier.'

'You think I'm not cut out to be a soldier?'

'I think you may have volunteered for the wrong reasons. But, you're a good staff officer and I don't want to lose you. I'll settle for that.'

Mark gave a wan smile. 'I'm glad I still have something to offer, sir.'

'You have indeed, Captain, and you can start by conveying my orders to the *Caroline*. But make sure that she sails without you.'

A fond smile lingered on the General's face as he watched Mark ride off towards the city docks. The man was almost young enough to be the son he'd so long yearned for, he reflected. Something that twenty-three years of marriage to his beloved Rachel had not blessed him with.

The attack on the British that night proved indecisive. The *Caroline*, after drifting quietly down the mist-cloaked river, opened fire on the unsuspecting British at 7.30 that evening. Soon after, the American troops attacked the other flank, but after several hours of confused fighting in the dark, both sides disengaged, as if my mutual consent.

Jackson withdrew his troops closer to the city, where he carefully selected a new defensive position. The British advance had been blunted but they remained, camped among the fields of cane stubble by the Villere plantation, to await reinforcements.

General Jackson had learned well from his experience at the Battle of Horseshoe Bend, where the powerful breastwork thrown up by the Creek Indians had made a lasting impression on him. He put this knowledge to good use in selecting the right position to defend New Orleans. The defensive line he chose was the Rodriguez canal, a ten foot wide dry ditch which cut at a right angle across the narrow plain that ran all the way to the city. The plain was bordered on the south side by the Mississippi, whilst its north side was protected by an impenetrable cypress swamp.

The following day, Mark was instructed to accompany the General along the canal and advise on the positioning of artillery. On his arrival, he saw that the whole length of the canal, a distance of over a mile, was a hive of activity. Hundreds of men, working in relays, were digging out the bed of the canal which was only four feet deep. As the canal was deepened, the mud taken out was used to build a rampart on one side to form a strong defensive line against any frontal attack.

Mark found General Jackson, sleepless and drawn, moving restlessly up and down the line giving directions and encouragement. 'Well, what do you think, Captain?'

'It's an excellent defensive line, sir,' Mark said admiringly. 'It could be made almost impregnable to a frontal attack-'

'It will be when the ramparts are high enough and strong enough. I've asked the plantation owners to let me have all the field hands they can spare and I've sent out men to commandeer every pick and shovel in the area. We'll work round the clock until it's completed.'

'If the British have any sense they won't let you finish it sir,' Mark said. He pointed across the plain to the Villere plantation. 'They're only two miles away and unless my glass is lying, they must have over four thousand troops camped in the stubble fields over there.'

'They're too disorganised and we'll make sure they stay that way,' the General said confidently. 'Besides, they haven't any heavy guns.'

It was just as well, Mark thought. The *Caroline* and the *Louisiana* would make easy targets out there on the river and would be highly vulnerable to cannon fire. It would only be a matter of time before the British brought up heavy guns; the Royal Navy would see to that he felt sure.

'Well, Captain, you've seen the line. What do you recommend?' The General's impatient voice interrupted Mark's deliberations.

'Twelve or thirteen guns should be enough, sir,' Mark said, quickly collecting his thoughts.

The General looked surprised. 'We'll need more than that, surely?'

'No, sir. The defensive line is perfect. I must compliment you on that.' Mark spoke without sounding ingratiating. 'As you can see, sir, the plain narrows to only nine hundred yards in front of the canal. That's where the British will be massed when they come within range. Allowing for the spread of grapeshot and canister, thirteen guns will give each cannon a seventy yard field of fire. That's more than adequate, sir, especially as we'll be using canister at short range.

The General still looked a little dubious. 'Well, if you're sure, Captain, I'll leave you to position the guns and instruct the battery commanders.'

'Do you want me to take charge of the artillery, sir?' Mark asked tentatively.

'No, Captain.' The General spoke firmly, 'You know my views on that,' he added gently. 'Report back to me when the guns are in place. I have other work for you.' With that he moved on down the line, issuing orders to his staff and shouting encouragement to the men as he went, his tall, thin frame exuding a restless, infectious energy.

As Mark stared at the retreating figure of the General he finally realised that Jackson was right. He'd been deluding himself thinking he could fight his own countrymen, but some perverse pride and a confused loyalty had prevented him from admitting it. He shuddered at the thought of what might come if the British were foolish enough to attempt a frontal attack on such a strong defensive position. At eight hundred yards, each cannon would fire round shot, inflicting the first casualties. From two hundred and fifty yards, it would be grape shot; a canvas bag filled with lethal iron balls. Then, from one hundred yards, it would be canister; tin cylinders packed with half pound leaden shot that would cut a murderous swath through the advancing columns of troops. At the same time, there would be a continuous and devastating fire from thousands of rifles and muskets. And the American backwoodsmen were some of the finest marksmen in the world.

Mark tried to shrug off his foreboding by throwing himself into a frenzy of work, but his depression remained. He was tired of war and the suffering it caused. Above all, he was sick of the sheer futility of it all; that two nations with a common ancestry and speaking the same language should engage in such conflict was completely beyond him.

*****

474

On Christmas Day, Major General Sir Edward Pakenham, brother-in-law of the Duke of Wellington, arrived at the Villere plantation to take command of the British troops. He immediately brought up more guns and two days later, his gunners had their first success. The *Caroline*, which been a thorn in the British flank since their arrival, was blown up in spectacular fashion and the *Louisiana* almost suffered the same fate. Jackson watched anxiously through his telescope as the *Louisiana*'s crew took to their boats and towed the ship out of range.

The loss of the *Caroline* was a blow to Jackson, for his tactics had been to harry the British from the river and send in raiding parties at night to keep them unsettled and awake. He wanted a tired and dispirited enemy. But he still had the *Louisiana* and she proved her worth the next day when the British advanced along the plain towards the mud ramparts behind the Rodriguez canal. Her raking fire helped to break up the advancing columns of redcoats. Seeing his men hopelessly pinned down, Pakenham was forced to call off the attack.

It was now clear to the British commander that without heavy guns, he would never breech the American lines. He decided to wait until the Royal Navy could bring up some of their heavy cannon and they duly obliged. After three days of superhuman effort, dragging the guns through the swamp, they delivered ten 18-pounders and four 24-pound carronades to a delighted Pakenham. On New Year's Day, 1815, he was ready to try again. He now had twenty-four guns in place, in hastily prepared positions dug overnight, eight hundred yards from the American line. As the early morning fog suddenly lifted, they opened fire on Jackson's unsuspecting men as they were preparing for a New Year's Day review.

Jackson rushed from his new headquarters at the nearby Macarte plantation and stood behind the mud rampart watching the British through his telescope. 'They must have brought up their guns during the night,' he growled, handing the telescope to Mark.

As he focused the glass, Mark saw that the British batteries were poorly protected. Earth filled sugar casks had been used to build up the parapets. 'They've been too hasty, sir,' he murmured. 'Sugar casks are the last thing I would have used to protect the guns.'

'Why, Captain?'

'Because they'll splinter, sir. They won't stand up to our cannon and as every navy man knows, wood splinters are more lethal than round-shot. '

Mark's assessment proved to be right. The British guns made little impression on the strong, mud ramparts of the American positions, though some damage was done to the Macarte house. In contrast, Jackson's heavy guns soon found their range and began to pulverize the poorly protected British batteries. By three in the afternoon Pakenham's guns were silenced. The uneasy lull that followed was soon broken when a band struck up Yankee Doodle and a ripple of cheers rang out along the American line.

Mark turned to the General. 'I don't think they'll make another frontal attack, sir.'

'Why do you think that, Captain?'

'Because it would be suicidal. Our defences are almost impregnable; they'd lose too many men.'

'I'd be inclined to agree with you if we were facing a clever, experienced commander like Wellington,' Jackson said. 'But we're not,' he added. 'We're facing the Duke's brother-in-law and that, Captain, is the critical difference.'

'Because he's a poor General?'

'He's certainly no military genius. He's probably a General because of money and connections. I suspect he's got more courage than common sense.'

'But he must have some good officers to advise him. Any staff officer worth his salt will tell him that it's sheer folly to attack such a strongly held position without first enfilading the rear.'

'So you think they'll try to outflank us, eh Captain?'

'Yes sir. By crossing the river and advancing along the other bank.'

'They'll need a lot of boats for that and I don't see any.' The General sounded sceptical.

'If the Royal Navy can drag 18-pounder guns weighing over two tons through miles of cypress swamp they can just as easily bring up boats.'

'You have a touching faith in the Royal Navy, Captain.' The words were spoken kindly and not meant to censure.

476

'I think it would be wise to reinforce the other bank, sir, just in case,' Mark urged. 'The *Louisiana* is now too vulnerable to gunfire to be any use on the river. I suggest we strip out her guns and use them to set up batteries on the other bank.'

The General thought for a moment and then nodded. 'But not all her guns, Captain. I'm going to set up a second defensive position behind the canal on this side. We'll need some extra guns for that.'

'It would be better to strengthen the other bank, sir,' Mark persisted. 'We'll need all the guns and men we can muster over there, if we are to avoid being outflanked.'

'I can't spare any men until the Kentucky Volunteers arrive. We'll just have to make do until then.'

Mark pointed to the mud ramparts lining the Rodriguez Canal. 'Our defensive line is barely a mile wide, sir. That will only allow for about fifteen hundred men to load and fire in comfort; yet we've more than three times that number. They'll be standing three deep waiting to fire.'

'That's exactly the way I've planned it,' the General said, smiling in anticipation. 'With each line firing in turn, we can keep up a continuous fire.'

'Always assuming the British will be foolish enough to make a frontal assault, sir,' Mark cautioned. 'We may regret it if they decide to attack along the other bank.'

'They won't, Captain. They'll come this way.' Jackson spoke with confidence. 'I think General Pakenham is impatient to become Governor of Louisiana. He's keen to loot New Orleans under the legal guise of claiming prize money. He's anxious to reap the spoils of war and we've held him up too long already.'

'I hope you're right, sir,' Mark said resignedly.

'I know I am, Captain. Pakenham's greed and ambition will prove greater than his patience or common sense, you'll see.'

Work went on to strengthen the canal embankment and two more defensive lines were started nearer to New Orleans. As the days passed, Mark felt certain that the British would not attempt a frontal attack on such a strongly held position. He watched the preparations

477

in the British camp with interest and noted the steady build-up of supplies and reinforcements. Something was bound to happen soon, but precisely what and where he wasn't sure.

On the third of January, the long awaited Kentucky militia arrived adding another two thousand three hundred men to Jackson's forces. When informed that some of them were without guns, Old Hickory was astounded. 'I've never seen a Kentuckian without a gun, a pack of cards and a bottle of whisky in my life,' he snorted, shaking his head in disbelief.

Three days later, Mark watched from the mud ramparts as the General trained his telescope on the British camp. 'What do you make of that, Captain?' Jackson murmured, handing the glass to Mark.

Mark focussed carefully on the British positions, scanning the area surrounding their camp. 'Looks as if they're making ladders, sir. They're also gathering heaps of cane or something.' He sounded a little puzzled.

'They're making scaling ladders and using the cane stalks to make fascines to cross the canal. I was right, Captain,' Jackson went on triumphantly. 'Their main assault will be on our position here.'

Mark continued to scan the British positions. 'They've also brought up boats, sir, and it looks as if they're cutting into the levee so that they can launch them into the river.' He lowered the telescope and turned to the General. 'I think they intend to attack along the other bank of the river, sir.'

'It will only be a diversion; an attempt to draw off some of our troops. The main attack will be on this side.'

'If they capture our guns on the other bank, they can turn them on our own line,' Mark said. 'Our defences are pretty thin over there, sir.'

The General took another long look at the British camp, and then shook his head. 'No, Captain, the main attack will be here. They wouldn't have gone to the trouble of making so many scaling ladders and fascines otherwise.'

At dawn the following day, a faint breeze stirred the mist that had settled over the white frosted stubble fields in front of the American lines. As the first streaks of daylight appeared in the sky, the mist began to clear, slowly at first, as if reluctant to usher in the day. Suddenly, a rocket exploded high in the air sending out a shower of silver fragments. It was the signal to start the attack.

From out of the mist-shrouded fields the massed ranks of the British troops could now be seen tramping steadfastly towards the grim ramparts which lined the Rodriguez Canal. White cross-belts gleamed against scarlet tunics and glistening bayonets bristled among the tightly packed columns of marching men.

General Jackson had been summoned from his headquarters at the nearby Macarte plantation house and was already on the ramparts, encouraging his men, when Mark joined him. The clearing mist now exposed the advancing British troops and at five hundred yards a long brass 12-pounder on the left of the line opened fire. This was immediately followed by an explosive roar as the rest of the American artillery opened up.

Along the line, Jackson's diverse army was awake and ready. The 7th Infantry and New Orleans militia were placed nearest to the river, whilst regulars of the 44th Infantry, Carroll's Tennesseans and General Adam's Kentuckians held the centre. General John Coffee's hard bitten sharpshooters were behind the ramparts nearest to the swamp and a mixed bag of troops, sailors from the *Caroline* and Laffite's buccaneers manned the guns. The whole length of the breastwork was jammed with men; a line of riflemen and musketeers standing ready on the firing step with two or three lines of men waiting to take their place.

Mark's eyes began to smart as the acrid smoke from the guns drifted across the line. They were now firing grape and canister, cutting swaths through the advancing British troops. He heard General Jackson's voice through the smoke. 'Aim at their cross-belts.'

On command, the riflemen of Kentucky and Tennessee, mostly skilled backwoodsmen, aimed and fired a crashing volley before stepping down to reload.

The second rank immediately leaped up onto the firing step, awaiting the command.

'Aim! Fire!'

Then the third line was up and aiming. 'Fire!'

479

The effects were staggering. Mark watched with dismay as the Redcoated British troops began to fall by the hundreds, cut down by the murderous, belching cannon fire and the continuous and accurate volleys of rifle fire. It was sheer slaughter and Mark felt his loyalties being ripped apart as he watched his countrymen being shot down in their hundreds before his eyes. The men coming up from behind had to step over the bodies of their fallen comrades. The columns halted and reformed, then faltered again. Finally, they wavered and broke ranks, streaming back to the rear.

Hardened veterans of the Peninsular campaign, they had never experienced such concentrated and lethal firepower before. Three British generals, including their Commander-in-Chief, Sir Edward Pakenham, had been cut down on the field of battle and now, leaderless, they were in full retreat. It was still only eight-thirty in the morning.

Pakenham's plan of attack had been too ambitious and far too complicated. It required intricate movements of large groups of men and equipment at night in order to deny Jackson's riflemen visible targets. Colonel Thornton and 1,400 men were to cross the river and capture the American batteries and turn their fire on Jackson's own defences along the Rodriguez Canal. Two columns of troops were to advance across the fields in front of the American lines, using the pre-dawn darkness as cover: one thousand two hundred men under Major General Keene along the river, and two thousand one hundred men under Major General Gibbs along the edge of the Cypress Swamp. The scaling ladders and fascines, which had earlier been taken to the advanced redoubt, were to be collected by the 44th Regiment who were to lead General Gibbs' advance.

The complex plan proved to be a disaster from the start. Thornton was four hours late launching his boats as there was too little water in the canal and the levee wasn't cut deep enough. When he finally shoved off, with only a third of his force, the current swept them much further downstream than planned. Worse was to follow. The 44th Regiment misunderstood their instructions and failed to bring up the ladders and fascines in time. As a result, Gibbs' column began their advance without adequate equipment to cross the Rodriguez Canal and scale the high mud ramparts on the other side. The two regiments, for which Pakenham had waited to reinforce his army, were never used. The 7th and 43rd Regiments, two of Wellington's best, were held in reserve under General Lambert and could only watch in dismay as the bloody fiasco unfolded.

Pakenham was forewarned of the likely difficulties and his aids urged him to call off the attack. But his impatience had clouded his judgement and he would not be moved. He ordered the attack to begin and committed half of his seven thousand veteran troops in a brave, but suicidal frontal attack on Jackson's almost impregnable position, defended by his hotchpotch army of more than five thousand determined men.

Had the British been better led, the outcome might well have been different. As it was, the British suffered more than two thousand casualties, including nearly three hundred who were killed in the assault. Ironically, Colonel Thornton's attack across the river was highly successful, but a disconsolate General Lambert, who had now taken command, ordered him to pull back.

General Jackson's casualties were light, only thirteen killed and some forty wounded or missing. He was also wise enough not to pursue the enemy and risk exposing his men. Mark watched, with a growing sickness inside him, as the dispirited British troops retreated back to their camp, leaving the stubble fields littered with dead and wounded Redcoats. As the plaintive cries of the wounded drifted across the cold morning air, he bitterly regretted the foolish whim that had caused him to volunteer in the first place. He tried hard to control his choking emotions but with little success until a sudden stir of excitement among the General's staff caught his attention. It was a messenger from the other bank with bad news.

'The British have overrun our batteries, sir. We need reinforcements urgently.'

'Have they captured our guns?' For the first time Mark detected a note of alarm in Jackson's voice.

'Yes, sir. But we managed to spike them all first.'

'Thank God for that. At least they can't use them to fire on our flank.' He turned to Mark. 'You were right, Captain. I should have sent more men across earlier. I pray to God we're not too late.'

'I think we were both right, sir,' Mark said, trying hard to force a smile.

There was an anxious wait as troops were hastily despatched across the river and a general sigh of relief when news came back that Thornton had withdrawn.

For the next ten days an uneasy truce settled over the battlefield before the British moved back to the bayou during the night, leaving their campfires burning to fool the Americans. On 25th January, the British fleet sailed out of Lake Borgne, taking with them the riddled body of General Pakenham, pickled in a hogshead of rum.

Rumours were now rife that Britain and the United States had made peace. The peace treaty had actually been signed in Ghent on Christmas Eve, two weeks before the attack on New Orleans, but news of this had not yet reached America. It was not until the evening of 11th February that the British sloop-of-war *Favourite*, still flying the flag of truce, slipped into New York harbour carrying copies of the treaty for ratification.

The battle for New Orleans was fought in ignorance of the peace treaty and had, therefore, been a needless waste of lives. However, it proved to be one of the most decisive battles in the history of America and one which would have momentous consequences. Though Jackson's victory had come too late to have any influence of the peace treaty itself, it strongly influenced the way in which it was interpreted and applied. It helped to legitimize the Louisiana Purchase in the eyes of a previously sceptical international community.

The elimination of British power in the area also seriously weakened Spanish influence in the Gulf, leading to its early demise. Jackson's unconstitutional attack on Pensacola was conveniently overlooked by Washington and what little protection the peace treaty gave to the Indians was ignored by the General, never a man to obey orders he found uncongenial. He just kept moving the demoralized Indians westwards. After all, he was now a national hero; the only one the country had. In the coming years, he would put his new found fame to good use.

Jackson's victory at New Orleans would pave the way for the future expansion of the United States, ultimately to the Pacific coast. But above all, the war had given the Americans a new sense of unity based on self-confidence and with this new found national pride would come respect from abroad. The ex-colony had now become a nation to be reckoned with.

RETRIBUTION

CHAPTER 48

On the soft summer evening of June 21st, 1815 Mark stood by the rail of the London bound sail ship *Tontine* as she edged her way slowly up the Thames. Aloft, the American flag fluttered briefly in the weakening breeze and the sails slowly filled, as if trying to find strength for the final part of the long voyage.

Even during his service in the Royal Navy, Mark had never seen so many ships of differing size, type and nationality in one place. For four miles from Deptford to London Bridge the forest of masts seemed to be continuous. Crowded wharves and warehouses lined both banks of the river and even at this time of day, the river pulsated with a restless energy.

'A lovely scene, eh?'

Mark turned to see a fellow passenger. Lieutenant Fitzsimmons, who was wearing his army uniform for the first time since leaving New York. 'Yes,' Mark answered, smiling. 'Nothing like a busy port to attract a man's attention.'

'I suppose it appeals to some people,' Fitzsimmons said dismissively, 'but that,' he went on, pointing beyond the north bank, 'is much more interesting.'

Mark's eyes followed the direction of the pointing finger and saw the classical City of London skyline, with its numerous stone belfries, reaching up into the evening sky. Away to the west, and dominating the scene, rose the magnificent dome of St Paul's, crowned by its golden cross standing three hundred and sixty-five feet above the ground.

'London's the most fascinating city in the world,' Fitzsimmons continued, 'and a damned sight more exciting than anything in Canada or America.'

Mark nodded politely. 'I'll have to take your word for it, since this is my first visit. I was born and raised in the north of England.'

'Then you must let me introduce you to some of her pleasures, my dear fellow. I have a few days before I leave to join my regiment in Flanders.'

'That's very kind of you, but...' Mark's intended protestation was cut short by the amiable lieutenant.

'I insist, my dear fellow. Come ashore with me and we'll discuss it over supper.'

'But I've already arranged to stay on board tonight and disembark in the morning.' Mark had nowhere to stay in London and another night on board seemed the best solution.

'Then I'll stay and keep you company. We'll drink some more of that Yankee captain's wine and get our money's worth from the voyage, eh?'

Mark acquiesced with a smile. Suddenly, and much to his surprise, he found himself beginning to like this deceptively languid young officer. Yet, at the beginning of the voyage, he'd found the man's arrogance and foppish gentlemanly ways utterly distasteful. But now he'd come to realise that beneath the aristocratic manner, lay a generous heart and a shrewd mind.

They had both embarked on the *Tontine* at New York; Mark after a long journey from Tennessee and the lieutenant after travelling from Canada, where he had been recovering from his wounds. Undeterred by this painful experience of war, Fitzsimmons was anxious to rejoin his regiment in Flanders, now that Bonaparte was back in France following his escape from Elba. The thought of fighting under the command of Wellington, who'd been appointed Commander-in-Chief of the Allied army, filled him with excitement.

At first, Mark had been tempted to travel steerage. He'd been used to roughing it at sea and the cost was only thirty-one dollars, whilst a cabin cost one hundred and seventy-five dollars. However, cabin passengers had food and wine provided whereas those travelling steerage had to supply their own food and provisions for up to seventy-two days, even though the voyage was usually completed in half that time.

It wasn't that Mark was short of money. His one hundred and twenty-four dollar enlistment bounty had been untouched as had most of his army pay. There was also the substantial credit facility that Henry had arranged for him at the Boston bank, but hardly used.

Mark had not answered his father's letters; at first because of the shock of Jane's death and the manner of it, and later because he did not wish to compromise Henry when he ultimately returned to England to seek his revenge. His father was, therefore, unaware of his son's homecoming.

Had it not been for General Jackson's personal interest in his problem, Mark might well have stayed in America and allowed his mental wounds to heal. But Old Hickory would have none of it. 'You were betrayed and treated shamefully,' he'd growled, bristling with anger. 'You'll never be able to live with yourself unless you confront the blackguard and do whatever must be done.' Then, placing his arm around Mark's shoulder he'd added, gently but firmly, 'You can't walk away from it, however unpleasant it may be.'

Mark assumed the General was right and had accepted his advice with fatalistic resignation. But then, in matters of honour, Jackson displayed a belligerency that sometimes bordered on paranoia. Nevertheless, Mark was deeply grateful to his mentor whose kindness had given him American citizenship and, with the help of the General's friends engaged in land speculation, title to more than two thousand acres of prime Alabama land at less than two dollars an acre, with payment spread over four years.

Jack had tried hard to dissuade his friend from returning to England. The three hundred and twenty acres they had each received from the American government on their discharge from the army were adjoining half sections. The additional acreage purchased by Mark now formed a large, continuous estate that presented an exciting challenge and the promise of vast profits from cotton, especially now that England and America were at peace. Jack relished the prospect but knew, being the junior partner, that he would need all Mark's leadership and support. 'It's not worth going back and opening up old wounds,' he had pleaded.

But Mark remained adamant. 'You stay and take charge of things here, Jack. I'll be back within a year, I promise.'

'I'm not cut out to run an enterprise like this on my own,' Jack had protested unhappily. 'I may have been brought up on a farm but I don't know anything about business and financial matters.'

'You won't need to, my friend. It will take a year to clear the land and build cabins and barns. I'll be back by then. '

Jack soon realised that Mark's mind was made up and had reluctantly agreed to his friend's proposals. Mark drafted a plan of action for Jack to follow and arranged for adequate finance to be made available to tide things over until he returned. He felt suddenly glad that he'd taken the time and patience to teach Jack the rudiments of reading and writing during their time spent as prisoners of war. At least they could communicate by post, slow though this would be.

But now that he was back in England, Mark's qualms began to resurface. Though he still hated Roland for what he'd done and remained determined to seek redress, he sometimes detected a faint weakening in his resolve for punitive action. The feeling for revenge as a cold obsessive hatred was something which did not come naturally to him and he found it difficult to sustain his anger.

There were times when he despised himself for this and since his arrival in England he'd found that, instead of feeling vengeful, he was suddenly consumed by an urgent need to see Jane's child.

It was strange, he reflected, how he always thought of the baby as Jane's child; not as Jane's son, or even as their son. The bitter memories of that terrible evening nearly five years ago still remained. Above all, the vision of an evil Roland gloating in his obscene satiation had been seared into his mind. Perhaps it was this nightmare that had clouded his paternal instincts making him feel ambivalent towards the child. But maybe the shock waves of his trauma were also beginning to wane, he reflected. Hence his growing urge to see the child. Michael would be four years old now and, regardless of whether he or Roland proved to be the father, the boy was still Jane's son.

From Henry's letters, Mark knew that his father would bring the boy up as if he were his own son rather than a grandson. This would provide stability and the child would want for nothing. Michael would also see Ralph as an older brother and not an uncle. It was this knowledge that the boy would be well cared for that had, in the past, allowed Mark to put aside any feelings of responsibility. But now he realised that he must face up to his obligations, and his recognition of the situation suddenly made him feel happier.

That evening, as he took supper with Lieutenant Fitzsimmons and the captain, Mark felt strangely elated. He couldn't understand why and after a while, ceased trying to find the reason and allowed his new found feeling of euphoria to have full rein.

Fitzsimmons noticed Mark's change of mood. 'You look damned cheerful tonight.'

Mark grinned. 'Aren't I always?'

'Indeed not. For most of the voyage you hardly smiled and your conversation was less than sparkling.' Fitzsimmons note of disapproval was softened by a hint of humour.

'Then my improved disposition must be due to my being back in England,' Mark concluded nonchalantly.

Fitzsimmons eyed him curiously. 'Have you been away long?'

'Almost five years.'

'Living in America?'

'Yes.' Seeing the continuing look of curiosity on the lieutenant's face Mark added, 'Assessing the country's prospects and acquiring some land.'

'To farm?'

'Yes. I intend to grow cotton.'

Fitzsimmons became more interested. 'If I may be so bold, how much land did you acquire?'

'A little over two thousand acres.'

Fitzsimmons was impressed. 'That's a good deal of land.'

'Not by American standards,' Mark said. 'You can buy undeveloped land from the American government for two dollars an acre; sometimes even less.'

Fitzsimmons did a quick mental calculation. 'Good God! That's less than nine shillings an acre in English Sterling.'

'Yes,' Mark agreed, 'but it usually needs a lot of work before it can be properly cultivated.'

Fitzsimmons nodded. 'And how much cotton can you harvest from two thousand acres?'

'At least a million pounds, assuming we get the average yield per acre which is usually between five and seven hundred pounds of cotton.'

'And what price do you expect your cotton to bring in the Market?'

Mark hesitated. He was beginning to feel a little uncomfortable under the constant barrage of questions. He went on cautiously. 'Now that the war is over, I think the price of cotton will rise to perhaps twenty-five or even thirty cents per pound.'

Fitzsimmons did another quick mental calculation then exclaimed, 'Well I'll be damned! That's a quarter of a million dollars per crop or fifty-five thousand pounds Sterling.' A low whistle of admiration escaped from his lips.

'But that's a gross profit,' Mark countered, trying to play down the exciting prospects of his venture. 'There's a lot of expenses and direct costs to be offset before you can arrive at a true profit. And the crop can always fail,' he added as a parting shot.

'So can all crops, dear fellow,' Fitzsimmons said airily. My father owns twenty thousand acres, but we can't grow anything as profitable as cotton. Not that it concerns me,' he added, smiling. 'I'm the youngest son so, to placate his conscience, father bought me off with a thousand pounds a year and the purchase of my commission.' There was a note of sadness in his voice.

'It doesn't seem fair.' Mark said, trying to sound sympathetic.

'Luck of the draw, dear fellow,' Fitzsimmons shrugged then went on to explain. 'Oldest groomed to be squire, second son into the Church and the third fed to the army. Still, it could have been worse.'

'In what way?' Mark asked.

Fitzsimmons laughed. 'Can you imagine me as the village parson!'

Mark grinned back. 'No. Indeed I can't.'

Later, after the captain had excused himself to attend to his duties, Mark and the young lieutenant relaxed over another bottle of claret. Fitzsimmons leaned back in his chair and fixed Mark with a quizzical smile. 'You're travelling on to Newcastle, I believe?'

'Yes. My father's in the coal trade. He's a partner in a firm of coal fitters.' It wasn't what Fitzsimmons had asked but Mark knew it was what he wanted to know.

Fitzsimmons looked blank. 'Coal fitters?' What, dear fellow, are they?'

'They act as sales agents for the colliery owners, Mark explained. The firm also has a working lease on two collieries and owns several collier brigs.'

'I see,' Fitzsimmons murmured, beginning to lose interest. 'Not as exciting as your American venture, eh? Coming from a long line of aristocratic landowners, he disdained trade, though he would happily marry an heiress to a trade fortune if it so suited him. But then that was how many families of ancient lineage had survived when, on succession, some reckless son had gambled away the family fortune.

Shortly before eleven o'clock that evening, Mark took his leave of Fitzsimmons and, despite the Lieutenant's protests, made his way unsteadily to his cabin. A drunk and disapproving Fitzsimmons scowled after him and muttered, 'Bloody poor company and no damned stamina.'

At about eleven o'clock that same evening, some two miles further upriver, a chaise-and-four was charging furiously over Westminster Bridge and after turning into Parliament Street, proceeded up Whitehall towards Downing Street. Inside the carriage and still wearing his blood-stained uniform, sat Major the Hon. Henry Percy, one of the few of Wellington's aides-de-camp to survive Waterloo without a serious wound. Two captured French eagles poked incongruously through the carriage window and four French flags were draped across the upholstery inside.

It was something of an anti-climax to learn that most of the cabinet were dining at Lord Harrowby's house in Grosvenor Square for, inside a purple velvet sachet given to him by a dancing partner at the Duchess of Richmond's Waterloo Ball, Major Percy carried the Duke of Wellington's dispatch giving news of his great victory over Napoleon Bonaparte.

An excited crowd followed the coach to Grosvenor Square and then on to St James Square, where the gallant major presented the French eagles to the Prince Regent, who was attending a ball. Outside, a large and growing throng gave loud huzzas and sang "God Save the King." In the City, weary newspaper compositors began to set up their headlines in block type; 'COMPLETE OVERTHROW OF BONAPARTE'S ARMY. OFFICIAL BULLETIN'. After twenty-two years of almost continuous fighting, war-weary Britain was ready for peace.

It was soon after dawn when Mark went ashore and headed for the Coal Exchange in Lower Thames Street. A thin mist hung over the river, clinging in wispy tendrils to the forest of masts and rigging which stretched along the river bank. After making some enquiries, he was directed to the captain of a Shields collier brig that was waiting to discharge its cargo at the Pool and booked a return passage to the Tyne. A guinea to the captain of another brig about to sail for the Tyne that day ensured that Rory MacGregor would be informed of Mark's pending arrival.

CHAPTER 49

The collier brig *Felicity* slowly began to heel as she wore round onto a broad reach and headed for the entrance to the River Tyne. The stiff southerly breeze was raising a heavy swell on the bar and Mark had to hold on to the weather shrouds to steady himself. His excitement rose as he picked out the ruins of Tynemouth Priory and the castle gatehouse perched on the cliff tops to the north. Closer to hand, on the rocky promontory of Priory Haven stood the grim outline of Spanish Battery.

After clearing the bar, the brig's motion eased as it entered the calmer, sheltered waters of the river mouth and edged slowly towards North Shields. Mark could now follow the transit between the Low Light and the High Light above the town which marked the shipping channel. Soon they were past Clifford's Fort, which guarded The Narrows, and into the main anchorage where the brig rounded up and dropped anchor. The river was crowded with ships of all types, from barques and brigantines to the sturdy foys engaged in the coastal trade and in every direction the ubiquitous collier brig. Here, the wherries from every part of the river loaded and unloaded; keels piled up with coal came alongside the colliers to cast their loads and foy-boats and ferries darted in and out among the anchored ships, like fat water beetles skimming the surface of the river.

Mark's preoccupation with the scene before him was interrupted by the *Felicity*'s captain. 'Looks like you've got a welcoming party, Mr Standish,' he said, pointing to an empty keel that was fast approaching the brig. The keel was carrying a single square sail to take advantage of the favourable wind and Mark admired the expert way she was being handled. He watched as the giant bearded man in the stern holding the large steering oar called out an order. Immediately, the two men standing by the mast began to lower the sail. The keel carried her way to the side of the brig before rounding up and coming smartly alongside. It was at that moment, with a sudden happy surge of recognition, that Mark found himself looking down into a pair of smiling blue eyes and heard the voice of Rory MacGregor. 'Welcome home, bonnie lad!'

Colin's grinning face emerged from beneath the lowered sail. 'Hallo, Mark,' he said, then leapt up like an athlete from the deck of the keel and casually vaulted over the brig's rail. The two men looked at each other for a brief moment before embracing in a mutual bear hug.

You haven't changed much,' Mark said with a grin.

'Nor you,' Colin answered.

Mark smiled wistfully. 'I feel a lot older. It seems like a hundred years since we fished and sailed our boats at Barras Bridge.'

'Aye, it does that,' Colin said, his eyes sparkling as the boyhood memories came flooding back. 'The glorious first of June when we beat the French, eh? I remember you were always Captain Collingwood.'

Only because you always insisted on being Admiral Howe,' Mark retorted.

'Naturally. I come from a long line of keelmen,' Colin said with a cheeky grin. 'Everyone knows that keelmen make the best seamen.'

'I hope the Navy doesn't force you to prove it one day,' Mark said quietly, recalling his own experience.

'Aye, so do I Mark. But a keelman learns to watch out for the scurvy press gang and not rely on his protection. Anyway, now that Boney's been defeated, the Navy will start laying up ships again. Rory reckons there'll soon be a glut of seamen looking for a collier berth.'

At this point their conversation was cut short by a stentorian bellow from Rory in the keel below. 'If you two would stop cackling like a couple of fishwives, we might have enough tide to take us back to Newcastle.'

Mark grinned at Colin. 'He hasn't changed much either. '

After taking his leave of the collier captain, Mark collected his bag and followed Colin over the rail and down on to the narrow side-deck of the keel. The open hold was empty and looked cavernous. On the order from Rory, Colin and the other keel bully hoisted the sail and, with Rory at the steering oar at the stern, they sailed into the middle of the river to take full advantage of the flood tide. The wind had backed and was now blowing from the east, greatly assisting their progress. Mark estimated that with the wind and tide in their favour, the keel was making well over four knots over the ground.

'Should make Sandgate in two hours if the wind holds,' Colin said, noting Mark's interest.

It was nine miles from Shields to Newcastle and Mark settled down to enjoy the trip. He suddenly realised that twenty years had passed since he'd last sailed on a keel during his boyhood days with Colin. It seemed a larger vessel than he remembered, forty-two feet long with an enormous beam of nineteen feet giving the keel a fat, oval shaped appearance that belied its nimbleness. The hull was dominated by the large open hold amidships, leaving space only for a small decked area at the bow and stern linked by the narrow side decks used to work the boat.

The River Tyne was the rich main artery that fed the black gold of the great northern coalfield to the prime markets of London and Continental Europe. As always, the river was bustling with activity but, despite the heavy traffic, they made good progress upstream. Mark noted that there were still large areas of the river bank that remained rural and picturesque, but the intrusions of industry were becoming more manifest. The ballast hills were larger and there seemed to be more coal staithes lining the banks. In some places, attracted by the abundance of cheap local coal, expanding manufactories crowded the shores. Grimy works producing glass, soap, soda, iron, lead and copperas, emitted clouds of black smoke and noxious vapours which rose to foul the summer sky.

Rory sat in the stern of the keel holding the long steering oar under his arm. His legs dangled through the hatch which led to the huddock, a small storage area beneath the afterdeck which served as a cabin. Mark saw his gesture and moved aft to join him. 'Things are changing, Rory. Seems to be more staithes taking colliers instead of keels.'

'You're an observant young fellow,' Rory said appreciatively. 'Still don't miss much do you?'

Mark smiled. 'You forget I helped run the brotherhood five years ago. The pitmen and keelmen were always close allies.'

'Still are, but the coal trade has changed a lot since then,' Rory said. 'Now, the best seams are in the lower Tyne basin and most of the bigger pits are below bridge. They prefer to load direct into colliers. Only the pits above bridge are still forced to use keels and only

497

because they can't squeeze a collier under it.' His voice was heavy with sarcasm.

'The fitters still own the keels and employ the crews, don't they?' Mark asked. And keelmen still have to sign an annual bond, just as the pitmen are forced to do?'

'Yes.'

'Well, with a financial investment like that, aren't the fitters committed to using keels?'

'Aye, but the pit owners aren't. The premium market is for large coal, so loading directly into colliers means less handling and less chance of breakage.'

'And less cost if you don't have to pay for keels,' Mark added.

Rory's eyes blazed with anger. 'Perhaps, but the pit owners have had some rich pickings during the war, Mark. They say there's been thirty new winnings, yet there's less work for keelmen. It can't be right.'

'It's unfair,' Mark agreed, trying to sound sympathetic. 'But loading directly into colliers where possible does seem to be a logical development. You can't stop progress.'

Rory exploded. 'Forcing keelmen and their families into the workhouse is not my idea of progress,' he roared, 'and we can do something to stop it.'

'Like what?' Mark asked, taken aback by Rory's sudden outburst.

'We can make life difficult for the owners. Withdraw our labour if necessary.' Then, as his anger subsided, he continued in a voice chill with determination. 'If we have to, we'll destroy the staithes.'

'You'll be playing right into the owner's hands if you allow them to goad you into breaking the law,' Mark cautioned. 'They'll bring the wrath of the authorities down on your heads; arrests, imprisonment and the leaders black-listed. Is that what you want?'

'Of course not, but there's no other way. There's no rights for the likes of us in this society, you of all people should know that. How can we trust in the law when the very magistrates who are supposed to uphold it, the likes of Forster, can get away with monstrous acts of injustice like......' Rory broke off in embarrassment as he realised the sensitivity of his clumsy tirade. He silently cursed as he saw the flicker of pain in Mark's eyes. 'Och, I'm sorry laddie,' he said wretchedly.

Mark tried to shrug off the sting from this unintentional wound with what he hoped was a nonchalant smile. 'No need to apologise, Rory. You've suffered as much as I have.'

'Perhaps, but then I've had my revenge...' Once more Rory stopped in confusion, again silently cursing himself for compounding his error. He grinned sheepishly at Mark and reverted to the vernacular to hide his embarrassment. 'Being tactful is no' ma strong point, ye ken. '

Mark smiled back. 'It never was, Rory and I hope it never will be.' He paused, then went on quietly. 'My turn will come, though. That I promise you.' He was surprised at the strength of feeling in his voice, echoing his new found determination.

'I'm sure it will, Mark,' Rory said softly, his eyes glinting with approbation. 'And if you need any help.....,' his voice trailed off, leaving the obvious unsaid.

Mark discerned a strange look on Rory's face, a mixture of sympathy and encouragement that seemed to be willing him on. It was almost as if he were being challenged. He wondered just how much Rory knew about the terrible events of his betrayal five years ago. There had always been a close friendship between Rory and his father which he assumed still existed. But, he thought, Henry would surely have no knowledge of the traumatic events which had followed his arrest; only that Forster had handed him over to the Press. Yet, he had a strange feeling Rory knew more than that.

Mark suddenly wondered if Jane had confided in Henry before her death, then quickly dismissed the idea. Jane was far too sensitive a person to discuss something so private and harrowing; unspeakable events which, in her eyes, would be the most shameful experience imaginable. But, there was something in Rory's demeanour which was disconcerting and this made him more anxious about his homecoming. All at once he felt uncomfortable. There were questions he needed to ask about the circumstances surrounding Jane's death. He still found it hard to accept that it was suicide; yet the uncertainty clung on stubbornly in the recesses of his mind.

The keel had now rounded Whitehill Point and Mark could see a broad expanse of water, about a mile wide, on the south shore where the tiny River Don entered the Tyne.

'Jarrow Slake,' Rory said, interrupting Mark's thoughts. 'Looks nice when the tide's in but it's all mud at low water and smells like a midden in hot weather.'

Mark forced a grin. 'I can well imagine.'

'Those are the Jarrow ballast hills,' Rory went on, indicating the high mounds on the west side of the Slake. 'That's Jarrow colliery over there and the waggonway down to the river. You can see more than two miles up-river from here, past Hebburn on the south bank and Wallsend on the North.

Mark could see that the colliers lying at the staithes at Jarrow were loading directly from the spouts. He could also see a cluster of masts further up river at Hebburn and assumed they too were colliers loading at the Hebburn staithes. It was the same picture on the north bank at Percy Main colliery and up past the huge Willington ballast hills, where the staithes serving Willington and Wallsend collieries lined the river.

Mark recognised that what he saw was progress and sadly, realised that Rory was fighting a battle that could not be won. New pumping technology had allowed the development of the Tyne basin and with it the creation of some of the greatest and deepest of Tyneside's collieries. All were below bridge and some were working coal more than one thousand feet below the surface. Sinking costs must have been enormous, he thought, and it was not surprising that the owners were circumventing the expensive use of keels. It made sound economic sense, but with Rory in his present mood he wasn't prepared to pursue the matter.

The keel was now approaching Wallsend and they sailed in close by the lofty, stout timbers that supported the deck of the staithe. Mark pointed to a strange looking structure that straddled the end of the waggonway on the edge of the staithes above. 'What's that?' he asked.

'It's a bloody coal drop,' Rory growled. 'I suppose you'd call it another bit of progress,' he added scathingly.

Mark ignored the provocation. 'What's it supposed to do?'

'Watch and you'll find out.'

As Rory spoke, Mark could see a chaldron waggon moving by gravity along the slope of the staithes. A man on the rear of the waggon controlled its speed using the long handled brake and the waggon disappeared inside the hump-backed shed at the end of the staithes. Suddenly the waggon reappeared. It was now resting on a square timber frame which was suspended between two long timber arms that were hinged to the base of the staithes near the waterline. Ropes controlling the drop were attached to the upper end of each timber arm and led back over pulleys inside the humped-back hut then down to two large weights suspended beneath the staithe.

Mark watched as the hinged arms of this strange contraption swung out in an arc over the river, like the lowering of some huge medieval drawbridge. The chaldron waggon was now suspended directly over the hold of a collier brig that had been carefully moored in position off the staithe. At this point, a man on the collier's deck drew the bolt at the base of the chaldron waggon which gently released its fifty-three hundredweights of coal into the brig's hold. When the waggon had discharged its load, the weight of the counterbalances slung beneath the staithe was sufficient to raise the empty chaldron waggon back to the deck of the staithe.

Mark was impressed by the sheer simplicity of this clever device, though he was not sure as to what it achieved. 'It's all very ingenious, Rory, but using a spout would surely be easier.'

'True, but spouts cause more damage to the coal. As you see, the drop takes the waggon right down to the collier's hold before the coal is released. That reduces breakage.'

'Is this the only one?'

Rory nodded. 'Aye, but there'll be others soon. More nails to drive into the keelman's coffin.'

'You see little hope for the future then?' Mark asked gently.

'Och, it's no' as bad as that.' Rory tried to sound confident but his voice lacked conviction. 'The Tyne's a difficult river, especially for the bigger ships like collier brigs. We're lucky today; we've got an easterly to blow us up-river, but the prevailing winds are westerly. Ships have to weather Whitehill Point after passing Shields and if they manage that, there's Bill Point at Walker which is even more difficult.

501

Then there's sandbanks and shallows everywhere because, fortunately for us keelmen, Newcastle Corporation won't spend money to improve the channel.'

'Sounds to me as though you've little to worry about, then,' Mark said reassuringly.

'For now, yes, but the coal trade and the shipowners are pushing hard for improvements. It's only a matter of time before they get them. They're a powerful group and they'll force the Corporation to do something, eventually.'

'So there is no future for the keelmen?'

'Above bridge, yes, but not below. Och, Colin will see his time out I'm sure, but after that,' Rory lowered his voice to a conspiratorial whisper. 'I know you can keep a confidence, Mark, so I'll tell you something that I would never admit to anyone else, not even Colin. There'll be work for Colin and his generation but not for the next.' There was a deep sadness in his voice that Mark found strangely moving. After a pause, he continued. 'Keelmen are a dying breed, my friend, but as long as I'm their leader, it will be a slow death, that I promise you.' His voice rose with determination. 'I'll fight the bastards all the way.'

'I'm sure you will, Rory, and I admire your courage.' Rory's despondency suddenly vanished and he gave Mark a broad grin. 'No' a word to Colin, mind ye.'

Mark smiled back. 'You have my promise.'

After this, they sat for a while in silence as the keel approached the most hazardous part of the river. 'That's it,' Rory said, pointing to the north bank. 'The infamous Bill Point. A curse to shipping but a blessing in disguise for the keelmen.'

Mark's eyes followed the direction of Rory's outstretched arm and saw a huge wedge of wooded land that jutted into the river, like the beak of a giant bird. 'I can see now why they call it Bill Point,' he said.

Rory nodded in silent confirmation. 'You can see how far the point thrusts into the river at the very spot where the stream makes the sharpest turn. That's why it's so difficult for shipping and its height makes it impossible to sight any vessels coming in the opposite direction. Until it's too late, that is,' he added with a broad grin.

Mark smiled at Rory's wicked sense of humour. 'Bill Point must be the patron saint of keelmen, then?'

Rory pretended to be shocked. 'That would be idolatry, my friend. The Church would never canonize a hill. You have to be a human and usually long dead at that.' An impish smile slowly crossed his face. 'But keelmen aren't so fussy, especially as the Church usually sides with the coal owners. Anyway, we need all the help we can get.'

After rounding Bill Point, the keel ran before the wind past St Anthony's. Here, the river turned North West for the final two miles past Felling and St. Peter's before reaching Newcastle.

Rory looked questioningly at Mark. 'We'll be at Sandgate in half-an-hour.'

Mark nodded. 'No welcoming party, I hope.'

Rory looked affronted. 'Of course not,' he snapped. 'Your letter made it clear that your return should be kept secret. Only your family and mine know you're back in Newcastle.'

Mark instantly regretted his flippant remark. 'I'm sorry, Rory. It was foolish of me to question a friend. Especially a man of your integrity.'

The apology quickly defused the misunderstanding. 'Och, I know you didn't mean it, laddie,' Rory said with a smile. 'No offence taken, either,' he added, anxious to excuse his own ill-tempered response.

There was an uneasy silence before Rory spoke again. 'You're glad to be home, then?' It was an innocent enough question but it unsettled Mark. 'In some ways yes, although in others….' Mark left the rest unspoken, but he knew Rory would understand.

'There's a lot of unfinished business to attend to.'

'Yes, I know.'

'And not only at North Moor,' Rory said pointedly.

Mark sighed. 'Just what are you trying to tell me, Rory?'

'You're father's a good man, Mark. He's also a very rich man since Ivison died.'

'Rich?' Mark was astonished. He knew his father had earned a comfortable living as Ivison's junior partner after leaving North Moor Colliery, but he had very little in the way of assets. 'Are you sure?' he asked.

503

'Aye. Mr Ivison died last year and your father was the major beneficiary in his will. Henry inherited the bulk of the estate: the fitting firm, two collieries, four collier brigs and several properties. There was also a considerable amount of cash and a partnership in a Newcastle bank. He was a very clever old gentleman, was our Mr Ivison.' Rory spoke with genuine respect and admiration and added. 'He was also the only owner I had any time for, apart from your father.'

The news of his father's good fortune should have made him happy, Mark thought, yet it left him feeling oddly disconcerted. 'I suppose it was the least Ivison could do to reward my father's misguided loyalty to him,' he said, unable to stem a faint resentment he still felt inside.

Rory's face clouded. 'What do you mean by that?'

'My father left Newcastle to avoid compromising his employer's reputation, didn't he? Ivison was seeking election to the Aldermanic bench of the Corporation, remember? Not many men would sacrifice themselves and their families for an employer.'

'Your father's different to most men. He's one of that rare breed; a man of honour.'

'Then why didn't he consider the feelings of his family? It broke my mother's heart having to leave Newcastle. It almost broke mine, too, being forced to give up school and leave my friends behind. Even after all these years, I still feel a little bitter.'

Rory shook his head, sadly. 'You're being unfair to him, Mark. It was your Uncle William who betrayed your father and caused three good men to be arrested and sent to prison. One later committed suicide.'

The sudden revelation caught Mark unawares, sending tingling shock waves through his body. 'That surely can't be true,' he gasped in stunned disbelief. 'Uncle William wouldn't have betrayed his own brother-in-law?'

'I'm afraid he did just that,' Rory said grimly.' Then he went on to betray me,' he added.

The pieces of the jigsaw were now coming together in Mark's mind. 'I think I'm beginning to understand,' he said. 'And you took your revenge when you came out of prison?'

504

Rory maintained a stony silence to the question, but Mark felt he already knew the answer. Surprisingly, he felt little outrage, only curiosity. With his own betrayal yet un-avenged, how could he condemn Rory? 'Was it worth it?' he asked.

'Yes,' Rory said. Then looking Mark firmly in the eye he added, 'It took courage, but you've no idea how much satisfaction it gave me.'

The fervour of Rory's studied reply shocked Mark. It also carried a message that was not lost on him. 'I hope you're right,' he said quietly.

'Your mother had courage too,' Rory went on. 'It was a brave act to stand by Henry the way she did.'

Mark shrugged. 'I don't know what else she could have done in the circumstances. She never quite forgave him, though, nor you. I think you know that.'

'Yes, but she held you together as a family and that helped your father to fight back.'

'Perhaps, but it was a high price to pay.'

Rory gave a deep sigh. 'I suppose if anyone's to blame for all this sorry mess, it's me. I asked one favour too many.'

Mark smiled. 'You always were a strong influence on him; a bad one, my mother would have said. She didn't really like you, Rory.'

'I know. She was a perceptive woman and knew that Henry's sense of honour and loyalty could be easily manipulated.' He paused and gave a sheepish grin before adding, 'Especially by the likes of me.'

A shadow of sadness crossed Mark's face. 'I wish I'd known all this before,' he said wistfully.

'Why? What difference would it have made?'

'I might not have gone down the pit.'

'Why did you, then?'

Mark thought for a moment. 'I suppose if I'm being honest, it was to spite my father.'

Rory looked puzzled. 'How could that hurt him?'

'Because he always promised my mother that he'd keep me out of the pit. I made him break that promise.'

Rory nodded. 'That explains a lot,' he said quietly.

505

They sat in silence for a while before Mark spoke. 'Doesn't my father's new found wealth and power put something of a strain on your friendship?'

Rory looked surprised. 'No. Why should it?'

'Well, you are on opposite sides of the fence, so to speak.'

'Only in trade matters and we don't let that interfere with our personal relationship.'

'Come on, Rory,' Mark chided. 'There must be major differences between you?' The friendship of two such disparate men had always intrigued him and he was anxious to learn more without seeming to pry.

Rory deliberated for a while before answering. 'No, there aren't. It's true your father's become a power to be reckoned with in the coal trade, but he's also by far the best employer in the northern coalfield. He draws up annual bonds that are fair to both pitmen and keelmen which explains why men queue up to sign for him at the binding.'

'Is it still held in October?' Mark asked.

'No. In 1811 it was changed to April, thanks largely to your efforts,' Rory said pointedly.

Mark gave a wry grin. 'Then I achieved something after all.'

Rory nodded. 'More than you realise. Anyway,' he continued, 'your father employs good viewers and honest keekers at his pits. He also listens to the men and tries to put right any just grievances. If a man fails to keep his bond, he doesn't have him arrested and brought before the Magistrates, which infuriates the other owners, of course.'

Mark laughed. 'I'm sure it does. All this doesn't surprise me after what he's been through, though I don't imagine his business methods will sit well with the other owners.'

'No. The bigger owners, like the Grand Allies, respect him for his honesty and business acumen and pretend to overlook the fact that he was once a pitman. But the hardliners, such as Forster, hate his guts.'

'I expect the feeling's mutual,' Mark said.

'More than likely. They say there's been some fierce rows between them at the Coal Owners Association meetings, with Secretary Buddle having to prize them apart.' Rory's exaggerated account wasn't too far from the truth.

Mark reflected for a moment. 'So Forster still has a lot of influence in the trade?'

'More than ever. Owns two other pits besides North Moor, thanks to the money Roland's wife inherited after her father died. Had to make Roland a full partner, though.'

'Is Forster still a Magistrate?'

'Old Duncan Forster, yes. Why do you ask?' Rory was curious.

'Just wondered,' Mark answered guardedly, seeing the look on Rory's face.

Rory grunted, but said nothing.

Changing the subject, Mark asked, 'Has Roland any children?' He tried to sound casual as he spoke Roland's name.

'Two, I think,' Rory replied, 'boy and a girl.' He closely scrutinised Mark's expression before venturing, 'You'll be seeing your own son for the first time, soon.'

Mark gazed at the passing river bank for a while before turning to answer. 'Yes, I will,' he said flatly, and saw the sadness in Rory's eyes as he spoke.

'He's a bonny lad is young Michael,' Rory went on, doggedly ignoring the signal. 'Just like his mother. '

Mark knew Rory meant well but it was the wrong thing to say. He'd agonised for years about the child, ever since Henry's devastating letter had reached him in America. With the passing of time he had managed to come to terms with his grief but, try as he may, his feelings towards the child had remained strangely ambivalent. His suffering had left a coldness in his heart that was alien to him. One part of him wanted to love the boy as his own; the other to reject him for fear that he might be the son of the man he hated.

Seeing Rory's discomfort, Mark forced a bleak smile. 'Perhaps he'll grow up to be as handsome and intelligent as his father.'

Rory turned away. 'I'm sure he will,' he said.

Mark wished he'd kept his mouth shut.

The keel was now abreast of the Friar's Goose colliery pumping engine, which stood on the south shore of the river about a mile or so east of Gateshead. Deep in thought, Mark gazed absently at the two vapour columns that rose above the huge engine house; one of black smoke from the boiler fire, the other of white, escaping steam. The

507

sounds of the engine could be heard across the water as the huge pumping beam rose and fell, groaning and sighing with each stroke, in its efforts to discharge one and a half million gallons of water from the pit each day. But little of this registered in his mind as he pondered over his homecoming and wondered why he should feel so nervous at the prospect of meeting his family again.

'I don't suppose they're worth a penny?' Rory's voice cut through Mark's reverie.

'You're right, they're not,' Mark responded with a wan smile.

'We'll be home in fifteen minutes anyway,' Rory went on, cheerfully. Then, in a voice full of warmth and understanding, he added, 'Go easy on your father, Mark. He's a good man and he loves you. He moved heaven and earth to try and get you back from the navy, you know.'

A soft sigh of resignation escaped from Mark's lips. 'I'm sure you're right, Rory, only …..' He paused trying to find the right words. 'I wish he'd shown the same loyalty and determination when he left North Moor Colliery to join Ivison.' There was a trace of bitterness in his voice despite his efforts to conceal it.

'Och, you're no' being fair, laddie.' Rory's exasperation made him bristle and lapse into the vernacular again. 'Your father was still grieving for his wife and he had a new baby son to look after. He saw a chance to redeem his promise to Mary and take you out of the pit; provide a future for both of you that she would have been proud of.'

'Yes,' Mark agreed, 'but at the expense of Wilf, Sep and all the men who had put their trust and faith in him. It was too high a price to pay, Rory.'

'For heaven's sake, man!' Rory exploded. 'That was over twelve years ago. You don't still hold that against him?'

'I try not to, but somehow it keeps creeping back into my mind. It's unworthy and inexcusable, I know, yet.... 'Mark's voice trailed off in despair.

'You've changed, Mark. I've never thought of you as a vindictive man.'

'I ignored the letter I received when I was a prisoner of war in America because I was too traumatised. I could have replied but I just let my wounds fester. Perhaps I am vindictive.'

'And perhaps you're not,' Rory snapped. 'Rancour is a corrosive emotion, Mark. If you lock it away inside you it eats away your soul. '

You want me to forgive and forget?'

'Yes, if you put it like that. At least discuss your differences, whatever they are. I think they go back more than twelve years.'

'Damn it, I've tried,' Mark said angrily. I've tried because I still love my father and,' he broke off in confusion.

There was an awkward silence before Rory said, 'I'm sorry, Mark. I only wish there was something I could do to remove whatever it is that still stands between you.'

'I wish you could too, Rory,' Mark answered forlornly. 'I don't know why, but there's always been something perverse in our relationship. There was a loving bond between us when I was a boy, but somehow we lost that when we went to North Moor. Then, shortly after my mother died, we suddenly became close again; closer than we'd ever been before. It was probably because we both needed something to hold on to in our misery. And it could have lasted, Rory, if only Ivison hadn't turned up with his thirty pieces of silver.'

Rory snorted. 'Now you are being vindictive, Mark. It's not true and I think you know it.'

Mark shrugged. 'Perhaps you're right, but if only Ivison had stayed away from North Moor things would have been different and possibly happier.'

Rory shook his head. 'For you, Mark, perhaps. But what of Henry and young Ralph? Aren't you being a little selfish?'

'I suppose I am if you look at it in that light.'

'Then for pity's sake why don't you, Mark?' Rory pleaded. 'You're putting all the blame on Ivison and your father when most of it should be on your Uncle William's head and mine,' he added.

Mark gave a despairing sigh. 'I'm sure you're right, Rory, but I'm too confused to think logically at the moment.'

Rory smiled. 'Well then,' he said gently, 'Go easy on your father, like I told you. Things will work out in time, I promise you.'

The keel was now past the Ouse Burn and heading for a spot called the Swirle, where a small tidal stream ran into the river at Sandgate. On a quiet order from Rory, the square sail was lowered and the keel gently nudged up onto the soft mud of Sandgate Shore. Mark stood up and took a deep breath. He was home at last.

CHAPTER 50

Mark heeded Rory's advice and the reunion with his father went surprisingly well. After the initial few moments of nervousness they embraced warmly then, as the shyness which constrained them began to ease, any remaining inhibitions quickly evaporated. Suddenly, they were smiling and talking excitedly across each other in a scramble to catch up on the news of the past five years.

'This calls for a celebration drink,' Henry said, breaking off and placing two glasses and a decanter of brandy on the desk. 'I don't normally imbibe when I'm working, but I'm happy to make an exception on this occasion.'

The reunion was taking place in Henry's office on the Quayside which, being late afternoon, was the place where Mark thought his father would most likely be found. He also wanted their first meeting to be confined to just the two of them, without the distraction of having other members of the family present.

Henry poured two large measures of brandy and handed a glass to Mark. 'Welcome home, Mark,' he said, raising his glass. Then, his voice choking with emotion, he added, 'It's a moment I've longed and prayed for these past five years.'

Mark warmly acknowledged the toast and felt his emotions rising as he looked across his glass and saw the expression of intense happiness on his father's face. 'I thought I'd call in here first so that we could have a private chat before I meet the rest of the family.'

'That was very thoughtful of you, Mark. I'm glad you did; gives us a chance to catch up on things.'

Mark nodded and smiled back fondly at his father. He relaxed and looked around the elegant partners' room that had once belonged to Ivison and was now used by Henry. It seemed a natural progression, he thought and probably well earned.

His gaze finally returned to his father and he saw that the passing years had been kind to him. The dark curly hair was now streaked with grey giving him the distinguished look that befitted his new found status. The waistline had thickened, he thought, but this was cleverly hidden by a well cut swallow tailed coat, beneath which was a loose frilled shirt and a voluminous neckcloth. Mark also noted that, unlike some older men, Henry had discarded breeches in favour of the fashionable slim fitting trousers, which were now all the rage. It was a piece of frivolous information that he remembered from his fleeting contact with the blades of London and caused him to smile.

'Is my nose running?' Henry asked, intrigued by Mark's stare.

Mark laughed. 'No, father, I was just thinking how well you look. I somehow expected you to look older.'

'Well, I'm past fifty you know, and I'm beginning to feel it, too.'

'You probably work too hard, father. It's not in your nature to take things easy is it?'

'Your Aunt Ellen certainly thinks I work too hard. Always trying to feed me up to compensate. Damn good cook, too,' he added, patting his thickening waist to emphasise the point.

'So she's still looking after you all then?'

'Yes. Got her hands full, what with me and the two boys. She's been like a second mother to them since...' Henry's voice suddenly trailed off into an awkward silence.

Mark saw his father's confusion and sensed this might be the moment to try and exorcise the ghosts that still haunted their relationship. He was glad they were alone, for he needed answers to questions which had long festered in his mind.

'There's no need to feel embarrassed, father,' he said, struggling to find the right words to ease the situation. 'We can't keep running away from the past, can we?'

Henry gave a smile of relief in acknowledgement. 'No Mark, I think it's about time we sought ways of coming to terms with it.'

Mark nodded in agreement. 'My thoughts, too. Aunt Ellen seems to have found her way by making amends for William's treachery. I think mine might prove a little more complicated.' It was an undeserved censure, however unintentional.

There was a sharp intake of breath from Henry. 'Your Aunt Ellen knows nothing about William's duplicity. Neither were you supposed to know.'

'Rory told me. He thought I ought to know.'

'I wish he hadn't.'

'So do I, father. I would rather have heard it from you. '

512

Henry sighed. 'There's no point in opening up old wounds, Mark. Rory should have let matters rest.'

'He suffered four years in prison for it. He had every right to tell me and I'm glad he did.'

'I still think it was none of his business.'

'You're being uncharitable, father. Rory was defending you. He thought that by explaining just what really happened all those years ago, it might help me understand your motives for acting the way you did.'

'And did it help?'

'Yes, it did.' Mark held his father's eyes. 'It would have helped even more if you'd told me yourself at the time, though.'

'Yes, I can see that now, but at the time....' Henry broke off in exasperation.

'But you must have told mother about William, surely?'

'No.'

The word hit Mark like a bombshell and there was a surprised pause before he could bring himself to continue. 'I think I'm just beginning to appreciate how bewildered and frustrated she must have felt. And I thought I was the only one who didn't understand. It explains a lot.'

'What do you mean?'

'Why mother was so unhappy at North Moor.'

'Telling her about William wouldn't have helped. She hated living in a pit village and hated the pit.'

'Yes, but there was more to it than that.' Mark retorted, his mind still struggling to find a satisfactory explanation. He looked sadly at his father. 'Something died between the two of you when we moved to North Moor. I could feel it then, young as I was, and I blamed you without quite knowing why.'

'Was that why you insisted on going down the pit? To spite me?'

Mark forced a wry smile. 'I suppose it was. It never occurred to me that I might be hurting mother even more.'

'Because you were too young to realise.'

'I was then, but not later. If I'd known you were trying to redeem your promise to keep me out of the pit when you accepted Ivison's offer, I might have understood.'

'So Rory told you that too?'

'Yes. He was angry when I suggested that you'd let Wilf and the men down by accepting Ivison's offer.'

Henry gave a crooked smile. 'It was more than a suggestion at the time, if I remember correctly. Your accusation hurt me more than you know.'

It was Mark's turn to look contrite. 'I suppose we both made mistakes, father. Perhaps we're equally to blame for all our misunderstandings over the years.'

Henry looked hesitantly at his son. 'Whatever happened in the past never lessened my love for you, Mark.'

'Nor mine for you father,' Mark responded with sincerity.

'Then this mutual purging of souls has been worthwhile,' Henry said, allowing himself to relax a little. 'I'm beginning to feel better already.'

'I think I do too, father. But now we've finally cleared the air, no more holding back, eh?'

'You mean the truth from now on?'

'Nothing but. Not even white lies.'

Henry smiled. 'You drive a hard bargain, Mark, but you have my word on that.'

'Good, because, Mark paused, wondering how he could soften the next question.

Henry sensed the dilemma. 'You may as well come out with it, Mark. No holding back you said.'

There was a further pause before Mark continued. 'There's something I must ask you, father.'

Henry had a sudden premonition of what the question would be and his heart sank. 'Go on,' he said, trying hard to sound normal.

Mark looked firmly into his father's eyes. 'Why did Jane commit suicide?'

A look of misery clouded Henry's face and he looked away. It was a while before he could answer. 'I think she was very depressed,' he said at last. 'After your capture, she worried herself sick and as the weeks went by without any news, she thought you would never return. Then, after finding she was pregnant, she convinced herself that you were dead.'

514

'But I wrote to her before I left England and again from the West Indies. The letters were addressed to you to give to her. She must have known I was safe.'

'There were no letters, Mark.' Henry spoke, almost in a whisper. He watched, feeling helpless and wretched, as the pain became etched on Mark's face. After a short pause he went on, 'After Michael was born, Jane became worse; sort of retreated inside herself as if she wanted to shut out the world.'

Mark shook his head angrily. 'What you've told me would not make her commit suicide. There's something else, isn't there?'

Henry could not hide his dismay as he tried desperately to protect his son from the unpalatable truth. 'No, Mark, there's nothing more to add, I promise you.'

'You promised me the truth from now on, father. No more lies, remember? You can't even tell the white ones convincingly.'

Henry averted his eyes. 'I'm sorry Mark. I have your best interests at heart and I don't think any useful purpose will be served by my telling you.'

'I think I should be the best judge of that.'

'It will only cause unnecessary anguish, for both of us.'

'You told Rory, for God's sake, so why can't you tell me?' It was a long shot but it would explain Rory's subtle innuendoes during the keel journey from Shields. The look on his father's face told him he was right.

Henry was mortified. 'Rory has awesome powers of persuasion,' he muttered unhappily. 'I was in the depths of my despair when he drew it out of me.'

'Drew what out of you, father? If you won't tell me then I'll have to ask Rory. Is that what you want?'

Henry sighed, accepting defeat. 'No, Mark, that's not what I want. I can see you won't let matters rest and I suppose you have every right to know. You'd better have some more brandy first,' he went on, pushing the decanter across the desk. 'What I am about to tell you is extremely unpleasant.

'I think I already know the worst, father.'

'No, Mark. I'm afraid you don't.'

Mark gave a brittle laugh. 'Then you'd better tell me.'

Henry took a deep breath. 'First, let me say that I know what happened on the night you were taken by Forster and his gamekeepers.' He paused to let this sink in, watching as the shock registered on his son's face.

'Everything?' Mark asked in a stunned voice.

Henry nodded. 'Everything.'

'But how can you possibly know unless...' Mark's mind raced furiously, 'Unless Jane told you herself. Did she?'

'Eventually, yes. She wrote to me before she died.' Henry avoided the emotive word suicide. 'She told me everything that happened, but I already knew.

'How could you have known before Jane wrote to you?' Mark asked in surprise.

'Forster's agent, Gibson, told me. He came to see me two weeks after you were taken.'

Mark still looked puzzled. 'How could he have known. He wasn't at the cottage that night.'

'No, but he was by the stable yard when the two gamekeepers brought you back. He was curious, so he decided to question them. By that time, they were ashamed of what they'd done and were worried about their involvement. They were only too glad to unburden themselves to Gibson once they'd been spotted.'

'He didn't intervene, though.'

'No, but he made sure that Duncan Forster knew what his son had been up to. He possibly thought it might help you.'

'Well, I can assure you it did not.'

'I'm well aware of that now, Mark. In fact it probably made matters worse.'

'In what way?'

'It was Duncan Forster's idea to hand you over to the press, not Roland's. He sent a groom to Newcastle to deliver a letter to the officer in charge of the press gang. Then, that night, he had you shipped down the waggonway in a chaldron waggon to the staithe on the Tyne. That was the agreed rendezvous. Roland was entrusted with a hundred guineas to hand over to the lieutenant in charge to make sure you were put aboard the receiving tender immediately.'

Mark gave a sardonic smile. 'That was more than Judas got.'

516

'Yes,' Henry said, ignoring the cynicism, 'but Roland's act of betrayal involved three men. You see, it was his idea to have the two gamekeepers pressed as well, not his father's.'

'And both Reid and Crombie died still thinking it was old Duncan Forster who'd sold them out,' Mark said, wryly.

'Duncan Forster was furious when he first found out,' Henry went on. 'But he soon realised that, for once, Roland had acted sensibly in order to protect their family interests. The only independent witnesses had been removed from the scene, so it would only be Jane's word against the son of a gentleman and magistrate, if she decided to bring charges.'

'Damn it! Wouldn't Gibson testify?' Mark's anger was soured with the bitterness of his memories.

'I tried to persuade him but he refused. Said it would only be hearsay and wouldn't hold up in court. He was right, too,' Henry added.

'Then you should have taken Jane to see a lawyer yourself. You could have afforded it.'

Though Henry was stung by Mark's censuring tone, he had no wish to force a quarrel. 'I did everything I could, Mark,' he answered stiffly. 'It wasn't easy, you know.'

Mark realised he was becoming over emotional and adopted a more placatory note. 'I'm not blaming you, father. I know it can't have been easy for you.'

Henry acknowledged this with a relieved smile. 'The problem was that Jane refused to talk about what happened that night. She wouldn't even talk to Dora about it and you know how close she was to her mother. The fact that I knew placed me in a very invidious situation, Mark. I was being torn apart watching her suffer.'

'Then why didn't you just tell her that you knew?' Mark asked reproachfully. 'After all, she was your daughter-in-law and it may have helped her. It might even have saved her life.'

A look of pain registered in Henry's face as he relived his dilemma. When he spoke, his voice was strained with anguish. 'I could see she felt humiliated and was deeply traumatised by what had happened. Every time I tried to draw her out she simply cut me off and withdrew into her own world. I thought her depression might lift a little with the passing of time, especially after the baby was born. But she seemed to get worse and became even more remote. There were times when Dora thought her behaviour was very strange.'

'Do you think she was losing her sanity?'

Henry shook his head. 'I think she was in deep shock, but not insane. She had sacrificed herself to save the man she loved and had been cruelly betrayed by the man she hated. Enough to unhinge the mind of any normal person.'

'And you think that drove her to suicide?' Mark asked, though still not prepared to believe it.

'No,' Henry answered quietly. 'I told you there was more.' He leaned down to open the bottom drawer of his desk and took out a small, oak deed box which was bound with strips of burnished brass. He fumbled nervously with the key as he opened the box and took out a letter. 'I think you'd better read this,' he said, handing it to Mark.

Mark saw that the letter was addressed to Henry, and a lump rose in his throat as he recognised the handwriting as Jane's. His hands trembled a little as he opened it and began to read.

'Dear Henry,

I'm afraid this letter may come as a shock to you and cause you some grief. Please believe me that I do not set out to do this deliberately, but rather in the hope that you may understand what I am about to do and that you may even find it in your heart to forgive me.

My greatest wish is that I could share your hope that Mark is still alive, but my heart tells me otherwise. Deep inside, I know he is dead and I cannot face an eternity of waiting for something that I know will only end in further tears and disappointment.

On the night that Mark was taken I gave myself to Roland Forster; not willingly, but in exchange for a promise that Mark would be allowed to go free. In retrospect, it was foolish of me to trust a man like Roland, who has no concept of honour and is depraved beyond belief. I kept my side of the bargain, but he did not keep his. So, I sacrificed my virtue in vain.

It was a wicked deceit which only an evil person like Roland could conceive. It involved the two gamekeepers who had captured Mark and who, no doubt, had been coerced and corrupted by their Master. I was allowed to witness Mark's escape, not knowing that another trap

518

had already been laid to recapture him. So my act of shame was to no purpose, though I did not know it at the time.

Soon after, I discovered I was pregnant, but by whom I am not sure. I would like to think it was Mark, but my heart tells me otherwise.

For a while, I found I could live with my shame, partly for my baby's sake, but mainly in the knowledge that my sacrifice, however vile, had saved Mark's life. I realised that he need never know and that, in time, with his love to help me, I could possibly come to terms with what I had done.

After Michael was born, my premonition that he was Roland's child seemed to be confirmed. I could see nothing of Mark in my son, and although I've tried my best to be a good mother, I somehow cannot feel for him the proper mother's love he deserves. This makes me even more ashamed of myself.

Yesterday, I was walking by the woods near the cottage, carrying baby Michael, when Roland suddenly came riding out from the trees. I tried to ignore him but he just laughed at me. He insisted on looking at baby Michael and asked if it were his, speaking in a callous, offhand way which provoked me. I called him a coward and a man without honour, which made him angry.

He took his revenge in the most cruel way by telling me what actually happened on the night Mark was taken. How he had duped me into allowing him to have his way with me and how the gamekeepers had forced Mark to watch everything. Then, he said some humiliating things about me and asked me why Mark would want to return to a slut like me, even if he survived the war. It is a question I still cannot answer and it constantly haunts me.

In time, I might have come to terms with being raped, for that's what it really was. But I cannot live with the knowledge that my shame was witnessed not only by my husband, the only man I ever loved, but also by two strangers.

You may find it hard to forgive me for what I did then and even more so for what I am about to do now. So when you pray for Mark, as I know you often do, perhaps you can find it in your heart to include a small prayer for me.

One final request, dear Henry. Please take care of baby Michael for me. He is the one innocent party in this sorry affair and deserves a loving home and a future with some hope and opportunity. This I know you can give him.

Your loving daughter-in-law,
Jane'

Mark's hand was shaking when he handed the letter back to Henry. He felt the warm trickle of tears running down his cheeks and brusquely wiped them away with the back of his hand. He looked at his father and saw his own poignancy reflected in Henry's eyes. 'It was knowing I'd witnessed her humiliation that drove her to it, wasn't it?' He said bleakly.

'I think the letter makes that clear,' Henry replied, his voice soft with sympathy.

'Yet the irony of it all is that our love could have survived,' Mark went on, his voice choked with emotion. 'In time, we could have been happy again, despite our misfortunes. '

Henry just nodded. He wondered if Michael's constant presence would have allowed the past to be forgotten, but said nothing.

'It wasn't really suicide, was it?'

It was the question that Henry had always dreaded, yet it still took him by surprise. 'I'm not sure I know what you mean,' he lied.

'It was really murder,' Mark said flatly. 'Jane was murdered by Roland Forster and as the law stands, he can't be punished for it.'

'He didn't murder her,' Henry said gently. 'He did some terrible things, Mark, but he didn't commit murder.'

'Not in law, perhaps, but his loathsome actions brought it about. He murdered her spirit, butchered her self-respect and destroyed her will to live. In my book that's murder.'

Henry could only stare helplessly at his son, watching the look on Mark's face harden as it turned from anger to implacable hatred. 'Don't do anything foolish, Mark,' he pleaded.

I can't stand idly by and do nothing. Do you expect me to live with the knowledge that an evil man like Roland can go unpunished after what he's done to me and my family?'

I know how you must feel,' Henry said, his voice edged with concern, 'but taking the law into your own hands is not the answer.'

Mark looked hard into his father's eyes. 'Then tell me what is,' he challenged.

Henry was at a loss to reply. 'I'm not sure,' he said awkwardly, struggling to find an answer. 'There must be some legal redress surely? Perhaps we should talk to a lawyer.'

Mark appreciated his father's concern and this softened his anger a little. He had no wish to add to Henry's obvious discomfort, so he pretended to go along with Henry's suggestion. 'You may be right,' he said, trying to sound reluctantly won over. 'Perhaps we should see a lawyer.'

Seeing his father's relief he added, 'Let me think it over for a few days.'

'Good,' Henry replied, relaxing visibly. 'Let me know when you've decided and I'll arrange an appointment with John Roberts. He's a good friend as well as a good lawyer.' He paused and looked anxiously at Mark. 'You won't do anything hasty in the meantime, I hope?'

Mark forced a smile. 'No, father, I won't,' he lied. There was no point in involving his father in what he was now determined to do. In fact, he thought, the less Henry knew of his intentions the better, for he would only feel compromised and unhappy. If he needed any help, the man he would turn to would be Rory MacGregor.

Mark approached the meeting with the rest of his family with a feeling of excitement tinged with apprehension. His five years absence now seemed like a lifetime and he felt something of a stranger. Michael would be four years old now and his brother, Ralph, nearly seventeen, almost a man.

He felt a twinge of regret as he thought about Ralph. Even allowing for their age difference, they had never been really close in the way that he thought brothers aught to be, and this saddened him. For some inexplicable reason, he had blamed Ralph for his mother's death. It was an irrational feeling he knew, yet somehow it had lingered right through Ralph's early childhood at North Moor. Later, the feelings of reproach lessened but never quite died until Mark had married Jane. After that he saw little of Ralph and lost the opportunity to make up for the lost years. He wondered if it would now be too late.

It was only a short distance from the coal fitter's office to Ivison's old house, further along the quayside, where Henry and the family now lived, Mark noted that it was one of the few remaining houses that still served as a gentleman's residence. Most of the others had been converted to commercial use to cope with the expanding needs of trade and industry. Many of the wealthy merchants who once lived in the quayside had long since deserted the area for the more fashionable parts of the upper town.

'Not quite what it was twenty years ago, but I like it here,' Henry said, as if reading Mark's mind. 'Only a few of us left, though,' he went on. 'Most of the people with money have moved up into the town, especially around Westgate. Places like Hanover Square and Clavering Place, where they have a fine view up the river, and more recently to Charlotte Square.'

'You have a nice view of the river from here,' Mark said, pleased that his father had not succumbed to social climbing. 'I think you did the right thing to stay.'

'I'm glad you think so,' Henry beamed, pleased that his son approved.

As they walked past the Grey Horse Inn, a quaintly attractive and popular hostelry, Mark watched the scene of seemingly chaotic bustle. It was always like this, he remembered, with ships discharging and taking on cargo along the length of the quay, often lying two and three abreast.

As they neared Sandgate, Mark could see the fine old house that now belonged to his father. The two square oriels with their latticed casements, set one above the other on the first and second floors, stood out over the pavement and were supported by two graceful pillars which flanked the entrance. It was a beautiful and comfortable house, Mark thought, and he could see why his father had refused to move to the more fashionable parts of the town.

Mark was greeted at the door by a tearful Aunt Ellen who gave him a warm hug. This surprised him, making him feel guilty about his earlier remarks to Henry.

'My you've changed,' she said, wiping away the tears that threatened to trickle down her cheeks. 'Come in, both of you. I've got a lovely meal ready and everyone's dying to meet Mark.' She closed the door and followed them inside, clucking with happy chatter like a mother hen with her chicks.

Mark smiled at her. 'You must be psychic, Aunt Ellen. I'm absolutely starving.'

'I'm not a mind reader, Mark. Your father sent one of his clerks round to tell me you were home. That was nearly an hour ago,' she added, looking pointedly at Henry.

Mark intervened. 'I'm sorry, Aunt Ellen, it was my fault. I kept father talking too long. It was selfish of me.' He caught Henry's appreciative eye and gave a surreptitious wink in acknowledgement.

'Never mind, you're home now and that's all that matters,' Ellen responded, suitably mollified. 'The clerk brought your bag, Mark. It's up in your room if you want it. I've put a bowl of water and a clean towel out for you. Dinner will be ready in ten minutes, so don't be late,' she said, departing for the kitchen.

Henry grinned at Mark. 'I think you'd better do as you're told, like the rest of us.'

Dinner was served in the elegant first floor dining room which overlooked the river. The last of the evening sun shone through the large oriel window, casting shadowy patterns of the latticework onto the polished floor.

Standing at the window, Mark could see the clutter of ships moored alongside the quay, some of them still unloading even at this late hour. Across the river, the town of Gateshead rose steeply from the Hillgate Quay and he picked out the large square tower of St Mary's Church outlined against the evening sky. Absorbed in his thoughts, he did not hear his father enter the room.

'It's a lovely view, isn't it?' Henry said. 'One of the reasons why I didn't move up into town. '

Mark turned and smiled. 'I don't blame you. It must also be convenient living virtually over the shop, as it were.'

'Yes. Thirty years ago almost everyone did. Now, it's only the poorer tradespeople and nostalgic traditionalists like me.'

Mark's response was interrupted by the arrival of his brother, Ralph, closely followed by an agitated Aunt Ellen propelling a very shy four year old boy into the room. 'Go and say hello to your father,' she instructed.

Michael nervously approached his father and shyly held out his hand. 'How do you do, father,' he said in a formal, well-rehearsed voice.

Mark's first reaction was to sweep the boy up and give him a hug, but for some strange reason he refrained. Perhaps it was the look of apprehension in the child's eyes that held him back; he wasn't sure. Instead, he took the proffered hand and said, awkwardly, 'I'm very pleased to be home at last. I would have returned earlier to look after you, had I been able.' As he spoke the apprehension in the boy's eyes increased to something like terror and he turned and ran back to Aunt Ellen, clutching at her skirts.

There was an embarrassed silence which was quickly broken by Aunt Ellen saying, 'Dinner's ready, so if you'll sit yourselves down we can start serving.' As she spoke, two maids entered the room carrying dishes of hot food and the tension began to ease. Mark suddenly realised that any anxieties about his homecoming had not been confined to himself. The worried expression on his father's face when had greeted Michael confirmed that.

During the meal, Mark tried to study young Michael without making his interest too obvious. He saw that the child's eyes were blue and his hair the colour of light sand. He was reminded of Jane's golden tresses and laughing blue eyes and felt a twinge of grief clutch at his stomach. Glancing again and again at the boy during the meal, he could not detect any of the signs he was looking for. Young Michael, he thought, bore no resemblance to himself.

An air of expectancy, courteous and restrained, persisted during the meal and Mark realised that the polite conversation could barely hide his family's growing curiosity. It was Ralph whose patience was the first to break. 'Aren't you going to tell us what you've been doing these past five years, Mark?'

Mark smiled enigmatically at his brother and said, 'Fighting for and against King and country.'

'Doesn't that make you a traitor?' Ralph asked in surprise.

'Depends on your point of view, Ralph. I was taken prisoner by the Royal Navy when I was pressed into service against my will. After

524

fighting for England for nearly two years, some of it bloody and dangerous, I was taken prisoner by the Americans. When I learned that Jane was dead, I decided to fight for America. Now I'm an American citizen.'

'Under English law you could still be hung if you're caught.'

'Only if the authorities knew I fought for the Americans. I trust my own family won't tell them.'

'Of course not,' Ralph said, looking a little pained. 'I just wanted to point out the danger.'

'Now that the war's over, I doubt if the authorities would be interested in taking any action,' Henry interposed. He was uncomfortable with the way the conversation was leading and did not, in any way, regard Mark as a renegade. Indeed, he saw his son as something of a hero, having already listened to his escapades of the past five years.

'You're quite right, father,' Mark said. 'Unless, of course, someone forced the issue by making a formal complaint. To do that they would have to know what I was up to in America, so anything I tell you is in strict confidence.'

'And what were you up to?' Ralph asked, aching to know.

Mark looked slowly around the table, wondering just how much he should tell them. His eyes finally rested on his father, the only one, apart from himself, who knew the full story, and he saw encouragement in Henry's eyes. He decided to tell them almost everything, leaving out only what took place inside the cottage on the night he was captured. 'It's going to be quite a tale,' he said, 'and young Michael here is going to be fast asleep long before I'm finished.'

'You're quite right,' Aunt Ellen said, taking her cue. She turned to Michael and took his hand. 'It's getting late, dear, and long past your bedtime. Your father can tell you all about his travels in the morning.' With that she rose and led a tired and disappointed young Michael round the table to say goodnight to everyone, before gently ushering him out of the room. When she returned, the candles were lit and a bottle of port was on the table.

With the candlelight sending flickering shadows across the panelled walls, Mark began to recount his story. He started by telling of his

525

capture and handing over to the press gang, followed by an account of his subsequent service in the Royal Navy. There was anger in the telling at first, but this slowly died as he began to narrate his experiences in America with General Jackson. At this point, a subtle note of pride gradually crept into his voice.

Mark's audience were spellbound and it had grown quite late by the time his account was complete and all the questions had been answered. Ellen was now tired out by all the excitement and Henry felt equally drained by having to pretend surprise as Mark's story was retold to him. They both decided it was time to retire for the night, leaving the two brothers to continue their conversation. 'I expect you two have a lot to catch up on,' Henry said with a smile as he left the room.

Ralph, looking very surprised, waited for the door to close. 'It's the first time he's let me stay up this late, 'he said.

'Well, you'll be seventeen in a couple of weeks, won't you? When I was your age.....' Mark suddenly felt silly and stopped.

'I was working down the pit, fourteen hours a day,' Ralph completed with a grin. They both burst out laughing.

'How did you know I was going to say that?' Mark asked.

'Because I've heard it so often from father,' Ralph answered, still grinning.

'I didn't realise I was becoming so pompous in my old age. '

'You're not really that old,' Ralph said, 'or are you?' he added mischievously.

'Twenty-nine,' Mark said sternly, 'and don't you forget it.'

'You sound like the archetypical elder brother. Heavy-handed too, I might add.'

'Yes, I should have taken you in tow years ago.' Mark said looking fondly across the table at his brother. 'It's sad to think that I've wasted so many years neglecting our relationship, Ralph. The difference in our age was no excuse.'

'They say it matters less as you get older.'

'I hope you're right.'

'I'd like to put it to the test,' Ralph ventured shyly.

'So would I,' Mark responded.

526

The two brothers clasped hands across the table and a new and happier chapter in their relationship was about to begin.

CHAPTER 51

In the weeks that followed, Mark renewed his acquaintance with the old town of Newcastle, walking the streets each day as he contemplated his future. To his delight, he found the town as vibrant as ever, with a restless energy that seemed to pulsate through every street and market. It was also growing fast, chafing at the confines of the mediaeval walls with their massive, obsolete gates that now only served as a hindrance to traffic. Since his boyhood days twenty years ago, several gates had been demolished and he felt a sad ache of nostalgia that Pandon Gate, Close Gate, Sand Gate, Pilgrim Street Gate and the massive West Gate, had all disappeared for ever.

It was September before Mark finally found the courage to visit North Moor. He had postponed the decision many times afraid that, far from exorcising any ghosts, a visit would only stir up more unhappy memories. But his desire to see Jane's grave eventually overcame his fears and on a fine, autumnal morning, he hired a horse and headed north from Newcastle. After crossing Barrass Bridge, he turned right into the Longbenton road and feeling happier with his decision, spurred his horse into a canter.

After his long absence, the sight of North Moor Colliery unsettled Mark and as the memories, good and bad, came flooding back he began to feel tense and unhappy. The bad memories were quickly drowning out the few good ones leaving him feeling depressed and confused. He began to wonder if coming back had been such a good idea after all.

Approaching the village, he saw that the old, grim pithead looked strangely deserted. No smoke belched from the depths of the shaft and the winding gear was eerily still. The engine house presented a forlorn picture with the absence of escaping steam and the clanking and sighing of the beam engine.

As he drew closer, Mark saw that the old pit was now derelict and the shaft had been boarded in. Weeds were beginning to sprout in the raff-yard which had once rung to the sound of smiths, engine-wrights, joiners and masons. There were gaps in the weatherboarding of many of the old colliery buildings and the cracked beech rails of the disused waggonway ran like parallel scars through the overgrown cinder horse-track. The old pit had clearly been abandoned in favour of the two new shafts that had been sunk during the five years of his absence. He could see the headgear of the two new pits, about a mile or so to the east of the village.

Mark dismounted and led his horse across the raff-yard to the building that was once used to stable the waggonway horses. He tried the door and it swung open to his touch. He saw the long line of stalls and caught the faint, stale smell of horses which still lingered in the air. He led his horse inside and tethered it in one of the stalls before leaving and closing the stable door securely behind him. He did not want to draw attention to himself and a man on horseback was always a focus for curiosity in a pit village like North Moor. It would be more prudent to walk and he could pick up his mount on the way back.

The original cottages that were nearest to the old shaft had been badly built and poorly maintained. They now displayed the same forlorn, rundown appearance as the abandoned pit. Most of the houses immediately adjacent to the pithead were empty and the walls were starting to crumble. Mark could see that the village had expanded considerably, but all the new cottages had been built in a long, straggling line eastwards, following the new pits.

Mark noted that the condition of the houses improved the further he walked away from the old pithead and judging by the smoke coming from the chimneys, most of them were occupied. He passed the chapel that also served as a Sunday school and was pleased to see it was still lovingly maintained. Another fifty yards on and he came to the cottage where he had spent his early years in North Moor. It was now the home of young Jed and his family, according to Henry. He smiled to himself for still thinking of his brother-in-law as "young Jed". He must be turned twenty-four now, with a wife and two children.

The cottage next door to Jed's was still occupied by Wilf and Dora and her youngest son, Jim. The door was closed, so Mark quickly walked past and strode out for North Moor village and the churchyard where Jane was buried. He decided he would call on Dora on his way back, by which time Wilf, Jed and Jim would all have finished their shift at North Moor colliery.

There appeared to be no one around the churchyard as Mark drew near and he saw that the church door was closed. Slipping quietly inside the gate, he followed the well-trodden, tree lined path that wound its way through the churchyard. He remembered exactly where his mother was buried and he knew that Henry had laid Jane to rest in the adjoining grave. His heart began to beat a little faster as he approached the spot and saw the fine headstone that marked his mother's grave. His grief became bitter when he saw the small flat stone, which was all that Henry had been allowed to place on Jane's grave. It bore the simple inscription. Jane Standish, 1788-1811. Only Henry's substantial bribe had achieved this much for, in the eyes of the church, Jane had sinned against God by committing suicide.

Both graves were well tended and Mark suspected that Dora was a frequent visitor. He knelt down and said a silent prayer, for he felt this would have been the wish to both Jane and his mother. But he was not a true believer any more, for he had suffered too much to be able to sustain his faith. He reasoned that no loving, caring God could allow Roland's evil deeds to go unpunished; yet the man continued to prosper. He could come to terms with man's inhumanity to man in the heat of battle, but not acts of calculated cruelty aimed at inflicting maximum pain on the victim.

The sun was now quite warm and the dampness had gone from the grass. The churchyard was peaceful and the only sounds were the singing of the birds and muted animal sounds from a distant farmyard. But there was no peace in Mark's heart, only a growing hatred for the man responsible for Jane's death. After an hour spent by the graveside, he rose and left the churchyard by the same way he had entered.

It was still too early for Wilf and Jed to have finished their shift so Mark took the rough road that led to the cottage he had shared with Jane. It was situated about two miles from the village and as he drew near, his pace faltered. It was another ghost he felt he had to lay, yet his heart cried out for him to turn around and go back to North Moor. But some stubborn instinct made him carry on.

When the cottage came in sight it looked deserted. Walking up to the door, Mark saw that the house was empty and judging by the poor state of repair, he suspected that it had not been occupied since Jane's death. He went to the window, where he had been forced to watch her terrible ordeal, and found the anguish inside him almost too much to bear. Memories, vivid and real, came flooding back, searing his mind. It proved too much and he turned and ran back down the road, sobbing and almost blinded by his tears.

He found himself back at the church before he managed to control his emotions and self-consciously blew hard into his handkerchief. Driven now by instinct, he took the path that skirted North Moor Hall, peering through the screen of trees at the ornamental gardens which bordered the drive leading up to the great house. Suddenly, a horseman appeared riding from the Hall towards the gate. As the figure drew nearer, Mark saw that the rider was Roland Forster, and the anger that had been simmering inside him all day, finally boiled over.

It did not occur to Mark at first, as he walked back to North Moor Colliery, that the day's events had finally steeled his resolve to seek revenge. But gradually, the anger clarified his mind and he knew what he must now do. Subconsciously, he had programmed himself for retribution and North Moor was the most fitting place to bring this about.

As he entered the street leading to Dora's house, there were obvious signs of activity which indicated that the hewers were home from the pit. In every cottage, tired men were washing the coal dust from their bodies. Without warning, a door would open and a bucket of dirty soap-suds would be hurled out into the street. Mark grinned as he avoided an unwanted ducking. Little had changed, he thought. Pitmen had always had a fetish for cleansing themselves after every shift. It was as if the symbolic act of washing removed the stigma of their bondage for a short while.

There was a delighted scream of surprise when Dora answered his knock. 'I can't believe it,' she gasped. Then turning, she shouted inside, 'It's our Mark, Wilf. He's back home.'

'Then don't just stand there, woman,' Wilf shouted back. 'Bring the lad in.'

531

Wilf, stripped to his shorts, was towelling himself vigorously as he turned to greet his visitor and Mark felt the damp embrace of Wilf's fervent welcome. Then young Jim stepped forward and shyly shook his hand.

'I'd better slip next door and let Jed know you're here,' Dora said. 'My, he will be surprised.' With that she hurried out to pass on the good news.

Two minutes later, Jed came bursting in. 'Mark, me old marra! Welcome back.' He grinned broadly as he pumped Mark's hand. 'It's been five years; what have you been up to?'

Mark smiled back. 'It's a long story, Jed. Difficult to know where to begin.'

'Then you can sit down and tell us while you're eating,' Dora interceded. 'We're just about to have our dinner.'

Mark caught the aroma of meat and pastry and it brought back memories of his first meal at North Moor, eighteen years ago. 'Still making your delicious meat and potato pies eh, Dora?' he said, feeling his mouth starting to water in anticipation. He realised that it was seven hours since he had last eaten.

'Aye, and there's some singing hinny as well,' Dora added, pleased with Mark's compliment.

'Now that's an invitation I can't refuse,' Mark responded with a smile.

Everyone sat down at the table whilst Dora served up large portions of her mouth-watering pie. Then, with his eager audience hanging on every work, Mark again recounted his exploits in the Royal Navy and his subsequent experiences in America. He said little of the night he was taken at the cottage, for he knew the truth would be as painful to the Hindmarsh family as it had been to Henry, and would serve no useful purpose.

Later, over thick slices of singing hinny washed down with hot, sweet tea, the conversation turned to more general matters. No one mentioned Jane, or the manner of her death, but Mark sensed that she was in everyone's thoughts. It was as if the family were politely waiting for him to resolve the silent impasse by broaching the subject first.

Mark finally decided to break the ice. 'I'm grateful to you for tending the graves,' he said, turning to Dora.

'You've been to the churchyard, then?' she said in surprise.

'Yes, I went there this morning. It's a very peaceful spot.'

'I think so too. I go there every Sunday to tidy things up.'

'I'm glad you do, Dora. A graveyard must be a lonely place if nobody cares.'

'Jane has your mother to keep her company now,' Dora said blinking back a tear. She rose quickly and busily began clearing the table before disappearing into the lean-to at the back of the house. The faint sounds of her sobbing could be heard over the clatter of plates being placed in the wooden washing up tub.

There was an awkward silence before Mark spoke. 'From what I can see it looks as if the Forsters are prospering,' he said, changing the subject.

'Aye, thanks to the money that Roland's wife brought into the family.' Wilf said. 'She's a right tarter too, by all accounts,' he added. 'Insisted that Roland should be made a full partner before she'd part with a penny. Had it all drawn up legal like before they got married.'

'I bet that didn't please old Duncan Forster,' Mark said with a grin.

'No. But he needed the money and could see that Roland's wife was wearing the trousers - and still is, so they say.'

'Well, the money seems to have worked wonders for North Moor Colliery.'

'Saved Forster's bacon, I'd say. They were able to sink another shaft and go after the coal under the land they stole when the common was enclosed.'

'Was it successful?' Mark asked.

'Yes, but only after they'd sunk a hundred and fifty feet below the old pit levels?'

'Why was that?'

'The old pit had reached the fault line. So Forster decided to sink a shaft on the easterly side of the dyke where the borings showed a continuation of the high main.'

'And he was right?' Mark asked.

'Yes. He found the main again. Five feet thick and as good a quality as Wallsend. Duncan Forster's a bloody awful owner to work for, but he has a nose for coal.' There was a note of grudging respect in Wilf's voice.

'So where does Roland live now?' Mark asked.

'Still at Northmoor Hall,' Jed interjected. My wife's cousin works in the kitchen there, so we get all the gossip,' he explained. 'They say all his wife's money went into the partnership to save the pit when the workings hit the fault line. Couldn't afford a stylish place of their own so they stayed on at the Hall.'

The news sent a glow of anticipation through Mark. It meant that Roland was not just visiting the Hall when he had seen him that morning and having pinpointed his enemy, he could start planning his next move. 'I bet they're just one big happy family,' he said, sarcastically.

Jed laughed. 'According to my wife's cousin, they're always arguing up at the big house. Roland's still a womaniser and drinks too much. His wife knows it and so does his father, but neither of them can do much about it now that he's an equal partner.'

'Does he run North Moor pit?'

'No. He leaves that to old Wilkins. He's terrified of the pit and hasn't been underground since he was made partner.'

Mark smiled contemptuously. 'So nothing's changed since the explosion. His father had to horsewhip him below even then.'

'Aye, but there's been two more explosions since you've been away Mark,' Wilf cut in. 'Fifteen more widows and all of 'em evicted, save those that had kids of working age.'

'I thought it was agreed that widows could stay on,' Mark said angrily.

'The Forsters still run things and they do as they like. '

'And the Brotherhood did nothing?'

'There isn't a Brotherhood any more, Mark. The owners saw to that after you left.'

'I didn't leave, Wilf,' Mark corrected. 'I was taken.'

'I know, I didn't mean that,' Wilf said, becoming flustered. 'But without your leadership the Brotherhood just fell apart.'

Mark was appalled at the news. 'All those years of hard work wasted, just when the men were gaining their self-respect and confidence.' He spoke more in sorrow than in anger.

'It wasn't your fault, Mark. If anyone's to blame it's me and Sep for not holding the men together. We did try though.'

'If anyone's to blame it's the owners,' Mark retorted, his anger rising again. 'Why is it that men as evil as the Forsters continue to prosper?' Is there no hope for justice in this world?'

'They'll get their just deserts one of these days,' Wilf said, 'especially that arrogant young bastard Roland.'

'Indeed he will,' Mark agreed, speaking with icy determination. 'I fully intend to see that he does.'

Wilf and Jed looked startled at Mark's response but said nothing. The conversation gradually drifted to less contentious matters before it was time for Mark to leave. Wilf and Jed accompanied him back to the old pit where he had left his horse and when they reached the raff-yard, Mark turned to Wilf. 'No word of my visit to anyone,' he warned, 'you too, Jed,' he added.

They both nodded their agreement as if knowing what he had in mind.

'You'll be coming back though, won't you?' Jed asked.

'Yes, but I don't want to draw attention to myself so it will probably be an evening visit - after dark,' he added, to emphasise his point. An idea was beginning to take shape in his mind.

'You planning something?' Wilf enquired, seeing the look of concentration of Mark's face.

'Yes, but it's best you don't know the details.'

'Why.'

'Because the less you know, the less you're likely to be involved.'

But you want some help from us, Jed said, as if understanding Mark's intentions.

'Yes. I need some information about the pit.'

'Go on,' Wilf said. 'What do you want to know?'

'First, is the old pit still safe?'

Wilf and Jed exchanged puzzled glances. 'It's dry if that's what you mean,' Wilf said. 'The new workings are a hundred and fifty feet below the old seams so that water drains into the new pit and is pumped up from there.'

'What about firedamp?'

'I don't know. Some of the old workings were stopped off when the pillars were robbed years ago. Forster's kept the airways open in the rest because he plans to take out the remaining pillars, before closing the old pit off.'

'So it's connected to the new pits?' Mark said, his excitement rising.

'Yes, by a staple that runs down to the new workings. But the wastemen don't like working in the old pit because the airways aren't very good.'

'Is the old shaft still operational?'

'Depends what you mean by operational,' Wilf said, frowning. 'It's only been used for ventilation since the winding engine and the pumps were taken out.'

By now Jed was unable to control his curiosity. 'Why are you so interested in the old pit, Mark?'

Mark smiled enigmatically. 'Like I said before, the less you know the better.' Seeing Jed's disappointment he gently added, 'It's for your own good, Jed.'

Jed shrugged. 'Whatever you say, Mark.' His admiration for Mark had grown to hero-worship when they were trapper boys together, especially after the pit explosion. Without Mark, he knew he would never have got out alive. Over the years, the idolisation had diminished but the respect and friendship remained as strong as ever.

'I'm sure you'll let us know what you're up to in your own good time, eh Mark?' Wilf said, curbing his own curiosity.

'Yes, provided it doesn't compromise you in any way,' Mark answered cautiously.

'Then is there anything else we can do to help?' Wilf asked.

'Can you get me a plan of the old pit? It must have changed a bit since I last worked there.'

Wilf rubbed his chin thoughtfully. 'I'm not sure, but if I can't, I'll sketch one out for you. It didn't change that much after you left,' he added. 'The workings just moved further out from the old shaft until we hit the fault.'

536

This news pleased Mark and his confidence grew as he led his horse from the stable. 'I'd like to know what Roland's up to these days,' he said, trying to sound casual.

'In what way?' Wilf asked looking puzzled.

'His movements during and after work; where he goes, what days, times and that sort of thing.'

'He doesn't seem to spend much time at the pit, that's for sure. Mind you,' Wilf went on, 'we're underground most of the time and that's one place you'll never find our Mr Roland.'

'Spends most of his time with Mrs Alder when he's not fornicating in Newcastle,' Jed said, grinning wickedly at the thought.

'Who's Mrs Alder?' Mark asked.

'A very luscious young widow,' Jed said, his hands making enormous mound shapes on his chest.

Mark smiled. 'I see what you mean. He hasn't changed much, has he?'

Wilf blushed as he turned to Jed. 'How do you know all this?'

'Just gossip from below stairs at the Hall,' Jed replied.

'Your bloody cousin again,' Wilf snorted.

'It might be gossip but she's usually right,' Jed said, rising to the defence of his relative.

'That could be very useful,' Mark intervened. 'Do you know where Mrs Alder lives?'

'Forest House, I think. It's a big stone house on the Killingworth to Benton road.'

'Do you think you could find out how often Roland visits her and on what days? Also the days he goes into town?'

Wilf and Jed exchanged quizzical glances. They were now beginning to suspect what Mark was up to, but said nothing.

Mark decided to be as frank as he dared without compromising them. 'He's not going to get away with what he did,' he said quietly. 'I don't what to involve you, but I need your help.'

'We can't spy on the man, if that's what you mean,' Jed said. 'Not while we're working down the pit every day.'

'No,' Mark agreed, 'but your wife's cousin might be able to supply the information I need.'

Jed looked doubtful. 'I'm not sure that we should involve her, Mark.'

'You don't have to. Just try and draw the information from her as part of your family chat.'

Seeing that Jed was about to demure, Wilf intervened. 'What do you want to know, exactly?'

'I need to establish if there's any pattern in Roland's movements. That's all I ask.' Mark looked hard at both men, trying to will their support.

Wilf turned to Jed. 'That shouldn't be too difficult,' he said, forcing the issue. 'It's the least we can do after what Mark's been through and we owe it to Jane.'

'Aye, I suppose so,' Jed agreed. 'I'll see what I can do. '

As Mark led his horse past the old shaft, he stopped to examine the close boarding which surrounded it. He saw that there was a door which he assumed allowed entrance for any maintenance work that might be required until such time as the shaft was permanently sealed off. It would probably be locked but that would not be a major obstacle to what he had in mind. He decided he would take a closer look on his next visit.

Wilf seemed to read his mind. 'When will you be back, then?' he asked.

'In a couple of weeks,' Mark replied.

'A night visit?'

'Yes. Like I said, I don't want to attract too much attention to myself.'

Wilf nodded. 'I see what you mean.'

Jed held the horse's reins until Mark was safely in the saddle. 'You'd never make a cavalryman,' he said, noting Mark's lack of horsemanship.

'Just as well I was pressed into the navy and not the army, then,' Mark responded, smiling wryly.

Wilf stepped forward and placed his hand on the saddle. 'If you need any help when the time comes, you only have to ask,' he said quietly.

Mark realised that Wilf was now aware of his intentions and his offer to help meant that he also approved. 'Thank you,' he said, 'I appreciate your offer, but this is something I have to do myself.'

Wilf's eyes showed understanding. 'I'd feel the same myself in your position,' he said, 'but the offer still holds.'

'I know, Wilf, and I'm grateful. I'm proud to have you as a friend. Both of you,' he added, turning to Jed. With that, Mark nudged his horse's flanks and guided it out of the pit yard towards the Killingworth road.

The man standing in the shadows waited until Wilf and Jed had left the raff-yard before stepping out into the open. He wondered what the trio had been up to and his eyes narrowed as he contemplated the mystery. The horseman looked vaguely familiar but he could not quite place him. What was going on, he wondered. Perhaps he should mention this to Mr Forster.

Scratching his head in bemusement, the man continued his journey to the isolated cottage on the outskirts of the village where he lived. Keekers like Mulligan were the hated lackeys of the owners and, for their own safety, were forced to live like outcasts outside the pit communities on which they preyed.

CHAPTER 52

In the weeks that followed Mark's plans for his revenge began to take shape. He made several secret visits to North Moor Colliery and listened carefully to the information provided by Wilf and Jed making coded notes which would later be destroyed. A pattern was now emerging on Roland's movements and lifestyle, the significance of which caused Mark to smile with quiet satisfaction.

It was clear that Roland still hated and feared the pit and, seemingly, went to great lengths to avoid going underground. On the few occasions that he did, it was on the insistence of his father, Duncan Forster, whose increasingly ill-tempered and despotic behaviour brooked no argument. Roland feared his father's wrath more than his own terror of being underground.

Early in December Mark visited North Moor Colliery again to put the finishing touches to his plan of action. He carried with him a special lock picking tool which he had obtained from a rather disreputable character recommended by Rory. 'Used to be a locksmith but found thieving more profitable,' Rory had informed him with a sly grin.

Arriving at the disused old pit, Mark made his way carefully across the deserted, weed grown yard to the empty stables, taking care not to be seen. Then, after stabling his horse, he walked over to the elevated weather-boarded shed which enclosed the old pit shaft and the adjoining coal screens. The building had been secured to keep out trespassers and the heavy wooden access door was locked. After checking to make sure he was not being watched, Mark set to work on the door lock using his newly acquired tool. The lock yielded with surprising ease and he went inside, carefully closing the door behind him.

After a few moments Mark's eyes became accustomed to the gloom inside. He could see the stout beams supporting the winding gear which rose to pierce the roof through the open section directly above the shaft. From the last of the evening light which filtered through the gap Mark could see that there was no rope attached to the pulleys. No doubt the heavy, valuable rope had been removed when the shaft was closed and the winding engine taken out for use in another pit. Disappointment overwhelmed him. Without access to the shaft bottom his plans were doomed.

Mark's dismay quickly gave way to relief when he spotted the block and tackle arrangement that must have been installed as a temporary measure to allow access to the shaft for inspection and maintenance.

The block and tackle was attached to a stout beam fixed across the shaft so that the banksman could lean on it to pull in a corfe of coal for unloading. An empty wicker corfe was attached to the huge coil of light rope leading to the pulley arrangement. Mark knew that the corfe, some three feet in diameter and over two feet deep, was designed to hold six hundredweight of coal. It would easily take the weight of two men.

Unslinging the large canvas satchel from his shoulders, he took out a small lantern, a length of thin line and a tinderbox. After completing the tedious process of kindling a flame, he transferred it to the candle inside the lamp, then tied one end of the line to the brass hook on the top of the lamp.

Using the beam for support, Mark lowered the lantern into the shaft and noted that the wooden brattice which divided it into the upcast and downcast sections, and the wooden tubbing which lined the shaft, were still in good condition. Being an old shaft, it was only some ten feet in diameter, but with the pumping and winding engines removed, it was not the cramped, fume choked pit that had struck terror into him when he had first descended its hellish depths as a boy. It must have been closed for almost ten years, he recalled, and was probably only being maintained for ventilation purposes and in the hope that coal from the pillars supporting the roof might be worked at some future date.

Satisfied with his examination of the top part of the shaft, Mark hauled up the lantern and placed it on the ground. Next, he picked up several large lumps of coal and threw them into the corfe tied to the block and tackle. Satisfied that there was enough ballast he took hold of the trailing rope and pushed the corfe into the shaft, allowing it to descend to the bottom.

When the trailing rope cased running through the blocks, he checked the amount of rope left at the surface. He guessed that less than half remained which meant that the block and tackle winding arrangement could not be operated from both ends of the shaft by one man.

Undeterred, Mark search around for a heavy piece of wood and tied it to the tail end of the remaining rope. He then threw the rope down the shaft. When the rope settled and hung taut, he tied his handkerchief around the rope by the block and tackle. Then hauling on the trailing rope until it slackened off on hitting the bottom of the shaft, he could measure how much additional rope he would need. He had guessed right. The rope was about thirty yards short.

Mark hauled up the corfe and replaced everything as he had found it. He cut a small piece from the end of the rope coil so that he could match the diameter with the new length of rope he would bring on his next visit. Splicing it on wouldn't be a problem, thanks to two years in the Royal Navy

It was now almost dark and only a pale, grey smudge marked the opening in the roof above the shaft. Mark looked at his watch and decided it was time to go. He crossed over to the door and, after snuffing out the candle, replaced the lantern and line inside his satchel. Locking the door behind him he paused, waiting for his eyes to adjust to the night.

It was completely dark when Mark left the pit yard and made his way towards the lights of the village. Arriving at Wilf's cottage, he knocked gently on the door and went inside, grinning as he caught the startled look on the faces of Wilf and Dora. 'I told you I'd be back for another slice of singing hinny,' he said, as Dora enveloped him in a welcoming hug.

'He only comes when he wants feeding,' Wilf retorted.

The room was warm and muggy. Heat from the banked up fire met the rising damp, causing condensation to form on the cold, whitewashed walls which glistened in the reflected light of the flames.

Dora placed three cups on the table and a plate of singing hinny. 'Sit yourselves down,' she ordered, as she poured hot water into the teapot from the large black kettle that was kept simmering by the fire. 'I'll just slip over to our Jed's and tell him you're here,' she said, smiling at Mark. 'I'll stay and keep Beth company, so you three can have a chat among yourselves.' With that, she disappeared through the back door leaving a draft of cold air to mark her departure.

Mark looked questioningly at Wilf. 'Sounds as though Dora thinks we're up to something?'

'Aye. She's an intuitive woman,' Wilf answered tactfully. 'Mind you, I haven't told her anything,' he added pointedly, seeing the look on Mark's face.

'There's nothing to tell, is there?' Mark countered.

A crooked smile crossed Wilf's face. 'If you say so, Mark, but Dora isn't the only one with intuition.'

Another cold blast of air announced Jed's arrival. He stood at the open door beaming at Mark.

'Come in and shut the bloody door before we all freeze to death,' Wilf snapped.

Jed grinned and closed the door. 'Somebody's in a right bad fettle,' he said, winking at Mark as he crossed to shake hands. 'I hope you rode out on that nag of yours, Mark. It's not a night to be walking back to Newcastle.'

'I keep telling you, Jed. It's not my horse. I hire it from the livery stable. I've left it at the old pit yard, safe from prying eyes.'

'I don't know why you're so secretive,' Jed complained. 'You've every right to come and go as you please.'

'He has his reasons,' Wilf cut in. 'Just leave it at that and drink your tea before it gets cold.'

Mark smiled his appreciation at Wilf. 'Any more news?' he asked.

'Aye,' Wilf responded. 'A bit of good and a bit of bad – depending, of course, on how you look at it.

'The good news?' Mark enquired.

'I've got a plan of the old pit workings.' Wilf delved into his pocket and took out a folded sheet of paper which he began to unfold on the table in front of him. 'There, plan of the old pit,' he said proudly. 'That's what you wanted.'

Mark could hardly hide his delight. What had seemed a simple request had proved to be far more difficult than any of them had thought. 'Where did you get it?' he asked.

'From old Sep,' Wilf replied. 'George Wright was killed when the waste fired last week. Sep's been made wasteman in his place.'

Mark received the news with a mixture of sadness and concern. A wasteman's job was to inspect the airways and galleries of the worked out area of the pit and keep them safe and in good order. It was a task usually given to older, more reliable men with years of good pit experience behind them – men like George and Sep. But it could also be highly dangerous, as George had found to his cost. In switching from hewing, Sep was taking on a less arduous job, but one that was considerably more hazardous.

'Sounds as though the old pit's in a bad way,' Mark said. 'Is that the bad news you mentioned earlier?'

Wilf nodded, 'Aye. It's riddled with blowers and full of firedamp. They've had to seal off some of the workings on the north side – that's where George was killed. Your father was right, Mark. Forster took out too much coal in the first working. The pillars that are left are not strong enough. The creep's pushing up the hill and causing more blowers.'

'Then why was the pit left open?' Mark asked. 'Surely it would have been cheaper to have it laid-in?'

'Forster still thinks he can take out more coal by robbing the pillars.'

'Not if there's creep in the workings,' Mark said. 'Too bloody dangerous.'

'Pitmen's lives mean nowt to Forster,' Wilf said caustically.

'How do the wastemen get into the old workings? There's no winding gear at the old shaft.'

Wilf smiled. 'You've had a look, then?'

'Yes, on my way in.'

'Thought you might.' Wilf's finger pointed to the plan. 'There's a stable here that heads down to the new pit workings, which are a hundred and fifty feet lower on the other side of the fault. The stable connects the two pits and there's a ladder inside the shaft which the wastemen use. '

'Interesting,' Mark said, staring thoughtfully at the plan.

'I don't know what's in your mind, Mark, but I'd keep well away from the old pit if I were you. Sep reckons it's ready to fire anytime. They've built a door to seal off the staple until the gas clears.'

'Does Sep think it will clear?'

544

Wilf shrugged. 'It might if the atmospheric conditions are right. No one's bothered that much since they've put in a door to stop the gas seeping through the staple into the new workings.'

Mark was dismayed at the news, for the gas could seriously jeopardise his plan. He knew that changes in atmospheric pressure could work wonders with pit ventilation, but it was something he could not rely on. He saw Wilf's enquiring look and decided to change the subject. 'Roland still calling on that rich widow?' he asked, looking at Jed.

'Every Friday night, regular as the church clock,' Jed said, 'but he doesn't just call on her,' he added with a lewd grin.

'Do you know what time he leaves?'

'Aye, just before ten o'clock.'

Mark looked surprised. 'How can you be so precise?'

'Because our luscious young widow gives her maid the night off, but she has to be back at the house by ten. The other servants don't live in, you see.'

'I do see,' Mark said. 'No prying eyes. But how can you be so certain that Roland leaves just before ten o'clock?' he persisted.

Jed sighed and began to explain. 'The maid is a friend of my wife's cousin. They lived next door to each other in North Moor before starting in service together. They still keep in touch and exchange gossip. The maid has a boyfriend who works at Killingworth pit, and he walks her home every Friday night.'

'And?' Mark insisted, his patience wearing thin.

'They have to wait around kissing and cuddling until Roland goes home, don't they? Just before ten o'clock, like I told you,' Jed added peevishly.

'Thank you,' Mark said, giving Jed a weary smile.

'Mind you,' Jed went on, ignoring Mark's hint of sarcasm, 'our Mr Roland doesn't keep such civilised hours on Saturdays. Lucky if he's home by dawn some weeks, and so drunk he can hardly stay on his horse.'

This was the final confirmation that Mark needed. He now had a choice of two nights for the execution of his plan. In some respects, he thought, Saturday night might prove the easiest, in that Roland would be drunk and less capable of defending himself. On the other hand, it

545

would mean a long wait and, being Saturday, a greater chance that other revellers might be using the road. No, it would have to be a Friday, he concluded and having made the decision, felt a little happier. But the gas in the old pit still worried him.

On his return to Newcastle, Mark studied the plan of the abandoned workings and pondered long and hard on the unexpected problem of firedamp in the old pit. He recalled that the terrifying explosion which he had experienced as a trapper boy, had been to the north of the main pit roadway, but in the intervening years much would have changed. And with creep setting in, the pit would be even more dangerous and unpredictable anyway. He put the plan away and wondered whether he should abandon his scheme altogether, or go ahead and take the risk.

In December the old Assembly Room in the Groat Market was crowded for the demonstration of George Stephenson's safety lamp to the Literary and Philosophical Society. Many prominent members of the coal trade were present, including some leading coal owners and colliery viewers.

Mark was impressed by the confident demeanour of Stephenson who, after overcoming his initial nervousness, displayed a level of self-assurance bordering almost on arrogance. Stephenson's dialect was stronger than Mark had expected and this was probably why he allowed his young friend Nicholas Wood, an apprentice viewer at Killingworth colliery, to explain the workings of the lamp - afraid perhaps that such a distinguished audience might not fully comprehend his own rough speech.

Nicholas Wood began the presentation, using bladders of gas to demonstrate the effectiveness of the lamp. George Stephenson stood by, silent at first, but increasingly intervening as his impatience with Wood's performance mounted. Eventually, he took over the presentation himself. Not a man to hide his light under the proverbial bushel, Mark concluded.

Afterwards, Mark waited while Henry talked to a group of business acquaintances. After a few minutes the discussion suddenly became quite heated and Mark could see that his father was struggling to hold his anger in check. He was about to intervene but changed his mind when the conversation returned to normality. When Henry detached himself from the group and made for the door, Mark followed.

'What was that all about?' he asked when they were outside.

'The Sir Humphry Davy faction says the man's a charlatan,' Henry said.

Mark looked puzzled, 'Which man?'

'Stephenson, of course.'

'What makes them say that?'

'He's an uneducated pit worker with no knowledge of chemistry. They think he's stolen Sir Humphry Davy's ideas and passing them off as his own.'

'That's a very serious accusation, father. I hope they have some proof.'

'Seemingly his ideas weren't working and his first two prototype lamps were failures.'

'That isn't proof, surely.'

'No, but there's some pretty damning evidence against him, even if it is only circumstantial.'

'Such as?'

'Let me explain,' Henry said. 'While you were away, Mark, there was a terrible explosion at Felling Colliery in which ninety-two men and boys died in the most horrendous way. Afterwards, a society was formed to look at ways of preventing explosions in mines. Two prominent churchmen, Dr Gray and the Reverend Hodgson, are members of the society's committee and they persuaded Sir Humphry to try and find a solution to the problem. Within two months he'd found the answer with his invention of a new safety lamp.'

'So, seemingly, has George Stephenson,' Mark observed.

'Yes, but the sudden success of his third prototype, the one he demonstrated tonight, looks suspicious to the Davy faction.'

'Why's that?'

'On the 30th October, Sir Humphry wrote to Gray and Hodgson, enclosing to both a paper outlining the results of his research into the problem. He asked them to treat his findings as confidential. In spite of this, some manuscript copies of the letter were circulated to a small number of viewers. On the 9th November, Sir Humphry read his paper detailing his discoveries to the Royal Society and so, must have established priority for his invention.' Henry paused, looking challengingly at Mark. 'Don't you agree?'

Mark nodded. 'I suppose so.'

'Well, on the 10th November, I attended a public meeting of the coal trade in Newcastle. Hodgson was there and he read out Sir Humphry's paper to the meeting. Said it was no longer confidential as the newspapers had already published news of Sir Humphry's success. And who else do you think was at that meeting?'' Henry paused to give dramatic effect to his revelation. 'Stephenson's supporters, of course. Only then did it become public knowledge that Stephenson was also experimenting with a safety lamp.'

'It has been known for two people to have been working on the same invention at the same time, father.' Mark did not see the matter in the same dramatic terms as Henry did.

'I agree, but we heard tonight that Stephenson's first and second lamps were unsuccessful. Yet within weeks of details of Davy's lamp being made public Stephenson had his third lamp made exactly along the principles outlined in Sir Humphry's paper. A coincidence? I think not, Mark.'

By now they had reached the house on the Quayside and Henry had settled into a mood of quiet frustration. Mark could not quite understand why his father was so concerned. It did not seem to matter who invented the safety lamp, as long as it reduced the danger of explosions that were ever present in the deep, fiery pits of the great northern coalfield.

As he lay in bed that night, Mark's concern was not about who invented the safety lamp, but how soon he could lay his hands on one.

CHAPTER 53

The New Year celebrations to mark the start of 1816 were marred by atrocious weather. A rapid thaw accompanied by strong winds and heavy rain, caused the Tyne to flood. The quayside was inundated and several ships broke their moorings. Many cellars in the lower part of the town were flooded and Henry bemoaned the loss of much food and drink that had been stored beneath his own house.

At supper a few days later, Henry was in an expansive mood. A bottle of vintage port which had been rescued from the flooded cellar was now being ceremoniously passed round the table.

Ralph cast a questioning glance at Mark who returned a baffled shrug. 'Are we celebrating something father?' he asked. Henry smiled enigmatically. 'I suppose we are, in a way.'

'Exactly what are we celebrating then' Ralph persisted.

Henry paused for effect, his expression still irritatingly obtuse. 'I've entered into a new partnership,' he said. 'We're going to reopen Walker Colliery.'

'But Walker pit is all worked out,' Mark said. 'It was closed five years ago.'

'I know,' Henry answered, 'but Thomas Barnes was a good viewer. He left half the coal in pillars to safeguard his men. Now, because of Sir Humphry Davy's safety lamp, we can reopen the mine and rob the pillars without the risk of an explosion.'

'Are the new safety lamps ready?' Mark asked in surprise.

'Yes. The first batch is on its way and should be delivered later this week.'

'Then it could prove to be a very profitable investment, father. You could recover thousands of tons of good quality coal at very low cost.'

Mark felt a rising excitement. His last remaining problem might now be solved if he could borrow one of his father's safety lamps.

Henry misread the look the Mark's face for interest in the new project. 'Problem is,' he said, 'I'm getting too old for all this extra work and responsibility. I need a new partner, someone who can take over the reins in due course.'

'Young Ralph's your man surely. It's his last term at Bruce's Academy and he's keen to join you.'

Henry looked crestfallen. 'And so he shall but I'd hoped, now that you've come home that you might....' His voice trailed off in embarrassment and dismay.

'I'm sorry, father, but I must return to America,' Mark said gently. 'I would like to stay in England but you know that's not possible.'

The awkward silence that followed was broken by Ralph. 'I've got some preparation to do for school, tomorrow. If I may be excused, I'll go to my room.'

Henry nodded absently and Ralph quickly made his exit.

A long silence ensued before it was finally broken by Henry. 'What makes you so certain that you can't stay in England?'

Mark sighed. 'Because I was officially serving my country, even though I was pressed into the Royal Navy. During the war against the United States of America I was taken prisoner and chose to join the American army and fight against my own people. That made me a traitor, father. If found guilty, I could be executed.'

'But there were mitigating circumstances,' Henry protested.

'Do you really think Duncan Forster would acknowledge that? He would move heaven and earth to have me arrested and charged to protect his son. I could be the perfect solution to his problem if he knew I was back in England and he is a Magistrate with considerable influence.'

Henry looked utterly dejected. 'So you're determined to go back to America then?'

'Yes, father. I have a lot at stake and I can't leave everything to Jack my partner. There's two thousand acres of land to clear, a house to be built and a crop to plant.'

'What will you grow?'

'Cotton mainly. It's a good cash crop.'

'Isn't that risky? I thought you needed a special soil and climate for cotton.'

'You do for the long staple sea-island variety but not for the short staple plant.

'Is there much difference?'

Mark laughed. 'A lot, the difference between success and failure. The long staple can only be grown in very limited lowland areas but the short can be grown almost anywhere in the South. At one time, short staple cotton was not commercially profitable because of the high cost of separating the fibre from the seeds. But back in '93, a fellow named Ely Whitney invented a cheap cotton gin that reduced the cost of separation fifty-fold. So now, everybody's planting short staple cotton all over the South. Cotton mania, they call it. The nearest thing to Southern gold.'

Henry's interest quickened. 'With two thousand acres you should make a fortune.'

'Perhaps, but first a lot of work needs to be done and a good deal of money will have to be invested.'

'Perhaps I can help?'

'You have enough problems without taking on mine.'

Henry did not pursue the matter. Instead he made a mental note to look into the cotton trade. There could be some profitable avenues to explore in such a rapidly expanding market. 'You'll be taking Michael with you to America?' he asked, suddenly changing the subject.

The question caught Mark unawares and it was some time before he replied. 'I don't think so,' he said eventually. Then, seeing the look on Henry's face, he added, 'You seem surprised?'

'I am. I thought you'd want him to live with you in America. After all, he is your son.'

Mark's eyes turned bleak as he looked at his father. 'If he was my son, then yes, I'd take him with me when I return to America. But I'm not sure that Michael is my son.'

'But surely...' Henry's voice faltered, 'Michael is Jane's child. Surely that must mean something?'

Mark sighed in his frustration. 'Yes, and I'll always love him for that. But that's only half the love I can guarantee him and I'm desperately afraid that the other half might turn sour. Don't you see, he might grow up looking more like Roland and less like Jane - a constant reminder of...,' he broke off, trying to control his emotions. 'I don't think I could live with that,' he added flatly.

Henry struggled hard to find an appropriate response, but nothing came and he remained silent.

'You have to understand,' Mark persisted, 'the boy is better off living here with the family he knows and loves. It would break his little heart if I took him away now. Besides, there's no school back in Alabama - indeed, there may not even be a house, yet!'

Henry could now see the logic of Mark's argument. 'I suppose you're right,' he said, 'but you do realise that when he's older, he will want to make his own decisions?'

Mark gave a wan smile. 'Of course I do. He'll always be welcome if he wants to come to America.'

'He may want more than that, one day.'

Mark looked long and hard at Henry. 'I'll try to be a father to him if that's what he eventually wants,' he said. 'But God forbid that he ever learns the truth.'

The following morning Mark checked the state of the tide before leaving the house. He made his way eastwards along the Quayside and entered Sandgate's teaming, warren of narrow chares which formed the keelmen's citadel. If he had judged the tide correctly, Rory would now be at home.

Running eastwards, and parallel to the main street of Sandgate, was the Low Way which followed the bank of the river. It was a narrow street with even narrower chares branching off left and right. Some of the houses on the right backed on to the river and Rory had moved here for greater safety after his release from prison. A secret escape route led through concealed openings in the roofs to the house at the end of the row. This house had a balcony at the rear which overhung the river, with steps leading down to the water. A boat or keel was always kept moored there in case of emergency. Rory knew his free spirit would never survive another long incarceration.

Arriving at Rory's house, Mark knocked on the door and waited, catching a faint scent of the river before it was quickly overpowered by the yeasty odour from the adjacent Tyne Brewery. He heard Fiona's cautious voice behind the door and called out, reassuringly, 'It's me, Mark. I've come to see Rory.'

The heavy bolts were drawn and as the door opened, Fiona's anxious face broke into a welcoming smile. 'Come in Mark. Rory's expecting you. You'll want to be alone so I'm off to visit Colin.' Flashing him a quick smile she turned and walked away.

It was Mark's first visit to the house and the main living room was surprisingly larger than he had expected. A ladder led up to the loft space which he assumed was used as a bedroom.

Rory rose from his chair by the large range and greeted Mark with a firm handshake. 'Welcome, bonnie lad. You've come to collect, I expect?'

'If you managed to get what I asked for.' There was a trace of anxiety in Mark's voice.

'An unusual request, my friend, most unusual,' Rory said, stooping to reach under the table. He pulled out a hessian sack and dropped it in front of Mark. There was the sound of clinking metal as the bag hit the floor. 'Brings back memories,' Rory said bitterly.

Mark was mortified by his tactlessness. 'I'm sorry, Rory,' he stuttered. 'I should have known better when I asked for your help, but it didn't occur to me at the time.'

Rory laughed at Mark's discomfort. 'Only teasing you, bonnie lad, but I hope you have a better use for them than I had.'

'I have indeed, I assure you.'

'Care to enlighten me?'

'Best if I don't Rory. I don't want to leave any incriminating evidence pointing your way.'

'You can rest assured there's no chance of that,' Rory's indomitable confidence was back. 'But if you need any more help.....' He left the rest unsaid.

'I know and I appreciate that. But it's my fight, something I must do alone.'

The look on Rory's face reassured Mark that he knew and fully understood.

On Friday, Mark woke with a start from a troubled sleep, his body damp with perspiration and his mind still chasing the confused shadows of half remembered dreams. Shivering in the cold morning air, he pulled up the covers and lay staring at the darkened ceiling, trying to concentrate his thoughts on his plans for the crucial day that lay ahead.

The pale light of a wintry dawn showed patches of frost on the bedroom window and he felt reluctant to rise. In the past, he had faced many difficult dawns - the tense prelude before an action, crouched over a cannon on a crowded gun deck, or waiting for the order to fire on the field of battle with General Jackson's army. Worse still were the unwanted dawns that heralded grief filled days, alone and far from home. But then, he had been trapped in an environment of iron discipline and so could not run away from his fears. Now, he was his own man and free to choose within the dictates of his conscience. And he knew that only his personal resolve, stoked up by his hatred of the man who had destroyed his life, could motivate his actions on this fateful day.

Thrusting all thoughts of failure from his mind, Mark rose and quickly washed and dressed before going downstairs to join the family for breakfast. Soon afterwards, Henry left to attend to some business at the Exchange and Ralph rushed off to Bruce's Academy in Percy Street. It was a frustrating two hours later when Aunt Ellen announced she was going to visit the Flesh market and would be taking young Michael with her. This meant Mark would now have the house to himself for at least an hour.

He waited for ten minutes before opening the cabinet where Henry had placed the new safety lamps. They were part of a batch that Sir Humphry Davy had sent from London for testing in the local collieries. After carefully removing one of the lamps from its protective box, he placed it on the table for examination. Inside the box he also found a handwritten note explaining the workings of the lamp and how it should be used.

The lamp itself consisted of a circular copper cistern which contained the oil and wick. On top of this, a close-topped cylinder was fitted, about eight inches high, made of fine wire-gauge containing seven hundred and forty apertures to the square inch. This provided a cover that was permeable to light and air but impermeable to flame. Should any gas be ignited by the lamp, the excellent heat conduction of the wire-gauge would cool the internal flame to a level below the ignition point of the external gases. In effect, the flame would be quenched by the wire-gauge.

The lamp also acted as a crude warning device against the dreaded firedamp. In the presence of explosive gas, the flame would become surrounded by a large blue aureole as the indrawn gas combusted on entry. This gave the miner a clear visual warning of any danger. Mark smiled in appreciation at the ingenious simplicity of Davy's invention.

Returning the safety lamp to its protective box, he placed it in a large canvas satchel together with a tinder box, a bottle of lamp oil, six candles, a small brass compass and a large canteen of drinking water. Going to the kitchen, he added a loaf of bread and half a cheese before picking up the hessian sack given to him by Rory and leaving the house.

Slinging the bulging satchel over his shoulder and carrying the sack under his arm, he made his way along to a stable recommended by Rory for being discreet about its customers. Probably another one of his disreputable associates, Mark thought. After mounting the horse provided he rode slowly out of the yard with his satchel slung over his back and the sack hung across the front of his saddle.

Turning off the busy Shields turnpike and onto the narrow North Moor road, the traffic became much lighter. As the evening dusk settled in, the landscape slowly deepened into ever lengthening shadows. By the time he reached the old pit at North Moor it was almost dark, exactly as he had planned it.

After leaving his horse in a stall at the old pit stables, he carried the satchel and sack across the yard to the elevated pithead building and up the ramp that led from the base of the screens to the entrance. Taking the lock-pick from his pocket he quickly opened the double doors that gave access to the old pit shaft and moved carefully inside, closing the doors behind him.

Inside, it was almost dark and his fingers searched inside the satchel for the tinder box and the candles. After some brisk work with the flint and steel he kindled a small flame and quickly lit a candle. Then, after checking the flame for any tinges of blue that would indicate the presence of gas, he lit two more candles and placed them strategically around the pit shaft.

Next, he opened the sack and took out the two lengths of chain, each with a manacle attached to one end, and placed them in the basket attached to the temporary winding gear and began lowering it down the shaft for a test run. He needed one last check to be sure there were no obstructions that might scupper his plans. At just over seven hundred feet, the rope slackened as the weighted corfe reached the bottom of the shaft. With a sigh of relief, Mark hauled the corfe back up, leaving it suspended at the top of the shaft.

Finally, he took out the safety lamp from his satchel and after filling the reservoir with oil, lit the wick with one of the candles. Satisfied that the lamp worked well, he extinguished the flame and placed it in a convenient spot just behind the door along with the satchel. Then, he snuffed out all the candles except one, which he left burning in the most shaded place he could find. Hopefully, it would still be burning when he returned and he would not have to perform the tedious ritual with the tinder box in the dark.

Locking the doors behind him, Mark crossed the yard to the disused stables. His horse whinnied in anticipation as he led it outside before mounting and riding off in the direction of Benton and Forest House. He could only hope that Roland would not deviate from his lustful habits and keep his Friday night tryst with the young Widow Alder.

The place carefully chosen by Mark to carry out his ambush seemed ideal. It was a stretch of road that was narrow and straight, with a small plantation of trees on each side growing close to the road. He took up a position that provided perfect concealment, whilst allowing him a clear view of the road for a hundred yards in each direction.

It was a cold night with scudding clouds intermittently blocking out the faint light of a waning moon. Mark had left his horse tethered deep inside the trees behind him and well out of sight. It was also downwind of the road which he hoped would prevent its scent from being picked up by Roland's mount. He knew that complete surprise would be essential for the smooth and successful execution of his plan.

After making sure that his horse was both secure and content, he had returned to the roadside, carrying with him a length of thin rope, a stout wooden stave and two short lengths of strong cord. He tied one end of the rope to a tree on the opposite side of the road and led it back to his place of concealment. After stretching it tight, he adjusted its height above the road's surface until he was satisfied that it was right for what he had in mind. Noting the optimum height and angle, he carefully lowered the rope until it lay flat across the thick layer of rotting leaves that covered the road's surface. Using his foot, he spread some of the leaves over the rope until it was buried from sight, then returned to his hiding place.

Content at last, he settled down to wait for Roland.

The sound of loud voices and peals of ribald laughter slowly penetrated Mark's drowsy mind, jerking him back to full consciousness. Startled at first, then angry with himself for having dozed off, he concentrated his eyes in the direction of the noise. After a few moments, he picked out the silhouettes of two men progressing slowly along the road towards him, weaving erratically from side to side. With a feeling of relief, he realised that it was only two revellers returning home from the local tavern and somewhat the worse for drink. But, he chided himself, it could have been Roland and he might have slipped by without his knowing. From now on, he decided firmly, he would remain fully alert.

The night grew colder and Mark felt a numbness seeping into his body. Afraid to move, all he could do was to rise from time to time and quietly stamp his feet and flap his arms about in an attempt to keep his muscles from seizing up altogether. Occasionally, when the waning moon broke free from its cloud cover, he was just able to discern the position of the pointers on his watch. At the last check, they indicated ten o'clock - the time when Roland should be leaving Forest House. He guessed it was now about ten fifteen, so his quarry would soon be approaching the trap. His hatred rose to swell the excitement he felt, as the time for his revenge drew near.

Any lingering doubts in Mark's mind, as to the justness of his actions, were now extinguished. His hatred for the man who had deliberately caused him so much suffering completely obliterated any thoughts of absolution. He could neither forgive nor forget. As the minutes ticked by, his excitement intensified and with it, paradoxically, came a cold, calculating calmness born of the conviction that what he was about to do was right, even though it was unlawful.

An eerie silence had now settled over the deserted road. It was as if it too, had closed down for the night, allowing the nocturnal creatures of the wood free passage. Mark began to wonder if Roland had changed his routine and a feeling of disappointment and failure began to well up inside him. Nervous tension had wound him up like a spring and as the prospect of Roland's appearance began to wane, the resulting anti-climax left him feeling foolish and despondent.

He was on the point of leaving when he heard the distant sound of hoof beats coming towards him along the road. Suddenly, he was taut with anticipation again, straining his eyes in the direction of the sound as he desperately tried to recognise the approaching horseman. The clouds cleared momentarily, exposing the road to a weak glimmer of moonlight. This seemed to act as a signal to the rider, who spurred his horse into a trot as if expecting trouble. As the horse drew nearer, Mark recognised the man in the saddle. It was Roland Forster.

Mark froze. It was as if an evil, ghostly presence had suddenly manifested itself in front of him and the horse was almost past before he reacted. Pulling hard on the rope, he rose and keeping the line taut, he aimed it just above the head of the passing horse. Half drunk and still satiated with vivid memories of his night of sexual abandonment, Roland was relaxed and off guard. The rope caught him over his shoulders and slid up tight across his neck, dragging him out of the saddle like a cork being drawn from a bottle. He fell heavily, cracking his head on the road which cut short his cry of alarm.

'Touché,' Mark murmured, elated at his success and remembering how his own attempted escape all those years ago had been thwarted in such a similar manner. It was why he had planned it this way; a form of poetic justice. But the covering of dead leaves had lessened the effect of Roland's fall and he tried to sit up, emitting a low moan as he did so.

The moan was quickly cut short as Mark sprang across the road and delivered a vicious blow with his stave to Roland's head. He watched, ready to strike again, as his victim fell back and lay with his face upturned towards the night sky. As if on cue, the moon again broke free from the scudding clouds to reveal the prone, unconscious figure in its sickly light. A thin trickle of blood ran down the side of Roland's forehead and around his ear before dripping onto the leaf strewn ground.

Roland's horse had not bolted, but stood patiently waiting some twenty yards down the road. Mark led it back and tethered it to a tree whose branches overhung the road. Taking the two lengths of cord from his pocket, he tied Roland's hands and feet together before passing one end of the rope under his shoulders and knotting it into a bowline. Next he passed the other end of the rope over one of the overhanging branches of the tree and hauled Roland's inert, overweight body up off the road until it was high enough to manoeuvre across the horse's saddle where it lay, finely balanced, legs on one side with head and shoulders hanging limp over the other. This done, he roped Roland firmly in place and led the horse back through the wood to the spot where he had left his own horse.

Keeping clear of the road as much as possible, Mark rode back to the old pit at North moor, leading the second horse with the still unconscious Roland slung over its back. Once inside the pit head building, he was pleased to see that the candle stub was still burning and quickly used it to light the safety lamp. Then, after hitching the rope over the cross beam of the pulley frame, he hoisted Roland off his horse and carefully lowered him into the corfe that he had left suspended over the mouth of the shaft. It was a delicate operation and he had to bend Roland's legs under him, leaving him squatting in the basket with his head slumped over his knees.

It was fortunate, Mark thought, that Roland had remained unconscious during the transfer, otherwise his fear of the pit might have sent him berserk, probably with fatal consequences. He did not wish to have his plans thwarted at the last hurdle.

After tying the safety lamp to the rope just above the corfe, Mark slung the satchel over his shoulder and stepped gingerly onto the rim of the basket. Untying the rope, he held on to the fall, taking the strain of his own and Roland's weight, ready to start lowering the corfe. He only hoped that someone had designed the correct purchase for the tackle that would allow him to check their seven hundred and fifty feet descent down the shaft.

Taking a deep breath, he slowly began to pay the rope through the pulley block, relieved that it was not wrenched from his hand as the corfe gathered momentum. Keeping a steady hand over hand rhythm, he made a controlled descent, stopping when he felt the knot that indicated a depth of seven hundred feet. Here, he shone the safety lamp around, looking for the spot where the angled furnace drift intersected the shaft. He heaved a sigh of relief when he saw its shadowy outline just below him. They were now only fifty feet from the shaft bottom and the flame of the safety lamp still showed no trace of gas. The worst part was almost over.

On reaching the shaft bottom, Mark jumped off the corfe and taking the safety lamp, began to search the main roadway that led off from the shaft. He soon spotted what he was looking for - a putter's sledge. This was a wooden sledge, mounted on four small wheels instead of runners, used by the putters to drag a loaded corfe of coal along the low, narrow galleries that led from the working face to the rolley ways. The corves would be transferred by crane onto a rolley, a large flat cart mounted on rails and drawn by a horse, for the final part of its journey to the shaft bottom.

After lubricating the dry axles with a pat of butter taken from his satchel, Mark returned to the shaft bottom, dragging the sledge behind him. When he got back, he noticed Roland was showing signs of regaining consciousness, his body twitching inside the cramped confines of the basket. He quickly lowered the corfe onto the sledge and, using the rope harness attached to one end, began hauling his prisoner towards the abandoned and dangerous old workings on the north side of the mine.

CHAPTER 54

Sweating profusely and almost out of breath, Mark finally reached the area of the mine where he judged George Wright, Sep's predecessor as wasteman, had been killed. If his compass was reading correctly and his allowance for magnetic variation had been calculated accurately, then he was now standing in the most hazardous part of the old pit workings.

Roland seemed to have relapsed back into unconsciousness. He sat, wedged tight inside the basket, with his head and shoulders sprawled limply across his hunched-up knees. This made Mark's next task a little easier, as he could now risk untying his prisoner. After doing so, he took out the two lengths of chain and locked the manacled ends around Roland's wrists before passing the other ends around the timber roof supports at opposite sides of the roadway. Hauling on the chains, he managed to lift Roland high enough to kick away the basket from underneath him. He then padlocked the looped end of each chain, leaving his prisoner firmly secured to the roof supports and with his body spread-eagled across the roadway.

The movement seemed to act as a stimulant to Roland's brain, stirring him back to consciousness. His sagging jaw began to tense and his eyes slowly flickered open. Mark had placed the lamp on the floor of the roadway and he quickly stepped back into the shadows, out of sight. He stood watching his victim, waiting for him to comprehend his awful situation as he became fully conscious.

Roland's eyes were now open, and with the return of his mental faculties came the feeling that all was not well. A low moan escaped his lips followed by loud cursing as he wrenched frantically on the restraining chains. When this failed to attract any attention, he began to focus on the pale, shadowy outlines that showed up in the dim light cast by the Davy lamp, seeking clues as to where he was being held. Suddenly, the realisation came that he was deep underground inside a mine, and his instincts told him it was a pit that had not been in use for a long time. He began to panic, shouting into the shadows, demanding to know what was going on and threatening dire consequences if he was not released immediately. But Mark remained silent and out of sight, smiling to himself as he watched his enemy squirm.

Roland's arrogance and bluster soon turned to alarm as he began to comprehend the seriousness of his predicament. Chained up like an animal and seemingly alone, he was clearly the victim of some sinister plot. His alarm quickly degenerated into abject terror as his fear of being underground began to take hold. His head ached and he simply could not recall how he had got himself into the situation he was in.

But, he reasoned, trying hard to keep control, someone must have left the lamp burning. He looked closer at the light and recognised it as one of the new safety lamps invented by Sir Humphry Davy. This fact disturbed him even more, though he could not quite understand why. However, of one thing he was certain. His incarceration was not the result of some spontaneous action, but rather part of some carefully planned, well executed plot against him. But why, he wondered. His panic returned and he began to struggle violently against his chains, screaming obscenities at his unknown tormentor.

Standing in the shadows, Mark could see that Roland was now dangerously close to breaking point. If he drove him to insanity, then the pleasure of his revenge would be lost. More important, he would not find the answer to the one question that might eradicate the cankerous doubts in his heart and, perhaps, give him some peace of mind.

Pulling his hat down over his eyes, and raising his neck-cloth to cover his mouth, Mark stepped forward until his shadowy outline could be seen in the dim light cast by the Davy lamp. Roland's hysterical cursing suddenly stopped as he caught the movement. 'Who's there?' he called, his voice tremulous with anxiety.

'That need not concern you for the moment,' Mark answered, his voice muffled by the neck-cloth.

'I insist on knowing who you are and what this is all about,' Roland blustered, trying to hide his fear.

'You're hardly in a position to insist on anything,' the voice mocked back at him.

'Where am I, damn you! And who are you?'

'You're down the old pit at North Moor; that much I'll tell you. As to who I am, you'll just have to be patient for a while.'

'Why are you holding me prisoner like this? Chained up like some common felon.'

'Because that's exactly what you are,' came the taunting reply. 'And now you must answer for your crimes.'

Roland's newly found confidence was now rapidly waning. There was something ugly and menacing in the cold, detached voice coming out of the shadows. He had the strangest feeling that he had heard the voice before but somehow, this disturbed rather than comforted him. He decided to try a more conciliatory approach.

'If this is some sort of prank, then I think it's gone far enough. If you and your accomplices release me now, I promise to overlook the matter and take no further action.'

'It's not a prank and there are no accomplices.' Mark informed him. The humiliation of his enemy was giving him great satisfaction, but it wasn't enough. He knew he would have to frighten the truth out of Roland.

There was a short silence whilst Roland absorbed the information. His memory was now returning and he remembered being violently unhorsed on his journey home. After that, his mind was a blank until he regained consciousness and found himself chained like a felon, in the depths of what he now knew was the old mine. Yet one man surely couldn't have carried him underground on his own. It didn't seem possible. And the voice! He was more certain than ever that he'd heard it before, but the identity still baffled him.

His mind was now reeling and he could feel the pit closing in on him as his fear of being underground took hold again. Desperately hanging on, he decided to make one more attempt to try and stamp his authority on his captor. 'You're a fool to refuse my offer, you know,' he shouted into the shadows. 'Now you'll suffer the consequences of your stupid, insolent action. I shall personally see that you're hunted down and arrested for this. You'll dance on the end of a rope one day, mark my words.'

He waited for a response to his tirade, but the only answer was a taunting silence.

Suddenly, the light from the Davy lamp began to move away and soon he was in complete darkness. As his fear again began to overwhelm him he abandoned all hope of imposing any authority on his sinister, unknown captor. His threats now turned to abject pleading and his screamed entreaties echoed down the dark, deserted galleries of the mine. But there was no answer. Finally, overcome with terror, he fainted and hung limp in his chains.

Mark made his way towards the staple that connected the old pit to the new workings that ran eastwards, a hundred and fifty feet below on the other side of the fault. He was puzzled by the absence of firedamp in the old pit. He had kept a constant watch on the safety lamp but not once had he discerned a trace of blue around the flame which would indicate the presence of gas. Yet Wilf was certain that the pit was ready to fire and had warned him of the danger. There must be an explanation for this, he thought.

He found it when he finally reached the staple. Using his compass and the plan of the old pit provided by Wilf, he arrived at the staple and saw that the shaft door was open. He felt the gentle movement of air being drawn down into the shaft and realised that some attempt must have been made to ventilate the old pit. Probably, it was because of Duncan Forster's greed and his desire to protect what coal deposits remained, so that they could be worked at some future date. An explosion would have wrecked the pit and made the cost of reopening it prohibitively expensive.

However, Mark's mining experience made him realise that the velocity of the ventilating current was too weak and would be totally inadequate to clear the whole of the old pit of the volume of gas indicated by Wilf. The only explanation he could think of was that Forster must have sealed off most of the old workings in order to keep the main roadway to the pit shaft clear of gas.

Working his way back, he explored the galleries on the dangerous north side of the mine and, as expected, found they were all sealed off to prevent gas from the blowers leaking into the main roadway. Most of the stoppings had been made semi-permanent by bricking up the passageways. A few, however, were constructed out of timber with heavy self-closing trap-doors fitting inside the closely sealed timber frames. When the time came to reopen the pit, a new ventilating system would be installed and the doors reopened so that the accumulated gas could be safely vented from the waste.

Leaving the safety lamp several yards behind him, Mark carefully eased open the first trapdoor then quickly walked back to check the safety lamp. He saw that the flame was now showing tinges of blue, where there had been none before, indicating the presence of gas. As he progressed back towards Roland, he opened more trap-doors until he was satisfied that there would be a slow but steady build-up of firedamp in the main roadway. He then made his way back to Roland and after placing the lamp on the floor in front of him, took off the protective wire-gauze cover before stepping back into the shadows.

The light seemed to rouse Roland back into a state of consciousness again. His arms jerked on the chains, showering him with coal dust as he pulled himself upright. When his eyes focussed on the safety lamp, he saw that the cover had been taken off, removing any protection from explosion. He also knew that the old pit workings were highly dangerous and these two facts linked together ominously in his mind to rekindle his terror. Suddenly, he lost all control and began to scream. His body wrenched and twisted in a futile frenzy of panic until the iron shackles cut deep into his wrists. Blood ran down his outstretched arms, turning darker as it mingled with the coal dust before congealing in a dark, sticky mass into the cuffs of his fine linen shirt.

Eventually, overcome by exhaustion, his struggles ceased and his body began to slump. His mind was numb and his eyes became transfixed in a hypnotic gaze on the Davy lamp standing on the ground in front of him. The yellow flame from the oil wick now spouted occasional tinges of blue as it picked up traces of firedamp that was slowly seeping from the reopened trap-doors into the main roadway of the mine.

Suddenly, Roland's anger welled up and for a moment overcame his fear. His voice raged and echoed down the deserted galleries of the mine. 'Damn you! Why are you doing this to me?'

There was no reply; only a mocking silence. He began to sob, quietly at first, but gradually growing into an uncontrollable fit of hysteria until it was finally stilled by exhaustion. Now, the only sounds were the drip of unseen water and the faint, ominous hiss of escaping gas from some obscure fissure in the coal seam.

After a while, Roland could discern the shadowy outline of his tormentor who was squatting on his haunches, pitman fashion, against the wall of the roadway. He decided to make one more appeal for reason. 'In God's name,' he implored, 'what is it you want of me?'

'Truthful answers to some questions,' Mark replied. 'And as you mentioned God, you can regard it as a confessional; a purging of your soul,' he added sardonically.

'I'm not a catholic and I'll wager you're no priest,' Roland countered, relieved that his captor was talking again.

'No, I'm not a priest.'

'Then why should I confess anything to you?'

'Because you'll die with a sinful conscience if you don't.'

'And you also, damn you!'

'True, but then I'm prepared to die. And unlike you, I'm not afraid.'

'You're mad! Roland screamed. 'Put the cover on the lamp before the pit explodes.'

'Not until you confess your guilt and explain.'

'Explain what? Just what am I guilty of?'

Mark rose and moved forward into the light, revealing himself for the first time. 'Rape, betrayal and murder,' he rasped.

Recognition flickered in Roland's eyes. 'You!' he whispered. 'I thought you were...' his voice dried up as a spasm of fear convulsed in his throat. Now that he knew the identity of his tormentor, any hope that he might somehow stay alive quickly faded.

He groaned and slowly sagged on his chains in limp resignation. He listened anxiously to the faint, menacing sound of the escaping gas and his eyes returned, trancelike, to the naked flickering flame of the Davy lamp. He knew that Mark must have opened some of the trap-doors in the old workings, weakening the vital flow of ventilating air and allowing the accumulated firedamp to seep into the main roadway of the mind. It was now only a matter of time before the gas built up to an explosive level that would be ignited by the unprotected Davy lamp. He could only watch, like some helpless rabbit frozen in the stare of a predatory stoat, waiting for death to strike.

The flame of the unguarded lamp was now surrounded by a large, blue aureole, indicating the strong presence of gas. From his own pit experience, Roland knew what would happen if the gas ignited. Without warning, the narrow confines of the roadway would be filled with a blinding flash of light, followed by the roar of the explosion as the pit erupted. Then, the searing heat of the fireball would scorch the skin from his body, leaving the exposed flesh charred and blackened. There would be moments of unimaginable agony before death and he shuddered, involuntarily, as the realisation took hold.

Paralysed with fear, he lost control and felt the warm, wet patch at his crotch widen and spread slowly down the legs of his trousers. He began to whimper as he waited for the end.

Subjecting his enemy to this form of mental torture afforded Mark more pleasure than he would have obtained from handing out a beating. Yet something was still missing, for watching Roland suffer did not give him the full sense of satisfaction he was seeking. He desperately needed to resolve the doubts that had festered in his mind ever since the night of Jane's rape. But he could not bring himself to ask the vital question until he could be sure of a truthful answer, and for this he knew he must take Roland to the brink and destroy his arrogant spirit. With someone so unscrupulous and totally devoid of morals, it was the only way.

Suddenly, overcome by some hidden yet compelling instinct, their eyes met. Then, after a few moments, Roland's gaze returned, defeated, to the flame of the Davy lamp. When he spoke, all the fight seemed to have been drained from him. 'Put the cover back on the lamp,' he pleaded. 'I'll tell you everything you want to know.'

'How can I be sure you're telling the truth?'

'Because I don't want to die. You'll just have to trust me.'

Mark looked again at the Davy lamp. He noted that the blue aureole surrounding the flame had enlarged considerably. The concentration of gas was clearly reaching dangerous levels and the pit could fire at any moment. Yet, unlike the pitiful Roland, he felt no fear; only a strange feeling of exhilaration and power. He would make this pathetic, whining creature suffer, as he had suffered, before taking his final revenge. It would be a biblical justice, he decided - an eye for an eye. Justice that had been denied to Jane and himself.

Trembling with fear, Roland made one last attempt to save himself. 'Please!' he begged. 'Put the cover on the lamp before the pit fires. I've told you, I'll answer your questions - truthfully,' he added, anxious to reassure Mark of his integrity.

Roland's tone was one of such abject capitulation, that Mark relented. He leaned forward and replaced the wire-gauze cover on the Davy lamp.

'Aren't you going to close the trap-doors as well?' Roland asked, nervously.

'Not until you've answered my questions - honestly and to my complete satisfaction.'

Roland sighed and nodded his head in mute agreement. At least they would be safe for a while, now that the lamp was covered. 'I'll try,' he murmured, dejectedly. 'Just what is it you want to know?'

'You recognise who I am?'

'Yes.'

'And six years ago you raped my wife.'

'Is that a question or a statement?' Roland asked, regretting his words as soon as they were out.

'It's an accusation,' Mark warned icily. Being flippant won't help you. I want a truthful answer.'

There was a long pause before Roland replied. 'It wasn't meant to happen,' he said contritely, eyes averted.

'You planned it, you scheming bastard.'

'I didn't,' Roland lied, frightened by the implacable hatred in Mark's voice. 'It was something done on the spur of the moment. She's a beautiful woman - I couldn't resist the temptation.'

'Was a beautiful woman,' Mark corrected angrily. 'You raped her and, not content with that, you betrayed her. Then you lied to her; laughed in her face and destroyed the one fragile thread that kept her alive.' His voice rose with his anger, reverberating down the empty galleries. 'You murdered her, you cowardly bastard. By your deeds if not by your own hand. But you're still guilty as hell in my eyes, if not in the eyes of the law.'

'It wasn't like that,' Roland screamed back. 'You're making it sound worse than it was.'

Mark fought to control his anger. 'You're forgetting that you also betrayed Crombie and Reid, your two gamekeepers. Handed them over to the press gang along with me, remember? We spent time together, imprisoned on a stinking hulk of a receiving ship being treated like the vermin we shared it with. Do you honestly think they carried on lying to protect you?'

'The press took them. I had no part in it.' Roland pleaded, still desperately lying to defend himself.

'You had no intention of letting me escape,' Mark went on, ignoring Roland's lies. 'It was your sick idea to make me watch my own wife being raped, wasn't it? God, just how depraved can a man get!'

'I didn't rape her,' Roland persisted. 'Your wife wanted to see you escape. Women are capable of strange acts when the mood takes them, you know.' He now sensed a faint weakening in Mark's determination and, instinctively, his innate cunning told him to brazen things out.

Mark looked at him with unconcealed contempt. 'Are you suggesting it was her idea? To give herself to you in order to save me from prison? Do you really expect me to believe that?'

'Perhaps it wasn't such a sacrifice in her eyes,' Roland countered cunningly.

'She wouldn't have given herself to you willingly,' Mark responded hotly. But the poisonous arrow had found its mark and the seeds of doubt were sown.

'Why not? Most women find me attractive - I appeal to their erotic instincts.' Roland had spotted the chink in Mark's armour and was now determined to exploit it. It might be the one thing that could save him.

Mark's anger flared again. 'Jane despised you for the weak, bullying coward that you are. She gave you no encouragement when she was in service at the Hall, despite all your crude and unwanted attentions.'

'The spirited ones always do,' Roland parried venomously. His confidence was growing and he detected a hint of doubt creeping into Mark's responses.

These were not the answers Mark wished to hear. Suddenly, he felt he was losing control, his anger disintegrating into seething frustration. 'My wife would never have been a willing party,' he persisted angrily. 'Especially with someone like you whom she loathed.'

'But she might with someone else, eh? She saw little of you and spent a lot of time cooped up in that isolated cottage of yours. She must have been a very lonely woman.'

Mark's anger and frustration boiled over. 'Damn you, Forster. I won't have you insulting my wife's memory with your filthy innuendo.' He stepped forward and struck Roland hard across his face and immediately regretted his action. It was further confirmation that he was losing control of the situation.

Roland smiled back triumphantly through the trickle of blood seeping from the corner of his mouth. 'My word, Standish, I do believe you're jealous,' he taunted. He suddenly understood what his captor wanted from him. He was looking for some sort of absolution; seeking a confession from him that might exorcise the doubts that must have harboured in his mind since the night of the rape. By God, he thought, the man really is jealous and he was damned if he would give him the satisfaction of an honest answer.

Roland now doubted if his captor had the guts to go through with whatever he had planned, and with this knowledge his confidence soared. For, being totally devoid of scruples himself, Roland feared only those who he judged were equally unscrupulous. He had found Mark's Achilles heel and was determined to exploit it to save himself. 'You said you wanted some answers,' he goaded, watching carefully for Mark's response.

Mark now realised that there was little hope for an honest dialogue with Roland and he would have to live with his doubts until he could find sufficient inner faith to eradicate them himself. He had also lost the initiative and, much as he still hated Roland, he now knew he could not kill him in cold blood without ending his own life with him. That seemed a futile and cowardly gesture and would, at best, only be a Pyrrhic victory. Frustration welled up inside him turning his anger into bitterness.

'Cat got your tongue, then?' Roland's sarcastic tone cut through his gloom bringing him sharply back to reality. 'Don't you want to hear the truth? Or are you afraid of it?'

'You don't know the meaning of the word,' Mark responded curtly.

Roland decided to gamble. 'You're still not sure, are you? '

'About what?'

'Your wife.'

'I don't know what you mean,' Mark lied. Suddenly, he did not want to hear the truth anymore and Roland's probing was making him feel uncomfortable.

'You were there - you watched,' Roland persisted.

'I was forced to watch,' Mark retorted angrily. 'It was all part of your depraved plan to gratify your sordid cravings, wasn't it? You weren't content with just raping an innocent woman were you? You had to humiliate her with your sexual perversions so that you could satisfy that sick mind of yours.'

'Your wife wasn't so innocent,' Roland countered balefully. 'She made no attempt to fight me off, did she?'

'Because you promised her my freedom,' Mark protested furiously. You lied to her and she believed you. But you had no intention of keeping your promise because it would have spoiled your warped sense of pleasure. Do these crude, sordid acts give you a heightened orgasm or something?'

'Yes, they do actually,' Roland goaded. Most women are aroused by them too, you know. It unshackles their inhibitions and allows their secret fantasies to take control for a while.'

Mark's disgust exploded in anger. 'My wife wasn't like that,' he shouted.

Roland smiled provocatively. 'Wasn't she? You watched the so called rape, didn't you? You saw her smile - watched her climax? Were those the actions of an unwilling partner?'

'Lies!' Mark roared. 'Damned lies, all of it.'

'I think not,' Roland said triumphantly. 'What you saw on that day, Standish, was a woman taking her pleasure and enjoying it in a way she could never experience with you. That's what really hurts you, isn't it.'

571

As this final thrust struck home, Mark's control snapped. Without warning, he began a furious attack, delivering a flurry of heavy blows to Roland's head and body. Taken by surprise, Roland hauled frantically on his chains trying desperately to keep out of range. But there was no escape and as the punches exploded in his face, his body writhed and swayed in the restraining chains, bringing down showers of coal dust from the roof of the mine.

Eventually, the violent movements dislodged the head-tree wedge from the roof support, freeing one of the chains. Roland now found himself with one arm free and, using the loose end of the chain as a flail, he delivered a vicious blow to the head of his attacker.

The chain struck Mark across the face, splitting open his cheek and bringing him to his knees. Dazed and half blinded with blood, he was unable to rise and could only hold his arms above his head to try to ward off any further blows. Seeing his advantage, Roland swung the chain again and again, delivering blow after blow to Mark's unprotected head.

Suddenly, the other chain came free, dislodging the roof support with it and causing a small roof fall. Roland managed to jump clear but Mark, weakened by the fierce battering he had received, was slow to move away and was caught on the edge of the fall. He lay trapped by his legs under a pile of loose stone, unable to move.

On the other side of the fall Roland now found himself free, except for the minor impediment of a length of chain still shackled to each wrist. He moved to inspect the Davy-lamp which was still burning and saw that the flame was encased in a large, blue aureole, indicating that the gas was ready to explode. He failed to notice the large dent in the wire-gauze cover of the lamp, caused by the roof fall, which now rendered the lamp extremely dangerous. Picking it up, he set off in the direction of the staple, hoping to make his way down into the safer workings of the new pit. In his terror he started to run, causing the flame of the lamp to impinge onto the indented area of the wire-gauze cover which soon became red-hot. But in his panic, Roland was blissfully unaware of the danger this posed.

A hundred yards before the staple shaft there was a slight dip in the roadway, and it was here that a large and lethal concentration of firedamp had accumulated. As soon as the red-hot gauze made contact, the gas fired and the pit erupted.

Roland's screams were drowned by the roar of the explosion. He saw the blinding fireball and felt excruciating agony as his skin was scorched from his body. A sharp intake of breath sent an incinerating blast of heat deep inside him, turning his throat and lungs into a shrivelled, blackened mass. His life was mercifully cut short, but the few seconds it took him to die was an eternity of unbearable pain.

The roadway where Mark lay injured and trapped suddenly became dazzlingly bright, as the searing fireball blasted through the pit. The force of the explosion sent pieces of discarded equipment and debris hurling along the roadways and up the shaft, which acted as a pressure relief valve. Being trapped in the roof fall saved Mark from death or further injury, for the deadly fireball and the force of the blast were diverted over him by the barrier of fallen stone which acted as a shield. Fortunately, there were no further explosions. The only threat now remaining was the spread of the dreaded choke-damp which would fill the vacuum left by the explosion.

Lying on his back in the inky blackness, he explored the fallen debris with his hands trying to visualise his situation and judge the extent of his entrapment. His hand ached abominably and there was a throbbing pain in his cheek. But his trapped legs felt numb and he wondered if his spine was fractured.

He slowly began removing stones from around his waist, working carefully down to his thighs and trying hard not to disturb the rest of the fall. After a while he was able to sit up, sighing with relief in the knowledge that his back was not broken. He tried to pull himself free but without success, and gently began removing more stones from around his legs. Unexpectedly, his fingers touched something that felt like wood. He grasped it and slowly pulled it out of the rubble. It was a length of roof support that had broken off when the roof collapsed. Reaching forward again, he discovered that his feet were firmly trapped behind another length of timber which seemed to be keeping the main weight of the fall off his legs.

He lay back with a groan, desperately trying to think of a way to free himself before the insidious choke-damp caught him in its lethal embrace. Suddenly, an idea came and he sat up, he hands groping in

573

the dark until he found the length of roof support that he had pulled out of the rubble. Using it as a crude tool, he carefully worked it underneath the timber that was pinioning his feet. Then, using a large stone as a fulcrum, he slowly began to lever it up.

At first nothing seemed to happen, save for a dangerous flexing of the makeshift wooden lever. But he persevered and felt the restraining timber inside the fall move a little. Soon, he could feel the circulation returning to his feet. Pulling hard, he managed to free one foot and then the other before quickly rolling away from the fall. He lay listening to the ominous sounds of splintering wood as the rocks settled into the space vacated by his legs.

Mark's elation at escaping from the fall was muted by the pain he now felt in his right foot. As the circulation returned, so the pain increased and he concluded that it must be broken or badly bruised. He tried to stand up but his injured foot could not bear his full weight. The effort made his aching head pulsate violently, causing a painful stretching of the skin beneath the sticky mass of blood that had congealed on his face. A bout of nausea overwhelmed him and he sat down to take stock of his situation.

He knew that his greatest danger stemmed from the lethal spread of the dreaded choke-damp produced by the explosion. Finding his way quickly back to the pit shaft was now a matter of the utmost urgency. But the aftermath of the explosion had left him in darkness; injured and completely disorientated. He still had his compass tucked safely in his pocket alongside the map of the pit. But these were now useless without a light to study them by. In the dark, he could waste precious time travelling in the wrong direction in his efforts to reach the safety of the pit shaft. By then it might be too late, but he knew he had to try.

After making another painful attempt to walk he was forced to give up and began to crawl in what he hoped would be the right direction for the shaft. His progress was agonisingly slow, but he stubbornly carried on until he reached the first junction. He paused. Left or right, he wondered, then shrugged and turned right, continuing his slow, dogged crawl through the dark, forbidding galleries of the mine.

After what seemed like an age, but in fact was only minutes, his hand came down on something metal. He picked it up and felt its shape, his hands exploring the contours of the object, trying to identify

574

it. Suddenly, he gave a gasp of recognition. It was a steel mill, an old device used to provide light in the explosive areas of the mine. His spirits began to rise. The mill would greatly improve his chances of escape if only he could find a flint.

His hands searched frantically in the darkness around the area where the steel mill had lain. He gave a soft cry of relief when his fingers finally settled on the distinctive shape of the flint. He placed the leather belt of the steel mill around his neck ready to operate the mill. With one hand, he turned the handle on the brass toothed wheel which in turn, through linked gears, rotated a second steel wheel. At the same time, his other hand held the flint pressed firmly to the steel wheel and the resultant friction sent a shower of bright sparks cascading into the darkness.

Satisfied that the mill worked, Mark took out the map and compass from his pocket and placed them on the ground in front of him. Then, operating the mill vigorously, he was just able to read the compass card and take a bearing from the point of the fall. He felt a flood of relief when he realised he had taken the correct turning and was, in fact, heading in the right direction.

He continued his painful crawling, using the faint light from the mill to search for a suitable length of timber which he could use as a crutch. It would speed up his progress and might just keep him ahead of the spreading choke-damp. But each time he paused to operate the mill he could find nothing that might serve his purpose. Pit props were too long and too heavy, even if he could dislodge one without risking a fall.

He had almost given up hope when he came across a putter's sledge which had been smashed against the wall by the blast. In the faint glow cast by the cascading sparks, he spotted a length of wood from the frame of the sledge which he knew would be about four feet long - ideal for his purpose. After retrieving it, he rolled up his jacket and placed it over one end for padding before tucking the improvised crutch under his arm. His progress was now dramatically improved and his hopes began to rise as he entered the main roadway leading to the pit shaft. He was almost there.

When Mark finally reached the bottom of the shaft he was totally exhausted. Only hope and dogged determination had kept him going this far and he almost collapsed as he felt his way into the shaft entry. Leaning against the wall, he began to operate the mill as hard as he could directing the light inside the shaft. He was searching for the ropes left hanging at the bottom to enable him to escape to the surface. Again and again he operated the mill staring in disbelief each time. The ropes had vanished, blown up the shaft by the force of the blast. Without them, the seven hundred feet of shaft was unscalable. He was trapped!

Mark slumped wearily to the ground, his new found confidence suddenly gone. It was a bitter blow after coming so close to saving himself. Now he could only sit and wait for the end. But at least, he thought, his own death, unlike Roland's, would be painless. *For the insidious choke-damp was a gentle, if deadly, killer.*

CHAPTER 55

Wilf had spent a restless night anxiously prowling round the room, ignoring Dora's exasperated appeals to come to bed. Finally, he had sat down in a chair in front of the banked up fire and drifted off into a shallow, troubled sleep.

The sound of the explosion jolted him from his nap and he sat up with a start. Dora, too, was wide awake for, like most pitmen's wives, she had long since learned to recognise the dreaded sounds of underground destruction.

'The pit's fired,' Wilf said, putting on his coat. He lit a candle from the fire and placed it inside a lantern, then turned to Dora, 'I'll call on Jed and see what we can do to help. '

'Be careful, pet,' she answered, making no attempt to dissuade him. She knew all the able bodied men in the village would also be rising from their beds to offer their help.

Wilf was about to knock on his son's door when it opened. A bleary-eyed Jed tumbled out, pulling on his coat. 'Sounds like the pit's fired,' he said drowsily.

'Aye,' Wilf answered, but it's the old pit, I reckon.'

'How do you make that out?'

'Because it's four o'clock in the morning,' Wilf explained. 'Saturday morning,' he added pointedly.

A sudden look of understanding appeared in Jed's eyes. 'You think Mark's down there, don't you?'

'Never mind what I think,' Wilf said irritably. 'Let's get up to the old shaft and bloody-well find out.'

Lights were starting to appear in many of the cottage windows as they hurried towards the old pit yard. Wilf kept the shutter of the lantern closed, partly to stop the candle being blown out but mainly to avoid drawing attention to themselves. He guessed that people would assume it was the new pit that had fired and find their way there first. That would give him perhaps half-an-hour to examine the old shaft and try to find out what had happened.

When they arrived at the old pit yard, it was obvious that Wilf had guessed right. The wooden pithead building had been badly damaged and there were lengths of splintered cladding strewn around the pit yard. Wilf checked the stable first and saw the two horses moving nervously in their stalls. He knew then that Mark must have put his plan into action. A closer inspection of the horses revealed that one was a magnificent hunter carrying an expensive saddle, the sort of horse that Roland like to ride.

Quickly moving across the yard, they entered the damaged pithead building through the gaping doors that had been blown open by the blast. The scattered debris and the acrid smell reinforced Wilf's worst fears. If Mark had been below at the time of the explosion, there was little hope that he would have survived it. He moved across to the pit shaft and saw the blocks attached to the beam and the tangled mass of rope hanging over the shaft. His worst fears were now confirmed.

Tying the lantern to the beam, Wilf leaned over the shaft and peered down into the darkness, hoping he might see a light at the bottom. Disappointed, he looked around and saw the stubs of two candles which, he assumed, must have been used by Mark. He called Jed over. 'I think we'll light these two candles,' he said. 'Give us a bit more light while we try and untangle the rope.'

'Do you think he'll still be alive?' Jed asked.

'I don't know, lad, but I'm going to try and find out.'

'You're going down, then?'

'Yes. If he managed it, then so can I. But first, we'll have to unravel this lot,' he added, pointing to the tangled mass of rope.

It took them five minutes to free the rope and Wilf leaned over the shaft shaking the falls until he was satisfied that it had not snagged further down. He then studied the blocks for a moment before turning to Jed. 'I hope the bloody thing works,' he said, trying to sound confident.

'I'll go if you like,' Jed offered. 'I owe him one, you know.'

'No, lad. You've got a wife and young bairns at home. But thanks for the offer all the same.'

Wilf turned to grasp the rope, and then stopped in amazement. He could hardly believe his eyes. The rope was moving slowly through the blocks. Someone was hauling himself up.

He called to Jed. 'Quick, lad, give me a hand.'

*****

578

When he first heard the faint slapping sounds, Mark thought he was hallucinating; a reaction to the insidious effects of the enveloping choke-damp. He stood up wearily to investigate and began turning the handle of the steel mill, directing the sparks into the shaft entrance. At first he could not see anything but gradually, as his eyes adjusted to the faint light, he began to pick out two swinging objects. At first, to his befuddled mind, they looked like swaying serpents and it took several seconds for him to comprehend that the serpents were, in fact, two rope ends.

With a shock, he realised that they were the ropes attached to the pulley block at the top of the shaft. Somehow, they must have freed themselves and fallen back to the bottom. He hobbled painfully into the shaft entrance and felt for the ropes. When he found them, he held on tightly, afraid it might all be a figment of his imagination. Reassured, he quickly tied a bowline to one end of the rope, thankful that the navy had taught him how to tie knots in the dark, and slipped his uninjured foot inside the loop. Then, taking the strain on the other rope, he transferred his weight and pulled down hard, raising himself about two feet. He repeated the exercise and slowly began the agonising ascent up the shaft.

After only fifty feet he knew he would not make it to the surface. It was exhausting work and in his weakened state he did not have the necessary strength and stamina to see it through. He had planned to make the ascent sat in the relative comfort of a corfe, where he could have rested safely by hitching the rope around the handle of the basket. But, injured and without a proper light, there simply hadn't been time to look for one.

He was wondering how long he could hang on, desperately trying to find the courage to let go, when he felt himself being drawn up the shaft again. Surprised, he lost his hold on the fall rope and tensed himself for the expected plummet to the bottom of the shaft. But, to his astonishment, he continued on his swift ascent up the shaft, clinging instinctively to the other end of the rope where his foot was still wedged firmly in the loop of the bowline. Now, he could see a faint light above him and he thought he could hear voices calling down the shaft.

The light grew brighter and he felt strong, confident hands pulling him to safety. He heard a comforting voice echoing in his brain, 'You're safe now, Mark.' Looking up, he saw the relieved smiles on the faces of Wilf and Jed before passing out.

Between them, Wilf and Jed carried Mark across the yard and into the stables. 'Put him down gently,' Wilf directed. 'Poor bugger's out cold.'

'Will he be all right?' Jed asked anxiously. 'His cheek's split down to the bone and there's a hell of a gash on the back of his head.'

'He'll need stitching up, that's for sure,' Wilf answered. 'I think his foot might be broken as well.'

'He's lost a lot of blood,' Jed said, peering uneasily at the huge, congealed mass of blood that had spread down Mark's face and neck, before disappearing inside his shirt. 'Shall I get some water to clean him up?'

'We haven't time for that,' Wilf replied. 'Here, help me lift him across the back of Roland's horse. They lifted the still unconscious Mark, gently easing him across the horse's back until he lay balanced, face down, arms and legs hanging limply down each side.

'Doesn't look very safe,' Jed said dubiously.

Wilf looked thoughtfully at the horse. 'Nip across to the pit shaft, Jed,' he ordered. 'You'll find a canvas cover and some rope lying near the door. We can use it to tie Mark to the horse and the cover will hide him from any prying eyes.'

A few moments later, Jed coaxed the horse slowly out of the stable, the unconscious form of Mark now safely secured across its back beneath the canvas cover. Wilf followed, leading out Mark's horse which was still saddled. 'Up you get, lad,' he said pointing to the saddle.

'I'm not very good with horses,' Jed demurred.

'Neither am I,' Wilf retorted, 'but we haven't time to argue the point.'

Jed gingerly mounted the horse and Wilf handed him the reins of the horse carrying Mark. 'Take it easy. He's hurt bad enough as it is so don't shake him off.'

'Where shall I take him?'

'Sandgate. Rory MacGregor's house. It's the first one you come to in the Low Way, near the Tyne Brewery.'

'What about Henry?'

'At this stage, the less he knows about what's happened, the better. I'll go and see him later to explain.'

'You're going home, then?'

'Not just yet. There's a lot of clearing up to be done here first. Now, on your way!' He gently nudged the horse's rump and watched as Jed nervously rode off, with the other horse following contentedly behind.

Before the horses had cleared the yard, Wilf sprinted across to the pit shaft and began hauling up the rope until it lay, free of the blocks, in a pile by his feet. He knew it would only be a matter of time before Duncan Forster and his men arrived and he wanted to remove all evidence of Mark's visit.

He was about to start searching for any other evidence when he heard the distant sound of voices. He stopped and walked over to a point in the wall where a large section of the wooden cladding had been blown out by the explosion. Looking out, he could see in the distance the lights of many lanterns and flambeaux heading towards him. He cursed silently. Clearly, Forster and his men had soon realised that it was the old pit that had fired and were coming to investigate.

Quickly snuffing out the candle in his lantern, Wilf ran out into the yard. His eyes searched frantically for a hiding place and found one in the form of an old chaldron waggon that lay abandoned outside the carpenter's shop. Minutes later, he was out of sight as the dancing lights of lanterns and flaming torches lit up the yard.

Crouched in the bottom of the waggon, he could see through the cracks in the dried out timber and watched as Forster led a small group of men inside the damaged pithead building. Moments later, he reappeared by the gaping doors bellowing to the rest of the men standing in the yard. 'We've had trespassers in here and whoever they were, they were up to no good. I want every building searched.'

The men split up in pairs, each with a lantern or torch, and began searching every building, breaking down doors where necessary. A shout came from the stable block and a man came running out, 'Over here, Mr Forster. We've found something.'

Forster ran across and disappeared inside. Soon, curiosity got the better of the other man and they gathered excitedly by the stable door. This distraction offered an opportunity for Wilf to extricate himself without being seen. He quickly climbed out of the chaldron waggon and, keeping to the shadows, made his way silently out of the yard. Setting a brisk pace, he headed back to his cottage in North Moor and a warm fire. He needed time to think. He felt sure that Duncan Forster had found some incriminating evidence that the old pit buildings had been recently used. And if he had, all hell would break loose.

Sandgate lay dark and deserted as Jed led the two horses down to the Swirle. After tethering his own mount, he led the other horse along the narrow Low Way in the direction of the Tyne Brewery Wharf, catching the strong aroma of yeast and hops that hung in the still, night air. He stopped at the first house, noting that a light was still showing inside, and knocked gently on the door. Unsure that it was the right house, he waited anxiously for an answer, hoping that no undue suspicion would be aroused if it wasn't.

After a few moments, he heard footsteps followed by the sound of bolts being partly withdrawn, as if the person inside the house was undecided. 'Who is it?' It sounded to Jed like a woman's voice.

'I'm looking for Rory MacGregor's house. I was told he lived in the Low Way.'

'What do you want him for?'

'I'm a friend of his. I've got an urgent message for him.'

'Just a minute.' There were sounds of the bolts being fully withdrawn and the door swung slowly open. The woman holding the lamp shone it into Jed's face. 'Who are you?' she asked.

'My name's Jed Hindmarsh. Rory knows my father, Wilf Hindmarsh. We live at North Moor.'

The woman stood back to let him enter. 'I'm Fiona MacGregor, Rory's wife. You'd better come in.'

Jed pointed to the shadowy outline of the horse. 'I've got someone with me. He's injured and Wilf said Rory would help.

Fiona moved out into the road and held the lamp up to the unconscious figure slumped over the horse's back. 'Do I know him?'

'I think so.' Jed Lifted the canvas cover to reveal Mark's face.

'Fiona stepped back in surprise. 'Mark!' she gasped. 'How did this happen?'

'He was down the old pit at North Moore when it fired.'

'What on earth was he doing down there? He's not ....' she cut herself short. This was not the time to ask questions. 'We must get him inside, quickly,' she said, taking control of the situation. Going back inside the house, she called up the narrow staircase, 'Rory! I need your help.'

Early morning knocks on the door usually sent Rory straight up into the roof space, ready to enter his secret escape route. He was sitting there when he heard Fiona's call and came bounding down the stairs. Seeing Jed, his caution immediately returned and it wasn't until Fiona introduced him that he began to relax. When he saw Mark's injuries, a look of concern clouded his eyes. Undoing the rope that held Mark onto the horse, he lifted him gently into his arms and carried him effortlessly upstairs to the bedroom, where he lowered him carefully onto the bed. 'He really needs a doctor,' he said, 'but that will only cause questions to be asked. We'll just have to manage.'

'I'll get some water to clean his wounds,' Fiona said, turning to go back downstairs.

Rory and Jed began to undress Mark, taking care not to disturb the broken foot. When he saw the full extent of Marks wounds, Rory decided he must seek medical help. He turned to Jed. 'I've got to go out for a while. You stay here and help Fiona.' With that he disappeared down the stairs and seconds later Jed heard the front door slam shut.

When Colin MacGregor answered the urgent knocking he was surprised to see his father standing on his doorstep. Rory quickly explained what had happened to his bleary-eyed son, then asked, 'Do you know where Tom Shute lives?'

'One of the chars off Sandgate, I think,' Colin replied, looking puzzled.

583

'Can you find him for me?'

'I think so. What do you want him for?'

'He served as a surgeon's mate in the navy during the war. When you find him, bring him to my house.'

A look of understanding crept over Colin's face.

'Leave it to me,' he said. 'I'll find the drunken bugger wherever he is.'

'And sober him up if you have to.'

Colin grinned. 'A cold dip in the Tyne should do that.'

'Make sure he has his instruments with him,' Rory said as he turned for home. 'There's a lot of sewing needs to be done and we'll probably need a splint for the broken foot.'

When he returned home, Fiona had finished washing off the coal dust and cleaning out the wounds on Mark's head and face. 'I've sent for Jonas Shute,' he told her. 'Colin's gone to fetch him.'

Fiona was shocked. 'That old drunk! He'll do more harm than good.'

'He's a good surgeon,' Rory insisted, 'and Mark needs stitching if we're to stop the bleeding,' he added looking down at the fearsome wounds now exposed by the cleansing.

'Jonas Shute may be a good surgeon but only if he's sober,' Fiona retorted.

'We'll see that he is,' Rory answered calmly. He knew that Jonas was a good surgeon when he was sober, which wasn't very often these days. A budding apothecary back in '96, he had been struck down with smallpox and his young wife had lovingly nursed him back to health. Unfortunately, he passed on the infection to his wife and infant child, both of whom subsequently died. Stricken with remorse and consumed with guilt for surviving the very disease that he himself had brought home, he took his solace in drink. Lying in a drunken stupor in some riverside tavern a few weeks later, he was taken by the press gang and spent the rest of the war aboard a ship of the line. Here, naval discipline controlled his worst excesses and he rose to become a highly respected surgeon's mate. Then, after his discharge at the end of the war, he quickly went back to his old ways.

But what the hell, Rory thought. Naval surgeons, if nothing else, were experts at tending wounds, drunk or sober. Besides, after

584

listening to Jed's account, he could guess what had really happened at the old North Moor pit and he knew he must keep Mark's presence in Sandgate a closely guarded secret.

When Jonas Shute arrived he was far from sober, yet his hands were remarkably steady. After examining Mark he treated the head wounds and set the broken foot. Then, after dressing the wounds, he pronounced his patient as 'Broken but not beyond mending'.

'He'll be all right, then?' Fiona asked, a new tone of respect creeping into her voice.

'Most certainly, madam,' Jonas replied gravely, with only a hint of a slur in his voice.

'Thank God for that, Fiona said, exuding a sigh of relief.

Rory shook Jonas Shute's hand. 'A fine job, sir! Ye'll find a bottle of fine Scottish whisky downstairs. Please help yourself, I'll join you in a moment.'

'Most civil of you, sir,' Jonas acknowledged, moving rapidly towards the door, his face wreathed in a smile of pure joy at the thought of the whisky.

As soon as Jonas had left the room Rory beckoned to Colin. He'll be drunk again by the time he leaves, I'll see to that. When he does, I want you to take him to Murphy's house and lock him in the cellar.'

Colin looked surprised. 'He won't like that. He'll raise the roof when he wakes up.'

'Not if we keep him well stocked with liquor. I want him off the streets for a few days.'

'Why.'

'Because he'll blabber about Mark when he's in his cups, that's why. I want him out of the way until we can decide what to do with Mark.'

Colin nodded. 'I think you're right. Leave him to me. '

Rory now turned to Jed. 'Did you bring back the horse Mark hired from the livery stable?'

'Yes. I left it tethered by the Swirle.'

'We'd best collect it then. I'll get someone to take it back first thing in the morning.'

'I can do that,' Jed offered.

'No,' Rory said firmly. I don't want anyone to make any connection, however remote, between the horse and North Moor.'

'Fat chance of that,' Jed scoffed.

'Any chance could be risky for Mark,' Rory admonished sternly. 'Best if you make your way home before it gets light. Tell Wilf everything's under control here but to keep me informed as to what's happening at North Moor.'

'Nowt much ever happens at North Moor,' Jed said jokingly.

'It will laddie,' Rory warned. 'Believe you me, it will, and soon.'

After Jed's departure, the town lay still in the cold, pre-dawn darkness. After checking that Jonas Shute was safely locked up in Murphy's cellar Rory arranged for the hired horse to be returned to the livery stable. Next, he sent word to one of his trusted radical friends to collect Roland's horse, which was now out of sight inside a disused keel store. He was to take the horse well clear of the town and leave it tethered in some quite spot.

Then, with a sigh, he set off for the house on the Quayside to inform Henry of the night's events and break the news of his son's injuries.

When discreet enquiries made at Forest House revealed that Roland had left the young Widow Alder's house at ten o'clock, Duncan Forster sent out every available man from his estate to search the area. Mounted men covered the roads and tracks whilst those on foot scoured the woods surrounding North Moor. After three hours, all the obvious places had been searched, including the old pit yard, but with no sign of Roland. A more intensive search was ordered to be carried out as soon as it was light.

The discovery of fresh horse manure at the old pit suggested that two horses had recently been using the stables. This puzzled Forster. The block and tackle left over the old shaft, together with an enormous length of rope and burnt out candle stubs, indicated that someone had recently descended the shaft, and this worried him. Why would anyone want to risk their lives doing such a thing? And for what purpose? He realised it could not be Roland, for he knew that his son was terrified of going underground even in the safest and best regulated pits.

He shook his head in exasperation. There had to be a logical explanation, and he knew he would have to explore the old workings in order to find out. But, it would be dangerous, for they now knew that the explosion had occurred inside the old pit and that an ominous new build-up of gas was taking place.

Undeterred, Forster led a search party underground and entered the old pit via the staple ladder that led up from the adjacent workings of the new mine. He was accompanied by Wilkins, his head viewer, and a handful of carefully picked pitmen which included Sep Fordyce in his role as wasteman for the old pit. They carried three of the new safety lamps between them, hastily borrowed from neighbouring pit owners who were testing them.

'Hope the bloody things work,' he muttered as he entered the old workings through the trapdoor at the top of the staple.

'Sir Humphry maintains they're perfectly safe,' Wilkins responded encouragingly.

'Maybe,' Forster growled, 'but your Sir bloody Humphry Davy is safe in London, not poking around in the arsehole of a pit that's constantly farting firedamp. Not quite the innocuous, smelly little things that you let go underneath the bedclothes for your wife to sniff, eh Wilkins?' he added. He enjoyed shocking his strait-laced head viewer.

Wilkins ignored the rude provocation. He now knew why none of the ambitious young viewers ever stayed more than a year with Forster; which probably explained why he was now head viewer. No one else could stomach working with such a crude, heartless and vicious employer.

They worked their way slowly along the roadway that led from the staple, re-sealing the dangerous galleries that Mark had opened up as they went. When they came to the seat of the explosion, Forster was surprised that the roof was still standing. 'Someone seems to have deliberately interfered with the ventilation,' he said. He turned to Sep who, as wasteman, was responsible for the care and maintenance of the old workings. 'Were you aware of this, Fordyce?'

587

'No, sir,' Sep answered, in genuine surprise. 'The trap-doors and stoppings were all properly closed off when I checked them yesterday morning.'

'Then someone must have been down here on Friday night.'

Suddenly, the strands of coincidence were beginning to weave themselves together in Duncan Forster's mind and everything seemed to coincide with the time of Roland's disappearance. The items they had found at the top of the shaft and in the old stables, further confirmed his belief that someone had secretly entered the old pit workings. Somehow, willingly or otherwise, Roland had been involved, and this added to his growing fears for the safety of his son.

His thoughts were abruptly interrupted by a shout from one of the pitmen. 'Over here, Mr Forster.' He hurried over to where the man was shining his lamp on a crumpled form lying at the side of the roadway. Bending down for a closer look, he saw it was the body of a man lying face down on the ground. There was something vaguely familiar about it that, try as he may, he could not quite place. A cold premonition of doom slowly crept over him making him feel vulnerable and apprehensive.

He turned and called across to the other men to bring the remaining two lamps over so that he could take a closer look at the body. As they approached, they formed themselves in a loose circle around the body, which was now clearly illuminated in the light of the three Davy lamps. Forster turned the body over and recoiled with shock at the sight of the blackened mass that had once been a face. The eyeless sockets were shrunk into the charred, skinless flesh, leaving the face grotesque and unrecognizable.

A closer examination of the body revealed a manacle and a length of chain attached to each wrist. Could it be an escaped felon? Forster wondered, his hopes rising. A disused mine would be an ideal place to lie low. With food and water a man could remain undetected for weeks, or even months.

He began searching for objects or signs that might help him identify the body, but the heat had scorched most of the clothing, fusing it with the flesh beneath. He caught the glint of a chain across the burnt remains of what had once been a waistcoat. Pulling gently on the chain, what looked like a watch slowly emerged from the ashes of the charred cloth. This was no felon, he sadly conceded, for it was once a fine, expensive watch, though it was now warped and stained by the heat. He turned it over and could just make out some of the engraving on the back of the case, *To ..... son Roland,* followed by the date, *12-2-1798.* Anguish flooded through his body like a sword thrust, as hope was suddenly overwhelmed by grief. It was the watch he had presented to Roland on his twenty-first birthday nearly eighteen years ago.

Rory's account of the night's events left Henry completely numbed. 'I had a feeling that something like this would happen,' he acknowledged sadly, 'but it comes as a shock just the same.'

'We're still only surmising what might have taken place, Rory cautioned. From what Jed told me, neither he nor Wilf could be sure that Roland was involved.'

'Come now, Rory. I think you and I both know he was secretly planning something like this. He denied it when I challenged him, but that was because he didn't want to compromise me.'

'You're jumping to conclusions, Henry. It's one thing to plan something like this, but it would take courage and a cold blooded mind to see it through. Mark has the courage but...' he left the rest unsaid.

'I hope you're right. I would hate my son to be branded a murderer, however justified he may have felt.'

'There you go again, Henry, pre-judging the issue. We haven't got a body yet.'

Henry suddenly looked contrite. 'You're right of course,' he said. 'I'm just worried about him, that's all.'

'Whatever he may have done, the poor lad's injured and needs our help. And I've a feeling things are going to get a lot worse before they get better.'

Henry looked reprovingly at his friend. 'I think you know a little more about this than you're telling me, Rory. You were helping him, weren't you?'

Rory looked uncomfortable. 'Och, I couldna' say no, could I? I only helped so that he could cover his tracks. Sort of kept an eye on him, if you like. He didna' confide in me about what he was up to though,' he added somewhat disingenuously.

'Did you ask?'

'Och no, man. It was none of ma' business.'

Henry shook his head in disbelief. Rory's lapse into the vernacular was a sure sign that he was covering something up, but he knew it would be a waste of time to pursue the matter. 'I think I'd like to go and see my son,' he said softly. 'He may have recovered consciousness by now.'

Rory glanced out of the window to check that it was still dark. 'Aye, if ye must,' he agreed cautiously, 'but we'd better hurry while it's still dark. I don't want to risk your being recognised.'

'Why?'

Rory sighed. 'When a rich and prominent gentleman of the coal trade visits a keelman's house in Sandgate, tongues begin to wag. That's why.'

'But we've been friends for nearly twenty years, Rory.'

'Aye, but when did ye last visit me in Sandgate?' Rory asked gently.

Henry coloured in embarrassment: 'Yes, I see what you mean. People will wonder why and start asking questions.' There was an awkward pause before he added lamely. 'My absence wasn't intentional you know.'

Rory smiled. 'I do know. It's what ye feel in your heart that really matters. 'Come on then,' he said, anxious to change the subject. 'It'll be dawn inside the hour. Time we were on our way.'

Duncan Forster's rage was awesome to watch. Even his closest and most senior employees who had worked for him for more than twenty years, could not recall a more terrifying exhibition of his wrath. They had expected the pain and distress of mourning, but not this. Grief had been consumed by a burning desire for retribution. But, without a target on which he could direct his wrath, a helpless frustration was eating him away like a canker in his soul.

They stood, silent and afraid, in the library of North Moor Hall anxiously waiting for their employer to exhaust his spleen. No one

590

dared to interrupt and they kept their heads averted to avoid any eye contact. The young viewer who had led the search of the old pit workings was taking the brunt of Forster's acid tongue.

'Found no other bodies, did you say? Are you telling me that my son took himself down the mine, opened the trapdoors and then chained himself up to wait for the explosion?'

'There were no more bodies sir. We searched every part of the old mine and found nothing. Not even an arm, leg or any other part of the human anatomy.' The young viewer was trying hard not to be intimidated.

'Someone else was down there,' Forster roared. 'There isn't any other logical explanation. He's hurt too, whoever he is. We found blood all over the stable floor.'

'I agree, sir,' the young viewer responded calmly. 'And we found this.' He dramatically produced a scorched and battered lamp and put it down on the mahogany writing table.

Forster stared at the lamp. 'By God it's a Davy lamp. That proves that someone else was down there with my son. Someone who meant him harm.'

'Whoever it was must have escaped before the pit fired,' Wilkins ventured. 'That would explain the candle stubs we found around the old pit shaft.'

Forster's agent, Gibson, spoke up. 'It must have been carefully planned sir. It's not something you can do on the spur of the moment, is it?'

'No, b'damned,' Forster agreed. 'It would also explain all the fresh horse shit we found in the stables; more than one horse too, by the look of the hoof marks.'

There was a short silence while all this sank in. It was interrupted by Mulligan, the keeker. 'I've just remembered something, sir. It's been bothering me for quite a while.'

Forster glared at him. 'Well, what is it, man?' he said irritably.

'A few weeks ago, sir. I saw some men at the old pit poking around in the yard.'

'Did you recognise them?'

'There were three of them, I think. One of them I think I recognised.'

591

'Who was that?'

'Mark Standish, sir. That troublemaker who used to work here years ago.'

Forster froze as the unpleasant memories came flooding back. 'He was pressed into the navy, so I was told,' he said guardedly.

'Aye, he was, sir. But the war's finished long since. They're all home now, discharged. Those that survived, that is.'

'Did you recognise the other two men?' Forster cut in impatiently.

'No, sir. It was getting dark, but they looked like pitmen from what I could see.

A look of vicious hatred flickered in Forster's eyes as he pondered on this new information. When he spoke, his voice was iced with venom. 'I'm going to issue a warrant for the arrest of Mark Standish. If it was him, I intend to hunt him down and make him pay for what he's done to my son. I don't care how much it costs or how long it takes. I'll swear in a hundred special constables if needs be and, by God, I'll raise the biggest hue and cry this county's ever seen.'

CHAPTER 56

Mark had regained consciousness and was sitting up in bed by the time Rory and Henry arrived back at the house in Sandgate. Fiona was spooning warm soup between his swollen lips, gently coaxing him to swallow. 'It'll help you get your strength back,' she said softly. 'You've lost a lot of blood.' When she saw Henry enter the room she motioned him towards the bed and moved away.

Henry looked down at his son, trying hard not to recoil at the sight of the angry purple swelling that spread out from beneath the blood-stained bandage swathed across his face.

'Not a pretty sight, eh father?' Mark said weakly.

'I don't know,' Henry replied, striving hard to sound more jovial than he felt. 'The old face wasn't up to much, was it? The rearrangement might turn out to be an improvement.'

Mark responded with a wan smile. 'A handsome Standish, eh? Now that would be a contradiction in terms, if ever there was one.'

'Och, ye can't have both beauty and brains,' Rory cut in, helping to ease the situation. 'Unless, of course, you're a MacGregor,' he added.

Fiona flashed him a wicked smile. 'Aye, but even the MacGregor clan misses out on a generation or two,' she said pointedly.

Rory sighed. 'There's just no pleasing some folk, I reckon.'

'If I had any brains I wouldn't have made a mess of things the way I did last night,' Mark interposed. 'I've brought a lot of trouble down on you, I'm afraid.'

Rory's eyes caught Henry's as he turned to Mark. 'Would ye mind telling us exactly what ye were up to at North Moor last night, then? I think ye owe an explanation to your father, at least.'

'I think I owe one to all of you,' Mark corrected. 'I didn't want to involve the people closest to me, which is why I was so secretive. But I'm afraid things have gone too far now and out of my control. So, for everyone's sake, let me explain my stupidity in the hope that you might at least understand my motives.'

There was a short pause as Mark tried to gather his thoughts into some rational order. Then, he began to talk, explaining as clearly as he could the events leading up to the previous night and the terrible aftermath. He omitted only the explanation of his real motive for questioning Roland about the rape of Jane. It would have stripped his soul bare and he was too ashamed to admit his appalling lack of faith. He spoke dispassionately, not seeking to justify his actions, but leaving it to those in the room to make their own judgement. It was a painful re-living of the most horrific experience of his life and when he finished, he lay back exhausted on his pillows.

There was a long silence before anyone spoke. It was finally broken by a question from Henry. 'Did you intend to kill Roland?' His voice was little more than a whisper, as if he was almost afraid to ask.

Mark paused before answering. At first I did.'

'Then, unless he had the same miraculous escape as yourself, doesn't that make you a murderer?'

Mark was too stunned to reply and could only stare uncomprehendingly at his father's grim expression. What had happened at North Moor was a failure of courage on his part and with it, the negation of his murderous intent. How could his father still think of him as a cold blooded murderer? He shook his head in disbelief.

Rory could see that Mark was hurt by his father's uncompromising attitude and he turned angrily on Henry. 'Damn it man, you're his father. You should be supporting Mark, not accusing him. He had every right to do what he did.'

'Every right except in law,' Henry said coldly. Only the courts have the right to deliberately take a man's life.'

'Aye, for stealing a sheep when he's hungry,' Rory said caustically. 'And do you really think a blackguard like Roland would have admitted his guilt in a court of law?'

'No. '

'Then how can justice prevail unless you take the law into your own hands?'

'I don't know, Rory. But setting out to deliberately kill someone, purely for revenge, isn't the answer.'

'Not even someone as evil and guilty as Roland?'

Henry hesitated for a moment. 'Not even Roland,' he said, but his voice lacked conviction.

594

Mark, who had been listening in dazed disbelief, suddenly intervened. 'I think you're both missing the point,' he said, trying to calm the situation. His head was pounding and he just wanted to close his eyes and rest, hoping the problems might melt away. But he also desperately wanted to allay his father's doubts and convince him that he had not degenerated into some barbaric killer. So he continued, holding Henry's gaze as he spoke, his voice soft but firm. 'I said my first intentions were to kill Roland. I wanted to exploit his fear of being underground to break him down; make him suffer as I had suffered and force him to admit his guilt.'

'And did he?' Henry asked.

'Yes, but only to torment me with it. He even implied that it wasn't really rape - that Jane had been a willing partner. It was ironic, really. After all my careful planning, the tables were turned. It was me, not Roland, who was finally taken to the brink. Physically, he was my prisoner, but in mental terms I was his. I think he knew that I couldn't kill him in cold blood and he was right. Call it conscience or simple humanity. I don't know. I only knew that I couldn't go through with it.'

'Then why didn't you let it all stop there?' Henry asked plaintively.

'I tried,' father. 'It was my intention, after making the pit safe again, to leave him there until I could make my own escape. Once clear, I would have arranged for word to be sent to Duncan Forster so that he could release his son. But Roland kept on goading me until I lost my temper. We fought and Roland dislodged the roof supports causing a small roof fall. I was trapped and Roland ran off with the safety lamp. Then the pit fired and you know the rest. But if I caused Roland's death, it was certainly not intentional.

Henry sighed. 'Whether it was intentional or not, Mark, you were still responsible.'

'If he died,' Rory cut in. 'We don't know for sure do we?'

'That's a purely academic point, Rory. If he did survive, it's no thanks to Mark. He had an unhealthy thirst for revenge which I'm sure you kept well salted,' he added, looking piercingly at his friend.

Rory ignored the jibe. 'Och, you're still a pompous old ass, Henry. Have ye no compassion in your soul. I'd ha' been proud of the lad if he were my son.'

'That's because you're a hard man, Rory. But at least you're honest about it. I may have accepted things better if Mark hadn't lied to me about his intentions. It's the fact that everything was done behind my back that really hurts.

'I lied to you because I wanted to protect you,' Mark intervened wearily. 'If I'd told you about my plans it would have compromised you and judging by your reaction now, you couldn't have lived with that.'

'At least I would have had the opportunity to try and talk you out of it. Now, it's too late. What's done is done. One way or another, you've extracted your revenge and no doubt you're satisfied. But don't expect me to share, or even condone your satisfaction.'

'There's none to condone, father, if that gives you any comfort.'

'It does a little,' Henry said, softening.

Mark forced a wry smile. 'You were right about one thing though. Revenge isn't sweet at all. It's the most bitter and corrosive emotion I've ever experienced. And all the more so for having waited so long to find out.'

'Well, that's something positive, at least,' Henry said, softening a little further. 'Perhaps you should try and get some rest now while I talk with Rory. We must think about the future and see what can be done.'

Mark didn't argue. He knew he'd failed to convince his father and this saddened him. Suddenly, the feeling of estrangement that had clouded their earlier years seemed to be returning to sour their relationship again. It was the same invisible barrier that had descended when Henry left North Moor all those years ago. He'd accused him then of betraying the men's trust and now, no doubt, it was his father who felt betrayed. The irony of it all was not lost on him and it added a further knife twist to his wounded ego.

He was glad when everyone finally left the room. He wanted to think about his future, assuming he still had one, but his head throbbed and his mind was fogged with conflicting emotions. He lay gazing at the ceiling, and slowly sank into a shallow, tormented sleep.

*****

596

In the early morning light Henry made his way dejectedly along the Quayside, oblivious to the bustle of activity that was going on around him. Instinctively, he dodged past the stevedores and the unloaded cargoes that were piled up along the quay until he arrived outside his house where he paused, wondering how he should break the news to his family. Suddenly, the front door opened and Ralph came rushing out. He stopped when he saw Henry and grinned apologetically. 'Morning, father. Sorry I'm late,' he said, before dashing off again.

Henry called him back. 'I'd like a word with you, Ralph. Something very urgent has cropped up.'

Puzzled and a little worried, Ralph followed his father back inside the house. 'Is it bad news?' he asked anxiously. 'You look terrible.'

'I feel terrible,' Henry replied, leading the way into the dining room which was still set out for breakfast. He felt hungry but knew he couldn't eat until he had told everyone what had happened. 'Ask your Aunt Ellen to come in, will you? It's important that she hears what I have to say.'

Mystified, Ralph did as he was asked. When Ellen came into the room they all sat down at the table, looking expectantly at Henry.

'There's been an explosion at the old pit at North Moor,' he told them. 'Mark was involved and he's been injured. Not fatally,' he assured them quickly, seeing the look of concern on their faces, 'but bad enough, nevertheless. However, there's more to it than that,' he went on, 'and I think it's important that you all know the full facts about what happened. I must warn you, though, it's not a pleasant story.'

Henry then went on to an edited explanation of the events of the previous night culminating in his visit to Sandgate to see Mark. He deliberately omitted any references to Jane. When he had finished, he looked around the table, waiting for their reaction.

Ellen was the first to speak. 'Will Mark be all right? Is he badly hurt?' Her voice quivered with shock and concern .

'His injuries are severe, but not life threatening. I'm sure he will make a full recovery,' Henry said gently.

'But why is he in Sandgate and not here with us?' Ellen asked anxiously.

'Because Rory thought it would be safer for him.'

597

'He's in trouble, then?'

Henry paused, undecided what to say. 'I'm afraid so,' he said uncomfortably. 'But you mustn't concern yourself,' he added, trying to sound reassuring. 'I'm sure everything will be all right.'

Ellen was not fully convinced but she had other pressing thoughts crossing her mind. 'I must get back to check on Michael,' she said, hurrying from the room.

As soon as they were alone, Ralph turned to his father. 'There's something more, isn't there? Something you're not telling me.'

'Yes. I didn't want Ellen to hear all the unpleasant details. Not just yet, anyway.'

'I hope you're going to tell me.'

Henry looked distraught. 'I suppose you're entitled to know the truth about your brother.'

'That sounds ominous, father. Is the truth so unpalatable?'

'It is to me,' Henry said unhappily. 'You see, I think Roland Forster is dead and I believe Mark is responsible for his death.'

'You mean Mark killed him?' Ralph asked, in astonishment.

'I didn't say that,' Henry said, looking oddly at his son. 'I must say you don't seem too surprised at the possibility, though.'

'I'm not. After what Roland did to Mark, I'm not at all surprised. I'd probably have tried to kill him myself if he'd done that to me.'

Henry looked at his son in astonishment. 'He didn't deserve to die for what he did.'

'Being handed over the press gang and being forced to spend two years in the navy is the equivalent to two years hard labour in my book. It's even worse because Mark was never found guilty of any offence.'

'It's wrong to take the law into your own hands, Ralph.'

'Yes, but surely Mark wasn't in a position to go to law. We know Roland was responsible but there's no evidence and he would never have confessed.'

'We could at least have talked to a lawyer,' Henry persisted.

'Yes, and risk Mark being exposed as a traitor? After all, he did fight for the Americans for three years after he was taken prisoner. That's why he wanted to keep his homecoming a secret so he wouldn't compromise his family.'

598

'I suppose you're right,' Henry agreed wearily.

There was a strained silence before Ralph spoke. 'Do you think all this had anything to do with Jane's suicide?'

Henry's expression became tense. 'Why do you say that? Was it something Mark said?'

'No, but…' Ralph paused, 'It's just all that time not knowing what had happened to Mark, whether he was alive or dead. And all the extra responsibility of having a baby.'

Henry's tenseness began to ease. He sensed Ralph was still unaware of Jane's rape by Roland. 'I suppose it must have affected her in some way,' he said cautiously, 'but we shall never know. All of us who knew and loved her still feel it was some sort of mental breakdown, probably due to the stress of it all.'

Ralph looked perplexed. 'I suppose so,' he said absently. 'Must have been a tremendous shock to Mark, though when he eventually found out. Especially after all he'd been through. I don't think I could have coped with it.'

'And you think Mark has?'

'Mark's not a murderer, father,' Ralph said firmly. 'Whatever he may have planned, it wasn't murder. Mark couldn't kill someone in cold blood, that I know. Not even Roland.' There was a note of stricture in his voice which wasn't lost on Henry.

Henry felt a surge of guilt. He now realised he had been hasty in his assessment of Mark's actions and too quick to condemn. He also knew that there were other more personal and deeper emotions involved, which had clouded his judgement and made him act like the pompous fool that Rory had so rightly called him.

He had fervently hoped that Mark would let matters rest on his return and settle down quietly in Newcastle. A faint hope that had now been irrevocably dashed by his son's foolish actions. Now, Mark would be forced to flee the country, probably back to America. And young Michael, whom he'd come to love as his own son, would one day want to be with him; something he had secretly dreaded and tried hard to put out of his mind. Was this the real reason why he had been so angry with Mark, he wondered, offering only condemnation instead of love and understanding? It made him feel wretched and something of a Judas.

When Henry finally spoke again, his voice was suffused with remorse. 'I think I've done your brother a great disservice, Ralph, and I'm deeply ashamed of myself. I should have stood by him when he needed me instead of censuring him. All I was concerned with was my own selfish interests.'

Ralph had watched his father's melancholy reverie with growing unease and, seeing his distress, moved to comfort him. 'If you think you've wronged Mark, there's still time to apologise and make amends,' he said gently.

Henry smiled wryly, 'Yes, indeed there is. Perhaps I'd better go to him now and try to explain my appallingly selfish behaviour.'

Ralph shook his head. 'You're not a selfish person, father.'

'I am where Michael's concerned. That's been the main problem. I didn't want Mark to take him away from me.'

'But Mark had no intention of doing that,' Ralph said in surprise.

'How do you know?'

'Because he told me. He thought it would be better, for Michael's sake, if he were brought up here in England. If he took him back to America, it would be to a virtual wilderness with no house, few neighbours, no school and no woman's loving care to help him. It would have broken the little fellow's heart, leaving here, and Mark knew it. I think you knew that too.'

'Yes, I did,' Henry confessed. His feeling of guilt now rose to the point where it began to physically hurt. 'I think I'll go back to Sandgate now,' he said. 'I must talk to Mark.'

'I'll come with you, if you don't mind. Ralph said. 'I may not get the chance to see Mark again. Not in this country, at least,' he added pointedly.

Henry's look of acute contrition delighted Rory. He winked at Mark as he left the bedroom, leaving the two men to what he hoped would be a happy, if belated, reconciliation.

There was a long silence before Henry spoke. 'I've come to apologise,' he said awkwardly.

'For what, father?' Mark asked in surprise.

'For accusing you. For letting you down when you most needed me. For being obstinate and blinkered. For being a poor father. Shall I go on?'

'No, there's no need,' Mark answered, taken aback by it all. 'I deserved criticism at least for what I did.'

'But not outright condemnation. I misjudged you, Mark. I didn't appreciate just how much suffering you'd endured and the frustration you must have felt at seeing Roland still free, unrepentant and unpunished. I was too quick to censure you. I should have had a little more charity in my soul.'

Beneath the pain a surge of happiness coursed through Mark. He smiled up at Henry from the bed. 'After all the trouble I've caused, I'm not sure an apology is called for, father. But, if it will make you content and bring us back together again, I'm happy to accept.'

Henry beamed and laid his hand gently on his son's shoulder. 'It makes me feel very content indeed. You and I have wasted too much time in our lives already, Mark. Let's put what's left to good use, eh?'

Mark nodded. 'There's not a lot left I'm afraid,' he said sadly. 'You must surely realise now that I can never set foot in England again. Not after this.'

Henry's eyes clouded over. 'Yes, but we can write to each other. Who knows, I may even visit you in America,' he added, his voice choking with emotion. He knew it was unlikely at his age, but he wanted to reassure his son.

'I hope so, father,' Mark said, keeping up the pretence.

They stared at each other, smiling bravely as they tried to hide their emotions. Suddenly, Henry bent down and clasped his son in a fierce embrace. A tear rolled down his cheek and he turned his head away to hide his embarrassment.

'Let it go, father,' he heard Mark whisper and as he turned back, he saw that his son's eyes were also moist with tears.

They held on to each other for several minutes before Henry broke away. 'I feel a lot better for that,' he said, his voice gruff with emotion.

'Me too,' Mark acknowledged.

'We've been repressing our feelings for too long, you and I.'

Mark smiled ruefully at his father. It was an ironic sense of timing, he thought, that their emotional liberation had finally taken place at the point when his enforced exile was fast approaching, but he said nothing.

'A penny for them?' Henry said.

'Not worth it, father. We can't put the clock back.'

No,' Henry sighed. 'But that we could, eh? With hindsight we'd all be a lot wiser. Which reminds me. Your brother wants to see you.'

Mark wiped his eyes on the bed cover, trying to hide his conflicting emotions. 'Better show him in, then.'

Ralph sensed the new atmosphere of rapprochement as soon as he entered the room and smiled happily as he approached the bed. 'You look an awful sight,' he said, holding out his hand.

Mark clasped it firmly. 'You should have seen the other fellow,' he answered flippantly and immediately wished he'd bitten his tongue. Fortunately, no one seemed to notice his unintentional satirical slip, or if they did, they ignored it.

'I'm going to miss you, Mark, Ralph said, turning serious.

'And I you.'

'I wish I'd had the chance to get to know you earlier.'

'You were too young to appreciate me then,' Mark answered teasingly. 'Still, the age gap becomes less as you get older.'

'I've found that out these past few months,' Ralph acknowledged. 'I only wish we had more time.'

'So do I, Ralph, but I've only got myself to blame.'

'I fully intend to visit you in America, you know,' Ralph said, with an earnestness that took Mark by surprise. 'If you'll have me, that is,' he added.

'You'll be most welcome.'

'Good, because I really intend to come.'

'I know you will, Ralph,' Mark said fondly, 'and I'll look forward to it. Still, we have a little time yet. We'll see some more of each other before I go.'

'I'm afraid not, Mark,' Rory interrupted after quietly entering the room. Jed's just brought some bad news. Wilf's been arrested.'

*****

602

Jed had ran most of the way from North Moor to Sandgate and he collapsed, exhausted, as soon as Rory opened the door. It took several minutes for him to recover sufficient breath to be able to recount the details of Wilf's arrest.

'They came to the house about ten o'clock,' he said, still gasping for breath.

'And did they say what he was being charged with?' Henry asked.

'No. They just said they had orders to take him up to North Moor Hall for questioning.'

'Why?'

'To see if he had anything to do with Roland Forster's death, I suppose.'

Henry was stunned. 'His death, did you say?'

'Yes. The rescue party found him, or rather what was left of him, in the old pit workings.'

'Was he caught in the explosion?'

'Aye, burnt to a cinder he was.'

'Then how did they recognize the body?'

'Seems there was a pocket watch with some inscription on it, according to Sep.

'Was Sep with the rescue party?'

'Aye. He was there when they found Roland. He came to tell us just before they arrested Wilf.'

That added authenticity to the story, Henry thought, and his feeling of apprehension began to grow. 'Did Sep tell you where they found Roland's body?'

'Aye. He was lying near the staple that leads down to the new workings. He must have been trying to escape from the firedamp.'

'Did he mention anything else that was unusual?'

Jed thought for a moment. 'I don't think so, except for one of those new Davy lamps they found lying near the body. 'An' summat else,' he added, suddenly remembering. 'Sep said there were chains fixed to Roland's wrists. Made them think, that did.'

Henry nodded thoughtfully. 'Was there much damage done to the pit?' he asked.

603

Jed shrugged. 'Not a lot, according to Sep. The old gear that was left lying around was smashed up, but there was only one small roof fall.'

This news cheered Henry for it confirmed Mark's story. His son was not a murderer and he again felt guilty for having ever doubted him. 'Just one more question, Jed.' He paused to give added emphasis. 'Did you or Wilf have anything to do with what happened last night?'

Jed shook his head firmly. 'No, we didn't. We wanted to help but Mark wouldn't let us. Said the less we knew the better. All he asked for was information on the old pit and the like.'

'The like being Roland, I suspect,' Henry said dryly.

Jed ignored the remark. 'I think Wilf guessed what he was up to, but said nowt. That's why we headed straight for the old shaft when the pit fired. Everybody else thought it was the new pit.'

'Did anyone see you,' Rory asked.

'Yes. We tried to keep out of sight in case we were followed but there were too many people about. The explosion woke the whole village.'

'Thank God for that,' Henry said. 'At least you've both got an alibi with independent witnesses.'

'Aye, but it might have been better if there'd been time for Wilf to get rid of some of the things that were left lying around.'

'It certainly would. Was he disturbed?'

'Aye. Duncan Forster and his men came searching, so he had to hide until he could slip away.'

'Was he seen?'

'He doesn't think so, but he was there when they found fresh horse shit and all the other things like candle stubs. Forster knows that somebody had been using the old shaft, that's for sure. He must think it was Mark.'

'Why ?'

'Because he's issued a warrant for his arrest. He's swearing in special constables by the dozen, offering them five shillings a day. They're queuing up to join.'

Henry's heart turned to ice as the shock news sank in. Mark must have been recognized for Duncan Forster to have acted so promptly and so confidently. He knew the man well enough to realise he wouldn't rest until Mark was caught. Grief would cloud his judgement turning an issue of law into a personal vendetta. His son was now in extreme danger.

Rory had come to the same conclusion and quickly took charge of the situation. 'We've got to get Mark out of the country as soon as possible. He'll no' be safe in Newcastle.'

'Duncan Forster has no jurisdiction in the town,' Henry corrected. 'He's a Northumberland magistrate.'

'Maybe, but he'll seek the co-operation of the town magistrates and they're bound to help. Once that happens, we'll have the town watch and Forster's special constables crawling all over the place. And your house will be the first one they'll search.'

'I'll deny any knowledge of my son's whereabouts.' Henry answered resolutely.

'Och I'm sure you will, Henry, but they'll no' believe you. There's something else you can do, though.'

Henry looked baffled. 'What's that?'

'When they do come, try and delay them or confuse them. We need time, Henry. Even a few hours could make all the difference.'

'I'll do my best. But how on earth are we going to get Mark out of the country? If what you say is true Forster will seal off the town. We'll be lucky if we even get him out of Sandgate.'

'Leave that to me,' Rory said confidently. 'Jamie Drummond's collier brig, the *Lady Morag*, is lying at Shields. He's due to sail as soon as he's taken on coal. I've an idea how we can smuggle Mark on board.'

'Can Jamie Drummond be trusted?'

'I'd trust him with my life. Mark will be safe enough once we get him on board.'

Henry looked dubious. 'What happens if we do?'

'Jamie will see that he's put aboard a ship for America. There are regular sailings from London. It's his only chance, Henry.'

'He's right, father,' Ralph broke in reassuringly.

'But won't they be watching the Port of London by then?'

'Maybe, but it would take an army of men to search every ship leaving London. With Jamie's help, I'm sure he'll be safe.'

'I hope you're right, Rory. I dread to think what will happen if Forster gets his hands on Mark.'

'He won't, believe me,' Rory said, still undaunted by the problems that lay ahead. 'Now, if you don't mind, Henry, I've got things to do. I suggest you go home and try to act as normal as possible. And remember what I told you about delaying tactics because we'll need to buy some time.'

'I'll do my best,' Henry said, rising to leave. 'You're a good friend to have at a time like this, Rory MacGregor. I shan't forget it.'

'Och, awa' wi' ye,' Rory exclaimed, his dialect returning to hide his embarrassment.

Ralph was about to accompany his father when Rory called him back. 'There's something you can do to help your brother, but it might be a little risky.'

'Tell me what it is,' Ralph said eagerly.

'Hire a fast horse and ride to North Shields. When you get there, find a boatman to take you out to the *Lady Morag* and let Jamie Drummond know what's happened. Tell him I'll have Mark on board before he sails for London. Jamie won't take a penny for helping, so don't insult him by offering payment. But you'll have to find some passage money for the voyage from London to America. Now, off you go, both of you. '

As they walked back to the Quayside, Henry rummaged in his pocket and took out a bunch of keys which he handed to Ralph. 'Before you go to the livery stables, call in at the office and open up the strongroom. Inside, you'll find a small oak chest and the key to open it is there on the ring. Inside the chest you'll find a leather bag containing a thousand guineas and a hundred gold sovereigns. Take it with you to Shields and give it to Jamie Drummond to keep for Mark.'

'That's a lot of gold to hand over to someone you don't know, father.'

'If Rory trusts him then so do I. Besides, the bank's paper money will be of little use to Mark in America.'

Ralph shrugged. 'I suppose not.'

'Then off with you. We haven't much time.'

CHAPTER 57

Henry had been home for barely an hour when he heard thunderous knocking on the front door. Remembering Rory's instructions, he decided to ignore it and carried on eating his belated breakfast playing for time. The furious knocking continued until he heard the front door being opened followed by the sound of angry voices. A few moments later, an agitated Ellen appeared at the dining room door but before she could announce who was calling, an enraged Duncan Forster pushed past her and burst into the room.

'This is outrageous behaviour,' Henry said, rising angrily from the table. 'I must ask you to leave my house at once.'

'Not until I'm sure your son isn't hiding here,' Forster responded belligerently, holding his ground.

'Hiding?' Henry said in mock surprise. 'Why should he be hiding in my house? It's his home.'

'Because I've got a warrant for his arrest, that's why. '

Henry feigned shock. 'On what charge, may I ask?'

'Murder. The murder of my son, Roland,' Forster snarled. His eyes were filled with hatred and his whole being clamoured for revenge.

'That's the most ridiculous allegation I've ever heard,' Henry said, pretending to be offended. 'My son is not a murderer, nor a rapist,' he added, looking scornfully at Forster.

The intended barb struck home and Forster's rage rose almost to bursting point. 'I demand you hand him over,' he screamed. 'Otherwise I'll order my constables to search the house.'

Henry was unmoved. 'Let me see your warrant, first,' he demanded.

Forster reached down inside his pocket and after pulling out the official document, flung it down on the table. Henry calmly picked it up and after glancing at it, threw it back at Forster. 'This is Newcastle, not Northumberland. You have no authority here.'

Forster turned almost apoplectic with rage. 'I know he's here, damn you. I insist you hand him over, unless you want to be cited as an accessory.'

'He's not here, I tell you, and I won't allow you to search my house without proper legal authority. As a magistrate, you should know that.'

For a few moments, Forster remained speechless as he struggled to control himself. When he finally spoke, his voice was filled with implacable hatred. 'Alright, Standish,' he growled threateningly. 'But you'll regret this, mark my words. I'm on my way to the Mansion House and I can assure you that the Mayor, as chief magistrate of this town, will support me. When he does, I'll be back with the necessary power to search this house; and search it I will, from top to bottom. In the meantime,' he added warningly, 'my constables will keep a close watch outside, both front and rear.'

'I'm not your prisoner,' Henry said defiantly. 'I'll come and go as I please until you have a legal order that says otherwise. Now kindly leave my house.'

With a baleful glare, Forster turned and stormed out of the room. A few seconds later, Henry heard the sound of the front door being violently slammed shut. He stood for a few moments, looking through the latticed casements of the large oriel window at the retreating figure of Duncan Forster until he turned into Sandhill and was lost from sight.

As he turned away from the window, a feeling of helplessness overwhelmed him. The Mansion House stood in the Close, a mere four hundred yards away on the riverside above the bridge. There would be precious little time before Forster returned to search the house and he could not think of anything to delay or confuse him as Rory had requested. After an unsuccessful search of the house, Henry knew that Forster's attention would turn to Sandgate and Rory MacGregor, for the connection between the two families was too well known to be kept secret for long. The thought depressed him and left him feeling even more impotent.

Suddenly, an idea struck him, causing a sly smile to spread slowly across his face. Donning his coat, he went downstairs and opened the front door. As he expected, the house was being watched. Two men stood on the pavement a few yards away from the door. One sported a heavy cudgel and Henry spotted what looked like the butt of a pistol sticking out from beneath the jacket of the other man. They stood,

608

undecided, when they saw him so Henry ignored them and after closing the door, marched off briskly along the Quayside.

The man with the pistol recovered quickly and beckoned to the other man to follow Henry whilst he remained guarding the front entry to the house. Henry assumed that another two men were watching the back of the house and he paid no attention to the man who was now following him. After a few yards, he turned up one of the narrow chares that led off the Quayside and took a long, circuitous route to the adjoining district of Pandon, where he owned a small warehouse. He tried to look nervous and paused from time to time to look around, but always pretending not to notice the man following him.

The warehouse was located in Blythe's Nook, a crooked alley running off Pandon Street near the spot where the impressive Pandon Hall once stood. Arriving at the warehouse, Henry paused and looked furtively around him, again pretending not to see the man following him who had quickly squeezed into a doorway. Taking a bunch of keys from his pocket he opened the door and went inside, carefully locking the door behind him. The warehouse had not been used for years and the windows were almost black with grime. Henry was able to watch the man outside who, after trying the door, moved back up the alley and stood in a doorway to keep watch.

Henry waited an hour before leaving, locking the door behind him. He ignored the man in the doorway and made his way slowly back to his house on the Quayside. The man followed at a safe distance, looking very pleased with himself.

A small crowd had gathered at Henry's door and were being held back by the constables. Henry noticed that some of the men wore the distinctive watch-coats of the town watch, which indicated that whatever help the mayor may have offered, had been conditional on Forster accepting the town's jurisdiction in the matter. This was confirmed when he went inside and was confronted not by Forster, but by the captain of the watch.

The captain was cautious and deferential in his questioning, for he knew Henry to be a rich and influential figure in the town.

'I'm sorry you weren't here, sir, when we searched the house, but the matter was urgent.'

'And did you find what you were looking for?' Henry asked calmly.

'No sir, we did not.'

'You were seeking my son, I presume?'

'Yes sir,' the captain said, looking searchingly at Henry. 'May I ask if you know of his whereabouts?'

'He was here last night as far as I'm aware,' Henry lied, 'so I imagine he went out somewhere early this morning.'

'And you've no idea where that might be, sir?'

'No, I'm afraid I haven't.'

'You do realise, sir, that you'll be committing an offence if you try to help him escape. Your son has been accused of murder.'

'He may have been accused, captain, but he's certainly not guilty.'

'That's for a court of law to decide, sir, if you don't mind me saying so.'

Henry's response was cut short by a loud commotion in the street below. Looking out of the window, he saw the man who had followed him to the warehouse talking excitedly to Duncan Forster and pointing in the general direction of Pandon. Forster immediately called his men together and began issuing instructions.

The captain of the watch, who had also observed the scene below, quickly realised what Forster was up to. 'If you'll excuse me, sir, I think I'd better get down there and find out what's going on.' Calling his men together, they left the house and began taking charge of the volatile situation outside. Then, trying hard to keep a semblance of order, he marched both his own men and Forster's constables off in the direction of Pandon, followed by an excited crowd of onlookers.

Standing at the window above, Henry allowed himself a quiet smile of satisfaction as he watched the crowd disappear round the corner into Broad Chare. 'That should keep them occupied for a while,' he murmured to himself.

It soon became very clear to Rory that his earlier prediction was proving correct. All hell had indeed broken loose and the town was now full of armed men searching for Mark. No one could remember anything quite like it since the battle of Sandgate in '97, when Rory

610

and his keelmen had routed the invading force of police and militia; an event now anchored in local folklore.

After a suitable rest, Jed was sent back to North Moor to seek further news of Wilf.

'Keep your head down, bonny lad, and don't tell anyone what you've been up to,' Rory warned. 'If Forster finds out you've been visiting Sandgate, he'll soon put two and two together and come storming in here earlier than I'd like.'

'You expecting him, then?'

'Aye, but not just yet. With a bit of luck I'll have time to organise Mark's escape.'

'Aa'll wish ye luck, then,' Jed said, and after shaking Rory by the hand, set off back to North Moor.

As soon as he had gone, Rory called to Colin. 'Right, laddie, we've got work to do. Get your coat on.'

'Where are we going?'

'To see old Silas Nesbit, the undertaker.'

Colin looked astonished. 'Why?'

'To arrange a funeral, of course.'

'Who for?'

'You'll see when we get there,' Rory said, smiling enigmatically.

Never a man to accept a minor role in anything, least of all in the search for his son's killer, Duncan Forster had virtually commandeered the whole town watch. The captain and his thirty watchmen were soon firmly under his thumb and the town magistrate appointed by the mayor to oversee the search was too weak and indecisive to put up much resistance. Forster was like a deranged crusader, driven by an obsessive fury that frightened everybody into a submissive acceptance of his leadership.

The debacle of the abortive raid on the warehouse had incensed him and he now turned his wrath on the known associates of Henry. Deep down, he sensed that Sandgate held the key to a successful outcome and when all else failed, he decided to concentrate his men on a house by house search of the area. But first, he had to seal off all escape routes from the town.

With only one bridge over the Tyne at Newcastle, the next being more than twenty miles upstream, blocking off the roads proved relatively easy. Armed men were posted on the bridge and at every road leading out of the town. But Forster knew that the most likely escape route would be by river, probably in the hope that the fugitive could be smuggled on board some friendly ship. That was why Sandgate held the key.

After careful thought, he ordered a boom of armed guard boats to be placed across the river, upstream at Dunston and downstream across the narrows between St Peter's Sand and Friars Goose. He instructed Gibson, his agent, to make the arrangements and hire whatever boats and men were needed. For good measure armed guards were posted at intervals along both banks of the river.

Finally, in a flash of pure inspiration, Forster hired the revolutionary new paddle steamer, *Perseverance*, one of the two steamboats recently introduced onto the Tyne. The *Perseverance* was the local wonder of the age and, in terms of speed and manoeuvrability, could out sail anything else on the river. He would make it his command post once he took to the river.

Satisfied that all escape routes were now tightly sealed, Forster began to brief the remainder of his men for the onslaught on Sandgate. With extra volunteers recruited from the town, attracted by the generous five shillings a day, he now had almost a hundred men available for the search and arrest operation. And remembering the fiasco of the '94 pre-dawn action, he vowed to move in during the afternoon while there was still light.

This time it would be different. This time it would be successful.

Rory planned Mark's funeral with great care. The coffin was extremely strong and spacious, made out of highly polished mahogany with six brass carrying handles. A large air hole had been drilled at the broad end of the coffin to correspond with the position of Mark's face when he was lying inside it. During the funeral, it would be covered by a large wreath of flowers.

Word of the funeral had been widely circulated and virtually the whole population of Sandgate turned out to watch or take part. At half past three in the afternoon, the black draped hearse drawn by two plumed horses, moved off from the undertakers and headed for St. Ann's, the keelmen's chapel, where a memorial service was to be held. Six strong keelmen, acting as pallbearers, marched alongside the hearse where the coffin lay surrounded by a wall of flowers. Behind the hearse marched scores of keelmen, with a large crowd of women and children bringing up the rear.

The keelmen were dressed in their traditional costume of short blue coat and slate coloured trousers, cut tight at the knee and belled out below. They wore yellow waistcoat and flat-brimmed, black silk hats with black trailing ribbons. It was their formal shore attire

The atmosphere grew tense as the long funeral cortege moved out of Sandgate and into St Ann's Street. It slowly approached the junction with the New Road where a group of Forster's armed constables stood barring the way. The tension rose further as the hearse reached the junction and the pallbearers walk stiffened in anticipation of trouble. Then suddenly, the armed constables fell back, allowing the procession to pass unhindered. Colin, who was one of the pallbearers, heaved a silent sigh of relief. So far, so good, he thought. They were over the first hurdle.

After a short service at St Ann's chapel, the coffin was returned to the hearse and the cortege continued on its way, crossing the bridge over the Ouseburn and up the steep slope to the Ballast Hills Burying Ground. The cemetery was a small railed in area set among hills formed by the discharge of ballast over many years from ships returning to the Tyne. This was the spot chosen by the early Scottish Presbyterian immigrants of Newcastle, stern, unbending Covenanters of the time of the early Stuarts, to bury their dead and still used by the town's Dissenters.

Looking down to the Ouseburn Colin could see the keel moored near the Glasshouse Bridge. He raised his arm in a pre-arranged signal and received the correct acknowledgement from one of the keelmen standing on the deck. He smiled. Rory's plan seemed to be working perfectly.

As the mourners gathered round the hastily dug grave, Colin gave the signal for the coffin to be lowered. A long length of copper tubing, about one inch in diameter, was passed forward from the crowd and wedged tightly into the hole that had been drilled into the coffin lid. Then, holding the tube upright, Colin ordered the grave to be filled in. When this was done, the end of the tube protruded a few inches above the soil level and was quickly hidden by the flowers and wreaths that were piled on top of the grave.

Slowly, the mourners made their way down the hill and headed back towards Sandgate. Soon, the graveside was left empty and forlorn as the deepening dusk settled over the grey tombstones.

From his vantage point on the high ground above the New Road, Duncan Forster watched the funeral below with growing unease. His men were ready to enter Sandgate and begin the house to house search, but the captain of the watch still cautioned against moving in. 'There'll be a bloodbath if we're not careful,' he warned. 'Funerals always raise the emotions and there's a lot of women and children down there.'

Forster grudgingly agreed to delay a little longer but he could not dispel the uncomfortable feeling that something was wrong. The funeral, and in particular the timing of it, was too much of a coincidence and his suspicions were aroused. The keelmen must know they were trapped, he thought, and a large, solemn funeral was just the sort of delaying tactic that Rory MacGregor would use to play for time. It would be to their advantage, not his, if the search was delayed until after dark.

He was about to order the men to move in when, out of the corner of his eye, he saw a drunken looking waterman push his way past the constables and grab the arm of the captain of the watch. An earnest conversation ensued, conducted in hoarse whispers, and it was clear to Forster that the two men were well known to each other. After a few moments, the captain approached Duncan Forster. 'Arnold Jessop, there,' he said pointing to the waterman, 'reckons he's got some important information, sir. I think you ought to hear it.'

'Is he reliable?' Forster asked warily.

'I've known him for years, sir. He works as a wherry-man and lives in Sandgate. He's my key informer when I want to know what the keelmen are up to.'

'Is he indeed,' Forster said sarcastically. 'Hasn't done much to stop their nuisances and spout wrecking lately, has it?'

The captain ignored the jibe. 'I still think you should hear him out, sir.'

Forster shrugged and beckoned the man over. 'Well?' he barked. 'What is it you have to say?'

Jessop looked uncomfortable and glanced back at the captain. 'Aa knaa's where the man your lookin' for is, yor honour,' he said fawningly.

'Then spit it out, man. We haven't much time.'

Jessop gave an embarrassed cough and again looked at the captain of the watch. Taking his cue, the captain spoke. 'The mayor usually pays him for any information, sir,' he said apologetically.

'Does he, indeed. Well I only pay for information when it's proved to have been of some use. I don't buy idle gossip.'

'It's not gossip, yor honour,' Jessop intervened, looking hurt and disappointed. 'Aa'll end up wi' me throat cut if Rory MacGregor ivor finds oot.'

'The name Rory MacGregor seemed to galvanise Forster's waning attention. 'Then you'd better speak out, man,' he said suddenly becoming interested. 'I'll give you five guineas for the information and another five if we catch Standish.'

'Oh, yee'll catch him allreet,' Jessop said confidently. 'He's doon there,' he added, pointing to the funeral cortege moving slowly towards St. Ann's.

'Where, exactly,' Forster snapped impatiently.

'Why, in the coffin, yor honour. They're gannin to bury him up at Ballast Hills then dig him up later, when it's dark.'

Forster looked puzzled. 'He'll suffocate surely?'

'No, yor honour. They're gannin to fix a tube doon to the coffin so as he can breathe like.'

A look of understanding dawned on Forster's face So that was it, he thought. A typical MacGregor ruse. He'd been right all along to feel suspicious about the funeral. 'What are they planning to do after they dig him up,' he asked out of curiosity.

'There's a keel waitin' doon on the Ouseburn near the Glasshouse Bridge. It'll take him doon to Shields.'

Forster beckoned to Gibson, he agent, who was standing nearby. 'Pay the man five guineas,' he ordered. Then, turning to the captain he whispered, 'but keep the rogue under close guard, just until this is all over.'

The captain nodded. 'Shall we move in now, sir?' he asked.

Forster looked thoughtful. 'No,' he answered after a while. 'Let the funeral proceed as though we don't suspect anything. When it's over, we'll keep a secret watch on the cemetery and wait for MacGregor to come back and dig him up. That way we can bag all the accomplices.'

The pale light of a half-moon cast an eerie glimmer over the burying ground as the cloud cover began to thin. The score of constables crouched in their cramped positions behind the larger tombstones shivered, though not always because of the cold, as the spectral shadows of their fertile imaginations danced across the graveyard.

After waiting for two hours in the darkness the realisation slowly came to Forster that the resurrection party would not be coming. Something had gone wrong, though he couldn't understand what it was. Perhaps they had been spotted by the keelmen when they were taking up their positions. Whatever the reason, there was no longer any point in sticking to the plan. At least, he consoled himself, the man who had killed his son was now lying only six feet beneath him and that thought gave him considerable cause for satisfaction.

He stood up and called to his men to come out. This they did with relief and gratitude, stretching their limbs as they emerged from the shadows to join him at the site of the new grave.

'No point in further concealment,' he said and ordered the constable, with the blacked out lantern, to relight the other lamps. Soon, the new grave was surrounded by a pool of light as the constables gathered round in a circle. Mulligan, the keeker, used his feet to kick the flowers from the grave top, revealing the copper tube sticking out of the loose soil. 'Want me to pull it out, Mr Forster?' he asked, a cruel glint showing in his eyes. 'Save a lot of bother with the courts and all that.'

Forster contemplated the suggestion for a few moments and found it appealing. He couldn't think of a worse way to die, slowly suffocating inside the dark, cramped confines of a coffin lying under six feet of earth. Being pronounced dead by some incompetent doctor and being buried alive was a fear that haunted many sick people. Besides, he thought, Mulligan had a point. It would save going to court and avoid the risk that his son's killer might be acquitted. A trial would be risky and he knew Henry Standish could afford to retain the best lawyer for his own son's defence. Yes, better this way. He nodded to Mulligan.

It took Mulligan only a few minutes to loosen the copper tube and draw it out. The smooth surface of the copper offered little resistance to the loosely packed soil inside the grave and Mulligan laid the tube at Forster's feet, like a devoted dog bringing its master his slippers. Forster stared at it excitedly, savouring the agony that the man trapped below must now be suffering. Vengeance really was sweet, he thought, and in a way this was almost poetic justice.

Not knowing how long it took for a man to suffocate to death, he sent a small party down to the keel which was still moored in the Ouseburn near the Glasshouse Bridge. He might as well arrest the keelmen as accomplices, he thought, and with luck one of them might be MacGregor. But in this he was soon disappointed, for when the constables returned they reported the keel deserted.

It was starting to get dark when Forster's patience finally ran out. 'Open up the grave,' he ordered. Turning to Mulligan he whispered 'I can't wait to see the dying terror on his face. This is one death mask I'll always treasure.'

The thud of an iron shovel striking wood brought Forster out of his grim reverie. Ropes were passed down and tied to the brass handles of the coffin which was then quickly raised to the surface. Forster looked down gloatingly at the soil encrusted lid. 'Open it,' he ordered.

Crowbars brought for this purpose were quickly forced under the lid of the coffin. There followed the sounds of splintering wood as the lid was prised open. The circle of lights moved forward and Forster bent down to look inside the coffin. Suddenly, his expression froze and a strangled cry escaped his tightly drawn lips.

The coffin was full of stones.

CHAPTER 58

It had been a long and hectic day for Rory MacGregor, but danger was like food and drink to him and gave him the energy to sustain the long hours without becoming careless. He enjoyed the challenge of pitting his wits against the authorities and his planning on this occasion was as meticulous as ever.

The funeral arrangements had taken up most of the morning and runners had been sent to ensure that the required numbers of keelmen and their families turned out for the occasion. It was important that large crowds should be seen on the streets to help confuse and intimidate the blockading constables.

After calling together his lieutenants, an inner circle of keel skippers, Rory outlined his plans. The tough, loyal band of brothers listened with growing enthusiasm and when he had finished, their admiration for their charismatic leader knew no bounds. Now they would cheerfully follow him to hell and back if needs be, especially if it would put the authority's nose out of joint.

When everybody had been fully briefed on their individual roles in the day's coming events, the meeting broke up in a jaunty mood of optimistic defiance. Lookouts were posted at strategic points with a team of boys acting as runners. This gave Rory eyes and ears in every part of his Sandgate stronghold and fast lines of communication to warn him of impending danger.

Colin's task was to co-ordinate and lead the funeral cortege, acting as a pallbearer. He was about to leave when Rory called him back. 'A word before you go, Colin.'

Colin saw the familiar Machiavellian look on his stepfather's face and groaned. 'What now, Rory?' he said cagily. 'I don't like the look of that devious grin on your face.'

'Just a little errand before you line up the funeral,' Rory beamed.

'Oh aye?' Colin answered sceptically.

'Do you think you can find Arnold Jessop?'

'Shouldn't be difficult. He'll be drinking in the Half Moon by now.'

'Good. Then send in two of your lads to stand beside him. Near enough for him to hear them talking.'

'And what will they be talking about?'

'That Mark's being smuggled out in the coffin to be buried at Ballast Hills and dug up again after dark.'

'But he's not. The coffin's full of stones.....' Colin's voice trailed off as he realised what Rory was up to.

'You cunning old rogue,' he said, admiringly. 'You know Arnold Jessop's an informer, don't you?'

'Aye, so why not use him?'

'Why not, indeed,' Colin said, smiling at the thought.

As soon as Colin left the house, Rory turned his attention to the next part of his plan. He made his way to a small carpenter's shop near the Swirle, which was owned by a taciturn ex-keelman who had learnt the trade after being pressed into the navy during the war. Although he had risen to the rank of carpenter's mate, he was still angry at his loss of freedom and carried a bitter grudge against the authorities. For this reason, Rory knew he could trust him.

He smiled at the man as he placed a sheet of paper down on the bench. 'Do you think you can make that for me before it gets dark?' he asked.

The man looked at the drawing and after studying it for a moment, shrugged his shoulders. 'Don't see why not,' he said, 'provided the keel's handy, like.'

'It's lying out there in the Swirle,' Rory said gesturing towards the door. 'By the bridge,' he added.

'Well I'd best get started, then,' the man said casually. There had been rumours flying around Sandgate all morning and he sensed this was part of some plot against the authorities. He decided to ask no further questions.

'Some of my lads will pick the keel up after dark,' Rory said. 'The tide will be right by then.'

'So will that,' the carpenter said, pointing to the drawing.

*****

619

Rory returned home and sat with Fiona for a short while, explaining the events he had set in motion. 'It'll be a long night,' he said, 'but a satisfying one.' He wanted to warn and comfort her at the same time.

'It'll be a dangerous one too, Rory MacGregor,' she replied, not taken in by his casualness.

'Aye, it will lassie. I won't deny it, but I thought you ought to know.'

'I think I've known ever since they brought Mark here,' Fiona replied. She understood Rory only too well to know he would never desert a friend. The danger would only add excitement to the challenge. He would never change, she thought, nor she realised, would she want him to change. For it was this caring side of his nature that had always appealed to her and made her love him all the more. She rose and kissed him. 'Take care, my love. You're very precious to me, so don't you go off and do something stupid.'

'I won't. You're just as precious to me, you know.'

'I do know,' Fiona responded, her eyes shining. She felt his arms pulling her close. His kiss was gentle, filled with a tenderness that always surprised her coming from a man who was so strong, both physically and mentally.

Rory looked down at her, sighing as he slowly released her. 'Now, if you don't mind, I must go upstairs and see how our patient is getting on. There's a few things I need to explain to him.'

Mark had just woken from a long, dreamless sleep and lay staring at the ceiling. He felt much better and though his wounds were still sore, the debilitating headache had almost gone. He smiled when he saw Rory enter the room. 'You should have woken me earlier,' he said. 'It's time I moved on.'

'You will, Mark, all in good time. But Forster's men are watching all the roads out of Newcastle and he's got guard boats out on the river. So you're best off where you are at the moment.'

'But the longer I stay, the greater the danger for you and Fiona,' Mark protested.

'Let me worry about that. You're safe here for now and we'll move you down to Shields tonight.'

'How? You said the roads were being watched.'

'You'll be going by river.'

'But the guard boats…'

Rory cut him short. 'Och, they'll no' be a problem. Just trust me, Mark. I'll get you to Shields and see you safely aboard the *Lady Morag*. That's Jamie Drummond's collier brig,' he explained. 'Jamie's an old friend of mine and he'll take you to London and arrange a passage to America for you from there. There's a regular packet ship service to New York.'

'I still don't see how you can get me to Shields if all the roads are being watched and Forster's guard boats are blockading the river.' Mark persisted.

'Because I have a plan that I'm sure will work. But it's risky and a lot will depend on you.'

'In what way?'

'Can you stand being cooped up for four hours or more?'

'Rory, I was cooped up on a frigate for two years, remember?'

'Aye, but I'm talking about a really small place. Like a box measuring only seven feet by less than three and only two feet high. And it will be dark,' Rory added to emphasise the discomfort.

'Sounds like a large coffin,' Mark said, looking bemused.

'Aye, it is in a way,' Rory replied watching Mark closely. 'You'll be buried in the bilge of a keel with twenty-one tons of coal on top of you. Do you think you can handle that?'

Mark thought for a moment. 'I think I can,' he said, 'but how will I be able to breathe?'

'The box will have air holes with tubes leading out through the bilge into the huddock.'

'Will it work?'

'In theory, yes.'

'But you won't know until I'm buried beneath the coal. And if it doesn't….' Mark left the rest unsaid.

'Well at least you've had some practice,' Rory said with a grin.

Mark looked puzzled. 'In what way?'

'We buried you this afternoon.' Seeing the look of astonishment on Mark's face, Rory continued, 'I think I'd better tell you all about it.

*****

As darkness settled over the river, the keel was floated off on the rising tide which had lapped its way up the Swirle. Using the two large oars, the crew brought the keel round to the mooring post beneath the row of houses in the Low Way, which backed onto the river. Using Rory's escape route, Mark was helped through the roof space and down onto a small balcony above the mooring post, where he was gently lowered by ropes down to the keel moored below. Once inside the empty hold, Rory pulled a heavy canvas across the opening and opened the shutter of the blacked out lantern to reveal the hiding place.

When Mark saw the box which was fitted into the floor of the hold, he realised why Rory had been so concerned. The Tyne keel drew only four feet six inches of water when fully loaded with its twenty-one tons of coal and this allowed them to negotiate the many shallows that lay between Newcastle and Shields. Because of this, the floor of the hold was only two feet below the gunwale, a severe constraint which governed the size of Mark's hiding place.

The keel itself was just over forty feet long with an enormous beam of nineteen feet. To compensate for the shallow draught, no hatch covers were fitted to the hold and the coal was allowed to pile up on the open deck amidships, being held in place by wooden retaining boards raised above the level of side decks. When loaded, the keel looked as if she were carrying a huge wheel-less waggon on her deck amidships, heaped high with coal.

The keel was manned by a skipper and a crew of three; two men and a boy. The keelmen were known as keel-bullies, meaning keel brothers, and the boy was called a pee-dee. After loading beneath the spouts at one of the many staithes that pockmarked the banks along the tidal reaches of the river, the keel would drop down to Shields on the ebb tide propelled by a pair of oars and steered over the stern by a twenty-five feet long oar called a swape. If the wind was favourable, the crew would hoist a single grimy square sail set forward of the hold. The mast was stepped in a pivoting socket so that it could be easily lowered when passing under the low arches of the Tyne Bridge at Newcastle.

Mark's eyes were still fixed on the box when Rory's voice broke through his thoughts.

'You still willing to try it?'

'I think so,' Mark responded after a pause.

'I wouldn't blame you if you said no. Four hours could seem like a lifetime in there.'

'It's just the thought of being buried under all that coal, 'Mark said.

'Aye, I'd feel the same myself.'

'But it's the only realistic chance I have, isn't it?' Mark said, looking Rory squarely in the eye.

'Rory held Mark's gaze. 'Probably, but even so, I can't guarantee it. With a man like Forster, hell bent on revenge, you can never tell what he'll do next. He'll stop at nothing to find you, that's for sure.'

'Well, I've made my bed so's to speak, so I'll just have to lie in it.' Mark said pointing to the coffin-like box.

The pun brought a grim smile to Rory's face. 'You've got spirit, I'll say that.'

Mark shook his head. 'You're the one who's taking all the risks, Rory. I just want you to know I'm very grateful.'

'Och, it's no bother. I do this sort of thing every day.' Rory spoke nonchalantly, partly to hide his embarrassment and partly to reassure Mark.

Mark pretended to be heartened. 'Little more than a pleasure cruise, eh?'

'It might be, if you had a more comfortable berth.'

'Don't worry, I'm used to confined places. The navy only allows you eighteen inches to sling your hammock.'

'Well in you get, then,' Rory said, motioning to the box. 'Try it for size.'

Mark climbed in and lay down. When he looked up, he saw Rory's bearded face lit by the lantern and staring concernedly down at him. 'You still all right?'

'Yes,' Mark answered with more confidence than he actually felt.

'Good,' Rory acknowledged with a smile. 'Now, before I fasten down the lid, let me explain what we're planning to do. First of all, I should warn you that the lid forms part of the hold floor. It's a tight fit to stop any coal dust getting in and causing you trouble. But once the keel is loaded with coal, I doubt if you'll be able to hear much outside. By the same token, we'll not be able to hear you either, so there'll be no point in shouting. Just try and relax and go to sleep.'

'Exactly what I had in mind,' Mark lied.

'Once I've closed the lid, I'll give you five minutes to check that you're all right,' Rory went on. 'If you're happy, knock twice on the lid. If you're not, knock four times and I'll open up.'

Mark nodded his understanding and tried to look unconcerned.

'Once we cast off,' Rory continued, 'we'll sail the keel down to Dandy Gears and load her up. Then, depending on tide and wind, it'll be anything up to four hours before we can sail to Shields and cast the coal on board the *Lady Morag*. You'll be on your own.'

Mark nodded again. 'Don't worry,' he murmured, trying to sound relaxed.

'Right then,' Rory said crisply. 'Should be an interesting night. I've organised the biggest fleet of keels that's every sailed on a single tide to Shields. We're going to lead Forster and his men a merry dance, believe me. I think it's going to be a night to remember.

Dandy Gears was a wooden staithe standing on the North Shore a hundred yards downstream from the Swirle. The staithe had three spouts, one at the end and one at each side, which allowed three keels to load at once. Unlike most of the other Tyne staithes, it was not fed by a waggon way. Instead, coals were brought to the staithe by carts from a small pit in Shieldfield.

When Rory brought the keel alongside the staithe, he tied up beneath the vacant end spout and quickly exchanged places with the skipper of a keel lying at one of the side spouts. He knew that because of his long standing friendship with the Standish family, his own keel and the one skippered by Colin would be closely watched by Forster's men and he did not want to draw attention to the keel where Mark was hidden.

A line of horse drawn carts moved slowly along the staithe, each cart releasing its load into one of the three spouts before retreating to make way for others. A steady stream of coal cascaded into the waiting keels below and when they had taken on board the full load of twenty-one tons, they cast off and drifted out into the centre of the river to begin the nine mile journey to Shields harbour.

In the darkness of his cramped compartment Mark tried hard to relax, hoping that he might be able to doze off and cat-nap for most of the journey to Shields. Suddenly, the deafening crash of the coals hitting the floor of the hold startled him out of his wits, putting paid to any thoughts of sleep. Then gradually, the roar abated as the hold began to fill. Soon, the noise faded into a distant, subdued rumble as the last of the coals heaped themselves around the retaining boards surrounding the hatchway of the keel's hold. Then silence, heavy and intimidating, made worse by the knowledge that two of his five senses were now temporarily lost to him. He lay sweating in the claustrophobic darkness of his prison, struggling to control the feeling of panic that threatened to overwhelm him.

Duncan Forster now realised that his first intuition had been right all along. If his informants were telling the truth, most of the keelmen had gone upstream on the last of the flood to load their keels ready to drift down to Shields on the evening ebb tide. Only women, children and the elderly remained to defend Sandgate. There was no point in moving in now, he thought. The river held the key to his problem. And he also remembered that it was the women who had led the rout of the authorities in the '97 debacle and he had no wish to risk ridicule by adding his own name to the keelmen's legend.

After carefully weighing the odds, he finally decided to follow his intuition and concentrate his forces on the river. He called Gibson and Mulligan across. 'Where's that new-fangled steam boat you chartered?'

'She's moored at the Quayside,' Gibson replied. 'I told the captain to wait there for further orders. She's called the *Perseverance*, by the way,' he added.

'I won't need her name, Gibson,' Forster responded irritably. 'There are only two damn steam boats on the river so I can hardly miss her, can I?'

'I'm sorry, Mr Forster. I wasn't.....'

Forster cut him short. 'Never mind your grovelling apologies, man! Is she any good?'

The agent bit back an angry retort. As a professional man, he had his pride but he quickly saw that Forster was in a black mood. 'I don't think you'll have wasted your money,' he said, stifling his annoyance. 'She can out sail anything on the river, so I'm told.'

'I hope you're right,' Forster snapped. 'Are all the guard boats in position?'

'Yes, Mr Forster. The river's blocked at Dunston and St Peter's like you ordered.'

'Right, then. I'm going on board the *Perseverance* to direct operations from there. I've a strong feeling it's the river we'll need to watch. Our quarry's probably hiding aboard one of the keels, possibly disguised as a crew member. They'll be trying to get him down to Shields tonight; that I'm sure.'

'Begging your pardon, sir,' Mulligan interrupted, 'but I reckon he's too badly hurt to be working on deck. He'll be hiding down below somewhere.'

'Yes,' Forster said thoughtfully. 'I think you might be right, Mulligan. Better make sure that all the boats are properly armed. And,' he added as an afterthought, 'see that each boat has something to probe the coal. They might try the same burial trick again.'

'What about Sandgate, sir?' Mulligan asked. 'Are we still going in?'

'Forster thought for a moment. 'No,' he said firmly. 'Just keep a close guard on all the exits until daylight.

We'll leave the captain of the watch in charge here. I want the rest of you on board the guard boats.'

'That will leave us a bit thin on the ground around Sandgate,' Gibson warned.

'But enough for our purpose. The river's the place we must watch. I can feel it in my bones. I want you to stop and board every keel that tries to run the blockade tonight. No one's to be allowed through the boom until they've been thoroughly searched, is that clear?'

'Some of the owners and fitters might take exception to having their property interfered with, sir,' Mulligan ventured. 'Any delay could cost them money.'

'I don't give a damn,' Forster said dismissively. 'I want Standish found and arrested. Shoot him if he shows the slightest sign of resistance. It might save the cost of a trial. There's twenty guineas for the man who finds him.' Then turning to Mulligan he whispered 'and another fifty to the man who shoots him.'

Mulligan grinned and nodded. 'I'll pass the word around, sir, quietly like.'

As he led his constables towards the river, Mulligan felt the bulge of the pistol tucked inside his waistband. 'And I know who that lucky fellow's going to be,' he murmured happily to himself.

The light of the half-moon cast a pale shimmer across the wide expanse of water above the bridge at Newcastle. From a keel moored near the bank, in the shadow of Redheugh staithe, Rory watched with quiet satisfaction as the great fleet of keels filtered through the line of guard boats off Dunston. There was little attempt to hinder them, for they were entering the sealed off area, not exiting it.

Well over one hundred keels were moving downstream to join the fifty or more waiting below bridge. They came from the great staithes at Stella, Derwentheugh and Dunston on the south side of the river, which served the rich coalfields of North West Durham, carrying coals from the pits of Whitefield, Pontop, Tanfield and Ravensworth. Others had loaded at staithes on the North Shore at Lemington, Scotswood, Benwell and Elswick, where the spouts were fed with the output from Wylam, Walbottle, Holywell Main, Elswick and Adair's Main collieries.

'A fine sight, eh?' Rory murmured to one of his keel bullies.

'Aye, but aa hope the buggers aren't drunk the neet, otherwise it'll be hell gannin under the bridge.'

Rory smiled at the man but didn't reply. He knew his skippers better than anyone and they all realised that tonight would be very special. No, he thought, the drinking will be saved for the journey back upriver. And it would be a victory celebration, he vowed. 'Better cast off,' he ordered. 'We'll shoot the bridge while there's still some room.'

Half an hour later, it was pandemonium below bridge as the huge fleet of keels manoeuvred into position. Their bulky black shapes dotted the river from the bridge to the mouth of the Ouseburn, more than half a mile downstream. When Rory was finally satisfied, he gave the order to proceed which was quietly passed back from keel to

627

keel. All lights were doused, for he wanted to use the darkness to cause maximum confusion when they came down on the guard boats at St Peters. For the same reason, he had ordered complete silence to be observed, a rare thing for the normally boisterous keelmen whose banter and repartee helped to while away the boredom of the fourteen hour round trip.

Slowly, the great fleet drifted downstream, past the glass works that lined the St Peter's shore and on towards the narrows, where the river turned northwards towards Dent's Hole, a picturesque hamlet on the north bank. The ruddy glow of the furnaces at Hawks and Crawshay's Gateshead foundry soon faded behind them and as they approached the narrows, Rory could hear the clank and sigh of the huge pumping engine at Friar's Goose Colliery on the Gateshead shore. He could now make out the lights on board the line of guard boats that formed a boom across the river with the steam boat *Perseverance* in the centre. Involuntarily, Rory stiffened, bracing himself for the imminent clash. There was no turning back now, and he could only hope that his instructions would be carried out to the letter.

Duncan Forster and his constables manning the guard boats were taken completely by surprise as the huge mass of keels suddenly bore down on them out of the darkness, like a fleet of ghost ships, silent and menacing. The keels were sailing in line abreast, almost gunwale to gunwale, as instructed by Rory. Immediately behind the first line came others, each line sailing five yards astern of the one in front, so that the whole fleet formed a closely packed, unstoppable phalanx borne on the fast ebbing tide towards the thin line of guard boats.

After the initial shock of surprise, Forster immediately began to rally his men and ordered them to board and search the keels, threatening to shoot any keelman who resisted. But soon, the sheer weight of the keels pressing down on them broke through the line of moored boats and everything quickly disintegrated into a scene of chaos, with groups of men shouting conflicting orders at each other. Many of the watermen, who had been hired to man the guard boats, also lived in Sandgate and they had no stomach to fight their keelmen neighbours. So, it was left to the constables to board the keels and carry out the searches, the consequences of which proved disastrous. As landsmen, they were unused to the motions of small boats, even on the relatively calm waters of a river. They soon became easy meat, for the nimble keelmen who "accidentally" barged into them on the narrow, unguarded side decks of the keels.

Rory had instructed his men not to use undue force, for he wanted no deaths on his hands. But soon, dozens of constables were struggling and spluttering in the cold, dark waters of the Tyne, calling anxiously to their colleagues to help them out. The lanterns carried by the constables were another prime target for the keelmen, for without lights, Forster's men could not carry out a proper search and in the darkness; the narrow decks became an even bigger obstacle. As the confusion grew, Forster screamed new orders to his men, but without any effect. Seething with anger and frustration, he could only stand and watch as the keels began to slip through the widening gaps in the line of guard boats.

As expected, Rory's keel became an early target for a search. He made no attempt to hide and proved surprisingly helpful to Mulligan and his constables when they singled him out. But a thorough search revealed nothing suspicious and he was eventually allowed to proceed. His keel quickly caught up with the leading group of about fifty keels who had already broken through the boom. As soon as he joined them, the keels ran out their long oars and made all haste to extend their lead. Rory then turned and bellowed back to the remaining keels, telling them to obey the law and give the authorities every assistance. The darkness hid the wicked smile that spread across his face as he said it.

Immediately, things began to settle down and Forster's constables were able to continue their slow, painstaking search of the remaining keels. The keelmen no longer openly resisted, but still found various ways to continue their subtle obstruction and delay the search. Every minute counted if it allowed Rory and the keel carrying Mark to move further downstream towards Shields.

Forster's unease grew as the search dragged on. The keelmen seemed too docile all of a sudden, which was totally out of character. As his suspicions grew, he scowled into the darkness in the direction of the departing Rory and the small fleet of keels that were now moving fast downstream. 'I've a feeling we've been fooled, Mulligan,' he muttered angrily .

'In what way, sir?'

'Most of those keels that forced their way through haven't been properly searched,' Forster explained, pointing downstream. 'I think all this confusion was deliberately planned. That rogue MacGregor has some trick up his sleeve, I'll be bound.'

Mulligan scratched his head reflectively. 'I think you might be right, sir. He made sure we spotted him quickly and made no attempt to stop us searching his keel. In fact he was too damned helpful for my liking. Almost as if he wanted to attract our attention, like.'

'Damn it! That's exactly what he did,' Forster growled. 'He drew us away from where we should have been looking. The man we want is on one of those keels that broke through the boom.' He made a quick decision. 'Call off the search and get the boats together. We're going after MacGregor.'

Mulligan called the boats together and relayed the new instructions to the harassed looking constables, telling them to follow the *Perseverance* downriver. But, as events turned out, the new instructions proved difficult to follow. Somehow, as the boats and keels had milled about in the darkness and confusion, the keelmen had quietly removed the oars from the guard boats whilst the unhappy watermen had conveniently turned a blind eye. Now the oars were nowhere to be seen.

Forster quickly understood what had happened and reacted furiously. 'I want you to select the two largest boats,' he shouted to Mulligan. 'Put a dozen armed men in each. We're going after MacGregor.'

'But there's no oars, sir,' Mulligan protested.

'I know that, damn you. We'll tow the boats behind the *Perseverance*.'

'What about the rest of 'em, sir?'

'To hell with them, they can find their own way home. The important thing is to catch up with MacGregor.'

CHAPTER 59

Once clear of Forster's guard boats, Rory changed places with the skipper of the keel carrying Mark. Steering by the long swape over the stern, he led the small flotilla of keels down the Felling reach towards St Anthony's point where the river turned almost due east.

The wind was still too light and changeable to warrant hoisting the square sail so the keels made maximum use of the tide, keeping to the deeper water where the current was strongest. In the absence of a good wind, each keel was propelled by two oars, one over the side plied by the two keel bullies, the other, the long swape, held over the stern by the skipper where it could be used as an oar and a rudder. In shallow waters, two iron shod poles called "puoys" were used, one over each side. The two keel bullies started at the prow, thrusting their shoulders against the pole as they walked down the side decks to the stern. The puoy was then lifted and taken back to the prow for the exercise to be repeated. This process, called "setin", was carried out like a drill exercise with the movements timed and in unison, allowing the crew to keep up a steady rhythm for long periods.

All the while, Rory kept careful watch astern, for he knew it would only be a matter of time before Forster realised his mistake. When he did, he would come in hot pursuit, so every yard gained would be a bonus. He had not reckoned on Forster chartering the *Perseverance*, which had given his enemy a major advantage. Her speed and manoeuvrability could well tip the balance against him. But that, he thought, would add to the challenge and make it all the more worthwhile.

The thought lingered and made Rory smile as the flotilla rounded St Anthony's point. The river now ran almost due east for a mile until it reached the Tyne's major navigational hazard, Bill Point. Once they had rounded it, Rory would feel more secure. But it would seem a long mile with Forster in hot pursuit. He looked across the black swirling waters of the river, trying to pick out Colin's keel and saw him guarding the flotilla's rear.

631

The crews were now working to a good steady rhythm, calling across the water to each other in mildly bantering tones. 'Warhoe, theor! Warhoe! Ye should larn ti handle that fat tub iv yors.'

'Warhoe! Haddaway and shite, man!' came back the crude reply.

Much fun had been poked at the keelmen over the years, depicting them as slow, stupid and gullible. But no one ever questioned their loyalty to each other or their awesome drinking and fighting prowess, nor the fact that they were by far the finest group of sailors on the river.

The keels were now approaching the dangerous Bill Point, the high promontory that jutted south, deep into the river, at the very point where the stream turned almost ninety degrees to the north. The obstruction created a blind corner that had caused so many collisions, that it was now regarded as a major danger to shipping. Rory called to the pee dee to take hold of the swape and picked up a large, brass telescope. Holding one end to his eye, he swept the river astern of the keel, searching for signs of pursuit. At first he could see nothing to cause concern and was about to lower the glass when, suddenly, he caught sight of a dark object about half a mile astern. He focused closer, trying to steady the glass and concentrate his mind on the object in the lens. Then, a grunt of recognition was quickly followed by a quiet curse. The pursuing boat was the *Perseverance* and, judging by the dark shapes immediately behind her, she was towing two boats, probably full of armed constables, he thought.

Rory called across to the other keels to form a protective shield behind him. He watched as the keelmen sweated at their oars, straining to increase the speed of the heavily loaded keels. 'Oh for a good westerly,' he sighed. A favourable wind would make all the difference. He picked up the telescope again and focused it astern. The outline of the *Perseverance* seemed larger and he thought he could detect the faint phosphorescence of her bow wave. The small steam packet was reputed to do five knots through the water, which was much more than the keels could manage in the present conditions. With a strong and favourable wind, the differential would be considerably narrowed but, alas, the breeze remained obstinately too light to be of any practical use.

The bluff of Bill Point now rose close to port and Rory reached down into the huddock, the keel's apology for a cabin, and brought out a shuttered lantern which had been kept alight since leaving the staithe. Holding the lamp in the direction of Bill Point, he opened the shutter and signalled two long flashes. The signal was immediately answered by two acknowledging flashes from someone standing at the top of the headland. Rory next signalled four long flashes and received the same acknowledgement in return. He smiled and turned to the sweating crew. 'Won't be long now, lads. You'll see some fun and games shortly, even without a wind.'

The unmistakable sounds of a steam engine could now be heard drifting across the water in mocking confirmation that their pursuers were narrowing the gap. Rory cast a quick glance at the extremity of Bill Point, then looked back at the rapidly gaining steam boat. With luck they would round the point a hundred yards ahead of the *Perseverance*, he estimated, just about enough for what he had in mind.

As the keel rounded Bill Point, Rory saw with relief that his planned second line of defence was in place. At the same time a strong gust of wind suddenly rippled across the river, raising a cheer from the tiring keelmen. Rory nudged the pee-dee. 'I'll take the swape. You go for'ard and run up the sail. Let's hope that wind holds.'

The small flotilla had rounded the point and they could now see another fleet of about forty empty keels who were making the return journey upriver. Following Rory's instructions, they had anchored on the eastern side of Bill Point, awaiting the signal that would tell them to proceed upstream. That signal, Rory hoped, would ensure that they rounded Bill Point at the same time as the *Perseverance* made her appearance from the opposite direction. In the ensuing confusion, Rory hoped the *Perseverance* would be disabled enough to stop her or at least slow her down.

The faint moon was now blotted out by clouds as the light westerly airs stiffened into a good sailing wind. The returning keels were now able to hoist their square sails and sail close hauled towards Bill Point. Being empty, they moved surprisingly fast for their clumsy looking oval shape, their immense beam of nineteen feet making them stiff sailers. Keeping to a close formation, they rounded the point together then tacked in unison, presenting a wall of solid timber to the approaching steam packet.

In the darkness, the *Perseverance* was unaware of the obstacle ahead and carried on sailing towards the point. The sudden surprised cry from a crewman in the bow was the first warning the helmsman had of the danger ahead, but by then it 'was too late. Desperately pushing up the tiller, he tried to avoid the black shape of the keel that loomed up suddenly out of the darkness. There was a jolting crash that threw everyone onto the deck, followed by the tortured sound of splintering wood as the stem of the keel drove deep into the starboard side of the steam boat forward of the paddle. This was following by further bumps as the two boats being towed rammed into the stern, adding to the confusion. Forster tried to rally his men, screaming his orders over the sounds of escaping steam and the curses of the men who had been injured in the collision.

There was no such disarray among the keelmen, however, and the keels quickly encircled the stricken steam boat, forcing her into the shallows of the river. Rory's orders had been specific; to delay any pursuit at whatever the cost, though no one had expected a steam boat.

On board the *Perseverance*, chaos still reigned as men stumbled around the decks shouting and cursing, unable to comprehend what was happening. Forster was the first to recover and called for a damage report which indicated that the *Perseverance* was not taking in water. The damage had been confined to the hull above the waterline which meant that the boat was still safe and seaworthy. He shouted for Mulligan who came up nursing his badly bruised ribs. 'Cut the towline,' he ordered.

'But the men, sir,' Mulligan protested. 'We'll need them when we catch MacGregor.'

'Bring the six men who have muskets on board the *Perseverance*. The rest will have to fend for themselves.' Seeing that Mulligan was about to make a further protest, he cut him short. 'Don't you see, man? This is another one of MacGregor's ambushes. If we don't extricate ourselves quickly, we'll soon have that blasted fleet of keels that we left behind at St Peter's bearing down on us. That's exactly what MacGregor wants.'

Mulligan soon realised that Forster was right. But before they could break free of the encircling keels the huge fleet of loaded keels from upriver, helped by the freshening westerly, caught up with the paddle steamer and added to the chaos. The keelmen, who were the smartest seamen on the river, suddenly became awkward amateurs blundering around the *Perseverance* and preventing her from moving. But Forster was not fooled by the charade. Calling together his men, he ordered them to open fire on any keel that obstructed their path. Realising that he was serious, the keelmen reluctantly gave way, but not before a few ropes had mysteriously become entangled in the steamer's paddle wheels. After a considerable delay, the *Perseverance* finally broke free and again set off in pursuit of Rory MacGregor.

With a strengthening westerly and a fast ebbing tide beneath her, the keel made rapid progress down Bill Reach. Steering with the long swape over the stern, Rory noted their speed as they raced past the glowing forges of the Walker Iron Works before moving out to take the main channel past Walker Sand. When they reached the bend at Cock Row Sand, the stream turned east towards Whitehill Point, a straight stretch of river almost three miles long and known as the Long Reach.

Rory felt happier now as they sped past the shadowy outlines of the great staithes at Wallsend, Hebburn and Willington. As the moon broke free of the clouds, the wide expanse of Jarrow Slake opened up, its black swirling waters draining with the ebbing tide that would soon transform its four hundred acres into a vast sea of mud. Though not a superstitious man, Rory felt there was something sinister and foreboding about the place and he fought to suppress an involuntary shiver.

At Whitehill Point, the river turned north east for the final mile to the harbour at Shields. There was still no sign of the *Perseverance* and Rory allowed a soft sigh of relief to escape his lips. He began to hum a tune to himself as they approached the cluster of collier brigs that lay at anchor, waiting to take on coal. As he expected, the *Lady Morag* was the furthest downstream, ready to be the first across the bar after loading.

The flotilla of keels descended like a swarm of moths on the flaming, coal filled braziers hoisted out by the colliers to provide light for loading. Soon, a keel was tied up along each side of the waiting colliers, while the remaining keels stood off to wait their turn to unload. As the braziers flared and died in the wind, the arduous task of casting the coals through the gates in the colliers' bulwarks began. When the blackened, sweating shovellers had finished they cast off, allowing one of the waiting keels to take its place alongside the collier.

The speed at which the keelmen worked was astonishing and it was often said that one keelman could keep at least three trimmers busy. Rory and his crew, aided by volunteers, broke all records to release Mark from his cramped box at the bottom of the hold. When the hold floor was finally uncovered, Rory apprehensively prised opened the lid of Mark's "coffin" and held his breath. Seeing no movement he called out anxiously 'Are you all right, Mark?'

There was no answer.

The first ten minutes of his entombment had been the hardest for Mark to endure, fighting to control the panic that welled up inside him. But gradually, as the air continued to flow through the improvised ventilation system, his confidence returned and he slowly began to relax. Still weak and tired from his injuries, he eventually drifted off to sleep.

His slumbers were disturbed by a strange, disjointed dream of his boyhood days working underground at North Moor pit. In his dream, the pit candles threw no light and everywhere he went there was silence and total darkness. No one spoke, though he could sense the presence of pitmen and boys all around him, like unseen spirits. It was like a ghost pit peopled by the spectral victims of past pit disasters, as if they were unable to find peace and rest in their other world. When he was being drawn up the shaft, he could see no welcoming light at the top and his arms ached as he clung desperately to the rope. All around him he could sense other boys clinging to the rope and letting go, one by one, to fall silently to the bottom of the shaft. He looked up, searching for the light at the top of the shaft, but there was only darkness. His arms ached even more and he knew he would soon have to let go. He felt his hands slip from the rope and his stomach churning descent began. Terrified, he started to scream.

'It's all right, lad,' the voice said reassuringly. 'You're safe now.' 'Thought you'd never wake up!' Strong hands lifted him up and he felt the cool, salt laden air brush his cheeks. When Mark opened his eyes, he saw the bearded face of Rory MacGregor smiling down at him, his blue eyes sparkling in the reflected light of the collier's flaming brazier.

Mark was quickly carried on board the *Lady Morag* and taken below to the great stern cabin, which was bathed in the soft, yellow light of an oil lamp that hung from one of the deck beams. Rory introduced Mark to Jamie Drummond, the captain and owner of the collier.

'What a beautiful cabin,' Mark said, looking around appreciatively. 'Much better than my last one,' he added, glancing at Rory.

'Aye, it's a fine place,' Jamie acknowledged, 'but I'm afraid ye'll no' be seeing much of it just yet.'

'Banished to the forecastle, eh?' Mark responded jokingly, happy to be alive and safe.

'No, you'll join me in here as my guest in due course. But first, you'll have to spend a little more time in a rather less commodious place, I'm afraid.'

Mark groaned. 'Not another priest hole?'

'Something like that,' Jamie replied. 'It's one of the ship's old hiding places where a sailor could take refuge if the Navy's press gang came on board. They were always after prime collier seamen during the war.'

'I know,' Mark said. 'I met quite a lot of them after I was taken.'

'It won't be for long,' Rory said, adding his support to Jamie's argument. 'Just in case Forster tries to search the ship. Once the *Lady Morag* sails you'll be able to come out. '

Mark sighed. 'All right. Just show me where I have to go.'

'Not just yet,' Jamie said. 'There's time to say goodbye to your friends while I keep watch on deck.' He turned as he reached the cabin door. 'I'll find Colin and send him down.'

There was a short silence after Jamie's departure, broken by Rory making a noisy attempt to clear his throat. He looked uncomfortable and began to fidget. 'I'm not very good at this, Mark,' he began awkwardly, 'but I think what you did was right, so don't go having any regrets. Henry's a lucky man to have a son like you.'

'Thank you, Rory, but you're a lucky man too. You have Colin. He loves you like a father, you know.'

'Aye, and I love the lad, like a son. He was only a bairn when his father died so, in a way, I sort of took his place. He'll miss you, Mark.'

'And I'll miss him too, Rory. But he'll always be welcome to visit me in America. It really is a land of opportunity, you know.'

'I suppose it is and maybe one day he'll take you up on your offer. There's no future for a keelman anymore. We're a dying breed.'

'Well, let's hope it will be a very slow death, eh Rory? '

'It will if I have anything to do with it.'

'Yes, I'm sure it will,' Mark said as he held out his hand. 'I owe you more than I can every repay, Rory, and I'm very grateful. Without your help I'd be languishing in some stinking gaol by now.'

The two men looked at each other, unable to speak but mutually touched by the moment of farewell. Mark felt Rory's great paw clasping his hand and a broad arm encircling his shoulders. They stood for a few moments, their feelings expressed in their silent, emotional embrace, until the sound of footsteps broke their special rapport.

'That'll be Colin, I expect,' Rory said gruffly. I'd better get back on deck and see how the keels are doing. The sooner the ship's loaded the better.' With that he turned and walked towards the cabin door, blowing loudly into a coal grimed handkerchief. 'Safe journey,' he called, without looking back.

Colin entered the cabin as soon as Rory had left. He stood for a moment, smiling sadly at Mark. 'It'll be time to sail, shortly. Ship's nearly loaded.'

Still choked with emotion, Mark could only gesture to the long window seat that ran the length of the great stern windows and they both sat down.

'Some cabin, eh?' Mark said, when he finally recovered.

'Aye,' Colin agreed. 'Do themselves proud do these collier captains. Still, aa prefer the huddock of a keel me'sell.'

'Never had the yen to skipper a collier, then?'

'Not since we sailed our models at Barras Bridge when we were kids. They were nowt like this, though,' he added indicating the elegant cabin.

'No,' Mark conceded, 'but much more fun.'

'You'll be in America, soon,' Colin said, suddenly changing the subject.

'Yes. Alabama. There's a lot of work to be done when I get back.'

'Is it a nice country?'

'Yes. It's a lot bigger and a lot nicer than England. It's a land of opportunity, Colin. The promised land for those who are prepared to work.'

'Sounds good. I might want to join you there one day.'

'You'll be very welcome if you do. I really mean that, Colin.'

'Aye, I can see that. Will you write when you get there?'

'Of course I will. And I'll keep on writing. You see, part of me will still be here on the Tyne and in Newcastle. And a piece of my heart lies buried at North Moor, so writing will help keep all those parts alive.'

'And I'll write back,' Colin said proudly. 'That's one thing All Saints' taught me that I've never forgotten.'

Mark smiled wistfully as the distant memories returned. 'Yes, they were good days, weren't they?'

Colin's intended reply was interrupted by a bull-like bellow from the deck above. 'Sounds like Rory telling me my time's up,' he said with a wry grin.

Mark nodded. 'Better not keep him waiting.'

The two friends rose and after a brief hesitation, embraced each other, silently and emotionally, until they were interrupted by another bellow from the deck above.

'Best be off, then,' Colin said. Pausing at the cabin door, he turned and forced a smile. 'Good luck, Mark. I'll never forget you.'

Before Mark could reply, he was gone.

On deck, the trimmers had finished levelling the coal and the hatch covers were being closed. Up on the yards, the crew were loosening the sails as the last two keels, skippered by Rory and Colin, cast off.

639

Slowly, the brig began to move down river, picking up speed as the wind filled her sails.

Mark quickly recognised the tell tale sounds and movement of a ship under way and immediately opened the special panel of his secret hiding place. After stretching his cramped muscles, he limped his way up on deck and moved aft to join Jamie, who was keeping a wary eye on the helmsman. It was well past dawn and a thin, wintry sun lay low on the horizon seaward of the bar. The wind had also veered and was now blowing from the north west, though not as strongly as before.

Jamie gave him a welcoming smile. 'We're on our way, Mark. Not as much wind as I'd like, though. I was hoping to clear the bar before the flood strengthened.'

'Will there be enough water over the bar?' Mark enquired.

'Yes. It's a neap tide.'

'Well at least it won't be as strong then.'

Mark's knowledge of the sea brought an amused smile to Jamie's face. 'Rory said you'd spent some time in the navy.'

'Time I'd prefer to forget,' Mark replied, smiling back.

'Aye, I suppose you would.'

'There's a lot of colliers in port for January,' Mark said, changing tack. 'I thought most of the fleet laid up for winter?'

'Not so much as they used to. The demand for house coal gets stronger in winter so you get better prices. Besides, now that the canals have reached London, the Midland pits are in a position to take some of our trade.'

'I thought the north east coal owners managed to persuade parliament to put a duty on all coal brought into London by canal?'

'They did, but most of it is smuggled in anyway.'

Their conversation was suddenly cut short by a shout from the lookout aloft, who had been told to keep a careful watch astern. 'Deck there! Steam boat coming up dead astern.'

Jamie snatched up his telescope and scanned the river behind them. At first, all he could see were other colliers who were following them downriver towards the bar. Then, in the distance towards Whitehill Point, he saw the tall plume of smoke and recognised the familiar outline of the paddle steamer. 'Well I'm damned,' he said. 'It's the *Perseverance*. She wasn't disabled after all.'

Mark's melancholy suddenly turned to apprehension at the thought of being hounded again. 'She won't catch us now, surely?'

'It'll be touch and go unless the wind picks up,' Jamie said, shaking his head. He cupped his hands to his face and hailed the men aloft, ordering them to set the topgallants.

Then, hauling himself up on the ratlines, he shouted across the water to alert Rory, who was sailing off the larboard quarter with a small group of empty keels. Rory instantly understood the new threat and raised his arm in acknowledgement of the warning. He began shouting instructions to the other keels and in a matter of minutes they had manoeuvred themselves smartly into a new formation, sailing in close line astern along the north shore of the river in the classic battle formation of the Royal Navy.

Mark and Jamie watched with total bemusement. 'What on earth is he up to?' Jamie asked.

'I don't know,' Mark replied, 'but knowing Rory, he's got something up his sleeve.'

'I hope he has, because that bloody paddle steamer's getting a lot closer.'

Mark glanced over the stern and was shocked to see the *Perseverance* closing rapidly. He borrowed the glass from Jamie and focused in on the approaching steamer. Black smoke belched from the tall funnel, which was stayed like a ship's mast, and the water foamed beneath the churning paddle wheels. He counted more than a dozen men on her deck, half of them armed with what looked like muskets. He handed the telescope back to Jamie and watched in silence.

The *Lady Morag* sailed on, gathering a little more speed as the top gallants filled and began to draw. Sailing on a broad reach she passed Clifford's Fort guarding The Narrows which formed the entrance to Shields harbour. It was now less than a mile to the bar and the relative safety of the North Sea. But all the time, the *Perseverance* was rapidly gaining on the collier brig.

Soon, the dangerous Black Midden rocks appeared to larboard, their jagged teeth still exposed above the rising tide. On the promontory above, the huge guns of the Spanish Battery could be seen commanding the entrance to the river. A quarter of a mile ahead the seas were breaking over the shallow bar.

A shot suddenly rang out and Mark turned to discover that the *Perseverance* was now only two hundred yards astern and closing fast. 'That sounded like a warning shot, Jamie. I think they want you to stop.'

'To hell with them,' Jamie growled. 'The *Lady Morag* stops for no one unless I say so.'

'It's me they want, Jamie. I don't want to make any trouble for you.'

'You won't, because I'm not stopping.'

'But they're armed, Jamie. I don't want anyone to get hurt or killed. They'll try to board us as soon as they come alongside.'

Jamie smiled. 'I think not, my friend. Look!'

Mark's eyes followed the line of Jamie's pointing finger and an involuntary gasp of astonishment escaped his lips. He watched in awe as Rory's flotilla of keels bore away and, still in close line of battle formation, began to sail across the mouth of the river seaward of the Narrows, to form a defensive line between the paddle steamer and the collier.

'The man's a fool,' Jamie said fondly, 'but oh what a brave one.'

'What's he trying to do?' Mark asked anxiously.

'Watch and you'll find out,' Jamie responded cryptically.

The keels were now sailing so close, they almost overlapped each other. There was no way the *Perseverance* could break through this barrier without sustaining crippling damage to herself and she was forced to alter course to run parallel with the line of keels. Forster was standing on deck screaming insults at the keelmen and threatening to open fire unless they let the *Perseverance* through. But Rory simply smiled and pretended not to hear.

Mark frowned. 'I still can't make out what Rory's up to.'

Jamie grinned and pointed. 'The Herd Sand,' he said. 'Don't you see?'

Mark looked at the long stretch of sand lying just inside the bar which ran southwards for more than a mile. A sudden look of understanding appeared in his eyes. 'The crafty old rogue,' he said admiringly. 'He's going to run that bloody paddle steamer aground.'

'Aye, he's a devious bugger is that one, even for a MacGregor,' Jamie conceded proudly.

Mark watched in rapt fascination as the keels skilfully and inexorably forced the *Perseverance* southwards until she struck the sandbank. 'She's aground,' Mark shouted excitedly.

'She is indeed,' Jamie said contentedly. 'And it'll take half an hour at least for the tide to float her off.'

'We're safe, then?'

'We are, laddie. They'll run out of coal before they can catch us now.'

On the deck of the leading keel, the giant figure of Rory could be seen waving farewell. Then, drifting across the water, came the stirring sound of the Clan MacGregor war cry.

'Ard-Choille!'

The swell increased as the *Lady Morag* approached the bar. Half a mile astern, Mark could see the *Perseverance* still hard and fast on the Herd Sand. To the north, the lighthouse and the ruins of Tynemouth Priory stood out on the headland above Priors Haven, presenting a magnificent backdrop in the early morning sunshine. He felt a touch on his arm and turned to see Jamie pointing over the stern towards the promontory above the Black Middens.

'I think you'll need this,' he said, handing Mark the telescope. 'Up there on top, by the Spanish Battery,' he added.

Mark swung the telescope and focused in on the distant group of figures silhouetted on the headland above the Black Midden rocks. Ralph, mounted on his horse, loomed large and clear in the lens, waving and smiling. In a gig next to him sat Henry, his smile stiff and forced to hide his emotions. Steam rose from the back of the horse standing in the shafts, indicating a hasty journey from Newcastle. Next to Henry sat young Michael, squeezed in between a weeping Aunt Ellen on the other side of the seat.

It was only then that the finality of his departure struck home to Mark. It was the beginning of his exile, for he now knew that he could never set foot in England again. The realisation caused a cold knot to tighten in his stomach as a wave of nostalgia threatened to overwhelm him.

A cold wind was now blowing off the sea, causing his wounds to ache, but he held the glass steady, watching the figures on the headland until they became mere specks in the lens. He felt another touch on his shoulder and turned to Jamie holding out a knotted leather bag. 'Ralph asked me to give you this,' he said. 'But not until we were clear of Forster and his men.'

Mark thanked him and took the bag, feeling surprise at the weight of it.

'Best go below and put it with your things,' Jamie said kindly. 'I'll be down directly, then we can have some breakfast.'

Mark went below and sat on the seat that ran below the great stern windows of the cabin. He opened the bag and emptied the contents onto the seat beside him, taken aback by the shower of gold coins that cascaded forth. Then, he saw the letter lying at the bottom of the bag. He took it out and began to read.

'Dear Brother,

Father insisted that you should have some of your inheritance in advance, a gesture with which I fully concur.

The bag contains one thousand one hundred and fifty pounds in gold (one hundred guineas and one hundred sovereigns). The rate of exchange for the English pound sterling is four dollars and forty-four cents, so your gold is worth five thousand one hundred and six dollars. But take my advice, use only the New England banks. Most other state banks are suspect and their paper may-prove worthless if there should ever be a run (which I think there will be, one day).

I was serious when I said I would visit you, so build that house and plant your cotton. The American branch of the family dynasty is in your hands so go forth and multiply! And don't forget to write. God speed and good luck,

Your loving brother, Ralph

Mark stared at the letter for a long time before replacing the coins into the bag. Suddenly, his melancholy began to lift as he thought of the future. Ralph would be his physical link with England and there would be letters to look forward to. Maybe Colin would come out one day. His gaze shifted to the huge stern window and he watched the rippling wake of the collier stretching and fading astern. The cliffs of Tynemouth were now only a speck on the distant horizon.

CHAPTER 60

On a spring night in 1816, the New York bound sail ship Albany, forty-six days out from London, ghosted through the calm, misty waters of the Nantucket shoals off the coast of America. A phosphorescent wake of shimmering light marked her slow passage through the shallow waters.

In one of the cabins below, Mark slept, fretfully tossing and turning as the recurring nightmare once more took hold. Again, in his mind, he heard the tortured cries of his terrified victim reverberating through his troubled mind, making him cry out in his sleep.

Suddenly, his body stiffened as he awoke from his dream. He lay still for a while, listening to the reassuring shipboard sounds of creaking timbers and the slap of water against the hull. The pungent smell of bilge water assailed his nostrils and as his disturbed mind gradually became aware of his surroundings, he gave a long, audible sigh of relief. His body, soaked in sweat, began to cool rapidly causing him to shiver uncontrollably. He reached down and retrieved the blanket which had been thrown off during his turbulent sleep, then lay back in his bunk staring into the darkness of the cabin as he reflected on his future.

Soon he would be starting a new life in America, thanks to the love and generosity of his family and friends. Five thousand dollars would help restore the physical trappings of his broken life but no amount of money could compensate for what he had lost. His physical wounds had almost mended but the mental scars ran deep. Time's healing process was slow and he wondered if, at the age of twenty-nine, there would be sufficient years left to complete the cure.

From his own experience, he knew that he was about to enter a better and more egalitarian society than the one he was leaving behind in England. With the disastrous war between the two countries now ended, both England and America were anxious to make a fresh start so that they could maximise the opportunities that peace between them, and above all in Europe, would bring. But the pain of his exile still smouldered deep inside him and his thoughts kept returning to distant England, the land that still held his heart. His family and friends were constantly in his mind, for he desperately wanted to preserve their memory.

With the blanket pulled around him, he felt the warmth returning to his body, slowly easing the turmoil inside his head. He gradually relaxed and drifted off into a deep, tranquil sleep, for once untroubled by the traumas of his recent past. Slowly, the lines of pain that were etched on his face began to fade.

At nine o'clock in the morning, the cry of 'land ho!' rang out from the lookout aloft, sending a shiver of excitement among the passengers who were just finishing breakfast. Everyone immediately went up on deck to catch their first glimpse of land for seven weeks. In the hazy sunshine, the coast of Long Island could be seen in the distance to starboard and the passengers crowded the rails to watch.

Mark was the last on deck and the fresh morning air was like a tonic, raising his spirits for the first time since leaving England. During the voyage, he had struck up a friendship with a family called Cameron who were emigrating to America. He saw them standing together by the rail talking excitedly and pointing to the distant shore. It was their first sight of their new homeland. He watched with interest until the eldest daughter, Julia, sensing his gaze glanced across at him. Their eyes met for a moment and she smiled before turning away.

Something stirred inside Mark as he watched the morning sun glinting in Julia's long, golden hair. She reminded him of Jane but, to his surprise, the anguish he felt seemed more muted as the harrowing memories resurfaced in his mind. Perhaps in time, he thought, the pain of remembrance would diminish and make way for warmer memories of their brief happiness together. He suddenly felt happier and walked over to the rail, where he was warmly greeted by the Cameron family.

By the following morning, the ship had beat her way past Sandy Hook off the New Jersey coast and entered the calmer waters of the bay which led up to the Hudson. They were now only sixteen miles from New York and Mark, watching from the deck, quickly realised that he must make the most of the time remaining before they disembarked.

When Julia came up on deck he smiled and moved to meet her. She returned his smile shyly, but in a way that enchanted him and made his heart grow lighter. Soon, they were talking absorbedly to each other as they walked the deck, seemingly oblivious to the other passengers.

Mr & Mrs Cameron smiled knowingly at each other and kept discreetly to the other side of the ship.

Wheeling in the light airs above the ship's mainmast, a gull called out its welcome. The sound made Mark pause and he looked up. Something in the gull's strident cry seemed familiar, yet he could not quite detect what it was. He heard the call again and a smile of understanding slowly crept over his face. Of course.

'Ard-Choille!'

He turned back to Julia and saw the look of puzzled amusement in her sparkling blue eyes. 'I'm sorry, I was distracted by something.'

'Am I such poor company, then?' she asked, her eyes twinkling with mischief.

'No, of course not,' he answered hastily. 'It was just, for a moment, I thought I heard an old friend calling.'

Lightning Source UK Ltd.
Milton Keynes UK
UKHW010632150621
385545UK00001B/4